Torsten

The Call of the Ice Fields

The 13th Paladin

Volume XII

Translated by Tim Casey

Copy Editor: Neil McCourt
Proof Reader: James Bryan

To all of you who have supported me in my imaginings of this epic adventure…

Soon, it will have been accomplished…

*And remember –
there is nothing more enjoyable than experiencing a story for the first time*

www.tweitze.de
www.facebook.com/t.weitze
Instagram: Torsten_weitze

© *Torsten Weitze Krefeld*

Picture:
Petra Rudolf / www.dracoliche.de

German editor/proof reader:
Janina Klinck / www.lectoreena.de

The
Sun
Plains

Cape
Verstaad

The Screaming
Cliffs

The Ravenous Maw

The Bay of Whiteness

The
Ice Fields

The Bitter Bulwark

The Frozen Teeth

Jorath

Chapter 1

I spy with my little eye…something that's green and wet!

Keeping his eyes closed, Ahren frowned and dived into Culhen's mind in an effort to solve the riddle. Then he sighed, immediately recognising the memory to which his loyal friend had been referring.

The Weeping Valley, he thought, exhibiting his boredom with a little groan. *Yet again.*

Yup, praised the wolf, not at all put out by the Paladin's mood. *You're doing very well.*

It isn't exactly difficult, retorted Ahren impatiently. *The only things you ever think of are your acts of heroism – big and small. This is the eighth time that the Weeping Valley has come up.*

Culhen didn't reply, Ahren reckoning that his wolf was basking in the glory that had followed his retrieval of the Soundless Lute. The Forest Guardian opened his eyes and blinked up at the sun, whose rays were intermittently shining down through the scudding clouds. Ahren had a magnificent view of the roiling ocean through the front railings of the *Queen of the Waves,* the broad expanse of sea extending far into the distance. The ship was bucking like an unruly horse whenever another foam-peaked wave crashed against the steel-reinforced keel, causing the dark timbers of the vessel, not to mention Ahren's bones, to shudder.

As majestic as the scenery that surrounded them was and had been from the moment they had set off on the high seas, a certain ennui was now gaining the upper hand, compelling Ahren into playing silly, little games with his friends, whenever he wasn't training Hakanu. Culhen's idea of their fishing in each other's mind for specific memories had been entertaining enough at the outset – or at least until the animal's self-centred nature had ensured that Ahren was presented with one glorious deed after another involving the wolf.

Count yourself lucky that we're not under constant attack from Dark Ones, sulked Culhen, who had returned from his daydreaming and was now reacting to Ahren's thoughts.

Ahren nodded as he absently ruffled Culhen's fur. He was lying on the fo'c'sle of the *Queen of the Waves,* cuddled up against the wolf's flank. He silently chided himself for his own discontent. His friend was right, of course – they hadn't encountered a single Dark One since setting off from the city of cutthroats on their southerly course. This was mainly down to the fact that the area around Gol-Konar was primarily occupied by marauding pirates rather than the servants of the Adversary. No greedy cutthroats had accosted them, however, not least because Dahl-Rhi, ruler of the Pallid House was now, thanks to Ahren's generosity, commander of the entire city and had ensured that no pirate flags were appearing on the horizon. The Forest Guardian wondered if the next heavily laden merchant ship to traverse these waters would be as lucky.

I rather doubt it, suggested Culhen dryly. *Gol-Konar is still a long way from having become tamed.*

I suppose I should enjoy the boredom for as long as it holds, conceded Ahren. The heavily depleted crew of the *Queen of the Waves* had been bravely maintaining their southward course since their departure from the city, knowing full well that it wouldn't be long before the turbulent waters would be teeming with bloodthirsty Dark Ones.

We still have another week of peace, replied Culhen before letting out a big yawn. *At least, if Yantilla's report on the maritime enemy movements are still holding true.*

Ahren turned his body so that he could look beyond his wolf's tail and onto the main deck of the *Queen of the Waves*. There, the commander of the Ice Wolves, her eyes merciless and her voice sharp, was drilling those of Ahren's personal guards who had survived the latest battle. Among the troop of fifty or so men and women, Ahren spotted his apprentice, Hakanu, the lad's face red with effort. The young master had ordered the boy in no uncertain terms, out of a mixture of pragmatism and self-interest, to take part in the Ice Wolves' physical training sessions in addition to his own exercises – and it hadn't been long after their departure from Gol-Konar that Ahren had heard the crew joking among themselves that the young warrior from the Green Sea was even training in his sleep.

I only wish it were so, thought Ahren as he turned back to face the unquiet sea again. *It will be such a short time before Hakanu finds himself confronting the Adversary.*

Only one more Paladin to go, exclaimed Culhen, unable to hide his excitement as he made himself more comfortable by shifting his weight behind Ahren's back. *Once we find Yollock and bring him back, we will have all thirteen Paladins together. Then we will go into battle against the Dark god – a battle that will put into the shade all those other ones that have been fought in Jorath for eight hundred winters!*

And this time we won't erect a Pall Pillar to win us some time before taking on the Dark god again in the far distant future, added Ahren grimly. *This time it will come to a final conclusion – one way or the other.*

'No wonder that the sea is foaming as though a thunderstorm is about to break out,' said a cheerful voice beside Ahren as Khara stepped into his field of vision before flopping down beside him and against Culhen's flank. 'The waves have seen your face and have concluded that a tempest is riding on their backs.'

Ahren beamed at his beloved and drew her into his arms. The Swordsmistress then pulled at his cloak until she, too, was wrapped up in it, before pressing against the Paladin and sighing contentedly.

'This is lovely and warm. Now I understand how you can remain here at the front of the ship for so long despite the whistling wind.'

'The cloak only works properly if *my* body is sufficiently covered,' chuckled Ahren, gently reminding the warrior as he pulled his half of the charmed leather as far as possible over his chest. 'Which means that I spend most of my time freezing just as much as everyone else.'

Khara stroked his cheek and sighed. 'Isn't this peace wonderful?' she asked playfully, pointing out at the ocean.

Ahren chuckled. 'Why the good humour?'

'May not a lass simply enjoy the fact that for a change there aren't any ne'er-do-wells, cutthroats, assassins, or any other dishonourable riffraff hounding us?' asked the Swordsmistress with a sparkle in her eyes.

Ahren nodded. Gol-Konar had been a difficult experience for all of them, and each of the Forest Guardian's companions was dealing with the consequences in their own way. Khara, for instance, had played the role of a Swordsmistress banished from the Eternal Empire and eager to earn easy money. This had forced her, on occasion, to ignore her own personal code of honour. Ahren was firmly convinced that his beloved would much rather take on two dozen Dark Ones in battle than be forced to wear her Warrior Pin the wrong way around in her hair again.

'Are Falk and Trogadon still fleecing the crew?' he asked.

Now it was Khara's turn to nod silently.

Ahren chuckled. 'We have sailed on this ship so often that surely every mariner on board must know by now that the pair have centuries' of acquired deviousness when it comes in throwing dice.'

'The younger ones, especially, are still falling victim to the duo's trickery,' said Khara, her tone of voice suggesting that her mind was somewhere else entirely.

Ahren glanced sideways at her, realising immediately that the Swordsmistress was studying the fast-moving clouds and that her good mood had vanished. 'What are you thinking about?' the Paladin asked gently.

'Cochan,' she replied deliberately. 'Uldini contacted her this morning – he wanted to find out how things were around the Ring. I happened to be present and overheard how tired her voice sounded.'

Ahren instinctively tensed up. 'I thought there was a kind of stalemate,' he said anxiously. 'As far as I know, the warriors on the Ring and the creatures of the Obsidian Fortress are simply eyeing each other suspiciously from behind their respective high walls.'

'That's true,' said Khara, her eyes still fixed on the sky. 'But according to Cochan, complicated bane curses have been heard coming from the depths of the fortress for days now. Their incantation has resulted in both sorcerous illnesses breaking out among the soldiers *and* the manifestation of accursed fogs – in which several of our patrols have been unwittingly caught up only to immediately suffer broken bones – to name but two examples. Quin-Wa and her fellow Ancients are doing their best to dispel the unholy sorcery before it causes any more damage.'

The Adversary is testing our magical defences, said Culhen with a low whimper as he pushed his head affectionately against the worried Swordsmistress.

'It sounds like the Dark god is taking a more active role in the war than before,' said Ahren morosely. 'And it seems that he has recovered from the creation of his children.'

'Not yet,' countered Khara, shaking her head. 'Or at least, not fully. According to Uldini, these charms are nothing more than exercises to help the Adversary fully awaken.'

A shiver ran down Ahren's spine. The enemy would not sleep for ever. The entire protracted journey that the young man and his companions had undertaken had been dominated by what amounted to an elaborate game of cat and mouse involving their own little troop and the peoples of the creation on the one side, and the Adversary with his dark creatures on the other. Both parties had enjoyed numerous victories and suffered countless defeats, resulting in the deaths of kings, Paladins, and ancient beasts, not to mention countless men, women, and Dark Ones. It was nothing short of a miracle that Ahren and his friends had come so far, and that now twelve of the thirteen Paladins of the gods had united to wage war on the Adversary.

Although some of the Paladins are more battle-ready than others, interjected Culhen, sharing a fragment of memory with his friend in which Trimm was trying – and failing – to complete a solitary press-up.

Ahren rubbed his face and pulled Khara closer to him. 'It will all work out,' he murmured, reassuring himself as much as his beloved.

Khara nodded and closed her eyes, her arms firmly wrapped around him. Ahren watched the tempestuous heavens a while longer in silence, the rays of light piercing through the blanket of cloud like darting fingers before dancing on the turbulent waters. Having heard the latest news, he couldn't help thinking that he was looking up at some extraordinary being that had feelers of naked light with which it was testing out the waters around its hopelessly exposed prey.

The captain's cabin, situated at the poop of the ship, seemed terribly confined to Ahren as always, not merely because of its miniature size when compared to the vastness of the ocean, but also because of the sheer number of visitors that populated it every evening. Muai and Culhen only remained outside the little room thanks to be being bribed with considerable portions of meat and fish, yet it still felt narrow and sticky as Ahren squeezed between Khara and Hakanu on one side of the long, wooden table. The floor, ceiling, and walls of the cabin creaked and squeaked with every wave that hit the vessel while the wooden plates and bowls slid this way and that on the rough surface of the table, following the rhythm of the ocean. As the others took their places, Ahren glanced around the room so that he could quickly judge the mood of his friends and allies. Falk and Trogadon were chuckling quietly and counting their little bundles of coins – presumably their ill-gotten gains from the dice throwing. Nevertheless, the young Paladin didn't fail to spot the sadness in Falk's eyes, the separation from Selsena clearly affecting his erstwhile teacher. The Titejunanwa had stayed behind on the mainland with Haminul and Lanlion so that she could give support to the Bloodless, who had muttered vaguely about undertaking some sort of pilgrimage. Despite the protests of the rest of his companions, Ahren had simply nodded and wished his friend all the best with his plan. Clearly, the encounter between the Bloodless and the THREE on the bridge at Gol-Konar had affected the accursed Paladin more deeply than Ahren had originally thought. Whatever Lanlion's pilgrimage involved, it seemed that Falk's Titejunanwa felt that she would be of more assistance there than in the search for Yollock – which would, moreover, have involved the Elven charger being forced to spend moons on end in the belly of the ship, following which she would inevitably sink into the snow and ice and quite possibly hold up the entire group, anyway. None of these arguments had persuaded Falk that her decision was a wise one, however, and the old man was now carrying around his pain at being separated from his companion animal like an open wound – and anyone who knew the old Paladin well was all too aware of his suffering.

Which is why Jelninolan isn't scolding Trogadon, said Culhen, who was gleefully chewing on a bone that he had been bribed with. *She is allowing him and Falk to rip off the unfortunate mariners because it is a welcome distraction.*

Ahren looked from Falk to Trogadon, and then fixed his eyes on Jelninolan. The Elf seemed tired and drawn but otherwise happy, as she sat there wearily, gazing good-naturedly at the dwarf who had won her heart. She, like the others present, was carrying no armour or weaponry – fulfilling the silent promise that they had all made to one another. The first days of their voyage were to be a time of peace.

Ahren hoped that circumstances wouldn't force them to quickly abandon their unwritten agreement. He continued to look around the cabin, his eyes then drawn to Uldini, who was sitting at the head of the table, absently polishing off a bowl of stew while staring into the depths of the dimly glimmering *Flamestar*. The first among the Ancients seemed to be working non-stop, sending dozens of coded messages cleverly hidden in old Elven poems. The Adversary would either soon become an expert in the literature of the elves or he would be driven to despair in his attempts at deciphering the war reports he was receiving. To add to the confusion, Uldini made sure that every fifth embassage was unadulterated nonsense, thoroughly baffling anyone who was potentially eavesdropping on the sorcerous messages.

Khara poked Ahren hard in his side with her elbow. 'You're staring,' she scolded. 'Which is rude – even among friends.'

The young man reached for a bowl of stew, then concentrated his attention on Hakanu and Kamaluq, the young lad's fox. 'Have you made good progress with your lessons?' he asked the apprentice, the latter immediately shrugging his shoulders and filling his mouth with food.

'Yes, master,' spluttered the boy, shovelling yet more stew into his already full cheeks, presumably hoping against hope that there would be no more questions.

Ahren chuckled knowingly. 'Falk's descriptions of Dark Ones are an invaluable source of knowledge – and you must internalise them,' he said severely. 'I understand that reading reports of encounters with such creatures is not as exciting as weapons training, but it is undoubtedly an advantage to know *where* to plunge or throw your spear when it comes to specific Dark Ones, don't you agree?'

Hakanu said nothing, but the young warrior's red ears spoke volumes.

Ahren sighed. 'We will study several pages together later,' he added in a gentler tone. 'Perhaps some knowledge will lodge in that head of yours which you seem intent on filling to the brim with stew.'

This was met with general laughter around the table, at which point Hakanu finally stopped stuffing his mouth with food, while the resultant lightening of the mood caused Ahren to suddenly see the things around him differently. The cabin didn't seem quite so confined and sweaty – instead, it was homely, inviting and filled with warmth.

The power of good friends, commented Culhen sagely, sending his now good-humoured friend an image of a sleeping pack of wolves, the animals all snuggled closely together.

Ahren smiled, sent his wolf a message of thanks, then concentrated on his food again, a giveaway shimmer near his bowl revealing the danger the contents of his bowl were suddenly in.

'Kamaluq!' he said sternly as he raised a finger. 'No!'

Caught in the act, the disguised Shimmer Fox jumped off the table and retreated under Hakanu's chair. The apprentice lovingly threw a lump of meat down, which immediately disappeared as the fox gobbled it up.

'Muai's and Culhen's bad influence on him have finally spoilt him for once and for all,' laughed Trogadon as he wiped breadcrumbs from his beard. 'The little fellow has made stealing food from everyone else into a permanent game.'

'He is only practising,' retorted Hakanu, jutting his chin forward belligerently. 'The longer he can remain in disguise, the better.'

'And as far as I can see, your fox is equally adept at justifying his bad behaviour as *our* companion animals,' interjected Falk with a chuckle, causing renewed laughter around the table.

Ahren saw, thanks to the light from the hurricane lamp, his erstwhile master's eyes glistening with tears, and the young Forest Guardian felt for him. Lanlion had intimated that he would head to the northernmost part of Jorath, while they were all journeying to the southernmost point of the known world. Selsena and Falk would then be as far apart from one another as was possible.

'Where are Palnah and Trimm, by the way?' asked Khara curiously once the laughter had subsided.

'Back in their cabin,' smiled Jelninolan.

Ahren raised an eyebrow in surprise. '*Again?*' He had hardly seen the newly rescued Paladin and his soul companion since the *Queen of the Waves* had left Gol-Konar.

'Or one might equally say, *still*,' muttered Uldini absently, his eyes still focused on his crystal ball.

'This is the first time in ages that they have been able to be together for an extended period,' interjected Hakanu. 'It is perfectly understandable that they long to be in each other's company.' Suddenly, one could hear a pin drop as all heads turned to stare at the boy, whose face once more took on a belligerent look.

'And what do you know about such matters, boy?' chuckled Trogadon, peering at the apprentice from beneath his bushy eyebrows.

'More than you all think,' replied the young warrior matter-of-factly. 'The tents of my tribe have thin walls.'

This was met with more laughter, and Ahren decided to change the subject. 'When will the first escort be with us?' he asked, turning to Uldini.

The Arch Wizard looked up from the orb for the first time. 'Two Eternal Empire warships should reach us in three days' time. The *Xuan-Foi* and the *Lady Aruti*.' The Ancient's statement was followed by a pregnant pause. 'I expect that we will have the first sightings of Dark Ones in five days.'

'As soon as one of the Adversary's servants catches sight of us, this voyage will immediately turn into an unpleasant enterprise,' murmured Falk. 'The Dark god will throw every maritime danger imaginable at us.

If he fails to stop us before we reach the Ice Fields, his worst fears may be realised.'

'Thirteen Paladins united to take on HIM, WHO FORCES,' said Ahren grimly. A shiver ran down his spine as he said the words, and the faces of his friends displayed a combination of awe, anxiety, and yearning. The Forest Guardian had dedicated much of his young life to finding and forging all the Paladins into a fighting force, but many around the table had been attempting to defeat the Dark god for aeons.

'Our voyage south will resemble smashing through a barricade,' commented Khara. 'Are we ready for the task?'

'Absolutely not,' countered Falk, his eyes narrowing. 'Hence, the escort. Moreover, we will dock in Men-Hark so that we can increase the crew of the *Queen of the Waves* and complete any repairs that cannot be done at sea.'

'And more ships will join us,' added Uldini. 'The nearer we approach the southern end of Jorath, the greater the resistance we can expect. If the Dark god wants to destroy our army with his servants, then a heavily armed flotilla will be our response.'

'Our next stop after Men-Hark will be Cape Verstaad,' explained Falk. 'Which is where we will equip ourselves for the expedition onto the Ice Fields.'

'Would it not make more sense to take on everything we need in Men-Hark and then sail *directly* to the Ice Fields?' asked Hakanu. 'By docking in Cape Verstaad, we will surely be inviting the Adversary to position another attack force of Dark Ones between us and our final destination.'

'Good thinking,' said Uldini approvingly before shaking his head. 'Alas, the equipment that we are going to need is not available in Men-Hark.' The Arch Wizard raised his right hand and used his fingers to list off his points. 'Most important will be an ice-breaker – a ship that can create a path for us through the pack ice. That will save us from having to trudge many leagues in the life-threatening cold. We also need to hire sorcerers and mercenaries who will support us on our journey into the eternal ice. There are more than enough of both in Cape Verstaad.' The Arch Wizard shrugged his shoulders. 'Also, we are going to need several moons' worth of provisions that are as fresh as possible, and we cannot leave Cape Verstaad before the spring, the winter temperatures in the Ice Fields being deadlier in winter than during the rest of the year.'

Ahren scratched his beard thoughtfully. 'Sounds considerably more challenging than any of the journeys we have undertaken thus far.'

'The weather itself will be our greatest enemy in the Ice Fields,' commented Falk. 'We must be well prepared for it.'

'Maybe Jelninolan could help us?' suggested Trogadon, looking at the elf. 'With a Blessing of the goddess, for example?'

'I'm sorry, darling,' said the priestess regretfully. 'Nature may protect us elves from considerable hardship, but I can tell you – based on the experiences my folk have endured in the Icy Vasts in the north of Eathinian – that it is quite a challenge for us to survive in such a bitterly cold region.'

'In other words, our route is settled – first, we head for Men-Hark, then to Cape Verstaad, and from there onto the Ice Fields,' said Khara, summarising their itinerary.

'Past hordes of Dark Ones,' added Hakanu, his eyes gleaming with exciting, which elicited a concerned sigh from Ahren.

The silence that followed was eventually broken by Trogadon slapping his large palms together. 'This sounds like enormous fun,' he said, grinning from ear to ear. 'I don't know what you lot think, but I'm sure that a good layer of winter fat wouldn't go amiss, along with plenty of extra clothing.' With that, he reached for the large pot of stew, causing Jelninolan to clear her throat crossly as she looked critically at the dwarf's waistline. 'What?' he asked innocently as he began to shovel spoonfuls of the meat and pea mixture down his throat. 'This is all for a good cause,' he mumbled once his mouth was full.

Again, merry laughter filled the little cabin, and for one glorious moment, all Ahren's concerns for the future were banished from his mind.

The new day greeted Ahren with the loud rhythmical thundering of enormous waves crashing against the prow of the ship. It seemed to the Paladin as if the compact cabin that he shared with Khara had been transformed into a drum, which was being beaten at regular intervals by a cumbersome, malignant giant, causing it to spring up and down with considerable force.

Ahren swung his legs out of the bed and rubbed his eyes. His tongue felt too big for his mouth and his ears seemed to be taking mischievous pleasure in magnifying the sound of the waves as they transmitted it into the Paladin's head.

'I should never have drunk the schnapps that Trogadon brought with him from Gol-Konar,' he murmured. A glance at the empty side of the rumpled berth told him that Khara was already up and about. He got to his feet with a groan, only to fall back onto the bed with the violent shudder of the next wave.

Why don't you creep out on all fours? suggested Culhen gleefully.

It was only now that Ahren noticed the presence of the wolf in his head, the animal having secretly observed the awakening of his friend.

It works for me at any rate.

Oh, you're so funny. Ahren tried to come up with a quick-witted response, only for the next wave to sweep away any possible creativity on his part as it slammed unmercifully against the ship. Painfully slowly, he made his was as far as the door, managing to get his hand on the copper handle when Culhen spoke again.

Ahren... said the wolf slowly. *Your trousers.*

Cursing, the Paladin reached down for the piece of clothing that was lying on the floor. He struggled into the garment and muttered. *Thank you.*

I'm only protecting myself, the wolf replied haughtily. *After all, it won't do my reputation any good at all to have my Paladin stumbling around on the deck of a warship dressed only in his underclothes.*

Ahren rubbed his face with his hands to bring some life into his features, then made his way to the deck. He passed Falk's cabin, knocking on the door as he did so, but all he could hear from behind the heavy wooden door was loud snoring.

'Some people have all the luck,' he muttered, shuffling onward while keeping one hand stretched sideways so that he could maintain his balance as the ship lurched wildly. Finally, he reached the ladder up to the deck, and as the Forest Guardian climbed up it, his head and neck were met by a refreshing, reinvigorating blast of cold air which helped to blow away the worst effects of the previous day's alcoholic consumption.

'Here he is,' said Khara cheerfully once Ahren was standing on the deck. Standing on the fo'c'sle and grinning broadly from behind Trogadon and Hakanu, she beckoned him to approach. Both dwarf and boy were sitting cross-legged on the wet planks, the Forest Guardian blinking at surprise at their near naked appearance. Muai and Culhen were lying nearby, gazing curiously at the pair.

'What, by the THREE, is going on here?' grumbled Ahren, stomping over to his friends. Enroute, he greeted the Ice Wolves and mariners in a friendly manner as they struggled to maintain the *Queen of the Waves'* southerly course in defiance of the high winds and roiling sea.

This is such fun, announced Culhen once Ahren had joined his companions. *You bipeds come up with the most amusing ideas.*

The wolf had rolled himself up into a ball of fur, Kamaluq's head peering up from the comfort of the wolf's soft stomach, where the fox had made himself secure and warm. The little fellow was whimpering and gazing at Hakanu, wide-eyed.

'Do I even *want* to know what's going on here?' asked Ahren as he beheld his friends.

Khara gave him a peck on the cheek, her eyes sparkling with delight, while both Hakanu and Trogadon turned their heads to look at him as they maintained their sitting position. The dwarf seemed relaxed, almost disengaged indeed, as he sat there in the cold wind, his skin bedewed with salt water, but Ahren's apprentice was shaking like a wind-tossed leaf on a tree in autumn. His lips were blue, his fingers looked frozen and incapable of gripping onto anything anymore, and Ahren was sure that he could see frost, glittering in the lad's hair.

'Thi...this is ho...ho...how dwa...dwarves ha...ha...harden themselves against the wi...wi...wi...winter,' stammered Hakanu, turning to face the wind again. 'And anywa...wa...way, it's suppo...supposed to be goo..good against ha...ha...hangovers.'

Ahren squirmed with silent pity as he heard the stubbornness and pride in the words of the young warrior – a pity mixed with a considerable amount of frustration, not to mention his own guilty conscience.

'Go inside *immediately* and put on the warmest clothing you can find!' bellowed Ahren, his shivering apprentice immediately getting to his feet and hurrying away. 'Then you will come back here, and I will ensure that you will soon be bathed in sweat!' he roared after the boy.

Hardly was the lad out of earshot when he spun around to Khara and Trogadon. 'What do you mean by this?' he hissed in a low voice. 'Do you want to kill Hakanu? You know how determined he can be. He could have frozen to death!'

Trogadon drew up his bushy eyebrows and raised an arm defensively. 'One must always handle the young Titejunanwas with care,' said the dwarf, as a particularly large wave crashed against the prow of the ship, showering everyone on the fo'c'sle with spray. He wiped the droplets from his beard before continuing: 'The boy saw me sitting here and was intent on trying out the hardening exercise himself.' Trogadon shrugged his shoulders as he smiled at the young Paladin. 'In view of our ultimate destination, I thought that it wouldn't do any harm if his body learned how to cope better with the bitter cold.'

'And his spirit is well aware of how dangerous the place that we are heading for may turn out to be,' added Khara, crossing her arms firmly before her chest. 'Your apprentice will surely challenge the very wind itself, should it dare to challenge him.'

Ahren could do nothing but let forth a groan that truly came from his heart. Hakanu's instinct to want to prove himself before the whole world, his innate fearlessness, and his tendency towards impulsive behaviour undoubtedly made him a worthy opponent for any Dark One that crossed his path – but it also presented a grave danger to his *own* life. 'By the THREE, this lad has the potential to become the most self-destructive Paladin of all time.'

Trogadon let forth a gravelly laugh before nonchalantly getting to his feet. 'I can think of *others* who in the past might well have laid claim to such a title,' he said with a twinkle in his eye as he peered at Ahren. 'Indeed, only a few days ago, there was a Paladin who insisted on offering his life to a child of the Dark god.'

One point for the dwarf, commented Culhen as he sent Ahren an image of the battle with the obsessive Reik Silvercape.

The Forest Guardian pursed his lips irritably. His attempts at sowing discord between the enslaved Gol-Konarian ruler and the mysterious child of the Adversary, who had taken up residence in the conceited man's mind had ended in failure, almost resulting in Ahren's own death. In light of this, Trogadon's playful criticism was not too far off the mark. Ahren's instincts often led to risky actions on the young man's part – mostly, they ended in success – but when they didn't, the consequences were often fatal.

'Still, your little wager with Hakanu could have ended in his suffering frostbite,' he grunted after a pause as he attempted to shift the focus of the conversation back to his apprentice.

Khara waved her hand dismissively. 'I was keeping a good eye on him – he was in no danger at all,' she said casually. 'Believe me, we shivered harder in the cells of the Arena – and were only too happy to squabble over a couple of measly blankets.'

Ahren frowned and pulled Khara in close to him. She rarely spoke of her experiences in the Guitu-Arena, and he knew only too well that it troubled her when memories of that time broke through to her conscious mind. She nodded gratefully and snuggled into him.

'Where are the others?' he asked Trogadon, who was putting his clothes back on with deliberate slowness while enjoying the furtive glances coming from the female mariners.

'Still having breakfast,' replied Trogadon, nodding towards the captain's cabin. 'I wasn't hungry earlier,' he said with a grin. 'But now my head is clear and my belly empty. Shall we go down?'

Ahren's own stomach grumbled audibly, but he shook his head. 'I'd love to – yet I must get Hakanu into a sweat first.'

'*I* can do that,' said Khara quietly. 'I need to stop thinking about my past, and as I didn't participate in your revelry last night, I've already had my breakfast.'

'Well now – I'd hardly call it revelry, for we lacked both good music and good food,' countered Trogadon firmly, his still-present grin visible from behind his bushy beard. 'What we had yesterday was good, old-fashioned wassailing amongst friends – no more than that.'

Khara gave him a long, cold stare.

'We'd better go in,' suggested Ahren, suppressing a chuckle.

The dwarf was already hurrying silently off the fo'c'sle.

'I trust that Hakanu, having narrowly escaped death by freezing, is not going to succumb to heatstroke through over-exertion?' he asked Khara in a low voice, as he slowly extricated himself from her embrace, one hand gently resting on her silken hair at the nape of her neck.

The shadow of her past that he had seen in her eyes now vanished under the influence of his gentle teasing, the Swordsmistress playfully placing a finger on her chin while she stared up at the cloud cover above. 'I can't promise anything,' she said sardonically. 'Put it this way – I won't let him try anything that *I* wouldn't do myself.'

Ahren gave her a farewell kiss before following Trogadon, who had already swung the door to the captain's cabin open and run directly into Jelninolan. The elf looked her beloved dwarf up and down before grinning knowingly. Then she silently straightened the chaotic braids on his beard before walking past him towards Ahren, with whom she was rather less conscientious.

'I see that you're back in the land of the living,' she murmured as he approached the doorway of the warm and inviting cabin, through which the Forest guardian could see Uldini, Trimm, Palnah, and Yantilla making room for the dwarf at the table, which was heavily laden with bowls and plates.

'Unlike Falk,' said Ahren with an apologetic grin as he tried to pass the elf, only for her to stop him with her hand.

'All of us are dealing with the trauma of Gol-Konar in our own way,' said the priestess in a low voice. 'Please make sure that Falk and Trogadon lay off the dice throwing so that yesterday's experience remains a one-off.'

Ahren nodded. The elf's warning jogged his memory and he replied: 'It seems to me that Khara's mood has been quite unpredictable ever since we sailed from the city of cutthroats,' he said furtively. 'One heartbeat she is remarkably carefree and cheerful, the next she is moody and taciturn.' He bit his lower lip, hesitated, then continued. 'Could *you* have a word with *her?*'

Jelninolan smiled and nodded. 'I am certain that it was the inescapable sleaziness of Gol-Konar prompting unpleasant memories of her childhood in captivity that has caused this. If it is something else, I will let you know.'

Ahren hugged the elf gratefully, only to be interrupted by Uldini's whining voice.

'Are you coming in or what?' grumbled the Arch Wizard loudly from inside the cabin. 'Close the door, anyway. It's getting cold in here.'

Jelninolan winked at Ahren in farewell, and the young Forest Guardian quickly entered the room before fulfilling Uldini's wish. The cabin was a welcome haven of warmth and homeliness after the icy wind and the penetrating cold of the sea spray on deck.

'What's on the menu for breakfast?' he asked, rubbing his hands – partly in joyful anticipation of food and partly to drive the icy feeling from his fingers.

'Oatmeal gruel and some other thing,' muttered Yantilla, the commander of the Ice Wolves. 'And I cannot decide which I despise more.'

Ahren's hands stopped above the pot that was fixed to the table. '*That bad?*' he asked.

'Gruel is *always* horrible,' said Uldini dryly. 'And the reports of the resistance that we are to encounter soon are leaving a similarly bad taste.'

'It seems that evermore Dark Ones are gathering in the waters that we are to traverse on our voyage south,' added Trimm. The corpulent Paladin seemed to shrink with every word he spoke. His fear was almost tangible. Only when Palnah silently took his hand in hers did he sit up straight again.

'I still think that we can reach Men-Hark without engaging in too bloody a skirmish,' announced Yantilla, giving Trimm a cool, sideways look. 'The wonderful thing about having an ocean as a battlefield is that it offers so many possibilities for evasive manoeuvres. Even thousands of Dark Ones can do little more than keep their eyes fixed on a mere fraction of the water. We will need little more than a pinch of good fortune and a soupçon of skilled boatmanship and, hey presto – we will have broken through the enemy line, where it is particularly vulnerable.'

Uldini rubbed his bald pate and narrowed his eyes. 'We could employ our two escort ships as baits and confuse the Dark Ones considerably before…'

'Absolutely not,' countered Ahren categorically, even before the Ancient had formulated the rest of his idea. 'No bait. The danger that the vessels will be scuppered by hordes of Dark Ones is too great. There is no way that I am going to sacrifice mariners so that we can avoid a fight.'

'In which case, we, too, might be scuppered,' murmured Trimm ruefully.

Ahren frowned as he looked down at the fearful Paladin. Then he forced himself to soften his features before speaking in a gentle voice: 'Take courage, brother. Where is the Paladin, who stabbed Reik in the heart with a dagger when all seemed lost.'

'He has regained his reason,' whispered Trimm with a shudder.

Ahren said nothing to that. It would clearly take some time before the man who had disguised himself as a grandee would finally shake off his past.

Hopefully not too long or the war will already be over, interjected Culhen, who was now transmitting some images to Ahren of a sweating Hakanu, who was undeniably suffering under Khara's strict training regime. It was clear that the Swordsmistress had come up with exercises in which the apprentice's spear played a central role. At this very moment, the boy had to climb up the long spear – which was vertically stuck into the ship's timbers – without either the weapon tipping to the side or the young warrior sliding down the smooth shaft. The physical tension involved would have even proven a challenge to Ahren. Smiling, he turned his attention back to the conversation within the cabin.

'How great is the possibility that Aluna and Fjolmungar will be with us again soon?' he asked hopefully.

Uldini shook his head. 'The sea serpent suffered numerous serious injuries during the battle of Gol-Konar. Fjolmungar needs time to recover.'

'Can sorcery help us?' wondered Ahren, now clearly clutching at straws.

Another shake of the head from Uldini. Yantilla sighed disapprovingly before speaking: 'The two Ancients must rest, too, following the skirmish in the city of cutthroats,' she said, staring disapprovingly at the childlike figure.

'Anyway, every charm that we cast will make our position easier to identify,' countered Uldini defensively. 'The Adversary is sufficiently awake to be able to follow any charm back to its source – especially, if it is being used against one of his servants.'

Ahren pricked up his ears. 'So, *smaller* magical rituals, performed with *great* caution and at considerable *distance* from Dark Ones will still be *possible*, right?'

Uldini nodded hesitantly. 'We'll see what Jelninolan and I can come up with.'

Ahren understood that the Arch Wizard was not going to commit himself any further, but the answer had satisfied the young man sufficiently. He helped himself to a bowl of gruel while he weighed their futures up in his mind. It would all come down to a mixture of luck, cunning, and skill for them to reach Men-Hark unscathed.

Impressive. Culhen's comment forced its way into Ahren's mind, the young Forest Guardian then looking through the eyes of his friend and concurring. With his muscles trembling, Hakanu was clutching the end of his barely swaying spear, whose tip was stuck between two planks. The boy's feet were pressing into the round Deep Steel from the side, while his closed hands were closed around the end of the weapon.

Hakanu's torso was stretched forward just far enough over the end of the spear for the young warrior to keep the rest of his body in a state of balance.

He looks like a pigeon sitting on top of a belltower, added Culhen, thoroughly amused. *What will happen, I wonder, if I suddenly howl loudly?*

Don't you dare! retorted Ahren sharply. He was too impressed by the achievement of his student to allow it to be destroyed by Culhen's antics. Hakanu, had even managed to compensate for the rocking of the ship, caused by the waves.

'Very nice.' Ahren heard Khara's words through the ears of the wolf. 'And you will maintain your position until the sun has moved two widths of a finger across the sky.'

Hakanu gasped, his body trembling with the tension. 'But…' he began in protest.

'No *buts*,' said Khara categorically and with enough steel in her voice to forge a Dwarfish war chariot. '*Feel* your weapon,' she said firmly. 'Acknowledge its movements so that you can adjust yourself before it comes to losing your balance.' She gripped Hakanu's waist and moved his torso forward a little. Ahren saw how the boy immediately relaxed and his eyes opened wide in surprise. 'Feel the *centre* that you and your spear are creating. If you remain true to this point of harmony, then nothing will upset your serenity or succeed in wearing you out,' she added, continuing her lesson. 'Once you have internalised these truths, you will understand how little strength is really needed to perfectly execute an action.'

Ahren was yanked from the scene on deck by the door to the captain's cabin opening, followed by the departure of Trogadon, Yantilla, and Uldini – to be replaced by a blast of cold air together with the entrance of Muai and Kamaluq. Ahren chuckled on seeing the tigress angle for a piece of meat that had been carelessly left hanging from a plate on the table, which she easily got with a swipe of her paw, immediately dropping it in front of the Shimmer Fox's nose before attending to her own food. The young companion animal whimpered loudly in gratitude, then set about consuming the tigress's gift, the big cat looking down approvingly with her agate-coloured eyes as she guarded the little fellow, who was now gulping down the large chunk of meat.

'She has lived for such a long time and yet only *now* is she a mother – spiritually, at any rate,' murmured Palnah in a voice that was little more than a whisper.

'What was that?' asked the Forest Guardian, but already the Brajah had sprung up and was whooshing out of the cabin, her head bowed.

'Please, forgive me,' she said to Muai in a low voice. Then she slipped through the door, which was slightly ajar, closing the heavy hatch behind her.

'She didn't mean to hurt your feelings,' said Trimm. 'Her gift is to see things that others would prefer to hide – from themselves, mostly.'

'I can see how dangerous and powerful such an ability must be,' mused Ahren before pointing at Muai. 'And how unwelcome such truths must often be to the recipient.'

Trimm forced himself to smile. 'I think that the reason why she remained with Reik for so long was because he never gave the feeling that her gift was a curse. No matter how bad the truth was or how devastating the deception that Palnah uncovered, he accepted her unconditionally.'

Ahren couldn't but hear the pain in his opposite number's voice. 'Do not believe for a heartbeat that you are worth any less than that lunatic who held Palnah captive in a cave of attraction, borne out of sheer self-interest. He *used* her, and that was the only reason for his loving her.'

Trimm shrugged his shoulders awkwardly. 'You have no idea how it is with people who think little of themselves or their abilities. What others regard as a crumb, we consider a feast for the ages.'

Ahren pursed his lips. He had never heard anything so sad in his life. 'I am firmly convinced that you and Palnah will be able to show each other what true love really is. And that you will both understand your true value to the world.'

Trimm gazed into Ahren's eyes, immediately recognising a wild yearning. 'You are able to resurrect dreams that have long since been deemed dead,' he whispered over the sounds of the cabin walls creaking. 'Is *this* your secret? Is that why all Paladins follow you?'

Ahren shrugged his shoulders, thoroughly taken aback by the corpulent fellow's question.' 'Maybe,' he said, after a considerable pause. 'I am so much younger than the rest of you,' he added in a feeble attempt at explaining the situation. 'I believe that in this way I can remind you of many memories that have been buried over the course of your long lives.' Ahren nodded towards the door, and in that way vaguely at the still balancing Hakanu, whom Culhen had been observing with a mixture of disbelief and paternal pride for a considerable time now. 'Hakanu, too, has done me a similar service. We all need someone from time to time who can remind us of the person that we truly want to be.' He fixed his eyes earnestly on Trimm. 'Or the person that we *must* become, if the circumstances so require.'

'You mean, a Paladin rather than a grandee?' Trimm's voice was more of a plaintive cry than a normal question.

Ahren nodded thoughtfully. 'You must become a Paladin for a while, so that you can return to being a grandee later,' he said in a gentle voice. 'In the same way that I must be Paladin, before returning to the simple life of a Forest Guardian at some point in the future.'

Trimm nodded, his plump face now drawn and weary. He said nothing, Ahren then placing a reassuring hand on the man's shoulder. The two Paladins sat there in silence. They listened to the ship, to the waves, and to the calls of the sailors, while with every heartbeat that passed, the *Queen of the Waves* brought them farther and farther south, closer and closer to the next inevitable skirmish – where both Ahren and Trimm would have to fight side-by-side as Champions of the gods.

Chapter 2

The clouds had disappeared, but there was still a blustery wind when Ahren returned to the fo'c'sle where Jelninolan was teaching Hakanu various strike and thrust combinations, with Khara looking on serenely.

'You need to place your right foot further forward, otherwise the weight won't be evenly distributed,' said the elf in a severe tone.

'But I...' began Hakanu, only for Jelninolan to deftly whip the back of the apprentice's left knee with a speed that even took Ahren by surprise. The attack was not particularly forceful but was so fast that the young warrior's leg immediately gave way, his poor posture having been suitably punished.

Jelninolan twirled her staff swiftly around her hips, her weapon now whizzing towards the unprotected neck of the stumbling Paladin, where it came to a sudden halt a hair's breadth from his artery.

'That's enough for today,' she said, the corners of her mouth turned down with irritation. 'I am exhausted and in no mood for any more *back* talk.' As she walked past Ahren, she murmured, 'by the Three, he is *so* stubborn. The more he learns, the more difficult it is to teach him anything – he is so sure that he knows *everything* better.'

Ahren squeezed her arm in a gesture of compassion as she pushed past him, only for her to pause a heartbeat later.

'I had a word with Khara,' she whispered. 'Gol-Konar is indeed weighing her down – as it is us all.'

Ahren scratched his beard thoughtfully. 'Maybe it would be a good idea for everyone to stretch their legs once we get to Men-Hark. In that way, we will remind ourselves how daily life goes on in a civilised environment.'

'Well, I'd certainly like to stroll through the town,' chuckled the elf. 'I'm pretty sure that there will be enough time for that while the *Queen of the Waves* is being repaired.' She gave the young man a warm smile and departed.

'What were you two whispering about?' asked Khara curiously, once Ahren had stepped between her and his apprentice, who was now resting. Hakanu looked somewhat misshapen, his master then realising that the young warrior was now wearing *two* layers of clothing.

'We were discussing how we could free ourselves from the shadow of Gol-Konar, which is hanging over all of us,' he said evasively. Then he pointed down at Hakanu. 'Did my comment on possible heatstroke inspire you or why is he wearing so many garments?' he joked.

Khara grinned at him. 'My idea was that he should learn how to fight while wearing cumbersome gear,' she said. 'Once we are in the Ice Fields, all those who do *not* possess a magical cloak will have to dress warmly. Which will make us more awkward than we usually are.'

'Everyone keeps overestimating this garment,' said Ahren, rubbing his neck. 'During the siege of Hjalgar, I froze as much as anyone whenever my arms and legs were exposed.'

Khara looked at him severely. 'And therein lies its blessing. Where mere mortals require a blazing fire to warm themselves, all you need to do is to wrap yourself up in your cloak.'

'I think it would be no harm for me, too, to learn how to fight in heavy layers of clothing,' mused Ahren. 'Acquiring new skills never does any harm.'

'Good,' said Khara, satisfied. 'Then you can start by going through some training moves with Hakanu.'

Ahren quickly hurried below deck and put on more clothes. From the mariners' common room nearby, he could hear cursing coming from the sailors, combined with Falk's and Trogadon's triumphant laughter and the intermittent sounds of dice being rolled. Shaking his head, he awkwardly made his way back up, now trapped within what felt like armour several sizes too small for him, which was making it *very* difficult for him to move his limbs.

Khara's broad grin spoke volumes. 'Very nice,' she commented. 'The first thing I want the two of you to do is to attempt a practise skirmish, which will give you the chance to adapt your moves to the layers of clothing.'

Slowly and carefully, Ahren and Hakanu circled each other, eyeing one another suspiciously while wielding their weapons awkwardly. Ahren's heart sank at the realisation that his companions would additionally have to wear thick mittens once they were all in the Ice Fields!

He began with simple attack moves, giving the boy sufficient time to parry or evade the blows.

'It's a bit like training in water,' said Hakanu. The apprentice, for his part, went on the attack at the first opportunity. He concentrated mainly on a variety of thrusts – an approach which seemed, given the heavy clothing, the best option as far as the apprentice was concerned.

Ahren let one of his student's thrusts slip past him before stepping up to Hakanu, his Wind Blade pressed close against his own body but ready to stab. 'You're dead,' he said firmly.

Hakanu's face displayed a mixture of defiance and helplessness.

'You need to *vary* things more – even if this is difficult in your constrained situation.' announced Khara. '*Again!*'

The sun began to descend from its zenith while master and pupil continued to practise, their session punctuated by short breaks and good advice from the Swordsmistress.

'How come *you* know so much about fighting in layers of clothing?' asked Ahren after she had announced a new intermission. The sweat was streaming down his body, and he was sorely tempted to strip off the inhibiting layers of cloth and leather.

'There was one year in the Arena when I was forced to train in padded clothing,' responded Khara absently. 'I was still too inexperienced to avoid being wounded in skirmishes by sharp weapons, but already valuable enough for my captors to realise that it would be a complete waste of time and resources for me to be killed without the attendance of paying spectators.'

Having heard her words, Ahren was on the point of comforting the Swordsmistress, only to be taken aback by the action of his apprentice – as indeed Khara herself was – if the expression on her face was anything to go by – for the boy had embraced her impulsively and was squeezing her hard.

'Nothing like that will *ever* happen to you again,' he promised. 'Master Ahren and I will look after you from now on.'

Khara blinked slowly as she looked at Ahren over Hakanu's shoulder, the boy still clinging to her like a limpet. The Forest Guardian had to stop himself from laughing out loud, while struggling at the same time with his emotions. Whatever faults his young protégé had, the boy certainly possessed a good heart – something which didn't, however, save the lad from suddenly being flung through the air, Khara having ended the unexpected embrace with a rather impressive throw. Still, the lad didn't scream in surprise – another point in his favour as far as Ahren was concerned.

'I appreciate your offer, but for the moment, Ahren and I will continue to look after *you*,' chuckled Khara as she looked at the apprentice, 'but I *am* looking forward to the day when the situation will reverse itself.' Then she helped the boy, now sprawled on his back, to his feet.

'Should we call it a day?' asked Ahren, taking a swig of water from a flask. He pointed over at Muai, Kamaluq, and Culhen, who were snuggled up together, having dozed throughout the whole afternoon. 'Even our companion animals have given up peppering our minds with sarcastic comments.'

You move about like a gouty tortoise, replied Culhen sleepily, the wolf not having found the energy to put much effort into his critical insight, which he had repeated often enough over the recent past.

Ahren grinned. 'Culhen is unable to come up with new barbs, it seems.'

'One last practise fight,' Khara decided after some rumination, during which time she had been absently playing with her bracelet, which was singing in Ahren's head like the distant call of an anxious mother. 'The winner gets to rest, while the loser must keep training until the sun goes down over the yardarm.'

Hardly had Khara spoken when Hakanu's spear was already flying towards Ahren. The young master only managed to evade the attack because the boy had chosen his favourite opening gambit. Ahren squinted before going directly on the offensive. Strike, push, feint, jink…he used his entire repertoire to force the boy into submission, Hakanu's youthful exuberance compensating for his lack of experience. Ahren knew that he could win the fight by simply tiring the lad out – but he plumped in the end for a different, *invaluable* lesson.

Culhen, was all he said, transmitting his idea to the wolf.

His friend immediately awakened from his semi-conscious state and lifted his nose. Then he uttered a howl so terrifying and loud that one of the mariners tumbled down onto the deck from the shrouds in shock. Hakanu's immediate reaction was to flinch and glance over at the animal, Ahren then expertly placing the edge of his Wind Blade to the boy's throat.

'*Always* expect the unexpected,' he said with a grin. 'Nimble in mind, nimble in body.' Falk had frequently drummed the same saying into Ahren's head, and the young Forest Guardian was determined to sear the same knowledge into his own enthusiastic student's mind.

His apprentice looked up at him wide-eyed, seemingly shocked at his master's willingness to perform such a dastardly trick. But when Kamaluq leaped up in a blinding flash of light and whined belligerently, Ahren understood immediately that Hakanu had turned the tables with impressive, not to mention breath-taking speed.

Ahren heard first Hakanu spinning away from the weapon at his throat, then the whizzing of the spear. The young master quickly performed a backward roll while still trying to orientate himself. The furious Culhen, too, had been blinded and was unable to assist.

Ahren rolled back onto his feet, using his other senses to try and figure out where Hakanu was positioned. Khara offered him a fixed point, for he could sense where *she* was through her bracelet – which seemed to act as a kind of lighthouse for the God's blessing within him.

Following his intuition, Ahren concentrated on this feeling of connectedness, trying to explore it as best he could. The bracelet was singing mysteriously to him, and, as the morning drops of dew glistening on the taut lines of a spider's web reveal its existence, so too did Ahren's awareness of the presence of one, then two, and finally *all* the Paladins on board the ship slowly manifest itself.

He sensed the fearful Trimm, lying in the arms of Palnah within their cabin, he picked up on Falk's frustration, the older Forest Guardian combating his boredom and inner unease by mechanically involving himself in a never-ending game of dice, and finally he located the cockiness of Hakanu, the lad being directly behind him and certain of victory, with his spear at the ready and on the point of forcing his master to surrender.

The Forest Guardian performed another backward roll, a move that caused him to pass by his surprised apprentice, before quickly standing up directly behind the boy. Still with his eyes closed, he pressed his Wind Blade against the apprentice's throat once more.

'I win!' he exclaimed triumphantly.

'But...how...? stammered the young warrior, dropping his spear.

Ahren opened his eyes reluctantly, for they were still streaming with tears. Then he pointed at Khara's bracelet forged from Elven Phantasm.

'I don't quite know *how*, but in some mysterious way I can sense the gods' Blessings of all the Paladins in the vicinity. All I need to do is concentrate on Uldini's and Jelninolan's wedding gift.'

Khara stared down at the piece of jewellery on her wrist and blinked in surprise. 'I thought only *I* could do that,' she said, bemused.

Hakanu frowned before staring at the others, wide-eyed. '*I* can sense them too,' he whispered. 'Falk is now coming up the ladder, and Trimm…Trimm can feel something, too, I think.'

Falk's confused face appeared from below, and the door of the captain's cabin was flung open.

'What is going on out here?' demanded Uldini roughly as he floated towards them quickly, followed by the clearly curious Jelninolan. 'Someone here is weaving a charm net of extraordinary delicacy.'

'Why are two *blackguards* and this good-for-nothing Trimm tormenting my mind?' asked Falk grimly, having arrived on the fo'c'sle. 'And why are the two of you dressed up like a pair of second-rate strolling players who, not knowing what costume to put on next have resorted to dressing in *all* your disguises before performing your next – no doubt ludicrous –sketch?'

Blackguards, interjected Culhen gleefully. *That's a good description.*

Ahren decided to ignore the cantankerous old man for the moment, turning to Uldini and Jelninolan instead. 'It is Khara's bracelet. It seems to ensure that each of us can sense the others' gods' Blessing.'

The first of the Ancients looked at the elf in surprise, the priestess merely shrugging her shoulders.

'All *we* knew was that the bracelet would enable Khara to harness the unconscious calling that is transmitted between all the Paladins.' She took Khara's hand and looked thoughtfully down at the little treasure. 'I never thought for a moment that it would form a filigree charm net *between* the Blessings.'

Ahren could sense Falk's irritation even before he saw it written on the old man's face. 'Can you somehow direct it?' asked old man irritably, nodding towards Ahren and Hakanu as he did so. 'I worry enough about those two without them literally *haunting* me in my mind.'

'Khara, what exactly happened when the charm net materialised?' asked Uldini.

The Swordsmistress pondered for some heartbeats before responding. 'Ahren and Hakanu were practising close combat fighting. Then Ahren encouraged Culhen to utter a terrifying howl…'

'Thank you for that,' interjected Trogadon cheerfully, having joined the group of onlookers that was gathering around the Paladins. 'My heart almost stopped at the shock of it.'

'…then Hakanu got his revenge by commanding Kamaluq to cause a blinding flash of light,' continued Khara.

The young fox reacted to the sound of his name by becoming visible again – creating another sudden impulse of piercing light into the bargain. This was immediately followed by groans and curses while those present rubbed their aching eyes.

'The next one to perform a magic trick without permission will spend the following day as a tadpole in a used chamber pot,' growled Uldini threateningly once everyone was able to see again. Kamaluq quickly retreated with a terrified whine behind Hakanu, who didn't move a muscle, so fearful was the young boy. 'Continue!' barked the Arch Wizard, glaring at Khara.

'I, as everyone here can now fully understand, was blinded, and tried to orientate myself. It felt as though Ahren was silently calling me somehow and that the piece of jewellery was…*responding?*' She scratched her head uncertainly. 'I really don't know how to put it any better. After that, I simply knew where every Paladin on board was situated.'

'How exciting!' exclaimed Jelninolan. 'Uldini and I understood that it would take some time for the charm bracelet forged from Elven Phantasm to attune itself to you, but never in our wildest dreams did we imagine that it could create an autonomous charm net capable of linking up all Paladins in its immediate field of influence.'

'It's perfectly logical when you think about it,' mused Uldini. 'The gods' Blessings are instinctively drawn to one another so that they can join forces. After all, only when all thirteen Paladins combine in one unit, will they prove powerful enough to defy the Adversary once and for all. Our little gift has the function of a lighthouse, helping them to find each other.' He turned the palms of his hands upwards, a self-satisfied look on his childlike face. 'It is the Blessings themselves that create their own charm net thanks to their constant connection to Khara's bracelet, which provides the stable core.'

'All well and good,' countered Falk impatiently. 'All this arcane slapping on the back still hasn't answered my question – can one switch the damn thing off?' he tapped his temple in annoyance. 'I'm not going to get a wink of sleep with those three as clouds of light floating inside my head.'

Jelninolan smiled at Khara. 'See if you can suppress the searching feeling that the bracelet is emitting within you,' she suggested.

Khara closed her eyes, Ahren immediately understanding from her relaxed state that she had temporarily slipped into Pelneng. Immediately, the connection to her and the Paladins was broken.

'Oh, no,' said Hakanu sadly. 'Now it suddenly feels strangely empty in my head.'

'No surprise there,' quipped Trogadon, the rest of the onlookers immediately bursting into laughter.

Ahren, however, silently agreed with his apprentice. It *had* been a comforting feeling, sensing the presence of the other Paladins.

Well, if you ask me, it was nothing other than a very loud cacophony, announced Culhen. *Your head is unbelievably chaotic – even without the echoing of the other Paladin Blessings.*

The first mate shouted out his orders in no uncertain terms, and the mariners went back to their work, except for the unfortunate fellow who had fallen from the shrouds at Culhen's howl and whose badly bruised ribs Jelninolan was now treating. Trogadon and Falk retired to below deck again, while Uldini used *Flamestar* to further examine Khara's bracelet. Among the general hubbub, Ahren couldn't help but notice Trimm in particular, the unfortunate man staring out onto the ocean, his face suggesting that he had just been deprived of something very dear to him. Palnah was standing by his side, comforting him with soothing words. Ahren approached them both and peered quizzically at the corpulent fellow.

'What is bothering you?' the Forest Guardian asked uncertainly. 'Were you not able to sense us?'

'Oh, I *was*,' countered Trimm, close to tears. His words were little more than a whisper. 'I was so *close* to all of you. It was wonderful.' He swallowed hard. 'And now it is over.' Then he turned stiffly and walked away, Palnah still by his side.

Ahren watched his fellow Paladin with pity as the corpulent man disappeared below deck. The unfortunate fellow's fate had ensured that

Trimm's lot was to suffer in his role as Champion of the gods, while the scorn shown to him by the other Paladins had only increased his feeling of being ostracised – a feeling which had already established itself because of his natural cowardice. Perhaps this moment of having sensed his connection to Falk, Hakanu, and Ahren had been the first time in Trimm's life that he had truly believed himself to be an accepted and equal part of the Paladin federation.

Night came quickly following the event-filled day. Uldini had suggested that Khara and the Paladins spend the following few days practising with the Blessing Band – his new name for the piece of jewellery, which they now knew bound the Champions of the gods together. Following this advice, the companions had settled down and discussed their new discovery. Ahren's attempts to hold a conversation with Trimm came to naught, however, the troubled Paladin having locked himself inside his cabin.

Taking Culhen's advice, Ahren had decided to give the corpulent Champion of the gods some time alone, and now the Forest Guardian was standing on the deck of the *Queen of the Waves*, enjoying the peace and quiet that the evening had blessed the ocean with. The gusty wind had abated somewhat, the wavelets were lapping gently against the vessel, and although there was already a nip in the air, heralding the onset of autumn, it was simply too pleasant for Ahren to retire inside. Most of the sailors were at supper, so that the ship seemed deserted. Ahren was resting his arms on the fo'c'sle railing with his face against the breeze, enjoying the cool, clear peace, which was soothing him from within himself. Gol-Konar was drifting further and further away, something which pleased Ahren no end.

Then he heard a familiar voice from behind: 'Shouldn't you be eating with the others, Thirteenth?'

'Soon,' replied Ahren without turning to look. 'The same question applies to you, commander.'

'I am not hungry,' countered Yantilla, now standing beside him and mirroring his pose at the railing. 'I will neither eat nor sleep until I have the comforting sight of two warships accompanying us, one port and one starboard.' She paused for a heartbeat before continuing. 'You *do* realise that we might encounter Dark Ones at any moment? And that the *Queen of the Waves* has suffered damage invisible to the untrained eye, but so extensive that our depleted crew are tearing their hair out wondering what they can do?'

Ahren nodded. 'Our escorts will soon be joining us. The sense of loyalty, not to mention the obsession with duty common to the inhabitants of the Eternal Empire will ensure such an outcome.'

'And if the *Xuan-Foi* and the *Lady Aruti* have been sunk?' asked Yantilla doubtfully.

'Then Men-Hark will dispatch two more warships to accompany us,' said Ahren confidently. 'Sending us into the Ice Fields without escorts would dishonour those responsible for the Eternal Empire fleet. Heads would roll, whole families would be disgraced if we were left to fend for ourselves.' Out of the corner of his eye, he saw Yantilla shudder.

'Quin-Wa has created a truly strict regime.'

Ahren shrugged his shoulders. 'It has its strengths and weaknesses. Like every realm that I have encountered thus far.' He glanced quickly at Yantilla. 'What *really* brings you to me?' he asked gently. 'You could just as easily be looking out for distant ships from the aft deck.'

An extended period of silence followed, Ahren taking advantage of the time that Yantilla needed to mentally check in on Culhen. The wolf was sitting in the captain's cabin grooming Kamaluq with his tongue. Or at least the top half of the fox, who was now soaking wet, Muai having taken on the task of cleaning the little fellow from the tail up. It seemed that the two companion animals were involved in yet another contest, and their unofficial protégé was bathing in its consequences – quite literally.

Stop it now, scolded Ahren, his tone affectionate, however. *If the pair of you keep carrying on like this, the little fellow won't have any fur left by tomorrow.*

But it's Muai who won't stop, grumbled the wolf. *If I give up now, she wins.*

NOW, Culhen! Ahren's command was sufficiently blunt for his friend to pull in his tongue.

Muai purred contentedly and carried on grooming for a couple of heartbeats before releasing the mightily relieved fox from her care, the animal squeaking his delight.

Ahren saw how Culhen looked challengingly at a large piece of dried meat before making a charge for it, immediately followed by Muai, the two of them setting about to devour it from either end. It seemed that the next contest was already under way. Ahren wondered in all seriousness how the pair of them would last several moons at sea without driving each other completely mad, not to mention everyone else on board.

Finally, Yantilla spoke from beside him. 'Is he doing alright, I wonder?' asked the woman. 'Lanlion, I mean.'

It was now Ahren's turn to say nothing for a while before he finally replied: 'Why wouldn't he be?'

'He wants to travel across the country, and only the gods know where to – and I mean that literally!' she exclaimed.

Ahren supressed a smile. His tactic of remaining silent had worked. 'He can look after himself,' he said in as neutral a tone as possible.

'He is a *Bloodless*, damn it!' exclaimed Yantilla, pounding her fist on the railing. 'If he is recognised by the wrong people, he will have a mob chasing him down in no time at all. Or if he becomes thirsty, and goes astray, then...'

'I thought you liked to keep your life and loves simple,' interjected Ahren, stopping the commander's tirade in mid-flow as he raised his eyebrows and looked at her.

Her response was an impatient snort. '*Someone* has to take care of this melancholic numbskull if *you* won't,' she retorted.

Ahren decided that he had strung the commander of his personal guards along for long enough. 'You forget the two Titejunanwas that are accompanying him,' he said reassuringly. 'Haminul is a four-legged force of nature, while Selsena is wise enough to keep the three of them clear from any serious trouble.' He turned to the woman with the ash-blonde hair and placed a hand on her shoulder. 'The gods themselves have summoned Lanlion. How could he possibly turn *them* down?' He shrugged his shoulders casually. 'I am absolutely convinced that the stars that are accompanying them on their journey are positively aligned.'

Yantilla's face was the picture of chagrin as she looked at him. Ahren couldn't tell whether this was down to her concern for the welfare of the pale Paladin, who was growing physically more distant from her with every heartbeat, or whether she was furious with herself for thinking about Lanlion despite herself. The ex-mercenary was a complicated woman – that much was certain.

'Speaking of lucky stars,' said Ahren, squeezing her shoulder and grinning, 'why don't you look over there?' He nodded towards the east, where two tiny, dancing points of light had become visible on the horizon. 'If my eyes aren't deceiving me, those are the beacons on the main masts of two impressively large ships.'

'And about bloody time,' grunted Yantilla, clearly relieved. 'At least I'll get *some* sleep tonight.'

The promise that the two night-time beacons had suggested was more than fulfilled by the sight that greeted the travellers the following day. Ahren and his companions stood on the deck of the *Queen of the Waves* and looked in astonishment from the *Xuan-Foi* to the *Lady Aruti* and back.

We're all going to get cricks in our necks, commented Culhen.

The wolf was no less impressed than the others by the enormous warships, whose railings began a good four paces higher than the top of the *Queen of the Wave's* railing. The vessels had evidently been recently built. Never had Ahren seen ships of such magnitude. Each possessed an iron dragon's head jutting forth from the prow of its steel-reinforced keel, and Ahren was convinced that the elaborately decorated figureheads were designed for ramming enemy ships or larger Dark Ones. Smaller Dragon Bows were mounted on both sides of the vessels, while three enormous sails, each carrying the symbol of the Empress Cherry, billowed in the freshening wind. Dozens of sailors were going about their work on the escort ships, busily keeping the floating giants on course.

'Am I the only one here who thinks that bigger is *not* necessarily always better?' murmured Trogadon, tugging sceptically at the braids on his beard. 'Does anyone else feel that these two swimming soup bowls are just that *little* bit over the top?'

Falk sighed gloomily. 'Ships of this size were built once before during the Dark Days,' he said sadly. 'Those Grinder Ships were too unwieldy, and it only took medium-strength storms to capsize them.'

'*Tusk* Ships,' countered Uldini, correcting the old man. 'They were called Tusk Ships – on account of the tusks that jutted out of them at the prow with which they could gore Dark Ones.'

'Oh, yes – I think you're right,' murmured Jelninolan. 'Isn't it true that only two dozen of them were ever built?'

Uldini nodded.

'Let's *not* say that to the two captains, shall we?' asked Khara dryly, nodding down at the two dinghies that were being lowered into the water, each occupied by bodyguards surrounding a straight-backed figure in full dress uniform.

'The question is – why did Quin-Wa commission the construction of such monstrosities?' asked Trimm. 'She's old enough to remember the capsizing of the Tusk Ships.'

'Quin-Wa often does things that *she* thinks are right – because she is a know-it-all,' muttered Uldini. Ahren was unable to suppress a smile as he saw Khara look daggers at the Arch Wizard.

'I'm more interested in finding out what sort of cages those are on their main masts,' said Hakanu, using his spear to point at the upper third of the soaring wooden poles, both painted with tar and a good two paces in width.

Ahren spotted a small, copper-coloured box at the height of the top cross brace, with a tiny hole on one side resembling a dungeon window. He thought he could make out a reddish flickering from within it.

'This light reminds me of something,' he murmured. 'But *what*?' Suddenly, Trimm shouted in surprise.

'Elves!' he shouted. 'I swear I've just seen some *Wrath* Elves peering over the railing!'

'Of course!' exclaimed Uldini, slapping his forehead with the flat of his hand. 'This light that we see in the boxes – we know it from Dhalvantil.'

'*Blood Magic*,' whispered Khara. 'They are using Blood Magic to imitate the very sorcery that the Wrath Elves used to keep the Dark Ones at bay.'

'These are no warships,' said Uldini after pondering for some heartbeats. 'They are floating fortresses – resting places for the corvettes that will be doing the real fighting.'

Trogadon shook his head, his eyes reflecting his puzzlement. 'These charm lights only function effectively at night. They have hardly any effect during the day.'

Falk shrugged his shoulders. 'The most calamitous attacks on the high seas are the ones that one cannot see. If one can sleep peacefully during the hours of darkness and if one only has to contend with the enemy during daylight – well, that must be worth *something*.'

'I never thought I'd ever see the sorcery of the Wrath Elves on the navy vessels of the Eternal Empire – ships which have further been equipped with Dwarfish Dragon Bows,' said Uldini in wonderment as he floated over to Ahren. He placed a hand on the surprised Paladin's shoulder and squeezed it gently. 'The alliance of the different races is really functioning – much better, indeed, than during the Dark Days. Congratulations, my boy.'

Ahren suddenly felt a lump on his throat and was struggling to respond, but already Uldini had floated away and was greeting the first of the two captains to ascend the rope ladder that had been lowered over the railing for them.

'Enjoy the moment while it lasts,' murmured Falk with a wink from beside him. 'Uldini has handed out his annual rations of laurels in one go.'

Ahren could hear the pride in his erstwhile master's voice, and he quickly cleared his throat. 'We should join the captains,' he said, walking quickly away while surreptitiously wiping a tear from his eye.

My Paladin! announced Culhen proudly, the wolf leaping towards Ahren before walking majestically beside the young man, all the while enjoying the looks of amazement from the neighbouring vessels. *I always knew that you would eventually amount to something.*

'Did my master *really* unite all the peoples of Jorath?' asked Hakanu excitedly from behind – clearly having no time for discretion.

'He *did* have *help*,' laughed Khara.

'A *lot* of help,' added Trogadon with a chuckle.

'Not to mention plenty of *luck*,' concluded Falk.

Suddenly, Ahren was only too happy to be fulfilling the responsibility of greeting a naval captain from the Eternal Empire and exchanging formalities with him, for Hakanu's innocent question had provoked a barrage of mocking commentary from the Forest Guardian's so-called friends.

The man, who had now turned to look at him, was bald, had high cheekbones, and his face was so tanned and leathery that it almost appeared like an ill-fitting mask. He peered momentarily at Ahren with his pale-green, intelligent eyes, then looked past him before bowing low before Khara and speaking humbly to her in the Imperial tongue.

'May good fortune ever be by your side, Your Highness,' said the man in a raw voice, which was well-accustomed over the decades to shouting out orders over the roar of storm-tossed waves. He bowed again before Muai, the big cat slinking easily past Culhen, whose nose was now very much out of joint as the feline sunned herself in the captain's admiring look.

'Many thanks, captain,' said Khara with a polite nod as she positioned herself beside Ahren. 'As you can see, I have all the luck that I need *very* close by my side.'

Ahren grinned as the man pretended that it was only now that he had seen the Paladin.'

'Greetings to you, too, Prince Consort,' he said with a curt bow, then straightening up, pounding his chest sharply, and standing to attention. 'Captain Soe-Anum here to serve the assembled dignitaries and generals. The *Xuan-Foi* has arrived and will immediately act as escort to the *Queen of the Waves.*'

'Thank you, captain,' said Khara in reply. 'Please remember that we maintain protocol *unobtrusively* aboard this ship.'

The old man blinked in surprise, Ahren realising that his opposite number found it difficult to comprehend Khara's announcement.

The Swordsmistress sighed and dismissed him with a wave of her hand. 'That will be all, Captain.'

Soe-Anum saluted again, bowed twice, and retreated silently to the railing before descending the rope ladder to the dinghy.

'A traditionalist of the worst kind,' murmured Khara, linking arms with Ahren. 'I am sure that he only acknowledged you to be my consort because you are a Paladin. Otherwise, he would never have accepted an *Altuan* by *my side.*'

'A *what*?' asked Hakanu from behind them.

'An *Altuan*,' repeated Ahren. 'A person who is not native to the Eternal Empire.'

'Oh, right,' said the boy, his eyes darting from left to right and back again. 'And who were the generals that he was talking about?'

Ahren shifted uneasily before responding. 'Each Paladin is simultaneously a general. This is what has legally been agreed to by the signatories in our alliance – which gives *us* full command over any and every troop that we might need in the field of battle.'

Hakanu's eyes widened in surprise.

You shouldn't have told him, commented Culhen.

I know, said Ahren with a sigh. *But I couldn't hide the truth from him either.*

'You mean, *I* am a *general?*' asked Hakanu with such exuberance in his tone that Ahren inwardly winced. His apprentice pointed at the mariners on the ship. 'I can order them around the place now?'

'Theoretically, yes,' said Falk curtly as he gave Ahren a warning look.

'If you do so much as order a jug of water from one of them, I will instruct Uldini to place a curse on your vocal cords – do I make myself clear?' hissed Ahren as he stared darkly at the apprentice.

The latter's enthusiasm collapsed faster than a badly baked cake. 'Yes, Master,' he muttered sulkily.

'You want me to cast a spell on this fellow then?' asked Uldini, looking at Ahren with his arms folded and one eyebrow raised playfully.

'Leave the teasing for later,' murmured Jelninolan. 'Here comes the captain of the *Lady Aruti.*'

Ahren looked over at the far side of the deck, spotting a small, delicately built woman, who was wearing the same ceremonial uniform as Soe-Anum, but with an elegance that bordered on nonchalance. He saw a Warrior Pin glittering in her shiny black hair, while her general posture and the way that she held her head left him in no doubt that she came from a noble family. She approached the companions, stopped a respectful distance away and bowed low before those present.

'Captain Konitu at your service, assembled dignitaries – the *Lady Aruti* is in position and ready to act as escort.' The woman's voice was like smooth silk, beneath which a sharp knife lay hidden. As she straightened up, her piercing, grey-blue eyes keenly examined those opposite her with a speed that suggested a lively intelligence.

'Welcome aboard,' said Khara.

'Shall we dispense with the usual formalities?' asked Konitu, the others nodding their agreement with relief.

Ahren immediately relaxed. 'Excellent. I was afraid we were going to spend the next few weeks getting bogged down in questions of protocol every time we'd have a discussion.'

'You have already become acquainted with Soe-Amun then, Thirteenth,' said Konitu with a wan smile. 'Leave him to me, Paladin. We've known each other long enough for me to able to get through to him more speedily than even the princess.' She turned to Khara. 'No disrespect, Your Highness.' The self-confidence of the woman was quite startling, and Ahren noticed Khara observing her critically for a heartbeat before she nodded in reply.

'Can we *finally* find out what the purpose of these two colossal ships is?' asked Uldini impatiently. 'Quin-Wa mentioned nothing in her messages about floating fortresses or Elven Blood Magic.'

Konitu bowed respectfully before answering. 'It seemed that she wanted to surprise you, first of the Ancients. These Lantern Frigates are intended to be both a symbol of cooperation among the races as well as the linchpins of the western fleet.' She pointed up at the copper-coloured cages above them. 'The Bane Lanterns will guarantee us nocturnal safe passage through waters infested with Dark Ones.'

Jelninolan pursed her lips sceptically. 'A single flame per ship seems insufficient to me. Has the charm already been tested out?'

Konitu nodded confidently. 'Three nights ago, we successfully negotiated a swarm of Sabre Rays on our route here.'

Falk breathed in sharply on hearing mention of the Dark Ones.

The captain looked at him triumphantly. 'In fact, I even allowed my crew to play dice on deck *and* gave them extra portions of rice wine. Not once did the rays attempt a leap up from the depths.'

'Impressive,' said Uldini. 'How do you manage such effectiveness.'

'Well, now that we are in position, the Bane Lanterns will be lit every evening. I think it would be better if you simply observe their sorcery once the sun sets,' said the captain before quickly adding: 'I am no charm expert.' She pointed to her ship and then at the *Xuan-Foi*. 'We will flank the *Queen of the Waves* and in that way fend off any dangers – hopefully. May I suggest that you manoeuvre your vessel into the middle of your future escorts, aligning your prows with ours. The *Queen of the Waves* being paces lower than our ships, any creature that wants to board you will first have to swim past the Lantern Frigates to reach you. And they will come under attack from our Dragon Bows as they attempt their assault.'

'A good strategy,' said Falk admiringly. 'In that way we will merely be vulnerable from abaft, and only if the Dark Ones can swim faster than we can sail.'

Yantilla bellowed some orders to the officers under her, the Ice Wolves immediately positioning their crossbows on the aft deck, while also anchoring a broad shield wall into the ship's timbers. 'Let them come,' said the commander grimly. 'Our bolts may not be as big as those of the Dragon Bows, but I have some damn fine shooters under my command.'

Ahren couldn't miss the challenging look that the blonde woman gave the captain. It seemed that Muai and Culhen were not alone when it came to spontaneous duelling, no matter how pointless the exercise.

We merely spurn each other on, countered Culhen snootily. *It helps us to maintain our advantage over you cumbersome bipeds.*

Ahren grasped his wolf by the fur and ruffled it affectionately, the animal growling contentedly. 'We are grateful to you for your protection, Captain Konitu,' he said, hoping to have thereby nipped any tension between the two women in the bud. 'It would be best if you now returned to your ship and resumed command there.'

The officer retired with a fleeting bow. Hardly was she out of earshot when Ahren turned to Yantilla.

'If I had known that you were so easily impressed by the sheer size of a ship, I would have had one built for you,' he teased.

The commander snorted before leaving to help her Ice Wolves in the defence preparations.

'Very clever,' said Trogadon with a chuckle. 'Annoy the woman responsible for your personal safety, of all people.'

Ahren pointed his thumb surreptitiously at Khara, his eyes sparkling with delight. 'I survived it with her, anyway.'

'Would you like to lose your thumb, darling?' asked the Swordsmistress in a honeyed voice. 'If so, just keep pointing it in my direction.'

'Enough messing about,' grunted Falk. 'If there are Sabre Rays swimming about in these waters, we had better be battle ready.'

The old Paladin's warning had all the effect of a pail of icy water being thrown over Ahren's mood, and suddenly he was *very* serious. 'Why don't we take the opportunity now and practise with the Blessing Band?'

His suggestion having met with nods of agreement, all the Paladins and Khara dressed in full armour and, with their weapons at the ready, gathered on the fo'c'sle to sharpen their senses, so that in the event of future skirmishes each would be aware of the others' position without needing to look around.

The day progressed, Ahren noticing much to his delight that even the normally fearful Trimm was making a decent fist of things. The invisible

Paladin bond, made tangible to them all thanks to Khara's bracelet, gave Trimm the opportunity to learn from the others about how to trust himself more, giving him courage in a manner more effective than all the words of advice that the world could possibly offer.

Chapter 3

It was late afternoon when Ahren had a well-earned break, taking a draught of diluted wine by the side of the fo'c'sle. Falk was training Hakanu, while Trimm was being taught by Khara, so that the young Forest Guardian had a little free time to look out over the sea and observe the enormous ships on the port and starboard sides of the *Queen of the Waves*. The wind blowing into his face was southerly, the sky was a deep blue, framing the late autumn sun, and the ocean itself seemed gentle and even sleepy, as if the sea was weary from its exploits over the previous few days.

'How is he getting on?' asked a gentle voice to Ahren's right.

Ahren glanced over his shoulder at Palnah, who had positioned herself two paces away from him.

'Quite well,' said Ahren, turning to face her. 'The Blessing Band is giving him strength.' He nodded towards Trimm, who was listening with great concentration to whatever it was that Falk was quietly teaching him. 'The connection may be reminding him of the long-ago days before he became terrified of the world. Or it is allowing Falk to see Trimm the Paladin and not Trimm the coward in front of him. At any rate, the two seem to trust one another much more now.'

Palnah smiled. 'Are you sure that there wasn't a Brajah among your forebears?' she asked with a chuckle. 'You certainly know how to see into a person's heart.'

Ahren shrugged his shoulders. 'I cannot rule it out. My father came from the Borderlands and his background was…well…uncertain.' He looked at Trimm's soul companion more closely. The quiet woman had tied back her hair, which gave her a more open appearance than previously. 'You are no longer using your hair as a shield. I see that much, at least,' he said. 'But that still doesn't mean that I can read into your soul.' He chuckled at himself ironically. '*If* there was a Brajah in my family, then it mut have been centuries ago.'

Palnah stepped beside him and place her hand on his arm. 'You have a good heart, *and* you make every effort to keep it thus – no matter the burdens that weigh down on you. This is a rarity.' Her voice had changed and was now reverberating with the certainty that accompanied it whenever the Brajah made use of her gift of clear-sightedness. 'Other, lesser spirits, when confronted with the challenges of life, turn away from their ideals with excuses such as "I did what had to be done" or "I had no choice". But you try to achieve the impossible time and again, so that you can achieve the *maximum*.'

Ahren looked at the woman in surprise as she pulled back her hand with a smile.

'I apologise. The first time I physically touch someone, I immediately have a clear picture of their nature,' she said, the timbre of her voice once again sounding shy and retiring. 'However, it is seldom that the impression is so clear and impressive that I am forced to blurt out what I have seen.'

'We others must make do with traditional questioning rather than magical visions when trying to glean the truth,' said Ahren, having been moved and painfully embarrassed at the same time. The woman's assessment had thrown him off balance, and so he decided to take the bull by the horns. 'How are things with *you*, now that you are no longer Reik's plaything?'

Palnah looked down at the floor, hiding the pained expression in her eyes. 'Although our relationship was more one-sided than I was willing to admit to myself, it did begin with noble aspirations and genuine mutual feelings. Reik wanted to reform Gol-Konar.' She was struggling to find the right words now. 'He wanted to make it more secure. Not only for the inhabitants of the city but also for their neighbours. He dreamed of a metropolis of mercenaries, who would offer their services throughout Jorath and thereby give meaning and structure to the violence of their daily work.' She pursed her lips and paused for several heartbeats before continuing bitterly: 'The path was long and bloody. *Too* long and *too* bloody. Reik changed – he became unpredictable and ruthless. Then, when Askadar came to the city, Reik's moral collapse gathered pace.' She shook her head sadly. 'I should have noticed that this sorcerer was avoiding me so that I would not unmask him as a High Fang.'

Ahren cocked his head quizzically. 'What you said earlier about people abandoning their ideals…you *were* talking about Reik, weren't you?'

Palnah nodded. 'Reik and so many others, who wander around Jorath. It is too easy to blame outside circumstances for one's actions. Too few notice the high price that they pay when they resort to such excuses.'

Ahren was about to come up with some comforting words when sudden cries of alarm from the *Xuan-Foi* caused him to spin around. Falk and the other companions hurried over to him at the railing, everyone now peering at the sailors on the warship to see what it was that was concerning them.

'Look ahead!' shouted Hakanu, pointing at a spot in the water, two hundred paces in front of them. 'Are those dark *bodies* just below the waves?'

Ahren squinted to see better. He could make out triangular shapes that were gliding towards them with alarming speed. Each of them had to be a good six paces across, and they tapered towards the end of their bodies.

'Sabre Rays,' muttered Falk anxiously. 'All those *not* wearing armour, below deck, *now!'* he bellowed across the ship.

'But they're under water,' countered Hakanu, irritated. 'How could they possibly…'

His question was interrupted by the sight of a slender, black body breaking through the surface and soaring upwards a good dozen paces in a flowing pirouette, spraying drops of seawater as it spun its way heavenward.

Ahren saw the ray's blunt wings, which resembled a coat as they wrapped around it as the monster soared, as well as two, glimmering, evil eyes of smouldering red, not to mention the fleeting glimpse of a mouth on its underside, filled with hooked teeth. The last thing that emerged from the water was a sharp, malleable sting, which more resembled a fencing weapon than a natural limb.

With a dull, barely audible plop, the wings of the ray opened as it reached the zenith of its leap, the creature then floating on the wind currents towards the *Xuan-Foi.* This gave Ahren the opportunity to see the creature more clearly, its movements making an elegant – if terrifying – impression on him. Its flat edges shimmered a pale white in contrast to its oily black skin, the line of white winding around the ray's outline like a thin ribbon. Ahren was amazed to see that, despite its impressive length and width, the Sabre Ray was no more than a thin line in the sky when viewed from the side.

'This wind is ideal for the shoal,' said Falk grimly, nodding towards one of the Dragon Bows that the crew of the ship under attack had now tautened and swung around to counter the danger. 'I'm not sure that they will be quick enough to shoot it down.'

Ahren quickly unshouldered *Fisiniell* and took an arrow from the quiver on his back, but it was already too late. With a deadly silence, the ray flew over the deck of the *Xuan-Foi,* not two paces above the deck. Sailors threw themselves onto the planks as the large body approached, one of them, however, too slowly. At first, Ahren did not understand the enormity of what he had seen, the ray simply sailing *through* the mariner, slicing the unfortunate man in two, both parts of his body then spraying blood everywhere. The ray sailed on seamlessly – as though its victim had not been there at all. The Dark One flew over the edge of the ship, furled its blunt wings, and had dropped like a stone into the water before the crossbow operators had shot off their bolts.

'What happened?' gasped Hakanu.

'Sabre Rays get their names from the razor-sharp layer of bonelike material growing on the outer edges of their body,' said Falk, breaking the stunned silence that had followed the boy's query. 'They are even deadlier in the water, but their broad wingspan and their flat bodies ensure that they can fly in the air for extended periods.' He pointed over at the other ship, where the crew were hurriedly covering the body parts of their fallen comrade in sheets, which immediately turned red. 'The bone of this creature can even cut through iron once the beast has built up sufficient momentum. The only tactic that guarantees success is to duck when they approach and then slice the underside of their bodies with a blade as they pass over. One should, of course, beware their broad mouths and their sharp tail, both of which the rays use if attacked from below.'

'Make one mistake, and...well...' brooded Trogadon, nodding down towards the deceased.

'Precisely,' agreed Falk before brooding in silence.

May I say at this point that I can see several dozen of the creatures below the surface? asked Culhen, who was standing at the railing, too. *And that I would find it difficult to bite them from below should they happen to sail over me?*

'Have harpoons or similar weapons ever been used against the rays?' asked Hakanu. 'Anything that might slow the beasts and cause them to fall onto deck?'

'Then you will be left with a colossus weighing several hundred stone lying on the timbers, whose bony edges could slice you in two within the blink of an eye,' countered Trogadon. 'Of course, the rays will die once they are out of the water for long enough, but before that happens, they will hit and slice all around them.' The dwarf shuddered. 'The yarns relating to Sabre Rays are one of the reasons for dwarves *not* going to sea.'

'And I always thought it was because you lot sink like stones,' said Trimm with a crooked grin.

'I said *one* of the reasons,' grumbled Trogadon, staring down at the water beyond the railing. 'And pointing out the shortcomings of my folk to me at a moment like this is *not* very nice.'

Ahren was relieved that Trimm was now feeling confident enough to take part in the general teasing that was common to the group, but when another Sabre Ray leaped out of the water, he gestured to the overweight Paladin that he should withdraw. Trimm immediately sought safety below deck once it had become clear that the Dark One was flying straight towards the *Queen of the Waves.*

Ahren extended *Fisiniell* with a grim smile and aimed with as much precision as he could manage. The ray was little more than a black line as it approached the Forest Guardian, and when he finally let his arrow fly, the creature dropped sufficiently for the projectile to fly harmlessly above its black skin.

'Damn it!' cursed Ahren, only for a large bolt to fly in from the left, cleanly piercing the Sabre Ray with a loud smack, sweeping it easily from the sky. The dead ray landed in the sea with a splash.

A victorious cheer rose from the crossbow operators on the *Xuan-Foi* as they speedily re-tautened their weapon. Their thirst to get revenge for their fallen comrade was clear for all to see – and to hear, judging by the jubilant shouts of the mariners.

'It is always best to aim at Sabre Rays from their sides,' explained Falk. 'In this way, they only notice the projectile when it is too late, and they can no longer change direction.'

Ahren peered down at the water, spotting several of the deadly rays changing their swimming direction. 'According to Culhen, the sea is full of these creatures.' He hadn't quite succeeded in disguising the anxiety in his voice.

'Well, at least the Sabre Rays are just as stupid as a bucketful of Needle Spiders,' murmured Falk. 'The Adversary may be able to send them to attack us, but he is unable to steer them with any great accuracy. If they were able to launch a coordinated attack or focus their attention on the rigging, then…'

'That's enough now,' growled Trogadon, raising his hand in protest. 'I'd better fetch my crossbow before you ruin my sleep patterns with your horrific visions.' The dwarf stamped away, muttering under his breath. 'So much for playing dice,' was all that Ahren could make out.

'Only shoot when they leap!' shouted Falk after his stocky friend. 'They are far too fast and nimble underwater!'

'You'd better instruct the Ice Wolves and the crews on the Lantern Frigates as well,' said Ahren when he saw one of the Dragon Bows on the *Lady Aruti* being aimed down at the surface of the water.

Cursing, Falk began to wave his arms furiously as he roared out commands. 'I'd better instruct the two captains on what tactics to use when tackling these Sabre Rays.' The old man shook his head impatiently. 'I knew I should have written about these sea creatures of the Adversary in my almanac.'

Hearing the low sound of wings unfurling behind him, Ahren was just quick enough to spin around and see a Sabre Ray gliding towards him. The creature had risen from the water close to the prow of the ship and was now on a low trajectory along the port side, from where it would reach Ahren in no time at all.

With a groan, the Paladin dived towards the centre of the deck, thereby just about evading the stinging tail of the creature.

Culhen, who had pressed himself low against the deck to avoid being sliced open, uttered a low whimper followed by an instinctive growl.

Let's hope that those beacons on the Lantern Frigates really do their job, was the message that the wolf transmitted to his friend. *If a thing like that emerges during the night, it will be impossible to take evasive action.*

Ahren struggled to his feet and looked around. The deck was almost devoid of people – only a skeleton crew was left, along with the Ice Wolf crossbow operators, who were giving the brave sailors cover. 'I think it would be best if we go below deck,' he said, overriding his own fighting instinct. 'I don't have many more arrows for *Fisiniell,* and this battle will not be decided in one day.'

Indeed, Ahren had the sinking feeling that the battle against the Adversary's sea creatures might take several moons.

The rest of the day passed painfully slowly. Every time that Ahren heard the quiet unfolding of the rays' wings, he feared that there would be more deaths, and after a few defensive manoeuvres all the Ice Wolves, along with the grumpy Trogadon, not to mention most of the remaining crew, decided to retire below deck. The bolts from the crossbows of the two companion ships were simply far more effective when it came to shooting down Sabre Rays, and the fewer persons there were on deck, the easier it was for the crossbow operators on the Lantern Frigates to shoot without risking injury or death to those on their own side.

The rigging and sails of the *Queen of the Waves* had been suitably adjusted, and now only the helmsman, a broad-shouldered, taciturn fellow was left on deck, making sure that the ship maintained her correct course. Whenever the wind changed direction or other things on the *Queen of the Wave* needed altering, he would bellow an order, the necessary crew then whooshing on deck to perform their tasks before disappearing back into the safety of the hull. Ahren silently thanked the deities for this sailor on the aft deck, for the previous captain of the *Queen of the Waves* had perished on the ship's voyage to Gol-Konar, and his successor was a fearful wretch, who seemed to spend most of his time hiding away. Ahren was now firmly of the opinion that the man would have to be replaced at the earliest opportunity.

On the other hand, the coward isn't meddling in your affairs or those of the other Paladins, mused Culhen. *Which means that you can do what you want.*

None of us is a mariner, countered Ahren. *I'd prefer to have a self-confident expert at the head of the crew.*

Then leave the navigational decisions to the captains of the Lantern Frigates, advised the wolf. *At least until we have reached Men-Hark and the* Queen of the Waves *has been whipped into shape again.*

'At least I got one of those damned creatures,' growled Trogadon as he stared into the storm lantern that lit up the captain's cabin, where Ahren and his friends had gathered.

'And you did it very well, darling,' murmured Jelninolan, praising her beloved, yet not quite able to hide the irritation in her tone. 'But we really don't need to hear you telling us for the eighth time.'

The loud twang of a crossbow at work was followed immediately by a cheer from the *Lady Aruti*.

'The shooters are improving all the time,' said Falk approvingly. 'Every second bolt is hitting its target now – while the rays are still leaping and before they begin their glide.'

'Maybe we should go on deck to hel—' began Hakanu, only to stop in mid-flow as Ahren stared angrily at him.

'Keep *reading*,' barked the teacher, the young warrior sighing sulkily before looking down to resume his study of Falk's almanac with its descriptions of various Dark Ones.

'The sun is close to setting,' said Uldini after a time, breaking the silence that had descended within the room. Everyone was now concentrating on the noises without. 'It won't be long before we find out if the Lantern Frigates' magic will amount to anything.'

'Am I imagining things or is it possible that a *tiny* part of you is hoping that the lanterns will fail?' asked Khara, looking at the Ancient, who was restlessly floating around the cabin. 'Perhaps because you played no part in their manufacture and are taken aback by Cochan's experiment?'

'Fiddlesticks!' snarled Uldini. 'Would I be calmer if I'd had a chance to examine those lanterns before risking our lives on their success? Of course, I would! But I am neither that proud nor that stubborn to desire that we be vulnerable to attacks by Dark Ones the moment the sun sets.'

'Time for us to eat,' said Trimm anxiously as he got to his feet. 'Nourishment drives away fear – that's one thing that I have learned over the years.'

'Then you must have been *very* afraid,' snapped Falk, glaring at the corpulent Paladin.

'I will go with Trimm and give him cover until he reaches the hatchway,' said Ahren, unshouldering *Fisiniell*. Then he stared at Falk. 'And we should all try to get used to this situation. If the reports are correct, then we are in for an extended maritime siege.'

A deathly silence descended on the cabin, and even Khara looked at him anxiously.

Now, that wasn't exactly a motivating speech, interjected Culhen, yawning as if to underline his point. *And woe betide if you forget to bring food for me and Muai. All this hanging around is making me hungry.*

Supper was completed in a mood of heightened anxiety, and all attempts on Ahren's part to lighten the mood with conversation were met with little more than half-hearted smiles. Hardly had the sun touched the horizon, when everyone gathered at the doorway of the cabin, which was slightly ajar, so that they could take turns to peek out to see what was going on.

Like a gaggle of godsday students hiding from the furious Keeper after having performed a prank, thought Ahren, utterly frustrated. *What a shower of Paladins and Ancients we are!*

Give me some room there, muttered Culhen, pushing his big head through the gap. *Ah – fresh air at last,* he announced, his nose taking in the outside scents. *It smells too much like Paladins stewing in their own juice in here.*

'It's beginning,' murmured Uldini solemnly, raising *Flamestar* so that it hovered before his eyes, enabling him to observe the lantern of the *Xuan-Foi* through his crystal ball.

'Be careful with your sorcery,' whispered Jelninolan anxiously. 'We don't want to inadvertently divert the light from an arcane beacon out onto the high seas.'

'As if those things over there don't emit magic too,' grumbled Uldini, only to gasp in surprise a heartbeat later. A Wrath Elf had nimbly scaled the main mast of the *Xuan-Foi* and quickly pulled back a bolt on the bronze box. The sides of the container immediately dropped open, revealing some kind of metallic flower, while a charm fire cast forth a reddish light from its centre – similar to what Ahren remembered from Dhalvantil – and sent it in all directions. The 'petals' of the structure were as smooth as mirrors, magnifying the glow as it spread out, ensuring that the area surrounding the ship was cast in a reddish shimmer, which reinforced the natural red of the setting sun.

'Those are *charm mirrors* within the boxes,' said Uldini, clearly impressed. 'Very similar to those from the Wizardly Domes. It's clear to me that Akkad had a hand in constructing these Bane Lanterns, using as a template the charm we used for inhibiting the spread of the Pall Cloud.'

'Look!' exclaimed Khara, stepping outside the cabin. 'The Sabre Rays – they are retreating into the depths of the sea!'

'Well, I'll be darned!' grinned Falk, looking on in amazement. 'The night belongs to us, then! No fearful hiding below deck or night-time ambushes! The next time I meet Quin-Wa and Akkad, I'll hug the life out of them.'

'I'm sure they'll be delighted,' commented Ahren dryly, although he, too was similarly relieved at the turn of events. 'So, shall we make the night our day, and the day our night? What do you think?' he asked the others. 'That's something we are already familiar with from the Forest of Ire.'

Trimm peered over at the two escort vessels. 'I certainly don't see anchors being dropped or sails being reefed. In fact, it seems that there are more mariners on deck now – and fewer soldiers.'

'The belly of those ships can hold many people, certainly. That's probably where the soldiers are,' mused Falk. It took no time at all for the Lantern Frigates to set sail, the old man nodding approvingly as he watched on. 'It seems as if our escorts have decided to use the safety of the night, too, to enable us to proceed with all possible speed.'

'I will go and alert the crew,' said Trogadon. 'Anyone who slept during the day, well, now's the time for them to earn their salt.'

While life returned to the deck of the *Queen of the Waves*, and the three vessels sailed southward, Ahren and Culhen paced the fo'c'sle, feeling the fair wind on their faces.

'Thank you,' the young man whispered to the current of air, his thoughts now very much with Quin-Wa, Akkad, and the Wrath Elves, all of whom had created this wonder.

Suddenly, the voyage to the Ice Fields didn't seem quite so threatening to him, his thoughts now moving onto the frozen land, from where there had been no news of Yollock for centuries, the Paladin presumably still searching for a wounded, angry dragon. Ahren rubbed his hands and shivered. The cold grip of winter was beginning to make its presence felt in the freshening night air. It was high time he put on his cloak.

Like a shimmering veil of blood, the two Bane Lanterns lit up the darkness of the night, transforming the sea into a murky black mirror and creating a border to another, unknown world.

'It seems that the charm light cannot break through the surface of the ocean,' said Trimm, positioning himself beside the pondering Forest Guardian. 'Fitting, somehow. We have the air for ourselves, while the rays keep ownership of the water.'

They were all to gather on the fo'c'sle to do a little fighting practice, and it was the corpulent Paladin who was the first to arrive, much to Ahren's surprise. He glanced at Trimm and raised a quizzical eyebrow. '*You're* early.'

The portly man shrugged his shoulders awkwardly. 'I suffer from cabin fever just as much as anyone else.'

Hmm, he spent rather a lot of time in his cabin with Palnah, commented Culhen, grinning wolfishly. Ahren's mind was immediately filled with an image of two rabbits frolicking in a field.

Drop it, chuckled the Forest Guardian. *Let the two enjoy their time together. And it's great that Trimm has turned up for training – despite having better things to do.*

'Two are already here,' laughed Khara as she gracefully ascended the steps to the fo'c'sle. 'Why don't we start with the pair of you while the rest are arriving? Without waiting for an answer, she closed her eyes, her bracelet immediately beginning to emit a subtle, milky light – just enough to give the illusion that a distant moon was casting its glow on the surface of the piece of jewellery.

Immediately, Ahren sensed where both Khara and Trim were situated without needing to look. 'How come I don't notice Falk?' he asked, taken aback.

'I'm still learning to control the range of the magic,' said Khara with a frown, her eyes still closed. 'Uldini says that it is necessary for me to extend the circumference of the charm net only as far as is necessary. He fears that otherwise charm-sensitive Dark Ones might locate us with greater ease.'

Ahren sighed. 'There is no light without shade.' Then he beckoned Trimm to get into position before raising his own Wind Blade. 'Let the dance begin,' he said with a crooked grin.

Trimm grinned in return, drawing two wooden daggers that Trogadon had carved for him, then sliding gracefully into an elegant pose, which Ahren would never have believed possible from such a portly fellow.

'The old moves are beginning to come back to me,' said Trimm, chuckling ironically at himself as he demonstratively raised his wooden knives. 'Even if it is better that I practise with toys for now.' And even while Ahren was preparing to reply, he launched into a sequence of flowing moves and thrusts.

The Forest Guardian received three hits to his chest before he could react, the practice daggers hitting powerfully off the young man's ribbon armour.

'Not bad,' said Ahren, taking a step backward.

Trimm shrugged his shoulders again, this time with a mixture of embarrassment and uncertainly on his face. 'That is all that I am capable of, I'm afraid. Without the element of surprise, I am rather hopeless.'

Ahren swiftly swung his sword down on the Paladin, his portly counterpart managing to stop himself from being wounded by crossing his wooden weapons before his face – which now took on a look of pure horror.

'Well, you certainly still have all your reflexes,' said Ahren light-heartedly. 'Much seems to be submerged, probably thanks to years of indolence, not to mention *this*.' With that, he pointed his blade at Trimm's large belly. 'I have no doubt that we can knock your stomach into shape within the next few moons.' Ahren refrained from commenting on the fact that Trimm was already more self-confident now than he had been even a few days previously. The delicate plant of courage within the fearful man needed to flourish in an atmosphere of calm seclusion.

Like a whelp, who discovers that they have teeth, commented Culhen, who had been watching the scene while snuggled up with Muai and Kamaluq in their usual spot.

Ahren wearily rubbed the back of his neck. *I am thankful for every individual step in the right direction,* he replied stoically. *There is no way that I will allow Trimm to go into the Ice Fields. Instead, he will be drilled in Deepstone until just before our assault on the Obsidian Fortress.*

When are you going to inform him? asked Culhen with a chuckle.

When his fear of the journey into the eternal ice has grown to the point that he will look forward eagerly to a couple of moons' backbreaking training, came the reply.

Very wise, said the wolf. *In fact, your idea is so good, it might easily have been my own.*

One by one, the other companions arrived, and it wasn't long before the night air was filled with groans, laughter, and colourful comradely curses – as if Ahren and his friends were displaying to the lurking dangers beneath the waves that they would *never* succumb to fear.

'What a view!' exclaimed Trimm fervently, spreading out his arms towards the coastline, now visible in the early morning light. 'Soon we will be in civilisation's warm embrace at last.'

The rest of the time before docking in Men-Hark was taken up with the usual on-board tasks before the port city finally stretched out before them, hardly illuminated at all, the autumn sun only breaking through the clouds with considerable difficulty. It was still another two leagues or so to the coast, and all were relieved that the Sabre Rays had remained behind once the three ships entered the calm waters of Men-Hark, where the local fishermen were trying their luck. The little cockleshell boats with their cheerfully waving occupants seemed terribly vulnerable on account of the Dark Ones lurking nearby, but streamlined patrol vessels, occupied by soldiers, and equipped with spears and harpoons kept guard near the defenceless fishing boats.

'It seems that every fisherman from the city wants to welcome their princess,' said Ahren, shaking his head. 'If you think that only two winters ago, Khara was a complete unknown…' he began, only to be interrupted by Trimm's loud chuckling.

'You still underestimate the power of the bards, *little brother*,' said the corpulent Paladin cynically. 'Even in faraway Cape Verstaad, Quin-Wa's fairy-tale of the mysterious daughter who was secreted away and brought up with great care, is being sung in every city tavern. Everyone wants to believe a story like that. Nobody wishes to hear the unpleasant truth of her childhood in the fighting arenas and of her condemned parents.'

Ahren was delighted to hear himself being referred to by his nickname again – the one that the other Paladins had given him years previously. Trimm was behaving more and more like his fellows – something that Ahren took as a very promising sign. The chubby Paladin would probably never equal Hakanu when it came to overweening pride, but this thought secretly pleased Ahren.

My heart wouldn't stand up to controlling two of them, he concluded, a shiver running down his spine.

By the way, isn't it time you took your whippersnapper down from the rigging? suggested Culhen, who had taken up position at the railing and was basking in the cheers of the admiring fishermen. *Khara has been putting him through his paces up there for a considerable period already. It may not be the best move for a Paladin to perform acrobatics in the shrouds for the entertainment of the masses.*

Ahren looked up, eventually catching sight of Hakanu, who was hanging upside down in the rigging just below the crow's nest, repeatedly pulling his torso up to his feet before dropping it back down again. Ahren's own stomach muscles burned at the mere sight of the exercise, but he couldn't help chuckling as an idea came into his head of how to ensure that Hakanu's pride didn't get the better of him during the upcoming ceremonial reception.

It worked with me that time, he said, reassuring Culhen, who seemed more than a little sceptical.

More and more people gathered as the ships approached the harbour, the citizens filling the broad, cobbled streets lined with pagoda-like houses, which were so typical of the Eternal Empire. Men-Hark was undoubtedly a wealthy city if the number of multi-roofed houses was anything to go by.

Ahren waved up at Khara, who was watching Hakanu's efforts from the crow's nest, then he tugged at his clothing and pointed at the crowds, who had by now broken into song. Khara indicated with a nod that she understood. Then she proceeded to release Hakanu from his task – only for Ahren to firmly shake his head. She stopped in surprise, quickly descending the rigging to join him.

'Shouldn't Hakanu put on *his* best clothing as well?' she asked.

Ahren shook his head. 'What do you think is going to happen if he, as the youngest of the Paladins, is praised to high heaven by the locals?'

'Hm,' she replied, scratching her head. 'That *could* be a problem.'

'Especially as there will be more than enough girls among the admiring multitudes,' added the young man.

Khara flinched. 'He'll hardly proceed ten paces without some angry father or indignant mother challenging him to a duel.'

'He will be dead by midday – *or* betrothed,' continued Ahren. Then he sighed playfully. 'If he could *only* make himself as invisible as his cunning fox.'

Khara glanced up at the boy, who was still continuing with his practice, completely red-faced by now. 'Should I not grant him a *short* break at the very least?'

Ahren shook his head firmly. 'I want to see him exhausted and sweaty by the time we dock. The less energy he has, the better.'

The couple went below deck together to put on their best garb, and by the time they re-joined their friends on the deck of the *Queen of the Waves*, the ship was gliding towards a long stone quay filled with crowds of people, who were lustily singing the Hymn of the Eternal Empress for all the world to hear. Ahren and his companions were now spick and span, their armour and weapons having been polished to a shine by means of a tiny magic spell, their hair, too, having been freshly brushed or combed. Ahren was well used to this type of sprucing up by now, and he had to admit to himself that they were a very impressive sight as they stood on the fo'c'sle, waving at the citizens of Men-hark. Much to the young man's surprise, Trimm seemed not in the least intimidated by the throng, and indeed the corpulent Paladin made a gracious impression in the noble-looking garment that Jelninolan had sewn together from the supplies of cloth that she had found on the ship.

'As a grandee, one often has the opportunity to bask in glory among one's people,' murmured Trimm quietly to Ahren as he noticed the Thirteenth observing him. 'Much more so than I ever did as a Paladin.'

On hearing the quiet note of pain in the man's voice, Ahren placed a hand on his companion's shoulder. 'These people are cheering the Paladins and the Ancients, who will free them from the Adversary's yoke.'

Khara, standing beside him, cleared her throat and raised her eyebrows commandingly.

'And above all, they are paying homage to their *princess,*' he quickly added.

Stuff and nonsense, interjected Culhen. *They are all here on account of me.*

The wolf's voice sounded dreamy, and he was positively wallowing in the cheering adulation. Ahren couldn't bring himself to inform his friend that the crowds looking up from the quayside had their eyes fixed firmly on Muai sitting regally beside him – the august companion of the Eternal Empress and protectress of her princess.

The ship made a squeaking sound as it bumped against the enormous stone jetty, Khara then gently squeezing Ahren's forearm. 'Shouldn't we think about releasing Hakanu from his task?' she asked.

The Forest Guardian looked up at the young warrior and grunted approvingly – the boy had been peering down from his upside-down position at the welcoming citizens of Men-Hark. Ahren let out a whistle and beckoned his protégé to come down, Hakanu almost losing his grip in his eagerness to reach the deck. Ahren sighed, any doubts he had regarding his treatment of the boy well and truly vanishing.

The *Queen of the Waves* having been safely moored and the gangplank lowered, the Thirteenth Paladin and his companions quickly walked across the swaying timbers towards a group of six people – clearly, the welcoming committee. Ahren saw four women and two men, exquisitely dressed and of impeccable bearing, each with one costly piece of jewellery, which could only be their individual Sigils, those objects that immediately identified their status within the Eternal Empire.

As they reached the six hosts, the singing of the Men-Hark citizens ceased, and Ahren was reminded of the iron self-disciple that was common to all inhabitants of the Eternal Empire. He also suddenly remembered the deep spirituality so typical of the Green Sea horse folk and he wondered if Quin-Wa, when she had been founding her empire, had taken note of her northern neighbours and adapted their mentality to her own purposes. The Forest Guardian couldn't help feeling that the more he saw of the world, the more he became aware of the invisible threads of cause and effect, which wove the various and very individual races of Jorath into a large and elaborate living carpet.

Stop philosophising, scolded Culhen, who was standing to attention, every inch the proud war-wolf. Somehow, his furry friend was managing to make his armour clatter impressively with the most miniscule of movements, thereby creating an even more heroic effect, although generally it was otherwise barely audible – even when he hurtled across the plains.

Khara stepped forward, and immediately the six dignitaries bowed deeply. Welcoming words were worthily uttered, followed by more bowing as, one by one, the honoured guests who would be stopping off in the cloud-covered city of Men-Hark were introduced.

When it was finally Hakanu's turn, the boy straightened up and prepared to state his name and rank only for Ahren to announce loudly: 'This is Hakanu, my apprentice. To pass the time, I am introducing him to the art of Forest Guardianship.' He gave Hakanu a piercing look. 'Please excuse his unkempt and sweaty appearance – the lad still has much to learn.'

The startled boy looked as though Ahren had stabbed him in the back – nevertheless, he did not protest, submitting instead to his fate as a menial pupil. Ahren was pleased to see how many of the young girls who had been admiring the boy suddenly lost interest in him, given his supposedly lowly status. Indeed, he was now being greeted with the barest of nods from the assembled crowd.

'Masterfully played,' whispered Falk into Ahren's ear. 'I was fully convinced that we would have to chain Hakanu up and keep him under armed guard so that he would not provoke half of Men-Hark to take up arms against him within half a day. Now that no-one is interested in him, there will be less opportunity for him to make silly mistakes.'

Ahren gave his humiliated apprentice an encouraging look, beckoning to the lad to stand by his side. 'Oh, I will do something better than chain him up,' he whispered to his erstwhile master as the boy approached. 'I won't let him out of my sight for a heartbeat.'

Their stay in Men-Hark was proving to be just as Ahren had imagined it would be. Gracious welcomes, a ceremonial meal in the house of the wealthiest family of the city, and laughing, friendly faces all around them. There was hardly a hint that the city was preparing for war. Only when he looked down at the harbour did it become immediately apparent. No sooner had passengers and crew disembarked when an army of craftsmen descended upon the ship, pulling it into a dry dock where the skilled artisans of the Eternal Empire set to work with such precision and efficiency that even Trogadon was impressed. Suitable timbers and metal fittings were already lying there at the ready, the latter emitting the tell-tale gleam of Dwarfish steel. 'When this ship sails away from Men-Hark, she will be more stable than she ever was,' said the blacksmith approvingly.

The afternoon was gradually yielding to evening as Ahren and Khara strolled through the streets of Men-Hark, both needing to stretch their legs and determined to take in the atmosphere of the harbour city together. Culhen and Muai walked proudly ahead, thereby ensuring a passageway through the citizens who looked in awe at the company. Kamaluq, meanwhile, was whimpering curiously, occasionally darting this way and that and clearly enjoying his first visit to the welcoming city. After a while, the Princess of the Eternal Empire sighed.

'How I would dearly love to see the inhabitants of this city go about their daily work,' she said regretfully. 'The fishermen would be fixing their nets and the traders offering their wares, while lovers would be whispering to the Empress under the blossoming Empress Tree, asking for her blessing so that they could become betrothed. Instead, we are being constantly bowed to and stared at in silence.'

'My poor but much-loved princess,' teased Ahren, hooking arms with her as she smiled at him wanly. Then he fixed his eyes on Hakanu. 'Well – what do *you* think of Men-Hark?' he asked. 'Is this how you imagined a city would be?'

The apprentice shook his head, his face an expression combining contemplation with not a little suspicion. 'Gol-Konar is the picture that every member of the horse folk has when they hear the words "city" and "civilisation". A place of death, far from nature – where everyone thinks only of themselves.' He waved his hand at the inhabitants and buildings that surrounded them. 'Everything is much *cleaner* than in Gol-Konar, and the people are much friendlier.' He paused, and Ahren was convinced that his protégé had finished, but then the boy continued: 'But for me it is only whitewash, covering the same rotten wood.' Ahren frowned and Khara gasped in surprise. 'So far, I have already seen at least a dozen people pleading for food or coinage.'

Ahren nodded. 'Those were beggars,' he explained. 'People who have no work and are dependent on the alms of others.' He himself had seen his first beggars after he had left Deepstone for the first time, and he well remembered how downcast he had felt to realise that there were those who existed as if in banishment, although they were surrounded by so many fellow humans.

'We have no such unfortunates in the Green Sea,' said Hakanu categorically, raising his head proudly.

Ahren knew his apprentice well enough to realise that the young warrior was now fixed in his opinion. The horse folk had their own unique view of the world, and it would take Hakanu a considerable time before realising that there was more than one way to live one's life.

'At least he is being true to himself,' whispered Khara, turning surreptitiously to Ahren. The Forest Guardian could hear the undertone of annoyance in her voice, however, at the fact that Hakanu had so easily denigrated the achievements of *her* people because of the presence of a few beggars.

'Perhaps we should head back to the others,' said Ahren, thinking of the opulent guesthouse where they were all being put up. It was said that the repairs to the *Queen of the Waves* would be completed by the following evening – and even though Ahren asked himself how such a thing could be possible, he knew that he could rely on the artisans of Men-Hark not to work beyond the deadline – after all, their personal honour depended on their punctuality.

Suddenly, Muai growled angrily and sprang forwards, scattering the curious onlookers in all directions. Ahren watched after the tigress, realising immediately what her destination was – a circular open space with a tall cherry tree at its centre. The tall plant was in full bloom – even though it was well into autumn.

'What's *that?*' asked Hakanu, rubbing his eyes in wonder.

'*That* is an Empress Cherry,' said Khara with more than a note of triumph in her voice. 'These trees, planted by Cochan herself, stand in every settlement throughout the Eternal Empire – one in each village, town or city.' The Swordsmistress stared commandingly at the young warrior. 'In times of peace the Eternal Empress can hear every word that is spoken beneath the foliage of these trees, provided that she herself is in the vicinity of such a tree. In this way, she has been there for the needs of her subjects over the course of many centuries.'

Ahren tried to remain impassive despite the fact the Khara had mentioned nothing of the shadowy uses which such trees had also been employed for. The magically created plants had played a crucial role during the invisible war against the Dopplers. A war that had determined many of Quin-Wa's actions over an extended period – including using the trees for spying on her own people.

By now, Muai was rubbing her head against the trunk of the tree and staring with her penetrating eyes at Khara. The Swordsmistress hurried forward, placed the palms of her hands against the Empress Cherry's bark, closed her eyes, and began to smile. Ahren and Hakanu exchanged puzzled looks before approaching Khara, who seemed to be listening to something. Muai was now lying down, her head pressed against the tree as she purred – it looked for all the world as if she was dozing in the heat of the midday sun in the height of summer. Ahren placed his own hands on the bark and closed his eyes.

...really hope that you're doing well, my love, and that the flea-ridden wolf isn't causing you too much bother.

Quin-Wa's words formed in Ahren's mind as though the Eternal Empress was standing right beside him, and the two of them were deep in conversation. Or rather, that she was conversing with *Muai*, the ruler now showering her cat with affectionate terms of endearment. Then the Ancient suddenly stopped in mid-flow.

Ahren – is that you? she asked. The tone of her voice had altered dramatically. *You might have warned me, little daughter.* It really felt as though her words were flowing directly from the tree and into the tips of his fingers.

I'm sorry, chuckled Khara. *I had my eyes closed and didn't know that he would catch up so quickly.* She paused, her next words being then more anxious. *It is very loud in my head,* she said. *And I'm finding it very hard to concentrate.*

No wonder, Quin-Wa replied feelingly. *I am using my connection to Muai to communicate with you through the Empress Cherry, while your mind is bound up with the bond that is keeping the Paladin and his companion animal together. You are not used to hearing so many voices in your head, especially as your spouse has insisted on eavesdropping.*

I am not eavesdropping, retorted Ahren brusquely. *I just didn't know what was going on.*

Is that Quin-Wa?! exclaimed Hakanu excitedly. *This is amazing!*

Even I am getting a headache now, countered the Eternal Empress, sounding particularly stand-offish in the presence of the apprentice.

Take your hands away from the tree – now! commanded Ahren in no uncertain tones.

But I...

NOW!

This is so unfair... The voice of the young warrior was then replaced by another one – more familiar to Ahren's ears.

Who are you talking to? asked the wolf, Ahren sensing that Culhen was pressing not only against his master but also the tree. *I can only hear your part of the conversation.*

The young man didn't fail to hear Quin-Wa's sigh. *Hello, Culhen,* she began before continuing more loudly: *I suppose it is too much to ask if I may be allowed to converse with my daughter and my beloved tigress alone?*

...Muai? Culhen's thoughts were a maelstrom of curiosity and barely concealed enthusiasm.

We can hear him, came the answer, as clear as a bell, in Ahren's head too. Somehow, the tigress had managed to give her thoughts a queenly echo, and it sounded as if she was uttering her judgement above the figure of a cowering supplicant. *And we take note that he does, indeed, speak as boorishly as we expected.*

Ah now, listen here... countered Culhen, his nose seriously out of joint. *I am better-looking, stronger, and smarter than you...*

The wee wolf may delude himself in self-aggrandising fantasies, but we know better—

THAT'S ENOUGH!

Quin-Wa's thought was like a tornado, sweeping Ahren's mind clear. *All those with more than two legs – SHUT UP!*

Muai's and Culhen's presence reverted to a sulky silence, and Ahren couldn't help noticing how similar the two of them were when they were annoyed by the same thing.

Khara, be so good as to explain to me where you are and what you're doing. Uldini's old-Elven is mediocre to say the least, and the coded messages that he keeps sending via Flamestar *are more confusing to me than they could possibly be to the enemy.*

We are in Men-Hark, reported Khara succinctly. *The* Queen of the Waves *is currently under repair in dry dock, your Lantern Frigates having safely escorted us here.*

Then they are working, Quin-Wa replied in a self-satisfied voice. *Very good.*

And where are you? asked Ahren. *Do you have any news for us?*

I am in Deepstone, was the Empress's surprising response. *I took the offshoot of the Empress Tree with me from the Eternal Empire and planted it here in the courtyard of the newly built Highstone Castle. The constant journeying damaged the young plant but having been safely placed with considerable sorcery in the fertile ground, its magic has blossomed successfully.* Her voice was becoming more irritable. *Justinian has insisted that I remain here.*

Why so, Cochan? asked Khara urgently.

The empress's next words took Ahren completely aback.

I am with child, she said angrily. *As is always the case with every female Paladin and soul companion that the deities can muster.*

The disgruntlement of the woman manifested itself in the form of a deep unease in the pit of Ahren's stomach.

It is as though the THREE are preparing for the next major defeat by breeding as many Paladin children as they can manage which they will let loose on the world.

Or perhaps the deep love and attachment between the Paladins and their soul companions are bearing fruit in a most natural manner, countered Khara. *There are always two sides to every story,* she added. *That is something that you taught me.*

You can gladly take my place and stagnate in this fortress if you like, muttered Quin-Wa irritably. *This town is swarming with Night Soldiers, over-attentive Paladins, and a plethora of magic charms. In fact, I'm quite sure it would survive a direct assault from the Adversary.*

Hopefully, that is something we will never have to find out, interjected Ahren with a shudder.

The mood of the agitated empress suddenly went from bad to worse. Snatches of memories, so powerful that they even managed to reach Ahren through the magical connection, suddenly passed before his inner eye – screams and blood and small, lifeless bodies were scattered around the place as heartless Dark Ones went about their barbaric work. The worst was the loss of young, innocent lives. He understood that he was experiencing the horrors of the Night of Blood – and all he could do was watch in silent dismay and compassion as the flood of images rushed past. The visions suddenly vanished as fast as they had appeared, leaving nothing behind but a terrible emptiness, which only slowly began to fill with thoughts again.

Oh, Cochan… began Khara, only to be cut off by the Eternal Empress.

A fleet is on its way towards you and will accompany you on your voyage south, said Quin-Wa, her voice flat. *It will help you to break through the many lines of Dark Ones that are gathering to prevent your progress. Please leave all acts of heroism to my sailors until you reach Cape Verstaad.* The Eternal Empress's self-confidence was returning with every word she spoke. *Oh, and before I forget it – Aluna will not be lending you her support. She is on the way here, to Deepstone – you can guess why.*

Ahren sensed that the connection with Quin-Wa was fast fading away.

Look after each other, said the ruler urgently, her presence continuing to dissipate. *If you happen to get lost in the eternal ice – well, you cannot depend on any sort of rapid assistance from outside…*

***

Revenge flew high above the clouds towards the south, hunting down that Paladin, who was supposedly spending his lonely time in the fields of the south. Revenge's father had given him the task of looking for Yollock, a task which he had taken on without hesitation.

On his journey over Jorath he had taken breaks from time to time, refreshing himself on those unfortunates, whose own vengeful feelings were powerful enough to attract him towards them. A farmer, who was obsessed by a family feud with his neighbour. A fisherman, who was convinced that his greatest rival secretly had it in for him. And even a brother, insanely jealous of his sister, who had been the sole beneficiary of their parents' last will and testament. Time and again, the child of the Dark god would visit these people, not leaving their souls until bloody revenge had been meted out on the object of their hatred – demanding as a price only the life force of those who had been filled with so much malice towards their fellow human beings. It was astounding how much vengefulness slumbered in the inhabitants of Jorath, and how petty the causes always seemed to be. It was enough for one person to have a different view of life for another to wish them dead.

If Revenge didn't have a task that needed fulfilling, he could gleefully satiate himself forever on those unfortunate creatures. But the south coast of Jorath had come into view, and the time for refreshments was over. Had the powers of his deceased siblings not divided themselves up between himself and Hate, he would have blanched at the sight of such a vast sea.

As it was, Revenge floated on – towards those icy shores, beyond which his prey was hiding from the world like a frightened rabbit.

Chapter 4

Ahren's companions had absorbed the news from Quin-Wa with mixed feelings once the young Forest Guardian and Khara had returned to the common room of the splendidly furnished guesthouse and related to the others their unexpected conversation with the Eternal Empress. With every pregnancy and new-born baby connected with the gods' Blessing of the Paladins, the threatening prospect of another Night of Blood grew. On the other hand, no-once could contain their joy at the prospect of their steadily growing family following centuries of deprivation in that regard.

'You should really have quizzed Quin-Wa on news of Onja and my daughter, you know,' muttered Falk for the umpteenth time.

'The connection was very difficult, and there were a lot of voices speaking over one another,' replied Khara regretfully, who was still rubbing her head and staring angrily over at Culhen and Muai.

The two companion animals had – once the Eternal Empress's voice had completely vanished – engaged in a bitter war of words until the Empress Cherry was no longer able to sustain the squabble. Muai's majestic, arrogant streak and Culhen's direct, conceited nature were like fire and water, and poor Khara's mind had been their battlefield.

'I, for my part, intend to enjoy our last full day on land tomorrow,' announced Trogadon, his powerful hands wrapped around a pitcher of rice wine that was resting on the main table, which was carved from precious wood.

'As though *you* won't drink on the high seas,' countered Jelninolan, her eyebrows raised disapprovingly.

'Of course, I will,' said the dwarf, completely unruffled as he raised the pitcher. 'But the alcohol *here* is sheer bliss. Once we've been *on board* for several moons, we will be drinking it out of sheer desperation.'

'We must prepare ourselves as well as we can for a long voyage full of dangers,' said Ahren earnestly, looking at the others. 'Make sure that you take what you need so that you are battle-ready and clear-headed.' He nodded towards Trogadon. 'That does *not* include barrels of rice wine. Do I make myself clear?'

The blacksmith gave an exaggerated salute. 'I promise on my love for this divine elf here that I will neither bring a single drop of alcohol with me on board the *Queen of the Waves* nor indeed have any brought on for me' he said solemnly.

'Which means that the barrels are already stored in the hold,' said Jelninolan coolly.

Trogadon scowled and stared down into his pitcher.

Trimm got to his feet with a yawn. 'The day has been long and filled with both hymns of praise and plenty of good food,' he said with an air of satisfaction. 'In other words, the waking hours have been precisely how I like them.' Then he took Palnah's hand, and she stood up with a smile. 'I shall crown it with the sensation of a large, soft bed filled with dreams of once more being in Cape Verstaad.' The couple left the room giggling, their heads close together like two young lovers.

Ahren then got up, intending to retire with Khara until his eyes fell on Hakanu, who was sitting there being surprisingly quiet. The lad was hiding something in his hands, and when Ahren stared angrily at him, the young warrior guiltily let his master see the object. It was a carefully folded parchment, on which were written symbols in the Imperial tongue.

Khara picked up the note, cocked her head and studied its contents. Then she gave it back to Hakanu. 'It is a message from the daughter of the house.'

'And what is written on it?' asked the boy shyly. 'I found it lying on the pillow of my bed earlier.' He pressed the note tightly to his chest. 'The writing looks picture-perfect, and it smells of flowers and grass,' he added.

Ahren saw that Khara was well aware of everyone's curiosity as she leaned down to the apprentice and whispered into his ear. Whatever it was that she had relayed, Hakanu's face turned crimson, and Kamaluq whimpered excitedly at the lad's feet.

'I propose that Hakanu sleep in Falk's room tonight,' said the Swordsmistress.

'Why do *I* have to save the boy from the delicate fingers of a self-confident girl,' protested the old man grumpily.

Khara went over to Ahren and took him demonstratively by the hand.

'Alright, alright,' muttered Falk, patting the free chair beside him. 'Come over here, lad,' he said to the now miserable looking Hakanu. 'Trogadon and I will introduce you to your first taste of vintage rice wine.'

'Should I really leave him in the care of *those* two?' asked Ahren doubtfully, Jelninolan having already stood up with a snort and left the room.'

Khara looked at him innocently. 'Of course, if you *want,* you can keep watch over him the whole night through,' she said. '*Or* we can follow Trimm's example when it comes to large soft beds, and so on.'

Tongue-tied and without looking back, the young man hurried out of the room, hot on the heels of the giggling Khara.

'I am going to miss this city,' sighed Ahren wistfully. The morning of their departure had arrived, and he and Khara were both getting dressed. It seemed to the Paladin that the previous day of idleness and togetherness had simply flown by. The advantages of civilisation were certainly not to be scoffed at, and although the Forest Guardian loved the freedom of nature, the benefits of Men-Hark's cultural life had been a welcome relief after the Green Sea and Gol-Konar.

He drew back the rice paper that covered their bedroom window, preparing to enjoy the fresh air, only to gasp loudly instead at the sight that presented itself to him.

'Look at that! he exclaimed.

Khara hurried to his side and whistled in approval. 'Cochan certainly wasn't exaggerating when she referred to a fleet,' she said hugging Ahren as she grinned broadly.

The Forest Guardian shook his head, unable to believe his eyes. From their second-floor guesthouse window, he had a perfect view of the harbour – and of the forest of masts that had appeared overnight! A dozen battleships – all reinforced with Dwarfish steel and armed with Dragon Bows – had anchored in the bay, while a veritable army of tenders were loading supplies onto the three-masters.

'*Fourteen* ships to escort us?' he asked, turning to look at Khara in disbelief. 'What must be lying in wait for us on the high seas for Quin-Wa to divert so much military support away from the supply lines in order to defend us?' He suddenly felt the heavy weight of responsibility on his shoulders, his concern reflected in the eyes of his beloved.

'Let's go down,' said Khara anxiously. 'The tide will soon be high, and if I am reading all the hubbub at the harbour correctly, the fleet will want to be leaving before it ebbs again.'

A similar atmosphere of departure had taken hold in the common room on the ground floor. There were bundles and boxes everywhere, and it seemed that both Trogadon and Jelninolan were in charge of the goods. Mariners from the *Queen of the Waves* snorted and panted as they carried the heavy boxes out, the double doors of the house having been fully opened. The gusty wind from the west had cooled the air within the house considerably, as if announcing to the guests that the time of comfort and homeliness was well and truly over.

'Get down to the harbour, the two of you,' said Jelninolan as soon as she spotted Ahren and Khara. 'The others have gone on ahead already – with the admiral.'

'*Admiral?*' asked Ahren, taken aback, just as Trogadon cursed and leaped to the assistance of a sailor who was on the point of dropping a heavy crate.

'Careful, my good man. The box is full of priceless blacksmith's powders *and* little crucibles containing alchemical materials that you would do well *not* to mix!' he growled, taking the crate from the intimidated man. 'Best if I carry it myself.'

'It would be even better if you packed the crucibles in separate crates,' interjected Jelninolan sharply.

'Yes, my love,' murmured the dwarf absently. 'Maybe I should leave some room near the ingots…'

Disgusted, Jelninolan threw her arms in the air, Ahren surreptitiously gesturing to Khara that they should make themselves scarce.

'It seems that the two of them have everything under control,' he whispered as they whooshed out of the guesthouse and into its fenced front garden.

'Let's hope that Trogadon doesn't accidentally set fire to everything…' began Khara before suddenly thrusting her finger sideways as if it were a dagger. She was pointing towards a stable with some horse boxes. 'There!' she exclaimed in alarm.

Ahren spun around, his hand on his Wind Blade, fully expecting an ambush from assassins or Dark Ones – but the truth was far, far worse.

Hakanu was standing in the shade of one of the horse boxes, his pose suggesting that he was in intimate conversation with a girl of about his own age. The two were only the width of a finger apart, the boy's eyes showing not a spark of reason – a commodity that was already rare enough when it came to the young Paladin. The apprentice was showing her the Deep Steel spear in his hand, his chest swollen with pride, and if the enchanted look on the girl's face was anything to go by, then the young man must have already babbled out the secret of his being a Champion of the gods.

'She is the daughter of the man who owns this guesthouse,' whispered Khara, quickly checking around her. 'If he should see them like that, without Hakanu having been formally introduced to her mother, and with no traditional gift from the guest, never mind the ritual four supplications before the statue of the Eternal Empress…'

The two ran as fast as they could to the pair of lovebirds, who were completely caught up in their own private world.

'Am I glad that I got to know you *outside* the Eternal Empire,' joked Ahren, his quip containing more than a germ of truth, however. When he saw Hakanu and the girl kissing, he grasped Khara's arm and immediately slowed down.

The Swordsmistress gave him a look that suggested he had stepped onto an anthill and said what a lovely, tickly feeling it was. 'What are you *doing?*' she hissed. 'Isn't this the very thing we were trying to stop?'

Ahren held onto Khara for another three heartbeats, giving her a reassuring look. Then he nodded contentedly. 'This way, they will both be left with *one* pleasant memory,' he said softly. 'I don't want to be unnecessarily gruesome, but…' He stopped in mid-sentence as Hakanu and the girl embraced more tightly, their kiss intensifying in passion. 'That's enough,' he muttered, both he and Khara then setting off again.

They had almost reached Hakanu and his admirer when Kamaluq whimpered loudly from the corner of the yard. The Shimmer Fox had clearly been standing guard, ready to alert his Paladin should danger arise.

Hakanu turned on his heels and stepped a good pace away from the blushing girl, Ahren silently admiring the lad for his reflexes – though not necessarily for his foresight.

'I *did* tell you the story of a certain red-haired mother with a large crossbow, who encouraged me to keep my distance from her daughter, the first time I left Deepstone, did I not?' he growled, beckoning his apprentice to come out of the stable. The boy nodded contritely before bowing his head. 'And that happened in sleepy Hjalgar,' added Ahren angrily. 'Here in the Eternal Empire, the rules are much, *much* stricter.' With a curt wave of his hand, he sent the young warrior down to the harbour, the boy managing to glance back with an apologetic look at the object of his affections.

Khara, meanwhile, gave the girl a severe telling off, the lass then bowing apologetically before fleeing into the house.

'Even though I *will* miss the soft bed in Men-Hark,' muttered Ahren as he shook his head sullenly, 'I will be only too glad to get Hakanu away from the temptations of the city.'

If the ships had seemed imposing from a distance, they were even more remarkable up close. The twelve Jade Galleons were only slightly smaller than the *Queen of the Waves*, but they were longer and also equipped with oars, which made for manoeuvrability in the event of a dead calm or if their sails were struck. Their long, pointed prows made for excellent streamlining, while their decks were teeming with soldiers.

Ahren stood with all his companions on the aft deck of the *Queen of the Waves* ignoring Hakanu's sulky look, not to mention the growling and squabbling of Culhen and Muai, who clearly hadn't settled their differences following their falling out at the Empress Cherry.

A middle-aged man was facing Ahren, his dark hair turning grey at his temples, which gave his striking, somewhat rough face an air of wisdom. His green-blue eyes were piercing, and his dark beard almost hid his broad mouth and pale lips.

Admiral Refelbek, who until very recently had been the King's Island ambassador to the Jade Palace, resembled a knotty oak tree that had been yanked out of the peace and quiet of a forest and replanted on a barren coastline. Apparently, King Blueground had ordered the admiral back into military service as soon as he had heard that the *Queen of the Waves* would be transporting her priceless passengers through dangerous waters without any high-ranking commander. And so, the ambassador, whose vast experience on the high seas was only equalled by his present perturbation at being restored to his old job, stood on the ship's aft deck finishing his report.

'On account of my rank and the dignitaries under my protection,' he continued, his raw, deep voice more suited to a Glower Bear – if such creatures were able to talk – 'and in accordance with the rules pertaining to the new alliance of the Jorathian races, I have been given the command of the fleet.' He made sure that he gave the companions equal attention as his eyes scanned from one listener to the next. 'I am keenly aware of the great age of some of my passengers. Should anyone here claim to be more skilled in navigation than me with my twenty years of ocean combat and wishes to take charge of the fleet, then be my guest.'

Quite taken aback, Ahren glanced at his friends, but they seemed equally disconcerted.

'No-one?' pressed Refelbek. 'Then I would politely ask permission to lead the fleet in the manner that *I* consider appropriate. Regarding questions of sorcery, I will of course yield to the expertise of the Ancients.' With that, the man bowed almost imperceptibly before immediately getting down to work, barking out commands to several mariners, who were to deliver the messages to the rest of the fleet, while he now completely ignored Ahren and his companions.

'We should let the good admiral get on with it,' said Trogadon somewhat lamely before making his way over to the captain's cabin. When he opened it, he froze before uttering low curses.

Ahren peered over the head of his friend and into what had been transformed into a war room, with all the attendant aura of discipline and severity. The table, around which they had always eaten together, was now covered with a sea chart, upon which stood fifteen small wooden ships, each of them secured to the map by means of a pin, their combination making up a complex pattern. The ship in the middle was painted gold, while two other vessels were red in colour, one to her port side and the other starboard, and each halfway between the main ship and the outer perimeter of the formation.

'Well, our admiral is certainly diligent, I'll give him that,' said Trimm, tugging uneasily at his sleeve. 'Even if I am going to greatly miss this room as it was.'

'What I miss is the anonymous officer who was previously in command and who never bothered us at all,' muttered Falk irritably. 'What was his name again?'

The silence that ensued was eventually broken by Khara. 'We should find ourselves another place on board as soon as possible where we can meet undisturbed – otherwise, this sea voyage is going to be even more uncomfortable than it was going to be.'

'I, for my part, am delighted at the competence and enthusiasm exhibited by our admiral,' said Palnah, Ahren and his companions staring at her in surprise. The woman gazed at them with the serene, all-knowing look that she always exhibited whenever she spoke with the power of her gift. 'He is concerned for the welfare of every one of his charges, from the mightiest of Paladins to the simplest sailor.' She cocked her head. 'And he is fully determined to return to his ambassadorial post in the Jade Palace. He will only succeed in his ambition if he fulfils his task by bringing us safe and sound to the Ice Fields.'

    'Thank you, Palnah. Now I trust this man's ambitions *much* more,' said Uldini, sighing contentedly. 'Justifiable self-interest. A motivation that drives one to remarkable achievements.'

    Jelninolan glared at the childlike figure. 'Sometimes your heart is as dark as your skin.'

    'Thank you, my dear,' replied the first of the Ancients serenely. 'But let us stop exchanging compliments and take Khara's advice before Admiral Refelbek gives us a snug little refuge in the bilge.'

By the time the sun had set on the horizon, the fleet was already on its southward course. Ahren had made himself comfortable in the crow's nest of the *Queen of the Waves*, still amazed by the sight of so many Jade Galleons surrounding her. During the afternoon, Refelbek had established a sequence of signals, which would transmit his commands from ship to ship, either by the light of lanterns at night or by flags during the hours of daylight. This also enabled the quick relaying of information from the perimeter of the fleet back to the command vessel. Now, signal lights on the starboard side of the escort formation were flashing on and off in sequence. The admiral's command ensured that the ships corrected their positions, thereby continuing to ensure that they were protecting the *Lady Aruti* from all possible attacks. Ahren slowly turned on his axis, watching the position lanterns of the fleet in the weak light of the moon, which was now high in the cloudless night sky. The travel formation of the ships revealed a simple elegance, Ahren immediately understanding its purpose. In the middle was the *Queen of the Waves*. On her port side sailed the *Xuan-Foi*, while the *Lady Aruti* accompanied her to starboard. The twelve Jade Galleons surrounded these three vessels in an oval formation which was wide rather than long when viewed from on high. Ahren understood the admiral's rationale – the Lantern Frigates could protect every other ship from attack by means of their Bane Lanterns, the *Queen of the Waves* having the added benefit of receiving light from both magical sources. The Jade Galleons, for their part, formed a sort of shield wall against attacks from all angles, it being impossible to predict where an assault from Dark Ones might spring from.

Ahren now heard quiet singing coming from below, and when he looked down, he made out seven Ice Wolves sitting on the deck passing around a leather skin which – he was certain of this – didn't contain water. Ahren chuckled as he listened to the untrained voices of the singers, who were attempting some sort of Eternal Empire drinking song that they had picked up on their travels, and which they were now doing their level best to remember. The innocence of their clumsy rendition appealed to him, the melody combining with the rise and fall of the waves to create a harmony that was lulling him to sleep...

'Where *is* Trevers, by the way?' asked one of the Ice Wolves suddenly, another verse of the song having been pleasingly mangled. An immediate silence followed, Ahren now finding himself waiting for a response.

'Invalided out,' said a woman's voice curtly. 'Some bastard animal ripped off his arm in Gol-Konar. The thing that the nasty sorcerer was riding on.'

'Damn hard luck,' said a third Ice Wolf. 'Trevers had a good singing voice. And he was bloody great with the crossbow. He'd have had great fun with those weird rays that flew over the deck.'

'Nah – he wouldn't,' interjected another soldier. 'Trevers wasn't a fan of fish.'

The Ice Wolves guffawed.

'Do ye know who it was who saved my life in the bay that time?' asked the woman, immediately providing the answer without waiting for a response from the others. 'The young fella that the Thirteenth has taken under his wing.'

'I think his name is Hakana,' said the man who had initially asked about Trever's fate.

'Ha-ka-*nu*,' corrected another woman in the group. 'And he is our Paladin's apprentice. So, you'd be better off learning his name, idiot.'

'Anyway,' continued the first woman forcefully, 'listen to me story. I'm doing me best to deal with one of those ugly bastards who's attacking me with two knives – none of those piddling throwing knives, mind you – we're talking about a common or garden cutthroat here. What do I do but trip over a corpse and lose me own weapon. I fall to the ground and scrabble around, looking for me bloody blade like someone who's only been soldiering for a wet week, while this ne'er-do-well throws himself at me with his weapons and a nasty laugh. I think to myself, that's me done for, but do ye know what happens next? A spear comes flying in from nowhere and nails the good-for-nothing to a fishing boat. The boy – I'm talking about Hakanu now – comes running past me as though there wasn't sheer bloody carnage going on all around him, yanks his spear out of the wood *and* the corpse and murmurs something like: "I need to work on that". I tell ye, the lad seemed invulnerable – the way he was standing there, completely fearless.'

Ahren gritted his teeth with both frustration *and* pride, having heard the story. When it came to Hakanu, both emotions seemed inseparable.

'What I'm trying to tell ye is this – I would go to war for this lad, anytime and anywhere. He has just as much courage as the Thirteenth, and by the THREE, we are going to need people like him.'

Her conclusion was met by murmurs of agreement, while Ahren bit his lips and mused. Trying to drum caution and wisdom into his apprentice was proving a difficult if not impossible task. But perhaps there was some way of getting Hakanu to realise for himself that a combination of daring and common sense would be no bad thing.

'My...*what?*'

Hakanu's voice veered between disbelief, pride, and something which sounded like uncertainty – much to Ahren's relief. Even the sun, now high in the sky, seemed to be laughing down on the boy who was standing before his master on the fo'c'sle of the *Queen of the Waves*, open-mouthed.

'Your bodyguards,' repeated the Forest Guardian, completely unruffled, as he pointed at the four Ice Wolves who had willingly agreed to look out for Hakanu's safety in any future skirmishes. 'They will follow you, wherever you go and be either the shield at your back or the vanguard of your attack – whichever you command.'

'Uh,' muttered the apprentice, overwhelmed by the news. Ahren couldn't help but feel very proud of himself and his idea.

No need to exaggerate things, warned Culhen. *Your pathetic human nose cannot smell it, but your protégé is on the point of having a panic attack.*

Only one more little push and I'm done, said the Paladin, reassuring his wolf. Then he spoke aloud: 'You are now responsible for the lives of these four. They are soldiers of great courage, but they are neither Paladins nor Ancients. So, behave in such a manner that they will survive the next battle.' He nodded to the four volunteers, who saluted sharply before turning to Hakanu and introducing themselves proudly yet amicably. The look on the apprentice's face, however, almost suggested that Ahren had given him sole responsibility for the protection of a pair of fluffy Roc chicks, upon whose survival the continuation of the enormous breed of birds now rested.

'We should give them their own name,' whispered Trogadon and nodding towards Hakanu's bodyguards once Ahren had joined the rest of his friends. 'How about the Ice Whelps", he added with a gravelly laugh.

'These four are established warriors,' countered Falk indignantly. 'Something like the Whelp Wardens would be better.'

'Are you sure that you aren't placing too much pressure on Hakanu?' murmured Khara. 'He looks as though he's going to jump into the water and seek refuge on one of the Lantern Frigates.'

Ahren refrained from looking over at the boy, for the last thing that he wanted to do was to yield and reverse his decision. 'My apprentice's heart is in the right place, but his head is in the clouds,' he announced. 'He risks his own health without hesitation, and he sees all of us as some sort of immortal heroic figures, who survive everything, no matter what we are confronted with.' He waved his hand vaguely towards the young warrior. 'Now, however, he has four normal soldiers, whose wellbeing is under his direct control. This will teach him to act in a more measured way in the heat of battle.'

Falk nodded approvingly, Ahren breathing a silent sigh of relief at the fact that his erstwhile master at least was not expressing doubts. 'It worked with Ahren, anyway,' said the old Paladin, wiping the sea spray from his beard. 'And the Ice Wolves weren't even my idea.'

'A great leader is contained within the body of the boy,' said Palnah in a low voice, Ahren and his companions then staring at the woman in surprise.

'Are you certain?' asked Trimm sceptically. 'Hakanu is…well…*simple*, if you know what I mean.'

'Hey,' protested Ahren, albeit half-heartedly. 'That's *my* apprentice you're talking about.'

'I said a *great* commander,' smiled Palnah. 'Not a *cunning* one. He is more likely to inspire rather than guide.'

Ahren nodded. 'Last night I heard the Ice Wolves talking about him. His courage inspires loyalty worthy of that shown to a Paladin.'

'Then you had better hope that Hakanu doesn't change your four Ice Wolves into hot-headed swashbucklers,' teased Uldini. 'Or you will have five of them to keep an eye on.'

Ahren glared at the Arch Wizard, who remained unruffled, however. 'Thank you for belittling even my smallest triumphs, Uldini,' muttered the Forest Guardian.

'You're more than welcome,' replied the childlike figure, grinning broadly. 'That's what friends are for.'

Four peaceful days passed by, during which time Ahren gradually grew accustomed to the multitude of ships, while Hakanu came to terms with his responsibility for the bodyguards. The four soldiers had given themselves the name 'Fox Guards' and they practised day and night with their fledgling leader. Ahren was particularly pleased by the fact that Hakanu had sought his and Falk's advice concerning the art of war on several occasions during this short time.

Ahren was standing on the aft deck, beside the admiral, who generally stayed close to the helmsman. The young Paladin listened absently to the barrage of commands that the serious-looking man was giving to two signallers. The pair of mariners, a woman and a man, were both bathed in sweat as they attempted to pass on Refelbek's complicated messages by waving their cloth flags at the neighbouring vessels.

Ahren watched the proceedings for a while before turning to the admiral and asked in a low voice: 'Are these constant course corrections *really* necessary?' The male signaller had issued his third order in a row, his message being conveyed to the farthest Jade Galleon on the starboard side.

'Yes,' replied Refelbek curtly, glancing briefly with narrowed eyes at the Paladin. Ahren could tell that the man was not at all happy at the fact that the Forest Guardian was not on the fo'c'sle or in the little storage room that Trogadon had appropriated as a gathering place for the travellers. 'But not for the reason that you think,' added the admiral with a sigh, Ahren continuing to look at him with a quizzical look and a polite smile. He pointed his chin towards Hakanu and the Fox Guards. 'What do you see over there?'

'My apprentice, training for battle.'

'Precisely,' said the admiral, before bellowing out more commands, which immediately caused a flurry of flag waving. 'I am doing the same.'

Ahren frowned, Refelbek having fallen silent after his short answer. 'You are *training?*' he asked in disbelief.

The admiral nodded impatiently. 'The Thirteenth Fleet has only now been formed,' he said. 'The crews are not yet accustomed to each other. Many Knight Marshes signals are alien to the sailors from the Eternal Empire – *or* they have another meaning.' He interrupted his explanation to roar at the signalwoman, who had waved her flag in a broad arc above her head. 'From left to right, dammit!' he yelled. 'Or do you want the *Xuan-Foi* to collide with one of the Jade Galleons?'

The blushing woman quickly reversed the direction of her red flag, Refelbek now grunting approvingly.

'There you go! That wasn't too hard!' Then he turned to Ahren again. 'As you can see, we *all* need to practise – and that includes *me*. The captains from the Eternal Empire are familiar with different command structures, and even though I know many of the formalities that I must weave into my normal commands, it is essential that I make no errors in the heat of battle or good men and women will end up paying for it with their lives.' Then the admiral turned demonstratively away from Ahren and issued his next command.

I take it I am dismissed, thought Ahren, taken aback. He then sought out Culhen's mind.

The man is simply protecting his pack – we must respect him for that, said Culhen, who was lying below deck on a pile of blankets and giving Kamaluq a thorough grooming. The fox, who was splayed out on his back, was enjoying having his stomach licked clean. Muai had snuggled in beside the wolf, and even when sleeping, with her head against Culhen's back, she looked majestical. It seemed that the argument between the pair had been settled or at least suspended for the time being.

You're probably right, Ahren admitted. *I can hardly blame the admiral for looking after the welfare of those under his command.*

Did you hear what he called the fleet? asked Culhen gleefully.

The Thirteenth Fleet, the young man replied, rolling his eyes. The pride exhibited by his furry friend was burning like a beacon in his own head.

Maybe he's given it that name because we are looking for the last, in other words, the thirteenth of the Paladins, teased the animal in a shamelessly obvious attempt at accusing Ahren of overweening conceitedness. *You must not always assume that everything revolves around you, you know...*

The deafening sound of a horn blasting high above the deck brought Culhen's jibe to a sudden halt, Ahren quickly turning his head to look at the now cursing Admiral.

'Enemy contact,' muttered the Admiral to the Forest Guardian before yelling up into the crow's nest: 'Status?!'

'Sabre Rays ahoy!' shouted the seawoman from on high. 'An enormous shoal. And Pallid Gulls wheeling above them.'

Refelbek groaned. 'Two species of Dark Ones together,' he growled. 'Not good.' He felt for his telescope, which was stored in a slim leather bag that hung from his shoulder and beckoned Ahren to accompany him. 'We'd better go and get a good look at them,' he said grimly.

Ahren followed the admiral through the anxiously whispering crew to the main mast of the ship, Refelbek then climbing the shrouds with surprising agility. It took all the Forest Guardian's skill to keep up with the man, and he silently admitted to himself that the admiral understood the practical side of being a sailor very well indeed. Hardly had they made their way into the crow's nest, the seawoman having made room for them by descending the shrouds, when Refelbek took out his telescope and looked through it towards the south. Even with the naked eye, Ahren could make out an enormous area of water filled with dozens, if not hundreds of swimming triangular shapes. The white birds flying in dizzying circles over the region boded ill, too.

Without saying a word, the admiral passed the telescope to Ahren, who looked through it, his stomach already feeling queasy. He sensed Culhen looking through his eyes and that the wolf's unease was just as great.

There are so many of them, commented the animal, perusing the scene that had revealed itself to Ahren. Thousands of gull-like creatures with oversized beaks were racing in seemingly erratic zigzag patterns through the sky, some of them hundreds of paces high, others a mere three hands above the sea, which was teeming with Sabre Rays. Already having familiarised himself with the sea creatures, Ahren concentrated his attention on the flying enemy. They had the general appearance and size of seagulls which had been pecked at and even somewhat shredded, but it was their misshapen heads that Ahren particularly noticed. Their pallid beaks looked as though they belonged to far larger predatory birds, seemingly consisting of some bonelike material that was remarkably porous and pitted.

'Is that spittle dripping from the gulls' beaks?' asked Ahren with a frown as he continued to look through the telescope.

'You mean, you don't *know?*' countered the admiral in surprise. 'I thought you Paladins were more than familiar with *all* the Dark Ones.'

Ahren lowered the telescope and gave Refelbek a tortured smile. 'Many of my brothers and sisters have centuries of experience under their belts, but I have not been a Champion of the gods sufficiently long to be able to rattle off the names of all the Dark Ones in existence. And I have been rather busy ever since my Naming, so that I still have some gaps in my knowledge.'

The admiral chuckled, the new expression on his face giving the generally dour looking man a much more sympathetic appearance. 'Pallid Gulls are not particularly dangerous in battle,' explained the admiral. 'They are not as nimble as Swarm Claws and possess no life-threatening attributes apart from their beaks.' He tapped his mouth. 'It is their spittle that makes them so despised and feared by all of those who spend their lives on the high seas.' He turned on his axis, seemingly looking for something in the ship's rigging. Finally, he stopped and spoke with a grunt of confirmation. 'There,' he said, pointing at the heavy beam, which held up the front sail of the *Queen of the Waves*.

Ahren peered through the telescope, locating after some searching a light spot, seemingly old and weathered, on the otherwise dark wood. 'What am I looking at?' asked the Forest Guardian warily.

'The untreated speck of a Pallid Gull's spittle,' said the admiral, the young man lowering the telescope again to look at his opposite number in bafflement. 'The secretion that Pallid Gulls extrude from their beaks is caustic,' explained the admiral grimly. 'Not so much that it will kill you in battle, but powerful enough to cause further damage to wounds already inflicted, or to eat away at unprotected skin and clothing. But the greatest danger of the spittle is the long-term damage it can do to wood, canvas, and ropes.' He pointed at the fleck that Ahren had spotted on the yard. 'A Pallid Gull must have sat there some years ago for a few dozen heartbeats.'

Ahren gazed with rising fear at the cloud of Dark Ones, wheeling about erratically on the horizon. 'If we don't do something about those gulls, our ships will be literally dissolved to nothing under our very feet.'

The admiral nodded grimly. 'It will, of course, take several days or possibly even weeks, but, alas, we require at least two moons before we reach Cape Verstaad.'

'Which means we need everyone on deck capable of using a bow and arrow or a crossbow,' concluded Ahren in a low voice.

'And that's not all, Thirteenth,' said Refelbek fiercely, pointing at the foaming waters to the south.

Ahren cursed. 'The Sabre Rays will leap too, won't they?' he asked anxiously. 'While we are busy dealing with the gulls, the swimming monsters can cut us to shreds as they glide above the deck.'

The admiral nodded. 'I fervently hope that the Champions of the gods are as effective as their reputations have led us all to believe them to be.'

'I can't take it anymore,' groaned Trogadon, rubbing fresh sand into his smoking beard from a bucket that was standing at the ready.

The red light from the Bane Lanterns cast an eerie shadow on the weary face of the dwarf, who plopped down on a coil of rope that was lying on the *Queen of the Waves'* main deck. 'It's been like this for three days. Three days of gull hunting while having to dodge the rays all the time.'

'The worst thing of all is that even in death, the creatures cause damage,' said Falk, kicking a lifeless Pallid Gull overboard. The timbers where it had ended its life were crackling and cracking like a smouldering fire. Ahren threw a handful of sand on the affected area, the sounds then gradually dying out.

'At least Refelbek had the wherewithal to bring this mixture on board,' said Khara, pointing at the wooden buckets, which were situated everywhere on the ship. The Swordsmistress was splattered with blood, but following the latest skirmishes Ahren had established that it wasn't her own.

'Others were not quite so far-sighted,' interjected Trimm, pointing north to the disappearing hurricane lantern of a Jade Galleon. The ship had suffered considerable damage over the course of the day, Refelbek eventually ordering the vessel to return to port. 'Three days, and we are already down to fourteen,' added the corpulent Paladin grumpily.

'You're forgetting the human cost caused by the rays,' added Falk gloomily. The *Queen of the Waves* alone has lost two mariners.'

'And an Ice Wolf had an arm ripped off,' murmured Ahren sadly. 'I saw the ray approaching, but my arrow was too late.'

'You must husband your munition, lad,' advised Trogadon. 'I need time to forge new arrows for *Fisiniell*.'

Ahren pointed at a normal bow that was lying on the deck near the railing. 'I'll use that one and the arrows that suit it for the gulls. But whenever I hit a ray using *Fisiniell*, the results are fantastic.'

'I still don't understand why Jelninolan and Uldini don't simply sweep away the gulls with their sorcery,' said Hakanu, exhausted. 'One decent whirlwind and we would be freed of this plague.'

'Firstly, they have from the outset been trying to heal the wounded,' replied Ahren in a severe tone. 'And secondly, they fear – quite rightly – a trap. HE, WHO FORCES knows that we are here – his horde of Dark Ones making life difficult for us are testament to that. Uldini and Jelninolan are convinced that he is waiting for them to cast more powerful magic so that he can then turn it against us. Anyway, they want to be ready in case the Dark god tries to attack us with his own black magic.'

'A sorcerous stalemate, then' said Trimm. 'With each side waiting for the other to make the first move.'

'And with every day that the Sabre Rays and Pallid Gulls continue their assaults, the greater becomes the likelihood that Uldini or Jelninolan will have to intervene,' added Khara.

Puh, muttered Culhen, who had just come on deck with Muai, both wishing to stretch their legs. *We're not going to let gangs of flying and swimming riffraff get us down.*

Ahren shuddered when he saw the corroded mouths and paws of the two large companion animals. After the first day, both he and Khara had banished the pair to below deck, their repeated contact with the Pallid Gulls having had too damaging an effect on them. Kamaluq walked awkwardly over to the wolf and licked his maltreated paws although Culhen had already done the same thing with his healing saliva.

Who is my good fox? You are my good fox, said Culhen, Ahren smiling at the good-natured thoughts of his furry friend.

Kamaluq had become quite the hero, having used his flashes of light at regular intervals under Hakanu's command to blind dozens of low flying Pallid Gulls, not to mention the occasional Sabre Ray that happened to be gliding over the deck, the ship's defenders then being able to wreak havoc on the disorientated Dark Ones. The fox was still too young to perform the feat more than a dozen times per day, but that didn't lessen the affection showered on the young fox by the crew or the pride that Culhen felt for *his* protégé.

'We should have something to eat and then get some sleep,' said Ahren to the others before staring out at the distant Bane Lanterns, whose invaluable light allowed them to enjoy the precious rest that they so desperately needed. The sky swarmed with screeching bodies, which had gathered beyond the red sheen, but not a single Dark One dared to enter the protected zone that the Blood Magic had created and within which the fourteen ships cowered like a flock of terrified sheep.

Or rather, fleeing sheep, thought Ahren, correcting himself as Refelbek roared out several commands in succession, the Thirteenth Fleet then proceeding at full sail and in close formation in the hope of gaining as many priceless leagues as possible before the sun rose again, bringing with it another day of energy-sapping skirmishes.

Chapter 5

Ahren's bloodcurdling scream rang around the deck as a drop of caustic spittle from a dying Pallid Gull landed in his left eye. Spinning wildly around, he struggled towards the hatch which led below deck, simultaneously sensing how Culhen was waking the slumbering Jelninolan in her cabin with his urgent whining.

It felt to Ahren as if his eye was on fire, and it was only through sheer instinct that he evaded an incoming Sabre Ray, rolling away from the glider and casually cutting off the creature's whipping tail with his Wind Blade. The pain in his eye socket penetrated deep into his skull, and he was gripped by fear as he imagined what would happen should he lose the use of his eye completely.

Culhen, too, was panic-stricken, the wolf now literally pushing the groggy elf along the passageway until they came into the line of sight of the Paladin, who was stumbling down the steps.

'My eye…' he groaned, and when the elf gasped in horror and began running towards him, he fell heavily against the wall.

'Keep your hand away from it!' said Jelninolan urgently, quickly unhooking the canteen of healing water, which she now always carried on her belt since she had perfected the curative spell. 'Let me examine the damage.'

It took Ahren considerable effort to pull his fingers away from over the damaged eye, and when Jelninolan quickly pulled back the eyelid, he had to stop himself from hitting out at her in pain.

'How bad is it?' he asked fearfully, now realising that it made no difference whether the eye was open or closed. He could see nothing anymore – neither shafts of light nor even dark spots.

Jelninolan didn't answer, slowly pouring the entire contents of her canteen onto the wound. It felt to Ahren as if a cooling wave was washing through the injury as the burning in his eye socket gradually lessened. The priestess murmured a charm and placed her hands on the left side of his face.

'Close your eye,' she said. Ahren did as he was told, and a numbness set in around the damaged area, which remained after Jelninolan had finished casting her spell. Ahren couldn't open his wounded eye, and his trembling fingers moved protectively back up to his face.

'*Don't!*' hissed the elf, quickly grasping his hand. 'Don't,' she repeated in a gentler voice as she pushed Ahren's arm back down. 'You must not touch the eye. Keep it closed as well or it will never look out onto the world again.'

Ahren froze – as if stung by the paralyzing bane of a High Fang. '*Never...?*' he stammered. What was a marksman without the keen judgement of his dominant eye?

Easy now, interjected Culhen, the presence of the wolf resting on Ahren's furious thoughts like a warm, woolly blanket. *Listen carefully to what Jelninolan is saying.* With that, the animal pushed himself against Ahren's back so that the Paladin could snuggle against him.

Ahren looked pleadingly up at Jelninolan's face with his working eye and dug his fingers into the comforting fur of the wolf behind him. 'Tell me – how bad *is* it?' he asked, this time trying to keep as calm as possible.

'It's bad,' replied the elf through gritted teeth. Then she gave him a reassuring smile. 'But not hopeless. For starters, I have charmed the area around the injured eye into a state of inertia so that you *cannot* open it. It is vitally important that it has a complete rest and that you place no demands on it.' She looked at him sternly. 'Which means no fighting, and no moving around on deck without a decent dressing on the eye.' She touched his knee before gracefully getting to her feet. 'This wound will take weeks to heal, and any further damage to the eye will lead to certain loss of sight. I am going to get a clean bandage and other things necessary to protect your injury from outside harm. Don't move – understand? Even if this ship sinks beneath us, you are to stay put until I have finished with you.'

Ahren nodded. 'Thank you,' he whispered. It took all his self-control not to touch his eye. The sudden realisation of his own vulnerability made him feel weak and exhausted.

Hurried footsteps caused him to turn his head. Khara came into his restricted view, the Swordsmistress stopping suddenly and gasping. Her face exhibited naked fear as she covered her mouth with her hand in alarm. 'Ahren...' she murmured before running to him.

'I will be fine,' he said quickly, hugging her awkwardly as she knelt beside him.

'*If* he looks after himself,' said Jelninolan, appearing in the passageway with a bundle of dressing. 'Ahren has been extremely unlucky, and yet at the same time more than a little fortunate. The corrosive hit his pupil, so if I hadn't been on board, he would certainly have lost his eye, and the caustic spittle might even have penetrated through to his brain.'

Dizziness overcame the Paladin, and he pushed hard against the large wolf, who had reacted with a whimpering on hearing the elf's words. An agonised scream from a mariner on the deck above resembled a macabre answer to the priestess's warning, the priestess now skilfully wrapping the right half of Ahren's face with a thick, rough bandage.

'Every day I will examine the eye and wash it out with healing water,' she explained before holding Ahren's chin firmly and staring at him severely. 'And in the meantime, you avoid performing any sort of heroics until I tell you otherwise. Understood?'

'Of course,' replied Ahren immediately. His fear of being permanently handicapped was contesting with his guilty conscience at being unavailable to help in the defence of the fleet for the next while.

'I will make sure that he doesn't get anywhere near the fighting,' promised Khara, and when Ahren looked at the Swordsmistress, all hope of assisting vanished.

The following weeks were torture. Ahren was literally imprisoned in the belly of the ship, with the unyielding Culhen as keeper of the dungeon. Only at night, and under the protection of two Ice Wolves bearing large shields, was Ahren allowed up on deck, where he could train his archery skills with his right eye and simultaneously get some fresh air. He also checked out the damage to the fleet, which was increasing by the day, as was the casualty list among the mariners.

Uldini and Jelninolan worked tirelessly, treating as many injuries as they could, the elf even resorting to creating another healing basin on board the *Lady Aruti*, just as she had done during the battle for Hjalgar. She was making every effort to come to grips with the sheer number of wounded defenders.

The seemingly never-ending battle against the Dark Ones drained the crew members, both physically and mentally, and Ahren's conversations with his friends became shorter and shorter as the skirmishes dragged on. Strangely enough, it was Trimm and Refelbek who were the most fruitful sources of information regarding the latest news from on deck. The admiral did not personally involve himself in the fighting, but instead coordinated the movements of the fleet from his cabin in the aft deck, while Trimm sought safety below deck, not having sufficient armour. He spent much of his time comforting the distraught Palnah, who was suffering under the influence of her gift's dark side. Clearly, she could sense the shadow of death, which accompanied the relentless skirmishes on the Thirteenth Fleet, the emotional turmoil causing her to seek refuge in some kind of spiritual twilight zone.

The only glimmer of light, literally, was the progressive recovery of Ahren's eye. By now, Ahren had been allowed to replace the dressing with an eye patch. Uldini would occasionally shine a beam of light for what seemed like an endless length of time onto the injured eye, using *Flamestar's* magic to help restore it to its former condition.

Jelninolan had announced the previous day that Ahren would be fully cured within one or two weeks, the Forest Guardian's enforced apathy beginning to yield to an almost uncontrollable thirst for action. Now he was standing on deck in the darkness of night with Falk and Trogadon acting as guards while he watched his surroundings keenly.

'How is Khara?' he asked uneasily, Trogadon's powerful hand landing with a slap on the young man's forearm.

'The same as she was ten heartbeats ago, the last time you asked,' growled the dwarf wearily. 'She only suffered a small cut to her face today, and she will be here soon.' The dwarf pointed at a shadow in the water, which was dancing on the waves. 'Look over there! That must be the tender bringing her back from the *Lady Aruti*.'

Ahren breathed a sigh of relief. 'Every time one of you is wounded…' he began, placing his hand meaningfully on his eye patch.

'I know, lad, I know,' responded Trogadon in his gravelly voice.

The dwarf looked yearningly at the frigate, the shine of her Bane Lantern giving the illusion that she was covered in a bloody shroud. The enormous vessels with their high hulls reminded Ahren on nights like these of those ghost stories that sailors would talk about during their night watches, tales of crews on ghost ships haunting the oceans, having been inflicted with some terrible curse.

'How long has it been since you have seen Jelninolan?' asked Falk compassionately.

'Two weeks,' sighed the dwarf. 'Whenever she isn't filling her healing basin with new strength, she sleeps, her labour being so exhausting.'

'Refelbek says that if it wasn't for her and Uldini's help, six ships would already have fallen by the wayside,' interjected Ahren. 'The pair are certainly keeping our fleet alive.'

'And yet, every day more Dark Ones arrive to attack us,' grumbled Trogadon. 'A never-ending flood of them.'

Ahren gritted his teeth and said nothing. Not for the first time did the Forest Guardian wish that there were more than two Lantern Frigates accompanying them. They were coming across evermore chunks of debris from sunken ships, silent witnesses to the destructive power of the enemy. The Thirteenth Fleet was being harried on its voyage south while being systematically cut off from any sort of reinforcement that was rushing to its aid. He felt compassion for those luckless mariners who were under attack in the same way that the Thirteenth Fleet was – but with the added disadvantage of being attacked both day *and* night.

'We should reach safety in twenty days or so,' murmured Ahren. Soon they would arrive at the southern end of Jorath's west coast before veering east towards Cape Verstaad – or so Admiral Refelbek had told him some hours earlier when Ahren had requested information regarding the progress of their voyage.

'But first we have to navigate our way past the Screaming Crags,' muttered Falk as he peered out to sea. 'One of the largest known nesting sites of Pallid Gulls.'

'And why didn't some bright spark of an Ancient sink those rocks into the sea centuries ago if I may ask?' grumbled Trogadon as he pulled at his beard, which had several burn holes in it now, thanks to the spittle of the Pallid Gulls.

Falk shrugged his shoulders. 'According to Uldini, the crags are part of an underwater mountain range and are particularly big. Exploding them would cause a tsunami that could destroy every coastal community.'

'And if we simply go on shore and travel the rest of the way to Cape Verstaad on foot?' asked Ahren.

'That won't alter the fact that we will still need the Thirteenth Fleet as soon as travel into the Ice Fields,' replied Falk with a sigh. 'Unless you believe that the Adversary will cave in once we have arrived in the city of a thousand thrones.'

'I thought that Cape Verstaad was governed by *fifty* grandees,' interjected Trogadon grumpily. 'How come there are a *thousand* thrones in the metropolis?'

'The bards like to guild the lily,' countered Falk with a chuckle.

'I wager whatever is left of my beard that a huge force of Dark Ones is waiting for us at the Screaming Crags,' muttered the blacksmith. 'It would be stupid of the Dark god *not* to pick a region full of underwater reefs, and rocks inhabited by Pallid Gulls as the location for one of the first decisive battles.'

'I think we are all in agreement with you on that,' said Ahren dryly. 'However, look on the bright side – if we can manage to get past the Screaming Crags, then we will surely reach Cape Verstaad at least.'

'Why didn't Yollock pick a relaxing beach off the west coast of the Sun Islands as his refuge?' sounded a familiar voice from just below deck. It was Trimm, who then came up through the hatch to join the others. 'I shudder to think,' continued the corpulent Paladin, 'that you are going to all this effort only to end up disembarking onto a deadly desert of ice.'

'How *considerate* of you,' snarled Trogadon. 'You are very welcome to accompany us if you wish.'

Trimm had known for weeks already that he was not capable of tackling a journey into the Ice Fields and therefore wouldn't be going. The realisation hadn't saddened him either – a fact which irked some of his companions more than others.

Ahren placed a reassuring hand on the squat dwarf's shoulder before turning to Trimm. 'How is Palnah?' he asked the Paladin, who was panting after the exertion of climbing the stairs.

Trimm's deep concern was evident on his face. 'Not good,' he said glumly. 'In Gol-Konar she was mostly sheltered within the confines of the Blood Red Palace, away from the horrors of that nefarious city, but now she is caught up in a maelstrom of blood, death, and despair.' He shook his head. 'I never knew that her gift could trouble her so much. I thought that she was able to see into the heart of a being – and that was it.'

'Sorcery and ever-present death have *never* been equal partners,' mused Falk. 'Some of the most horrific creatures in Jorath have been formed from the malevolent interaction of these two powers.'

Ahren couldn't help thinking of how the Swamplings had originated – creations of the unfortunate amalgamation of deathly sorrow and goblin magic. 'Do we know what will be waiting for us at the Screaming Crags?' he asked dolefully.

Falk shook his head. 'No-one who has sailed to this region over the past few weeks has lived long enough to deliver a report.'

The thud against the outside of the hull provided a welcome distraction for Ahren and he quickly went to the railing to peer down at those on the tender below, immediately spotting Khara. She looked up at him with a mixture of weariness and relief.

'You'd make a half-decent pirate now with that eye patch,' she called up with a faint smile.

'He's a few feathers short if you ask me,' grunted Falk with a chuckle, remembering back to the time that he had played the role of Captain Featherbeard on the Cutlass Sea. It was at times like these that Ahren asked himself if, in another life, his mentor would have happily chosen a career as a buccaneer.

Khara clambered up the rope ladder, Ahren flinching when he saw the dark rings under the eyes of his beloved. 'You look terrible,' he blurted out, unable to stop himself.

Khara, however, winked at him. 'You *really* know how to charm a girl,' she teased. Then her face became serious. 'Jelninolan is shattered. With smaller injuries – like mine – she uses magic that draws its source from *within* the patient. A good night's sleep and I'll be right as rain.'

Ahren held her close for several heartbeats before guiding her to the hatch. He had worried enough for one night. Only time would tell what they were going to encounter at the Screaming Crags, and the Paladin was grimly determined to be ready to fight – whenever that day arrived.

'That's painful,' groaned Ahren, blinking the tears out of his left eye, which was already feeling the soft evening rays of light.

'I told you that you should wait another few days,' scolded Jelninolan, holding the leather eye patch that Ahren had worn for so long now.

Ahren blinked again, enjoying – despite the pain – the anticipation of soon being able to see perfectly again. He hugged Jelninolan impulsively, causing the weak elf to groan. 'Thank you,' he murmured into her ear.

'You're welcome,' she replied equally quietly before reattaching the patch. 'Keep protecting your eye for a *little* longer so that you will be ready for action.'

Ahren released the elf from his embrace and looked around curiously. They were all standing on the fo'c'sle of the *Lady Aruti*, in whose hull the priestess had placed her healing basin, and the view from the enormous ship was breath-taking. 'It's like standing in a crow's nest,' said Ahren, enthralled by the vista. He was enjoying the gentle breeze on his face and, now that his patch was back on, the glow of the setting sun in the clear blue sky, which would soon be replaced by the scornful light of the Bane Lanterns. Even though it was the onset of winter, the air was comfortably warm, the deep south following different rules to those of the countries in the middle of the continent.

'Then you shouldn't miss the opportunity of climbing up *there*,' laughed the elf, pointing up to the big basket, dizzyingly high, at the top of the main mast. 'It's like standing on a swaying mountain top.'

Ahren hugged the exhausted elf a second time before she disappeared below deck to take care of her other patients. Then he approached the main mast, passing by Hakanu and Captain Konitu as he did so, the boy and the woman busily evaluating the latest damage to the Lantern Frigate. In the weeks that Ahren had been forced to spend below deck, his apprentice had won the respect of all the captains in the fleet. The young warrior had helped the neighbouring ships on several occasions in crisis situations, flinging his spear and wounding gliding Sabre Rays in mid-flight. The lad's shoulders had bulked up during this time, and he diligently continued his training every day after the relentless skirmishes, while others fell into their bunks, exhausted. Trogadon's notorious weights were now just as much a part of the apprentice's routine as those back-breaking exercises in the shrouds that Khara had introduced the young warrior to at the outset of their voyage.

Hakanu's urge to prove himself drove him on relentlessly, but the boy's motivation seemed to have shifted its focus markedly, much to Ahren's delight. Hakanu's stunts were still as daring as ever, but now they seemed aimed at maintaining the health and safety of his fellow fighters rather than at simply trying to kill as many Dark Ones as possible and in the most spectacular manner imaginable. As far as Ahren was concerned, this was a very important step in the right direction – especially as not one of the Fox Guards had been lost since the establishment of the group. Yantilla had even reported to Ahren that the number of Ice Wolves petitioning her to join the Fox Guards was growing all the time.

'...indeed, we are under the impression that the gulls are now particularly targeting the protective boxes of the Bane Lanterns during their daylight attacks,' explained Captain Konitu, causing Ahren to stop in his tracks.

'Why do you think that?' he asked, turning back to face the apprentice and the captain.

'The spittle stains have been increasing for some days now on the metal casing around the Bane Lanterns. They are very easy to identify, Thirteenth,' explained Konitu, bowing slightly. 'Furthermore, my crew have seen an increasing number of gulls sitting in the vicinity of the main mast over the past four days.'

'Is this possible, master?' asked Hakanu, wide-eyed. 'I thought that the gulls were notorious for their *dull* intelligence.'

Ahren scratched his beard as he pondered. 'We have seen no signs of there being a High Fang among the attackers. This is one of the few advantages of fighting at sea. And the only Dopplers that we know to exist are the remaining children of the Adversary,' he mused. 'It *is* possible that the Dark god's controlling power has grown in the meantime, so that he can awaken vague impulses in the gulls, thereby creating a more targeted approach on their part, and...well...that would be bad news, indeed.' Ahren felt a queasiness in his stomach as he imagined what carnage a Glower Bear or a Blood Wolf could wreak if controlled in such a manner. All the Dark Ones in Jorath would suddenly become dramatically more menacing – especially the more deviously clever ones. 'I need to talk to Uldini about this,' said Ahren, drumming his left thigh nervously with his fingers. The Arch Wizard had been lying in a deep sleep whenever possible since the skirmishing had started, in an attempt at conserving his energy. Should he rouse the sorcerer straight away or wait for the Ancient to wake up?

Uldini has just staggered past me on his way to his cabin, said Culhen helpfully from the belly of the *Queen of the Waves*. *He seems to be sleepwalking through over-exhaustion.*

Then I'll leave it until later, Ahren decided, thanking the wolf for his assistance.

'Didn't you want to go up there?' asked Konitu, pointing up at the crow's nest.

Ahren nodded with exaggerated enthusiasm. 'Maybe I will be able to see the Screaming Crags,' he added, the confidence in his voice disguising the fact that he was, in fact, feeling like a godsday student attending his first festive ball.

The captain squinted her eyes and looked up at the heavens. 'With a bit of luck you *will*, Thirteenth,' she said before reaching for her telescope and handing it to him. 'Would you be so kind as to report back to us should you see anything of importance?'

Ahren nodded, securing the precious instrument to his belt. He was about to begin his ascent when he was joined by Hakanu.

'I'll race you to the top, master!' exclaimed the lad, immediately climbing one of the ratlines attached to the tall timber pole.

'Why does *everyone* want to make climbing up to the crow's nest into a contest,' muttered Ahren, following his apprentice up the shrouds.

Hakanu already had a slight edge and, of course, the strength of his growing body, but Ahren had the greater experience combined with a longer reach. Still, the young master was surprised by how out of breath he was when he finally arrived at the basket's edge several heartbeats before his protégé.

'Well done,' he said, praising the young warrior while trying to draw breath as quietly as he could. 'If you keep practising, you may well beat me in, say, ten to twenty years' time.'

Hakanu thrust forth his chin belligerently, and Ahren groaned inwardly. He knew all too well that the apprentice would add several more training exercises to his regime over the next few evenings. He quietly swore to himself that he, too, would do some additional climbing routines.

Your apprentice is really driving you forward, said Culhen smugly. *I must say, I find that most edifying.*

You're beginning to sound as haughty as Muai, countered Ahren, the wolf sulking silently after that.

The Forest Guardian pulled himself over the edge and into the crow's nest of the Lantern Frigate, the bucket being a good five paces across, making it just as over-large as everything else on the ship. He nodded at the saluting mariner who was keeping watch, then turned to face the east.

While Hakanu gasped in astonishment behind him, the young master calmly allowed the view to work its wonders in silence.

Jelninolan had not been exaggerating. The vastness of the sea below was fantastic to behold, while every movement of the ship was magnified considerably in his lofty position. Being stuck up here in a storm would certainly be nerve-wracking. Fortunately, the heavens, so near to where he was standing, were free from clouds, while the wind was pleasant enough.

Hakanu positioned himself beside his master with and grinned broadly. 'This is how the mother of the winds must have felt when she swept across Jorath.'

Ahren allowed himself to be infected by his protégé's enthusiasm and nodded vigorously. 'It really is breath-taking,' he called out before demonstratively taking the telescope from his belt. 'Will we see what surprises lie in store for us?'

Hakanu nodded, and as if responding to a secret command, the pair of Paladins suddenly became serious. Ahren's pulse quickened as he peered through the glass with his good eye, scanning the east, which had become their new destination now that they had circumnavigated the west coast of Jorath. Despite the encroaching gloom, the horizon was still clearly visible, and it wasn't long before the Forest Guardian found what he had been looking for – a line of snow-white rocks with an unbelievably filthy surface completely devoid of plant life, thanks to generations of brooding Pallid Gulls having nested there – not to mention countless more of Dark Ones that populated the rocks. Ahren saw that many of the Pallid Gulls were badly wounded from the saliva of their neighbours, and he could also make out what happened to the flesh of those that had succumbed to their injuries. It seemed that the screeching chicks were indifferent to the source of the meat that was delivered to their open beaks.

Ahren managed to suppress the nausea that was rising within him, trying, instead, to feel some sort of compassion for the tortured birds. They were, after all, as much *victims* as they were servants of the Dark god.

Ahren then scanned the waters between the rocks for signs of Sabre Rays, his efforts being duly and generously rewarded. But much to his dismay, there were other shadows visible. These were slim and speedy, yet also enormous.

'May I look, too?' asked Hakanu, Ahren nodding absently. He handed his apprentice the telescope and pondered over what it was that had caught his eye. It seemed that the Adversary had another baleful surprise in store for the Paladins.

He was still wondering what the creatures could possibly be when Hakanu pulled the telescope away from his eye and looked in terror at Ahren. 'A se..sea...mo...mo...monster has just leaped out of the water!' he stammered.

Ahren had never seen his apprentice so stunned before.

'It was at least ten paces long!'

Out of the corner of his eye, Ahren noticed that the mariner with whom they were sharing the crow's nest seemed to understand the trading language of the new arrivals, for he glanced from one Paladin to the other with a look of horror on his face.

Ahren cursed quietly and took the telescope from his apprentice's trembling fingers. 'Let me look again,' he said grimly.

'Aren't those Monster Eels, master?' asked Hakanu, who was slowly regaining his self-control. 'I think I read about them in the good Falk's almanac.'

Ahren gritted his teeth, partly because of the growing enthusiasm evident in the boy's tone, but also because of the terrified groan of the mariner, who would doubtless spread Hakanu's news, thus ensuring that the entire Thirteenth Fleet would be in the know before the night was through. He waited impatiently in the hope of getting a better look at one of the swimming shadows, and when one of them finally leaped out of the water, Ahren cursed heartily at the precise picture that presented itself. A bullish, almost square-headed monster with a wide, narrow mouth filled with protruding teeth had broken through the surface and soared up in a high arc before diving elegantly back into the ocean, tearing apart with its powerful jaws an unfortunate Sabre Ray.

'A slim, snakelike torso,' murmured Ahren, trying to sound as casual as possible. 'Total length between eight and ten paces, bony head, mouth full of carnassial teeth...yes, those are certainly Monster Eels,' he said, slowly lowering the telescope and muttering oaths under his breath.

'So, I'm *right* then?' asked Hakanu excitedly.

'Yes,' said Ahren, his wan smile exhibiting his approval of the boy's educational progress, at least. 'Even if the term Monster Eel is somewhat inaccurate. Strictly speaking, they are moray eels which have grown unnaturally large thanks to the Dark god. Hence, the insatiable appetite, which causes them to devour the Sabre Rays. A Monster Eel that isn't constantly feeding starves to death within days.'

Hakanu blinked in consternation. 'That's not particularly clever of the Adversary,' he said. 'Not only is he losing rays, but the eels are cutting themselves on their bony prey.'

Ahren bit his lower lip anxiously. 'One way or another, we are clearly meant to come to grief at the Screaming Crags,' he said after some heartbeats. 'Even if HE, WHO FORCES is willing to sacrifice a whole army of his servants in the process.'

'Why don't we simply steer clear of the area?' asked Hakanu doubtfully.

Ahren was glad that his apprentice was at least considering the option of avoiding a future battle. With a heavy heart, he repeated the answer that the admiral had given him when he had asked the same question only a few days before.

'The detour would be too onerous, and the danger of the Dark god summoning yet more of his monsters too great. Anyway, we shouldn't sail *too* far south. There is a current down there, which separates the southern sea from the frozen shores of the Ice Fields. Ships that are sucked into it are pulled away, inevitably ending up in an area known as the Ravenous Maw.'

'Oh, right,' mumbled Hakanu, crestfallen. Clearly, becoming lost without trace did not belong to the list of heroic deeds that excited the young boy's brain.

'And anyway, we are going to have to defeat these Dark Ones if we want to keep the supply routes along the coast free,' mused Ahren. He looked through the telescope one last time before coming to a decision. 'If we continue to travel at this speed, we will reach the Screaming Crags in the early morning,' he said anxiously. 'We had better speak to the admiral. I think I have an idea of how we can avoid a considerable number of skirmishes.'

'This is foolhardy in the *extreme*, Thirteenth,' said Admiral Refelbek.

Ahren could positively feel the disdain in the voice of the man who was now leaning back at the captain's table, around which Ahren, his companions, and Yantilla had gathered.

'Passing through the Screaming Crags at night would mean negotiating them practically blind. The light from the Bane Lanterns makes the waters appear black, thereby hiding underwater reefs. Furthermore, the protective sheen will force us into a more compact formation, which will only intensify the difficulties of such a manoeuvre! We risk losing the *entire* fleet to the rocks, should you stubbornly insist on avoiding Dark One assaults in the manner you have described.'

'He is right,' said the wan-looking Uldini, the Arch Wizard hardly able to keep his eyes open. 'You are merely exchanging one evil for another.'

Ahren rubbed his temples as he looked around the table for support. 'We would take in the sails tonight and proceed the rest of the way to the Screaming Crags during the course of tomorrow,' he said, repeating his argument stubbornly. 'Then, with the onset of dusk, we would meet the army of Dark Ones, moving through them under the protection of the Bane Lanterns.' He spread out his arms in a gesture of helplessness. 'What is our alternative? Literally fighting a sea of dark Ones during the hours of daylight while at the *same time* trying desperately to avoid the underwater reefs.'

'Which we would at least be able to *see*,' countered Trogadon, glancing apologetically at Ahren. 'Personally, I would prefer an intact hull rather than one that has been sliced though by sharp underwater rocks. That would undoubtedly help me make it to the coast without having to walk with my heavy frame along the seabed.'

'Still, we cannot dismiss Ahren's points out of hand,' mumbled Jelninolan, who was so tired that her voice was slurred. Her eyes were closed, but it seemed that she had been listening carefully. 'Uldini and I are completely exhausted and will hardly be able to involve ourselves in the battle. Despite this, we will be ready to do our bit on the *Queen of the Waves*, helping where we can. The fewer the number of casualties that result from our passage through the crags, the better.'

'I am sure that it will come as no surprise to everyone sitting around this table that I am in favour of the plan that involves fewer skirmishes,' said Trimm with a faint smile as he turned to the sceptical looking admiral. 'How often have you sailed through the Screaming Crags?' asked the corpulent Paladin.

'Many times,' admitted Refelbek, scratching his chin. 'So often, in fact, that I know the passage like the back of my hand.'

And the other captains?' asked Ahren hopefully.

'At least as often as I have,' conceded the admiral hesitantly. 'You must not forget that the waters belong to the Eternal Empire. Until recently, during the conflict with the Sunplains, the coastline to the west of Cape Verstaad was a war zone, and therefore the waters were sailed through as often as they were fought over.'

'In other words, we have the choice between a full-scale battle and a cloak-and-dagger night-time voyage around a few reefs which everyone in this fleet is familiar with,' commented Falk. 'So, why are we even discussing this?'

'We are not *discussing* anything!' snapped Refelbek. 'You lot are sharing your highfalutin' ideas and suggestions with me, and then *I* will decide which ones – *if any* – I will subject *my* fleet to.'

Falk furiously bit his lip. Ahren could see the vein on the old man's temple pulsating angrily.

'Why don't we let the admiral mull over the advantages and disadvantages of both strategies in peace and quiet,' he suggested hastily. 'He can give us his decision later.'

Falk opened his mouth, but Trogadon poked him hard in the stomach and shook his head vigorously. The companions streamed out of the narrow cabin and into the still young evening.

Hardly had the door closed behind them when Falk exhaled forcefully. 'I admit that as a Paladin – and therefore as a general – I am spoilt,' he growled angrily, 'in that when I make a *suggestion*, I expect it to be *implemented!*'

'Refelbek is an *admiral,* remember,' chuckled Trimm quietly. 'Which means that he ranks higher than you do on the high seas. Or are Paladins now generals *and* admirals?'

Uldini shook his head. 'Not officially. Very few of the Champions of the gods were qualified mariners. Fisker and Luna could certainly lay claim to the rank, but they aren't here.'

'Let's hope that Refelbek will take the bull by the horns and go for the night voyage,' said Yantilla. 'My Ice Wolves could certainly do with some protection.'

'The admiral is a smart man, who is simply unused to sharing his authority with others. He will do the right thing,' said Khara, then stretching with a groan. 'Well, I don't know about you lot, but I'm going to lie down. If we really *are* going to end up sailing through the night, then tomorrow may well end up being a *very* long day.'

'Or very short,' added Trogadon with an air of foreboding, a heavy silence then descending on the companions as they made their way to their cabins.

Ahren was awakened by the loud calls of industrious sailors and the characteristic sounds of canvases being taken in.

'The sails are being furled,' said Khara beside him in the dark as she snuggled in close, sighing contentedly. 'It seems that Refelbek has overcome his inner struggle and listened to us.' Soon she was breathing deeply and regularly again.

Ahren kissed his beloved gently on her forehead and stared up towards the ceiling through the impenetrable blackness that surrounded them in their cabin.

He sensed that Culhen was awake, too, listening to the sounds that were echoing from the deck. Through the eyes of his friend, he could see that the companion animals were lying on the fo'c'sle, in their usual ball of snouts and paws. The wolf was watching quietly as the sails gradually disappeared until only the silhouettes of the gently bobbing ships lay indolently on the silent waters.

Refelbek has picked a good location for his manoeuvre, announced Culhen. *The current here seems almost non-existent. We are hardly moving from the spot.*

Ahren now understood why the admiral had been so hesitant earlier. Bringing an entire fleet simultaneously to a halt and maintaining that formation for a whole night was surely no easy undertaking. And the next night, he would have to guide fourteen ships through a passage riddled with underwater reefs. The young Paladin felt an ever-growing respect for the man.

If only Fisker and Aluna were here to advise us, thought Ahren with a sigh. *They would surely have come up with a better plan than mine.*

We all work with what we have been given, teased Culhen. *After all, I had to make a genuine Paladin out of you, remember?*

Ahren could sense the undercurrent of genuine affection in the wolf's jibe and found himself smiling in the darkness. *How are you?* he asked gently.

I am bored, restless, and even a little afraid, came the unexpectedly honest reply. *I miss not being able to move about. I may as well tell you this now – as soon as we get to Cape Verstaad, you are not going to see me and Muai for a few days. I am going to accompany her around the place until my paws fall off!*

You will get more than enough exercise when we arrive in the Ice Fields, said Ahren, comforting his friend. *And I can well understand your being afraid of the next night that awaits us. Cooped up on board these ships while the waters around us are seething with Dark Ones and the skies are infested by Pallid Gulls isn't exactly my first choice as the ideal way of spending a night at sea either. If everything works out as I hope it will, my plan should spare us the majority of skirmishes.*

But at least you have a bow and arrows that you can use, as well as hands with which you can grasp things, complained Culhen in a surprisingly forceful tone. *I am completely dependent on the seamanship of the crew. If the ships split on the reefs and sink, how are Muai, Kamaluq, and I going to save ourselves? Unlike you humans, we can't drag ourselves onto a piece of wreckage and paddle to the shore.*

Ahren flinched. Never before had he realised how it felt for the companion animals to be imprisoned on board ship. No wonder that Selsena had preferred the option of accompanying Lanlion rather than submitting herself to moons of this torture. *I promise you that I will do everything in my power to protect you – and all the living creatures on the ships – from perdition,* said Ahren fervently. *And that as soon as we have broken through the blockade of Dark Ones, I will give you a thorough grooming.*

Culhen's agitated mind began to calm somewhat, Ahren then adding with a smile: *Remember when we were fleeing the Needle Spiders in the Southern Jungles?* he asked. *And you let me tumble down a waterfall?*

Oh, yes, came the joyous reply. *The face on you would have made even the deities laugh...*

Ahren and Culhen then proceeded to spend half the night revelling in the memories of their previous adventures and, especially, of the animal's heroic deeds. Slowly but surely, both the self-confidence and dignity of the wolf re-established themselves – two traits that made Ahren's friend a rock of reliability in the young Paladin's tumultuous life.

When they both finally fell asleep, they had smiles on their faces.

'Well, you can knock me down with a feather!' exclaimed Falk as he and Ahren stared at the spectacle playing out in front of them.

All the companions were standing in formation with the Ice Wolves – who were holding shields aloft – on the fo'c'sle of the *Queen of the Waves*, watching a massive cloud of Pallid Gulls rising in the sky and then heading towards the fleet. Their birds were so packed together that the lowest ones were inevitably being wounded by the spittle dropping from above before crashing onto the water and being greedily consumed by the Monster Eels, swimming just below the surface. The approaching army was a veritable tsunami, threatening to overwhelm the fleet, and Ahren was now fully convinced that *his* tactic would soon prove to have been the right one. Nervously, he looked over at the setting sun, the fierce ball of fire looming out from behind some straggling clouds and casting the sea in an ominous, golden-red sheen.

'This truly is a breath-taking sunset,' murmured Khara, who was standing with her weapons drawn, nervously looking at the heavenly body. 'But I *do* wish the sun would set rather more quickly today.'

'Why did we start sailing so early?' asked Trogadon anxiously, checking his heavy crossbow yet again.

'So that we reach the Screaming Crags at precisely the right moment,' replied Ahren in a strained voice. 'Refelbek needs the last remaining light to figure out his starting position for a successful passage between the underwater reefs once night has set in.'

'There's always a catch,' grunted Falk before breathing in sharply. 'They are reaching the first of the Jade Galleons,' he added. 'Let us hope that she bears up…'

Falk's words fizzled out into an uncomprehending silence as the ship literally disappeared beneath the plummeting seabirds. Simultaneously, the water around the galleon exploded as both Sabre Rays and Monster Eels launched an attack on any screaming crewmembers who were standing on deck. While the rays engaged in their typical gliding manoeuvres, the snakelike Dark Ones shot out of the water like arrows, closing their jaws around any sailor that was standing too close to the railing, and then disappearing with their squirming victims beneath the spray, the surface of the water turning red in no time at all. Meanwhile, fumes could be seen rising from the ship's framework as the spittle of countless Pallid Gulls performed its deadly task. The occasional whizzing arrow or bolt dispatched by the despairing defenders killed a few rays, eels, and gulls, but with every heartbeat the unwanted outcome of this skirmish seemed to become ever clearer.

'This is utter carnage!' exclaimed Trimm hoarsely…we must do *something!*'

The front galleon had already veered off course, her ripped sails now falling from the creaking, steaming masts, while ropes ripped, and the first of her timbers began cracking under the corrosive.

Ahren could only stand there and watch in utter helplessness. Meanwhile, behind him Refelbek screamed out a single command, which was then transmitted to the other ships by a sharp, penetrating blow of a bugle instead of the usual flags. Dragon Bows sang, while both arrows and thick bolts whizzed through the air, resembling dozens of hornet swarms as the rest of the ships caught up with the seriously damaged front vessel and furiously dispatched their long-range artillery on the ball of Dark Ones.

His eyes moist, Ahren, too, participated in the shooting once it was apparent that there were no sailors left on the deck of the stricken vessel that he might accidentally hit. His companions, either cursing or in grim silence, shot at the swallowing, screeching, and ravenous blood-spattered Dark Ones, which began to scatter under the relentless volley of bolts and arrows raining down on them. Ahren saw to his surprise that many of the projectiles being launched from the Jade Galleons to the front were burning before slamming into the timbers of the stricken ship. Fires were breaking out everywhere, and soon there was a furious spitting sound as the flames turned into a veritable conflagration, greedily consuming every inch of the dying vessel as well as any Dark Ones that were in or on the ship.

Ahren looked over at Uldini, who was hovering grimly behind the Ice Wolves, but the Arch Wizard merely shook his head. 'There was no magic in play here,' he said, perplexed.

'It was lamp oil,' said Khara flatly. 'They soaked the whole ship in lamp oil, for they knew that, as they were the vanguard, they didn't stand a chance anyway.' She turned her head and looked over at Refelbek. 'And *he* knew that he would have to lure the Dark Ones to the vessel so that as many of the monsters as possible would be consumed by the firestorm.'

Ahren stared over in disbelief at the admiral, who was standing at the wheel, his face grim and his eyes filled with tears as he bellowed out order after order, his voice only betraying the hint of a tremble. 'He *sacrificed* the ship and her *entire* crew.' His own voice was quaking with horror and rage. 'They were the bait to distract the Dark Ones, which *he* could then destroy.'

There was a cracking sound, and Ahren turned to look once more at the sea. The Jade Galleon had finally split asunder, her smoking wreckage spreading out on the surface of the water. Countless Pallid Gulls rose into the air, screeching and burning, only to suddenly lose power before plummeting helplessly into the sea. The ocean seemed to consist of nothing other than burning wood and wildly swimming Dark Ones, the latter either desperate to flee the chaos of the flames or eager to approach the next two Jade Galleons, which were now moving closer to the *Queen of the Waves* and guarding her from the front.

Ahren gasped as he prepared inwardly for another massacre when suddenly there was a loud creaking sound as the Bane Lantern boxes opened out, the shining light from within them then masking the rays of the dying sun. Screeching and snarling, the army of enslaved creatures sought the safety of distance, and a cry of triumph arose from the decks of the fleet, the route to the Screaming Crags now suddenly open before them. The last, smouldering timbers of the destroyed Jade Galleon floated on the water like macabre celebratory fires, lending the entrance to the reefs a solemn, almost morbid feel. Refelbek yelled out command after command, and the entire fleet – ship by ship – began to slowly turn course like a cumbersome giant until it was ready to proceed along its course, manoeuvring between the numerous, dangerously jagged rocks.

The first leg of their passage had been completed, but when Ahren looked at the burning pieces of driftwood – all that was left of a once-proud vessel and her valiant crew – he could think of nothing else but of the high price that they had already paid. And who could tell what tribute the Screaming Crags might yet demand of them?

Chapter 6

The darkness of the night started where the light of the Bane Lanterns ended – as if they were surrounded by a pitch-black dome.

Every defender stood at the ready, not only on the *Queen of the Waves*, but on the other ships too, the vessels resembling spectres in a feverish, blood-red dream. Admiral Refelbek issued commands in the gloom from time to time, his messages being conveyed to the other ships by means of light signals.

The pale, sickly-looking rocky reefs would manifest themselves like the broken teeth of some dreadful sea monster whenever they were caught by the light of the Bane Lanterns, the Pallid Gulls that rested on them then rising into the night sky, screeching their displeasure and circling balefully before retreating to the safety of the shadows beyond the sorcerous light-field, landing again on the cauterised rocks once the fleet had passed. Now and again, the head of a particularly aggressive Monster Eel would emerge from the water, only to dive into the depths again with a snarl of indignant fury.

Ahren and his friends sat on the damp timbers among the Ice Wolves, not one of them having dared to speak since the onset of night, for they all silently feared that to do so would break the uneasy peace that the Bane Lanterns had caused to settle on the dark waves of the sea.

Eventually, Khara broke the silence. 'How many reefs have we already passed?' she whispered.

The companions were all sitting back-to-back, their weapons resting on the planks at their feet. The rest of the ship's defenders were sitting in similar formation, the little groups painfully aware of the dangers that surrounded them. On hearing the Swordsmistress break the uneasy silence, which seemed to have resembled an unuttered curse, they turned anxiously to look at her. Even Ahren waited and listened expectantly – as if he were expecting all hell to break loose in reaction to the words that his beloved had murmured.

He shook his head at his own anxiety before whispering in response: 'Refelbek said that we will certainly have to fend off some attacks tomorrow before we are finally safely beyond the reefs – and as it is roughly halfway through the night, I would imagine that we have reached the midway point, more or less.'

Khara reacted with a sigh. 'A pity. Muai is slowly losing her nerve, which is in turn making things difficult for me.' Then Ahren felt her shudder against him. 'And now she is scolding me for having told you how she is feeling.'

'Distract her with happy memories,' he advised. 'It always works with Culhen.'

'Maybe,' said Khara. 'I know very little of her life before the Eternal Empire was established. It might be exciting to learn more about the Dark Days.'

With that, she fell silent, Ahren knowing that she would be occupied for the rest of the night. He decided to follow his own advice, sinking into Culhen's mind, and cheering up the anxious wolf with a few of the animal's tales of derring-do where the canine was – of course – the hero.

The wind was so sudden and unexpected that Ahren understood immediately that the source of the gusts could not be natural. It began as a scornful, shrill howl in the distance, which approached with incredible speed, churning up the ocean as though it was some sort of invisible water giant running on top of the waves. The first vessels to be caught up in it were the galleons closest to the coast. They lurched violently from port to starboard, their crews uttering cries of terror although they remained unharmed.

'Damn and blast it,' snarled Uldini, awakening from his slumber and quickly bringing *Flamestar* to blazing life. 'The Adversary!'

The Arch Wizard had time to say no more, for the squall was moving with lightning speed, like a wildcat leaping from ship to ship, and already it had reached the *Xuan-Foi*. Like the other vessels, the enormous Lantern Frigate was tossed this way and that by the sudden wind – but with one significant difference, which caused Ahren's hairs to stand on end. The Bane Lantern flickered like a candle in the wind for a heartbeat, sparked in all directions, and was then extinguished in the blink of an eye!

Ahren wanted to yell out a warning, but already the evil magic was sweeping over the deck of the *Queen of the Waves,* pushing him down onto the timbers like an incorporeal hand intent on squeezing the life out of him.

PALADIN!

It was only one word that had been spat out into the raging wind, one solitary word, but filled with all the hatred that the Adversary possessed towards his enemies and laced with an element that Ahren clearly recognised – *fear!*

Then the wind was gone, moving forcefully onto the *Lady Aruti*, where it extinguished her Bane Lantern too. A dark laugh, lacking any hint of humour, rang out over the Thirteenth Fleet, disappearing with the dying howls of the mysterious squall into the darkness of the night.

For a few shocked heartbeats there was a dead calm on board the ships, but then a new sound broke the silence – the whooshing and flapping sounds of thousands of wings, and the splashing of water as heavy bodies pushed their way forcefully up through the surface of the water!

'ATTACK!' bellowed Ahren full-throatedly, before adding totally instinctively, "PALADINIM THEOS DURALAS!'

Khara gasped behind him, the presence of the other Paladins flaming to life within Ahren's consciousness. Falk, also behind him but to his right, barely three paces from the railing, was picking up his shield and sword. Trimm was scurrying below deck, his tactic fuelled by self-preservation. Hakanu had his spear at the ready in one hand, while with his other, he helped a Fox Guard to their feet. And then there was Khara, no Champion of the gods to be sure, but mysteriously bound up with the others thanks to the bracelet that she was wearing.

For the briefest of moments Ahren luxuriated in the feeling of unity that the trinket had called forth within him, but then the Dark Ones were on top of them like a wave of horror.

Ahren's Wind Blade zinged out of its scabbard, and with one swing the Forest Guardian sliced three Pallid Gulls in two, while simultaneously dodging a Sabre Ray. The monster was struck from the side by a hurtling bolt, which slammed it off course and sent it crashing onto the timbers.

Khara somersaulted over the creature as it began to hit out wildly in all directions, the two blades of the Swordsmistress creating a veritable mosaic of death as they repeatedly stabbed the flesh of the Sabre Ray while she flew in an arc over the monster.

Ahren heard a furious hissing sound behind him, but in no time at all Trogadon was beside him with his hammer, and by the time the Paladin turned, the dwarf had already smashed his weapon onto the skull of an attacking Monster Eel. The beast fell back into the water as if struck by a thunderbolt, Trogadon then peering down to look.

'How I *hate* eels,' he grunted. Then all hell broke loose.

Pallid Gulls, Sabre Rays, and Monster Eels formed a murderous web of spittle, sharp blades, and killer fangs, almost causing Ahren to lose his bearings.

But *only* almost.

The Paladins and Khara danced about the deck, each one aware of where the others were currently positioned. Parries were blindly carried out to defend a companion, the flanks of friends were intuitively defended, and more than one life-saving thrust was delivered when a member of the group found themselves in the line of attack of a Dark One.

Thanks to the patch he was wearing, Ahren could see nothing through his left eye, but the connections created by the Blessing Band gave him a strategic seventh sense – an awareness of the battlefield, which more than compensated for the handicap. All around him, mariners, monsters, and Ice Wolves were fighting and dying, but the Paladins and the Swordsmistress formed a core of stability in the maelstrom of destruction.

'Jelninolan!' exclaimed Uldini suddenly, Ahren instinctively fighting his way through to the Arch Wizard. 'We must ensure that the lanterns are re-lit!'

'Only the Wrath Elves can do that,' countered the Storm Weaver, Ahren only aware of where she was because of her staff, which was spitting out sparks in every direction as it slammed into Dark Ones, sending them flying into the night, no matter how large and powerful the monsters were. Ahren recognised her magic from a vision that Jelninolan had shared with him in Deepstone so long ago, and he shivered at the memory of it. The elf had clearly modified the Chains of War charm to such an extent that she no longer needed to have the shackles wrapped around her arms but was simply using her staff as a focus. He was all too aware of what this sorcery entailed – Jelninolan was on the verge of an Unleashing!

'This is a *coordinated* attack!' roared Falk over the sounds of battle. 'There must be a High Fang in the vicinity, directing the Dark Ones! We need to find him before we can no longer withstand the onslaught!'

Ahren sensed his master being struck in the back and violently thrown forward by a Sabre Ray. The jarring sound of the monster's bonelike blade on the Deep Steel had a uniquely dissonant ring when compared to the screams of the defenders, the omnipresent screeching, and the snarling of the enemy. Ahren knew that his mentor was uninjured, and he breathed a sigh of relief only to perceive Hakanu being grabbed by a Monster Eel that plucked the boy up off the deck like a rag doll.

'No!' gasped the Forest Guardian as he began to run, sheathing *Sun* and unshouldering *Fisiniell*. The air was filled with Pallid Gulls, he could only use his right eye, and his view was so limited by the inadequacy of the moonlight that he could hardly aim properly. In fact, visibility proved unnecessary. He simply *sensed* through the Blessing Band and shot the arrow to half a pace above where he had located Hakanu. His reward was two Pallid Gulls being skewered right through, followed by a scream from Hakanu as the wounded Monster Eel let go of the boy, the apprentice then beginning to plummet downwards towards the seething water, filled with Dark Ones.

As if to mock Ahren, the Pallid Gulls created a space whereby the young man couldn't fail to see his protégé dropping beyond the far side of the railing, a member of the Fox Guards throwing himself against the wall of wood in an attempt to grab Hakanu with his outstretched arm.

'I have you, sir,' gasped the man, ignoring two Pallid Gulls that were beginning to peck at his face with their spittle-dripping beaks. Ahren wanted to run to the Fox Guard's aid, but he was roughly pulled around from behind, not by the enemy, in fact, but by Trogadon, whose furious face was speckled with blood.

'*I'll* help him,' roared the dwarf, pushing Ahren out of the way. 'Your job is to find this High Fang!'

'The lanterns will first have to be put back in service!' yelled Uldini, who was hovering above the deck, turning any Pallid Gull that came too close to him into ashes with the net of sparks that surrounded him. *Flamestar* was glimmering erratically, resembling a dying candle, and leaving Ahren in no doubt but that the Ancient was weakening fast. 'Their light will win us time and ensure that the defenders of the fleet will no longer have to manoeuvre themselves blindly in the dark.'

'Let's split up!' gasped Jelninolan, her voice betraying her exhaustion above the sounds of skirmishing. 'I will make my way over to the *Lady Aruti* – Uldini, you go to the *Xuan-Foi.*'

Uldini scowled unhappily and pointed over at Jelninolan. 'Assist her on the *Lady Aruti,*' he instructed Ahren urgently. 'Before she expends her energy to the point of utter exhaustion.'

Ahren struggled past Khara, who was gracefully using her blades to deadly effect, and also Falk, who was busy protecting the elf. 'What can I do?!' he screamed above the chaos as he shot down a Monster Eel with *Fisiniell,* the creature's eyes having been fixed on another potential target.

'Come to *me!*' gasped Jelninolan, the staccato-like glimmering of her staff clearly beginning to wane.

The right sleeve of her robe was ripped up to her shoulder, revealing the filigree armour beneath, which Trogadon had presented her with when he had confessed his love for the elf. Seldom had Ahren seen the priestess look so martial, and the sight filled him with fear and foreboding.

'I am a couple of spells short of an Unleashing,' muttered Jelninolan through gritted teeth. 'But what I have should be sufficient.'

'Sufficient for what?' asked Ahren only to suddenly feel as if a powerful, invisible hand was grabbing him and yanking him forcefully upwards. Then he was flung through the night sky, his body painfully colliding with several Pallid Gulls as he quickly placed his hand over his healthy eye. Through the chinks between his fingers, he could see the hurricane lanterns of the *Lady Aruti* getting ever bigger, the realisation then dawning on him regarding what was going to happen next. Gritting his teeth, and tensing up his muscles, he landed hard on the embattled deck, somersaulting several times while simultaneously drawing *Sun* with his free hand, and slicing through the stomach of an incoming Sabre Ray. Hardly had he rolled to a halt and pulled himself to his feet when Jelninolan was already flying towards him like a shooting star, her sparks flying in all directions, the icy expression on her face indicating in no uncertain terms that the elf was about to perform an Unleashing. Ahren could see a similar flare in the distance as the little figure of Uldini split the night sky, the childlike figure flying towards the *Xuan-Foi.* As he had promised, the Ancient was going to lend his assistance to the Wrath Elves on the ship, while Jelninolan and Ahren would create the breathing space necessary in order to create the ritual Blood Magic which would bring the Bane Lanterns back to life.

Ahren saw a spindly Wrath Elf with a protective circle of mariners around him, who were in turn surrounded by the scattered bodies of more than four dozen slain comrades. 'Take that!' muttered Ahren, shooting at a ray which was heading straight for the defensive group.

Jelninolan pointed at the elf, immediately causing the haggard figure to float upward. He let out a frightened cry as he rose higher and landed on the rigging near the extinguished bane fire. 'I must hold him up there,' gasped Jelninolan as she looked over at Ahren, while still aiming her floating charm upward, the Wrath Elf then shakily beginning his ritual to resurrect the bane flame. 'Protect him until the lantern is burning again.'

The soldiers and sailors of the *Lady Aruti* gathered around the sorcerous elf and the Forest Guardian in a concerted effort to shield them from the attacks on deck, while Ahren began dispatching arrow after arrow, felling two or three of the flying gulls with every shot. His right eye was sore through weariness, and he missed his targets on several occasions. Although the Forest Guardian had practised with his good eye for several weeks, his accuracy was now far from perfect.

Meanwhile, the spindly Wrath Elf up in the rigging was doing his best to perform the ritual, his efforts being hampered, however, by the fact that he was being constantly peppered with caustic spittle, Jelninolan's levitation charm slowing him down, too.

The sweat was rolling into Ahren's eye as he continued to shoot until he reached back to his quiver one more time and found that it was empty. Time seemed to stand still as he and the Wrath Elf exchanged looks, several Pallid Gulls suddenly swooping down on the now unprotected figure. With a curt nod in Ahren's direction, the Wrath Elf pulled out a short knife and stabbed himself hard in the forearm, aiming the fountain of spraying blood at the magical apparatus. There was a hissing sound, as if of flesh being cooked over too hot a flame, the red fire of the Bane Lantern then flaring up and burning the figure of the Wrath Elf to a cinder within a couple of heartbeats.

Ahren gasped in horror and turned his eyes away, so great was the intensity of the flame, which seemed to transform the night into a day of fiery red.

That was the very moment when Ahren caught sight of a cowering figure, hiding behind the jagged peak of one of the spittle-stained crags.

It was a human face with three eyes, and teeth growing uselessly from the tops of its ears.

The High Fang!

Ahren acted instinctively and with lightning speed. In one flowing movement, the Forest Guardian pulled an arrow out of a dead Pallid Gull, set it on the bowstring and dispatched it, making sure to calculate his aim according to the vision afforded by his right eye. His target had only enough time to watch in surprise as the projectile flew a distance far greater than a normal arrow would before it sank downwards, landing cleanly in the High Fang's third eye. Above Ahren, the light of the Bane Lantern had reduced to its normal intensity, the Paladin pleading silently to the THREE that they honour the Wrath Elf with the dignity that he deserved for having made the ultimate sacrifice so that no worse damage would befall the Thirteenth Fleet.

The Dark Ones fled in droves from the Bane Lantern's circle of light, but when Ahren looked down at the waters around him, the cheer that he was about to let forth stuck in his throat. Two more Jade Galleons had been split asunder, the Forest Guardian understanding immediately that their captains had deliberately steered the vessels between the *Lady Aruti* and the wave of Dark Ones, only to be literally ripped apart. Behind him, Ahren heard cheers of jubilation, and when he turned around to look, he saw that the second Bane Lantern had been lit and was casting its light out into the night.

'Saved,' he murmured as if in a daze before going over to Jelninolan, who was weeping tears of sorrow and relief.

'Good,' she said, her voice belying the emotions that were churning up within her. 'Very good.'

With that, she began to fall like an autumn leaf, Ahren catching her before she hit the deck. He laid her gently against the main mast and shouted for a blanket. Yielding to the tugging in his head, he opened his mind to Culhen's vision, the wolf now standing at the railing of the *Queen of the Waves*, looking over at the *Xuan-Foi*. Ahren's heart sank as he saw the flotsam strewn on the sea's surface.

How many, he asked anxiously.

Four, was the painful response. *Four Jade Galleons are now succumbing to the ocean's embrace.*

Seven. The word was almost too much to comprehend. Seven galleons in total had been lost on their passage through the Screaming Crags. *Would it have been better to have sailed during daylight?*

Are you mad? countered Culhen. *We would never have survived the Dark Ones. If the battle had lasted the whole day, we would now be at the bottom of these infested waters.*

Ahren leaned wearily against the railing and closed his eye. The war was becoming ever more gruesome, and he knew all too well that this battle had been merely a pale shadow of what had occurred during the Dark Days, and of what would surely happen again.

Time to finish all this before it becomes too unbearable, he said silently, clenching his fists. *Time to find the last Paladin.*

The sun was little more than a faint ball behind the blanket of grey cloud the following morning – it almost seemed as if the orb was reluctant to reveal the true scope of the destruction that had befallen the Thirteenth Fleet. The turbulent sea had even gone one step further, ensuring that all signs of destruction had vanished from its surface. The Screaming Crags lay half a league behind, and no matter how hard he tried, Ahren could not make out a single piece of wreckage around the cauterised jagged rocks in the distance. The screeching of the Pallid Gulls perched on the naked peaks, the ugly noise being carried towards the ships by gusts of wind, was the only reminder of why the area was so named.

'And to think that ships *really* sailed through there every day,' muttered Trogadon as he joined Ahren at the railing. The dwarf had a pipe in the downturned corner of his weary mouth, the Forest Guardian immediately finding the familiar smell of the strong tobacco comforting.

'Pallid Gulls were nothing more than a nuisance until recently,' said Ahren. 'Refelbek told me that they behaved in exactly the same way as other gulls until only a few years ago. A nuisance but never deadly.' He sighed. 'And they have been acting far more aggressively towards our fleet than to any other ships.'

Trogadon chuckled quietly, a gravelly, humorous sound that belied his exhausted look. 'And I wonder why *that* is?'

Ahren slowly exhaled as he tried to alleviate the uneasy feeling in the pit of his stomach. He had begun the day with his customary *Twelve Greetings to the Sun* in an effort to come to terms with the grief that he felt over the loss of so many lives. Once he had repeated the exercise eight times, he had at least regained the steely determination that had brought him this far.

'The Adversary launched a direct attack and came up short,' he said firmly, looking at Trogadon, whose eyes managed to sparkle with pride. 'When his spirit touched me yesterday, I could sense his hatred – *and* his fear. This is no normal sea voyage. It is one of the last opportunities for the Dark god to stop us Paladins from taking him on as a united force.'

'If you look at it like that, we've made a pretty good fist of things,' commented Trogadon before patting Ahren on the shoulder. Then he pointed with his pipe at the now calm sea and the screeching gulls in the distance, 'But why aren't the birds following us? And where have all the rays and eels gone?'

'They have headed south,' muttered Uldini, the weary Arch Wizard floating over to his friends. 'Have you grown roots here at the railing?' he asked Ahren with his normal, biting humour. 'You're spending all your time out here at the prow of the ship.'

'I have spent weeks on end below deck,' replied Ahren, pointing meaningfully at his left eye. 'Every time I go back down the hatch, I feel claustrophobic.'

Who are you telling? grumbled Culhen, not for the first time playing the stowaway in Ahren's mind. *And don't forget that you promised me a thorough grooming.*

Ignoring his wolf for the moment, – after all, Culhen wouldn't give him any peace anyway until he was holding a comb in his hand – Ahren looked at the Arch Wizard. Uldini's face was wan, his eyes sunken, and his hands were trembling. 'You should be lying in a deep sleep, like Jelninolan,' said the young man with a frown.

'She has, thanks to her ceaseless healing efforts, been weakened considerably more than me,' replied Uldini, although Ahren knew full well that *Flamestar* had been similarly at work during the day whenever there had been a peaceful moment on deck that had allowed for Sun Magic to be implemented as a curative method. 'The two of us agreed that I should recover in the normal manner, so that I can ensure that we safely reach Cape Verstaad.' He nodded back towards the Screaming Crags, now little more than a bad memory on the hazy horizon. 'It seems that it will not be long before I find my desired peace.'

'You said that the water creatures have swum off to the south?' pressed Trogadon, anticipating Ahren's question.

Uldini nodded. 'We aren't the only ones licking our wounds. I suspect that the Adversary is not as powerful as he wants us to believe he is. Not yet. The wind last night took a lot out of him – even if that isn't so obvious to the lay person. Blowing out the Bane Lanterns must have drained him significantly.' Uldini looked at the sea beyond the starboard side. 'The Dark god is gathering his troops somewhere off the coast of the Ice Fields – and we are going to have to do the same in Cape Verstaad.'

Although Ahren shivered at the thought that the decisive sea battle still lay ahead of them, he controlled his breathing and let the fear slide off him as if he were discarding an old, shabby coat. 'We are safe for now,' he said, forcing a smile. 'I don't know about you lot, but I am going to spend the rest of the day grooming my wolf – and I won't stop until my arms fall off me.'

A joyful howl echoed up from the hull of the ship, while Ahren's friends burst out laughing.

'You know what?' said Trogadon, cocking his head as he mused. 'That's put an idea into my head.'

Ahren could hardly lift his weary hands, but he was happy and contented, nonetheless. The sounds of laughter and song were echoing from all the ships, and a smell of roast meat filled the air. Trogadon's brainwave had been to collect all the spare food from the ships' holds, with which he organised a celebration on the decks, both in honour of their victory over the Adversary *and* the fact that they were still alive to tell the tale. Admiral Refelbek had been somewhat sceptical at first, but Ahren was sure that the tobacco, which Trogadon had given the mariner and which the sombre man was now enjoying as he puffed away on his pipe had more than a little to do with permission finally having been granted.

Uldini had cooked the meat with *Flamestar's* assistance, having already plundered the slumbering Jelninolan's reserve of herbs. The celebrations were sure to be a success now that the remaining rum supplies were being distributed. The crow's nests were populated by volunteers, who kept a look out for danger while their comrades below partied, and so the fleet floated gently eastward towards Cape Verstaad, now not far away at all, while the sun cast a cheerful light on the ships' festivities.

Trogadon was teaching a Dwarfish drinking song to a group of eager mariners, the sound of which resembled the noisy crashing of rocks tumbling, while Ahren, his eyes closed, snuggled against Culhen's silken soft fur as he listened to Khara humming the catchy melody, the Swordsmistress resting in the warmth of his embrace. The coast was now near enough for the characteristic aroma of rich vegetation to occasionally waft over to them – a smell that Ahren had until now only associated with the Southern Jungles and the Cutlass Sea. He had to remind himself, not for the first time, that *winter* meant something quite different here in the deep south of Jorath than it did in his home place. He opened his eyes and caught sight of a line of palm trees, decorating the jagged coastline. He was also enjoying the fact that he could at last manage without his eye patch. Today, as with every day, he had continued his ritual of taking off the leather cover and carefully looking out into the daylight. Now, as if to reinforce the festive spirit, he had allowed his left eye to finally withstand the rays of the sun. Ahren vowed to continue training his right eye anyway, so that he would be better prepared for possible future injuries.

'Is this how our lives will always be in the future?' he asked finally, Trogadon having launched into yet another drinking song. 'Good food, the laughter of friends, and an almost unbearably long peace?'

'We can find that out together,' murmured Khara, snuggling in closer to the Paladin. 'Enjoy this moment.'

Ahren squeezed her in response as he felt Culhen's soft fur behind him, the satisfied wolf being now more relaxed than he had been in moons. Then, seeing Hakanu approaching, he sat up as much as the weight of his beloved would permit.

'How are you?' he asked quietly once his apprentice had sat down beside him. The pain in the young warrior's eyes was impossible to miss, and Ahren sensed that the boy's suffering was not only because of the bandage-covered bite marks peppering his protégé's back, which the Monster Eel had inflicted on him before almost consuming him for its supper.

'Frerik is dead,' said the apprentice morosely. Kamaluq immediately hurtled towards the boy, throwing himself onto the lad's lap, before rolling himself up into a ball and gazing loyally up at his Paladin. 'It was a Sabre Ray that caught him when he was trying to shield me.' Hakanu began to absently stroke his fox while gazing into the distance. 'He had been looking forward to entering the bond of matrimony, you know,' he murmured. 'His beloved is fighting at the Ring. She comes from the Ice Islands and has twice been decorated for bravery in battle.' The boy sighed. 'Frerik used to say that not everything is bad in this war. That it brings people together, who would otherwise never have met. And that everyone works towards a common goal, putting their petty differences aside in the process.'

'It sounds as if Frerik was a wise man,' said Ahren, feeling a stab of guilt in his chest. He had hardly known the stocky fellow, an Ice Wolf who had volunteered to serve in the Fox Guards as one of Hakanu's protectors.

'And he was always unruffled,' added Hakanu with a nod. 'With ice water in his veins – that's what his beloved always tells him…' he sobbed, '…sorry, I mean *told*,' he corrected himself.

Ahren placed his hand on the boy's shoulder and squeezed it gently. 'We save as many as we can – but we also need help,' he said, remembering as if it was yesterday the same thing being said to him by his companions. 'And those who help us, do so because they believe that it is a good thing, risking their lives for others when it becomes necessary.' He looked earnestly into Hakanu's eyes. 'And sometimes they pay the ultimate price, leaving us behind with our grief.'

'But why *him?*' asked Hakanu, despairingly. 'Why not *me?* What makes *me* so special? Is it only because *my* father was a Paladin that I am allowed to live while my friend must *die?*'

The singing and laughter of the sailors nearby provided an unfortunate backdrop to the boy's agony, and Ahren would have liked nothing better than to scream at the revellers to shut up. Instead, he gathered himself and remembered the lessons that he, himself, had learned over the previous few years.

'We Paladins bear a burden – and this consists of more than our war against the Adversary,' said the Forest Guardian in a gentle voice. 'It also comes from the fact that others are willing to sacrifice themselves so that we may continue to live. So that the war ends. So that the loss of all those who have offered themselves up since the First appeared in Jorath will not have died in vain.'

Hakanu's eyes began to radiate a new understanding – like a blossom flowering in the alluring light of a spring morning. 'So that Frerik will not have died in vain?' whispered the apprentice, Ahren picking up on the undertone of steel in the timbre of the boy's voice.

Ahren hugged the boy, Khara mumbling irritably at being disturbed in her slumber, and Kamaluq whimpering irately as he unwillingly jumped off Hakanu's lap. Both Paladins chuckled quietly.

'One last lesson,' whispered Ahren into his apprentice's ear. 'Find joy and strength in days like today, for this is indeed what we are fighting for – for joy in life, for the feeling of humanity that finds its expression in the sound of communal laughter. Gather these good memories, and they will shine like beacons during our darkest moments. And be grateful to all those who willingly walk with you on your journey.' Then he released the overwhelmed boy, who nodded solemnly before getting to his feet and going over to the three remaining members of the Fox Guards. Observing the straight back and unhurried walk of his apprentice, Ahren realised that Hakanu had grown that little bit more into his role of Paladin.

You really know how to lay it on thick, commented Culhen before yawning loudly.

You know what Hakanu is like, Ahren replied, filled with pride for his protégé. *I wanted to make sure that he got the message before his heroic pride got in the way.* He nodded over at the lad, who was now standing proudly with one foot on a coil of rope, gesticulating wildly and undoubtedly relating yesterday's adventures of derring-do to his three listeners.

Say what you like about him, countered Culhen in Ahren's mind, *but calling Hakanu indestructible is putting it more than mildly.*

Ahren watched the young Paladin for a while longer, then beckoned over the mirthful Falk, the inebriated Yantilla, as well as both Trimm and Palnah.

'Come here and sit yourselves down,' he said cheerfully. 'Let us celebrate.'

Snorting and sweating, Ahren lowered his Wind Blade and wiped the perspiration from his brow. For days now, there had been barely a hint of a breeze, and the warm air was hard to bear, even on deck. Were it not for the natural ocean current carrying them slowly but surely eastward, progress would have been reduced to nothing. Admiral Refelbek had assured them that the undertow would carry them all the way to the Bay of Cape Verstaad, and Ahren found himself repeatedly glancing at the nearby coastline to see if there were any signs of the wealthy trading city. He squinted his eyes and thought he could make out something glittering to the east, only to be roused from his musings by a playful prod to his overarm.

'No daydreaming now,' said Khara, taking up the opening position that she always used when beginning a practice session. 'It was *you* who wanted to be in top form when we reach Cape Verstaad, don't forget. Concentrate on your exercises.'

'Slavedriver,' mumbled Ahren with a smile.

The Swordsmistress was bathed in sweat, too, as were their other companions, who had followed the example of the young couple and were scattered in pairs around the deck, exhausted. Uldini, meanwhile, was floating amongst them, nodding appreciatively like a satisfied taskmaster. The weariness that had been evident on his face had all but vanished.

'Cape Verstaad is a place where outer appearances are of paramount importance,' said the Arch Wizard, repeating his warning words of the past few days. 'In other words, keep pushing yourselves sufficiently so that the grandees of the city will take you for the heroic figures and creators of legends that you are.'

The Ancient's speech was underlined by the frustrated panting of Trimm, Ahren frowning with pity for the fellow. Yantilla had personally taken on the responsibility of managing the grandee's training regime, and the weeks of hard conditioning were at last beginning to show results.

'She should be careful that he doesn't collapse altogether,' mused Ahren, glancing over at the commander and her breathless victim. 'I'm not sure if our gods' Blessing protects us from heatstroke.' Then he ducked under Khara's guileful thrust, his beloved having hoped to take advantage of his brief inattention.

'If anyone is going to suffer from heatstroke, then it will be those two,' chuckled Khara, pointing her Whisper Blade at Muai and Culhen while still holding Ahren at bay with her Wind Blade.

So...warm..., mumbled Culhen, twitching one of his four paws, all of which were pointing straight up in the air. The two large, furry companion animals were lying in the prow of the ship, trying to cool themselves with any breeze and spray that managed to make its way to the fo'c'sle.

'Ha!' exclaimed Trimm, his face red with effort as he suddenly turned and ran to the railing, ignoring Yantilla's protests. The corpulent man smiled blissfully. 'Ah, my beloved Cape Verstaad, the heart of civilised society and citadel of sorcerous studies.'

Uldini snorted in disapproval at the Paladin's last words, but Trimm seemed not in the least put off. He turned and beckoned both Ahren and the others to join him at the railing.

'Come closer! One never forgets seeing the City of a Thousand Thrones for the first time.'

'Why does Cape Verstaad call itself that?' asked Ahren, coming to a halt beside the serenely smiling Paladin.

'Because everyone who lives there is a king or queen,' said Trimm dreamily.

'As long as they have enough gold,' interjected Uldini sarcastically. 'Otherwise, they are mere beggars.'

'Sounds like every other city then,' commented Trogadon, unimpressed.

By now, all the companions had gathered at the prow and were craning their necks to see what it was that was enchanting Trimm so much.

Give us a bit of room now, complained Culhen as he and Muai found themselves surrounded. *Here are two melting companion animals who would like to survive the day!*

Palnah joined Trimm, who beamed at his soul companion. 'Soon you will see your new home,' he announced proudly. 'And by the THREE, you will want for nothing there!'

Ahren had seldom seen the Paladin behaving so exuberantly, and it struck him that he liked this aspect of Trimm's personality. He exchanged looks with Falk, who seemed equally surprised. It seemed that the corpulent Paladin's chosen domicile had a positive influence on Trimm – who was known locally as Salman Tilderius, the Thirty-fourth Grandee of Cape Verstaad. It may not have ignited his courage, but it certainly had done wonders for his joie de vivre. Ahren had only heard a little about Trimm's earlier existence as a Paladin, but the tales of his mortal fear of Dark Ones combined with the scorn shown towards him by the other Paladins suggested to Ahren that Trimm had fled from his own personal, never-ending nightmare, finding in Cape Verstaad his paradise. The Forest Guardian silently vowed to be open and accommodating towards Cape Verstaad, even if he already knew from Uldini and Falk that the city was far from perfect. No place where the wealth of a person took precedence over personal qualities could ever be that.

Ahren caught sight of a golden sparkle, and Trimm sighed happily. This must have been what the infatuated Paladin had spotted earlier.

'Behold the Golden Council of the Grandees, the centre of power in the southern Sunplains!' announced Trimm, Ahren seeing after a little searching, an onion-shaped cupola soaring high above the coastline, which seemed to be made from pure gold.

Trogadon whistled through his teeth and scratched under his helmet. 'You can thank your lucky stars that we dwarves live so far north,' he murmured, deeply impressed. 'Otherwise, we would certainly have tried to seize that chunk of gold for ourselves.'

'But you are doing that already,' chuckled Falk. 'With one trade agreement after another – and each one in *your* favour.'

Trogadon grinned. 'I suppose you're right.'

'Is the cupola really made out of pure gold?' asked Khara sceptically. 'That seems not only wasteful to me, but also *very* impractical.'

Trimm smiled and shook his head. 'It's only made up of gold plates – each a good forearm thick,' he said, Hakanu gasping in disbelief.

'There isn't enough wealth in all of the Green Sea to afford more than a handful of these plates,' he said in consternation.

'And yet you want for nothing,' interjected Ahren admonishingly. 'Don't allow yourself to be dazzled by Cape Verstaad's splendour before we have even arrived.'

'Says he, who couldn't get his fill of the Silver Cliff the first time he saw it,' teased Trogadon. 'Nothing beats showing off one's wealth a little. If the grandees want to decorate their homeplace with a little gold, that's their business.'

'Oh, no-one *lives* in the Golden Council,' smiled Trimm, enraptured. 'That is the place where we meet when we need to discuss matters.'

Ahren looked at his fellow Paladin as if the latter had lost his mind. Then the coastline gave way, revealing the bay of the trading city, Cape Verstaad.

'Incredible,' whispered Hakanu, Ahren finding himself in silent agreement with his protégé despite his far greater experience in exploring the entire continent.

The vast metropolis stretched along the entire two leagues of the bay shore and was the same distance deep. Dozens of cupolas, like the one they had spotted already, were now visible on the city skyline. Ahren was convinced that there had to be more people living on this patch of earth than in all Hjalgar.

The magnificent residences of the grandees were all individually decorated, creating a colourful potpourri of decadent opulence, which dominated the cityscape. Ahren saw slender towers studded with jewels, and palaces with breath-taking motifs made from delicate mosaic work. Some depicted stylized coats of arms, others presented heroic scenes with glorious warriors or great sorcerers.

From a distance, the roads seemed to be made of white stone, and even the most modest dwellings were at least two stories high, decorated with artistic ironwork on their doors and windows. In front of this backdrop, there were streamlined boats and large ships made from precious timber, all moored and floating peacefully on the turquoise water. Ahren was sure that some of the sails were made of silk, confirming Khara's suspicion that pomp and outer appearance took precedence over sensible practicality in this magnificent city.

To the innocent observer, the hundreds of fishing boats bobbing up and down on the outer margins of the bay seemed to be hiding from the glitter, far from the ornate stone pier which the Thirteenth Fleet was now approaching. To Ahren's surprise, he could see neither defensive weapons, nor any sort of floating boom that could prevent access to the bay should there be an enemy assault.

'How do they defend themselves here?' he asked, puzzled. 'The truce and subsequent alliance between the Eternal Empire and the Sunplains are only very recent developments. But I can see no sign of the war having had any effect on Cape Verstaad.'

'Do you see those slender towers over there?' asked Trimm, pointing at a series of elegant, white, regularly spaced structures lining the bay, each one probably five paces across and at least fifteen paces tall and all with a pointed roof on top.

'Are those the residences of the lesser nobles?' asked Hakanu. 'Twenty people or so could easily live in each one of them.'

Trimm looked pitifully at the apprentice, refraining, however, from expressing whatever it was that he thought of the boy's idea. 'In every one of them,' he explained proudly instead, 'lives a Battle Wizard – a graduate of the Academy of Arcane Power – each of whom has learned the art of casting fire with his hands. The top alumni from the sorcery school are granted such a tower in perpetuity as well as a very generous salary – on condition that they vow to protect both the harbour and the city. Whoever sails into this port is at the mercy of the grandees.'

'Why does it *always* have to be fireballs?' muttered Uldini irritably. 'Whatever happened to *creativity?*'

'It's no wonder that Cape Verstaad produces almost exclusively battle magic,' added Falk, shaking his head sadly. 'From the very first days of their education, the students only have one goal in their mind – to live in one of these towers.'

'Anyone who doesn't manage to get into the Flaming Company still has a good chance of being taken on by one of the grandees as a personal sorcerer or joining one of the resident mercenary groups, who work in the interest of the grandees,' added Trimm. He cocked his head and examined Hakanu keenly. 'You could certainly live the high life here with your magic spear if you attached yourself to one of the grandees,' he said, his eyes sparkling cunningly. 'One that you already *knew* and *valued*, perhaps?'

Hakanu looked at the Paladin, raising an eyebrow as he did so. 'You're not talking about *yourself* surely, are you?' he asked mischievously, Ahren struggling not to break into a smile.

'Have you just been defeated by Hakanu in a battle of words?' chuckled Khara, looking at the corpulent man. 'The same Hakanu, who pondered aloud if he could stab a wave of the sea to death if he only threw his spear hard enough?'

'I was tipsy when I said that,' grumbled the young warrior irritably.

'Whatever,' growled Trimm, miffed. 'Cape Verstaad knows very well how to protect itself and how to defend its interests. Even the Sun Emperor remains polite when he presents us with his demands.'

'Because you always acquiesce in the end,' interjected Uldini gleefully. 'You know very well that if the Sun Court was to send in its legions, then neither your sorcerers nor your mercenaries would be able to bail you out.'

'We have always been able to come to agreed compensatory sums when it came to stilling the greed of the Sun Emperor,' muttered Trimm haughtily. 'And if you lot are going to do nothing but criticise my highly esteemed homeland, then please stop peppering me with silly questions and let me enjoy the view instead.'

On hearing the unmistakeable hurt in his fellow Paladin's voice, Ahren gave a warning look to the others before changing the subject. 'Which of these buildings is *your* residence?' he asked, genuinely interested.

'As if *he* would own a palace,' whispered Hakanu, shaking his head.

'The small one over there,' replied Trimm modestly, pointing at a magnificent building with a simple white cupola and two extensive residential wings built of white marble, one on either side of the main building. The palace might at a stretch have been considered modest were it not for the fact that every nook and cranny of its exterior was decorated with extensive gold inlay that was even visible to the naked eye from the ship.

'Well, I must say that second to Quin-Wa you are definitely the wealthiest Paladin that I know,' said Trogadon appreciatively, pausing for a heartbeat before adding, 'and it would be an *honour* for me to discuss a trade agreement with Murgamolosch – that is, if your offer still stands.'

'Just as well that Jelninolan isn't awake to hear how you're hawking your colony,' snarled Uldini with a sharpness that was particularly cutting. Ahren wondered if Trimm's undoubted wealth was a thorn in the Arch Wizard's side.

'I am *helping* my colony,' retorted Trogadon, his mood having suddenly become serious. 'We must trade with one of the seafaring nations, and it is high time that King's Island understood that the dwarves of Murgamolosch have other options and are not necessarily dependent on the ships of the Knight Marshes.'

Trimm and the dwarf were soon engaged in a lively and detailed discussion concerning prices, delivery times, and a multitude of other commercial details, while the others, clearly uninterested, gradually dispersed to various parts of the deck. Ahren beckoned Uldini with a nod to follow him to the mid-deck, where the Paladin sat down in the shade of the main mast, the Ancient joining him with a scowl.

'Why do you disapprove of Trimm's wealth so much?' asked the Forest Guardian, coming straight to the point.

'Because Cape Verstaad is our overweight and battle-shy friend's centre of power,' replied Uldini meaningfully, looking at Ahren expectantly.

The Paladin blinked, a look of incomprehension on his face. 'And?'

Uldini's eyes rolled with such superiority that it took all the Forest Guardian's self-control not to nail the Ancient's robe to the mast with *Sun*. 'What I mean is – if Trimm decides that he'd rather *not* go to the Ring, and if we try to compel him to, then he will have enough influence in Cape Verstaad to start a mini-war.'

'But…but he surely wouldn't do that,' responded Ahren, perplexed. '*Would* he?'

'*You* tell *me*,' Uldini murmured, nodding towards the merchant Paladin, who was bargaining enthusiastically with Trogadon.

Trimm seemed a new person as he cheerfully engaged in haggling, throwing numbers at his Dwarfish trading partner and gleefully making counter offers – not at all like the fearful Champion of the gods that Ahren was so familiar with.

'Does he look as if he is going to want to give up his cushy existence here and risk losing his life at the Ring? I think not. The fact that we are not taking him with us to the Ice Fields suits him down to the ground, for it will give him the chance to develop a plan unhindered, which will prevent his journeying to the Ring. Mark my words – the more power he wields in Cape Verstaad, the harder it will be to persuade him to leave it all behind.'

Ahren watched the Arch Wizard as he floated away like a wandering spectre, who had issued his final words of foreboding. Then the Forest Guardian turned his attention again to what was going on at the *Queen of the Waves'* prow. It was with mixed feelings that he observed Trogadon and Trimm shaking hands solemnly. The corpulent Paladin's eyes sparkled triumphantly, Ahren suddenly seeing a man used to issuing orders and who had banned the word *no* from his vocabulary. He was looking at the Grandee Salman Tilderius – and it was a sight that didn't appeal to him one little bit.

Entering the harbour of Cape Verstaad took longer than expected, as berths first had to be freed up to make room for the damaged ships in the fleet. Apart from the numerous luxurious cogs and caravels of the trading city, there was also a multitude of other trading ships in the harbour basin, which were either travelling east or west, bringing their wares from faraway lands to harbours that were just as distant, where they would peddle their exotic wares. Admiral Refelbek had insisted that the fleet would not be spread out across the entire bay, and as a result it wasn't until the sun began to set that a sufficiently large pier became available where the remaining ships of the Thirteenth Fleet could be berthed, and all the necessary repair works undertaken over the next few weeks. Following age-old tradition, the admiral ordered that the *Queen of the Waves* be the last to be moored, and it was only once the oil in the ship's lanterns ran out that the restless companions would be allowed to disembark.

Ahren stood on deck in the twilight and allowed the impressions of this strange city to wash over him without yet having walked its broad streets. Cape Verstaad was decorated with elegant lanterns that were positioned on the walls of houses, on bronze pedestals, and even in the crowns of the ornamental palm trees that were arranged in orderly lines. Ahren found this odd, as surely an unwelcome gust of wind would set the plants on fire, but then he reckoned that a solution to this problem had somehow been found, given the outrageous wealth that was on display everywhere.

Maybe they aren't real palm trees at all, but lifelike wrought iron representations, snarled Culhen, whose mood was dark, to say the least. He had deliberately settled down before the retracted gangplank, thereby making his impatience clear for all to see, for the wolf simply couldn't understand why the admiral hadn't immediately given the passengers permission to leave the ship. Of course, their eventual disembarkation had to fulfil the requirements of an adequately formal celebration, and the last thing that Ahren wanted was for Culhen and his feline friend to roam the streets of this strange city at night before the enormous Ice Wolf had been presented as an ally, with all the attendant pomp and ceremony, to at least half the city residents, Culhen yielded – not without protest – to the wishes of his Paladin.

You have to understand, said Ahren wearily. *I just don't want a nervous guard – never mind, an over-enthusiastic Battle Wizard – to see either you or Muai as the enemy and attack.*

As though I wouldn't emerge the victor in such an encounter, complained Culhen.

It is considered rude to bite city guards or sorcerers when one is a visitor, explained Ahren with growing concern.

Stupid humans with their stupid rules, sulked the wolf, snorting loudly before covering his nose with his tail. *And stupid admirals.*

Ahren heard steps behind him and turned to see Trimm walking lightly up to him, Ahren gazing in amazement at his fellow Paladin's white, silken robe, decorated with gold stitching and presenting the merchant's corpulent body in a flattering light. 'Grandee Tilderius,' said the Forest Guardian, bowing ironically.

'Honourable Thirteenth,' his opposite number replied, nodding, too. Then he positioned himself beside Ahren and glanced at Culhen. 'Is he *still* kicking up a fuss?'

Culhen snorted again, sparing Ahren the necessity of responding.

'I see you have had a new robe delivered to you already, but where is your tomcat?' asked Ahren instead. 'His name is Eken, isn't that right?'

'He didn't want to come,' explained Trimm, shrugging his shoulders. 'My friend is *very* lazy.' Ahren looked at him in disbelief, the grandee then laughing cheerfully. 'Oh, that is perfectly normal for us,' he said. 'We each make allowances for the other's little weaknesses and are never offended.' Trimm straightened his robe. 'Although Eken could simply have allowed himself to be carried here when I had these rags brought from my palace.'

Ahren raised his hands in resignation. 'I must admit that it's going to take me a while to get used to the fact that your position as grandee is more than a mere title. In Gol-Konar it immediately spelt trouble, and at the very least would have meant our expulsion.'

Trimm laughed patronizingly. 'My dear Ahren, that is perfectly understandable, of course. You have never been to Cape Verstaad, *and* you come from Hjalgar, where pover—' The Paladin stopped in mid-sentence, Ahren now staring balefully at him. 'Please forgive me,' he said meekly in Trimm's normal tone of voice, which the Forest Guardian was familiar with. 'It doesn't take one long to fall into one's old habits here.'

Suddenly, Uldini's warning was all too present again in Ahren's mind, and he found himself unable to ignore the Arch Wizard's sceptical tone: *The more power he possesses in Cape Verstaad...* Ahren shook his head and forced himself to smile, albeit weakly. 'Why don't you first explain to me why your streets are so white?' he asked. 'The roads don't look as if they are made of stone. Is it sand?'

'Almost,' said Trimm with a crooked grin. 'Powdered mussel shells. Solid enough to walk on, yet easier to remove than sand.'

'Remove?' asked Ahren irritably.

Trimm nodded absently. Once a year the streets are swept clear of them, and then new mussel shells are sprinkled in their place.' He waved his hand. 'This is how one gets rid of the dirt that has collected on the roads over the course of the period.'

Ahren pursed his lips and said nothing. It seemed that problems in Cape Verstaad were never solved in the simplest manner when a more expensive one was possible. He briefly considered posing a question regarding chamber pots, but then thought better of it as he would doubtless be finding out soon enough anyway. 'What are Palnah's first impressions of her new homeland?' he asked instead.

'Oh, she finds it charming!' replied Trimm quickly. 'At least, I *think* she does,' he added with considerably less certainty. He shrugged his shoulders again. 'If there is anything that she doesn't like, I will have it changed.

The self-confidence with which the corpulent Paladin alluded to his power and wealth reminded Ahren again of Uldini's warning. 'And what if the climate doesn't suit her?' he asked cautiously. 'You cannot simply change that.'

Trimm fixed his eyes on Ahren and stared at his fellow Paladin in such a manner that the young master felt as if he had been somehow found out. 'Then we will probably leave Cape Verstaad and begin our lives somewhere else,' he said slowly. 'At the *Ring*, perhaps?'

'Em,' muttered Ahren, but Trimm waved his hand dismissively.

'Uldini has mistrusted me ever since he learned of my title,' said the grandee, his voice once again carrying with it an air of authority. 'I gave up trying to please *him* a long time ago.' His eyes were still locked on Ahren's 'And I have always felt that I have had no *need* to try and please *you*. Or am I mistaken?'

Ahren shook his head, annoyed at himself for having allowed the seed of doubt to be planted in his head. 'You are my brother,' he simply said.

'Good.' Trimm's curt response might as easily have come from the voice of the sun king. 'Then I am sure *you* will trust *me* to put *my* plans in effect for preparing *your* expedition into the Ice Fields as smoothly as possible.'

Ahren frowned at the grandee's peculiar formulation, nodding silently, nevertheless. Trimm mirrored the gesture, a look of triumph in his eyes. Then the corpulent Paladin turned and disappeared below deck, leaving a thoroughly confused Forest Guardian in his wake, who was wondering if his fearful brother would really be capable of withstanding the siren song of power once he inevitably found himself in its inviting embrace.

Chapter 7

Ahren stepped onto the ground of the opulent city for the first time, his feet making a crunching sound in the warm sunshine that cast its light on wealthy Cape Verstaad.

It seemed that every citizen of the metropolis had made their way down to the harbour to greet their honoured guests. Dozens of minstrels had struck up the air of *The Champions of the Gods* once Ahren had disembarked, the throngs of people cheering jubilantly. Servants dressed in coloured livery waited in position at the large, gold-inlaid sedans made from sycamore wood, raising the vehicles as soon as the visitors had stepped into them. Their lavish procession was led by exotic animals – a proud bird, for example, which fanned its colourful tail feathers in a most impressive manner, or a most peculiar horse, whose body was covered in black and white stripes – the creatures with their gold-embroidered reins presenting the newcomers to the jubilant crowds as they processed solemnly along the streets.

As if a two paces tall Ice Wolf wearing magnificent Deep Steel armour weren't enough of a sensation, said Culhen haughtily as he walked beside Ahren, enjoying the attention immensely, nonetheless. *But perhaps these creatures in front of us are going to by our midday meal,* he added, licking his chops.

I thought that you and Muai were going to stretch your legs by immediately going for an extended run once you stepped onto dry land, teased Ahren. *Why are you still here with all these admiring eyes looking at you then?*

Muai insisted on hanging on, said Culhen, quick as a flash. *I thought I would give in to her wishes and wait for the end of the procession. Until the fuss has died down a little and there is space on the city streets again – if you see what I mean.*

Ahren decided to let the wolf off the hook, concentrating on his surroundings and his friends behind him, instead. Khara was in the sedan immediately to his rear, the Swordsmistress smiling at him when she spotted him looking at her. Behind her were Falk, Jelninolan, Uldini, and Hakanu. The apprentice was so wide-eyed and sitting so proudly that Ahren couldn't stop himself from laughing out loud – luckily, he was drowned out by the boisterous cheering. Even Yantilla was in a sedan, looking for all the world as if she would challenge anyone that dared to question her being so cossetted – and indeed even the Forest Guardian was surprised no end.

Then Ahren spotted Trimm, who was sitting on a twin-seater with Palnah beside him, the white-timbered vehicle resembling a portable throne for two. A dozen servants were carrying the couple on their shoulders, and it seemed to Ahren that the grandee and his chosen one were raised considerably higher than the Paladins, the Ancients, and the other dignitaries. As he directed his eyes forward again, he looked for a heartbeat at Uldini, who was staring right back at him with piercing eyes that seemed to say, *I told you so. His alienation from us is already beginning.*

Ahren quickly faced the front, concentrating now on the crowd that was parting before them as the procession approached and would close once the companions had passed through. By now, he was very familiar with such ceremonial welcomes, and he smiled, nodded, and waved in the manner expected of him. A part of him was wondering when precisely he had become accustomed to being honoured in such a manner, while another thought niggled at him simultaneously – namely, the striking differences in these people that were greeting him so jubilantly. He had certainly expected the wealthily garbed merchants, and the nobles who were being carried in their own sedans, but behind them, like a wall of deprivation and poverty, was a veritable army consisting of beggars, undernourished workers, and gaunt-looking mercenaries. Ahren remembered Falk's comment on the gulf between the rich and poor of Cape Verstaad, and indeed it was impossible to miss – the contrast was so extreme that Ahren had the feeling that citizens of two completely incompatible cities were cheering them on.

At least they are all happy to see us, interjected Culhen, who was giving out slobbery licks to the excited onlookers, especially to the little children with their eagerly outstretched hands, the youngsters being held out to him by their proud parents.

Ahren looked out for signs of whipping or any other draconian measures that might have been meted out to the commoners, but all he could see were genuinely happy faces – people, it seemed, who had worked hard all their lives for very little reward. Their meagre earnings kept these citizens captive more effectively than any rod could.

And here come the grandees, interrupted Culhen, bringing his friend back to the here and now.

Ahren saw a long procession of similar vehicles to the one that Trimm and Palnah were sitting in, except that many of these ones were studded with jewels, their framework being made with precious metals. Upon them were sitting, lying or standing figures dressed so ostentatiously that the nobles of King's Island itself – if they had happened to be standing in the crowd – would surely have crept into the next hole in the ground, embarrassed by their own relative plainness.

Like a bolt out of the blue, Ahren suddenly understood that there was a kind of metaphorical secret war being waged between the wealthy of the north and their counterparts in the south of Jorath, in which the soldiers were not people but trade agreements and where victories came in the form of annual profits.

Their war is just a game, interjected Culhen. *Not one of them would dare set foot on the walls of the Ring.*

Which is why they have their mercenaries, added Ahren grimly.

The Cape Verstaad grandees nodded and bowed, but only slightly, at the distinguished visitors as they were carried past in their opulent sedans while the music of the minstrels and the loud cheering of the other citizens continued to fill the air. The looks and gestures of the grandees suggested to Ahren that the city leaders believed they were performing a benevolent favour by offering up their precious time – even if no more than a fleeting moment – to the Paladins. Indeed, hardly had these high and mighty leaders of the city been carried past when they veered off the main avenue and disappeared down an adjoining street and into the most exclusive part of the city with its grand and opulent residences.

Like kings throwing alms at a beggar, thought Ahren as he shook his head in disbelief and looked over at Trimm. He merely shrugged his shoulders in return, and it was suddenly clear to the young Paladin that they were in a difficult dilemma. They would need all the support they could muster from within the city if they were to equip their upcoming expedition sufficiently, and above all prove victorious in the expected battle with the Dark Ones, now lurking in the waters to the south of Cape Verstaad. Trimm was their key to this self-enamoured group of people, who were so wealthy that they even gave the sun emperor a permanent headache with their demands and power games. But the more Trimm allowed himself to be sucked into their machinations, the greater the danger would be of his turning his back on his life as a Champion of the gods, the communality of the Paladins then inevitably falling apart.

'Then we will simply force him,' hissed Falk. 'It won't have been the first time.'

Ahren and his friends were standing and whispering to each other having stepped off their sedans. The companions found themselves in an enormous front garden with splendid plants and broad paths. They had to crane their necks to take in Trimm's palace in its entirety, Ahren reckoning it to be over one hundred paces across, with its cupola soaring a good thirty paces above them. The master of the house was preoccupied with helping Palnah down from the palanquin that the couple had been transported on, and Ahren took the opportunity to share his and Uldini's doubts with the others – in the hope that his friends would dispel them.

'Force is *not* the answer,' murmured Khara. 'Trimm is beginning to trust you Paladins again. I can sense it through the Blessing Band whenever we are practising.'

'*He's* beginning to trust *us?*' whispered Falk. 'It's *me*, who's slowly coming to terms with the fact that Trimm isn't *completely* useless. If he hadn't saved Ahren in the bay of Gol-Konar and killed Reik then...'

'But he *did,*' interjected Ahren in a whisper. 'And you are confirming what Khara senses and what I know, deep in my heart – if the Paladins don't all pull together and trust one another implicitly, then how, by the THREE, are we going to be able to bring the Adversary to his knees?'

'Yes, *indeed,*' said Uldini in a tone of voice that made a shiver run down Ahren's back, 'how *are* you going to manage that?'

The Forest Guardian didn't fail to notice Falk shaking his head almost imperceptibly, and he wondered what precisely the Ancient meant with his comment.

'We must not lose Trimm to Cape Verstaad,' said Ahren decisively. 'The Paladins have to remain united.'

'Very well put, *little brother!*' Ahren immediately recognised the deep voice behind him, the Forest Guardian spinning around in amazement to see a familiar figure emerging from the shade of one of the many opulent palm trees which decorated the front garden of the palace.

'*Bergen?*' asked Falk, taken aback, Ahren looking in disbelief at the broad-shouldered wildly-grinning, charismatic Paladin who was striding quickly towards them with his arms spread out in welcome. The Ice Lander had a few more wrinkles on his face than Ahren remembered, but both his deportment and his sparkling eyes suggested a positively youthful exuberance which had not been visible during their last meeting.

'Boy, but it's lovely to see you again,' boomed the man, laughing uproariously and giving Ahren such a bearhug that the Forest Guardian gasped and spluttered.

'By the THREE am I glad that I'm wearing my armour,' snorted Ahren, slapping his fellow Paladin on the back in the desperate hope that he would be let go. 'A Glower Bear's embrace is gentler than yours.'

Another guffaw. 'Don't be like that,' chuckled Bergen before finally releasing Ahren from the steel clamp of his effusive and hearty welcome. One by one, the others were subjected to the dubious pleasure of Bergen's hug, but when he arrived at Trimm, he suddenly paused.

'Is this *your* palace?' he asked the Paladin, who was eyeing Bergen critically if not with outright hostility.

So what if it is?' came the truculent response. 'Have you any objections? Are you telling me that a Paladin shouldn't possess such a property, but should spend his time going from tavern to tavern, killing Dark Ones or bandits for monetary reward?'

Bergen narrowed his eyes, and Ahren was on the point of stepping in between them to nip any hostility in the bud when suddenly the Ice Lander threw his head back, laughed uproariously again, before embracing Trimm and lifting him off the ground effortlessly. 'Good for you!' he exclaimed cheerily. 'I always said that you had more within you than you believed possible. Only, I'd never have believed that one of your talents was to acquire immeasurable wealth.'

Falk positioned himself beside Ahren and scratched his beard in confusion as Bergen greeted Palnah with a low bow and some well-chosen words, engaging the quiet woman in some easy conversation, during which she visibly relaxed.

'This is not the Bergen of the Brazen City,' said Falk, stunned. 'This is the Bergen that I *used* to know – before the Night of Blood scarred him for ever.'

Ahren could hear the undertone of envy in the voice of his mentor, which was always there whenever he spoke of the Ice Lander, who was beloved wherever he went. The ease with which Bergen won loyalty and fidelity from his fellow humans was in stark contrast to Falk – whose stoical, quiet, and occasionally prickly personality sometimes made him seem stand-offish.

Then Bergen stopped in front of Hakanu, eyeing him with a critical eye, only for Ahren to suddenly jump forward as if someone had dumped a pail of freezing water over his head.

'Oh, no!' the young man exclaimed, panic-stricken as he shoved his way between the pair of them. 'No, no, *no!*' He grabbed Hakanu by the shoulders, shook him vigorously, and began lecturing his apprentice, who was staring, awe-struck at what the lad presumably took to be a luminous figure from a heroic saga. 'He is a *bad* man! Do *not* talk to him, and don't believe a *word* that comes out of his mouth!' he scolded, while everyone around him laughed gleefully. 'It doesn't matter what stories he tells, they're all *lies,* and they *never* end well!'

Bergen burst out laughing, stood beside the panic-stricken Forest Guardian, and placed a comforting hand on his shoulder. 'Don't worry, little brother,' he said affectionately. 'I'm not going to take your apprentice away from you.' Ahren dropped his arms and looked pleadingly at Bergen. 'Please don't fill his head with tales of courage and bravado. It's taken me so long to get him to think before he acts.'

Well, insofar as Hakanu is capable of thinking, added Culhen cheerfully as he rubbed his head against the Ice Lander's back. *It's so nice to see Bergen again.*

The broad-shouldered Paladin laughed again and placed an arm across Hakanu's shoulders. 'You seem to me to be a clever, self-confident young fellow,' he said good-heartedly. 'One or two stories aren't likely to do you any harm, isn't that right?'

'Appearances can be deceptive,' interjected Trogadon dryly before handing Bergen his little metal canteen.

The Ice Lander drank down the liquid in one go, then handed the receptacle back to the dwarf. 'Ah, Trogadon, my *dear* friend! Let us enter Trimm's mansion and find something else to drink while I tell this young lad of how I felled two Glower Bears with one blow of an axe…'

The trio quickly marched towards the enormous open front door of the property, before which liveried servants and mercenaries in shining armour were positioned in readiness to welcome their lord and master but who were now looking uncertainly over at Trimm as the three figures simply pushed their way through them. The corpulent Paladin waved his hand in a gesture of annoyance, Bergen, Hakanu, and Trogadon then proceeding unhindered before disappearing inside the enormous palace.

'I love Bergen like a brother,' said Falk, non-plussed, 'but why, by the THREE, is he here at all?'

'There's only one way of finding out,' replied Ahren crossly, nodding towards the entrance. 'And if we can stop Hakanu from falling back into his old heroic idiocies, then that suits me down to the ground.' He looked demandingly at Trimm, who promptly regained his composure, linked arms with Palnah, and strode towards the ostentatious doorway.

'Welcome to your new home,' said the merchant, looking lovingly at the woman beside him. 'I *do* hope that you will like it here.'

With the rustling of silk and the clanking of Dwarfish steel, the assembly of servants knelt and bowed before Palnah, now thoroughly taken aback.

'But...' she stammered. 'But it really isn't necessary. Please rise.'

The servants rose in unison, pressing the palm of their left hands to their hearts.

'Would m'lady like to see her apartments?' asked a young woman, smiling warmly.

'Uh...yes?' said Palnah, glancing uncertainly at Trimm.

He nodded and grinned. 'The days of you having to ask your consort for permission to do things are over,' he murmured. 'Do as you wish. As long as you are happy, then all my troubles will have been worth it.'

Dumbstruck, Palnah simply nodded before being led away by the handmaiden. Trimm wiped a corner of his eye with his thumb, then turned to the others. 'May I invite those of you who are *not* intent on plundering my wine cellars into my humble home?' he asked, and without waiting for an answer, he strode in, every inch a grandee again.

Khara linked arms with Ahren and craned her neck to see inside the palace for the first time, while Uldini muttered under his breath. Looking beyond Trimm, Ahren could make out marble floors, delicate oak carvings, and more gold than could possibly be good for an entrance hall. He glanced over at Falk, who rolled his eyes at the wealth of their brother.

We'll be off, then, said Culhen hurriedly. *Now that we're not being admired anymore – sorry, I mean, now that the streets are no longer thronged – we urgently need to get the feel of grass under our paws again.* Then he and Muai fled into the city, doubtless with the intention of setting off on a hunt and avoiding the necessity of taking part in the tour of the residence. The prospect of being the subject of more cheering from the gradually dispersing crowds surely influenced the canine's decision, too.

'Let's get this over with,' sighed Ahren to the others as Trimm began to explain every detail of his home, from the artists who had done the plastering, to the quarries from where the marble had originated. It wasn't long before Ahren regretted not having gone with Bergen, Hakanu, and Trogadon.

'And this is my guest parlour,' said Trimm proudly before coming to a sudden halt. '*You?!*' he gasped, horrified, Ahren quickly rousing himself from the semi-conscious state to which he had fled in order to bear the grandee's never-ending descriptions of the building's furnishings.

They were standing in an opulent, circular room, a good eight paces in diameter, whose walls and ceilings were decorated with brass mirrors, which strengthened the sunshine coming down through light shafts above them to such a degree that it seemed to the Forest Guardian that he was being accosted by the blinding rays of a hot summer's day. There were some black-leathered seats in the centre of the room, on one of which sat…*the First!*

Suddenly wide awake, Ahren stared open-mouthed at one of the oldest living beings in all Jorath. The man, with his archaic armour and rivetted medals, seemed to be the personification of a war veteran, and when he got to his feet, he became, in his expansive, clanking metal sheets a walking force of nature. To Ahren, the First seemed unalterable no matter what happened, and it was this consistency that had, to a large extent, given him an air of invincibility – like an impenetrable protective wall.

'Good day to you all,' he boomed, the unmistakable tone of authority audible in his voice. 'I have come as requested,' he added, nodding towards Uldini.

'Very good,' said the Ancient, floating over to the Paladin. 'I wasn't sure that you would be able to get away, but I am delighted that you have made it here in good time.'

'*You* called him here?' asked Falk, taken aback. 'How come we didn't know about it?'

Uldini shrugged his shoulders. 'It was unclear as to whether the First would accompany us to the Ice Fields – that's why I didn't mention it.'

By now, Ahren had recovered from the shock, and he gave the age-old Paladin his hand. 'It is good to see you again,' he said sincerely. 'If I'd had to listen to yet another story about the joys of plasterwork in niches or the transport routes of Dwarfish basalt, I would have burned this palace to the ground.' He then looked apologetically at the dumbstruck grandee. 'Nothing personal,' he added, 'but it's just that I am a humble Forest Guardian, and a hut under a few trees is perfectly fine for me. Even Jelninolan has slipped away under the excuse of being exhausted – and *that's* saying something.'

Trimm wasn't listening, however. He was still standing there open-mouthed, staring at the First like an oversized mouse, paralysed with fear before a cat about to pounce. Clearly, he hadn't heard what Ahren had said. The veteran, too, stared back at the shivering grandee with his penetrating eyes. It was time for Ahren to intervene.

'That's enough now, First,' he said firmly to the age-old Paladin.

'Very well,' growled the soldier before looking away. 'Trimm has understood my message.'

'You...you?' stammered the grandee, turning to look at Ahren before clearing his throat nervously. '*You* tell the *First* what to do?' He stared at the Forest Guardian as if he had unmasked a Doppler.

'I wouldn't put it like *that,* exactly,' replied Ahren, breaking into a crooked smile, the age-old Champion of the gods doing precisely the same. 'We know each other well enough by now not to tread on each other's toes – unless it is absolutely necessary.'

'That's one way of putting it,' chuckled the First.

Only now had Khara recovered from the shock, throwing herself into the man's arms, the First then laughing and spinning her around. 'What a lovely surprise!' she exclaimed.

'Khara, my dear,' he said. 'It really is such a pity that I missed your bond ceremony. Mind you, maybe that wasn't such a bad thing, for I surely would have talked you out of hitching up with this poor excuse for a Forest Guardian.'

'I can hear you, you know,' interjected Ahren snippily. He would never understand the closeness between Khara and the seasoned warrior. Still, they had protected each other during the Hjalgarian campaign, and he would forever be in the First's debt for that service.

'Are you now Ahren's soul companion?' asked the man, holding her by the shoulders now with his arms outstretched so that he could examine her critically. 'Could the THREE really have been *so* cruel?' The sparkling in his eyes died down once he noticed that the atmosphere in the room had suddenly grown colder.

'We do not know the answer to that question,' said Ahren truthfully. 'But everything seems to suggest that Khara is a normal mortal who has had the misfortune of falling in love with a Paladin.'

Khara's expression betrayed the inner turmoil she was feeling, which was eventually transformed into a cheekiness that Ahren felt was a little too contrived. '*Who* is *normal* here?' she asked, flashing her eyes at him before releasing herself from the First and positioning herself beside Ahren.

'I think that it would be right to say that there is no-one in this room who could be described as "normal", My Queen,' replied the Forest Guardian, pecking her on the cheek before turning to face the First and Uldini again, the latter having grown increasingly impatient at the greetings and subsequent chatter. 'Why don't the two of you tell us why you and Bergen are here?' suggested Ahren, changing the subject.

'Very simple,' said the First, folding his arms in front of his chest. 'Dragon hunting.'

'Could you be a little more specific?' asked Falk, rolling his eyes.

'At last – a few *sensible* questions,' grumbled Uldini, floating to the middle of the room, where the light illuminated him from all sides. 'We know that Yollock went off after Four Claws centuries ago with the intention of slaying the dastardly dragon. The monster was last sighted flying towards the Ice Fields.'

'The fact that Yollock hasn't returned doesn't tell us very much,' said the First, taking over from the Arch Wizard. 'Either he is dead, which is highly unlikely, for then we other Paladins would surely have sensed it…'

'…unless the vast distance between the Ice Fields and the continent meant that his demise echoed unheard,' interjected Uldini argumentatively, Ahren realising that the pair must have squabbled over this matter previously.

'How probable is that?' asked Ahren, ignoring the uneasy feeling in the pit of his stomach. Was it possible that they were travelling to the most hostile region in all creation in search of nothing more than a skeleton?'

The First was calmness personified as he turned to Trimm. 'How long have you been playing the merchant in Cape Verstaad?' he asked in a bored tone.

The grandee made sure to adopt a worthy pose before he answered: 'For a long, long time,' he said vaguely. 'One does not become a grandee overnight, and I had to start at the very bottom. I took on many identities over the centuries, with the help of which I gradually amassed my fortune.'

'And you changed your appearance every time?' asked the First, before waving his hand dismissively. 'Do you know, I really don't care how you managed to neglect your sacred responsibilities to the deities. At least you were creative, something which can't be said of Falk. He wasted his time staring into the bottom of wine tankards.'

'You were about to tell us what inferences you have drawn regarding Yollock's location,' said Falk, coughing with embarrassment.

The First nodded, his face the picture of concentration. Ahren was certain that the age-old Paladin was not in the least bothered by the fact that he was upsetting both Falk and Trimm. The warrior was as unswerving as an avalanche of rocks, which crushed to pieces everything that it could not carry along. 'If Trimm spent the whole time in Cape Verstaad, then he would certainly have sensed Yollock's death.' He turned irritably to Uldini. 'Can we not knock that possibility on the head, for once and for all?'

The Ancient raised his arms in a gesture of capitulation. 'By all means,' he grumbled. 'It's not as if I *wanted* the old swashbuckler to have snuffed it.'

'Which leaves two possibilities – either Yollock is missing in action in the Ice Fields...or he is still hunting this dragon.'

Ahren blinked in surprise, while Khara expressed his disbelief with an incredulous '*whaaat?*'

'Yollock trained the very first Forest Guardians,' said Falk, shaking his head firmly. 'No way would he ever be missing in action – and especially not over centuries. If anyone knows their way out of the land of eternal snow and ice, then it is him.'

'Precisely,' added the First, satisfied. 'So, let us stick with the dragon hunting.'

'Even if it means my repeating the question,' interjected Khara, still incredulous. '*What* do you *mean?* He has hardly spent hundreds of years hunting down a dragon that can easily fly away from him anyway.'

The First looked sternly at Khara. 'I have slaughtered countless Southern Dragons that came under the control of the Adversary. Hence, I think I can judge the situation well enough.' His voice softened. 'There are ways and means of stopping a dragon from flying, and as Four Claws was badly wounded when he flew into the Ice Fields, he might well be in what is known as a Dragon Sleep – a state in which his wounds can heal.'

'A sleep like that can last for many years,' added Uldini.

'Centuries?' asked Ahren.

'Not normally,' admitted the First, tapping his helmet, which was in the form of a dragon's head. 'But I wager that we will find Yollock engaged in dragon hunting. It's the only logical conclusion.'

'Marvellous.' Ahren's comment dripped with sarcasm. 'Slaying a dragon is still on Hakanu's "to do" list.'

The First's eyes sparkled with interest. 'Your apprentice if I'm not mistaken?' he asked. 'I'm sure it will be an absolute pleasure to meet him.'

'Hm,' said Ahren, smiling weakly. 'I'm not so sure about that.'

'Of all the mutton-headed, obstinate, idealistic Paladins that I've ever had the misfortune of coming across…' cursed the First for the umpteenth time.

Ahren was sitting with the veteran, Trogadon, Falk, and Yantilla on an enormous terrace situated on the roof of the western wing of Trimm's palace. The sun had already gone down, and the moon shone on the intricate coloured mosaic that framed a large pool where reed roses floated invitingly on the water for anyone who might be tempted to go bathing. They had all made themselves comfortable on the surrounding divans and were listening with varying amounts of amusement to the age-old Paladin's tirade.

Ahren reacted to the First's choice of words with equanimity. 'Hakanu isn't perfect, but his heart is in the right place.'

'Remember those words,' said the veteran caustically, 'for they will make a good epitaph on his *gravestone!*'

'You were similarly harsh in your criticism when it came to Ahren, don't you remember?' said Falk. 'If I recall correctly, you accused *me* of having failed in my duties.'

'That was different,' muttered the First, crossing his arms angrily.

Ahren took advantage of the man's defensiveness and changed the subject – after all, he secretly agreed with the First's analysis. Hakanu still had a lot to learn, and the war was approaching its decisive moment far too quickly for his protégé to develop into the perfect Paladin before the lad found himself facing the Dark god. Then again, thought Ahren, who of them was perfect? 'Trimm, too, was considered a hopeless case, and look what he has achieved,' said the Forest Guardian, gesturing to the palace below and behind them.

The First snorted angrily. 'He had several centuries to gather a pile of money together,' he said dismissively. 'If you have enough time, that is no great achievement. During the chaos of the Dark Days, I had several opportunities to conquer Jorath had I wished to do so.' The man stared out into the night, Ahren seeing a mysterious expression on the veteran warrior's face. 'Luckily for all the wealthy of this world, I am above such trivial game-playing.'

Yantilla stopped raising her wine tankard in surprise on hearing the Paladin's words, and now she stared at him like a rabbit would a snake. 'Now you're exaggerating,' she gasped, then glancing at Falk for support.

'There is a *grain* of truth to his claim,' the old man said, scratching his beard ruminatively. 'All the important generals of the various tribes listened to the commands of the First. Had he found the right words, he would perhaps have been able to unite them and make Jorath into one mighty empire. The THREE know that the Paladins of the time would never have stood in his way.

'Why did you decide against it?' asked Ahren out of a certain morbid curiosity. It was a shock to him that the war leader would have turned his back on the opportunity to unite all the military forces of Jorath under his control.

The First did not respond initially, concentrating on enjoying the wine that he was supping from his tankard before murmuring, 'well, Trimm *does* have taste, I'll give him that.' Then he took a deep breath and fixed his eyes on Ahren.

The Forest Guardian had the feeling that he was looking directly through the eyes of the veteran and into the distant past that they were now talking about.

'The pragmatic reason is that it would have attracted too much attention. One single empire means one law for all, the same values, the same treatment of all the subjects. The suppression of the inevitable rebellions might have taken perhaps one, two centuries, during which time the Adversary would have taken every opportunity to rain on my parade.' The First shook his head. 'A militarily controlled Jorath would have been too dangerous for him, leaving me with two wars to fight – one against him, and another against my subjects.'

A shiver ran down Ahren's spine on becoming reacquainted with the ruthlessly analytical aspect of the First's personality – that same trait that could easily have turned Hjalgar into a massive conflagration when the centaurs had invaded the Forest Guardian's homeland.

Ahren was distracted by the yammering of Trimm, who was walking through the front garden of his palace, pleading in exasperation with Palnah, who was discussing with Jelninolan and Khara the proposed changes that she had suggested regarding the – to her eyes – overblown and tasteless palace furnishings. One by one, the companions on the roof terrace turned their heads to peer down on the drama unfolding below, none of them able to stop themselves from chuckling. From what Ahren could hear, not much more would be left of Trimm's domicile than its foundations. The Forest Guardian and his companions exchanged grins before the First returned to the subject in hand.

'Of more importance, however, was a simple truth,' he said, referring to his plans of conquest. 'Jorath consists of so many races, all of them completely different to each other and likely to squabble more than one can possibly imagine. A single enormous empire would have destroyed this diversity and made us far more predictable and easier to second guess.' He laughed grimly. 'For much of the time, one half of the alliance against the Adversary did not know what the other half was up to.' The First again sipped at his wine before concluding: 'A little chaos at the right time is worth more than total control.'

'I'm relieved that you possess a philosophical streak,' mused Falk. 'Otherwise, you would have been ruler of Jorath when I was born.'

'Indeed,' brooded the First. 'And you would all now be my subjects.'

An uneasy silence descended on the group, finally broken by Trogadon's quiet singing. The dwarf was sitting with his own tankard of wine, looking up at the moon, his eyes expressing the inner calm he was feeling.

'What sort of a song are you singing?' asked Ahren curiously.

Falk came up with the answer even before the blacksmith had the chance to explain. 'It is *The Song of the Lost Brothers*. It is a lament for the dwarves who turned their backs on tradition and now make up the Wild Clans.'

`Yantilla looked at Trogadon in surprise. 'And I always thought that you respect those who build lives for themselves far away from the Dwarfish fortifications.'

The blacksmith finished his verse, then smiled at the commander. 'For me it was never a *sad* song,' he murmured. 'More a source of comfort during the time that I believed I would never earn an Ancestry Name.' He cocked his head and mused. 'Now it reminds me of how far I have come, and that there are many ways of achieving personal freedom.'

'Says he who has to win a war against a god in order to gain permission to take the female of his dreams as wife.' It had been Uldini who had spoken, the childlike figure now floating up from the shadow of the stairwell.

'How long have you been lurking there?' asked Ahren, feeling strangely spied upon. It seemed like forever since the last time he and his companions had chatted so freely about all sorts of things that had come into their heads.

'Long enough to realise that no-one has come up with an idea of how we can get Trimm back to thinking rationally if he stays on here,' grumbled Uldini before pointing his thumb back over his shoulder at the slightly tottering figure behind. 'By the THREE, our exuberant friend here has made no effort at doing so, at any rate.'

'*Falk! Trogadon!*' bellowed Bergen, stepping onto the terrace with several carafes of tempting looking wine. 'Why did you abandon me in the cellar? I found…uh…five…' he stumbled forward, the receptacles clinking off each other, '…*four* of the best vintages I've ever had the honour of trying out.'

'You fell asleep after the wine-tasting,' said the dwarf, his eyes gleaming. '*And* with one arm wrapped around a wineskin. We didn't want to disturb you.'

'That wa..was ve…very *nice* of you,' mumbled Bergen, carefully placing the carafes on the marble table. Then he plonked himself on a divan and blinked owlishly at the others. 'What were you talking about?' he asked.

'Nothing *important*,' teased Uldini, Ahren sighing in annoyance.

'We were discussing how there is more than one way to climb a mountain,' said the Forest Guardian, glaring at Uldini. 'For example, how a Paladin unsuited for fighting but capable of amassing a fortune might help us to achieve our goal.'

The Ancient snorted. 'Do you *really* believe that Trimm has worked his way up to being a grandee so that he can help the war effort? And if so, how do you imagine he can do so? By inviting the Adversary to a decadent supper?'

Ahren frowned angrily. 'Why don't you just *ask* him?' he asked forcefully. 'Then he will no longer have the cloud of suspicion hanging over him.'

'Well, if *I* was waiting for an imminent battle and was terrified,' interjected Yantilla, much to Ahren's surprise, 'then I would seek out as much help as I could get.' She looked from Uldini to Ahren and back. 'Preferably enough help so that I would not have to fight myself.'

The Arch Wizard was aghast. 'The Paladins must confront the Dark god in *person* on the field of battle. An army of mercenaries won't be of any use in that respect.'

Yantilla nodded. 'But they can eliminate any Dark Ones that are in situ *between* Trimm and the Adversary.' She placed her hand on her chest. 'We Ice Wolves perform such a function – when we are *allowed* to.'

Ahren flinched at the woman's little barb, and she glanced at him before continuing.

'Perhaps Trimm is purchasing the support from his mercenaries – a support that we Ice Wolves offer the Thirteenth out of loyalty. But a shield is a shield no matter why it is raised when protecting innocent lives.'

'Puh!' muttered Uldini, but Ahren could see that the Ancient was contemplating what had been said. 'This place is turning you all into philosophers as far as I can see.'

Ahren gazed at the terrace with its pool in the centre, the moon shining down on the reed roses. From time to time, the sounds of laughter wafted up from the lantern-illuminated city below. The nighttime view of the metropolis was breath-taking, many of the Cape Verstaad palaces catching the moonlight on their adorned cupolas and roofs – indeed, it almost seemed as though they were in direct competition with the stars above.

'There are worse places to consider the mysteries of life,' he said.

'Well said,' said Bergen loudly, the Paladin now slumped on his divan and looking particularly sleepy. 'Those who leave behind their families seek comfort in the arms of their friends.'

Ahren stared steadfastly at the blonde Paladin, suddenly understanding why Bergen was so *despairingly* merry. 'What's her name, then?' he asked bluntly. 'Your soul companion, I mean.'

'Carlai,' the broad-shouldered man replied, smiling sheepishly at having been found out. 'She is in Deepstone, where the Blue Cohorts are protecting her and her fellow soul companions.'

'It will be crowded in the castle with all the other guards and Night Soldiers,' mused Falk. His grin suggested, however, that it was a relief to him that Onja and her baby were being looked after by the forty well-armed men and women who each possessed a soupcon of the god's Blessing that Bergen had so generously given them.

'She will give birth in one or two moons,' said Bergen. 'Leaving her was the hardest thing I have done in centuries.'

'Then why are you here?' asked Trogadon. 'Not that I don't appreciate your company, mind!'

Bergen fixed his eyes on the dwarf, laughter lines appearing around his eyes. 'Are you really asking why an *Ice* Lander would accompany you into the *Ice* Fields?'

'Forget it,' grumbled Trogadon, reaching for one of the full carafes.

Ahren felt unexpectedly relieved with the knowledge that someone that he implicitly trusted and who knew their way around the eternal ice would be among their number. Uldini had planned on hiring guides for their expedition, but Bergen's presence gave Ahren a warm feeling of security. 'I am delighted that you will be helping us,' he said simply.

'Not a bad idea at all,' admitted Uldini grumpily. 'But first, we need to gather up as much armour and support as we can while we are in Cape Verstaad.'

'That should be no problem,' said Trogadon, shrugging his shoulders. 'After all, we will be heading off to collect the last Paladin so that he can keep his appointment with the Adversary.'

'Out of *stock?!*' Uldini repeated in a voice so harsh that it might have broken rocks asunder. 'This is the greatest merchant city in the south and you have *no* fur clothing in *stock?*'

The merchant facing the Ancient and Ahren stooped so low that it seemed to the Forest Guardian as if he wanted to hide behind his wooden counter. 'I do apologise, Tahiri,' said the man hurriedly. 'But all the supplies were purchased weeks ago.'

'By whom?' growled Uldini, Ahren exchanging concerned looks with Khara and Hakanu, who were also accompanying the Arch Wizard on his Cape Verstaad shopping spree.

Uldini had insisted on embarking on the expedition without Trimm's assistance, for he still did not fully trust the fearful Paladin. The Forest Guardian was curious about the everyday activities of the city, anyway, and so he, Khara, and Hakanu had dressed themselves in light, loose robes, taking on the roles of bodyguards to the Ancient. Of course, their disguises were totally inadequate for anyone in the know who might be hunting for them, but they were sufficient to fool others and allow the friends to get to know the metropolis a little better.

'Em, the honourable Grandee Hekatlon,' said the merchant, nervously replying to Uldini's question. 'They say that he is planning an expedition to the Ice Fields and has been buying armour for weeks now, as well as hiring specialised mercenaries.'

Uldini uttered a succession of colourful curses before beckoning Ahren and the others to leave the merchant's spacious shop, where all sorts of things were stored in crates, barrels, and roles of oilskin.

On reaching the exit, Ahren could hear once again the many voices haggling loudly outside, the alley being full of vendors' stalls and small shops. The smells of exotic herbs and spices, and the screeching sounds of multi-coloured birds from the isles of the Cutlass Sea, all of them in their wrought-iron cages and waiting to be sold, combined with the heat rising between the whitewashed, flat-roofed houses, not to mention the lively chatter of buyers and sellers all created an exciting maelstrom of sensations, which Ahren needed some time to acclimatise to following all those weeks at sea.

'This is the third merchant already who has given me the same answer,' muttered Uldini through gritted teeth. 'It stinks to high heaven of intrigue on the part of the grandees.'

Ahren looked anxiously at the Ancient. 'Do you believe that they have deliberately purchased everything that *we* need for our journey to the south?'

Uldini snorted. 'Well, that is what *I* would do if I wanted to force the competition into making concessions.' The Arch Wizard threw his hands in the air irritably. 'It seems that our plans were seen through too easily, and the grandees want to withhold the provisions we need until we pay the price they demand, no matter how exorbitant.'

'Could it simply be a coincidence?' asked Hakanu, Ahren recognising the innocence of youth in the lad's question.

'Let me *think*,' sighed Uldini, looking at the apprentice. 'How *likely* is it that a gang of fat cats, who have at most ordered three exploratory missions into the Ice Fields over the past few centuries will now want to send such an *enormous* expedition – in the middle of a war, no less – that they end up having to purchase *all* the necessary provisions available in the city?'

Hakanu, however, continued to look quizzically at the Ancient. Ahren forced himself not to smile at Uldini's sarcastic tone, while Khara couldn't stop herself from snorting in delight. The apprentice waited for the Ancient's response to his own rhetorical question, and when the Arch Wizard realised that his sarcasm had rolled off Hakanu like water off a duck's back, the sorcerer floated a little away, cursing in exasperation.

'It *isn't* very likely,' said Ahren, deciding it was time to come to his apprentice's assistance.

'I see,' was Hakanu's concise reply, Ahren then noticing the young warrior's eyes sparkling with humour before the boy turned and followed Uldini.

'Am I imagining things or did Hakanu deliberately rile Uldini?' whispered Khara.

Ahren scratched his stubble in surprise. 'I think you might be right. He really *is* learning things.'

Khara nodded surreptitiously in Kamaluq's direction, the young animal leaping enthusiastically around Hakanu 'And what if it is our sweet little *fox* who is doing the learning?' she whispered. 'Remember how radically you changed once Culhen had learned how to hold real conversations with you?'

Ahren looked at his beloved in wide-eyed surprise. 'But of *course!*' he whispered. 'Kamaluq is taking control of his thinking!'

Khara smiled and shook her head. 'Aren't you being a little hard on your apprentice?' she murmured.

Ahren shrugged his shoulders. 'As long as Hakanu acts with a bit more sense, I couldn't care less which of them has come up with the correct idea.' Then he gave Khara a fleeting kiss.

'Are you lot coming or what?' muttered Uldini grumpily, turning to look back. The Ancient had floated some distance down the busy street already and had Hakanu in tow. 'Or will I go back to Trimm on my own and—.' The eyes of the Arch Wizard suddenly widened as he spun on his own axis, sparks of light now flashing between his trembling fingers. '*High Fang!*' he snarled, the words hitting Ahren like a thunderclap.

The Paladin and Khara raced towards the Ancient, simultaneously casting off their cloaks and drawing their weapons. The throng of merchants and buyers scattered in panic, everyone searching for cover in the surrounding shops or behind market stalls, the most agile of them clambering up onto the flat roofs of the lowest houses on the street.

'Where?' asked Ahren tensely, once they had reached Uldini, who was scanning the scene in all directions, while Hakanu was already on high alert, his spear ready for action in his hands.

The Ancient's eyes scrutinised the terrified crowd, his finger then pointing forward at a wealthy-looking merchant in a blue-white robe, who was trying to make herself as small as possible behind a group of six armed men and women. '*Her!*' gasped Uldini, fishing *Flamestar* out of his bundle, so that it would draw the sunlight to its core. Ahren, Khara, and Hakanu hurtled towards the merchant, who quickly withdrew into her shop, barely escaping Uldini's spell, which had blazed forth from his crystal ball as a flaming beam. The façade of the building began to smoulder, smoke rising from where the light hit the wall.

'Don't just *stand* there, you fools!' screamed the High Fang from inside at the dumbstruck mercenaries. 'Earn your salt! One hundred gold coins for anyone who can bring me the head of the boy.' This was immediately followed by the sounds of jars cracking from inside the shop, adding to the screams of the panic-stricken and cursing of the merchants and residents.

By now, Ahren had almost reached the six guards, but his hope that they would easily make way had been dashed by the generous reward offered by the High Fang, the defenders puzzled faces hardening as they drew their weapons.

'Out of the way,' growled Ahren. 'In the name of the Paladins!'

None of the mercenaries reacted, Ahren now staring at three sabres and two pikes, as well as at a woman who was holding a dagger in each hand, with more weapons hanging from the sash that she was wearing.

'I am a knife-thrower from Gol-Konar. You lot had better pis—' she began, only for Hakanu's spear to whizz pass Ahren before nailing the woman against the façade of the house, the weapon penetrating so deeply into the stone that the apprentice was unable to call it back with his sorcery.

Ahren leaped forwards to keep the mercenary to the left of the door in check, while Khara dealt with the ne'er-do-wells to the right. The mercenaries hadn't even flinched on witnessing the death of their comrade and now prepared for an assault on the Paladin and the Swordsmistress. Two each lunged towards Ahren and Khara, the fifth, meanwhile, pointing his sabre at Hakanu in an effort at preventing the apprentice from pulling his weapon both out of the stone wall and the dead woman.

'They are isolating us,' hissed Ahren in warning, as a woman with a pike and a sabre-holding man pushed in towards him, covering each other with their weapons at the same time. The fellow concentrated on countering Ahren's attack with lightning quick parries, the woman, meanwhile, seeking out openings in the Forest Guardian's defence so that she could skewer him with her pike. The Paladin was amazed by the mercenaries' fighting skills, and after several failed attempts at ending the skirmish in his favour, he decided to alter his tactics. He abandoned any attempt at attacking the sabre swinger, luring him and the woman instead with several cunning feints in the hope of getting the woman to break cover.

Khara, meanwhile, had become the personification of a steel-bladed whirlwind, forcing her two attackers to concentrate solely on remaining alive. The fact that they were doing so successfully, spoke volumes for their ability. Hakanu, on the other hand, was playing a deadly game of cat and mouse with the fifth mercenary by repeatedly reaching forward to grasp his spear only to leap back with equal speed to avoid the sabre of the wilding grinning man.

'Uldini!' shouted Ahren anxiously, one eye on his apprentice and the other squinting at his two attackers, who were doing their level best to slaughter him. 'A bit of help would be *more* than welcome!'

'Sorry,' replied the Arch Wizard through gritted teeth, the sorcerer now several paces behind the Paladin. 'I still haven't fully recovered my strength, and this house is being protected by a refined charm. It seems that the High Fang is planning something, and I would like to forestall whatever it is she has up her sleeve.' As if to reinforce his point, there was another cracking sound from inside the building – as though the woman was creating some sort of escape route for herself.

Ahren glanced at the house for the briefest of moments – the doorway of the shop seemed to have some sort of deep shadow hanging there, which stopped anyone outside from seeing what was going on within.

Cursing, Ahren pretended to be distracted by what he had seen, lowering his Wind Blade just enough for the pike carrier to risk stabbing her weapon at his face. The steel point shimmered in the sunshine and became ever greater as it filled Ahren's field of vision. Only at the very last moment did he swing his arm in an upward parry, slicing off the tip of the woman's long weapon, the spinning piece of steel cutting his right cheek as it flew away.

Ahren groaned as the warm blood began to run down his face as the sabre swinger now prepared to ruthlessly stab the young man in the abdomen. Unable to lower his upraised Wind Blade in time, the Forest Guardian half-turned on his own axis, past his enemy's weapon and using his spin to gracefully run his Wind Blade, now directly in front of his face, along the back of his attacker.

Even as the man screamed in agony and dropped his weapon, Ahren continued his turn until he was standing directly opposite the woman with her topless pike. He stabbed her in the right shoulder, and with a groan she dropped her useless weapon, sinking down at the wall of the house as she raised an arm in a pleading gesture for mercy.

Having thrown a look at the woman which suggested that she should on no account test his mercy, Ahren then turned this attention to aiding Khara and Hakanu. His apprentice was at the opposite end of the skirmish and unreachable for the moment. The Forest Guardian, therefore, uttered a loud cry of fury and leapt towards the pike carrier who was assailing Khara. The powerful man flinched in shock, raising his weapon defensively. That was all the distraction that Khara needed. She easily broke through the cover of the sabre swinger, who was now fighting on her own, the Swordsmistress slipping past the heavily bleeding woman to attack the fifth mercenary, who was doing his best to impale Hakanu.

'Give up!' yelled Ahren at the brawny, spear-holding mercenary as he pointed at the inside of the house with his chin. 'You will die *here* and *now* if you stand in the way of the Champions of the gods!'

The man's eyes studied Ahren's weapon and armour for a heartbeat before widening as the mercenary finally understood who it was that was facing him. His spear fell to the ground with a clatter, the final sabre-swinger immediately following her companion's example, letting go of her weapon as it if were a red-hot poker before raising her hands in a gesture of surrender.

Hakanu, out of his mind with fury, slammed his fist into the man's jaw, sending him unconscious to the ground. The boy's left hand had a nasty cut, and his left shoulder was similarly gashed. It seemed that the apprentice had done all in his power to protect his weapon hand from the sabre swinger's attacks.

'Pull your spear out of the wall,' commanded Ahren, his voice sounding rawer than intended, so concerned was he for the safety of his apprentice.

Meanwhile, a low cry emanated from the interior of the house, followed by hectic clattering sounds that grew ever louder. The unnatural shadows receded from the shop's doorframe, Uldini then giving a gasp of satisfaction. 'And about time,' he muttered wearily. 'Now – go *get* her!'

Ahren and Khara stormed into the shop, only to stop just as suddenly when they found that they were standing ankle-deep in a liquid that gave off a distinctive odour, which the enemy charm had disguised up to this point. Before them stood the High Fang, surrounded by an enormous pile of smashed vials, and holding a burning lantern in her hands. The eyes of the woman blazed fanatically as she raised the lamp above her head and snarled at Ahren: 'Burn in the name of the one worthy god!' Then she hurled the lamp to the floor, the pool of oil immediately igniting.

Ahren turned back to the doorway, shoving Khara out to safety in no uncertain terms, the flames already reaching him and licking up his armoured boots. With gritted teeth, the Forest Guardian leaped out of the deadly trap, the flames now consuming the inside of the house in their deadly embrace.

'Too *late!*' he heard from behind as he gasped in a heap on the ground, the High Fang then adding in an agonized cackle as the inferno began to burn her to a cinder: 'You have come *far* too *late!*'

Chapter 8

'How many?' asked Uldini impatiently as Jelninolan stepped out onto the palace rooftop terrace, the companions having selected it as their meeting place.

The air was humid and sticky. Ahren looked longingly at the inviting pool nearby, his nagging unease having been the only thing that had prevented him from diving into its cool water as he and the others had waited in nervous anticipation for Jelninolan to reveal the information from the charm net that she had cast regarding how many other High Fangs were abroad in the city.

'Seventeen at a minimum,' said Jelninolan morosely. 'Probably more. I recognised dozens if not hundreds of bane charms in the city. There are many sorcerers and even more wealthy families residing in Cape Verstaad, all of them intent on hiding their secrets – whether worldly or magical – from prying eyes.'

'We should have reckoned on that,' grumbled Falk. 'Anyone who cannot hurl a fireball still manages to earn a decent living here once they've mastered a few disguise spells.'

'This day has brought us little good news,' said Khara, succinctly if bleakly. Once they had returned to their base, they had engaged in earnest discussion until dusk. The smoking ruins of the dead High Fang's house was still visible in the distance. 'The grandees are preventing us from getting access to the materials that we need, and there are High Fangs hiding everywhere in the city.'

'Not for much longer,' said Uldini coldly. 'Jelninolan and I will first smoke out the High Fangs, and then I will take the grandees to task.'

'May I suggest that *I* deal with the grandees?' asked Trimm, who was resting alongside Palnah on a divan and looking remarkably relaxed considering the latest news. Indeed, to Ahren's eyes, his fellow Paladin almost looked smug. The Forest Guardian was immediately, and despite his best efforts, filled with doubt again concerning the merchant, not least because of Uldini's obvious distrust.

'What are you thinking of, precisely?' asked Trogadon, who was polishing his blacksmith's hammer and presumably already imagining how he would use it to put the accursed High Fangs out of their misery.

'I'm thinking of holding a reception,' explained Trimm, Ahren raising his eyebrows in surprise at the unexpected response. 'A little feast in my palace, to which all the grandees of Cape Verstaad will be invited.'

'A *reception?*' echoed Bergen, similarly taken aback. 'But why?'

'Oh, for several reasons,' said Trimm airily as he smiled enigmatically. 'For a start, the grandees are going to present us with *demands* – and if we acquiesce to said demands, they will give us the equipment that we need for your expedition.'

'I still don't understand why it's so important,' grumbled Trogadon, peering up from his hammer. 'Thick clothing, enough to eat, reasonable shoes, and off we go,' he continued, shrugging his shoulders.

Bergen groaned and covered his eyes. 'Where will I begin?' he muttered. 'It has to be the *right* clothing, unless you want your own sweat to saturate the leather, which will mean – despite the fact that the material is supposed to be protective – you will *freeze* to death.' He pointed at his face. 'Any exposed skin must be rubbed with animal fat to protect it against the cold – but if you apply the wrong sort, your skin will begin to crack after a few weeks like the dry earth at the height of summer. Generally, injuries are a matter of serious concern in the eternal ice, because your blood will freeze after a few heartbeats, and your body will quickly drop in temperature on account of the wound. Then there is also th—'

'Alright, alright,' said Trogadon, raising a hand defensively. 'Then let's buy the right blankets and whatever else we need.'

'There is more to it than that,' countered Uldini sulkily. 'I have my eyes on two specialist ships. They are known as "Flame Bellies". Their prows are reinforced with steel plates, and they have a special chamber beneath the fo'c'sle. A specially trained magician can heat the plates sufficiently, causing the pack ice which the ship smashes into to melt. Wind Sorcerers can in the meantime keep the sails billowing so that the vessel is able to push her way through the Ice Fields.'

Falk whistled through his teeth approvingly. 'That would save us several moons of journeying wearily on foot. It's no wonder that you wanted to stop off here.'

'And anyway, the Thirteenth Fleet certainly will need reinforcements if the Adversary is lying in wait for us somewhere along the way to the Ice Fields,' added Trimm. 'We will need the support of the grandees for that, too. Another reason why carousing with them in private is a good idea. I wouldn't be at all surprised if word has gotten out that the High Fangs, which Uldini and Jelninolan intend to unmask over the next few days, are in the vicinity of the grandees. And it is not beyond the realms of possibility that it was the High Fangs themselves that came up with the idea of supply shortages before whispering into the greedy ears of certain distinguished ladies and gentlemen. The uncovering and expulsion of the High Fangs will cause considerable uncertainty among the city rulers. If we promise to tell the Sun Emperor that the grandees have simply fallen for High Fang's intrigue and that it was *not* their own plan to stymy the Paladins' journey, the city fathers might be more willing to lend us a willing ear.'

'That sounds like good old-fashioned blackmail,' said Yantilla.

Trimm shrugged his shoulders. 'It was they who started it by withholding the supplies. We are simply playing them at their own game.'

Much to his dismay. Ahren noticed a gleam in Trimm's eyes which immediately raised his suspicions again. The corpulent Paladin was plotting something else as well, but whatever it was, he was keeping it to himself. The Forest Guardian was torn between confronting Trimm or saying nothing. He decided on the latter option. Speaking now would only add to Uldini's suspicions. The young Paladin would make do on keeping a good eye on Trimm for now.

'Then our next moves have been decided,' said Khara, anxiously getting to her feet. 'Uldini and Jelninolan will deal with the High Fangs, Trimm will organise an informal parley with the grandees, and the rest of us will concentrating on achieving top physical fitness.'

'Again?' muttered Falk.

Khara pointed at a welt on Ahren's cheek which Uldini had magically patched up. 'If you think it is unnecessary, why don't we simply get indolent and fat over the next few weeks? Then we will end up rolling like snowballs on the Ice Fields once we get there,' she countered provocatively, 'making us easy pickings for any mercenaries we might encounter.'

'Alright, alright,' countered Falk defensively, before wagging a finger. 'The days will belong to *you*, young lady, but *we* will reserve the nights for drinking and singing.'

'Agreed,' said Khara with a grin, Ahren knowing his beloved well enough to realise that the old Paladin had just made a *very* big mistake.

Khara's command was as rigorous as it was effective. From dawn to dusk, they all sweated, snorted and engaged in combat, thereby increasing the effectiveness of the Blessing Band and making up for the limited physical activity that had been afforded to them during their moons at sea. Part of their daily routine involved an extended run through Trimm's palace gardens, and after the first week Ahren was convinced that, thanks to the relentless physical training, he knew every leaf of every plant in the portly Paladin's demesne.

Culhen and Muai had returned from the hunt two days previously, the wolf's presence lightening Ahren's mood considerably. The animal was enjoying life and hence was a true source of spiritual strength. He gave Ahren a boost every time the young Paladin felt like giving up during a particularly difficult exercise – whether the young man *wanted* his friend's support in his head or not.

Trimm would sneak away from time to time, whenever his advice was needed regarding the upcoming reception, while Palnah began to take on her role as lady of the house with increasing ease, no longer running to the corpulent Paladin every time a decision had to be made, but instead taking her own initiative in matters of a domestic nature. Indeed, Ahren suspected that she was making full use of the special gift that she had – namely, her ability to read the minds of anyone in her vicinity like an open book. Trimm beamed with pride at the increasing independence that Palnah was exhibiting, and Ahren was convinced that the two would make a striking couple in Cape Verstaad society once the Brajah had fully settled into the daily life of Cape Verstaad.

It was the evening of the eighth day following the start of the High Fang hunt that the Arch Wizard announced on the roof terrace: 'That is that. Cape Verstaad is now officially free of High Fangs.'

'Are you sure, Uldini?' asked Ahren wearily. The sun had just set, the welcome drop in temperature only beginning to have a soothing effect on the young Paladin's aching muscles. Khara had, indeed, kept her word, so that the nights were free from toil, but Ahren and his friends were able for little more after the day's hard training than to lie on their divans and listen to the night sounds of the city below before falling asleep through sheer exhaustion.

'*We* are absolutely certain,' interjected Jelninolan firmly. 'Over the past few days, I have familiarised myself with the bane charms that have been developed against magical spying and which are being currently taught in the local sorcery school. I have adapted my charm net sufficiently to circumvent the new methods. This evening, I got an overview of the entire city and did not locate a *single* remaining High fang.'

'How many did you catch?' asked Trogadon sulkily, the dwarf still very much peeved at the fact that he had not been allowed to accompany the Ancients on their hunt. The pair had headed off with Yantilla's Ice Wolves, having concluded that the troop would be sufficient to deal with any High Fangs that would choose fight rather than flight.

'Eight in total,' said Uldini through pursed lips. 'Every one of them put up such bitter resistance that we were unable to take any of them alive.'

'We came across considerable evidence of High Fangs having gotten rid of evidence, such as incinerated documents,' added Yantilla, looking piteously at the worn-out companions on the divans. 'Any High Fangs that were in a position to do so, had already fled the city.'

'The important thing is that the High Fangs are gone,' muttered Uldini with an air of defiance. 'The names and descriptions of those that made a run for it have been sent out in all directions along with the news that there is a considerable bounty on their heads.' He gleefully rubbed his hands. 'They will not find peace anywhere until the war is over.'

'One less problem to deal with,' said Hakanu, relieved.

'I'm not so sure about that,' countered Jelninolan hesitantly. 'The High Fangs may be gone, but their plans are still in existence.'

Ahren raised his head, immediately groaning at the pain in his neck muscles. 'What do you mean?'

'Don't you remember Trimm's theory? There must be a connection between the High Fangs and the grandees who purchased all the supplies and hired the people that we need for our expedition to the Ice Fields,' said the elf.

'What are you saying? Was it the High Fangs in the city that planted in the heads of the grandees the wonderful idea of obstructing our search for Yollock unless we fulfil their demands?' asked Bergen.

'Precisely. Trimm was right in that regard,' confirmed Uldini with a grimace. 'The High Fangs must have urged the grandees to up their prices more and more – in the hope of driving a significant wedge between us and Cape Verstaad.'

'I still find it completely absurd that the grandees even considered this idea for a moment,' said Hakanu. The young warrior was Khara's most ardent student and had been throwing himself into every exercise with gusto – as if the war would be won as long as he came out first in every routine.

He might well see things like that, interjected Culhen, who was sitting by the pool, cooling his front paws in the water. *He's probably imagining all the time what will happen in the upcoming battle if he isn't strong or fast enough to save one of you Paladins.* The wolf looked knowingly over at the Forest Guardian. *He has been training with even more determination ever since he lost a member of his Fox Guards.*

Ahren peered at Hakanu, trying to observe his apprentice with unprejudiced eyes. The young man's features seemed serious, the lad listening intently to what was being discussed. Even if Hakanu didn't quite understand all the consequences of what had been said, he still radiated a conscientiousness which seemed to be like a shell protecting his undoubted courage. Suddenly, the lad seemed more like a steely Paladin and less like a hot-blooded whippersnapper eager to win instant recognition. Hadn't Falk, too, failed to spot the development in Ahren's personality during his own apprenticeship? And wasn't *that* why the old man had been repeatedly taken aback by his protégé's actions?

'As far as the grandees are concerned, their actions are based on an over-riding logic,' Trimm was saying, referring to the High Fang plan. 'Cape Verstaad is in the process of change.' He looked at Ahren. 'A change in which the Paladins, and especially Ahren, have played a considerable role.' When everyone looked quizzically at the corpulent man, he sighed before continuing. 'I'm talking about the trade routes,' he said, Uldini immediately reacting by slapping himself on the forehead.

'Of course!' exclaimed the Ancient. 'Cape Verstaad is the point where the shipping lines from east and west meet one another. Officially, trade between the Eternal Empire and the Sunplains used to be forbidden, merchant vessels from the Knight Marshes having to dock in Cape Verstaad if they wanted to get to the Eternal Empire, and vice versa.'

Trimm nodded. 'And all the time, smuggled goods found their way into the harbour of our city,' he said cunningly. 'Goods from every corner of Jorath were to be found here, the wealth of the city growing every day – until now, that is.'

Khara nodded, realisation dawning on her weary face. However difficult the training was that she inflicted on the others during the day, she too took part in every exercise. 'The commerce between the Eternal Empire and the Sunplains is legal again,' she said. 'The Fortress Belt is being dismantled, and with that the border between the two empires will eventually fall. New trade routes will materialise in the interior once the war is over.'

Bergen let out a long whistle through his teeth. 'Cape Verstaad will lose considerable influence over the next few decades,' he said, 'not to mention its principal source of wealth.'

Trimm nodded, his face resembling that of a teacher, satisfied that his dullard pupils were, indeed, making progress. 'I am certain that the whisperings of the High Fangs found all too welcoming ears because the grandees are anxious about their futures. Nothing encourages a person to take dubious decisions like the fear of uncertainty,' said the corpulent Paladin.

'When is this unholy reception of yours going to take place?' asked Uldini grumpily. 'I want to give these grandees a good talking-to so that we can proceed with our preparations.'

'In two weeks,' replied Trimm casually, 'which gives us more than enough time,' he added, cutting off Uldini, who was about to protest. 'You shouldn't enter the Ice Fields until the onset of spring anyway – otherwise, the pack ice will be so thick that no Flame Belly in the world will be able to break its way through it. Remember – the region beyond the southern straits follows its own rules.'

When Ahren considered the dangers and uncertainties that would be lying in wait for them on their upcoming journey, he concluded that another fortnight under the sun sounded like a rather attractive proposition.

'Such a lot of fuss and bother,' growled Trogadon, Ahren silently agreeing with the dwarf.

Night was beginning to fall as the pair stood at the entrance to the imposing palace, staring at the front garden bedecked with lights. Each individual palm had no less than three elaborately designed lanterns, the marble carriageway was surely swept a dozen times a day, while petals lay freshly strewn on the broad path which snaked its way through the lush green lawn. There had to be at least a hundred liveried servants forming a guard of honour, the immaculate white of their uniforms accentuated by gold embroidery.

The two friends proceeded along the path to the summer pavilion, an enormous candle-lit room with a roof of leaded windows within which the crews of three ships had taken their places. Servants stood at the ready in every nook, ready to show to their seats those guests who simply couldn't follow the illuminated pointers of lanterns and candles which indicated the way.

'Even a blind person would find this feast,' added Trogadon, adjusting his clothing. 'And look at the state of us! I'd much rather sneak into Trimm's wine cellar and stay there until this nonsense is over.' His statement almost sounded like a question, as he glanced at Ahren hopefully.

'You want to leave me on my own to strut like a peacock?' countered Ahren, glaring at his friend. 'Absolutely not!'

Trogadon angrily crossed his arms, the black silk garment that he was wearing rustling audibly, while his silk floppy hat, also black, slipped sideways on his head. Ahren forced himself not to laugh before surreptitiously adjusting his too tight silk, green trews.

'But why does everything have to be silk?' he murmured without thinking, only for Trogadon to quote Trimm in an exaggerated manner:

'Silk is the standard material of the Cape Verstaad dignitaries. Only a peasant or the hoi polloi would wear anything else to a feast graced by all the grandees of the city.'

'Indeed, you are right!' interjected the corpulent Paladin cheerfully from the end of the path. 'Now follow me, you two. Receiving the guests at the entrance is a gesture of servility which we can ill afford today.'

'Can I strangle him?' muttered Trogadon. 'Even just a little bit?'

'He's helping us,' murmured Ahren, giving his friend a warning look. *At least, I hope he is,* he thought, Culhen immediately interjecting.

Well, I think this feast is already a great success, said the wolf as Ahren and the dwarf followed Trimm into the summer pavilion.

Within the rotunda – which was a good forty paces in diameter – were long tables filled with an amazing variety of dishes – some of the delicacies causing Ahren to frown in puzzlement. Quite apart from the plates of meat and exotic fruit, he saw small balls of ice, in many different colours – as if ingredients had been added to the tiny globes of frozen water. Trimm assured him that the prepared ice would taste sweet, but Ahren politely declined. If he got thirsty, he would simply drink water or wine. Why would he want to put *ice* into his mouth?

He looked over at the companion animals, who were lying resplendently on enormous cushions covered in silk, the creatures having been bathed, perfumed, and groomed by dozens of diligent servants. Muai resembled a queen holding court as she gazed at the assembled guests through half-closed eyes, Culhen seemed to be in his element, while Kamaluq had retreated behind his disguise.

The fat, redhaired tomcat with black paws and dark markings on his face which made him look like a racoon, had to be Eken, Trimm's companion animal. He was fast asleep on his cushion, thereby giving the impression that he was bored with the occasion, which was no different to all the other evenings he suffered on a regular basis in the palace. Ahren had never encountered such a passive companion animal before. Although this was the first time that Eken had met Culhen and the others, he was clearly uninterested in either the animals or the other Paladins. There was no sign of Bergen's companion animal, the falcon Karkas, but Ahren knew that the raptor was shy when it came to humans and preferred to keep to himself whenever the Ice Lander was in company.

'Bold fox,' hissed the blue garbed Hakanu as Ahren and Trogadon reached the middle of the room, the apprentice then hurrying over to the disguised Kamaluq, who immediately became visible again with a flash of light before demonstratively turning his back on his friend.

'The little fellow seems to be slowly growing up,' said Khara, approaching Ahren in her normal clothing, her beloved eyeing her enviously.

'Why are you allowed to go around in comfortable garb while I have to suffer in a tight-fitting green silk doublet?' He arched his back and groaned. 'I'm sure that Trimm has reinforced it with wire to prevent me from daring to slouch a little.'

'Firstly, I *always* look good, which means I don't need any special clothing,' said Khara, grinning cheekily. 'And secondly, my robe is made from Deep *Silk*. And as we all know, silk is…'

'…the standard material for dignitaries,' said both Trogadon and Ahren, finishing the Swordsmistress's sentence in unison.

'Exactly,' chuckled Khara.

'But why does everyone have to wear a different colour?' asked Ahren, pointing at Falk and Bergen, who were standing together, the former dressed in golden-yellow silk, the latter in light blue.

'This is a little embarrassing,' explained Trimm, clearing his throat. 'Most of the grandees are…how should I put it…well, a little *slow* in some respects. For them, those who don't come from the southern Sunplains all look the same, and they quickly forget the faces of people they have just met. The different colours will help them to differentiate between you all.'

'So, we can allow ourselves a bit of fun this evening by swapping costumes?' chuckled Trogadon, only to quickly become serious again when Trimm glared at him.

'There is a lot resting on this reception,' warned the corpulent Paladin, who was decked out in a substantial waistcoat and with what resembled a crown on his head, which looked suspiciously as if it was made from Deep Steel. 'This evening, we are going to lull the grandees into revealing their precise intentions to us.'

'I thought we were going to blackmail them?' replied Trogadon, causing Trimm to immediately flinch.

'Yes,' sighed the Paladin. 'That too – only later.'

Ahren looked the grandee up and down, wondering for the umpteenth time what it was that the man was planning. How many of his personal goals did, in fact, coincide with those of the other Champions of the gods? Ahren's eyes wandered over to Uldini, the Arch Wizard nodding knowingly, as though the childlike figure could easily read Ahren's own doubts in the Forest Guardian's frown.

And, indeed, he can, interjected Culhen ruthlessly. *Your face speaks volumes.*

The young man quickly adopted a stoic demeanour before making his way over to the First, who was standing there like a tower of strength, wearing the red garments that had been assigned to him as if it were armour, an inch thick.

'Well,' said the war veteran in a low voice, once Ahren was beside him. 'Has Trimm revealed to you how he intends to *shirk* his calling as Paladin this time?'

Ahren narrowed his eyes and looked through the open windows into the night, past the twenty or so servants who were fanning air into the interior of the large room and trying to keep the temperature at a bearable level. 'Why does *everyone* assume that he will baulk at fulfilling his responsibilities,' he asked with a force that he had not intended. 'Trimm is fearful – not irrational. He is fully aware that this war can only come to a successful conclusion with his help.'

The First looked mockingly at Ahren. '*You* have never delayed performing an unwelcome but necessary duty until every last alternative has been exhausted, have you?' he asked. 'Or even *procrastinated?*'

'Not if waiting would cost people's lives.'

'Nor have you ever experienced the same level of fear as Trimm has. I know what happens to him when he falls victim to panic. We *all* do.' With that, the soldier got to his feet and strode over to Falk before Ahren had a chance to respond.

The Forest Guardian looked out into the impenetrable darkness of the night again and wished that he didn't have that niggling doubt regarding Trimm's trustworthiness. Finally, he silently swore to himself that he would not give in to his own misgivings but continue to put his faith in his fearful brother. He turned and made his way over to Hakanu.

'Master,' said the young warrior, his eyes glittering. 'Have you seen how beautifully arranged everything is?'

Ahren couldn't help smiling at the naïve astonishment of his protégé, who reminded the Forest Guardian of himself in younger, more innocent days. 'You like it then?' he asked.

Hakanu nodded, then hesitated before finally shaking his head ever so slightly. 'Everything is nice to *look* at,' he whispered. 'But there is nothing *living* here. Everything is so dead and...well, *inert*.' Hakanu was clearly struggling for words. He then cocked his head as if he were listening out for something. 'This room is diametrically opposed to the moral compass and belief system that *I* grew up with,' he said woodenly – as if he were reading awkwardly from a scroll. 'Yes, that's precisely what I mean,' he concluded proudly, as though he had completed a performance with which he was particularly satisfied.

Ahren looked long and hard at his apprentice, the boy then shifting uneasily from one foot to the other. 'It was Kamaluq who put that sentence into your head, wasn't it?' murmured the Forest Guardian.

Hakanu blushed. 'He's helping me to understand things that other people are saying, and also things that I'm *feeling*.' He scratched the back of his head helplessly. 'Only sometimes he speaks in such a weird way that I can't follow him.'

'Then tell him that, and he will find more suitable words,' replied Ahren, smiling at his protégé. 'What you just said there sounded as if you had listened once too often to Uldini expounding on magic theory. How are you going to learn from the fox if you don't have a common language?' He paused for a couple of heartbeats before continuing: 'If you understand each other, then he will be able to learn from you, too.'

'*He?*' asked Hakanu incredulously. 'Learn from *me?*'

Ahren chuckled. 'When it comes to courage and endurance, then we could *all* learn from you,' he said, squeezing the apprentice's shoulder.

Hakanu beamed at him and then turned to Kamaluq, who was now honouring the guests with his visible presence. The clever fox looked at Ahren, the Forest Guardian now rather proud of the fact that he had given his protégé and the companion animal something to ponder over.

I must admit, I'm looking forward to seeing how Cassobo and Kamaluq will communicate with each other through Sun Shimmer for the first time, said Culhen gleefully as he stretched out on his soft cushion. *Our little monkey always prides himself on his cleverness. I can't wait to see his face when he realises that Kamaluq has a better way with words than he does.*

You're such a gossipmonger, countered Ahren with a grin. *Maybe you should...*

He lost his train of thought as he heard the sound of many steps approaching along the path leading to the sun pavilion, indicating the arrival of the first of the grandees with their entourages. If the clothing of the Cape Verstaad rulers had seemed extravagant during the procession at the harbour, they were now displaying nothing less than unadulterated opulence.

One woman was wearing a gossamer dress of emerald chains held together by silken cords, the Forest Guardian being in no doubt but that her servants would have to cut her out of her garment after the feast, for he could make out no fasteners.

Fans of pure gold seemed to be the standard accessory, expanded at will so that everyone could see the diamond-studded grips and the interwoven threads of Deep Steel which strengthened the thin metal material.

Decorative weapons adorned the broad, jewel-encrusted belts of the guests, and whenever a hand was placed on one of the grips, Ahren could see from the unnatural positioning of their fingers that the grandees had absolutely no idea of how to wield the weapons, should they suddenly have to use them.

Despite the heat, many of the esteemed guests were clad in voluminous cloaks which billowed at every hint of a breeze from the servants' fanning at the windows. Ahren thanked the THREE that Trimm had spared them from wearing the cloaks that Onja had sewn for them, and which was now their standard wear during many official engagements.

'Do I see a dead rat under the nose of that man over there?' asked Bergen, who had wandered over to Ahren before pressing a golden goblet of wine into his friend's hand. 'And that chap over there is definitely wearing a wig.'

'Hush,' whispered the Forest Guardian, turning away so that neither the grandee with the rampant moustache nor the other with his ill-concealed bald pate would see him grin.

'My dear *friends!*' exclaimed Trimm, hurrying to the centre of the room so that he could receive the stream of guests and present the Paladins as if they were exotic wild animals that he had recently captured.

Ahren glanced over at Culhen and wondered how much self-control it had cost Trimm not to place the Champions of the gods on podiums with velvet cushions.

It's far better up here than you think, said Culhen generously, yawning long and demonstratively so that the grandees could behold his fangs in wonderment, flinching from them as they shivered in awe. Yet, as far as Ahren could see, not one of the rulers of Cape Verstaad seemed to be aware of the fact that those jaws could bite them in two, were the wolf to be vexed.

'Ahren, the long yearned for Thirteenth Paladin,' announced Trimm, the Forest Guardian bowing slightly as he was greeted with polite oohs and aahs. The young man's blood began to boil, however, for the men and women glanced at him with no more than passing interest, and they seemed to consider that the Champions – whom the gods themselves had chosen to take on the Adversary – were little more than a troupe of strolling players. He heard the conversation turn in no time at all to the rising price of leather, and its increasing scarcity in these days of war. When a lady with far too much powder on her face asked if the defenders of their beautiful high Ring around the Pall Pillar might not fight with padded *cloth* jerkins instead, Ahren clenched a fist and moved in towards the ever-swelling throng of grandees.

'Take it easy there,' said the First, nodding towards the goblet in Ahren's hand. 'You'd want to drain that first before hitting one of the city rulers on the head with it.'

'Did you not hear what they are saying?' hissed Ahren. Then Hakanu was beside him, placing a hand on his arm.

'You must calm down, master,' said the young warrior. 'Don't do anything rash now.'

The warning, from Hakanu of all people, hit the Forest Guardian like a pailful of freezing water, Ahren nearly stumbling backwards in surprise. Luckily, Khara was already on his other side, taking him by the arm.

'What a beautiful night it is,' she said in a loud voice. 'Would my spouse like to accompany me into the garden?' Then she led Ahren out into the relative darkness of the busy ornamental garden, lit by lanterns. 'Is everything alright?' she asked in a low voice. 'I'm fairly sure there was murder in your eyes.'

'Never in my life…' spluttered Ahren. 'Never in my *life* have I encountered such *ignorant* people. Compared to these grandees, the princes of the Knight Marshes are the personification of good-hearted benevolence! These characters care for nothing beyond the trivial worries in their own little world – the only thing that interests them is whether they can gain possession of another chest of gold tomorrow!'

'And *because* they look after their fortunes, they are able to sponsor half the salaries of the Sun Legions, don't forget,' said Khara reassuringly. 'If you remember the wealthy families of the Eternal Empire, their horizons stretched no farther than their own spheres of influence. The only difference was that they expressed their superiority with somewhat more politeness.'

Ahren nodded as he tried to regain his composure. 'But they are so self-centred,' he said. 'At this very moment, I can hear through Culhen's ears one of the grandees suggesting that a truce be reached with the Adversary so that fewer of the Cape Verstaad labourers will be conscripted.' The Forest Guardian spoke on through gritted teeth. 'Now another one is suggesting that the Sun Emperor pay lower salaries, so that more of the potential recruits will stay at home and continue to work in Cape Verstaad.' Exasperated, he threw his hands in the air. 'It doesn't seem to strike him that he can achieve the same effect by simply offering *higher wages.*'

'Would you like to tell him that yourself?' asked Khara with mock seriousness. 'So that he will relieve us of the soldiers that we so desperately need?'

Ahren chuckled despite himself, the young couple then walking further into the garden. 'I really must learn to accept the customs here,' he said, chiding himself. 'After all, I have come across conventions on my travels that were even more peculiar than the ones here.' He wrang his hands in a gesture of helplessness. 'It is just that we are so near a possible victory.'

Khara nodded. 'Only one more Paladin.'

'Only one more Paladin,' whispered Ahren, echoing his beloved.

Khara embraced him, and it was as if new strength flowed into him. They stood there for a while, pressed close together and saying nothing.

'Thank you,' he finally murmured, releasing himself from her.

'Ready to face the grandees a second time?'

Ahren nodded solemnly. 'I know what is awaiting me this time,' he said with a smile. 'It can hardly be *that* bad.'

'You are gritting your teeth again,' murmured Bergen surreptitiously as he glanced sideways at Ahren, the Paladins now standing together with Khara, Jelninolan, Uldini, and Trogadon behind Trimm and looking for all the world like a pack of particularly well-behaved hounds, while the merchant described in a stilted manner the obstacles that he and his friends had encountered during the preparations for their expedition.

The evening was well advanced by now, and the self-centred attitude of the assembled grandees was driving Ahren almost out of his wits. Indeed, one elderly lady with more diamonds on her necklace than one would find on a decent crown asked him if he would be willing to sell her his gods' Blessing, as there was a good-for-nothing nephew in her family who 'could do with a decent job.' At another point, a gaunt man stepped up to Ahren and suggested in a conspiratorial whisper that the Forest Guardian might prolong the war into the year after next. It seemed that the man had wagered a large amount of money on just such an outcome and if he were to win, he would make sure that Ahren's future would be financially secure. The fact that the man continued to possess all his teeth following *that* suggestion was a source of some pride to the Paladin.

Watch out! murmured Culhen urgently. *I think things are about to get interesting.*

Ahren forced himself to relax his jaw muscles and concentrated on what was unfolding around him.

'...and, indeed, I am sorry to inform you, my honoured guests, that all of the armour *and* the competent personnel for such an undertaking are in the august hands of some of you present here tonight,' said Trimm, concluding his speech.

'Oh dearie me, how regrettable,' replied an old man, whose strands of snow-white hair reached down to his ears. 'I, myself, have only recently acquired several dozen ice-hardened mercenaries together with a Flame Belly ship and several extremely resourceful magicians who specialise in fanning favourable winds.' He looked at Trimm, his wide eyes full of feigned sympathy and his tone almost jubilant. 'The house of Heklaton would like to do nothing more than be of assistance to the honourable Champions of the gods in their ongoing military campaign.' This was followed by a thin smile aimed at Ahren and the other Paladins, causing the Forest Guardian to grit his teeth again until Bergen gave him a subtle kick in the shin. 'Alas,' continued the Grandee Heklaton, 'all of our resources are currently on a training exercise on one of the smaller islands off the Ice Fields, and I have no idea of when it will be over.'

'This is regrettable indeed,' said Trimm in an oily voice. 'Could we persuade you to send a sorcerous message to one of the magicians on board with the request that they return forthwith?' asked the corpulent Paladin without batting an eyelid. 'Perhaps we could grant you...a *favour* in return?'

'What an interesting thought, my dear Salman,' countered Heklaton, as though the counteroffer had come completely out of the blue. 'Let me think for a moment...'

Ahren's patience was increasingly stretched as the evening dragged on, a succession of grandees taking the opportunity, under the guise of helpfulness, to place demand after demand on the host. Trimm maintained his equanimity, nodding politely without making any mention of the High Fangs that had been uncovered, nor even of the urgency of he and his companions' mission. Another thing that struck the young Forest Guardian was that all the grandees addressed Trimm with the name that he used in the city. It was apparent to him that the portly Paladin had made sure that his true identity had not been revealed beyond the decks of the Thirteenth Fleet. It was apparent, too, that Uldini was growing increasingly anxious at the fact that they were not blackmailing the grandees in return, the Arch Wizard looking on more than one occasion in alarm at Ahren and his companions.

Suddenly, Trimm clapped his hands and bowed slightly before his guests. 'How *rude* of me,' he said. 'Here we are, standing around until deep into the night and gossiping like washerwomen.' This was met by polite laughter from the grandees. 'Why don't you give me the opportunity to discuss with the Champions of the gods and the two Ancients the generous offers of help that you have showered me with?' He smiled so warmly that Ahren felt nauseous. On whose side *was* Trimm?

If he is representing us, then he is acting in a human manner, commented Culhen, the canine being similarly confused. *In other words, in an unnecessarily complicated manner.*

On hearing Trimm's words, the grandees openly rubbed their hands with glee and exchanged triumphant looks. The corpulent Paladin bowed again and asked submissively: 'Would it be at all possible to call a full meeting of the Golden Council? And as soon as tomorrow? Then, once we have discussed the offers being made on both sides, we can officially seal our agreement on the matter.'

The grandees hesitated for a moment, before mumbling their assent to Trimm's proposal. There was yet another bow from the corpulent Paladin before he indicated to his fellow grandees that they could go if they wished. Then he waved them out with a broad smile until they were all out of sight.

'None of them wanted to be the first to go, for fear of missing something important,' chuckled Trimm to himself. 'Even just seeing the looks on their faces made this whole exercise worthwhile.' He turned to face his companions, flinching when he noticed Ahren's murderous look.

'What – was – *that* – then?' snarled Uldini, sparks flying between the Arch Wizard's fingers.

'I think that this evening was highly successful,' said Trimm with an innocent look on his face, Ahren privately admitting to himself that the Paladin was holding up well considering the furious faces that were glaring at him. There was only a hint of a quiver in his voice, and his trembling knees were hidden well enough under his wide robe.

'What are you planning, Trimm,' asked Falk in a cutting voice. 'Or would you prefer if I called you *Salman?*'

'How by the THREE did you manage to keep your identity as Paladin secret in this city?' interjected Jelninolan, her voice laden with suspicion.

Trimm suddenly looked decidedly glum. 'With gold,' he replied. 'And with the help of the admiral, who limited any comings and goings to and from the ships for fear of the fleet being sabotaged by either henchmen of the High Fangs or by over-exuberant grandees.'

'Let me guess,' said Trogadon. 'You planted the idea in the admiral's head so that you wouldn't have to bribe every sailor in the fleet.'

'A true grandee,' said Bergen mockingly. 'Why pay the simple people when one can simply lie to their officer.'

Ahren was taken aback by the sudden change in atmosphere, the others seemingly all too willing to believe the worst of Trimm.

'You said that you wanted to put the grandees under pressure for their closeness to the High Fangs,' said the First. 'Instead of which you lent every one of them a benevolent ear as they set out their demands. One of the grandees even called for the overthrow of the Sun Emperor and for the establishment of Cape Verstaad as the new capital of the Sunplains.' The old warrior stepped menacingly forward, Trimm retreating in fear immediately. 'I should put you in chains today, for tomorrow you will entrench yourself behind the power of the grandee assembly, making a civil war inevitable if we want to get your lily-livered self away to the Ring.'

Ahren looked helplessly from one companion to the next, torn between his instinctive belief in the goodness at the heart of people and the many clues that suggested that Trimm's cowardice was coming back to life.

'What is your plan?' asked Ahren in a loud voice, overriding the suspicious murmurings of his friends. His question resembled Falk's, except this time there was no hint of accusation, of suspicion, or of prejudice. Every syllable carried with it a genuine curiosity as to what it was that the corpulent Paladin had in mind. 'Has it something to do with the fact that Palnah is not here tonight?' he pressed, Trimm still looking aghast at the First and not responding to Ahren's questioning.

'It's true,' murmured Khara, surprised. 'Mind you, I thought I caught sight of her occasionally. Strangely enough, she was wearing a veil.'

'Trimm?' asked Ahren insistently. 'You must provide us with answers or else live with the consequences of the conclusions that we will draw for ourselves.' Still, he refused to pre-judge his fellow Paladin, appealing to him instead as a brother.

'What will he come out with now?' snarled Uldini when Trimm finally opened his mouth to speak. 'That this is all a misunderstanding and that we must not worry or some such rubbish.'

'This whole situation reminds me of when we hunted a horde of Gloom Wings – oh, it must have been thirty years before the Dark Days ended,' said Falk, Trimm flinching guiltily. 'They were eagle-like Dark Ones that have long since become extinct. Trimm was supposed to help us eliminate the Gloom Wings that time, but with the excuse of seeking out reinforcements, he made himself scarce. Instead of the promised assistance, a rag-tag of bribed woodcutters appeared and led us a merry dance while our *brother* here, escaped by hiding in a vegetable cart.'

'You didn't really want me there anyway,' replied Trimm, the tremble in his voice audible as he uttered his weak excuse.

The young master took a step forward and raised his hand in warning, his face stern. 'We are *not* going to waste time talking about past failures,' he said firmly. 'That might only make things awkward for *everyone,* and it would take at least half the night to list off my own particular mistakes – even though *I* haven't lived for centuries.' Ahren made sure not to focus on anyone in particular, but the heated atmosphere cooled markedly and was replaced by a ruminative silence. Satisfied, Ahren nodded towards Trimm. 'What did you want to say?'

'Uh,' began Trimm weakly before clearing his throat and continuing: 'You can all trust me, and I know what I'm doing,' he mumbled with a grimace, as though he imminently expected a sound thrashing.

Ahren rolled his eyes as the angry mutterings from Falk, Uldini, Bergen, and the First grew in volume. 'Please tell me that you have more to say than this,' pleaded the Forest Guardian. He stared into the grandee's eyes in the hope of seeing the truth hidden behind the man's fear and shattered self-confidence.

'But that's about it,' countered Trimm, wringing his hands. 'My plan has been maturing since before you were born,' he said, turning to Ahren as if they were the only ones in the room. 'In fact, it has been in existence since I turned my back on the Pall Pillar.'

'You mean, since you turned your back on all of *us,* don't you?' growled the First.

Trimm pushed his chin forward belligerently, his rage gaining the upper hand over his fear for the briefest of moments. 'Me and just about every other Paladin, too. Or have I misunderstood Ahren, and he *didn't* have to search for his brothers and sisters all over Jorath before uniting them into a fighting force?'

Ahren stepped in between the First and Trim so that they could no longer glare at each other. 'Khara,' he said in a gentle voice. 'Would you be so kind and concentrate on your bracelet?'

Almost immediately, Ahren sensed the Paladins behind his back and the cowering Trimm to his front. It seemed as if there was a veritable chasm between the grandee on one side and Falk, Bergen, and the First on the other, while Ahren himself stood with one foot planted on each side of the gorge, his Blessing the only thing that was connecting him to the corpulent Paladin. 'You have a *plan?'* he asked, pressing Trimm again.

The man nodded, and Ahren sensed his uprightness through the Blessing Band.

'And this plan will not hinder us in our war against the Adversary?' Another nod, but after an almost imperceptible hesitation.

Ahren squinted. 'And you don't want to tell us about it because we are not going to like it?'

Another nod, yet Ahren could sense fear rising within Trimm like a wall of fire, which hindered the Forest Guardian from making out other emotions or intentions coming from the corpulent Paladin. 'You think that we will stop you if we know the truth?' asked Ahren in the most neutral voice that he could manage.

Again, Trimm nodded, his fearfulness seeming to swallow him whole, as though he were succumbing to the naked hostility that the Paladins were showing him. Ahren turned his head towards Khara, the Swordsmistress immediately understanding. A heartbeat later and the Blessing Band effect had dissolved, the Forest Guardian now concentrating once again solely on Trimm.

'Carry out your plan,' he said to the sound of loud objections, which Ahren drowned out determinedly. 'And remember that *I* am depending on you.' By now he was almost shouting: 'All *Jorath* is depending on you!'

Wide-eyed, Trimm gazed at Ahren, the Forest Guardian recognising a mixture of surprise, relief, and even a hint of guilt in the grandee's look. 'Thank you,' whispered the merchant, bowing ever so slightly, then quickly exiting the summer pavilion before anyone had a chance to stop him.

'What are you *doing?*' snarled Uldini, setting off to float after Trimm, only for the Forest Guardian to stop him.

'Leave him be!' snapped Ahren. 'He should prove himself.'

'But —,' began Falk only for his protégé to cut him off with a firm gesture.

'He *must* prove himself,' said Ahren urgently. 'The whole lot of you are stuck in the past, but I want to believe that Trimm is far more than an opportunistic coward. We defied Gol-Konar for him and Palnah. And it was Trimm who laid Reik low in the end.'

'Because he was forced into a corner and had no other choice,' said Falk with a sigh. 'You only got to know Trimm as a petitioner in need. Here he has the chance to keep as great a distance from us as he pleases, delaying his participation in the war for as long as he can.' Falk pointed towards the exit. 'You have seen how the grandees operate, and the way that he buttered them up. The list of demands that we have heard even before they will raise a finger to help us is as long as the *Queen of the Waves*!'

'That's enough,' said Ahren, exhausted. 'Please – I've heard enough.' He beckoned Hakanu to him, the latter stepping up to his master with a look of pure distrust. 'I am going to go for a night-time stroll through Cape Verstaad with my apprentice, so that I can explain to him that the Champions of the gods are better than their behaviour just now suggests. That we truly *have* earned the term "brotherhood" and that we *never* exclude any of our members without giving them the chance to make up for any mistakes that they may have made.' Ahren looked his fellow Paladins in the eye. 'Trimm will never be a fearless warrior.' He pointed at Hakanu. 'And my apprentice will never be an ingenious strategist.'

'Master?' asked his protégé, looking for all the world like a puppy that had been doused with a pail of water.

'I will never abandon my impulsiveness, even if means my comrades having to rescue me from time to time,' continued Ahren. 'Just as the First will never be a poet or Falk an exuberant dancing juggler.'

'He's been forced into juggling on many an occasion, but never of his own volition,' interjected Trogadon cheerfully, and when Ahren saw the first flickers of smiles appearing on his companions' faces, it was as if a heavy load had been lifted from his shoulders. The icy mood was melting. Then the First began to speak.

His wings no longer beat
His heart it is still
The dragon in defeat
Lieth dead upon the hill.
My future 'tis in ashes
Ne'er forget the beast's gashes.

Everyone looked at the veteran in astonishment as he proceeded to walk in silence towards the door before stopping beside Ahren and briefly placing his hand on his fellow Paladin's shoulder. 'Never think that you *know* a Paladin who has seen the aeons come and go,' he whispered. Then he marched out, calling without looking back over his shoulder: 'And what about the promised stroll? *Real* Paladins walk together, never alone.'

The mood was strange among the little group as they walked through the illuminated streets of Cape Verstaad. The Paladins strolled silently in the middle, with Jelninolan, Trogadon, Khara, and the companion animals making up a sort of protective ring around the Champions of the gods. It almost seemed to Ahren as if everyone had to come to terms with a defeat, licking their wounds although none of them had suffered any physical injury. Many mental scars, however, had been ripped open, and Ahren fervently prayed to the gods that Trimm would not stab his dagger into their fresh wounds.

Your pack is strong, said Culhen. *Because it has a strong Alpha.*

Sometimes I wish that we were more like you animals, admitted Ahren wistfully. *Then Khara and I would raise our own pack of whelps and there would be no more war.*

Don't say things like that, countered Culhen in mock horror. *If you were all animals, then who would serve me my regular dish of roast meat?*

Ahren sensed the wolf's full belly, into which what seemed like half the meat served at Trimm's reception had disappeared. Muai had bravely taken on the other half, both the elders, however, intercepting the tastiest morsels from the platters before feeding them to little Kamaluq.

'Master?' asked Hakanu in a low voice.

Seeing the boy's look of shame, Ahren walked forward quickly with him so that the other Paladins wouldn't hear.

'Yes, Hakanu?' he murmured.

'Will I really *never* be a good strategist?' asked the young warrior sadly. 'If this is so, then I will lead many good men and women under my command to their deaths.'

Ahren smiled and drew the surprised boy to him. 'Your heart is as mighty as your courage,' said the Forest Guardian. 'And the understanding of your fox trumps both. The gods are wise and have sent him to you as advisor. When you can't think of what to do next, Kamaluq will come up with the solution that you are seeking. Your conscience will take care of the rest.'

Ahren's honest words seemed to sweep all troubles from his apprentice's face, and not for the first time, the young master was astounded at Hakanu's natural disposition.

'It was wonderful, how you defended Trimm,' said the young man enthusiastically. 'Tomorrow, he will undoubtedly impress us with his great plan, and then the others will never doubt him again!' Hakanu's voice was possessed of such pure conviction that Ahren was almost brought to tears.

'So it will be,' he said in a low voice to his apprentice. 'Yes – so it will certainly be.'

Hakanu beamed for a moment before cocking his head as Kamaluq engaged him in mental conversation.

Well, Hakanu will never be cursed by excessive brooding, interjected Culhen dryly. *If only his fox knew how lucky he is!*

Ahren let his apprentice carry on his conversation with the fox, moving away from the other Paladins and towards Khara. 'The mighty Champion of the gods has remembered his wife after all, and deigns to give her some of his attention, I see,' she teased, giving her beloved a peck on the cheek.

'It is expected of me, honourable lady, to grace you with my presence,' replied Ahren in an exaggeratedly haughty tone, for which he received a playful dig in the ribs.

'You have spent too much time in the company of these grandees,' joked Khara before becoming more serious. 'Much of what you have said this night may well cause chaos tomorrow. The unity of the Paladins has never been so tested.'

Ahren nodded. 'Trimm *appears* to be our weakest link. Not because he lacks courage, but because he is not getting the necessary support.' He ran his hand anxiously through his short hair. 'It is almost as if the gods want to test us Paladins through Trimm's fearfulness. As though we must prove ourselves worthy of our Blessing by each of us accepting who we are.'

'Have you been promoted to Keeper now?' asked Khara, her eyebrows raised. 'That almost sounded like a sermon.'

'I'm being serious,' countered Ahren. 'You, too, could feel through the Blessing Band how great the gulf between Trimm and the others has become.'

She nodded. 'It was as if our practice routines over the past few moons hadn't taken place at all.'

Ahren looked longingly up at the moon – as if in search of the answers to his questions. 'Tomorrow, Trimm must fill in the void that has lain between him and the other Paladins for centuries,' he murmured, almost pleadingly. 'And it will hardly be possible without them being willing to help.'

'And what if they *don't?*' whispered Khara.

Ahren looked over at the First, Falk, and Bergen, all of whom were humming an enigmatic song as they walked, arms linked, down the deserted streets of Cape Verstaad. 'If my faith in Trimm has been misplaced,' he sighed, 'then the Adversary will eventually be confronted by thirteen Paladins somewhere – but they will no longer be a united force.'

Chapter 9

'It's as if we are marching into battle,' joked Trogadon, patting his beloved hauberk. 'My hammer in my hand, and my armour rattling with every step – this promises to be a good day!'

Ahren didn't share his friend's enthusiasm. Trimm had surprised them that morning with the request that they present themselves before the palace in full armour and carrying their weapons, as though he was expecting blood to be shed before the celestial orb would reach its zenith.

Hardly a good sign, said Ahren to Culhen, who was lying beside him, panting heavily.

You're telling me, grumbled the wolf. *Who do you think is going to have to carry you to this stupid Golden Council any moment now, sweating like mad under a layer of Deep Steel?*

Ahren was about to utter a retort when he saw the horses that would carry his companions being led to the opulent palace entrance. There was even a pony for Trogadon. All the animals had expensive saddles of the choicest leather, the equines' pedigrees doubtless stretching back to before the Dark Days. There was only one sedan visible, and it was the same white vehicle that had borne Trimm and Palnah on the procession from the harbour.

'Why do I believe that Trimm has only provided us with horses so that we can immediately make our escape from the city once he has pulled off his little ruse?' asked Falk suspiciously.

Clearly, Ahren's speech had not succeeded in changing the old Paladin's opinion, the younger Forest Guardian suspecting that it was only the others' respect for him that was stopping them from simply tying up the corpulent Paladin immediately, making sure to gag his mouth before hauling him away to the Ring.

If our corpulent friend lets us down today, then his chicanery will ensure that everyone's respect for me will diminish, thought Ahren glumly.

This is no time for losing self-confidence, interjected Culhen. *Either put your faith in him, or don't and take immediate action. A pendulum constantly swinging from side to side never finds rest.*

How did you come up with such a pearl of wisdom? asked Ahren, amused.

You're not the only one who can choose their words wisely, snapped the animal, but the Forest Guardian was suddenly aware of a memory in his four-legged friend's mind involving an old woman in an Eternal Empire marketplace. Culhen had absorbed her advice while dozing in his cage when he had been playing the role of a Dark One in Uldini's troupe of strolling players.

'Here he comes,' grunted Bergen.

Ahren turned around and saw Trimm with Palnah at his side approaching the group of friends. The slender woman was, like her corpulent companion, dressed in white and gold, while a veil of golden threads hid her face completely. Her shoulders seemed to be cramped, she was leaning her head forward, and her knuckles were white as her hand clutched Trimm's right arm.

'Are you well, madam?' Ahren asked Palnah as the grandee couple walked past him.

'Only a little nervous,' she responded, her voice trembling from behind her veil.

Trimm smiled reassuringly, stroking the hand of his soul companion as he led her to the sedan, which was surrounded now by eight heavily armed mercenaries, all wearing white-enamelled plate armour. 'It will all be over after the full meeting of the grandee council. Then we will be safe,' murmured Trimm conspiratorially, Ahren's hair standing on end at the words of the corpulent Paladin.

He took a deep breath and threw a warning look at his fellow Champions of the gods, silently urging them to refrain from making comments. Much to his surprise, it was Khara, who whispered to him: 'Am I imagining things, or is Palnah behaving in the same manner as when she was forced to stay by Reik's side?' The distrust in her voice was unmistakable. 'I don't like this. What is Trimm demanding of her that has made her fall into her old pattern of behaviour?'

'*Trust*,' said Ahren, reminding himself as much as the Swordsmistress. 'This is what it is all about today. So let us maintain our trust in Trimm until we have good reason to withdraw it.'

Khara nodded hesitantly. 'I'm still going to keep an eye on Palnah,' she said determinedly, Ahren nodding in return.

By now, Trimm and the Brajah had climbed onto the two chairs of the sedan, the guards then hoisting the vehicle onto their shoulders.

'Please get onto your mounts,' said Trimm before clicking his tongue.

Eken came out from behind one of the palace pillars and trotted along the marble tiles before purring and rubbing himself against Muai's right foreleg. The tigress looked down at the fat tomcat and narrowed her eyes.

Khara giggled. 'She can't decide if she should give him a good licking or crush him under her front paws. Although Eken is a born charmer, he is willing to do anything to ensure that he gets what he wants. There was one occasion when he lured her into combatting a Glower Bear so that he could help himself to her bowl of food while she struggled with the Dark One.'

'Come on now, my boy,' said Trimm, encouraging the tomcat to approach him. Today is for *your* benefit, too, you know, and I'm going to need you beside me in case we have to…well…*improvise*.'

The grandee couldn't resist glancing at the other Paladins as he finished his sentence, causing Ahren to shiver instinctively before he quickly sat into the sweating wolf's saddle. As though his move had broken an invisible spell, the other companions got onto their mounts too and, following Trimm's instruction, arranged themselves in a line behind the sedan. Then the grandee clapped his hands once, row after row of mercenaries immediately appearing from behind the archways of the low palace outhouses and taking up position on either side of the companions' column.

'There are at least two hundred men and women,' muttered Trogadon as he looked anxiously at them. 'Why do we need so many?'

'*We* don't need them at all,' prophesied Uldini darkly. 'But our dodgy grandee might well use them to protect himself against *us* if we don't agree to whatever ominous plan he has up his sleeve.'

Ahren sighed. Uldini was far too much a power seeker himself to be able to keep his suspicion of Trimm in check, especially as the Arch Wizard had no idea of what the portly Paladin's machinations amounted to.

'These mercenaries are simply a demonstration of strength,' said Trimm airily – as though the little army around them was nothing worth talking about. 'Each grandee will bring their own modest escort. This will ensure that the negotiations will remain peaceful, and no-one will start whetting their knives in public.'

'Why don't we bring the Ice Wolves along, too?' asked Bergen sceptically. 'Now *that* would be some demonstration of might.'

'Ah,' replied Trimm, licking his lips. 'They have been amusing themselves for days in Cape Verstaad. We cannot simply wait for them all to arrive back here.'

Ahren's unease was increasing all the time. According to Yantilla, the Ice Wolves were residing in one of the palace's barracks. Although now that he thought of it, he hadn't seen the commander herself for a couple of days.

Maybe it is a mistake to let Trimm have his own way, said Culhen. *We still have the chance of getting the necessary supplies by using a little gentle force – we could simply storm a warehouse and take what we need. Then we can scarper onto the* Queen of the Waves, *leaving this city of intrigue behind us.*

Do you believe that the Champions of the gods should take what they want like thieves and plunderers? countered Ahren irritably while shaking his head. *I suspect that such an approach would simply provoke an immediate and violent response from the grandees. You saw what they were like last night. In their world, nothing matters but their own self-interest.* He paused before continuing. *If we have no other option, we will, however, revert to your plan.*

The troop of soldiers began to move, Ahren and his friends now riding through the freshly swept streets of Cape Verstaad. The Paladin saw many residents sitting on the flat roofs of their houses, while others gathered in the little parks and large market squares, some even perching on high carts.

'All eyes are fixed on the Golden Council,' commented the First. 'An official, *full* assembly of the grandees is a rare event, and the decisions reached during such meetings always have grave consequences for Cape Verstaad. *Everyone* wants to keep an ear out to find out what is being talked about.'

Trogadon laughed ironically. 'The palace is good five furlongs from here. How are these poor souls going to hear *anything* regarding the grandees' discussions?'

'Just you wait,' said the First enigmatically. 'I have to admit, it's pretty impressive.'

Uldini snorted. 'Nothing more than second-rate sleights of hand.'

Ahren was curious to find out more, but then he noticed another group of armed mercenaries on a parallel street, also moving towards the Golden Council. They were surrounding a sedan, which seemed to be made from polished amber and was occupied by an elderly grandee and a young woman. Ahren was sure that he recognised Elven decorative work on the outside of the vehicle. Clearly, the pockets of the grandees were deep enough to even employ sorcerous artisans from Evergreen. He gave Jelninolan a questioning look, the priestess immediately pursing her lips disapprovingly.

'The house of Mekra-Thur,' she said darkly. 'Three or four centuries ago, when Cape Verstaad was gaining considerably in influence and wealth, Eathinian concluded that it would be a wise move to make some friends here.' She frowned. 'Our artisanship seems to have lasted considerably longer than the amicability that had been promised.'

'Look! There's another army on the march,' said Hakanu in astonishment. 'And *another!*'

'Ten thousand soldiers or more – their sole function being to show off the grandees,' muttered Bergen through gritted teeth. 'We could certainly do with *them* at the Ring.'

'And those are only the honour guards,' added the First. 'You will find many more mercenaries in the outskirts of the city, employed by the grandees whenever they feel the need to protect themselves and their own interests – mostly from one another.'

Ahren suddenly understood how valuable Cape Verstaad's support could be against the Adversary, and why the Sun Emperor was willing to allow the grandees so much autonomy. Any ruler that had to choose between being given generous tributes consisting of dozens of chests filled with gold or a bloody civil war would undoubtedly plump for the first option.

'This palace *is* imposing, I'll say that much,' murmured Trogadon from behind Ahren, the Forest Guardian now concentrating on their destination as the building loomed ever larger before them. The numerous palaces were more tightly packed together the nearer they approached the seat of power, something which Ahren was already familiar with from King's Island, but the golden cupola, gleaming in the midday heat and shining on Cape Verstaad like a second sun, put all the surrounding buildings in the shade.

'We are not the first,' said Ahren, awed by what he saw. The street they were proceeding along opened into an enormous plaza which surrounded the Golden Council, the area already full of honour guards attached to the grandees who had arrived earlier. The atmosphere among the eight thousand or so men and women ranged from disciplined to amicable, the Forest Guardian noticing on several occasions, pairs of soldiers – each from different households – exchanging gold coins.

'Soldiers and mercenaries are the same wherever you go,' chuckled Bergen. 'Gambling is in their blood. If they're not betting on the outcome of the General Assembly now, then I'll eat a Pallid Frog.'

'Yuck!' exclaimed Jelninolan, the Ice Lander guffawing before exchanging pleasantries with the grandees' mercenaries as the mounts trotted onward.

Falk was riding beside Ahren and nodded enviously towards Bergen. 'Give him a day or two and he'll have them all eating out of his hand.'

Ahren grinned. 'I thought you'd come to terms with Bergen's way of doing things,' he said genially.

Falk grunted. 'Of course,' he said with a hint of shame in his voice. 'But it doesn't mean that I like it.' The old man suddenly became serious. 'There are a *lot* of weapons and shields all around us. Are you still convinced that we should give Trimm a completely free hand? If he really does go behind our backs, or if something else goes wrong…'

'…we will find a solution,' said Ahren, grimly completing his mentor's sentence. 'The grandees are hardly going to incarcerate us and try to make an alliance with the Adversary like Reik did in Gol-Konar. If the worst comes to the worst, they will simply expel us from the city.'

'And Trimm will remain here like a fat spider lurking in his net until he feels like helping us,' retorted Falk.

Ahren had no time to point out the futility of engaging in yet another discussion on the matter, for a gong sounded from within the Golden Council, two enormous golden doors then swinging open. The impressive building was made from white sandstone and circular in form. It was a good ten paces high at least, the striking golden cupola sitting on top of it. The first of the grandees were carried on their sedans from the safety of their guards before disappearing within the building.

'And we're off,' murmured the First as Trimm and Palnah were also carried forward, Ahren and his companions following the grandee and his soul companion to the enormous entrance of the structure, which dominated the broad plaza surrounding it. The Forest Guardian and his companions dismounted, Ahren struggling hard not to gape in amazement at the splendour that awaited them within the Golden Council.

Boy, oh boy, said Culhen. *That sure is a whole heap of gold.*

The entire building consisted of only one room, Ahren and his similarly awestruck friends now entering on the heels of Trimm, who was joking in a low voice with a fellow grandee. The cupola of the council soared forty paces and more into the heavens, its interior replicating its exterior by being entirely covered in gold plates, with the addition, however, of a multitude of ornate engravings, which Ahren immediately recognised as magical symbols.

Eight sorcerers, all of them dressed in sky-blue robes, stood at regular intervals on the top row of the opulently decorated, dark marble tribunes which formed ascending rings, so that all the grandees participating in the General Assembly could look at their counterparts opposite them. The tribunes were divided into generous, semi-circular boxes with velvet seats, the grandee with their partners – if they had one – sitting in the middle, their sedan carriers operating now as bodyguards, taking up position around their masters, while their specially invited guests sat in the row behind the grandees. Each council member had arrived with at least twenty invitees, and it wasn't long before the chatter of many voices filled the room, the enormous cupola magnifying the sound considerably.

Trimm headed for one of the boxes, midway up the tiered rostra, plonking his heavy weight on a throne-like seat at its centre with Palnah settling down beside him. Ahren and his companions divided themselves up on the cushions behind the corpulent Paladin, and the Forest Guardian began to look around and listen curiously. He noticed the advisors of individual grandees gathering in little groups to make deals, form alliances, or issue veiled threats. The general anticipation of great power shifts was palpable in the rotunda, a lust for more wealth and power apparent with every hastily spoken word.

'The vultures are dividing up the spoils before their prey has even been slain,' muttered Falk disdainfully. 'See them staring at us. We might as well be roast pigs with apples stuffed into our mouths, wating to be gobbled up.'

Well, isn't that just great, complained Culhen. *Now I'm hungry again.* The wolf had positioned himself demonstratively to the left of their box, while Muai was on the right side, glaring threateningly at anyone who came too close.

Once the old grandee who had spoken at Trimm's feast the previous evening took his seat in his own box, he picked up an ornamental hammer and banged it hard onto a special podium that was set up in front of him, an immediate silence descending on the large room. Only the occasional murmur could be heard, Trimm taking advantage of one such hushed conversation to whisper to his companions: 'That is Grandee Ilnelus Heklaton, the first among the grandees. He is given the honour of opening the General Assembly, and he is the only one permitted to make suggestions that have consequences so far-reaching that they go beyond the borders of Cape Verstaad. In this way, the city manages, at least officially, to speak with one voice and to sing from one hymn sheet, as it were.'

'The three hundred and seventy-fourth General Assembly of the Cape Verstaad grandees is hereby opened,' said Ilnelus in a feeble voice, Ahren, nonetheless, being able to understand every word. The grandee frowned, however, and gave a signal to one of the sorcerers standing at the edge of the cupola, the eight men and women in their sky-blue robes turning as one and placing their hands on the gold plates from where the convoluted magical symbols spread out, covering the entire inner surface of the cupola. The runes began to shimmer in an ever so faint blue, causing Uldini to audibly snort.

'The sleight of hand begins,' he grumbled.

'The three hundred and seventy-fourth General Assembly of the Cape Verstaad grandees is hereby opened,' repeated Ilnelus, and this time his voice filled the room so powerfully that it seemed that one of the gods themselves was addressing the city powers. The man's words echoed back into the chamber from the open doors, Ahren recognising immediately that every resident of the city on the bay was able to hear the man's words effortlessly.

'That explains why all the citizens of Cape Verstaad had gathered out in the open,' said Khara excitedly. 'Thanks to the magic, they can follow everything that's said in here.'

'Indeed, you are right,' murmured Trimm, glancing back nervously at the Swordsmistress. 'But the magic doesn't distinguish between the person who is officially allowed to speak and those who do not have the floor. Therefore, I strongly suggest you keep your voice down unless you want every Tom, Dick, and Harry outside to be listening to your commentary.'

'Amateurs!' scoffed Uldini petulantly as he looked from one sorcerer to the next, all of them concentrating hard on their work. The Arch Wizard made sure to keep his voice low, however.

'We have gathered here this day to decide how *our* modest city may be of assistance in the war against the Adversary, who has erected his Obsidian Fortress in the far north,' continued the Grandee of the House of Heklaton. 'Here in this hall are also some of the Champions of the gods, sent forth by the deities, who have been pursuing *since time immemorial* the holy task of freeing us mere mortals from the age-old evil that has been tormenting us for far too long.'

Ahren immediately noticed the speaker's tone, the grandee subtly placing the responsibility for the war – and the fact that it was still being waged – on the Paladins. Hakanu, who was sitting beside him, was about to leap up and protest, but the Forest Guardian quickly shook his head and placed his hand on the lad's shoulder. 'This is *not* the Green Sea,' he murmured. 'They have other customs here. And please remember that Fists-like-Iron, your foster father, put forward similar arguments against us when we were among your chieftains.'

'It has come to the ears of the grandees that the Paladins need help so that they may find one of their own, who is lost in the eternal ice of the south,' interjected a young grandessa, who could hardly have been more than twenty summers. 'And that they have made *no* preparations, but expect *us* to provide everything, willy-nilly, for their madcap enterprise!' She looked through half closed eyes at Ahren and his fellow Paladins. 'Criminally *irresponsible* if you ask me – considering the responsibility that they bear.'

Now Ahren, himself, clenched his fists, noticing, however, that the First was nodding, as though the young woman was simply confirming something that he had already suspected.

'Furthermore, an armada of Dark Ones are gathering in the waters south of Cape Verstaad,' announced a swarthy grandee, who seemed to have a predilection for jade, his clothing being peppered with it. 'It seems that the fleet of the Paladins *failed* to eliminate the creatures, who are now preparing a counterattack should the planned expedition approach the Ice Fields. Ergo, these people are demanding more from us then simply warm clothing and a Flame Belly ship. They want to assimilate *our* fleet into theirs!'

Angry cries indicated the assembled grandees' views on the matter.

'What *I* would like to know is this,' interjected another grandee, too far away for Ahren to properly see. '*What* is a Champion of the gods doing on the Ice Fields in the first place? Is he simply *hiding* from the task he has been assigned?'

A murmur of outrage spread throughout the cupola, as genuine as the youthfulness of the heavily made up grandessa two rows in front of Ahren.

'It seems to *me* that Grandee Salman Tilderius, thirty-fourth in rank among us here present, has become the voice of the Paladins and is pleading their cause,' announced Ilnelus, looking directly at Trimm. 'Am I correct in this regard?'

The corpulent Paladin got to his feet. 'This is indeed correct, sir,' he said, his voice loud enough for the magic to echo forth his words to the multitudes throughout the city. 'I met the Thirteenth on one of my trading expeditions in the far west and suggested to him that I convey to my fellow grandees what the Champions of the gods needed in their search for their missing brother.'

'Would the Thirteenth Paladin kindly rise and confirm that Salman Tilderius speaks on his behalf and on behalf of the other Champions of the gods?' asked Ilnelus, Ahren then hesitantly getting to his feet. Trimm gave him a pleading look, and the Forest Guardian reminded himself of the silent promise that he had made – not to condemn Trimm because of his history.

'This is so,' he said simply before sitting down again.

'How *exactly* did you meet the Thirteenth Paladin?' asked the woman, who had previously accused Ahren and friends of negligent preparations.

'He was busy overthrowing the sovereign of an independent city sate,' said Trimm, Ahren immediately gasping in horror. '*And*, may I add, that he was completely successful in his mission. Reik Silvercape was slain at the hands of a Paladin.' A nervous whispering immediately ensued within the chamber.

'That's…' stammered Ahren towards his companions. 'That is a complete distortion of the facts! We were only in Gol-Konar because of Trimm! And the Paladin that he has just spoken of was none other than himself!'

'I told you so,' replied Uldini in a resigned voice. 'I warned you again and again.'

'A female assassin now rules in Gol-Konar, who looks upon the Paladins favourably,' continued Trimm blithely. 'The city of cutthroats is more dangerous than ever.'

Ahren blushed a deep red as he heard Trimm play fast and loose with the truth in the space of a few sentences. His eyes strayed to Palnah, but the woman was simply sitting there beside her Paladin, her shoulders hunched, and her head bowed, her face hidden by her golden veil. Had Ahren been wrong about Trimm. Had he been wrong about Palnah, too?

'Since the Paladins have already displayed ruthless aggression towards rulers who have opposed to their will, I have taken precautions and arrested their so-called Thirteenth Fleet, not to mention the elite mercenaries, going by the name of *Ice* Wolves, who have accompanied them,' added Trimm mercilessly, Ahren now feeling as though he was falling into a bottomless pit. 'This assembly has the necessary room to manoeuvre and can immediately demand the appropriate compensation for providing both logistical *and* military aid to the Champions of the gods.'

This was greeted by polite applause, and Ahren could see self-satisfied expressions on the faces of the grandees – even on Trimm's. *Bartered and betrayed,* he thought bitterly.

Will I give Trimm a lesson? asked Culhen scornfully. *He'll change his tune soon enough once his arm is between my teeth.*

Violence isn't going to get us anywhere, countered the Forest Guardian, now thoroughly crushed, nonetheless. *If we react by opposing the Golden Council, for example, we will merely be affirming his presentation of us as power-hungry tyrants, ready to bloodily depose every sovereign that stands in our way. We must fight our way out of the city – we have no other choice.*

Images of Gol-Konar flashed through Ahren's mind, sent to him by the furious wolf. *It worked once before, didn't it?*

Ahren exchanged looks with his friends, their faces, too, expressing the same hopelessness that he was feeling. The First glared at him in silent rebuke, which suggested that whenever – not to mention *however* – they got out of this situation, the young man would be in for a severe dressing down.

'The conditions regarding any potential support on the part of Cape Verstaad for the Paladins have already been informally put together and conveyed,' said Ilnelus, revelling in the growing discomfiture of the supplicants before him. 'This was all discussed yesterday. Among other things, the Southern Sunplains are to be peacefully ceded to the control of this assembly, *and* we shall have sole trading rights over all goods imported from the Eternal Empire.' The man's voice betrayed an almost childlike glee – as if he was a spoilt brat who had only now been presented with the beautifully carved hobby horse that he had been demanding ever since the previous Winter Festival. The grandee had absolutely no need for the things that he was demanding - he was simply revelling in having ripped them out of the hands of those he was supposedly negotiating with.

'If the Golden Council is in agreement, we can spare ourselves the reading out of the individual demands and simply come to an immediate vote on the matter,' concluded Ilnelus in a self-satisfied tone, lifting the hammer which would, when slammed down on the table, shatter any hope that Ahren and his friends might have of quickly resuming their search for the missing Yollock.

'One moment,' said Trimm, the tiniest spark of hope igniting in the breast of the young Forest Guardian. 'As everyone assembled here already knows, the winnings earned through the concessions that will have been confirmed by this vote will be divided up according to the relative ranks of the grandees here present.' Trimm took an audible breath and exchanged a quick glance with Eken, who was sitting attentively and with his ears pricked up on his Paladin's lap and purring contentedly. 'As it is *I* who have taken up negotiations with the Champions of the gods and led them to a conclusion satisfactory for Cape Verstaad, I request a formal re-assignment of *my* rank in accordance with grandee tradition.'

Ahren groaned inwardly. Trimm was greedily trying to increase his sinecure, taking full advantage of his treacherous betrayal of the Paladins' cause.

'This request is indeed in order,' said Ilnelus generously. 'We shall now re-evaluate the rank of Salman Tilderius, thus far the thirty-fourth among the fifty grandees.'

Trimm got to his feet and beckoned Palnah to do the same. Then he spoke in a loud voice. 'My negotiating skills, *and* my ability to say the right thing at the right time prompted the Paladins to choose me to be their speaker before this assembly. This has led to today's vote, which will ensure the future wealth of the city for decades, if not for centuries to come.' He looked triumphantly around the chamber, Ahren now wanting to do nothing more but smash his fist into the portly Paladin's face. As Trimm grinned, some of the grandees tossed flat, white stones onto the circular floor in front of the tribunes, among them Ilnelus, his generous gesture being met with quiet applause.

'The more of these stones that land on the floor, the higher Trimm's rank will be,' muttered Uldini, barely containing his fury.

Ahren counted fifteen white counters on the dark marble circle that made up the centre of the chamber, directly beneath the cupola. So far, Trimm's act of betrayal had not paid off for him. The grandees of Cape Verstaad were, it seemed, as miserly amongst themselves as they were toward others.

'I would further like to point out that I have been in negotiations with the new ruler of the city of cutthroats and have successfully concluded an agreement with her,' continued Trimm, Ahren shaking his head in total disbelief.

When had the corpulent Paladin dreamed up all this subterfuge? He had only regained consciousness a short time before the *Queen of the Waves* had sailed away from the amoral city. Had he really managed to speak to Dahl-Rhi or one of her representatives during that timeframe?

'The pirate ships to the west will refrain from attacking our trade routes on condition that we hire them as escorts for our freight cogs. This will guarantee us yet more security and financial gains – of special benefit to those of us who carry out our trade along the west coast of Jorath.' This statement was greeted by amazed murmurs as six more stones were tossed onto the floor by clearly delighted grandees.

Trimm then pointed at Trogadon and exclaimed: 'Furthermore, I have negotiated *sole* trading rights with a new Dwarfish colony on the Cutlass Sea! Behold, Trogadon, the bearer of an Ancestry Name, who has given me his word that there is a plentiful supply of precious stones, gold, silver, and even...' he paused dramatically, and now one could hear a pin drop in the large chamber, '...*Deep Steel!*'

Tumultuous applause and loud cheers filled the air, while Trogadon gripped the handle of his hammer so hard that Ahren was sure he was going to crush it. The look of naked fury on the dwarf's face suggested that Trimm might well feel the full weight of the heavy artefact eventually, but the grandee was relishing the moment as more counters were thrown into the ring. Ahren could now count more than thirty expressions of favour. Uldini's prophetic words were now haunting the young Forest Guardian, who recognised the full truth of the image – Trimm, the fat spider, louring in his web of intrigue. Ahren could do nothing but stand there and watch as his recreant brother listed out his achievements – brought about through chicanery and disloyalty – the grandee's exaggerated misinformation leading the portly Paladin closer and closer to the centre of Cape Verstaad's power.

Trust, he scolded himself, his inner voice weakening all the time. *You wanted to trust him!*

'My dear friends,' said Trimm loudly, the noise in the chamber gradually dying down so that it was now possible to hear the cheering of the citizenry through the open doors. 'You are honouring me in a manner that I would never have believed possible, and modesty would normally force me to take my seat at this point...'

Uldini snorted audibly.

'...but my pride in my future wife compels me to continue speaking.' He beckoned Palnah to lift her veil, the nervous woman straightening up noticeably beside him.

Ahren noticed how her hands were shaking, and he wondered if Trimm had betrayed her, too, so that he could move up the rankings another couple of places in his duplicitous power grab.

'For you *must* know that this enchanting creature is a *Brajah*, with an ever-alert mind and sensitive ears. Ears which she used to great effect yesterday evening during my little reception while she wandered among you guests unbeknownst to you all. Afterwards, my dear friends, she confided to me one or two juicy secrets that she had had...well...*overheard.*'

Once again, the chamber was filled with murmurs, whispers, and surprised expressions – although this time there was no cheering.

'And, indeed, it will be easy for her to continue standing by my side, using the sharp blade of her gift to separate truth from lies.' The corpulent Paladin's demeanour changed from amicable to threatening as his eyes scanned the listeners. Seven more stones – most of them belonging to grandees who were not so well-heeled – flew in high arcs, landing in the middle of the floor. The expressions on the faces of Trimm's newest supporters betrayed a mixture of naked terror and fawning obsequiousness.

'Rank twelve,' murmured Khara. 'At least, Trimm is making *everyone* here pay, not just us.'

'Last but not least,' exclaimed Trimm, his words causing a general groan within the chamber, 'it is my sad obligation to have to inform this assembly and the entire citizenry of Cape Verstaad that our glorious city was infested by Dark Ones.'

This was met by a silence so stunned that Ahren could hear the cries of dismay from the populace outside, the sound being carried in through the open doors.

'Happily, *all* these nefarious servants of the Adversary have been either eliminated of forced to flee, thanks to the assistance of the two honourable Ancients here present – Jelninolan Storm Weaver and Uldini Getobo. The latter has the ear of none other than the Sun Emperor himself and is one of my personal allies.'

Three more discs clattered onto the floor, cementing Trimm's meteoric rise.

'Why not,' grumbled Uldini, a look of resignation on his face. 'Why *not* make me your complaisant accomplice?'

Ahren understood the childlike figure's reaction only too well. Trimm had not only stabbed them all in the back, he had also twisted the blade several times and was now gleefully stamping on their prostrate bodies as they lay there, helpless on the ground.

'Indeed, it has come to light,' continued Trimm, Ahren now despising the corpulent Paladin's voice more than anything else in the world, 'that the aforementioned High Fangs had sought out the company of several easily malleable grandees, who then took what can only be described as *highly questionable* decisions. There is no point in naming names here, I believe, and submitting the gullible victims in our ranks to public displeasure.' It was clear from the gleam in Trimm's eyes that he intended to make full use of his knowledge concerning those grandees who had been complicit by implicitly threatening them with exposure.

While five more discs were thrown in by terrified-looking grandees, Bergen groaned in frustration as he covered his face with his hands. 'At *last*, he is blackmailing them with his knowledge of the High Fangs,' he complained. 'But for what purpose? For just a tad more power?'

Trimm's eyes were now firmly fixed on the young grandessa, who only a short time earlier had been gleefully painting the Paladins in as bad a light as possible. The young woman was clutching her white stone as if her life depended on it.

'That is Claudmil Ergenthron,' whispered Uldini, the Arch Wizard clearly mesmerised – despite his best efforts – by Trimm's power grab. 'Her house ranks number two. Because Ilnelus supported Trimm in the first round – when he was certain that our treacherous friend was perfectly harmless – her vote is the only one yet to be cast and hence can make Trimm the principal grandee of Cape Verstaad. If she withholds it, then he will remain as second in command, while she will climb to the top position in the city.'

Ahren leaned back and observed the young lady, who was glaring belligerently at Trimm, her chin thrust forward defiantly. Never, ever would this woman spurn the opportunity to seize power in Cape Verstaad.

Trimm nodded, gave an understanding smile, and made as if he were to sit down. The face on the Grandessa of the House of Ergenthron formed into a triumphant grimace when suddenly the corpulent Paladin paused and raised a pudgy finger. 'Just one more minor detail that I suppose I *should* reveal to the General Assembly,' he said theatrically before drawing forth two daggers from beneath his cloak and crossing them before his chest. Then he bellowed, his voice echoing around the chamber and out onto the streets of Cape Verstaad: 'My name is Trimm Askvuur, and *I* am a *Paladin!*'

Ahren sat bolt upright in his seat, he and his friends exchanging questioning looks. What was Trimm trying to achieve with this revelation? Was he now going to exploit his status as Champion of the gods to achieve the final stone so that it would land alongside all the others on the cold, hard floor beneath the cupola, under which he had already secured his status as the second most powerful person in the city?

'And, alas, as Paladin, I am forced to declare that Cape Verstaad has significantly *impeded* us in the course of the war,' said Trimm, suddenly speaking in the severe tone of a judge about to pronounce the harshest of judgements. 'The presence of High Fangs was tolerated among the elite circles within this city, while the Paladins were denied equipment essential to their quest – the quest of ensuring the existential survival of Jorath itself. *And,* ladies and gentlemen, even the unity of the Sunplains was threatened.' Trimm looked almost pityingly over at Claudmil. 'I fear that the next Principal Grandee of Cape Verstaad will have to do a lot of explaining to the league of Jorathian leaders, and especially to the Sun Emperor, once they have received the sorcerous messages from me and allies, the messages that I will have to send as soon as this session has ended – especially the message describing the so-called *loyalty* shown by this city, the wealthiest city of the south.'

Trimm's rival stared back at him before reacting to the white stone in her hand as if it were burning hot. With a furious cry, she hurled the disc away from her and sent it clattered onto the floor, where it rolled along until it came to a halt beside its forty-eight comrades.

Trimm gave a thin smile, then made his way over to Ilnelus's box, humming all the while before politely asking the grandee: 'How many stones are lying down there in the centre of this venerable hall?' Then he nonchalantly cast his own stone to where the others were lying.

There was a pause for several heartbeats. Then the old man spoke: 'Fifty,' he said icily. From outside, Ahren could hear cries of consternation and surprise. 'This is nothing less than a coup d'état,' he added quietly as Trimm took the hammer out of the man's wizened hands.

'Oh, yes,' replied the corpulent Paladin in a voice equally as low. 'Indeed, it is.' He tapped the instrument once on the former Principal Grandee's armrest. 'And every one of you has played your part.'

It took some time for the grandees of Cape Verstaad to recover themselves and become used to the fact that a Paladin was now head of their city. Trimm played absently with the hammer in his hand, smiling fondly from time to time at Palnah, who responded in kind. Her nervousness had clearly been solely down to her anticipation of how events before the assembly would unfold, for now she was as relaxed and happy as she always was by Trimm's side.

'What is he going to do with his power?' asked Ahren, looking at his companions. When he had put precisely the same question to Trimm, the only response had been a tight-lipped smile. While the grandees prepared to vote on their demands regarding the Paladins, it seemed to Ahren as if Trimm himself was somewhat at a loss as to what should happen next. Eken kept rubbing his head against that of his corpulent companion, and the young Paladin was certain that the pair of them were engaging in lively conversation.

Finally, Trimm let the hammer do the speaking, and an expectant silence fell over the room.

'Would anyone like to formally express the original conditions demanded of the Champions of the gods and thereby draw the wrath of the continent upon them?' asked Trimm in a honeyed voice as his eyes scanned the assembled grandees.

No-one moved an inch.

'Excellent,' said the newly assigned Principal Grandee of Cape Verstaad. 'Then I will instead put the following proposal forward for a vote – our city will *immediately* put all our logistical, miliary and magical means at the disposal of the Paladins here present so that they may journey onto the Ice Fields and continue their search for their missing brother, whose recovery is essential to the final elimination of the Dark god. Any costs incurred will be borne equally by the fifty grandees.' Trimm looked around the assembly, adding in a voice low enough so that the magic wouldn't carry his words beyond the cupola: 'By the way, it was *me* who stabbed Reik Silvercape in the heart when he resisted us Paladins.' He looked thoughtfully down at his weapons. 'It's funny, but I can't remember which of these daggers I used to kill him.'

Once again, a barrage of white stones flew through the air, Trimm carelessly throwing his own after them. 'Unanimously passed,' said the corpulent grandee, winking over at Ahren. 'Whoever would have believed it?'

Ahren sighed wearily. It was as if all the Forest Guardian's strength had been sucked out of his bones as he slumped back on his seat. His rage and frustration at Trimm's supposed shabby treachery had suddenly evaporated, leaving behind a feeling of emptiness, shame, and regret. Ahren had demanded of Trimm that he prove himself, and this is what the grandee had indeed done – although in a most perfidious and nerve-wracking manner.

'I further propose that we provide all the citizenry of Cape Verstaad with free food to support them in these uncertain times and as a reward for the invaluable service they have already done,' continued Trimm, the grandees grumbling in disapproval, albeit in voices low enough for the people outside not to hear them. 'These costs, too, will fall to the grandees – although I hardly think this will prove too taxing given the future earnings that will accrue from the new trade agreement with the Dwarfish colony.' Again, he played with his daggers. 'The vote, please,' he said. A loud clattering ensued. 'Unanimous again,' announced Trimm in a loud voice, cries of jubilation sounding throughout the city, the loudest cheers coming from the poverty-stricken outskirts.

'What a harmonious gang of grandees,' murmured Trimm, glancing over his shoulder at his companions, all of whom were shaking their heads in disbelief. 'Do you think I could persuade them to rename the city? How about Trimm Harbour? Or Trimm's Bay?'

'Don't overdo it,' warned Uldini sternly. 'So far, everyone has won. We are getting our equipment and ships, you are acquiring a city that you can toy with all you like, the workers have enough to eat at last, and your little trading arrangements with Gol-Konar and Murgamolosch will enrich the grandees even more, so that even the Sun Emperor will choose to ignore any idle gossip about Cape Verstaad having desired to claim full sovereignty.'

'You are right,' said Trimm, grinning broadly. 'One should always stop when everything seems perfect.' He nonchalantly slammed the hammer down on the armrest of his chair. 'The assembly is hereby concluded. May we all meet again – once the Dark god has been destroyed by the valiant Champions of the gods.'

Ahren could only silently concur with Trimm's final words, the jubilant roars from without the council chamber confirming that now all Cape Verstaad stood behind them – even if it had taken some remarkable detours to bring them to this point.

'Was this your real plan all along?' asked Ahren late that night, as he and Trimm stood alone on the rooftop terrace of the palace.

The moon was low on the horizon and would soon disappear altogether, the rest of the companions having already retired to bed. Trimm had been the recipient of copious apologies during the course of the evening, with more than one tear being shed as the rift between the Paladins was settled for once and for all. Ahren was sure of one thing – after today, the corpulent man would be known as Trimm the Devious rather than Trimm the Coward, and he couldn't help smiling at the thought before he continued to speak.

'You explained to us earlier that you didn't want to give us any clues because you wanted our horror at your supposed treachery to be genuine, but that wasn't the only reason, was it?' the young man pressed.

'No,' admitted Trimm with a sigh. 'As I've already said, I have spent decades preparing for this day – for this one vote, when I would be holding all the aces and could thereby ascend the ranks of Cape Verstaad to the very summit at meteoric speed.' Trimm shrugged his shoulders. 'The fact is that you and your friends gave me enough ammunition to move to within inches of my goal.'

'*Our* friends, not merely *mine,*' said Ahren, correcting his fellow Paladin.

'Maybe,' murmured Trimm with a smile. 'If they can forgive me my ham acting in the assembly today. Especially Trogadon.' He frowned. 'And Yantilla. Keeping the Ice Wolves in detention must have cost her an absolute fortune in terms of liquor for every one of her soldiers.'

Ahren guffawed. 'I am sure that the pair of them will find the necessary consolation in your wine cellar.' Then the Forest Guardian became serious again. 'But you have evaded my question. I want to know what your plan is, not about how you wished to become the Principal Grandee.'

Trimm shifted uncomfortably from one foot to the other. 'Uldini was right, in fact. I wanted to use Cape Verstaad as a shield for whenever you were going to come to collect me.' The man's face took on a horrified look. 'The idea of having to combat the Dark god…the very thought of it is unbearable to me.'

Ahren nodded understandingly. 'And why the change of heart then? You are now head of the city. You could simply have us thrown into the bay.'

'Because of Palnah,' said Trimm after a couple of heartbeats. 'I want to create a better world for her. One where there is no war.' He looked at Ahren almost shyly. 'And because of you – or rather, because of your faith in me.' He took a deep breath and looked out into the night, the sounds still echoing across from the celebrations in the workers' district on the outskirts of the city. 'It has been a long time since anyone has trusted me implicitly.'

Ahren slapped him on the back in a gesture of camaraderie. 'I must admit that I did have misgivings concerning your motivation on more than one occasion. But from now on you won't have to struggle so much to win the trust of others.'

'Apart from the grandees,' chuckled Trimm. 'But I can live with that.'

Again, loud laughter split the night sky, and Ahren pointed at the light from the bonfires in the distance. 'Why the free food? Was it only to win over the common folk as Uldini suspects?'

Trimm shook his head. 'I have felt sorry for these poor souls ever since I have begun to make my way up through the ranks – they lead such wearying lives, one and all. Sure, I could have reduced the contributions of the merchants – in which case I would possess a few more influential friends. But we Paladins are supposed to help those who cannot help themselves.' Again, he shrugged his shoulders. 'This is my way of fulfilling this task. Others can assist with sword or bow while I will use my money bags – after all, that is where my talent lies.'

Ahren looked out to sea and pondered the fact that it was now only the Dark Ones lurking in the waters that was preventing them from getting to the Ice Fields. Trimm had done what he could with his purse. Now it was time for those Paladins who wielded weapons and shields to do their bit – again.

Chapter 10

The new Cape Verstaad under Trimm's control turned out to be a true paradise for the Paladins and their companions. Whatever Uldini and Bergen needed for the expedition, their wishes were granted, whether it was blankets made from special beaver fur or strange shoes that had nails under their soles.

Even Admiral Refelbek had no complaints to make when Ahren paid the man a visit two days before their planned departure. The harbour of the mighty merchant city was still teeming with boats, but now military order reigned supreme in the western part of the large bay, while the chaotic comings and goings of the trading ships were confined to the eastern side. The Thirteenth Fleet had expanded to well over thirty ships, thanks in large part to the war carracks, which normally represented Cape Verstaad's interests at sea – squat, agile vessels with heavy crossbows mounted to the fore and aft decks, each one almost the size of a Dragon Bow. There were a further four splendidly furnished ships among the reinforcements – these had been the personal property of individual grandees who had hurriedly pressed them into service under the control of the Paladins.

They probably belong to families that were closer to the High Fangs than advisable, said Culhen, who was studying the new fleet from the dockside, his tongue lolling, while Ahren, Khara, Bergen, and Falk were already standing on the deck of the *Queen of the Waves,* listening to the latest updates from the admiral concerning the upcoming expedition.

Why don't you join us? asked Ahren curiously. *Or have you suddenly become seasick?*

I will only board this ship when it becomes absolutely necessary, the wolf replied worthily. *And for your information, Muai and I are going to go hunting this afternoon. We want to stretch our legs thoroughly before we are locked into this floating wooden box again.*

Ahren nodded. *You may as well head off straight away,* he suggested. *The admiral is so fond of his own voice that I can't help thinking that he and Uldini are related.*

The wolf barked once in gratitude. Five heartbeats later the animal was swallowed up in the hubbub of daily harbour life.

Ahren heard a cough beside him that expressed an artful mixture of politeness and indignation. 'You *are* still listening to me, Thirteenth?' asked Refelbek, in a tone suggesting that he already knew the answer.

'Apologies,' said Ahren cheerfully. 'You were saying?'

'That we are expecting the arrival of two Flame Belly ships tomorrow,' repeated the admiral tersely. 'Which means that nothing stands in the way of our setting sail with the following day's high tide.'

Ahren squinted and stared out at the smooth waters to the south. 'How long will it take us to reach the Ice Fields?' he asked.

'Three weeks,' replied Falk. 'Assuming the weather is favourable.'

'*And* providing we are not attacked along the way,' interjected Uldini with a frown.

'The Lantern Frigates have certainly proven themselves,' said Refelbek, nodding towards the two newly repaired ships with the Bane Lanterns fixed to the top of their masts. 'I have personally decided on the formation in which the fleet is to proceed. The circle of light provided by the two frigates will be sufficient to protect the entire naval flotilla – even if it means that the helmsmen and -women will have to keep the tightest of courses to ensure that the larger ships don't take the wind out of the smaller ones' sails.'

'You need not worry about such details, Admiral,' said Uldini, shrugging his shoulders. 'Each individual ship from Cape Verstaad will have six to eight sorcerers on board. Including those who have perfected the conjuring up of winds.'

Ahren was taken aback at the number that Uldini had mentioned, and he whistled through his teeth in surprise. 'In all Hjalgar there are hardly any magicians other than the Keepers, yet in Cape Verstaad one can find them by the hundreds. It hardly seems fair.'

Uldini laughed ironically. 'Firstly, Cape Verstaad now has more inhabitants than your homeland, and secondly, they pay their sorcerers so much that none of them want to leave here.'

'That is, if you don't count those who are attracted by the chance of earning easy gold,' interjected Khara, who was sitting on a coil of rope, dangling her legs in a somewhat bored manner.

'And we know where *they* end up,' muttered Falk grimly. 'Either on the pirate ships of the Cutlass Sea or in Gol-Konar.'

'I have wondered about something for a long time,' said Admiral Refelbek, looking over at Uldini curiously. 'There are very few sorcerers in the Jorathian army or navy. Does the talent for magic go hand in hand with a love for gold?'

Uldini scowled, his face looking as if he had bitten into a lemon, Ahren then finding it impossible to suppress a grin. 'You forget, honourable Admiral,' retorted Uldini in a prickly voice, 'that Cape Verstaad is the only place that contains a central school for sorcery. Nine out of every ten magicians are trained here.'

'And if Cape Verstaad teaches a young person anything, then it is about the advantages of wealth,' added Khara through pursed lips.

'Precisely,' concurred Uldini defiantly. 'And it therefore pleases me to inform you that it is only very rarely that *Ancients* emerge, who have learned their magical arts in this city. It seems that all this opulence deadens the hunger necessary for discovering the greatest mysteries of sorcery.'

Ahren was all ears now as he looked keenly at Uldini. The sorcerer had never described to them the moment when he had unearthed the mystery of agelessness for himself. The childlike figure saw the Paladin peering at him and promptly floated away with a fathomless expression on his face. Clearly, there were some secrets that Uldini would rather take to the grave than share.

'Sorcerers here, warships there,' said Bergen after a few heartbeats, breaking the silence that had descended on the little group. 'We can take it as given that the Adversary will put up stubborn resistance before we even reach the Ice Fields. He will either blow the lanterns out again, or he will have some other fiendish plan to turn the tables on us.'

'We are as well prepared as we will ever be,' mused Falk. 'We shall have to overcome this final obstacle, come what may.' He scratched his beard, the look on the old man's face making Ahren uneasy. 'It's what will happen *afterwards* that is worrying me more. Trying to locate Yollock in a vast desert of ice could turn out to be a real problem.'

Ahren pointed at Uldini, who was now floating above the stern. 'Surely he or Jelninolan can cast a charm net to try and locate our missing comrade,' suggested Ahren.

Falk shook his head. 'Only once we are close enough to Yollock. But the Ice Fields are vaster than the entirety of the Sunplains. No sorcerer's charm net can spread so wide – nor do Uldini and Jelninolan together have the necessary power.'

Khara frowned. 'Are you saying that we have no point of reference?' she asked irritably. 'I thought that all the Ancients had feverishly searched for the vanished Paladins before the Pall Cloud appeared. Did *their* combined charm net not even suffice?'

Falk shook his head. 'Charm nets are never completely reliable. Especially not if they have to spread across large areas of water.' He nodded towards the city. 'Trimm, for example, was able to hide beneath the echoes of the many charms that are uttered in Cape Verstaad on a daily basis – in this way, he was never discovered. The Father of the Mountain was also beyond reach on his icy peak.' Falk gave a crooked grin. 'It never occurred to the Ancients to search for the Paladins in the lofty heights.'

The more Ahren learned about magic, the more he understood how limited this power really was. There seemed to be more rules and regulations than at a Dwarfish clan gathering, and the further the spells radiated from their creators, the more likely they were to fail. 'In other words, we know nothing regarding Yollock's whereabouts?' he asked.

'Not quite true,' said Bergen. 'Firstly, he certainly isn't hiding out on the outer edges of the Ice Fields – otherwise, the Ancients would have at least sensed through their charm nets whether he is alive or dead. Secondly, certain reports over the centuries have made their way back to the mainland confirming that members of the *Hisunik* tribe had seen a white-haired, sullen *Beraal.*'

'Sorry, a *what?*' asked Khara, taking the words out of Ahren's mouth.

Bergen grinned. 'The *Hisunik* are a folk whose villages lie on the coasts of the Ice Fields, and their livelihoods depend on fishing and seal hunting. Theirs is a meagre and lonely existence, and if I were to hazard a guess, I would say that there are no more than three or four dozen *Hisunik* villages on the Ice Fields. They categorise all people who come from the continent as *Beraal*, which roughly translates as "ephemeral".'

Refelbek grunted in surprise. 'Do these savages give *us* this nickname because *they* live so long?'

'No,' replied Bergen solemnly, looking earnestly at the admiral. 'But all Jorathians who travel onto the Ice Fields either return home very quickly or die within a very short time on the icy plains.'

'Ephemeral indeed,' mused Ahren.

Bergen slapped him hard on the back. 'Don't you worry about a thing. I know a little bit about cold weather, and our equipment is first rate. The grandees have provided us with an additional dozen experienced guides, and with two Flame Bellies, we will be able to breach the ice sufficiently so that we can take a third ship along, carrying more equipment and mercenaries.'

'*Mercenaries?*' asked Ahren sceptically. 'What will we need them for?'

Bergen pointed towards the south, his face now drawn and serious. 'You remember our suspicion that Four Claws is still out there? The more armed men and women we take with us onto the eternal ice, the better the chances that this will not turn out to be the final journey of the Thirteenth Paladin.'

On hearing those words, Khara grasped Ahren's hand, the latter responding in kind by squeezing her fingers. There was no doubt that Hakanu would be overjoyed at the prospect of taking on a dragon, but the thought of such an adventure filled Ahren with anxiety. If he had to confront a power-hungry god at the end of his travels, then the THREE could at *least* spare him an encounter with the most dangerous living creature that Jorath had ever seen.

***

Revenge was hungry and weary. The journey south had been onerous, the clouds upon which he had allowed himself to be driven had blown this way and that. It had been so long since he had enjoyed humanity's petty discords. It was invigorating to watch Revenge's victims nurturing their own personal hatreds as if they were tiny flames, growing bigger and bigger until they ignited into an unstoppable desire to destroy a fellow human for some supposed slight or other.

Revenge wallowed in the memories of having the taste of blood on his tongue, and in the emotions that bubbled up in his hosts, once they realised what they had just done. Some felt instantly triumphant before becoming possessed by a feverish desire to destroy the next target of their rage. Such people were never satiated by their hatred, distracting themselves from their own shortcomings by constantly finding fault in the people that they saw around them. These individuals were particularly delicious as far as Revenge was concerned, for he could feast on them repeatedly before they fully understood the horror of what they had done – before he left them, shattered and lifeless.

Most of his victims, much to his chagrin, were simply plagued by that most boring of feelings, remorse – once they had carried out their vengeful action and were standing over the bloody remains of their enemy. The child of the Dark god tended to slaughter the remorseful with an element of disdain. After that, he would always seek the safety of the clouds to continue his travels southward, always keeping an eye out for his next feast.

But in this desert of water and stupid fish, there was no nourishment for him. Revenge thirsted, nay lusted to taste the scorn of another rational creature again.

The child of the Dark god was drowning in self-pity when he suddenly sensed the presence of his creator. Father was undoubtedly suffering from exhaustion, but his message was clear, and his Will was the hungry child's command.

SEARCH...SEARCH...SEARCH IN THE DEPTHS!

***

The air was filled with the screeching of seagulls and the shouts of countless mariners making final preparations for the voyage under the critical eyes of the officers. The sun cast its warm beams from a cloudless sky and the bards played the popular songs that Uldini had taught the locals so many years before. Resourceful hawkers sold sugared fruits and light wine to the spectators, who thronged the quayside and the beaches that lined the bay of Cape Verstaad, everyone wanting to witness the imminent departure of the fighting force as it set sail in its quest to find the one remaining Paladin of the gods who was still missing.

Trimm and Palnah, in contrast, stood among the assembled city grandees in a grand pavilion on the largest pier of the harbour and watched how the ships formed a complex pattern, the *Queen of the Waves* in the middle.

Ahren found himself humming along to the melody of *The Lad and his Wolf* as he stood on the aft deck alongside his friends and Admiral Refelbek, waving from time to time at the jubilant masses on land.

'Someone is clearly enjoying the heroic ballads,' chuckled Trogadon, who was lighting his pipe with its sweet-smelling tobacco. He puffed away contentedly before pointing the stem at Ahren. 'Should I ask one of the bards to accompany us on our voyage?' he asked with a grin. 'It will surely lead to the immediate composition of yet more gems concerning the Thirteenth Paladin and his glorious deeds.'

'You're only jealous because no-one has written a song about you,' teased Ahren, who was, nevertheless, secretly annoyed at the fact that he couldn't get the simple melody of the ballad out of his head.

'There certainly *is* a song – and what a composition!' the dwarf replied, grinning broadly. 'The masterpiece goes by the title *Heart of Sapphire and Hurricane Soul*. Admittedly it is dripping with schmaltz, but it serves its purpose.'

'Weren't we going to remain schtum on the matter until we were certain that it would be played?' asked Jelninolan irritably.

'Now I'm *really* curious,' interjected Khara with a chuckle. 'What is this song all about?'

'Yes,' snarled Uldini, 'what, indeed? I don't remember ever having told the bards anything about a song concerning a certain Dwarfish blacksmith.' The Arch Wizard put his hands on his hips and glared at Trogadon and Jelninolan. 'The whole *point* of all this caterwauling was to raise morale among the hoi polloi and to endear them to the Paladins and the alliance of the nations – *not* to claim all the glory for a pair of scandalous individuals *and* to obtain a limitless supply of free beer in the taverns.'

Trogadon's eyes lit up. 'Now that you mention it, I have no objections to such side effects.' Despite Jelninolan rewarding him with a clip on the ear, he laughed uproariously.

'I have, indeed, heard this ballad,' said Refelbek. 'An emotionally stirring story of a Dwarfish blacksmith and an Elven priestess…' His voice trailed off as he looked from Trogadon to Jelninolan and back again. '*Oh…*' he added before trailing off.

Ahren raised his eyebrows in surprise, Jelninolan looking decidedly pleased with herself as she said: 'Because Trogadon and I are *not* allowed to enter the bond before the war is won and our union officially recognised by the leaders of our folk, we have decided to make things easier by tipping the balance in our favour.' She looked coolly at her listeners, allowing the aura of her power to radiate as she continued to speak. 'If the dilemma of our forbidden love can melt the hearts of simple soldiers and noble alumni the length and breadth of Jorath, it might cause the Dwarfish elders to remember and every Elven sage to announce what it was that we have been promised as a reward for our labours.' With that, she took Trogadon's hand and walked majestically away to the stern of the ship, so that everyone could see them.

Ahren listened in disbelief as the bards let their songs fade away to nothing, only to strike up a hymn of love, combining Elven harmonies with the stomping rhythms of Dwarfish drinking songs, the two forms coming together in an infectious, powerful union.

'Now *that* was clever,' said Bergen with a smirk, waving his finger in warning before Uldini's nose just as the Arch Wizard opened his mouth to speak. 'I don't want to hear the slightest hint of disapproval from you,' said the Paladin energetically. 'It was you who started using songs as a weapon. That couple are only following in your footsteps. And you hardly want to chastise them for wanting to protect their own love for each other, do you?'

Uldini pursed his lips, Ahren observing that the Ancient was appraising the mood of his companions before deciding whether to let the matter drop or not.

Ahren resolved to set an example by immediately positioning himself beside Trogadon. Then he drew his Wind Blade, held it over the hand-holding couple, and beckoned the other Paladins to assemble around the pair of lovebirds.

'*Really?*' grunted the First, his face suggesting that the Forest Guardian had asked him to sit down with a Glower Bear and discuss any differences that they might have over a nice cup of tea, but when Falk and Bergen each grabbed an arm of the veteran, the old soldier yielded. Hakanu hurriedly joined them, grinning broadly, and soon the Paladins' weapons formed into a protective roof of blades over Trogadon and Jelninolan, the gesture ensuring that a jubilant cheer rose from among the citizenry of Cape Verstaad.

Ahren was sure that he saw Trimm and Palnah wiping their eyes in the shade of their pavilion, and as he stood there for a while longer, keeping his Wind Blade raised over his two friends and thereby publicly declaring his blessing regarding their love, he remembered the last conversation that he'd had with his corpulent brother.

'What are you going to do now?' Ahren had asked the grandee in a low voice as they were boarding the *Queen of the Waves*. 'You can't stay here forever, you know.'

Trimm had smiled and shrugged his shoulders in a strangely enigmatic manner. 'I am the Principal of the Grandees. I have achieved my goal here. And for this reason, I will do exactly what Uldini expects of me – only in a completely different way to what he imagined. I shall *indeed* hide behind as many mercenaries as I can gather in Cape Verstaad…but then I will take them with me to the Ring, so that they can protect me and Palnah until there are no more Dark Ones between me and the Dark god.' Trimm had made a great effort to maintain a dignified demeanour, but the fear in his eyes had been unmistakable. '*That* will be the moment when I, dressed in the thickest Deep Steel armour that the dwarves will have been able to forge, shall join the rest of you, and when you will hopefully keep me alive for long enough until we are standing face to face with the Dark god. Then we will slay him together – however that will happen.'

Ahren had embraced his brother, and likewise the smiling Palnah, who was becoming more like a ruler every day and less resembling the intimidated concubine of Reik that she had once been. Yet, although Ahren was leaving Cape Verstaad in the hands of Trimm and Palnah with a good conscience, he could not get Trimm's final words out of his head.

'*However that will happen,*' thought Ahren fretfully as he lowered his Wind Blade, now that the crowds on the shore were beginning to disperse, the ships having completed their final preparations for departure. *Whatever did he mean by that?*

Ask Uldini or one of the other Paladin, who fought against the Adversary that time if it's bothering you that much, muttered Culhen dismissively, the wolf having taken up his usual position on the fo'c'sle with Muai and Kamaluq. *I, for my part, intend to enjoy the cheering of the few remaining happy humans for as long as possible. And you should do the same. This moment will be your last look at the comforts of civilisation for some time to come.*

Ahren decided to leave any further questions for later, for Admiral Refelbek had blown into a large bugle, the piercing sound being echoed by the captains of the Thirteenth Fleet. The sails were unfurled and what sounded like a low sound of thunder filled the bay as dozens of ships began to move in a slow, stately manner.

'The Thirteenth Fleet,' announced the admiral before immediately correcting himself. 'Nay,' he proclaimed solemnly. 'The Thirteenth

Armada is on course. May the winds and waters of the south be merciful to us.'

Ahren sheathed his Wind Blade, and as he turned, his eyes looked away from the receding bay, from its impressive houses, clean streets, and colourfully dressed residents. Instead, they fixed themselves on the southern horizon, the young Paladin imagining the white vastness of the Ice Fields, where Yollock had been lost without a trace for centuries now. The Forest Guardian in him delighted at the opportunity of exploring a new world completely unknown to him, of facing new challenges, and of a final search. The Paladin in Ahren rejoiced at the symbolic significance of their successful return. For, should they find Yollock and bring him back to Jorath, then only one remaining mission awaited them – the final battle against a self-proclaimed god.

The creaking of the rigging and the flapping of the sails in the steady wind were the only sounds that Ahren heard as he stood on the deck of the *Queen of the Waves* on the third night of their voyage, peering thoughtfully up at the moon, which came and went behind the silhouettes of the surrounding vessels as the ship gently rocked. Since they had set sail, more than twenty sorcerers had conjured up a favourable tailwind while another ten took care of the condition of the sea, ensuring that the waves were no more than ripples, the sea now almost resembling a smooth mirror.

The Thirteenth Armada was sailing due south, and nothing seemed to be standing in their way. Only occasionally did lookouts on the lead vessels report sightings of Dark Ones, but the servants of the Dark god seemed to be permanently on the retreat. Ahren knew better, however, and he could see by the looks on his friends' faces that they, too, were equally anxious, the uneasy feeling in his bones driving him on deck night after night so that he could check on the Bane Lanterns, which cast their reddish light over the entire armada. He was certain of one thing – this was the calm before the storm.

The two precious Flame Belly ships held their positions between the Lantern Frigates and the *Queen of the Waves*, the bulky ships looking even more aggressive in the unnatural glow of the magical flames than they did in the light of day. The massive two-masters with their heavy, steel battering rams at their prows both displayed figureheads in the form of a dragon. The sails were not particularly tall, but they were certainly broad, and the ships planks were strikingly thick. Each of the two ships had a pair of Wind Sorcerers, who took it in turns to cast their spells, enabling the two vessels to maintain their course day and night.

'Ah, the wonders of magic,' said Uldini, suddenly appearing above Ahren and causing the young man to flinch. The Arch Wizard floated down until he was looking the Forest Guardian straight in the eye. Clearly, Ahren was not the only one watching out from the armada at night. 'Ships that are not really made for the high seas, are being pushed beyond their limits by the will of individuals. The vessels and the sorcerers are thereby creating something big, something *sublime.*'

'Like the THREE did that time,' said Ahren, returning the Arch Wizard's stare.

'Precisely. Like the gods did when they created Jorath as we know it,' said Uldini before squinting and peering questioningly at the young man. 'What is going through your head?'

Ahren waved vaguely northward. 'Trimm said something which worries me. Something that has thrown up some questions.'

Uldini snorted. 'I find that much of what Trimm says is questionable.' Then his features softened. 'But I must admit that his political chicanery during the General Assembly of the grandees was masterful. Both the gold *and* the troops of Cape Verstaad will be invaluable to us when we finally fight our way through the Obsidian Fortress.'

'To kill HIM, WHO FORCES,' murmured Ahren with a threatening undertone.

'Indeed,' replied Uldini before sighing. 'Stop beating around the bush, Ahren. What is it that you want to know?'

'Do we know *exactly* how we are going to slay the Dark god?' asked the Forest Guardian anxiously. 'Trimm didn't seem to be certain. Are *you?*'

Uldini grimaced and bit on his lower lip, Ahren not liking one little bit the look of deep concern on the Arch Wizard's face. 'Theoretically, yes,' said the childlike figure. 'Your gods' Blessings are supposed to merge as soon as you come face to face with the Adversary in battle and you have made him vulnerable to your weapons.'

'*Supposed to?*' pressed Ahren. 'In other words, you are *not* certain?'

'It has never been attempted yet,' said Uldini with a tortured smile. 'HE, WHO FORCES understood masterfully how to avoid a gathering of all thirteen Paladins during the Dark Days.' He sighed loudly. 'When, however, the twelve surviving Champions of the gods fought against him after the Night of Blood, he was weakened in their presence to the point where we Ancients were able to erect the Pall Pillar around him. Hence, it is only logical that the thirteen of you together should be able to decrease his power sufficiently that you can kill him.' He hesitated for a heartbeat before adding: 'Somehow.'

Ahren winced. That one final word was enough to undercut any confidence that had been built up in the Paladin by what Uldini had said beforehand. 'We need to be certain of what is to be done,' grunted Ahren darkly. 'It isn't as though we are going to have a multitude of opportunities.'

'Belsarius occupied himself with this very question in his time.' As always, Uldini's voice became dreamy when he spoke of the visionary sorcerer who had been first among the Ancients before the childlike figure had succeeded to the position. 'If he found the solution during his lifetime, he certainly never had the chance to tell us.'

'And what is *your* plan?' asked Ahren, Uldini shaking his head energetically in response.

'First, let us find Yollock,' said the sorcerer, speaking with self-confidence again. 'Then we will gather the Paladins and Ancients in Deepstone – or to be more exact, in Castle Highstone.' Uldini rolled his eyes as he always did whenever he mentioned the less than original name of the fortification containing the pregnant soul companions and Paladins who were being guarded by elite guards, Night Soldiers, and recently even the Blue Cohorts. 'Together we will think of something.'

'Are we not simply conjuring up a second Night of Blood?' asked Ahren sceptically.

To his surprise, Uldini merely shrugged his shoulders. 'We will not be able to avoid the danger of a second Night of Death – unless the Paladins *don't* come together. The Adversary will undoubtedly send for his ablest assassins as soon as he senses that the Thirteen are gathered in one place. You keep forgetting how afraid he is of you when you are united.' The Arch Wizard looked up at the moon. 'The only thing we can do is prepare for this final battle as best we can. By the time we arrive, Highstone will have been transformed into a fortress of steel and magic, the like of which has never been seen before – you can be sure of that.'

'But…' began Ahren, Uldini raising a hand to stop him while at the same time gazing at him kindly.

'No buts,' he said. 'One step at a time. This is how we have managed this epic journey up until now, and this is how we will conclude it – understood?'

Ahren nodded hesitantly. 'I will drop the subject until we are back on the mainland again.' He stared hard at Uldini. 'But by then, you had better have a couple of solutions at the ready, for unravelling the mysteries of creation is *your* area of expertise.' He pointed at himself before adding with a smile: 'I, for my part, will simply pepper Dark Ones with arrows or skewer them with my Wind Blade.'

'*And* make life difficult for me at every opportunity,' added Uldini with a grin.

'The gods have given each one of us a role,' announced Ahren in a mock-serious tone. 'It is hardly my fault that I play my one so well.'

The following days were accompanied by leaden-grey clouds and a persistent drizzle, both of which dampened the mood of all the mariners and seemed a harbinger of ill tidings. Ahren was convinced that not a single soul among the armada was in any doubt of an imminent sea battle.

The companions were sitting together in the cargo hold of the *Queen of the Waves* – which had been converted for their private use – listening to Refelbek and Yantilla. The ex-mercenary leader had given the Ice Wolves the task of strengthening the watch on the various decks for the duration of the voyage and she was co-ordinating the incoming reports from the other ships. The admiral seemed to have nothing against the fact that the gaunt commander had become his unofficial right-hand woman – indeed, he seemed delighted to have her assistance, given the sheer size of the naval fleet for whose manoeuvres he was responsible.

'The horizon is now teeming with Sabre Rays, Monster Eels, and even the occasional Carapace Whale,' said Yantilla, playing absently with the hilt of her weapon. 'It cannot be much longer until the assault – otherwise, the Dark Ones will start eating each other alive, such is the lack of space beneath the waves.'

'*Carapace* Whales?' asked Trogadon, ignoring the dry humour of the gaunt woman. 'That name sounds more than ominous.'

'Grey whales with masses of barnacles on their unbelievably thick skin,' said Bergen, scowling. 'The barnacles are so closely packed together that they form an effective shell, which protects the whales from attack. One of the Adversary's more elegant creations.'

'It depends on how one defines *elegant,*' retorted Jelninolan, nauseated. 'Only one in ten of the Carapace Whales is strong enough to reach maturity. The others sink to the seabed under the sheer weight of the barnacles, where they suffer an agonising death.'

'Which is why these creatures are so rare,' added Refelbek. 'I, myself, have only ever sighted one during all my years at sea.' The serious man shivered. 'The monster ate the entire crew of a ship, which it had a short time earlier holed by ramming into her.'

'The sorcerers of the armada should take care of the whales,' said Uldini grimly. 'We can deal with the other Dark Ones by using arrows, bolts, and harpoons, but we must leave the Carapace Whales to the magicians.'

Refelbek nodded while Yantilla made a note on a little slate. 'This means that the crew of the armada will have to tackle the Monster Eels and the Sabre Rays without magical support,' she mused.

'And they will have to simultaneously give the sorcerers cover,' interjected Falk solemnly. 'Which will be no easy task.'

'Should we divide ourselves up onto different ships?' asked Khara. 'In that way we can give significant support…'

'On *no* account!' said Refelbek decisively. These thirty-three ships are only surrounding us to protect the *Queen of the Waves*, which also means protecting those of us on board her. If you were all to split up, it would defeat the whole purpose of this armada.'

'What if the Adversary strikes again?' interjected Hakanu, Ahren secretly pleased at his apprentice's reasonable question, which contained none of the exaggerated heroism that was more typical of the boy.

'Jelninolan and I will be at the ready,' said Uldini. 'We have installed bane charms on the Lantern Frigates, which should protect the beacons from sorcerous attacks. All that we need to do now is to activate them at the *right* moment, for they are only effective for a few days, and they will cost us considerable strength once put into effect.'

Ahren frowned as it became apparent that the upcoming sea battle would yet again be one of these conflicts where he would have to spend a lot of the time looking helplessly on at others determining the weal and woe of their journey, the innocent paying for their onward journey with blood.

At least we will be able to secure the deck of the Queen of the Waves *alongside the Ice Wolves and the Fox Guards,* said Culhen, consoling his friend.

Ahren looked over at Yantilla, Culhen's commentary having reminded him of the question that he had already planned on asking. 'How are the newcomers getting on?' he queried, referring to those from Cape Verstaad who had volunteered to join the two troops that the wolf had mentioned.

'Very well,' replied Yantilla. 'Their fighting skills have shown themselves to be adequate, and their dedication to the defence of the Paladins cannot be questioned.' A fleeting smile flitted across the commander's face. 'We now have eighty-three Ice Wolves and nine Fox Guards.' She glanced over at Bergen, Falk, and the First. 'Furthermore, I should mention that I have been asked about bringing back into use the Bear Sentries, the Dragon Wall, *and* the Falcon Watch.'

While the First shook his head, Bergen laughed uproariously. 'Thank you, but I already have my Blue Cohorts – and they are more than enough to keep me awake at night.' He cocked his head and grinned. 'Although, I *do* wonder why people always talk of bears when they think of me.'

'Because you eat and drink like a brown bear after hibernation,' said Falk, before gesturing politely yet dismissively towards Yantilla. 'I could order hundreds of soldiers from my barony to appear. If I had wanted more protection, then I would have gotten it. More bodyguards always mean more complications. This armada is proof positive of that.'

'Are you *still* of the opinion that we should have stolen away on one ship?' asked Jelninolan incredulously. 'Despite *all* the Dark Ones out there?'

Falk frowned. 'Yes, I still am,' he replied. 'With your help and Uldini's we would have been able to camouflage a Flame Belly ship before the eyes of the Adversary, isn't that so?'

'Perhaps,' said Uldini in a cutting voice. 'It *might* have worked. 'But if the Dark god had blindsided us somehow with a ruse, then it would have been one cumbersome ship against an army of Dark Ones.'

Falk opened his mouth, Ahren suspecting that the old Paladin was about to list off his objections, but after a moment of silence, Falk nodded. 'There are almost three thousand souls on board our ships,' said the Forest Guardian grimly. 'And we are steering them into the middle of a massacre.'

Ahren empathised with his erstwhile master. Then he noticed the pleading look on Hakanu's face as the young boy gazed at him. 'I'm sorry, lad,' said the Paladin regretfully. 'There are no feints here, no clever tricks that we can use to protect the lives of our soldiers. The enemy knows our destination and where we are situated. There is no place on the sea where we can hide, and the Dark Ones are faster than us. This battle is unavoidable.'

Hakanu nodded, the determination on his face giving him a more mature appearance than befitted his age. 'Then we must prepare well,' he said, picking up his spear. 'I will be outside training with the Fox Guards.' He stepped out of the room, and a short time later the sound of stamping feet could be heard coming from the deck.

'Don't you want to follow him?' asked Khara in a low voice, but Ahren shook his head.

'At the moment,' said the Forest Guardian morosely, he too being troubled by the inevitable and imminent loss of life, 'I really have *no* idea of what I should say to him.'

At noon, two days later, cries of alarm could be heard coming from the fleet's lead ships, the vessels nothing more than hazy silhouettes on the water, thanks to the relentless rain. The light conditions being so poor, a decision had been taken that the Bane Lanterns should burn during the day as well, the dreadful weather proving a blessing in that respect at least, for the magic continued to protect them despite the sun, which was hidden behind the leaden clouds above.

Ahren was standing, wrapped in his cloak, on the prow of the ship, taking in some fresh air when he was suddenly witness to the strangest of dramas. The foremost ships of the armada shuddered as if struck from the starboard side, the Forest Guardian looking on in disbelief as the war carracks, now listing violently, struggled to hold course. Sailors rushed hither and thither on the decks, adjusting the sails of the rolling vessels. Believing the fleet to be under attack, Ahren looked frantically at the mariners on his own ship, but all he could see were stoical faces continuing to stare south even when the next ships of the armada were shaken by the same phenomenon.

'Prepare to enter the Ravenous Maw!' thundered Refelbek, hectic activity immediately ensuing on board. Ahren ran between the rushing mariners, who were busily taking in a sail here and unfurling another sail there.

'What's going on?!' yelled Ahren through the teeming rain and chaos, the admiral acknowledging his presence with a curt nod.

'We are reaching the Ravenous Maw,' said Refelbek. 'An ocean trench so unimaginably deep that according to legend it would take a sinking ship a full year to settle on the floor of this underwater ravine.'

More ships were pulled to the portside, then rolling this way and that beneath the cries of their crews until they resumed their course. Ahren reckoned that it would be the turn of the *Queen of the Waves* within the next dozen heartbeats, and he held onto the railing in preparation.

'Current, hard starboard!' yelled Refelbek, the ship suddenly shuddering violently as if an invisible giant had grabbed the prow of the *Queen of the Waves* and was yanking it violently to the left.

Some of the sailors cut knots, others pulled hard at taut ropes, and two winches creaked in protest as several crewmembers hauled them as fast as their sweating, aching bodies would permit.

For the unknowing Ahren it seemed almost like a miracle as within a few moments the sails above him turned in a most intricate manner. The masts of the *Queen of the Waves* groaned alarmingly, and for a moment Ahren feared that they might snap. The ship tumbled like a drunkard as it rolled violently from port to starboard and back again until she finally came to a rest before resuming her southerly course even though it seemed to Ahren from the position of the sails, that the wind ought in fact to have been carrying them southwest.

'That was a *current* that shook us so violently?' asked Ahren disbelievingly.

Refelbek wiped the sweat and rain from his brow before nodding. 'It is the strongest sea current known to mariners,' he said. 'Any ship that fails to counter it, is swept out to the Ravenous Maw in the far east, never to return.'

'Where does this current come from?' asked Ahren curiously, hearing loud cursing from below deck, the first sullen faces of his companions appearing at the hatch leading below deck.

Refelbek shrugged his shoulders. 'One suspects that it has to do with the water temperature,' he said. 'It is cold in the Ravenous Maw – so cold that we are going to see our first ice floes soon.'

Ahren looked at the admiral, wide-eyed. This morning, the pail raised from the sea for washing had contained comfortably warm sea water. 'Is this sea ravine the line between the warm climes of the south and the cold surrounds of the Ice Fields then?' he asked.

Refelbek nodded, then put on a pair of mittens. 'If you weren't wearing your extraordinary cloak, you wouldn't be asking me this, Thirteenth.'

'Damn it, what *was* that just now?' grumbled Trogadon, now stamping towards them on the fo'c'sle, Ahren's other friends in his wake. 'And who told the sun to go off duty? It's colder here than in a Dwarfish storeroom.'

Noticing that there were little clouds of steam emanating from the blacksmith's mouth, Ahren tested the temperature by pulling back the hood of his cloak and uncovering his hands. It took him no time at all to break off his experiment.

'It *is* cold,' he murmured.

Wonderful, commented Culhen, the wolf sticking his head out of the hatch before stepping up into the open. *At last, a temperature ideal for someone wearing fur.* Then Ahren's four-legged friend shook his head in disgust and turned back. *Let me know when the rain eases off,* he said, disappointed. *I don't want to be listening to complaints about stinking wet wolf the whole night through.*

'A little forewarning would have been appreciated,' muttered Falk, rubbing an impressive bump on his forehead.

Refelbek seemed completely unperturbed. 'I *did* shout,' he said. 'But experience suggests that it is better for passengers to remain in total ignorance below deck when approaching the current of the Ravenous Maw. Too many have gone on deck out of curiosity, wanting to observe the spectacle from the railing only to fall overboard, never to be seen again.'

'Have you been down in these parts before?' asked Uldini, rubbing the rainwater off his bald pate. 'I would never have expected an admiral of the Knight Marshes to have sailed so far south.'

'Two or three times,' said the man vaguely. 'The Ravenous Maw was particularly useful in times of war if one wanted to get quickly from west to east – while at the same time evading both the ships of the Eternal Empire *and* those of the Sunplains, the two navies skirmishing repeatedly on the south coast of Jorath.'

'A daring manoeuvre,' commented Bergen, testing the waters by throwing a wooden bowl overboard only to see it being pulled violently away by the current below. 'Freeing a ship from these waters takes some skill and is surely a risky undertaking if one travels with the current for a period.'

Refelbek said nothing, merely nodding in response.

'How long will we need to traverse the gorge?' asked the First.

'Until we reach the pack ice,' said the Admiral, much to Ahren's surprise. 'The current reaches to beneath the Ice Fields.'

Ahren shivered. 'If anyone falls into the water along the coast of the Ice Fields…' he began.

'…then they will be pulled under unmercifully and lost forever,' said Refelbek, concluding the young man's sentence with an unapologetic nod. 'The same thing applies to holes in the pack ice, by the way. If you fall in, you are sucked down beneath the surrounding ice.'

'Do you know something,' said Trogadon, wringing out his sodden beard, 'I now fully appreciate these Flame Belly ships that are going to lead us through the pack ice.'

Ahren nodded, now understanding all too well why Uldini had insisted that they make every effort in Cape Verstaad to gather as much equipment as possible. He silently thanked Trimm, now so far away from them, who had established through his plan the best possible conditions for their search on the Ice Fields.

'I assume that we are safe here – am I right in thinking that?' asked Falk, looking out through the rain at the barely visible horizon in the distance. 'I mean, the Dark Ones will find it just as difficult to manage the current as our ships.'

'Alas, no,' said Refelbek. 'The current gets weaker, the deeper one goes, and hence, as creatures of the sea, they are far better able to cope than a fleet of battleships.'

'That explains why we haven't been attacked yet,' said the First stoically. 'We have had the advantage until now. But here, above the gorge, manoeuvrability is an issue, and anyone who falls overboard will be forever lost. The perfect conditions for the Adversary to be victorious.'

'Then let us go below deck and prepare for battle,' concluded Ahren. 'From now on no-one is to go about above deck without armour, weapons or sorcery.'

His command was greeted by nods from his companions, and one by one Ahren and his friends went down into the belly of the ship to arm themselves for the upcoming battle.

Ahren had just finished preparing himself when he saw Trogadon and Jelninolan approaching Hakanu and pressing into the surprised boy's hands a bundle wrapped in oilskin. 'Best wishes for the Spring Festival,' said the blacksmith awkwardly. 'Even if it is only celebrated a week or two later in this region.'

'We went shopping in Cape Verstaad,' said Jelninolan as Hakanu opened up the cloth, revealing two objects. One was a backplate made from Dwarfish Steel and was clearly the companion piece to Hakanu's breastplate. The other was a silver glove, Ahren recognising threads of Deep Steel, which formed into a complex pattern. 'Using what we found, we created these gifts for you.'

Trogadon pointed at the backplate. 'I think we will all sleep easier, if no-one can simply stab you through the ribs from behind anymore.'

'Thanks for putting it so well,' murmured Ahren, a shiver running down his spine.

'Alas, there was not sufficient Deep Steel to forge complete armour, so I improvised a little,' added the dwarf with a grin. 'If we really *do* end up having to hunt down a dragon in the Ice Fields, please ensure that it can only bite you from the front.'

'That's *enough*,' growled Ahren, images of Hakanu's horrific demise now competing with each other in his imagination.

'Thank you,' said the young warrior, trying on the new piece of armour. 'That will reassure my Fox Guards, too, who are always having to cover my back.'

'They will still do so,' countered Ahren quickly. 'A bit of steel covering your shoulder blades is not the same thing as having eyes at the back of your head. Don't get too cocky, lad.'

'Perhaps the glove will reassure you,' said Jelninolan, smiling at the Forest Guardian. 'It is a very simple example of Elven sorcerous art, but considering the little time and material I had, I am very proud of it.'

Hakanu slipped the glove over his hand and then moved his fingers experimentally. 'It's a perfect fit and looks quite nice,' he said politely, his voice nonetheless reflecting his bafflement.

The elf smiled forgivingly. 'Pick up your spear,' she said. The apprentice reached for his weapon, his eyes widening in surprise as the pattern on his glove lit up as soon it made contact with the engraved spear, making it seem as if the remnants of moonlight had been woven into the Deep Steel threads.

'The glove will reinforce your magic,' explained Jelninolan. 'It is attuned to your spear, meaning that from now on it will be much easier for you to throw the weapon – and for it to return to your hand.'

Hakanu raised his weapon over his shoulder to test out the glove, only for Ahren to leap forward with a groan. 'Please – do *not* test out your spear inside the ship, lad!' he scolded. 'I can already see myself having to explain to Admiral Refelbek why a hole has suddenly appeared in the hull of the *Queen of the Waves*.'

'There are two empty barrels on deck which had been used for storing food,' said Trogadon, rubbing his hands with glee. 'Why don't you use those as targets?'

Hakanu nodded enthusiastically and hurried after the chuckling dwarf.

'They're like little children,' said Khara, grinning.

Ahren turned to Jelninolan and gave her a big hug. 'Thank you,' he murmured. 'Anything that stops Hakanu from running headlong into the front lines is like a gift from the gods.'

The priestess smiled and was about to reply when there was the sound of heavy wood splintering, followed by jubilant cheers from both Trogadon and Hakanu.

'It seems to me that the glove is operational,' commented the First dryly. 'Maybe the greenhorn will remain sufficiently far back from the line of battle so as not to be hacked into a thousand pieces. Unless he still needs to be chewed up by a Carapace Whale before he finally learns his lesson.'

Ahren sighed bitterly. 'Could you all *please* refrain from talking the death of my apprentice into existence?' he asked, the Forest Guardian now at the end of his tether. When at last a merciful silence descended on the room, he breathed a sigh of relief – only to hear more splintering followed by another cheer from Hakanu.

'Now I really *am* unbeatable!'

Chapter 11

The attack began so suddenly that at first Ahren didn't know what was going on. One moment, the ocean was non-descript beneath the leaden clouds, the teeming rain peppering the choppy waves, only for the ocean to suddenly seethe with Dark Ones while the sailors on the foremost ships shouted anxiously.

Ahren peered southward through the diffuse light of the chilly day and spotted a line of Sabre Rays gliding in formation above the decks of the leading war carracks.

This cannot end well, said Culhen anxiously, the wolf having abandoned his usual curled up position on the fo'c'sle and joined his friend at the railing. *There is no place on deck where they can evade the attackers.*

Ahren looked on in dismay as countless soldiers and mariners threw themselves down on the planks while the living echelon of Dark Ones flew towards them, any contact likely to cause serious injury to those on board. Suppressing a groan, the Forest Guardian saw the stings of the rays whipping down between the prostrate soldiers, and even from a distance, he could see blood spraying up in all directions. Some of the Dark Ones were slit open from below by swords and boathooks, but those creatures sliced in mid-flight aimed, even in their struggle to remain alive, straight for the unfortunates on deck, causing as much bloody mayhem as possible. By the time the surviving Sabre Rays dived into the water again, only every second defender was able to get to their feet.

'This is a massacre,' murmured Ahren tonelessly, the warning bugles of the armada then blasting from all directions. Waves of dark, identically shaped, gliding bodies washed over the decks of the surrounding ships, leaving bloodied corpses in their wake, Ahren looking over at the dying lights of the Bane Lanterns, their beams having been ineffective, anyway, in the pallid gloom of the rain-soaked day.

They waited until our sorcerous fire could no longer protect us, he thought. *But how is it that the Sabre Rays are working in such a co-ordinated manner?*

It must be the work of a High Fang, mustn't it? asked Culhen running from one side of the fo'c'sle to the other so that he could peer down into the water in all directions. *But how is that possible? How can he survive out here on the cold high seas, not to mention the Ravenous Maw? Surely, the current alone would have pulled the High Fang away.*

Ahren was about to reply only for an array of shiny, oily creatures to break through the surface of the ocean close to the prow of the *Queen of the Waves*, shooting into the air with a deadly elegance. Instinctively, Ahren reacted by unshouldering *Fisiniell* and planting in quick succession three arrows into the Sabre Ray rising directly before him, the creature being stunned by the force of the impact and falling backwards into the spray. 'Come to me, Culhen!' he roared, and when he heard hurried footsteps from below, he yelled: 'Stay below! For the love of the THREE, the rest of you, stay *below!*'

Two more arrows shot harmlessly over the Dark Ones, the creatures having minimally altered their flying altitude to evade the projectiles. As they approached with their deadly outer edges, they tried to close the gap that Ahren had created in their formation, gliding from left to right as they neared the Forest Guardian and his loyal wolf. Ahren gritted his teeth and pushed himself in front of Culhen, glaring at the Sabre Rays coming ever closer.

Ahren... the wolf protested, but the Paladin had already dropped his bow and drawn *Sun*. He stared coldly at the ray that was swerving towards him and forced himself to glide into Pelneng.

The wall of steel, he replied, raising his blade above his head.

You want to parry this thing? asked Culhen incredulously. *Can we not simply throw ourselves down on the planks or make a run for the hatch...?*

No time, countered Ahren, and then the moment of truth was upon them. The *Wall of Iron* was simply a masterful sword manoeuvre, converting the momentum of an overhead two-handed strike into a vertical parry, bringing the incoming object to a dead halt just in front of the body. Originally conceived as an emergency strategy when taking on a particularly heavy weapon, Ahren had never been the defensive move's greatest fan. Khara never used it during her two-handed displays, and the Forest Guardian generally preferred to dodge his enemies' blows when possible. He hadn't practised the *Wall of Iron* for moons – or even years.

And now he wanted to put his faith in this uncertain technique against an enemy for whom it had never been invented.

No, Ahren! said Culhen. *Lie beneath me and let us hope that my armour will protect us against the spikes!*

The red, glimmering eyes of the Sabre Ray approaching them burned like two unholy candles, Ahren's field of vision now taken up by the monstrous creature that was making its silent downward glide.

Three paces.

Ahren took a deep breath, filling his lungs with as much air as possible.

Two paces.

The Paladin gripped the hilt of his Wind Blade. *Be hard as steel but don't seize up.* He remembered Khara's stern advice. *The strength must flow.*

One pace.

The blade-like gristles of the creature neared his chest like the swinging scythe of a giant. His Deep Steel ribbon armour would perhaps withstand the impact, but the ray would slide along him and up to his neck...

Half a pace.

Ahren let his Wind Blade sink vertically at the very moment that the Sabre Ray, expecting a feint, twitched its stinger.

The blade hit the hard, sharp gristle dead on, Ahren releasing the stored air in his lungs in the form of a quick, explosive scream while simultaneously compressing all his energy into his arms and wrists.

Into the *Wall of Iron.*

Thanks to the momentum of the ray, the sharpness of *Sun,* and the tension in Ahren's flesh and bones, the beast was sliced cleanly in two. For a heartbeat, Ahren lost his balance and Pelnang shattered as several hundred stone of muscle and its accompanying inertia collided with his body, but then he felt Culhen's head in his back, his loyal wolf supporting him from behind to keep him from falling.

I am here, said the animal worthily, and never had Ahren heard more wonderful words. *I will hold you up.*

It's working! exclaimed Ahren, his weapon plunging further and further into the enormous creature, whose momentum was contributing to its own death. To Ahren's left and right, meanwhile, the deadly line of gleaming bodies continued their glide through the unequal skirmish, the young man ignoring the blood and whatever else was spurting over him as he continued to maintain his parry until the two halves of the Sabre Ray landed with a smack on the soaking deck of the *Queen of the Waves*.

Gasping, Ahren stood there, allowing his body some time to recover once the danger had passed, before turning round. It was as if he had to order all the muscles in his body to free themselves of the tension he had imposed on them, and when he finally managed to look at the remaining rays, he found himself staring at open-mouthed, wide-eyed mariners. Many of those on deck had fled to the safety of the gap that Ahren had created with his Wind Blade, while Ahren's friends stood by the hatch that they only now climbed through.

'Master...' gasped Hakanu, nodding weakly at the dissected ray. 'You...you...slew...'

The First reacted before Ahren had a chance to speak, the veteran prodding with his forefinger the armoured chest of the apprentice, who was bursting with pride. 'Don't. You. Even. Think. Of. Imitating. That. *Ever!*

Ahren could only silently agree with the old Paladin, while fervently hoping that Falk wouldn't storm over and scold his erstwhile apprentice for his cavalier behaviour in front of the assembled crew.

'For the *tenth* time,' said Ahren in the safety of Refelbek's cabin, 'none of it is my blood.'

'What on earth were you thinking of?' hissed Khara angrily. 'Employing the *Wall of Iron* against a beast weighing hundreds of stone? It's almost impossible to perform the parry against a heavy weapon, let alone an enormous Dark One.'

'Culhen was with me,' replied Ahren reassuringly. 'And anyway, I had no other choice.'

'Well, at least the bards will have something else to sing about – assuming we get out of here alive,' said Trogadon, opening the door of the cabin wide enough so that he could peer outside. 'They're still moving along out there,' he grumbled before closing it again.

'We are incapacitated,' announced Refelbek grimly, looking around the overcrowded cabin in which Ahren had sought sanctuary, along with his companions and any sailors who hadn't managed to flee below deck before the Sabre Ray attack. The stench of the blood seeping under the door was almost unbearable, while the air within the room was suffocatingly sticky. From time to time, Ahren heard the heavy scraping of sharp gristle against the wood as Dark Ones glided alongside the outer walls of the cabin. 'Every ship is currently progressing without a single sailor on deck,' added the admiral anxiously. 'The ships' wheels are firmly fixed with rope, but it is only a matter of time before the vessels start colliding – now that there is no-one to react to unexpected changes in our course.'

'Can we ignite the Bane Lanterns?' asked Falk, looking at Uldini and Jelninolan.

'Alas, no,' said Uldini.

'Or to be more exact, we *can*, but it is too bright for the magical light to be effective,' added Jelninolan.

'And what about rain clouds?' asked Bergen, looking at the elf. 'So that the fires of the Wrath Elves can perform their noble, life-saving mission with sufficient darkness?'

'You're talking in a roundabout way,' complained the First. 'Is Karkas in your head again?'

The Ice Lander nodded. 'He is sitting on top of the main mast, and what I can see through his eyes is causing me as much fear as it is him.'

'Using rain clouds would cost us a lot of energy,' said Jelninolan. 'And it could only be a temporary solution. We are still at least three days from the Ice Fields. There is no way that I can maintain a bad weather front for that long.'

'A short-term solution would suffice, as far as I am concerned,' countered Refelbek. If we cannot steer our ships, the Thirteenth Armada will soon be a tangled wreckage of sinking ships – all of them on their way to the Ravenous Maw.'

'Thank you for putting that image into my head,' grumbled Trogadon. 'We dwarves *always* sink to the seabed – as you all well know. And that is a *very* long way down, here of all places.'

Jelninolan produced her Storm Fiddle and looked over at Uldini. 'If the Adversary attacks…'

'…I will know how to defend us,' said the Ancient, finishing the sentence with considerable gravitas. 'Even if I have to evacuate a ship and perform an Unleashing.'

'Something else that no-one wanted to hear,' said Trogadon irritably, nodding toward the fearful faces of the mariners in the room, who were whispering anxiously to one another.

'There is another question that we should ask ourselves, the answer to which may provide a genuine solution to our problem,' said the First, staring at the nervous mariners, who lowered their eyes and fell silent. 'Where is the High Fang that is controlling these rays? They are incapable of launching such a co-ordinated attack of their own volition.'

'Might there be a spy on board one of the ships?' asked Khara, Uldini groaning with frustration as the sailors began murmuring again, this time casting suspicious glances at their neighbours.

'Jelninolan and I have, over several days, checked every single vessel several times with a charm net,' said the Arch Wizard. 'There are *no* High Fangs or Dopplers within the armada,' he added firmly.

'Then it has to be underwater,' said Bergen, shaking his head as if in disbelief at his own words.

'Is that even possible?' asked Hakanu.

Uldini narrowed his eyes and nodded indecisively. 'It would have to be a High Fang who accidentally received the gift of being able to live below the surface whenever the Dark god touched him.'

Falk snorted in disbelief. 'So we are looking for one among how many? A thousand? Ten thousand?'

'*I* would hide a unique commander, who would present a decisive advantage in a specialised battlefield for as long as possible – until I really needed them,' said the First in his familiar coldly analytical tone. 'High Fangs do not age as quickly as normal humans. He or she could have been swimming around in the ocean for a *very* long time practising their skills on individual ships without our knowing of their existence.'

'The Dark god is afraid that we are going to reach the Ice Fields,' said Ahren. 'I could clearly sense it when his magic swept over us, extinguishing the Bane Lanterns. If he really does have such a High Fang among his servants, then he is going to put them to use here and now.'

Using his new glove, Hakanu impatiently grasped his spear, which was lying on the admiral's table. 'Right then, Jelninolan is going to conjure up a storm, the Lantern Frigates will keep the Dark Ones at bay, and we are going to slay this High Fang?'

'What a nice, *simple* plan,' said Bergen ironically, grinning at Hakanu, who nearly burst with pride. 'I'm all in favour of it.'

'Except that we cannot see what lies beneath the surface by the light of the Bane Lanterns,' interjected Khara. 'The sea is like a black mirror in their reflection. Have you forgotten?'

'Then we shall extinguish the lanterns ourselves,' said Ahren, the others staring at him as if he had suggested that they ride to the Ice Fields on the backs of the Sabre Rays.

'Would you mind explaining that to us in a little more detail?' asked Uldini in a sickly-sweet voice. 'Your suggestion seems well...somewhat...*hasty*.' Ahren was sure that it was only the fact that the mariners were listening respectfully which had prevented the Ancient from using more colourful language.

'The first thing that we will do is to secure the ships under the cover of the lanterns and the storm,' said Ahren, beginning to formulate his idea. 'Then all those with good eyes and the requisite long-range weaponry and fighting skills will climb up to the crows' nests of the armada and keep their eyes peeled for the High Fang, while we all pretend that the Bane Lanterns have broken down.'

'The High Fang will then – confident of victory – launch a fresh assault giving us *one* chance to locate him or her,' said the First, following Ahren's train of thought. 'One clean, well-placed arrow should suffice – and then we will have solved a very big problem.'

'Let me get my crossbow,' said Trogadon enthusiastically, but Jelninolan caught him by the beard as he was about to open the door.

'You're forgetting that we are really going to have to extinguish the Bane Lanterns for our deceptive manoeuvre, and that the Wrath Elves – who are the only ones that can light them again – are hiding below deck for as long the Dark Ones are slaying anyone who dares to come out into the open,' warned the elf. 'If we don't find the High Fang because he or she doesn't rise to the surface, then we could well cause our own downfall.'

'It has only been the Sabre Rays that have attacked us thus far,' said Refelbek, shaking his head. 'With this plan, you are to all intents and purposes inviting the enemy to send forth the Monster Eels and Carapace Whales to finish us in our vulnerable state.'

'It gives me no pleasure to say this,' countered Ahren dryly, 'but we could hardly be any more vulnerable than we are now. This High Fang is holding back the rest of his or her troops. Probably until the first of the ships sustains damage. A warship might well survive a Carapace Whale ramming her once, but two carracks that have collided with each other would be easy prey.'

'We should make the bait more tempting for the High Fang,' suggested Yantilla, who had been listening in silence up to that point. The gaunt woman was covered in blood, Ahren not daring to ask her if it came from one of the Ice Wolves. 'How about we *pretend* that two of the ships have collided with each other?'

This High Fang is a hunter, pondered Culhen. *And what is their prey in this forest full of ships?*

'The Queen of the Waves,' said Ahren in response to his wolf, his answer immediately earning him the undivided attention of the others. 'Our ship must be involved in this supposed collision. If that doesn't tempt the High Fang, then I really don't know what's what anymore.'

'Because we're not running enough risks as it is with this plan,' snarled Uldini sarcastically.

'We are jeopardising the survival of the entire armada as it is,' said the First matter-of-factly. 'Either we play it completely safe, or we do everything at our disposal to kill this High Fang.' The veteran nodded approvingly at Ahren, the Forest Guardian suddenly wondering if he had gone too far with his idea. Any plan that the First considered worthy was normally nefarious – and that was putting it mildly.

A heavy silence – but for the creaking cabin walls – fell over the interior of the room, until suddenly, they heard a distant cracking sound to the west.

Trogadon yanked open the door, immediately flinching as a dark body sailed over the deck directly in front of him. The dwarf raised his hammer, smashing it into the Dark One, sending it crashing against the mast, from where it fell onto the planks, thrashing and stabbing.

'Bastards,' grunted the blacksmith. 'If I only had enough time, I could slay them all from this doorway and…' His voice trailed off as he looked west.

Bergen cursed loudly. 'Karkas has seen two war carracks colliding,' reported the Ice Lander darkly. 'Their crews are trying to separate the ships…'

'…but Dark Ones are swarming around them like flies around a corpse,' said Trogadon, his voice as cold as ice. 'Both rays and eels are hurling themselves at anything moving on the decks.'

Bergen and Trogadon gasped simultaneously. Before either of them had the chance to speak, another crack sounded, which transformed into splintering and bursting.

'A Carapace Whale,' whispered Bergen. 'Carried along by the full force of the current, it rammed into where the two carracks were wedged together.'

Ahren didn't need to ask what was happening now. The horrified looks on the faces of his two friends spoke volumes. 'Jelninolan – please conjure up your tempest,' he asked calmly, a powerful melody immediately filling the room as *Mirilan's* hypnotic melody rose to the heavens, driving the clouds into a rage and transforming the incessant drizzle into a downpour. The world suddenly darkened, and even without Refelbek having to sound the signal, the creaking of the Bane Lanterns opening was audible to all.

Ahren turned to his friends and saw the same determination on their faces that he was feeling. 'Let us hunt down a High Fang,' he said in a low voice. Then he stepped out into the tempest with *Fisiniell* in his hand.

The first part of their plan had been effortlessly implemented, but this had been the easy part of the enterprise. Refelbek's signal lanterns had transmitted the intentions of the Paladins to the other captains of the Thirteenth Armada, and the remaining ships were as well protected by the Bane Lanterns as was possible, considering the powerful current of the Ravenous Maw. Meanwhile, the best marksmen and -women among the crews, whether with bow and arrow or crossbow, had climbed up the crow's nests from where they could lie in wait.

Ahren, Falk, Hakanu, Bergen, and Trogadon were all crouching in position high above the *Queen of the Waves*, holding their breaths and waiting for the point of no return. Soon Refelbek would give the signal to extinguish the Bane Lanterns while simultaneously causing his vessel to collide with the *Lady Aruti* in a feigned accident. Jelninolan would then immediately cause the tempest to die down so that the sun would break forth from behind the clouds, giving Ahren and the others the opportunity to spot in the sunlight the High Fang that they were certain was controlling the hordes of Dark Ones.

For a heartbeat, Ahren was filled with fear that they were on completely the wrong track, and that the behaviour of the Dark Ones was down to the direct will of the Adversary, who had ordered his rabble to hunt them down on the ice-cold waters, but then the young man calmed himself down with a simple piece of common sense – *if* the Dark god really was present here, then Ahren and the other Paladins would have sensed him by now. It was simply a High Fang at work – and all they need to do was to locate him or her.

Refelbek's signal sounded – three extended blasts of the bugle, each one fading out at the end – and immediately loud shouting emanated from the Lantern Frigates as the sailors expressed their feigned dismay at the now flickering Bane Lanterns. Simultaneously, the Wrath Elves quenched the runes on the brackets holding up the sorcerous fire and which protected the flames from conventional rain. Very quickly, the tempest did its work, the glimmering red which protected the armada being extinguished.

The yelling mariners on the ships' decks hurried down into the safety of the holds, Ahren unable to stop himself from chuckling at their exaggerated performance – these sailors would have no problem finding work as bards or strolling players if they wished to change careers.

'It's starting,' murmured Falk, nodding down at the first Sabre Rays shooting up out of the water to begin their deadly attacks. 'And now Refelbek is initiating his part in luring our prey.'

Ahren sensed the *Queen of the Waves* drifting to starboard and getting dangerously close to the *Lady Aruti*. Then the Forest Guardian dropped unceremoniously to the floor of the crow's nest as the two ships collided. The barrels that had been discreetly tied to the outside of the railing burst and splintered under the force of the impact, creating a sound suggesting that the damage to the two vessels was considerably worse than it was.

'We have sprung a leak!' bellowed Refelbek, ensuring that this voice echoed far across the waters, hopefully reaching its intended target. 'Tie up the ships and mend the hull, or we will all end up in a watery grave today!'

'Let's hope that the good admiral hasn't conjured up an ominous fate for us,' said Trogadon, peering over the edge of the crow's nest to see if he could spot the mysterious High Fang.

'Search, Karkas,' whispered Bergen, who was sitting cross-legged in the middle of the basket. 'Find what is hidden to us.'

Ahren, too, looked down at the churning waters, hoping that Bergen's falcon, who was circling high above them, would use the keenness of his eyes to catch sight of the invaluable prey, whose death might mean the survival of the fleet.

'If anyone sees him or her, react immediately,' murmured Ahren to the others while he concentrated his attention on the east. 'Who knows for how long the High Fang will be visible – so, shoot first and then call out.'

'But no over-hasty actions, please,' warned Falk. 'If arrows, bolts, and spears all rain down on the water from up here, our ruse will be revealed faster than one can say *missed*!'

'Speedy but precise,' murmured Trogadon, summarising the situation. 'In other words – same as usual.'

Ahren glanced quickly at Hakanu, but the face of the young warrior showed utter concentration and no sign of impatience. It seemed that his protégé understood the importance of their mission, and that the only important thing was that they kill the High Fang – it didn't matter a whit *who* performed the deed. Reassured, the Forest Guardian fixed his eyes on his section of the ocean again, listening to Bergen's mumbled words as he did so.

'Karkas sees movement below the surface,' said the Ice Lander in a dignified voice. 'That is one hell of an army of Dark Ones making its way towards us.'

Ahren narrowed his eyes, recognising shadowy movements in the water, but he was unable to make out details. The sun had not yet proved victorious over the abating storm, and the water seemed murkier than it really was. 'Come on, come on,' he whispered. 'What's keeping you, you stupid High Fang.'

'Well if *that* doesn't tempt him out, then I'm a Swampling,' muttered Falk sarcastically.

'Whale from the west!' warned Bergen, the others all immediately turning to look.

Ahren's heart missed a beat as he spotted the brawny shadow approaching at great speed. The Carapace Whale had to be at least fifteen paces long and almost half as wide. The pale skin of the creature was so pockmarked by barnacles that the monster seemed to have been afflicted by some terrible disease that had infected its whole body. Ahren felt a sudden wave of pity as he saw what the Dark god had inflicted on his servants to make them even more dangerous and deadly.

'It is going to collide with the *Lady Aruti* in twenty heartbeats,' said Falk, figuring out the speed of the beast that was gliding towards the mid-starboard side of the ship below the waterline like a travelling reef.

'We are lucky in misfortune, the Lantern Frigate being between us and this thing.'

Anxious cries echoed across from the tall ship to Ahren and the others, the Forest Guardian observing how the crew were furiously trying to prepare themselves for the inevitable collision with the colossus.

'Even if it's difficult,' warned Falk, 'keep your eyes on the water. With a little luck, the High Fang, too, will want to observe this spectacle and show their ugly visage.'

Ahren concentrated on his search again, but his eyes, as though they had a will of their own, kept glancing back at the approaching pockmarked whale. When the monster finally slammed into the wall of the Lantern Frigate with an almighty crash, the *Queen of the Waves*, which was tied to her, was also thoroughly shaken – so much so, in fact, that it took the occupants of the crow's nest considerable effort not to be thrown out of the large basket.

Ahren struggled to his feet once the ships had settled, then looked out to sea again. Monster Eels and Sabre Rays were breaking through the surface around the supposedly crippled ships, the whale, meanwhile, having descended into the depths again, presumably with the intention of launching a fresh assault.

'They are cutting us off from the rest of the fleet,' said Bergen grimly. 'From Karkas's point of view, the manoeuvre is obvious.'

Ahren perused the scene, recognising immediately what the Ice Lander meant. The sea around the ships was teeming with Dark Ones, and two more whales were smashing into ships, splintering timbers everywhere. While the solidly constructed Lantern Frigates could withstand a ramming relatively unscathed, the lighter war carracks suffered considerable damage with each impact. Their crews, unable to defend themselves, could only cower helplessly below deck, and it was clear to Ahren that with every moment that passed, the balance was tilting more and more in favour of the Dark god's army.

'Has anyone spotted anything yet?' he asked through gritted teeth as the first carrack split in two, a whale having rammed her a second time, screaming sailors tumbling into the water where Dark Ones and certain death awaited them.

'Not yet,' replied Hakanu, whose voice trembled with the same trepidation that the Forest Guardian was feeling.

'Stay calm,' said Falk, and Ahren was unsure as to whether his erstwhile master was addressing him or Hakanu. 'The mariners are doing their work, horrible as it may seem, so let us concentrate on doing ours. They are depending on us being successful, so keep staring down at the water and find this High Fang.'

Falk's soothing tone gave Ahren new courage, and he dedicated himself to fixing his eyes on the little portion of water below. A small shadow glided just below the surface, but even as Ahren was about to yell triumphantly, the Paladin recognised it as being the body of a sailor which the current of the Ravenous Maw was pulling away into the unknown.

Again and again, the sound of wood breaking could be heard as the pockmarked whales continued their dreadful work, and when two carracks almost simultaneously splintered like toys in the hands of an angry giant, Ahren resolved to abandon their plan.

Culhen pushed his way into the young man's mind, giving him the strength to carry on, however, while the wolf and the other friends, as well as the animal companions listened to the unequal battle from the *Queen of the Waves'* belly. *I will never, ever go to sea again,* complained Culhen, Ahren immediately recognising his friend's words as nothing more than a deliberate distraction.

To be honest, I think I've had enough of sailing, agreed Ahren anxiously. *At least, for as long as we cannot see the coast reasonably close by.*

No, continued the animal after pondering for a moment, *it has been decided. Once we get back to Jorath, I will never allow my paws to touch the deck of a ship again.*

By now, Jelninolan had caused the storm to abate, the sun beginning to break through the clouds, casting its golden rays on the surface of the water.

'Karkas can see something. 'The hoarsely whispered words of Bergen yanked Ahren out of his private conversation with Culhen. 'There was a humanlike outline in the water – I am sure of it.'

'Could it perhaps have been a corpse?' asked Trogadon without looking away from the ocean, his crossbow nonchalantly against his shoulder. 'For there are far too many of them floating about the place.'

'I am certain,' insisted Bergen. 'Look out towards the north-east for a particularly large Sabre Ray. A slim, manlike figure is hanging from its barb and allowing itself to be pulled along through the water.'

'That explains how the High Fang can resist the current over an extended period,' murmured Ahren broodingly.

'There – ahead!' whispered Hakanu excitedly, pointed to where Bergen had told them to look. 'I've seen him too.'

'Don't indicate,' growled Falk. 'Just throw.'

'He is far too fast,' said the apprentice, shaking his head. 'The ray is pulling him through the water at lightning speed.'

Ahren and the others stood in a semi-circle around Hakanu and looked down in the north-easterly direction close to the *Queen of the Waves*.

'At the stern,' whispered Bergen, Ahren then able to catch his first brief glimpse of their prey. A slim, almost gaunt figure was holding onto the tail of an over-sized Sabre Ray, which reached the length of eight paces or more. The unequal duo disappeared below the stern of the ship, the Paladins and the dwarf then scanning the water where they reckoned the High Fang and his unusual mount would appear again.

'Hakanu is right,' muttered Ahren, scowling. 'The pair are too fast for us to be able to hit the High Fang.'

'Then let us dispose of the Sabre Ray first,' said Trogadon, briefly stroking his crossbow. 'A bolt in the back will slow it down considerably.'

Falk shook his head. 'Then the High Fang will be forewarned, and he will disappear in the depths.

'Two salvoes,' said Ahren curtly. 'In quick succession.' He pointed at Trogadon and Hakanu, then at Falk and himself. 'The large missiles at the ray, then the flexible arrows into the High Fang.'

'Risky,' murmured Falk, his voice almost being drowned out by the splintering sounds from another escort ship, whose keel then snapped into three pieces. 'Let's give it a try,' he added immediately.

'Karkas sees the pair,' reported Bergen anxiously. 'They are circling us and the *Lady Aruti*. I think our High Fang is trying to assess the damage that was caused by our supposed collision.'

'Presumable he wants to be able to issue suitable orders to his whales,' growled Trogadon.

Ahren's nervousness increased. 'Then our ploy will soon be unmasked. 'If the High Fang sees that there is only the wreckage of barrels floating in the water...'

'He will be coming into view imminently,' interjected Bergen. 'At the stern of the *Lady Aruti,* in three, two, one...'

Ahren extended *Fisiniell* and stared at the area indicated. His entire world shrank to that tiny spot in the water, now glittering in the sunshine. He slipped into Pelneng, inhaling and exhaling deeply. Beside him, Hakanu raised his spear, Falk drew his bow, and Trogadon levelled his crossbow. Then the outline of the ray came into view and Ahren whispered: 'Falk and I will shoot the very moment that the High Fang lets go of the ray's barb.'

'My swift bolt will follow your powerful spear, lad,' murmured the dwarf to Hakanu. 'Your throw will be the signal for me.'

Hakanu breathed a 'yes', pulling his spear arm back. Ahren drew *Fisiniell* as far as possible, following the outline of the High Fang with the tip of his arrow.

'Now!' cried Hakanu hurling his arm forward.

At that moment, there was a deafening collision below, the Paladins and the dwarf being thrown up above the crow's nest as the *Queen of the Waves* bucked like an unbroken horse.

Water, thought Culhen, panic-stricken. *There is water everywhere here!*

Ahren sensed a feeling of weightlessness as his flight upwards slowed to nothing and he found himself in the merciless embrace of gravity again. Even as Culhen's eyes informed him that water was springing up through the floor of the hold where his friends were sitting tight, his own body dropped back into the basket and he landed painfully on Trogadon, who had slammed onto its floor below him. Fortunately, still having his wits about him, he grabbed the screaming Hakanu, who was falling out of the crow's nest, the painful yank as he prevented his protégé from tumbling to his death almost ripping his own arm off. With a groan, he pulled Hakanu by the leg, Falk and Bergen helping him to haul the deathly-pale young warrior back into the safety of the basket.

'What...' gasped the winded Trogadon, pulling himself to his feet. 'What was *that?*'

'Kamaluq is in a panic,' murmured Hakanu, horrified. 'He says we are sinking.'

Bergen shook his head in dismay. 'That had to have been a Carapace Whale,' he muttered. 'It must have rammed us from below.'

Ahren bent down to pick up *Fisiniell*, which was, luckily, still in the crow's nest. 'Your spear?' he asked Hakanu urgently. 'Did you already throw it?' If the High Fang had been warned, then their cause was lost. Yet, even with the sinking ship below them...

Jelninolan is playing against the surge now, announced Culhen, who was standing knee-deep in water. Ahren saw that many of his friends in the hold had suffered cuts, including Khara. They had all painfully hit the deck above them thanks to the collision. *Kill this High Fang,* urged the wolf. *Another ramming like that and we'll all end up in the monster's mouth.*

Ahren shuddered as he looked expectantly at his apprentice. 'Your spear?' he asked again.

'Kamaluq is so afraid,' whispered the young warrior, swallowing hard. Ahren saw how Hakanu was struggling to pull himself together. Then the boy stretched out his gloved arm. The apprentice's spear came flying almost perpendicularly back into his hand. 'It hit the deck,' mumbled Hakanu, his teeth chattering. 'The impact threw me off balance at the last moment.'

'Let us thank the THREE for small mercies,' said Falk vehemently before showing the others his empty hands. 'Unfortunately, my bow is somewhere down on the main deck.'

Ahren looked first at Bergen, then Trogadon and Hakanu. 'The plan remains the same,' he murmured defiantly. 'Karkas finds this High Fang – you two stop the ray.' He gripped *Fisiniell* harder. 'And I will finish off the bastard that is causing us so much trouble.'

The others nodded, Ahren then placing a reassuring hand on Falk's shoulder, the old man nodding encouragingly before sitting down beside Bergen so that he wouldn't be in the three marksmen's way. 'Let us complete the mission,' said Ahren, forcing himself then to wait patiently for Bergen's next call. The whale lurking beneath the *Queen of the Waves* could ram again at any moment, and then...

'West,' hissed Bergen. 'Directly west. He's heading straight for us.'

'Because he wants to watch our downfall from close quarters,' said Ahren grimly, extending his weapon. The outlines of the two creatures were clearly visible. The ray was pulling his human shadow towards the *Queen of the Waves* in an almost playful manner.

'Whenever you're ready, Hakanu,' whispered Trogadon, the apprentice's spear immediately whizzing forward, uttering a vibrating hum as the young warrior's throwing magic was amplified thanks to his new glove. 'Wow,' gasped Trogadon, immediately pressing the trigger. 'My bolt will hardly be able to keep up.'

Ahren took no notice of the ray, nor was he concerned whether his friends had hit their target. The only thing that interested him was the spindly human body stiffening at the precise moment that it released itself from the Dark One's barb. Ahren adjusted his aim one last time and let *Fisiniell* sing as the High Fang spun in the water and prepared to descend into the ocean's dark embrace.

Like a flashing length of silver, Ahren's Deep Steel arrow shot through air and water, then through flesh and bone. A heartbeat after the Forest Guardian had let go of his weapon's string, the scrawny outline of the High Fang was nothing more than a silhouette, now subject – along with all the dead mariners of the Thirteenth Armada – to the fathomless greed of the Ravenous Maw.

'Done!' gasped Ahren, grasping onto the rail of the crow's nest to keep his balance.

'Good shot, young man!' exclaimed Falk proudly, and for a brief, precious moment, they were master and apprentice once more.

'And no-one acknowledges *our* hits,' grumbled Trogadon, albeit good-naturedly. 'Both Hakanu and I caught the ray in its head.'

'Would you like a medal for it?' barked Falk, grinning broadly. 'You're supposed to be good with your hands. Well, make yourself useful and patch up this ship before she sinks.'

The dwarf looked demonstratively down at the water, where Sabre Rays and Monster Eels were looking for prey in an uncoordinated manner, with feuding among the Dark Ones breaking out in no time at all. The authority of the High Fang being now non-existent, only murderous instinct remained – and something else, which Ahren couldn't quite put his finger on.

Hunger, said Culhen, whose fear had been transformed into peeved irritability. *What you are looking at is hunger beyond measure. I bet you that the High Fang had driven his army onward for days on end without allowing them to feed.*

As if to underline the point, a Carapace Whale swimming close to the *Queen of the Waves* surfaced, immediately grabbing two contorting

Monster Eels with its toothy mouth before sinking into the dark depths of the Ravenous Maw. Like a neglected, overworked army of mercenaries, whose hated commander had fallen, the Dark Ones were no longer inhibited, tearing into each other with gusto, Ahren looking on in silent horror as the Adversary's horde ripped one another asunder.

'When the force is broken, nothing but chaos remains,' murmured Hakanu, Ahren glancing at this apprentice in surprise. 'An old saying from the Green Sea,' added the young warrior. 'It is supposed to remind us to always serve the deities *willingly*. Everything else ends in disaster.'

Ahren said nothing, contenting himself with placing his arm on his protégé's shoulder, the pair of them watching how two heavily armed groups of sea soldiers and sorcerers accompanied the Wrath Elves to the main masts of the Lantern Frigates. As dusk fell, the flames burned brightly again, their red glow hiding the horrific feasting that was continuing beneath the surface.

Seven carracks had been destroyed and the *Queen of the Waves* badly damaged. But Ahren comforted himself with the hope that they had broken the resistance of the Dark god sufficiently for them to continue to the Ice Fields unhindered.

***

Revenge glided deeper and deeper into the Ravenous Maw until even the darkness of the water yielded to the mysteries below, and strange, irreal lights – like a multicoloured firmament of the abysmal sea – illuminated the pitch blackness. Revenge sensed living beings in his midst, creatures that had never seen the surface of the sea, never having even ventured more than half a league upward. This was a realm of its own. Whether forgotten by the gods or simply a first attempt from the early days of Creation, it mattered to Revenge not a whit. The only thing important to him was the precious fire which was burning in an ever more violent glow of angry red that only he could see. He sensed its powerful outlines more than he could see them, but Revenge never worried about things such as size or danger. He slipped into the spirit of the slumbering being that had rested for so long on the ocean floor that it had become a part of the seabed. Eyes, several paces wide, opened as Revenge took his place in its red core, which glimmered in the primitive understanding of the beast and was a veritable *banquet* for this child of the Dark god. He seized the dark hatred of the monster, pulling and tearing at it until its toothy mouth turned and pointed upwards.

There, whispered Revenge almost inaudibly, communicating more through vague images than through language, filling the stupid beast's mind with his own thirst for retribution – transmitting his desire that retaliatory action be carried out against those responsible for the death of his brothers. *There they are – those who have earned your wrath.*

A powerful flap of the fin caused Revenge's new vassal to break forth from the ocean bed, and begin its cumbersome movements – like an avalanche, moving upwards now instead of rumbling down.

Revenge rode in the head of his newest weapon, up to that distant, distant world far away from the depths, rejoicing with every fin flap in the knowledge that he was being brought closer and closer to his unsuspecting victims.

Closer to their imminent demise.

Chapter 12

'She certainly isn't for the scrap heap, but I don't think we can describe her as perfectly restored,' said Trogadon, wiping the beads of sweat from his face with a rag and pointing at the planks, which had been nailed as reinforcements to the broken timbers on the floor of the damaged storeroom of the *Queen of the Waves*. The dwarf looked at Ahren and the rest of his companions, who were all standing in a circle around the spot where the whale had almost broken through. 'Two paces closer to the middle and the keel would have snapped like a cheap wooden sign in a barroom brawl.'

'Can we proceed on our voyage?' asked Refelbek, staring grimly at the area, five paces by eight, where his vessel was also being held together by thick steel bolts and Dwarfish tar.

'It would be better not to,' said Trogadon, scratching his sodden beard. 'The next storm could finish the *Queen of the Waves* off if these planks aren't able for the powerful waves.'

'Should we evacuate then?' asked Ahren, unable to quite shake off the feeling of suffering a defeat. He had experienced so much on this ship – good and bad – and abandoning her here on the ocean seemed wrong to him, no matter what his rational mind told him.

Ahren, said Culhen irritably. *Look at this damage. I'm waiting all the time for a Dark One to stick his head in.*

'We will take everyone off the *Queen of the Waves*,' said Refelbek, turning to face the Paladins present. 'Seeing as the pack ice is not too far away anymore, I propose that we transfer all those on board to one of the Flame Belly ships.'

'Are they not overcrowded already?' asked Falk sceptically. 'The stowage is already extremely limited on account of the magical chamber in the prow and all the expedition gear in the stern. Also, if I'm not mistaken, there is a contingent of mercenaries on each of these ships alongside the normal crew.'

The admiral nodded curtly. 'In a perfect world the two Flame Belly ships would melt the pack ice and the *Queen of the Waves* would follow in their wake. She would be narrow and nimble enough for the task, while her armaments would more than suffice. But because I am not going to permit you to sail on a badly damaged vessel, and the Lantern

Frigates rule themselves out on account of their width and weight, there is only one other option – to transport you on one of the war carracks.'

'Absolutely not,' said the First. 'One of those nutshells would capsize as soon as a Glower Bear sneezed in her direction.'

'Oh, come now – you exaggerate,' countered Bergen.

'Maybe,' admitted the war veteran. 'But precisely how many attacks from one of those barnacled whales did it take to split one of the Cape Verstaad naval vessels like a rotten melon?'

'Alright, alright,' muttered the Ice Lander. 'We can release a few of the mercenaries from the Flame Belly ships.'

'Not possible, I'm afraid,' said Refelbek, coughing apologetically. 'Grandessa Nabaltur, who lent us both vessels, insisted that her personal guards remain on board her ships. Clearly, she wants to bask in the glory, should your search prove successful.'

'What do *we* care?' barked the First irritably. 'Those of them who don't toe the line will be put on a tender and sent on their merry way back to Jorath.'

'The sorcerers driving both the Flame Bellies and the ram bows in the pack ice care,' said the admiral, shrugging his shoulders. 'They are on the payroll of Grandessa Nabaltur. Without their support, it will be up to Master Uldini and Lady Jelninolan to keep the ships above water.'

'Thank you, but no thank you,' replied Uldini promptly. 'We will simply divide ourselves up on the two ships – that way, there should be enough room for everyone.'

'We didn't want to separate, remember?' interjected Khara anxiously. 'We should stick to the plan.'

'The Ice Wolves will go to the second Flame Belly ship,' said Yantilla, who had been listening in silence to the conversation, as had been her habit recently. Ahren suspected that the gaunt woman's mind was often elsewhere – namely with a certain wan Paladin, who was roaming about somewhere in Jorath. 'There are not so many left now, and I will have no difficulty finding accommodation for them.'

Ahren shuddered. Over the past few moons, the risk of an untimely end had become an ever-present danger for the Ice Wolves.

Refelbek considered the commander's suggestion before responding. 'That should work,' he murmured. 'It will take a little time and plenty of complex fleet manoeuvres, but I think in one or two days enough room will have been made for us to evacuate most of the *Queen of the Waves*.

A skeleton crew of volunteers accompanied by a small escort will then sail the vessel back to Cape Verstaad, once all the preparations have been completed. Until then, the flagship must remain, insofar as this is possible, the heart of the fleet – that way, the morale can be kept high among the crews.'

'During the manoeuvres the other weather sorcerers and I will keep the sea calm,' said Jelninolan before leaving the cabin holding *Mirilan*.

'Then we had better start packing,' said Khara, pointing at Muai. 'I don't think my tigress is going to close her eyes even for an instant before we are off this ship.'

The big cat uttered a low growl, making it clear to everyone that Khara certainly wasn't exaggerating. The animal then strolled out the door and onto the deck with Culhen and Kamaluq in her wake.

We will wait by the railing until you all are ready to free us from this death trap, muttered Culhen curtly.

Ahren sensed the unease and helplessness behind the wolf's words, the animal having been condemned to unaccustomed passivity for moons now. *It's only another few days,* said Ahren, comforting his friend and feeling a sense of joyful anticipation on his own part. *Then we will be on the pack ice, and you can run around in front of the Flame Belly ships to your heart's content.*

The emptying of the *Queen of the Waves* proved far more complicated than Ahren had anticipated, for he hadn't considered the difficulties caused by the Ravenous Maw's powerful current. Dinghies were practically useless, the rowers being unable to battle their way forward whenever they wanted to go from east to west, which meant that the goods and people were instead passed from one ship's deck to the next, whenever the armada's formation enabled two vessels to come very close to each other.

Ahren was standing on the deck of the *Xuan-Foi* watching the ship's strict captain when Khara touched his hand and pointed excitedly towards the south.

'Is that the coast?' she asked.

Ahren craned his neck and shielded his eyes from the sun with his hand. In the distance he could make out a faint, mysterious glitter stretching along the entire horizon. He wasn't quite sure how to respond, but then Bergen sauntered up beside them with a broad grin and nodded at the white ribbon in the distance.

'The start of the Ice Fields,' he said cheerfully. 'And not a moment too soon. *Alina's Rage* is now being tied to the other side of the *Xuan-Foi*. By this evening we should be able to settle into our new quarters.'

'My admiration for Refelbek is growing with every day that passes,' said Ahren, finding it difficult to take his eyes away from the distant ice mass. 'If it was easier to pass us from one ship to the next – no less than five times – than to manoeuvre a Flame Belly ship alongside the *Queen of the Waves*, then maintaining the formation of our armada must be far harder work than I would ever have believed.'

'He didn't want us to have to pause in our voyage,' commented the First from his position in the middle of the deck. 'This saved us a full day's journey, *and* the Armada is still battle ready. Those are two things that I appreciate about this man – even if I found him initially to be most irritating.'

'You find everyone irritating,' countered Falk with a chuckle.

'Only those who don't do exactly as I say,' retorted the veteran cuttingly. 'And such people were few and far between in Jorath before Ahren turned up.'

The young Forest Guardian bowed ironically and for a fleeting moment he thought he saw a hint of a smile on the First's wrinkled face.

His aeons' old mission is coming to an end, said Culhen, the wolf barking impatiently at the sailors who were tying the ships to each other. *His joyful anticipation of locating the final Paladin must be a thousand times greater than yours.*

Or yours, added Ahren.

As long as I get away from this water, we can look for ten more Paladins as far as I'm concerned, said Culhen fervently before licking his chops. *Hopefully, we can go hunting on the Ice Fields. This dried meat is beginning to taste like rotten Pallid Frog.*

Ahren's thoughts began to turn to the next stage of their journey. The ocean challenges lay behind them now. Since the death of the High Fang, only the occasional Dark One had been spotted. The Ravenous Maw formed a natural barrier which those creatures had as little desire to negotiate as any other sea creatures.

Now a world of frozen water awaited them, where their greatest enemies could well be freezing temperatures and hunger. *And a dragon.*

The thought that he had tried so hard to suppress flashed through his mind. *If the First is correct in his analysis, then somewhere in the white vastness there is a decidedly cranky dragon.*

Ahren and his companions stared in disbelief at the compact cabin, almost fully taken up with hammocks and narrow bunkbeds. They had stuffed their belongings into any nooks and crannies they could find, but there was still an untidy mountain of their possessions in the middle of the little room.

'Well, this is going to be *really* uncomfortable,' muttered Trogadon, scratching his beard helplessly.

'Ahren and I will sleep in the hammocks in the centre of the cabin,' said Khara. 'Then Muai and Culhen can lie beneath us.'

Can't we go back to the Queen of the Waves? asked the wolf unhappily. *I promise that I won't mention the gaping hole in its side ever again.* The animal snorted and shook his head. *Yuck, what a stink in here! Do these mercenaries never wash themselves?*

Ahren glanced over his shoulder, spotting two of the uncouth fellows, both resembling bandits with their short spears on their backs as they eyed the new guests on board *Alina's Rage* with far from welcoming looks. Had it not been for the blue and black tabards that indicated they belonged to the house of Nabaltur, Ahren would have been convinced that he and his friends had been stranded in a den of thieves.

The two hired warriors were now blatantly ogling Khara from behind, Ahren immediately moving forward a threatening half pace towards therm. Immediately, they disappeared down a narrow, doorless passageway – a characteristic of the vessel's interior. There were twelve or so such cabins down in the steerage, all of them with thick walls and reinforced by steel struts, each little room filled to bursting with equipment and people.

'Don't start complaining too soon,' said Bergen with a groan as he heaved his rucksack onto one of the upper bunks. 'We are going to need every last bit of the nourishment and armour that is stored down here – and to be honest with you, I have no objections to having a few additional spear throwers on our side.'

Well, I would prefer my Ice Wolves, thought Culhen. *At least, they are house trained and well brought up.*

Ahren suppressed a grin and moved to step out of the cabin only to find himself facing another pile of rucksacks which were waiting to be stored in their cabin. 'You know what?' he said irritably. 'Culhen and I will sleep on deck. My cloak will keep me warm, and ever since we have sailed into colder climes, Culhen's fur has been flourishing like weeds.'

Good idea, agreed the wolf, trampling unceremoniously over the pile of possessions as he left the cabin. *As far as I can remember, the fo'c'sle is the only place on the ship with a little free space.*

Kamaluq and Muai sidled out into the passageway, Khara looking pertly at her Forest Guardian from the side. 'If you leave a little room for me under your cloak, then I will join you all. With all that fur around us and the magic leather as a blanket, we should be able to withstand any weather.'

'Not bad training for when you have to overnight on the Ice Fields, at any rate,' said Bergen with a grin. 'Also, it means that *we* will have more room here.'

To the sound of laughter from his friends, Ahren and Khara made their way to the hatch leading up to the fresh air. A squat, broad-shouldered warrior crossed in front of them. He had a moustache which was plaited at both ends, his shaven head providing a sharp contrast. The silver lining on his tabard suggested that he was one of the mercenary officers.

The man narrowed his eyes on seeing Ahren, then stopped and stood with his legs apart, straddling the passageway and clearly having no intention of getting out of the Paladin's way. 'So, *you* are the posh ladies and gentlemen who are the reason why we have all travelled to the ars—, uh…the *far e*nd of the world, is that right?' he snorted, his heavy accent Ahren recognising as typical of the Southern Sunplains.

'We are those who are honoured to have you accompanying us,' replied the Paladin diplomatically. 'And you are?'

'Hungry,' retorted the fellow, laughing at his own joke.

Charming, opined Culhen, who was already up on deck. *Should I come back down and shove him sideways with my muzzle? He might get the message then that he's nothing but a hindrance.*

'If he doesn't wish to introduce himself, then so be it,' said Khara coolly, clearly annoyed by the man's manner. She glided elegantly past both the Paladin and the mercenary, the latter watching her then in stunned silence. 'I will be waiting on deck,' added the Swordsmistress, glancing back over her shoulder and winking at Ahren before disappearing through the hatch.

'Well, tickle me pink,' muttered the sturdy fellow. 'She is more slippery than an eel.'

'Princess Khara is the bearer of a Warrior Pin,' said Ahren matter-of-factly. 'That gives her a certain authority.' He was immediately annoyed at himself for not being able to adopt a friendlier tone to this rough and ready fellow. He made another attempt: 'By the way, I am Ahren, the Thirteenth Paladin,' he added, smiling amicably and offering his hand.

The man reacted with a shrug of his shoulders. 'Posh gentlemen like to give themselves posh names,' he said dismissively. 'I couldn't care less who I am shedding blood for as long as the gold is right.'

Ahren blinked at the fellow, not knowing what to say in response. The stranger was surely an example of those people who couldn't think of a world beyond their own personal needs. If something wasn't immediately relevant to them, then it was of no importance whatsoever. 'You *do* know that we are at war with a god, don't you?'

'Balderdash,' said the warrior, shaking his head, his moustache plaits swinging wildly. 'That ne'er-do-well isn't a real god at all. He's only carrying *on* as if he is.'

Ahren was flabbergasted. 'Yes, but—'

'And if he is only *pretending* to be one, then might not the "Champions of the god" be frauds too?' asked the man, before spitting on the floor. 'Sounds logical, doesn't it? Maybe you don't *really* need thirteen of you to finish off the Adversary – only one *proper* warrior with a good weapon.' With that he casually tapped his spear

'You are welcome to test out your theory,' replied Ahren irritably.

The man waved dismissively. 'I'm earning my livelihood already by guarding the ship for the battle-axe Nabaltur,' he said. 'Someone else can construct a Pall Pillar or whatever as far as I'm concerned.' Then he stepped towards Ahren, clearly expecting the Paladin to make way for him.

Please can I bite him? asked Culhen sulkily. *Only long enough for him to understand his place?*

His place is here on this ship, replied Ahren, pressing himself against the wall to let the stranger pass. *And you know something? Maybe he will end up saving our bacon in the end – it doesn't really matter what his real motivations are or for whom he is fighting.*

Not if the gods are merciful, said the wolf darkly. *If I have to be saved by him, then I won't deserve to be called a companion animal.*

Ahren went up on deck and pulled back the hood of his cloak, hoping that the cold sea air would drive away his feeling of annoyance, which his unpleasant encounter with the squat mercenary had aroused in him. He looked around *Alina's Rage* and was surprised to see so few sailors. Then he spotted two sorcerers wearing bright-blue fur robes who were standing on the afterdeck, deep in conversation. Ahren ascended the low wooden steps, silently hoping that talking with them would be a friendlier affair.

'Thirteenth,' said the one of the sorcerers, bowing low in greeting. 'This is such an honour.' The rotund, dark-skinned man had seen thirty winters or so, and had a weather-beaten, open face which boasted a long and sharp nose. 'I am Captain Ounlamun, and this is my first mate and cousin, Harrebon.' He nodded at the younger and slimmer sorcerer by his side, who bore a slight resemblance to the older man.

'So, you believe the myth that I am a Paladin, do you?' asked Ahren somewhat sarcastically before immediately silently scolding himself for making such a petulant first impression.

Ounlamun laughed, however, while his cousin's face broke into a grin. 'I see you have met Master of the Mercenaries Deklar then,' countered the captain, shaking his head regretfully. 'Nothing is holy to him apart from what fits into his moneybag. If the world was to end tomorrow, he would do nothing but curse loudly at not having received his salary.'

'What a nice fellow he is,' said Ahren with a scowl.

'You should see him and Caldria when they are together,' said Harrebon, still grinning. 'Talk about hate at first sight!'

'I really must get to know this Caldria then,' countered Ahren with a smile.

'You will find her in the flame chamber in the prow of the ship,' said Ounlamun affably. 'She is the one who keeps our dragon heated.'

Did someone say something about dragons? asked Culhen nervously, Ahren's face then speaking volumes causing both sorcerers to guffaw.

'It's a nickname for *Alina's Rage*,' explained the captain.

'How did she get such an unusual name?' asked Ahren curiously.

Harrebon grinned yet again. Clearly, the man spent half his life with a smile on his face, the Forest Guardian feeling suddenly a little jealous of the sorcerer with his sunny disposition. 'Grandessa Nabaltur is blessed with a daughter by the name of Alina, who has inherited her mother's temperament. The old lady had these two Flame Belly ships built in honour of the striking qualities of her heir.'

'Alina's Rage and *Alina's Malice,'* added Ounlamun. 'It is self-evident that we wish our lady and mistress a long and healthy life.'

'And that we be allowed to settle up north as soon as her daughter takes over the running of the house,' added Harrebon, grinning even more broadly – if such a thing were possible.

Ounlamun raised a warning finger and the younger man fell silent. 'Should you need anything, Thirteenth, you will always find at least one of us here, for this ship would otherwise sink like a stone if a storm blew up and would hardly make progress even in calm seas.' He pointed at a magic circle that was burned into the wooden timbers of the deck, just behind the ship's wheel, within whose circumference Harrebon was standing. 'If neither of us is standing here, then you know that the ship is in trouble.'

Ahren nodded, bowed politely, and left them to their work. It seemed that at least the two sorcerers were genial, the Forest Guardian mentally resolving to steer clear of Master of the Mercenaries Deklar as much as he could, discussing any matters pertaining to the ship with either the captain or his cousin instead.

Master of the Mercenaries? muttered Culhen, Ahren then hearing the wolf's snort echoing across the entire deck. *What a pretentious title for someone with only a handful of fighters at his disposal.*

Leave it, Ahren replied as he climbed up to his wolf, Khara, and the other companion animals on the fo'c'sle. The wind was bitterly cold here, Ahren immediately covering his head with his hood.

'You're such a wimp,' chuckled Khara, who had made herself comfortable in the mountain of fur which Culhen, Muai, and Kamaluq had created. The wolf had lain down at the front railing, where he served as a windbreak, presenting enough of his stomach so that one could cuddle into him. Muai was lying across the Swordsmistress's legs, while the fox was snuggled up on her stomach, enjoying the fact that she was tickling him behind his ears.

'Well, *you* certainly don't look as though you need a magic cloak,' said the Forest Guardian with a grin before settling down beside his beloved, spreading his sorcerous garment so that they were both warm and snug.

'This is nice,' said Khara, sighing contentedly in her mummified state.

The sky began to darken under the mantle of night, while the Bane Lanterns resumed their fiery watch.

'Do you think Hakanu is jealous because we have his fox up here with us?' pondered Ahren.

Khara giggled. 'The little fellow always slips away to his Paladin at night and returns to Culhen and Muai when dawn is breaking. I think he is torn between Hakanu and these two clucking hens.'

Muai growled irritably in response, glaring at Khara with her green eyes, Culhen making do with a sulky *puh*.

The fox, on the other hand, looked almost pleadingly at Ahren, the young man then stroking him gently before picking him up and setting him down on the deck. 'Come on, then, little lad,' he murmured. 'Don't let anything come between a Paladin and his companion animal.'

Kamaluq whimpered once before hurrying off to the hatch.

Oh, it is so difficult once they have grown up, said Culhen wistfully, and when Ahren guffawed in response, the wolf punished his friend for the rest of the night by ignoring him completely in icy silence.

***

Revenge steered his new toy ever upwards towards the surface, drowning out the creature's instinct to avoid the lower water pressure with visions of voraciousness and envy. He wove the shadows of the ships above them into his primal host's dull consciousness, in the form of an illusory picture of a hungry shoal of whales.

They are invading your patch, he whispered. *They are taking your food. And yet, they themselves are nothing but nourishment for you!*

The monster that he was controlling reacted by flapping its fins and increasing its tempo, the suffering in its veins transforming itself into a rabid frenzy.

Revenge chortled with vengeful glee, delighting in the images of Paladins being ground to a pulp by giant teeth as they screamed and drowned in the ocean waters. He fixed his eyes on the ship above, which he knew contained the prey that he was seeking.

This shadow, he whispered. *Gorge yourself on this one first!*

***

Ahren was jolted out of his sleep by a cry of pain and was on his feet a mere heartbeat before Khara. He saw Jelninolan come tumbling out of the hatch, and the blood running out of her nose and ears seemed almost black in the reddish light of the Bane Lanterns. 'What the…?!' he exclaimed as he and his dumbfounded beloved hurried over to the elf, who had dragged herself over to the railing and was now looking down into the water.

'Ye gods!' she whispered, the rest of Ahren's companions now hurrying up on deck from the ship's interior, accompanied by a handful of sailors and mercenaries. The former seemed shocked, while the latter were standing around on deck in their underclothes, staring suspiciously at the priestess.

'We have people here who would like to *sleep*,' complained Deklar coldly. 'Having females on a ship is nothing but trouble – I've always said so – what with their constant screeching and wailing.'

Ahren was silently relieved that the dwarf was more concerned for the health of Jelninolan than the nonsense that the mercenary had spewed, the blacksmith making do with meting out a casual punch as he hurried past, which cost Deklar nothing more than losing a tooth and his consciousness.

'What's wrong, my heart?' asked the blacksmith anxiously, while Uldini stopped the elf's flow of blood with a tiny spell that he cast without the assistance of *Flamestar,*

'Danger…' murmured Jelninolan before collapsing in a heap. 'An ancient being…'

'A leviathan?' asked Ahren hesitantly, remembering a similar encounter on the Cutlass Sea.'

Jelninolan shook her head, then nodded. 'Yes…no…different…' she stammered.

Ahren was about to ask what the priestess meant when he was afflicted with a sudden, stabbing headache which almost caused his knees to buckle and give way. Everyone around him except for Trogadon groaned in pain, Uldini immediately causing *Flamestar* to come to fiery life. The golden rays drove the pain away, meaning that Ahren was able to think clearly again. He leaned over the railing, looked down, and instantly regretted having done so.

The Forest Guardian was certain that what he saw would remain with him to the end of his days, haunting him in the dead of night whenever sleep didn't come easily, and his infrequent dreams were filled with forgotten fears. A small, angry, red sun was blazing far below him in the water, lighting up a skull-like, scaled ancient creature, whose pallid eyes and grotesque jutting teeth were surely the personification of that fear which every man and woman felt who had ever fearfully traversed the oceans of Jorath asking themselves what was the worst sort of monster that lurked in the unknown, hidden depths of the ocean.

The dimensions of this monster were enormous, and in contrast to the peacefully gliding Leviathan of the Cutlass Sea, this creature from the dawn of creation was moving up towards the surface at speed.

Directly towards the fleet!

Ahren, whimpered Culhen. *Do something, Ahren!*

The panic and helplessness of the wolf was almost tangible, but the Paladin felt as helpless as his four-legged friend. How could he take on this *mountain* hurtling towards them?

'*Uldini!*' gasped Ahren, beckoning the Ancient to the railing. 'Please tell me that you can help with your magic.'

By now, Ahren's friends and some of the mariners had looked down into the water, too. The horror was evident in their faces, some of the sailors, both men and women, now sobbing quietly or throwing up.

Uldini floated momentarily over the railing, glanced down, and hurried back to the relative safety of the ship. 'Horrible little fiend,' he said, but the untypical quiver in his voice betrayed the unease of the Arch Wizard. 'Jelninolan…?' he whispered, but the elf merely shook her head resignedly.

'I am trying to communicate with him, but he is so *angry*,' she said, her voice quaking. 'As if our ships had hurt him terribly and he has come to seek his revenge.'

'You had better think of something quickly,' said Ahren, having peered down into the ocean again. The bony face of the predatory sea being was easier to make out now, and Ahren could see that the red sun that seemed to be leading the creature on was connected to it by means of a fleshy stalk. The being was so mysterious that it could just as easily have been the product of a feverish dream. Alas, it was all too real and coming closer all the time. Already, it was opening its mouth, and Ahren realised to his horror that an entire ship would fit easily enough into the monster's maw.

'Jelninolan, Uldini!' he urged. 'We must do something – now!'

The two Ancients were turning to him with looks of bewilderment on their faces when the impossible happened – the leviathan broke through the surface, causing a veritable flood wave as it did so, then swallowed the ship that it had been targeting in one go!

The literal shock waves of the attack created a deadly succession of peaks and troughs, which the cumbersome Flame Belly ships were only able to withstand because of the spells being roared out by the chanting Wind Sorcerers. While Ahren battled to maintain his balance, he was fighting against a terrible vision that had taken hold of his mind – a vision that was both unfathomable and agonising at the same time. The *Queen of the Waves* – and all who were on board her – was gone! Crushed and swallowed by this primeval beast that was now biting wildly right and left, using its tailfin to smash to smithereens one war carrack after another. The creature's body was enormous – at least sixty paces long, its back decorated with curved barbs, the remains of rocks sticking to some of them, reminders of the seabed from where it had risen to assault the Thirteenth Armada.

Ahren's mind was numb with shock as he tried to remember if the Ice Wolves had remained on board the *Queen of the Waves* or if they had been transferred to the other Flame Belly ship.

Uldini, standing beside the dumbstruck Paladin, raised *Flamestar* aloft, a powerful beam of fire shooting out from the crystal ball which, in view of the enormity of the opposition, seemed like nothing more than a spark trying to ignite a massive, rain-soaked oak tree.

By now, the First had climbed up to the sorcerers on the aft deck and was brusquely issuing orders. Immediately, they changed their incantation, *Alina's Rage* jolting suddenly forward – away from what remained of the armada and the raging leviathan, which was continuing to wreak havoc.

Ahren's numbness snapped like an over-extended thread, and he stormed up to the First. 'What do think you are *doing!*' he roared at the war veteran.

'I am saving us,' replied the old man, nodding out towards the foaming sea with its hardly recognisable ships. Now the fishlike monster was swallowing the rear of the *Lady Aruti,* Ahren having to look away as the sound of splintering timbers echoed across to them. 'It wasn't for no reason that the *Queen of the Waves* was the first vessel to be rammed. The Adversary set out to attack us with the leviathan. If we hadn't changed vessels because of the damage, then...'

Ahren felt dizzy as for a brief moment he observed the massive jaws wrapping themselves around the whole ship before...'

Stop! interjected Culhen wildly. *Your thoughts are leading us to despair, which can only hinder your decision-making.*

Ahren gritted his teeth and forced himself to look at the armada, now consisting of nothing more than fifteen ships. Then he drew his Wind Blade and positioned himself at the stern.

'What are *you* doing?!' shouted the First in alarm from behind.

'*You* saved us,' said Ahren dryly. 'And now I am going to save anyone that I can.' He raised his blade high and bellowed in as loud a voice as he could manage: 'PALADINUM THEOS DURALAS!'

***

Revenge revelled in his victory. Father's plan had worked, and the flagship of the Armada was in the belly of his compliant fool.

The beast continued wreaking carnage thanks to the whisperings of the Adversary's child, even though the splintering timbers and the lack of seabed water pressure was damaging the innards of the leviathan more and more.

Revenge gloried in the orgy of violence as he imagined himself returning home to father and reporting back the simultaneous demise of several Paladins.

Then suddenly a beam of light shot down from a solitary ship to the south. A beam that hurt Revenge to his very core, accompanied as it was by a cry that threatened to rip the child apart, so great was his fury.

'PALADINIM THEOS DURALAS!'

The Paladins were still alive!

Revenge prodded and pulled at the understanding of the slowly dying leviathan, aiming his enormous weapon on a new, southerly course. These accursed Paladins were laughing in his face!

They would pay for it – they would *all* pay for it by ending up in the belly of the monstrous sea beast.

***

'Well, isn't this great,' muttered Trogadon flatly. 'Now he's heading straight for us.'

'Did we want him to continue destroying the armada?' retorted Ahren defiantly.

'You *do* realise that this thing is faster than we are?' asked Bergen nervously, pointing at the huge waves that the racing leviathan was creating.

Ahren turned to Jelninolan beside him, the elf having gathered with the others on the aft deck. 'Can you assist the sorcerers with the sails?' he asked the Storm Weaver hopefully. He had acted without thinking, and he only prayed now that his impulsiveness would not mean their imminent demise.

'No. The sails would rip,' said the elf, much to his horror. 'But I *do* have an idea,' added the Ancient hesitantly, Ahren believing that he had never heard a more beautiful sentence in his life.

'This thing is getting closer all the time,' said Khara grimly. 'Whatever the idea is, can you put it into effect quickly?'

'And to think that we used to all be terrified of Fjolmungar,' said Trogadon airily. 'At least I was able to put *him* off for a little with a bolt. The shooting from the armada doesn't seem to have bothered this fellow here one little bit.'

'You talk too much,' grunted the First, glaring darkly at the dwarf.

'Only when I'm terrified,' was the blacksmith's quick response, accompanied by a shrug of his shoulders. 'And anyway, Jelninolan is going to rescue us all,' he added, glancing over at the priestess. 'Isn't that right, my heart?'

'I cannot injure the leviathan,' she said absently, setting *Mirilan* on her shoulder.

The leviathan was no more than five furlongs from them now and was looming like a towering cliff behind them. It took only another few heartbeats for the bow wave of the approaching monster to reach the stern of the ship, the vessel pitching further and further forward, struggling twice as hard against the waves that were hitting her from the front.

'Jelninolan,' urged Uldini, 'now it really *is* time that you started.'

The elf nodded and began to play. 'I am going to need your energy,' she said, the Ancient floating beside the priestess and placing his childlike hand on her left shoulder.

Jelninolan began playing a ponderous melody, which seemed to repeat itself again and again, it's ending blending seamlessly into its opening, and when the elf lifted her bow off her Storm Fiddle, the slow-sounding notes continued to play. Ahren gasped in astonishment when Jelninolan then began to make circular movements with the bow of her magical instrument as if she were stirring an invisible cauldron.

Or is she stirring an ocean? suggested Culhen, thoroughly impressed. *Look.*

Ahren's eyes widened in surprise as he saw how every circular motion of the elf seemed to create a swirl, precisely between the ship and the approaching leviathan.

'We must stop,' murmured Jelninolan as if in a trance, the First breathing in sharply in response.

'We are in the process of *fleeing*,' he barked. 'Stopping is hardly going to help matters.'

Ahren, however, bellowed out the command to the two Wind Sorcerers. He silently applauded them for obeying him without question, even though he had a sneaking suspicion that they considered any further attempt at escape to be impossible anyway.

Jelninolan's movements with the Storm Fiddle bow were now gaining in strength and speed, the melody adjusting its tempo accordingly – seemingly controlled by some invisible hand. The whirlpool behind the ship was becoming larger and deeper with every passing heartbeat, until it finally became a raging monster, threatening to swallow the leviathan whole.

There was something forced and driven about the behaviour of the giant creature, and Ahren was now no longer certain that the Adversary was behind the arrival of the primitive being. The scaly colossus fought its way through the swirling waters, finally passing the deepest point of the maelstrom with considerable effort, Ahren's heart almost stopping when he finally realised that Jelninolan's plan would ultimately fail.

'Child of Creation, listen to my voice!' whispered the elf. 'The gods have given you a home – return to where you came from forthwith.'

The tailfin of the leviathan was working non-stop, bringing the creature ever closer to the now loitering ship. The Wind Sorcerers had their hands full as they fought against the whirlpool's current so that the vessel would not herself fall victim to the conjured-up force of nature.

'Child of Creation, listen to my voice!' intoned Jelninolan once more, Ahren not failing to hear the exhaustion in the voice of the Storm Weaver. 'Into the deep with you, forthwith!'

The leviathan uttered a dissonant hissing sound, and the young Forest Guardian then saw blood spurting out of the creature's mouth and eyes, each fountain large enough to drown a fully-grown man.

'Into the deep with you!' said Jelninolan again, the echo of her power pushing through her command with such force that Ahren flinched instinctively. The leviathan continued to fight its way forwards, the teeth of the extraordinary creature no more than ten paces away from the railing at the stern. Ahren could see a splintered main mast sticking into the gum of the monster like a toothpick, and he squeezed Khara's hand with his, digging his other one into Culhen's neck fur, below the wolf's armour. It was as if he was gaping into the maw of a god who was threatening to swallow the whole world.

'CHILD OF CREATION, LISTEN TO MY VOICE!' thundered Jelninolan at the enormous, terrifying sea monster, the light and cold that the priestess was now emitting causing Ahren to groan in pain. 'INTO THE DEEP WITH YOU!'

A shudder went through the colossus, and Ahren was unsure as to whether it was the maelstrom that caused it to stop, or perhaps it was rather an invisible controlling ribbon that finally ripped thanks to Jelninolan's command, thereby granting the age-old creature its freedom. Suddenly, the leviathan gave up trying to fight, allowing itself to be drawn, slowly but surely by the powerful whirlpool, down into the deep.

Down into the deep where it belonged.

***

Revenge ranted and raved in the whirling waters, cursing beyond measure the pathetic creature that had freed itself from his control, thanks to the command of the elf priestess. The leviathan had been too stupid to feel genuine cravings for revenge, and because every moment on the surface of the water had been sheer torture for the primitive beast, it had been only too happy to choose peace and quiet over bloody retribution.

Revenge had given his all while trying to carry out father's plan, and his own strength was gone after all the whipping he had done, trying to propel the sinking colossus forward. He waited until the elf's whirlpool had died down before ascending like dark wisps of clouds in the dead of night.

Revenge had learned his lesson. He stretched his senses southward, searching for a spirit genuinely simmering with a desire for retribution.

When he found it, a deep, malicious feeling of satisfaction welled up within him.

***

The night was already retreating, and the moon little more than a faint memory on the horizon, which was shimmering a gentle pink, but still Ahren and his friends had not yet found peace. Together with their companion animals, almost all of them stood packed together on the fo'c'sle as they continued to talk of the events that had befallen them only a short time before.

'I still cannot believe that the *Queen of the Waves* and the admiral are gone forever,' said Hakanu, shaking his head.

It seemed to Ahren that his protégé had been hit hardest by the sudden loss of the ship and her crew. The apprentice's hands were shaking, while Kamaluq pressed into the legs of the young warrior, whining sympathetically. Hakanu's eyes seemed unnaturally big, Ahren wishing that he could ask Jelninolan to calm down his apprentice by magical means, but the elf was lying in a deep sleep, guarded in her place of slumber by Trogadon, who was crouching beside her.

Ahren simply could not find the right words to comfort Hakanu, so badly was he shocked himself by the staggering losses that they had suffered overnight. With Culhen's help, he had gone over the events of those terrible moments, when the leviathan had raged beneath the armada, and he had silently calculated the number of ships that had been lost to the ocean. It was certainly more than fifteen, which meant that hundreds of mariners and mercenaries would never again return home to their loved ones.

Again and again, the young man would gaze to the north, but there was no sign of the other ships in the armada. Whether forced back by the flood waves of the leviathan or dragged away by the current of the

Ravenous Maw, or simply because they were making their way back to Cape Verstaad, beaten and demoralised, the fact remained that *Alina's Rage* was totally on her own now, floating before the shores of the Ice Fields.

The only crumb of comfort that Ahren had found was thanks to the First, who had assured him that the Ice Wolves had been on the *Xuan-Foi* during the attack, and the Lantern Frigate had survived the leviathan's assault – unlike *Alina's Malice*, onto which the troop would have been transferred the following morning.

Ahren forced himself to put his own worrying aside so that he could concentrate on lessening Hakanu's suffering. 'We are doing all of this so there will be no more war with its associated deaths,' he said, his voice sounding hollow to his own ears. Bergen and Falk nodded in silence as they looked compassionately at the apprentice. Khara placed a comforting hand on the young warrior's shoulder, and even Muai pressed her head behind Hakanu's back for a moment.

'We were unable to help them,' whispered the young apprentice, staring down at the spear in his right hand. '*I* was unable to help them.'

'Welcome to reality,' said the First, his voice having the same effect on the silence as a hot knife slicing through a piece of butter. 'Sometimes, we Paladins can do nothing but survive and allow others to die in our place. No individual act of heroism in the world can stop an entire army, and no firm promise can prevent an avalanche from falling. The sooner you realise that not every battle consists of personal acts of heroism, the better. It would have made absolutely no difference if there had been a Swordsmaster or a spear virtuoso standing guard on the *Queen of the Waves* when the leviathan surfaced.' The war veteran fixed his steely eyes on the downcast apprentice. 'All their merits and skills meant nothing once the jaws of the monster closed. Which is why we Paladins must always be on our guard.' His eyes then turned to Ahren. 'You will probably have internalised this lesson once you have spent a hundred years or so exhausting yourself in an endless war.'

'You are so cruel,' complained Ahren despairingly.

'No – I am honest,' countered the First with a shrug of his shoulders. 'The hot courage of your apprentice must be cooled down before he becomes a capable leader possessing grim, cold determination.' The veteran turned away and walked towards the ship's hatch. 'I will go and stand guard over Trogadon. The fact that he knocked out the mercenary leader's tooth is sure to come back to haunt us.'

'Too true,' said Bergen, following the veteran, glancing over his shoulder apologetically at Ahren as he did so. 'This unique fellow that we're stuck with judges quickly and rarely forgives.'

'Thanks a lot,' groaned Ahren before turning to Hakanu, who was still looking down at his weapon. 'The First was unbelievably harsh with me, too, during our first meeting,' said the Forest Guardian reassuringly. 'He cannot bear it when others see the world differently to him. Alas, the core of what he says is undeniable. We cannot save everyone, and some threats are too much for any of us as individuals.' He gently took Hakanu by the chin, forcing the doubtful apprentice to look up at him. 'Which is precisely why the gods have created thirteen of us. So that we are never alone.' He pointed at Falk, Khara, the companion animals, and the unusually silent Arch Wizard. 'And we thirteen have formed friendships and alliances, which in turn have led to new unions.'

Hakanu looked deep into Ahren's eyes, the Forest Guardian convinced that the young warrior was absorbing every word that he was hearing. Here and now, Ahren was speaking *past* the courage, the stubbornness, and the clumsiness of his protégé and appealing straight to the lad's *heart.*

'All these humans, elves, and dwarves are standing by us in our struggle, merging into that which makes us Paladins truly stand out. It has nothing to do with our shining armour or our impressive weaponry, nor even with our loyal animals.

Ah now, here, complained Culhen, Ahren silently vowing that he would make it up to his four-legged friend by giving him a particularly generous grooming later.

'No,' he continued, turning the apprentice so that he was looking directly into the faces of the other. 'It is the *solidarity* that we have formed that accompanies us on our battle to save Creation – a solidarity that is the heart and backbone of our existence. The combined will of all the Jorathian tribes defying the Dark god – *that* is what we Paladins are creating.' Ahren nodded solemnly before finishing his speech. 'And what we are *together* is so much greater than each of us as individuals – a united force that no leviathan in the world can consume.'

Hakanu gulped, nodded weakly, and threw his arms around Ahren, before he started to sob silently, shedding copious tears. The Forest

Guardian had never seen his apprentice so vulnerable. He held the boy in an embrace while the sun began to shine on the horizon, sending a silent message that Ahren so desperately needed to hear.

No matter how dark the night, there was always a new dawn, and it was *always* filled with hope.

Chapter 13

'Welcome to the Ice Fields,' said Uldini, spreading out his arms as if to embrace the unforgiving desert of snow and ice, which stretched to the horizon.

Ahren heard these words with mixed feelings. Since leaving Evergreen, they had travelled through Jorath all the way from north to south, and now they were standing here, looking at the godsforsaken mass of ice ahead of them, which seemed too inhospitable for any living being.

Although the snow-covered pack ice sparkled in the bright sunshine, the rays had no hope of conquering the ever present cold. The air above what seemed like a seemingly endless field of white was particularly pure and clear, thereby accentuating the absence of any life forms on the closely packed icebergs, which appeared to be like a solid landmass from where they were looking. Now and again, however, a piece would break away from the edge of the pack ice, only to be swept away by the current of the Ravenous Maw.

Take closer heed, urged the wolf, turning his nose into the wind, upon which dozens of scents were suddenly apparent, some of them fresh, and some several weeks old.

There are definitely animals, added the wolf. *Dark Ones, too. There are a few scents that smell strangely unnatural.*

Ahren nodded mutely. He had expected that the Adversary would have played around with Creation here, just as he had done on the Isles of the Cutlass Sea. The more remote the region, the easier it was for the Dark god to create new servant mutations, only to cast them aside if they were of inferior quality. 'Let us hope that it won't be as bad as it was on Simian Island,' he murmured, immediately receiving concerned looks from his friends. He gestured vaguely towards the pack ice. 'Culhen smells Dark Ones.'

'Another reason for us to remain on this charmed ship for as long as possible,' said Trogadon before cocking his head. 'Now that we're on the subject, why precisely are we not sailing *directly* into the ice but simply maintaining our position against the current?'

'Because the Flame Belly still has to awaken,' said the captain from behind, Ahren turning to face the man. The Wind Sorcerer stepped up onto the fo'c'sle and pointed sheepishly down at the planks. 'Caldria still has to be informed that we have reached the pack ice so that she can begin with her work. I thought I might leave the honour of doing that to one of you.'

'If I didn't know any better, I would conclude that you are terrified of the woman,' said Falk with a grin.

Ounlamun shook his head yet shrugged his shoulders at the same time. 'Her heart is in the right place but the longer she is cooped up in the flame chamber, the grumpier she gets.'

Ahren shook his head irritably. Now that he thought of it, he had not yet seen this woman, who would be responsible for them making further progress. 'I will go to her,' he said, moving off, his curiosity having gotten the better of him.

'I'm coming too,' announced Trogadon. 'Bergen can guard Jelninolan on his own for a moment, and the change will do me good. If I have to drive away yet another mercenary who wants to ogle over her in her sleep...'

'It's a shame that the cabins in the belly of the ship don't have doors,' said Khara. 'Deklar's spear carriers are a rough lot. I always want to wash myself after one of them has looked me up and down.'

'The troop leader only recruits the scum of the earth for his unit,' said Ounlamun regretfully. 'On the other hand, their reputation as fighters is second to none. Grandessa Nabaltur thought it fitting to put Deklar and his gang on her precious ship, knowing that there very few others equal to the mercenaries in terms of fighting skills, while their reputation for being powerful, rough and ready fighters should be more than enough to put off thieves and pirates. You must remember, Flame Belly ships are invaluable vessels.'

'Just our luck to end up on the vessel carrying the rabble,' complained Khara irritably.

'Far from it,' countered the First curtly. 'I asked around before we left Cape Verstaad. The crew of *Alina's Rage*, too, enjoyed some notoriety. Which was why the Ice Wolves were going to be accommodated on her. That would have ensured some peace during the dangerous passage through the pack ice.'

Ahren sorely missed Yantilla and her loyal men and women, and he prayed that they were making their way safely back with the rest of the Armada to Cape Verstaad. Trimm would take good care of the Ice

Wolves after that – until Ahren and the others returned with Yollock. The Forest Guardian's bodyguards would hopefully be in no danger in the meantime. 'We must make do with what we have...' he began, only for an agonised howl to sound from within the ship, causing Hakanu to suddenly flinch.

That sounded like Kamaluq! exclaimed Culhen anxiously as he and the growling Muai hurried towards the hatch, followed by Hakanu, who had pulled his spear furiously from his back.

'This reeks of trouble,' muttered Falk anxiously, Ahren and the other companions quickly following, with the captain hurrying in their wake.

Even before the Forest Guardian began his descent, he could hear angry snarling and Culhen's loud growling, as well as cursing coming from more than a dozen men. A quick look revealed the passageway between the cabins to be crowded with people. Kamaluq was lying on his side and clearly in pain while one of Deklar's mercenaries was pinned to the floor beneath Muai's paws, Culhen keeping the fellow's comrades at bay with bared and threatening teeth even though the villains had all drawn their spears and were pointing them at the companion animals!

Hakanu shoved his way unceremoniously through the tightly packed passage, his eyes blazing with fury.

'This won't end well,' murmured Ahren to the others as he hurried down the steps. By the time he reached the bottom, Hakanu had already pushed his way forward to the mercenary under Muai's control, the boy now surrounded by a circle of spears – which didn't seem to bother him one little bit. The lad hurried over to Kamaluq, then gently and carefully picked up the young fox, the animal reacting with a low, heart-rending whimpering.

Deklar, too, had by now barrelled his way through from the other side of the passage and was snarly angrily: 'If those creatures don't release Mauk within three heartbeats, stab the lot of them!'

'WHAT IS GOING ON HERE?!'

The thundering voice of the First echoed with a thousand skirmishes' worth of life experience, and no matter how hard-boiled Deklar's mercenaries may have considered themselves, they all turned their faces in shock to look at the veteran, who was standing on the top step of the stairwell staring down at the spear carriers like a father glaring angrily at his unruly children.

'That fleabag attacked Mauk for no good reason!' snarled Deklar furiously, the only mercenary not to have lost his courage in the presence of the age-old Paladin.

'No good *reason?*' retorted Hakanu angrily, still holding the whimpering fox in his arms. 'This lowlife kicked Kamaluq because he was supposedly in the way. And he *laughed* as he did it!'

Ahren was convinced that it was only because his apprentice was so concerned with looking after his fox that the wrong doer was still alive. He quickly glanced at Uldini, who floated forward over the shoulders of the now intimidated spear carriers before placing his hand on the side of the injured animal. The fox snapped once towards the Ancient, but then his pained whimpering stopped, and the little fellow began to lick the childlike figure's hand.

'See?' murmured the Arch Wizard in an unusually gentle tone. 'It was only a few broken ribs. Nothing that Uncle Uldini wasn't able to fix.'

'Falk,' murmured Ahren, looking at his erstwhile master, who was now standing beside him on the stairs. 'The healing charm has clearly had an effect on our friend, and if it should come to a skirmish down here, then…'

'I'll take care of it,' said the old Forest Guardian, pushing his way through the mercenaries, and then carefully guiding Uldini towards the cabin, before which Bergen was standing with an axe in his hand, keeping watch over the sleeping Jelninolan. Ahren followed in Falk's wake until he reached Hakanu, who was holding the now chipper Kamaluq close to his chest while staring balefully down at the mercenary squirming uneasily beneath Muai's paws.

'Chastise your damned animal or I'll do it,' snarled Deklar, raising his spear.

The Wind Blade whizzed even before Ahren realised that he had drawn it. *Sun* severed the wooden shaft of the spear clean through, a hair's breadth above the thumb of the dumbstruck troop leader, the Forest Guardian's weapon being restored to its resting place on his back an instant later. 'You had better put your weapons away or we will have to draw ours,' said the young man in the shocked silence that followed, the mercenaries then immediately dropping their weapons – with the exception of Deklar, who glared at Ahren and seemed to be seriously considering whether he should attack the Paladin with the stump of his weapon.

Unimpressed, the Forest Guardian turned to his protégé. 'What should we do to this fellow?' he asked Hakanu in a loud, firm voice. 'It was *your* fox who was hurt, *you* should decide on his punishment.'

'*Punishment?*' gasped Mauk, still pinned to the floor by Muai. 'It's only a stupid fox…'

Hakanu drew himself up proudly, and at that moment Ahren found himself looking, not at an apprentice, not at a trainee Forest Guardian, nor even at a young Paladin warrior, but at a clansman of the Green Sea.

'Cruelty towards the offspring of Creation is punishable in only one manner,' he said in a serious voice. 'Muai, let him stand up.'

'If this boy touches even a hair of Mauk's head…' began Deklar in a threatening voice, only to be interrupted as the guilty mercenary got to his feet and Hakanu kicked him once, hard in the chest. The loud cracks of breaking bones echoed down the narrow passageway, while the agonised groans of the doubled-over mercenary that immediately followed caused his comrades to flinch instinctively.

'Maybe you will think twice the next time before meting out unnecessary pain,' added Hakanu in a ritualistic tone. 'Your guilt has been expiated and life goes on.' He stretched his hand out to the injured man.

Deklar took a step forward, interrupting Hakanu's gesture of reconciliation, only for Ahren's hand to move threateningly to *Sun's* hilt, the action seeming to prevent the troop leader from attacking the apprentice.

'It would have been better if *you* had thought twice before breaking the ribs of the best spear thrower in our ranks,' growled Deklar maliciously. 'Perhaps his pain will cause him to misthrow his weapon in the next skirmish,' he added, his eyes wandering over meaningfully towards Kamaluq, 'so that it will hit another target – quite *accidentally*, of course.'

Ahren was about to respond, but before he could think of what to say, Culhen rammed his helmeted head into Deklar's nose. Another cracking sound echoed, as did the sound of agonised groaning.

I swear by the THREE, the next time he or one of his bastards threaten Kamaluq, there will be hell to pay, muttered the wolf with such rage that Ahren could not but believe his four-legged friend.

'You lot had better make yourselves scarce now,' said the First, staring icily at the grumbling mercenaries. 'I have had commanders executed for less than what has occurred here. Threatening or harming a companion animal of the Paladins would mean in every Jorathian country the minimum of a spell in the dungeon. If we didn't need you now, it would give me great pleasure to have each and every one of you thrown into the icy waters outside. NOW, GET OUT OUF MY SIGHT!'

The warrior's words proved instantly effective, the mercenaries disappearing into their narrow cabins, although not without throwing accusatory looks at Ahren and Hakanu.

'Well, that really worked out *wonderfully* well,' commented Trogadon grimly, still holding his hammer in his hands and rocking aggressively on the balls of his feet. 'I can't think of anything better than making enemies out of a rabble of ne'er-do-wells in the confines of an overcrowded ship.'

'Let us go and visit this Fire Wizard,' muttered Ahren, trying to hide his rage as he turned towards the prow. 'The sooner this journey is behind us, the faster we will be able to rid ourselves of Deklar and his gang.'

***

Revenge lauded himself as he relished the pain in the ribs of his newest marionette. This Mauk fellow had been bitten by a dog whilst a child and had viewed any animal with fangs suspiciously ever since. It had been the easiest thing in the world to provoke him into kicking the fox so beautifully, and the result could hardly have been better. He sensed the festering desire for revenge within the mercenary against the Paladins and their companions, without the child of the Adversary having to do anything much at all.

Revenge gorged himself on the man's negativity like a predatory animal, fortifying himself on its nutrition while he observed one idea for retribution after another arising in Mauk's mind like rancid bubbles of air in a filthy mire.

The child of the Dark god made himself comfortable, fortifying himself on the burning desire for revenge emanating from the pathetic man. This chappie would undoubtedly prove useful. And once he had burnt himself out, why, there were another twenty vengeful mercenaries on board this ship of wonders!

***

The flame chamber ensured that Ahren quickly forgot his anger towards the mercenaries' attitude. Behind the circular, pitch-black oak door decorated all around with a charm circle, the Paladin encountered a bizarre sight. The floor, the walls and even the ceiling were covered in a layer of thin steel sheets, inlaid with intricate Deep Steel designs. Every rune and swirl connected to each other, forming a highly complex charm circle in the middle of the room at the frontmost part of the prow. The interior of the chamber was – despite a total absence of lanterns – lit up in a warm glow, as if dozens of candles were illuminating the cabin. And as if all this wasn't wonderful enough, in the middle of the masterful charm circle sat a sturdy old woman – snoring loudly on a wooden bunk!

'Well now, I wasn't expecting *this,*' murmured Trogadon, who had entered the cabin with Ahren, the rest of the companions hanging back and standing guard in case any of the mercenaries would try something foolhardy.

'There's even a chamber pot,' whispered Ahren, puckering up his nose, having checked the corners left and right of the round door once he had entered. 'And it's pretty full.'

'You're more than welcome to slop out, lad,' said the old woman in a shrill, quaky voice as she sat up in her bed, before blinking, stretching, and yawning to the point that Ahren could see down her throat. The sorceress scratched herself beneath what once must have been an elegant, red and silver robe, but which was now little more than a filthy tattered rag, hanging loosely over her round frame.

Now that the sorceress was sitting up, Ahren noticed that her hair was shoulder length on one side but shaven off on the other. A contorted talisman decorated her visible ear, while her eyes looked at Ahren with a weary but keen intelligence.

'Hm, neither of you look at all like cabin boys, so I think I would do well to withdraw my offer.' She stood up, trying to tidy her robe as she did so, only to abandon the effort with a shrug of her shoulders. 'May I ask you gentlemen to close the door behind you before formal introductions are made? The magic of the flame chamber does not flow properly when the door is ajar.'

Trogadon quickly did her bidding, Ahren noticing that the blacksmith seemed somewhat intimidated. The dwarf had clearly been reckoning on the occasional artisanal trick, but this cabin seemed to be a work of pure magic.

'I am Ahren, the Thirteenth Paladin, and beside me is Trogadon,' said the Forest Guardian politely, the woman then giving a slight bow. 'It is because of me and my friends that your services have been requested.'

'Caldria, the Blaze Mistress of this ship,' said their opposite number before heavily plonking herself down on her bunk again. She spread out her arms with an embarrassed smile. 'This here is my little fiefdom. This is where I breathe, sleep, eat, and shi—'

'Yes, indeed,' interrupted Ahren, glancing at the chamber pot. 'Are you telling us that you are never allowed to leave this cabin?'

The sorceress laughed on hearing the consternation in his voice. 'I am not a prisoner,' she said with a chuckle,' but I really have no desire to do double the amount of work.' She gazed at Ahren before cocking her head. 'You *do* know that almost every sorcerer in the world can only master one type of magic in their life, do you not?'

The Paladin nodded.

'And that we all strive to learn the most mightily impressive charm possible?

'What are you telling us?' asked Trogadon impatiently.

Ahren could sense the disillusionment in his friend without having to look at him.

The Blaze Mistress shrugged her shoulders again, which gave a fatalistic feeling to the words that followed. 'So, this position is only offered to those whose own magic amounts to nothing more than the heating of metal. This cabin draws from me every last spark of arcane energy that I possess, for as long as I spend in here, directing the force on my command towards the iron-plated prow on the outside of the ship. The fact that all these Deep Steel glyphs are already glowing is down to me having spent weeks on end in here, the chamber having collect plentiful supplies of Caldrian magic.' She pointed at the door behind the others. 'Which evaporates the moment I walk outside this cabin.' The old woman lovingly patted her bunk. 'Hence, I stay where I am so that we can make our way through the ice for as long as possible. Once the supplies are exhausted, I will only be able to bring *Alina's Rage* forward for no more than a few furlongs.'

'Then I thank you for your commitment and patience,' said Ahren politely. 'We have reached the pack ice and will need your services from now on.'

Caldria nodded impassively, Ahren sensing that the sorceress would have had nothing against another day of rest. 'As soon as the captain has decided on his course and gives me the command, this Flame Belly ship will become more than worthy of her name.' She looked expectantly at Ahren. 'The Ice Fields are large and our supply of magic limited. Where precisely shall we be going?'

Ahren looked helplessly at the sorceress, shrugged his shoulders helplessly, then left the cabin silently so that he could discuss the matter with his friends. Behind him he heard the sound of things rattling and Trogadon's voice. 'If you are bored, why don't we pass the time with playing dice?'

Captain Ounlamun looked pensively towards the south, his fingers drumming on the ship's wheel. The round-faced man, who was standing with Falk, the First, Uldini, and Ahren, had been pondering in silence the question of what course they would take for some time now. 'And you have no clue as to where the Paladin Yollock might be residing?' he asked Uldini for what had to have been the umpteenth time.

'No,' muttered the Arch Wizard through gritted teeth. 'Our charm nets have revealed nothing in the past, and my attempts at tracking him down now have also proven fruitless.' He nodded at his crystal ball and then down to the interior of the ship. *Flamestar* finds it difficult with all the water, and our Mistress of Charm Nets, is still in a deep sleep.'

'Where was Yollock last seen?' asked Falk, scratching his beard in consternation.

'In Cape Verstaad, when he announced that he was going to hurry after Four Claws,' grumbled Uldini. 'But you knew that already.'

'I mean afterwards,' replied the old Paladin mysteriously.

'You're thinking of the *Hisunik*,' muttered the First sceptically. 'Do you *really* believe that the folk memory of a simple village community made up of fishermen and hunters has lasted through all the centuries?'

Falk spread out his arms in a gesture of helplessness. 'What harm could it do if we don't know where we are going anyway? Look at it like this – even if Yollock's appearance isn't mentioned in the history of the village, we will surely find reference to the sighting of a dragon.'

Ahren nodded hopefully. 'Yollock will certainly have picked up the scent of the dragon in the *Hisunik* villages. Let us find the village that remembers Four Claws' overflight and we will also find the spot from where Yollock set off into the Ice Fields.'

'There is much in flux here,' said Ounlamun. 'The pack ice is moving – slowly, of course, but sufficiently that the village you are looking for might not give you a useful starting point anymore.'

'These people live from fishing and stalking, isn't that so?' asked Hakanu, who was ascending the steps to the fo'c'sle. 'Then their elders or their hunters will have internalised all the changes that have taken place in their land, so that they can keep in mind their old *and* their new hunting grounds as clearly as possible. Such would be the situation in the Green Sea at any rate. We can find out from them where the village must have originally been when the dragon flew past overhead.'

'That is a *lot* of ifs and buts,' countered Uldini.

'Do you have a better idea?' asked Ahren, and when the Ancient replied by scowling and shaking his head, the Paladin turned to the waiting Ounlamun. 'Then let us sail along the coast of the Ice Fields until we find a *Hisunik* village,' he said firmly.

The captain nodded, turning the wheel immediately as he called out commands. Then the plump man explained his plan: 'We shall first sail with the current, pulling hard to port, if necessary,' he said. 'It makes no sense to voyage for moons on end east against the pull of the Ravenous Maw, especially if we must leave the Ice Fields behind us again before winter sets in.'

'Don't forget that the seasons follow their own rules on the Ice Fields,' explained Uldini. 'Akkad is convinced that some unknown centre of power has this region in its grip, influencing its cycles of cold and warmth in some mysterious manner.'

'Which means we have *how long* to comb an entire continent of ice for one individual?!' asked Hakanu, taken aback by what he had heard.

'According to Akkad's calculations, we have five moons, providing that the weather is stable enough and the temperatures remain relatively high,' said Uldini. 'At most,' he added dolefully.

The First nodded. 'If we are unsuccessful in this time period, then we will have to return again during the next phase of good weather – which might not happen for many moons.'

Ahren narrowed his eyes as he imagined the fighting power of Dark Ones that would then be lurking for them in these waters. 'We will find Yollock, even if it means me having to dig through all the snow drifts of this country,' he said, his voice steely. And he meant every word.

The mood below was as foul as the air that Ahren had no choice but to inhale. Hakanu had hurriedly met him on the aft deck to tell him that he had to go to Khara in the cabin that the companions were sharing. Now he was standing there with his apprentice, while Bergen stood guard at the doorway, Jelninolan slumbered, and the Swordsmistress cast worried looks through the doorframe. The woollen blanket, which Bergen had hung at the entrance to the little chamber as a temporary veil, lay ripped on the planks.

'The mercenaries?' asked Ahren as he looked down at the torn material.

Khara nodded. 'One of these…*warriors*,' she spat out the word, '*accidentally* caught his spear in the blanket.'

'While a chamber pot was dropped just as *accidentally* outside our doorway,' grunted Bergen, pointing with his chin down at the timber boards, the stench for the most part almost certainly emanating from the unsavoury stains.

'We have sent Culhen and the other animals back up onto the fo'c'sle,' added Khara. 'Muai was almost uncontrollable. If one of the mercenaries had touched her, there would have been a bloodbath.' With that, the Swordsmistress placed her hand meaningfully on the hilt of her Whisper Blade.

A vision flashed through Ahren's head of Khara performing her elegant dance of death among the horrified mercenaries, almost causing him to smile. These fighters were still their allies until proved otherwise. As long as Deklar's men were on the right side during a skirmish with a couple of Dark Ones, he and his companions would have to suffer their relatively harmless chicaneries.

'None of you were attacked otherwise?' he asked in a low voice, his friends shaking their heads in response. 'I will try and reason with Deklar again,' said Ahren only for Khara to lay a warning hand on his forearm.

'I knew more than enough of his type in the fighting arenas,' she said. 'It's best to leave him and his ilk to cool down for a bit first.'

Ahren hesitated before snorting. 'To be perfectly honest, the last thing I want to do now is see this so-called troop leader.' He turned to Bergen and Hakanu. 'Khara and I will remain on deck with the companion animals,' he murmured. 'Hopefully, that will put off any mercenaries that are thinking of taking revenge on them. Will you be alright down here?'

His young apprentice demonstratively turned his spear around so that the blunt end was facing upwards. 'Jelninolan has taught me how to use *both* ends of my weapon when fighting. If those smelly good-for-nothings create trouble, I can ensure that they get a few welts before using the pointy end.'

The boy spoke loudly enough for his words to echo down the passageway, causing Ahren to groan inwardly. It seemed that the lad was only too eager to teach Deklar's men a few more manners. He looked pleadingly over at Bergen, the latter casually shrugging his shoulders, however.

'You can count your lucky stars that you have only experienced the First in his mellow state,' said the Ice Lander. 'In his darker moods, he would most certainly have long since tossed these unruly scoundrels overboard – and in full armour, to boot.' When the blonde Paladin noticed Ahren's puzzled look, he laughed good-naturedly. 'I have travelled long enough with fellow warriors to ignore childish provocations. As long as they don't try to hurt us in any way, I will be the voice of reason – well, at least until Trogadon can replace me. He was so vexed earlier that I had to kick him out of the cabin so that he could cool off. Apparently, this Caldria woman cleaned him out.'

Ahren nodded with a chuckle and made his way towards the deck, accompanied by Khara, only to meet Falk, who was coming from the opposite direction with a determined look on his face.

'What's the matter?' asked Ahren in alarm.

'Nothing, nothing. Merely a question of honour,' muttered the old Paladin, squeezing past. It was then that Ahren noticed the dice cup in his erstwhile master's hand.

The grey-haired Forest Guardian disappeared so quickly that Ahren could hardly make out the old man's final words. It sounded something like: 'Well, if you're going to tangle with *one* of us, then you're going to tangle with *both*.'

It was with mixed feelings that Ahren saw the first *Hisunik* village come into view almost two weeks later. On the one hand, there was at least an outside chance that they might get some clue as to where Yollock might have headed off to, while on the other hand, their voyage along the monotonous and seemingly endless desert of ice merely underlined how large the country was within which they had to locate the missing Paladin.

Ahren stood between Culhen and Khara at the railing of *Alina's Rage*, watching with concern how the crew of the Flame Belly ship lowered the gangplanks onto the enormous floe upon which the little hunters' settlement had defiantly put down its roots. All the companions, with the exception of Ahren, were muffled up in thick fur clothing, even Uldini, who resembled a hovering Glower Bear cub in his heavy garment.

Ahren's only concession to the icy southerly wind that had whipped itself up over the previous days had been a pair of leather gloves, which kept his hands warm for no longer than a dozen heartbeats before he found himself having to pull them back beneath his magical cloak. Now he was regretting not having accepted the offer of a woollen scarf to protect his face, for the cloak's charm only reached the tip of the Paladin's nose when he pulled his hood low down, an action that he had to constantly repeat in the biting wind.

'You're as jittery as a godsday student before their first Autumn Festival,' murmured Falk with a chuckle.

'Magic does have its limits, you know,' retorted Ahren. 'But I thought it might be a good idea if at least one of us moved in a manner *not* reminiscent of an overfed wolf.'

Hey! complained Culhen, using the tip of his nose to push Ahren's hood off his head. *Leave me out of it!*

While Ahren was cursing and pulling his hood back on again, he felt Khara's elbow in his ribs, which she had skilfully managed to manoeuvre between the ribbons of his armour while he was busy fixing his garment.

'So, *I* am cumbersome then, am I?' she asked provocatively, but Ahren had enough sense not to reply – even if the simple truth was that none of his friends in their winter garb would be as mobile in battle as they normally were.

Ahren concentrated instead on the snow-covered round houses of the *Hisunik*. Every one of the dwellings was dome-shaped, and each had a low, semi-circular entrance through which the residents would crawl in and out whenever necessary. There seemed to be no proper roads, nor even paths – at least, if one ignored the footprints in the snow. Here and there stood weathered wooden structures, Ahren reckoning that they had been built from driftwood. Cleverly knotted nets hung down from them, though how they were attached, he really couldn't say. As far as he could make out, every member of the tribe wore thick hide and fur to protect themselves from the elements, the young Paladin noticing how cleverly they tied the garments to their bodies so that no accidental rips or awkward movements would let the cold in. Their little eyes on their dark-skinned faces were barely visible, some of the tribe members even covering them with a thin veil.

'How can these people see anything at all?' asked Trogadon, shaking his head and nodding towards one of the blind-folded natives.

'We're going to need something like that soon enough,' said Bergen. 'The snow reflects the sun, and if you keep looking at the glittering whiteness, you can go snow-blind very quickly.'

'Well, isn't that just *great*,' muttered the dwarf. 'And I thought the sun would be our friend in this land of ice.'

Bergen shook his head and was about to speak, but by now the planks had been fixed with ropes and iron bolts to the ice, with Deklar and his men already pushing their way down the gangway.

'What's going on here?' asked Uldini, glaring at the captain, Ounlamun then shrugging his shoulders meekly before replying.

'Deklar asked for permission to disembark, and I couldn't refuse him,' explained the plump man in a low voice. 'Experience has taught me that his people are much more agreeable if they are given the opportunity to stretch their legs and engage in some bartering. The *Hisunik* concoct a nasty drink made partly from fish that has been hung for years, to which are added ice egret eggs and some sort of black lichen that grows in dark, dank caves.'

'That sounds…tempting,' said Khara, whose face had turned somewhat green, while the thought of trying the liquid almost turned Ahren's stomach. He dreaded to think how it would smell on board ship if the mercenaries really did procure some of the pitchers which two cheerful *Hisunik* had pulled out of one of the little, completely snow-covered houses. Loud bargaining could now be heard, with the mercenaries chortling, dangling before the natives all sorts of trinkets from the streets of Cape Verstaad. Here a glittering whirligig made from polished sandstone, there a necklace of inferior steel. Ahren could see how the mercenaries were having fun, exchanging the tat – which had cost them no more than five copper coins in their home city – for the alcohol that they desired so much. The *Hisunik*, nevertheless, seemed more than happy with their new possessions. The Forest Guardian observed with a frown how this only seemed to worsen the mood of the mercenaries, and he beckoned his friends to follow him.

'It seems that our new allies were hoping for a decent skirmish,' murmured Bergen, who was now behind Ahren. 'The fact that the *Hisunik* refuse to be provoked must really grate on Deklar and his henchmen.'

'This is only cut glass,' griped the troop leader to a young man, who was whooping with joy as he carried away a colourful shard, holding it up to the sky as he looked through it. 'It's worth nothing!' The mercenary shook his head. 'Bloody idiot,' he muttered, picking up two heavy pitchers.

'Please do not insult these friendly people,' said Ahren coolly. 'We are relying on their help.'

'They don't understand us anyway,' said Deklar, guffawing balefully. 'All they can do is spout incomprehensible nonsense full of clicking sounds.' Then he started to stomp back towards the ship, clearly intent on shoving one of the villagers out of the way in the process, thereby hopefully starting a fight. Hakanu pulled the smiling *Hisunik* out of the way and then bowed politely before the little man, who cheerfully reciprocated the action.

'Do you know, I think that I can actually understand a little of what I am hearing,' said Uldini, surprised. 'If I'm not completely mistaken, these people must have found their way here from the Southern Jungle a long, long time ago.'

'In canoes, you mean?' asked Trogadon incredulously. 'Across the wide sea and through the Ravenous Maw?'

'Curiosity always finds a way to make the impossible possible,' said the First in a surprisingly philosophical tone. 'Luck and a considerable degree of stubbornness help, of course.' He paused for a moment before continuing. 'And the ability to withstand the failures and deaths of hundreds of others who are seeking the same goal.'

'Whew,' said Bergen with mock relief before grinning at the veteran. 'For a moment there you were sounding far too optimistic for me, but you corrected yourself in the end.'

'Bergen, Ahren, and I will try to collect information,' interjected Uldini gruffly. 'The rest of you keep an eye on the mercenaries. We don't want them stirring up the villagers against us.'

'I am going back to the cabin,' said Trogadon. 'Jelninolan must not be left alone when these good-for-nothings return to the ship.'

'Kamaluq and Muai are guarding her,' said Hakanu, but the dwarf was already on his way.

'How is your animal companion now?' asked Ahren gently. 'Has he recovered from the shock?'

Hakanu nodded. 'He's beginning to develop a stubborn streak.' The apprentice looked down in embarrassment. 'He says he gets that from me.'

Ahren looked over at Culhen who was – and how could it be otherwise? – lying under a mass of children. 'We must thank the deities for their wisdom for having chosen our companion animals so well,' he said. 'Without Culhen I would never have lasted a summer performing my mission.'

'You'd want to be on your way now,' said the First roughly, a concerned look on his face. 'Before the mercenaries provoke a dispute and the *Hisunik* turn against us.'

Ahren nodded. He hugged Khara, waved at his other friends, and walked on with Bergen, Uldini floating beside them. 'Any idea of who we should ask first?' he murmured to his companions.

Uldini shrugged his shoulders, then spoke to the nearest villager, who was admiring a little silver flute that he had purchased in exchange for ten pitchers of alcohol. The man pointed at a house in the middle of the settlement, the Arch Wizard then flying towards it while Ahren and Bergen ran after him, eventually catching up with the childlike figure halfway along the route.

'You seem to know what's happening,' said the Ice Lander.

'I can't believe I'm saying this, but I am following the advice of Ahren's apprentice,' admitted Uldini, whose expression was hidden behind his thick, woollen scarf. 'He said that the oldest person in the village would in all probability have the greatest store of folk knowledge.' He pointed at the hut that he was floating towards. 'The woman living within is supposed to have experienced more than one hundred summers.'

Ahren was more than impressed by the fact that one could survive for so long in such an inhospitable environment. Then a thought struck him. 'Could she be a shaman? In other words, have magical skills?' he asked. 'That would explain why the *Hisunik* are not in the least afraid of a flying boy or a wolf the size of a horse.'

Bergen laughed good-naturedly. 'The *Hisunik* are a very simple folk. One is either their friend or their enemy. There is no middle ground. We came into their village with goods to be bartered and without drawing our weapons. Hence, they will be our friends until we do something that changes the situation. If we break the unwritten law of nonviolence, we will be cast out.'

'Life out here on the periphery of nothingness must only allow for simple truths,' mused Ahren. 'Just like in the Forest of Ire.'

'The *Hisunik* have no neighbours eyeing them suspiciously,' countered Uldini as they arrived at the entrance of the low house hardly taller than Ahren himself. 'Which means that they are apparently more open-hearted than the residents of the Forest of Ire – that can only be to our advantage.'

Bergen frowned and pointed up at Karkas, who was circling high above them. 'He says that almost all the mercenaries are back on board. Only Mauk and two of his pals are still bartering stubbornly.'

Ahren chewed on his lower lip. 'Hopefully, Hakanu and the others will keep a good eye on them. I really don't trust them.'

'The sooner we put our questions, the quicker we can get away again,' said Uldini. Then he shouted in through the entrance, speaking in the tongue of the Southern Jungle. A fragile voice responded from within, whereupon the Arch Wizard floated down to the ground and in through the low entrance, which hardly measured a pace across.

Ahren allowed Bergen to enter before him as he glanced at the three mercenaries, who were a hundred paces away or so, bargaining loudly with the villagers, who were examining the proffered trinkets with interest. He had an uneasy feeling in the pit of his stomach, but soon he was pushing his way in behind the blonde Paladin. Hopefully, the First and the others would ensure that the mercenaries behaved themselves.

***

Revenge, using the eyes of the bartering Mauk, watched how the Thirteenth Paladin, together with the annoying little sorcerer and the Ice Lander, disappeared into one of these weird snow huts, and he didn't like it one little bit. He had only heard snippets of their plan, but like every good hunter, he knew what they were up to – every hounding always began with a scent. And it was in Revenge's interest that this scent stayed as vague as possible, for he had many things still up his sleeve for weakening the Paladins. Regretfully, he sank his claws into Mauk's mind, twisting and turning his host's desire to wreak revenge. It was time to stop playing.

***

Ahren was amazed by what he saw once he had crawled into the house – for it was obvious that the building wasn't, in fact, merely snow-covered, but it consisted totally of snow!

Once inside the dimly lit interior he saw by the little flame of a stone oil lamp that the house consisted of a single circular cabin, roughly four paces in diameter. The entrance was the lowest part of the structure, and when Ahren got to his feet and gingerly pulled back his hood, he knew why. The warmth of the light and of the old woman wrapped in furs – who was sitting on a simple rocking chair – rose to the ceiling, not having anywhere else to escape to, thereby remaining trapped withing the snow dome. Although it was still cold enough for the walls not to thaw, Ahren was sure that one could easily sleep here the night if one was wrapped up in furs. The *Hisunik* had with an admirable elegance used what they had in abundance to create a protection against the cold.

They use snow to keep out the cold? How extraordinarily clever for mere bipeds, commented Culhen, who was cheerfully running on top of the pack ice with a crowd of boisterous children on his back, almost the entire village looking on – with, as far as Ahren could make out, concern and admiration in equal measure.

If you let one of their children fall, that will be the end of our sojourn in this village, warned Ahren, chuckling, nonetheless.

Me? asked Culhen, most put out by the warning. *Me let one of the children fall?!* And with that he leaped over a large snowdrift, which immediately provoked delighted laughter from atop his back, but loud groans from the parents looking on.

Just be careful, advised Ahren before turning his attention back to his own situation.

The old woman was examining Uldini and Bergen keenly from her rocking chair. Both had taken off their scarves, and Ahren quickly pulled the cloth from in front of his mouth so that the mistress of the hut could get a good look at his face. He could see in the weak light cast by the heavy, stone oil lamp standing in the middle of the floor that the dark, wrinkled skin of the white-haired woman hung loosely from her round face, which, remarkably, looked as if had seen no more than eighty winters. She pointed at her three guests, then said something in her language, the concentrated and serious look on the Arch Wizard's face suggesting that he understood only some of what she was saying.

'She's using words that don't exist in the language of the jungle,' said Uldini.

'Probably ones that they don't need there,' suggested Bergen helpfully, 'like ice or snow.'

The childlike figure nodded before pointing at the wall, the floor, and his breath before repeating some of the words that the woman had spoken. She nodded and smiled, Uldini looking particularly smug as he turned to Ahren and Bergen again. 'She says that the three of us shouldn't spend too long in here. Each dwelling has been built with a particular number of inhabitants in mind. If we dawdle here for too long, the inner wall will begin to melt.'

'I was wondering why you wanted us in here with you anyway,' said Bergen, shrugging his shoulders.

'Because you can help me with things that only an inhabitant of an icy country can understand, and because Ahren usually causes all resistance to crumble with his naïve looking eyes and his ability to make a short speech.'

'Thanks for the compliment,' said the Forest Guardian, completely unmoved. 'But we are wasting precious time here with your song of praise for me. Why don't you simply put the burning questions to this friendly lady here before the ceiling begins to shed tears?'

Uldini nodded before turning to the oldest villager again and spewing out a barrage of words in the Jungle language – not without waving his arms dramatically from time to time whenever a misunderstanding would arise between him and the old woman.

When the Arch Wizard made his arms flap up and down and he pretended to spew fire, it became clear to Ahren that this conversation still had a little way to run.

***

Culhen was thoroughly enjoying his time with the children, and he silently promised himself that he would spend his time after the war near a settlement with youngsters, so that he could play with them every day. Maybe a big village or a school or something like that...

Scornful shouts penetrated his sensitive ears, and immediately the wolf craned his neck towards where the noise was coming from. Something was unfolding near *Alina's Rage*.

***

'You had better go back on board.'

The boy had spoken with just the right mixture of politeness and authority as he attempted to cool down Mauk's anger. Revenge had caused the mercenary to drive away the last of the village barterers, and even his comrades had escaped from his dreadful humour, so that the embittered man was the only one standing between the Paladins and their friends.

'You *will not* tell me what to do!' screamed Mauk, quickly evading the hands of the Paladin who had all the medals tacked to his armour.

Revenge wallowed in Mauk's furious mind. The mercenary was no longer able to think straight, which gave the child of the Adversary the perfect opportunity to plant a germ of an idea into the hot-headed fellow's mind – an idea that could be put into practice immediately. The man's painful ribs – now healing ever so slowly – creaked as he drew a dagger and leaped towards Hakanu.

'I should never have bothered with your fox in the first place,' he snarled as he began to stab.

Chapter 14

Culhen heard a gurgling scream. The smell of blood filled the clear air with the dreadful certainty that a living creature had breathed their last breath. The villagers, who until now had been watching the wolf, pulled their children off his back as soon as he had reached them. Then Culhen raced onward, around the next snow dwelling, and...

He stopped and stood, rooted to the spot, staring at the scene in front of him.

Ahren, he said. *Ahren – you'd better come quickly.*

***

Revenge was more than satisfied with the result. He sent a final command into Mauk's mind, the latter then using whatever little strength he had left to hurl the dagger into the sea. There were so many other mercenaries now only too willing to be used, and after what had just happened, they would be ripe fruit for Revenge to pick whenever he wanted. He seeped into the ice, and from there down into the deep water below. Then he pushed his way through a tiny crack, back into the ship. Where he waited for his next victim.

***

Ahren cursed loudly as Culhen's thoughts and senses flooded his own. 'We have to go,' he muttered to Bergen.

'What? Why?' asked the blonde Paladin, then stiffening instinctively as Karkas presumably delivered the news. 'I understand,' he murmured.

'Why are you two whispering to each other?' complained Uldini, glancing over at them. 'I am still trying to extract important information here.'

'Then talk faster,' retorted Ahren grimly as he turned to the exit. 'For Hakanu has just stabbed Mauk to death.'

While shoving himself out into the open, the Forest Guardian heard Uldini's loud expletives behind him. Doubtless, the Ancient was thinking the same thing that he was – the simple rules of behaviour adopted by the *Hisunik* would hardly allow them to consider a murderer or a murderer's companions to be friends. Indeed, the deadly shedding of blood tended to end any form of hospitality in most parts of Jorath.

***

'*Mauk!*' Culhen heard Deklar's furious cry once the mercenary had emerged on deck on account of the noise and spotted the dead man lying in a pool of blood at Hakanu's feet. The apprentice was staring down at the body, a mixture of confusion and anger on the boy's face, while Khara, the First, and Falk instinctively formed a protective semi-circle around Ahren's apprentice as more and more angrily shouting mercenaries ran down the gangplank.

'This snotty-nosed kid stabbed our Mauk to death as if he were a worthless pig!' snarled the troop leader, glaring at Hakanu, who seemed unable to move as the blood froze on his gloves – nature herself seeming to want the dreadful deed to be visible for all to see. Spears were raised, the weapons of the companions whizzing out of their scabbards, too.

'Get back!' growled the First. 'Or by the THREE, this ice floe will turn completely red before a hundred heartbeats have passed.'

Culhen positioned himself beside Falk and risked a glance over his shoulder at Ahren, who was still crawling out of the snow house, a good hundred paces away.

I really don't like saying this, warned the wolf, *but either you start running as if all the Fog Panthers of Jorath were on your heels or you get your bow ready.*

***

Ahren wondered how he had inhaled enough air to curse loudly as he raced through the snow, but he found that the strength required to do so helped him to keep a cool head. Pelneng simply wasn't an option now. The Forest Guardian feared that it would cause him to make a cold-blooded calculation, ending the simmering problem of the disgruntled mercenaries by killing them all mercilessly in a bloody skirmish. Already, he could hear a little voice in the back of his head whispering to him that life would be so much easier if the mercenaries were simply eradicated…

Ahren shook his head as he ran. That wasn't an option. Ahead of him, he could see Falk, Khara, Culhen, and the First shielding the shivering Hakanu, while the furious mercenaries edged closer and closer to them. Ahren decided to heed Culhen's advice and to put it into effect, albeit in a modified form.

'What are you going to do?' yelled Bergen from behind as he saw Ahren unshouldering *Fisiniell*.

'Something that I should have done a long time ago,' said Ahren icily. 'I am going to send a warning.' Then he extended the bowstring and aimed with as much care as he could muster, given that he was seeing things through four eyes.

***

'This was cold blooded murder!' fumed Deklar, his voice hoarse with fury. 'First, the lout breaks Mauk's ribs so that he can't defend himself, and then he stabs him to death when none of us are nearby to help him. And he calls himself a *Paladin!*'

The troop leader spat onto the snow, Culhen smelling the man's hatred in the sweat that was pouring from the mercenary's pores.

'*He* attacked *me!*' exclaimed Hakanu, now gathering himself after the initial shock. 'Completely without warning. I could hardly fend him off, and it was only then that I drew my own knife…'

'A likely story,' spluttered Deklar sarcastically. 'And where is this weapon that Mauk attacked you with, you self-important Champion of the gods? I suppose that went up in a puff of smoke like your so-called honour?'

'He…uh…threw it away during the fight,' murmured Hakanu, his voice now weak, Culhen immediately lowering his head on hearing those words. The mercenaries wanted blood, and without the attacker's weapon, there was nothing which would persuade them that Hakanu was telling the truth. Already, the first mercenaries were withing striking distance with their spears, Culhen now preparing to leap into the ranks of the furious gang when he suddenly heard the familiar whizzing of an arrow. The missile landed with a crunch in Deklar's right thigh, causing the leader of the mercenaries to utter an agonised scream and collapse on the snow.

***

'THAT'S ENOUGH!' bellowed Ahren at the top of his lungs as he shot more arrows at the feet of the mercenaries, who hurriedly retreated until there were four paces between them and his companions. The ruffians stared wide-eyed at the onrushing Paladin. 'The next one who dares to take a step towards my apprentice will be nailed to the ice floe with arrows!'

'Nice one,' grunted the First as Ahren stormed passed the age-old Paladin and the others, but the Forest Guardian acknowledged the dubious complement with little more than a snort. Then he grabbed the groaning Deklar by the arm and lifted him up from the snow-covered ice so that he could look him directly in the eye. He leaned in until their noses were almost touching.

'*We* have conquered armies of Dark Ones on land and at sea, *we* have defied age-old fabulous creatures and the madness of the Forest of Ire, *we* have overcome the heat of the Nameless Desert and the oppressive humidity of the Southern Jungles!' He knew full well that he was still screaming but he didn't care. 'My friends and I have tamed an entire city full of miscreants, all of whom were far more frightening than you lot will ever be.' He kept his eyes fixed on the snarling troop leader, determined that he was going to win this particular battle of wills. Then he lowered his voice so that it sounded even more raw and threatening. 'No matter what you have heard about *me*,' he said in little more than a terrifying whisper, '*I* will only save those who do not get in my way.' The Forest Guardian than dropped his bow, the rage suddenly vanishing from his face as he drew his Wind Blade. 'Let me ask you this once and only once, Troop Leader Deklar: Are *you* my enemy?'

Are you sure about this? asked Culhen in the following silence while Deklar stared into Ahren's eyes, doubtless looking to see if the Paladin was merely putting on an act to intimidate the mercenary.

Yes, was Ahren's simple answer, the Forest Guardian then sending Culhen an image which the wolf understood – an Alpha was defending his pack by chasing a horde of Fog Cats. It mattered not a whit if one of the Dark Ones was to perish as long as the rest of them fled. The only thing that mattered was the safety of those in his care.

'I may not be your friend,' said Deklar at last, spitting sideways onto the snow, 'but this does not mean that I am your enemy.'

Ahren nodded and slowly lowered the man back down onto the ice. Then, just as slowly, he sheathed his Wind Blade, picked up his bow, and shouldered it. 'Hakanu,' he called out in a stern voice, keeping his eyes fixed on Deklar, who was now holding his injured leg with gritted teeth.

'Yes, Master?' The boy's voice betrayed an unusual amount of nervousness.

'Did you attack and kill that man without any good reason?' asked Ahren, his eyes now scanning the assembled mercenaries.

'No, Master,' came the reply from the young warrior. 'He attacked first and then threw his knife into the water when he collapsed.' Ahren had been hoping for just such an answer from his proud apprentice, and he could see the first signs of doubt in the eyes of the mercenaries.

Then we are finished here?' asked Ahren, looking at the roughnecks. 'Or do any of you see things differently?'

None of the spear carriers made a move to speak. Deklar, too, now being helped up by one of his men, seemed to have lost any desire to fight. The mercenaries retreated below deck, and as Ahren turned around to his friends, he spotted a wall of grim villagers approaching with accusing looks on their faces.

'We'd better make a move,' said Ahren with a sigh, quickly beckoning Uldini to hurry, the latter floating through the village in the distance. 'I don't think that they are going to be welcoming any more strangers for the next while.'

The *Hisunik* drove the companions away without uttering a word. The wall of villagers walked slowly forward, their every pace being mirrored in reverse by the visitors, who one by one ascended the gangplank, their banishers observing them with sad, serious eyes that seemed to be bidding a silent, reproachful farewell. Uldini floated around the villagers and onto the ship, Ahren being the last to step onto the deck before pulling up the gangplank in silence with Falk and locking regretful eyes with the *Hisunik* for one last time. The locals cut the mooring ropes with their sharp knives carved from bone, and even before the companions had gathered on the fo'c'sle, *Alina's Rage* was pulled away from the pack ice, thanks to the conjuration of the first mate and the current of the Ravenous Maw.

'Our first meeting with one of the tribes of the Ice Fields has been an absolute disaster,' said Khara gloomily. 'I would have loved to have learned more about the *Hisunik*.'

'The only thing that concerns us is this – did Uldini find out anything about Yollock or Four Claws?' interjected the First coldly. 'You can exchange pleasantries with the *Hisunik* to your heart's content once this war has been won.'

Uldini nodded distractedly, unable for the moment to look away from the body of Mauk, which was being covered by the villagers under a black hide as it grew smaller and smaller. 'That he dared to attack a Paladin like that...' began the Arch Wizard before turning to look at Hakanu, who was standing there, his face pinched and drawn. 'Did you really have to *kill* him?'

To Ahren's surprise, his protégé did not immediately become angry, the boy responding instead in a thoughtful tone. 'Had I anticipated his attack a heartbeat earlier, then possibly *not*. After all, his ribs had been injured already, and it was only a knife. But the stab towards my neck was so sudden that I reacted instinctively.'

'Mauk surprised us all,' said Khara reassuringly. 'One moment, he was disgusting the villagers with his behaviour, the next, he was trying to ram a knife into Hakanu's throat.'

'His stabbing manoeuvre was unhesitating and *very* skilful,' added Falk musingly. 'Mauk was determined to do his worst. It was only Hakanu's quick reflexes that saved the lad from certain death.'

'I'll go and help Trogadon,' said Bergen, turning towards the hatch. 'He needs to know why he's suddenly surrounded by a rabble of recalcitrant mercenaries.'

Uldini snorted. 'As if they were *ever* our friends.'

'I'd better go with him,' said Falk, moving away from the others. 'My raised shield in the doorway to our cabin will hopefully stop most of the mercenaries from trying anything stupid.'

'And what *did* your enquiries reveal?' asked the First, turning to face Uldini as the two Paladins disappeared below deck.

The Arch Wizard seemed lost in thought as he looked again towards the ever-shrinking village. Ahren could see that Mauk's body, wrapped in pelts, was being handed over to the sea.

The fur will become saturated and drag the body into the depths, explained Culhen. *The current will take care of the rest.*

Ahren nodded. A burial on land would have been well-nigh impossible in a land of ice, as indeed would a cremation have been. The sea, on the other hand, greedily accepted whatever it was offered. He shivered as he thought of all those bodies that had been tossed about among the destroyed armada, and he uttered a silent prayer that the gods would accept all the souls that had been lost during the long voyage.

'The elder could indeed tell me something about Four Claws' landing on the Ice Fields – and also, that it wasn't her village that the dragon had seen,' said the Arch Wizard, the others having gathered around him.

'Now that's what I call sheer good luck,' said Khara, relieved. 'And you found that out having spoken to only one person!'

Uldini scowled. 'The village that Four Claws discovered was less lucky. When he reached the pack ice, he was hungry, weary, and injured. His right wing was broken, and yet despite this, he had successfully traversed the southern sea.' The Ancient looked his companions in the eye before continuing. 'The first thing he did was to attack the first prey that he could find.'

'The *Hisunik*,' said Hakanu dolefully, Uldini nodding in response.

'There were only two survivors from this star-crossed village,' said the childlike figure, his voice peculiarly flat. 'A brother and sister who were just returning from the hunt and saw the massacre from a distance. They went their separate ways so that they could warn all the other *Hisunik*. He went to the west, she to the east. The story of Four Claws' landing is common knowledge now in every *Hisunik* village. Which is why the old woman was aware of the dragon.' She rubbed her eyes wearily. 'But she knew nothing of Yollock. It is said that the dragon flew to the Frozen Teeth in the south. That is the name of the mountains that soar up deep in the Ice Fields.'

The First had become unusually silent as he listened to Uldini's explanation. Then he spoke. 'Flying such a distance with a broken wing…' he began before shaking his head in disbelief. 'That must have caused him incredible pain. The nerves in the pinions of dragons are particularly sensitive and filigree. Making that sort of an effort having suffered such a terrible injury means that his wings will never fully recuperate. He must have been in dreadful pain ever since then.'

'You know a lot about dragons,' said Hakanu curiously, prompting Ahren to subtly gesture to his apprentice to not pursue the matter any further. Alas, subtlety was ineffective when it came to the young warrior, who asked blithely: 'Did you hunt and kill many of them?'

'My animal companion was a dragon,' said the First, an undertone of threat evident in his voice. He glared at Hakanu, who immediately flinched. 'She was the most noble creature in the world, and she died trying to bring a war to an end – a war that she'd had nothing to do with.' Then the veteran walked away, leaving the quaking apprentice in his wake.

'Not a good topic of conversation,' said Uldini superfluously, breaking the silence that had ensued.

'I...' murmured Hakanu, '...I'd better go and clean myself up. 'Mauk's comrades shouldn't see his blood on me for any longer than necessary.'

'I'll go with you,' said Ahren gently, but Uldini stopped him with a quick shake of his head.

'Then *I* will,' said Khara. 'Should the mercenaries wish to attack you, I can stop them – even without blades.'

Ahren sighed as he watched them disappear, then he went over to Culhen to snuggle up in his friend's fur, the wolf having settled down in his usual spot. The feeling of protection that the wolf radiated always revived him and gave him security.

'What did you want to talk to me about?' he asked Uldini, who had floated towards the young Paladin and landed beside him.

'It's nice and warm here!' exclaimed the Arch Wizard, who was now resting against Culhen, having even loosened his scarf a little.

Tell him not to get used to this, said Culhen majestically. *I am not a fireside, where everyone can warm themselves up whenever they feel like it. You and Khara are always welcome, of course – and maybe Hakanu.*

And what about Jelninolan? teased Ahren.

Her too, of course, admitted the animal after a little hesitation.

And Trogadon?

Well, alright. Him, too.

And what did poor old Falk ever do to you?

Culhen snorted loudly. *Alright, alright. Invite the whole lot of them as far as I'm concerned. But don't complain if there's no more room for you.*

With some difficulty, Ahren put his arm around his friend's neck and squeezed the wolf affectionately before focusing his attention on Uldini.

'What was that all about there?' asked the Arch Wizard suspiciously.

'Nothing,' said the Forest Guardian with a grin. 'Culhen is delighted that you are here.'

Pshaw, countered the wolf, settling his head down on his front paws.

'I see,' said Uldini, far from convinced. 'Mauk's attack has me worried.'

Ahren nodded. 'Me, too,' he agreed. 'Sharing this confined space with the mercenaries was difficult enough at the start, but now…'

'That's not what I'm talking about,' muttered Uldini. 'I mean the attack itself. A wounded mercenary assaulting a Paladin without reason – and doing so in the full knowledge that there are two more Champions of the gods, not to mention a Swordsmistress in the immediate vicinity? What lunatic would dare such a suicidal act?'

'People are capable of all sorts of things when they are furious,' said Ahren thoughtfully. 'Perhaps in the heat of the moment Mauk didn't think beyond killing Hakanu?'

Uldini scowled in disbelief. 'The two of them were by no means mortal enemies,' he countered. 'Sure, in a dark alley without witnesses and with a knife that could be rammed into the boy's back…yes, I could certainly see Mauk performing an assassination in such a situation. But to throw his own life away by trying to take a Paladin's?' The Arch Wizard shook his head. 'There is something rotten about all this.' He pointed back at the fast-disappearing *Hisunik* settlement. 'I wish I'd looked at Mauk's body. Perhaps that would have told me something.'

Ahren frowned. 'You don't think he was a High Fang, do you?'

Uldini shook his head. 'I would have sensed that,' he said firmly. 'I am thinking more of a poison or an illness. Something that would explain such a sudden explosion of violence.'

'You mean something like rabies?' asked Ahren sceptically. 'It certainly wasn't *that.*'

'I don't know what I mean,' said Uldini sadly. 'And that is the problem. Some kind of exotic poison? Are our provisions on board ship somehow contaminated? Or have the mercenaries brought some kind of rare disease on board which infects people without us noticing?' He waved his arms helplessly. 'All I can say is that I sensed absolutely no sorcery emanating from the corpse.'

'We will in all probability never find out what it was that drove Mauk into his state of madness,' said Ahren, trying to be reassuring. 'Perhaps it was nothing more than the wrong words at the wrong time in the wrong place.'

Uldini groaned in exasperation, then floated upwards. 'I'll see if I can awaken Jelninolan,' he said. 'She has more knowledge than me in the areas of illnesses and poisons.'

'Don't do that,' said Ahren firmly. 'Let her rest for as long as possible. When we leave *Alina's Rage*, she is going to need every ounce of energy that she possesses. As we all will.'

Uldini looked out at the ice in silence before finally reluctantly nodding. 'Keep an eye on those mercenaries,' he commanded. 'If you notice anything unusual, let me know. I will cast another charm net – just to be sure. Maybe we *will* find something.'

***

Revenge snuggled into the scorn of the blonde mercenary to which he had attached himself. He sensed the charm spell that the little wizard had concocted whoosh over the man's rational mind, but it was incapable of locating him, in his comfortable position. Revenge was the most incorporeal of the Dark god's children, an even more fleeting shred of mental power than Shadow had been. But Revenge's greatest weakness was also his greatest strength. Once his victim was intent enough on retribution, then Revenge was practically unlocatable within the mind of his puppet – no more than was a droplet of oil in a raging ocean.

Another thing – Revenge was learning all the time. He had withstood the temptation to settle down within the leader of the mercenaries, who was launching one tirade after another – about the Paladins, about everyone who was wealthier and more successful than he was, even about the gods themselves. The man ranted and raved over anybody and everybody who didn't share his points of view or his experiences of life. Revenge had realised that Deklar was much more useful if the child of the Adversary worked on him from outside rather than from within. As long as the raging, chunky mercenary commander drew all the attention to himself, then Revenge would have free rein to do as he pleased.

Deklar had just finished yet another monologue, giving Revenge a chance to open his own toy's mouth. 'What these stuck-up prigs need now,' said his puppet, 'is a little bit of *humility*. And *I* have something up my sleeve which will *really* annoy them…'

Revenge basked in the greedy shine of Deklar's eye. This was going to be so much fun!

***

'Are you alright?'

The question cut through the rustling of the sails, which were ensuring that the ship held a westerly course. Ahren had used the darkness of the late evening to step quietly towards the First, a shadowy figure at the far end of the aft deck staring out to the gloomy sea.

'Why don't you address that question to your apprentice?' asked the age-old Paladin without turning to face the Forest Guardian. 'After all, it was he who killed someone today.'

Ahren was not fooled by the First's attempt at changing the subject. 'Hakanu is robust,' was his calm reply. 'One of the advantages of his...recklessness.'

The First snorted. 'Stupidity, you mean!' he blurted out gruffly.

'What is it that is making you lash out like this?' asked Ahren, unperturbed. 'The First I know is much more self-controlled.'

The old warrior raised an eyebrow but said no more. Ahren positioned himself beside the veteran and he, too, gazed out to the sea behind the ship. He could wait.

The two of you look so alike at the moment, said Culhen, who had turned around with extra care so as not to awaken Khara. *As though the past and present of the Paladins are standing side by side.*

My, but we are being philosophical tonight,' murmured Ahren with a chuckle, teasing his four-legged friend.

There was fish for supper – but far from enough of it, complained the wolf. *Ergo, I am thinking about the world in general and its unfair treatment of loyal companion animals in particular. In this way I can attempt to ignore the rumbling in my stomach.*

Ahren grinned, allowing the animal victory in their little battle of words. Instead, he looked sideways at the First patiently until the latter sighed in annoyance.

'I take it you are planning on standing and staring at me for the whole night or until I speak,' he muttered coldly.

Ahren shrugged his shoulders, pointing back over his shoulder at the fo'c'sle. 'Culhen can keep me awake until morning with his complaints about the food,' he chuckled. 'It's not necessarily the *best* way of passing the time but it will help me keep you company until you yield.'

'The advantages of having a companion animal,' said the First, the bitter undertone in his voice reminiscent of an underground spring, pushing its way inexorably up through the hard rock of a mountain.

'This is all about your dragon, isn't it?' asked Ahren instinctively. 'This is why you came on this voyage – am I correct?' He cocked his head and looked the First up and down. 'Did Four Claws kill your companion animal that time?'

The First pursed his lips. 'You know nothing,' he snarled. 'None of you know anything. Either about me or about dragons or Four Claws or…' The warrior stopped and shook his head. 'We will find Yollock and slay Four Claws – if he is still alive. That is all that counts. You don't need to know any more.'

Ahren was sensible enough to say nothing for a while. The few words that the perturbed man had uttered were already an important starting point. The Forest Guardian's suspicion had been well founded – that the First had something personal against Four Claws. The dragon had fought for the Adversary – the only one of his species to have done so. Did the First see this as some sort of betrayal of his own beloved companion animal? Did he want to call Four Claws to account for the decision that the creature had taken?

Ahren frowned and made his weary way back to Culhen, Muai, and Khara. Certainly, a personal vendetta would be most untypical for the First. The young Paladin decided to consult with Falk on the matter as soon as possible.

When Ahren closed his eyes, he couldn't stop thinking of Uldini's suspicion – that Mauk's actions had made no sense. The Forest Guardian snuggled into his wolf and up to his beloved, vowing to put off solving the conundrums on board the ship until the following day. Then he fell asleep and dreamt that he was on an endless journey through a labyrinth filled with dangers in whose side passages and dead ends he kept meeting Dark Ones and vengeful mercenaries as well as Uldini, who was at his wits' end because something was amiss. Meanwhile, the words of the First kept echoing through his dreams – *You know nothing.*

Ahren awoke in the early morning to the creaking sounds of sails turning on their masts. The wood, canvas, and ropes seemed brittle in the cold, the skeleton crew of the Flame Belly ship stripping the ice that had formed on the structure of *Alina's Rage*.

Trying not to wake Culhen, Muai, and Khara, he turned his head to look at the land and was surprised to see that they were sailing into some sort of enormous bay that went deep into the pack ice. *Alina's Rage* turned sedately landwards until her prow pointed towards the deepest point of the bay, and then Ahren heard Captain Ounlamun bellow a command. The sails were furled a little until the ship had reduced her speed to such an extent that it almost felt as if she wasn't moving, with the innermost part of the bay still a good half league away.

'We must be heading right into the pack ice at last,' said Khara sleepily, having just woken up. She blinked and looked at the sight ahead.

The timbers beneath me are getting very warm, announced Culhen, shaking his head and yawing. Surprised, Ahren placed a hand on the fo'c'sle deck, and indeed, it was not as cold near the wolf as he would have expected.

'It seems that Caldria is getting down to work,' he murmured as he got to his feet and leaned over the railing to get a look at the steel plates on the outside of the prow. He couldn't see any difference in them yet, but the air above the dull-black plates was already shimmering. Curious, he made his way up to Ounlamun, who was on the aft deck chatting with Uldini and Bergen as he steered the ship.

'…and she assured me that we have gathered enough magic to last for three or even four weeks,' the captain said, completing his sentence.

Bergen seemed less than impressed. 'According to any vague reports that I have heard from the very few expeditions that dared to travel so far south in the first place, this length of time will only be enough to get us to the Frozen Teeth – at least to those directly ahead of us. If we need to travel to the western Ice Fields, we will only be able to proceed at a snail's pace. And we would need to factor in an additional two moons for our return journey if Caldria is only able to heat the prow for a fraction of each day.'

'I can help if the worst comes to the worst,' said Uldini thoughtfully as he waved at Ahren to come closer. 'I imagine that things are going to heat up for you lot on the fo'c'sle over the next while,' he added with a chuckle. 'But I warn you – it's also going to get wet.'

'What do you mean?' asked Ahren, but the Arch Wizard merely grinned and said no more on the subject. Instead, he addressed the captain again.

'Couldn't we head for more *Hisunik* villages and ask them if they know where Yollock might be hiding out?'

Ounlamun tapped with his fingers on the helm as he thought – the wheel barely moving as the sea was so smooth. 'From what I know, the Bay of Whiteness is beyond the last inland point where one might come across the *Hisunik*,' said the captain regretfully. 'And I don't see any settlements, so I think we're out of luck.'

'Might we not find a village further south?' suggested Ahren hopefully.

'Unlikely,' said Bergen. 'The *Hisunik* live mostly from fishing and are also happy to trade with the few ships that pass along the coast. Clearly, both are more or less impossible deeper in the pack ice.'

Ahren sighed. It would be sad if their encounter with the *Hisunik*, which had ended so badly, would end up being their only one. 'How far will the clue regarding the Frozen Teeth bring us?' he asked.

Bergen pulled a map – which was hardly worthy of the name – out of his pocket. It was a tattered piece of leather, upon which rough, smudgy lines and crosses had been drawn. 'This is the most accurate map of the Ice Fields that exists,' said Bergen apologetically, handing it to Ahren. 'As you can see, it is barely useable.'

Ahren looked in dismay at the rag he was holding. To the north, he could read *Cape Verstaad*, while beneath it were several wavy lines bearing the name *the Ravenous Maw*, and to the south were several crude markings which presumable represented ice floes. A half-moon on its back inscribed with the title *The Bay of Whiteness* could only be the geographical feature within which they currently found themselves. 'How come this bay exists at all?' he asked absently, his eyes still fixed on the chart. 'I thought the ice floes ensured that the entire coastline was in a permanent state of flux.'

'There is a volcano under the water here,' explained Ounlamun. 'Its heat keeps this part of the sea free of ice. Which also explains why so many seals live here.' He pointed at a multitude of bulky creature with large tusks, lying in their hundreds in the sun, near the edge of the ice, some of them diving into the icy waters only to reappear a few heartbeats later, snorting loudly. Culhen had already pointed out no less than three times that these seals looked decidedly tasty.

Ahren ignored the harmless sea creatures and stared at the captain in wide-eyed disbelief – as if he was listening to a sailor spinning a far-fetched yarn. '*A volcano?*' he asked. '*Under* the water?'

Bergen laughed. 'Such things exist,' he said, confirming the veracity of the captain's statement to the sceptical Forest Guardian. 'Near the Ice Islands there is an area called the "the Glowing Sea" because the ocean bed radiates a bright red light at night.' Bergen scowled. 'Alas, fishing there is impossible because the water is too hot.'

Not being sure if the two mariners were pulling his leg, Ahren concentrated on the map again. There were hardly any signs lower than the Bay of Whiteness apart from a few seemingly random crosses at the very bottom edge of the map where the Frozen Teeth were. 'This really doesn't tell us much,' he said gloomily.

'I know,' said Ounlamun with a shrug of his shoulders. 'Most of the expeditions from Cape Verstaad were little more than prestige ventures funded by wealthy grandees who wished to impress their fellow merchants. They usually did little more than pick up exotic creatures from the edge of the Ice Fields to prove that they had, indeed, made it this far. Then they headed home to warmer climes.'

Ahren had a queasy feeling in the pit of his stomach. 'Can you be more specific about these creatures?' he asked.

'Diving birds that can't fly, for instance,' explained the captain after thinking for a moment. 'There were some that looked rather cute, and then others who had teeth in their beaks and red feathers on their heads.'

'Dark Ones,' said Bergen without hesitation. 'We have suspected as much. Here, too, the Adversary must have deformed creatures and bent them to his will.'

'They say that there is also a sub-species of Glower Bear here, as well as Fog Panthers – but I can't be any more precise,' added Ounlamun regretfully. 'Trying to distinguish between what is true and what is self-aggrandizement when it comes to experiences here in the endless ice is well-nigh impossible. During my expeditions on *Alina's Rage*, I have never encountered Dark Ones, but Grandessa Nabaltur has never sent us more than a league into the ice.' Then he pointed south at the thick mass of ice ahead, which was still only a few dozen paces closer. 'Perhaps you should go and get your friends,' he suggested with a grin. 'Sailing into the pack ice is always quite dramatic.'

Ahren nodded and hurried below deck, squeezing past two glaring mercenaries as he did so. The fact that he quickly checked to see whether they had drawn their weapons depressed him. These people were supposed to be a support, but he couldn't help imagining them to be potential enemies.

The further he walked along the passageway towards their cabin, the stronger became the smell of rotten fish and eggs. Ahren felt like throwing up, covering his nose with a cloth as he reached his friends. They, too, were protecting their noses with rags as they murmured angrily to one another.

'These bastards poured the *Hisunik* schnapps in front of our cabin,' muttered Trogadon, his eyes flashing with fury. 'That is not merely an insult, but also an unforgivable waste of alcohol.'

'It was a mistake, of *course,*' added Falk, his tone of voice suggesting that he didn't believe a word of what they had been told.

'We were wondering if we should bring Jelninolan up into the fresh air,' explained Hakanu, scrunching up his face so much that it was easy to see that he was most put out – even with his temporary covering. 'She's asleep but looking a little sick.'

'Everyone out,' said Ahren firmly. 'From now on, the fo'c'sle will be warmed by the flame chamber, and it's time that we cleared out of here. We will have more room above, and with a few lengths of cloth and some oilskins, we can build some sort of tent. Maybe the mood will improve if the mercenaries can call the belly of the ship their own, and the two groups keep to themselves.'

'Good idea,' said Trogadon, picking Jelninolan up as if she were little heavier than a feather. 'Let's get out of here.'

Ahren helped to pack their necessaries, himself and Hakanu being the last to climb up on deck. A hissing sound could be heard at the prow, and a powerful cloud of mist rose from the ice directly before *Alina's Rage*. Uttering a curse, Ahren heaved the rucksacks onto the fo'c'sle before positioning himself with his companions, who had gathered at the railing and were watching the performance in front of them.

'Very impressive but also very damp,' commented Uldini as the swathes of mist billowed across the fo'c'sle and caused by the melting ice which the Flame Belly ship was crashing into, the frozen blocks groaning on impact.

Ahren reckoned their current speed to be no more than a moderate march, and he understood now why they had taken the detour to the Bay of Whiteness. They had covered the half league or so to the innermost part of the bay in almost no time at all – from now on they would need considerably more time to cover the same distance.

We are not a ship anymore but a slow coach, commented Culhen. *And not only that, but a blind one if the fog is going to continue to roll in on top of us.*

Ahren could only concur with his wolf. Of course, it had been considerably easier to sail south on *Alina's Rage*, especially as the ship was carrying all their provisions and important equipment, but the fog that was covering the Flame Belly ship now made it almost impossible to make out what was lying ahead of them.

'Hakanu, go up to the crow's nest!' commanded Ahren, his apprentice agreeing with a willing grin. 'If you notice anything unusual, please shout down to us first, rather than resorting to your spear.'

'I will go with him,' said Bergen. 'After all, Karkas is keeping guard over us all from above, and if he spots something from on high, Hakanu and I can look at it together without Karkas having to swoop down. He needs all the strength that he has in this cold. Without his Animal Blessing he would not be able to withstand these weather conditions.'

Ahren nodded, then turned to the rest of his friends. 'According to Ounlamun, there are rumours of Dark Ones being in the Ice Fields, and the cloud that *Alina's Rage* is creating must be visible a league away. I propose that the best thing we can do is to prepare for an eventual attack. Put up a tent on the fo'c'sle – one large enough for us all to sleep in at night. That way, we will all be able to react to any danger at short notice while also staying out of the way of the mercenaries.'

'You sound as though *you* are *not* going to help us,' muttered Falk as he glared at Ahren. 'Have you better things to be doing?'

Ahren nodded and grinned. 'I have an underemployed riding wolf here who is also an Ice Wolf. I need to find out if he will live up to his name.'

With a whimper and a joyful leap, Culhen was already standing beside Ahren, licking his friend's face exuberantly. *You are the best Paladin one could ever have!*

The dark steel plates of *Alina's Rage* glowed red-hot, melting the ice at the prow of the ship within heartbeats as the sorcerous wind in the sails pushed the vessel deeper into the yielding pack ice. Yet even more impressive than the sight of the smouldering colossus of wood and steel that created a cloud of fog which was surely visible in Cape Verstaad, was the fact that a good hundred paces behind the Flame Belly ship the ice was re-forming in the channel that had so recently been burned into the cold white blocks. Their voyage home would be equally as hard-fought.

Ahren felt queasy at this realisation. While sitting on Culhen's back, he made sure that his cloak was completely covering him. There was nothing here on the pack ice that would ameliorate the heartless wind, and the cold rising from below would have been unbearable were it not for his magic garment. He was suddenly aware of another advantage that the Flame Belly ship offered – standing on solid timbers was quite different to being on slippery ice.

Well, I love it, commented Culhen, the wolf running joyfully on the frozen mass like an excited puppy. *It's as if I was born to be on the ice.*

Strictly speaking, you were, Ahren replied, smiling from behind his woollen scarf. *Or at least, your conspecifics were before they were turned into Blood Wolves.*

Which means that I belong here, added Culhen, stunned by this realisation. *If we forget about all the detours, the Blessing of the gods, the war against the Adversary, and the Paladins – then this would be my home.*

To be more accurate, the Icy Vasts in the north of Eathinian, said Ahren. *I have no idea if this place also has Ice Wolves.*

But Culhen was no longer listening. Ahren realised, as he sank further and further into the mind of his friend, that the Ice Wolf was absorbing every sensation with a new intensity – as if the animal had been born again. The crunching of the snow beneath Culhen's paws, the whistling of the wind, the new, unfamiliar smells that wafted into the wolf's nostrils, or the crystal-clear air which suggested through its biting coldness that only the strongest could survive here – all these things touched Culhen so much that they revealed to him the core of his being, which until now had always been hidden from him.

Isn't this wonderful? said Culhen gleefully. *No distractions, just the joy of anticipating the next few days.*

Sounds lovely, agreed Ahren, who felt, nonetheless, that his friend was going a little too far. *I take it, then, that you will no longer be requiring roast meat, or a comfortable corner packed with soft cushions.*

Uh, countered Culhen, the Forest Guardian sensing how his wolf had been suddenly yanked out of his reverie. *You really are a spoilsport,* he complained before adding a heartbeat later: *Well, this is really great. Now all I can think about is roast meat!*

Ahren leaned forward and ruffled his four-legged friend's neck fur before hurriedly pulling his gloved fingers back under his cloak. *You are more than a mere Ice Wolf,* he said lovingly. *The gods have granted you more powers than your fellows – a craving for roast meat, for example.*

Ahren could see that Culhen was swallowing hard. *We really must talk about other things,* the wolf replied with as much worthiness as he could muster. *If the saliva drools out of my mouth, it will freeze on the spot.*

I thought that this place with its extreme temperatures would suit you down to the ground, countered Ahren teasingly.

Ahren? asked the wolf, sounding as sugary sweet as he could.

Yes, Culhen?

Shut up.

Together they circled the slowly progressing Flame Belly ship several times, Ahren sensing that Culhen was developing an ever-greater awareness of what lay beneath them. The wolf's paws were figuring out which layers of ice could easily take the combined weight of animal and rider, and where the never-ending layers of snow were covering the tiny but lethal fissures between ice floes. Ahren understood that the vast field of ice surrounding them was made up of countless floes that had either long since fused or recently been pushed together, leaving narrow gaps here and there which were lying in wait, ready to accept anyone unfortunate enough to fall through them, plunging into the lurking dark sea below, from where they would be pulled away forever by the current.

Ahren, look! said Culhen suddenly, the wolf's head jolting up, his ears pricked, his body tensed from nose to tail.

Ahren followed his friend's gaze and saw a white, shaggy animal disappear behind a snowdrift.

Was that a...a white bear? the Forest Guardian asked uncertainly.

I'm pretty sure it was, replied Culhen. *But if it was, then I've never seen a bear that big.*

Let us hope that it was a Dark One, countered Ahren, immediately sensing Culhen's irritation.

What makes you say that? asked the animal.

Ahren signalled to the wolf to return to the ship before explaining his rationale. *Because otherwise there could well be another version of the same type of bear in the area – only one that has been deformed by the Adversary and is therefore larger, meaner, and infinitely more dangerous.*

'What you saw was an ice bear. They are harmless as long as one leaves them in peace and doesn't try to take their food,' said Bergen, Ahren and Culhen having made their way back on board *Alina's Rage*.

'Sounds like Culhen,' interjected Trogadon, his quip being met by general laughter.

The companions were sitting in the comfortably warm tent that Falk, the First, and Bergen had constructed with lengths of cloth and oilskins. Several empty crates of various shapes and sizes, which Trogadon had pinched from the ship's stowage, served as temporary tables and chairs. The cleverly knotted materials ensured both that the warmth rising from the prow was trapped within the tent, and that the fog remained outside. It meant, too, that the companions would have to sleep close together, but at least they had fresh air and the necessary warmth to keep them from freezing to death overnight. For this reason, the atmosphere within the tent was relaxed and cheerful, while the fact that Jelninolan had woken up from her deep sleep as twilight fell merely added to the festive mood and the sense of community that they were all feeling. They joked, ate, and drank, and anyone looking at them from the outside would have taken them to be a group of revellers in a tavern rather than passengers of a ship, which was struggling to make her way south through the endless ice, journeying further and further from any civilisation.

'Take it easy with the wine,' said Uldini as Trogadon reached for another pitcher. 'Once our supplies are used up, there will only be water left to drink.' The Arch Wizard pointed meaningfully at the ice which surrounded them. The dwarf stroked the jug once, then reluctantly placed it back where he had found it.

'It would also make sense for both Culhen and Muai to start fending for themselves from tomorrow,' added Falk. 'We could then make our food provisions go a lot further.'

Ahren sensed the wolf's joy at the prospect of going hunting, but Muai growled irritably on hearing the old Paladin's words, fixing her green eyes on Khara as she did so.

'My tigress does not like walking on snow,' she said, rolling her eyes. 'It freezes between her pads, and then she has to nibble at her paws later to get the frozen water off.'

The First turned to Muai and gave her a steely stare. 'We all have to do things that we don't like on this journey. Would you like me to tell Quin-Wa that the all-powerful Muai is scared of a little bit of ice?'

The tigress stopped growling and turned her head demonstratively away. Then she curled up and pretended that she was asleep.

'Well, I must remember that trick in future. That will nip a lot of arguments in the bud,' said Khara with a grin. Much to Ahren's surprise, the First winked at the Swordsmistress.

'Despite all the harmony and comfort of our new lodgings, let us not forget how vulnerable we are on board this ship,' said Ahren sombrely. 'The light being cast at night by the prow of the Flame Belly ship is sure to attract all sorts of predatory animals – the largest of which may even be able to board the vessel.'

'Ahren is right,' agreed Bergen. 'We are no longer being protected by water. The next danger may be lurking in the immediate vicinity. Karkas can't watch over us at night, and he does need to sleep at some point.'

Ahren nodded towards Hakanu. 'Then you should alternate shifts from now on. Hakanu can be the lookout in the crow's nest at night, and he can sleep during the day, while Karkas can watch over us from daybreak onwards.

Muai and I can help, too, volunteered Culhen. *And when we swap, one of us can do circles of the ship while the other one is hunting or sleeping.*

'I have been told that both Muai and Culhen will keep watch, too,' Ahren announced to the others, at which point the big cat raised her head and looked witheringly at Culhen as if he were nothing more than a dastardly traitor.

'The rest of us will keep watch in shifts on deck,' added Falk with a nod.

Ahren could see that everyone was in agreement, and satisfied, he settled down, leaning into Culhen's flank. They now had a plan to counter possible attacks by Dark Ones, a destination that would hopefully bring them closer to Yollock, and a cosy place on board the ship where they could relax and be themselves.

All in all, the situation was much better than he had feared it might be.

***

Revenge had to admit to himself that he had underestimated the Paladins. Instead of reacting to the petty provocations of the mercenaries – as they would surely have done in the past – the Champions of the gods and their companions had retreated to the fo'c'sle, where their mood was much better than at any time since they had first boarded *Alina's Rage*. Revenge listened to the discontented mutterings of the men around Deklar, and a new plan formed in his mind, nourished by the grudge of the man in whose head he was currently residing.

By this stage, Revenge had leaped between six or seven of the most splenetic spear carriers whenever they had been asleep, leaving a tiny splinter of his own self in each one of them, which meant that he could easily swap between any one of them, depending on the situation. He had even surprised himself at the ease with which he could perform this newest trick.

The six having picked the same goals for their revenge fantasies, it had been child's play for the Adversary's child to create more than one puppet. The possibilities that had been created by his new power were endless, but Revenge was going to continue his little game of hide and seek for as long as it took.

He allowed his mercenary to get to his feet and leave the cabin without saying a word. Then he planted a little, *mean* idea in his puppet's head – namely, to keep an eye out for one *very* particular object.

Chapter 15

'That doesn't look good.' Ounlamun's friendly voice was at odds with the import of his words, but the dark line of clouds approaching *Alina's Rage* from the south spoke volumes.

'Is this weather normal?' asked Ahren, who was on sentry duty on the aft deck and watching Culhen, the wolf scampering around on the ice and clearly enjoying himself.

'Alas, yes,' replied the captain gloomily. 'Snowstorms are very common here in spring and autumn. However, we should be safe enough as long as we take in the sails and hunker below deck while the tempest is raging. Caldria will stop heating the prow and use the time to gather her strength. Hopefully, by the time the full force of the storm hits us, we will be completely frozen in by ice – that should give us additional stability. The last thing we want is for *Alina's Rage* to tip over in the powerful winds because the water around her has not re-frozen.'

Ahren nodded and looked over at the improvised tent that had served him and his friends so well over the previous nine days. 'I suppose we had better move lodgings again,' he said with a sigh. 'Hopefully, Deklar's men have calmed down a little.'

Now it was Ounlamun's turn to sigh. 'The story of Mauk's fate is nothing short of a tragedy. The man was always cantankerous, but attempted murder…' He clucked his tongue. 'Deklar will get a right earful once we get back to Cape Verstaad. Those who lose control over their people, are very quickly relieved of their positions as military leaders.'

Ahren pursed his lips and said nothing. He was all too aware of whom Deklar would blame for his problems. This storm was certainly going to prove uncomfortable for more than one reason.

'There are neither High Fangs nor Dopplers here,' said Jelninolan, her voice weak. Ahren, Falk, and Bergen had been spending the afternoon moving the companions' belongings below deck again. For the moment they were standing among crates and rucksacks on the fo'c'sle, Ahren having brought up with the elf Uldini's suspicion that something on board was amiss. 'Nor can I confirm any poisons or illnesses among the mercenaries,' murmured the Ancient. 'Every charm net that I've cast remains stubbornly silent. If Mauk was influenced by something, then certainly no-one else was.'

Ahren breathed a sigh of relief and picked up two heavy rucksacks, which he was going to carry below deck. 'Bergen!' he bellowed, looking up towards the crow's nest. 'The storm is nearly upon us! You and Karkas should come down now!'

'Give me a moment!' shouted the blonde Paladin from on high. 'Karkas has spotted something to the east – it looks like a pack of wild animals. He wants to get a closer look at them!'

Ahren frowned and looked out onto the ice, but he couldn't see anything. Muai was on sentry duty, while Culhen had gone hunting. Of course, the wolf was delayed, but this did not overly bother the Forest Guardian. Procuring food was much more difficult on the Ice Fields, both the big cat and Culhen spending much more time trying to fill their stomachs than was normally the case.

Ahren carried the rucksacks down to their old cabin, which was already uncomfortably full, dropping the luggage beside Khara, who was preparing a bunk. 'Can Muai see any creatures out there?' he asked in a low voice. 'Karkas believes that he has spotted something to the east of the ship.'

Khara seemed momentarily lost in thought before shaking her head. 'Muai hasn't noticed anything out of the ordinary – mind you, she's finding it difficult to see with all the whiteness.' She giggled before continuing: 'You're not supposed to know that, by the way.'

Ahren absently tapped the door frame with his fingers while he looked down the passageway towards the mercenaries' cabins. 'Are our...allies...behaving themselves?' he asked.

'Yes – so far,' said Khara from behind. 'But the glares that they are throwing us whenever they believe we are not looking are hostile, to say the least.'

The Paladin grunted and moved into the corridor.

'What are you going to do?' asked Falk, who was at that moment climbing down the steps, his arms laden with belongings.

'We cannot ignore Deklar's men for ever,' said Ahren, glancing back over his shoulder. 'If Karkas has discovered a threat, then we could certainly do with the mercenaries and their spears.'

Falk's look spoke volumes. 'Don't expect too much,' he said.

Ahren nodded, then walked past the three cabins which had been allocated to the mercenaries. He made sure not to look any of the men in the eye for too long as he tried to hide his true feelings towards the gang of roughnecks. On spotting Deklar, who was repairing his fur cloak, the young man stopped and politely knocked on the door frame of the compact cabin, which was full of men and their belongings. 'Can I speak to you for a moment?' asked Ahren, painfully aware of the brittleness and curtness of his tone.

'Is it to do with the storm?' asked Deklar in a bored voice and not bothering to look up from his handiwork. His nose was no longer swollen, nor could Ahren see any sign of bandaging around his thigh. 'This tear won't mend itself.'

The Paladin stopped himself from uttering a sarcastic response and spoke in a calm voice: 'There may be trouble ahead,' he said vaguely. 'A sighting to the east.'

Deklar looked up suddenly, as did the six other mercenaries in the cabin, all of them now peering at the Forest Guardian with the same suspicion. Their movements seemed strangely synchronized, causing a shiver to run down Ahren's spine. Deklar's men clearly worked well as a unit.

'I will come up,' said the troop leader, reaching into a chest. When he pulled out his hand, Ahren caught sight of an expensive looking telescope. Without uttering another word, the Paladin turned and made his way up onto the main deck of the ship, Deklar stomping loudly behind him.

'Bergen!' shouted Ahren, looking up the crow's nest once they were up on deck. 'Any developments?!'

'At least twenty fox-like creatures!' bellowed the Ice Lander from the lookout. 'But not the cute-looking normal ones. I'm talking about six-legged creatures with mouths filled with fangs. And they have *two* tails.'

'Snow Slashers,' said Deklar, spitting onto the planks. 'Encountered them during an expedition before I was hired by *Alina's Rage*. Dark Ones that were once snow foxes. Cunning and greedy, they always attack in a pack, but only if they think they are after easy prey – or when they smell blood.'

'Do you think that they will attack us on board ship?' asked Ahren, who had been pleasantly surprised by Deklar's professional attitude.

'Hard to say,' said the troop leader uncertainly, looking up at the threatening black clouds. 'If the storm gets bad enough for the Snow Slashers to seek refuge, then we might – if the worst come to the worst – suddenly find the creatures running around on the deck. I *have* seen them chewing their way through thick wood.' He looked meaningfully at the hatch.

'What do we do?' asked Ahren anxiously.

'Keep watch,' came the curt reply, which the Paladin had feared. 'At least four sentries on deck and two more at the hatch. We may have to fend off the pack before things develop into a skirmish in the belly of the ship. That means we will need eyes out here to warn everyone in time.'

Ahren nodded grimly. 'Then two of ours and two of yours, and one of each at the hatch,' he said. 'After all, we are going to have to learn to…work with each other.'

Deklar merely snorted and nodded curtly. Then he stomped back to the hatch, where he paused. 'Thirteenth,' he said without turning. 'Regarding Mauk…I don't know what got into him – assuming your apprentice is telling the truth.' This was followed by a pause, and just when Ahren believed that the man would say no more, the mercenary added: 'I am doing my level best to keep my men under control. Promise me that Mauk's final deed won't become known to Grandessa Nabaltur.'

Ahren took a deep breath, realisation and disappointment affecting him equally. Deklar was unusually reasonable because he wanted something from the Paladin, not because he had suddenly realised the error of his ways. 'So long as incidents like the one in the village or the one involving Kamaluq never occur again, I am ready to forget about the last few weeks – *and* providing that my friends arrive safe and sound in Cape Verstaad.'

Deklar grunted his approval and disappeared below deck, leaving Ahren behind to wonder if his conversation with the mercenary might make an alliance with Deklar's men a possibility, however fragile.

***

Revenge had listened in on the discussion between the troop leader and the Thirteenth Paladin. Immediately, he searched in the minds of his mercenaries for someone who had a score to settle. It didn't take him long. His marionette was already rubbing his hands with glee.

'Hey, Skiltous, did ya hear?' asked Revenge's plaything, the puppet approaching the afore-mentioned mercenary. 'They're looking to form a night watch for during the storm – up on deck. What d'ya say? Why don't we share the first watch? If I know Deklar, it'll mean extra coppers once this voyage is over for anyone who's volunteered.'

Skiltous looked at his opposite number in surprise. 'What kind of a tone is that?' he asked, taken aback. 'For moons, you've been accusing me of cheating at dice and saying that I've nicked your wages. And now this?'

'Ye're a good fighter,' lied Revenge's marionette with a shrug of his shoulders. 'An' I'd rather have you coverin' me back than one o' them highfalutin Paladins – them lot only care about themselves.'

'Well…alright,' came the hesitant reply. 'Tell Deklar that the two of us will do the first shift. But from tomorrow on, I never want to hear another word from you about my supposed cheating – do you *understand?*'

'That's a promise,' said Revenge's toy, without the child of the Adversary having to prompt him at all.

You'll never hear another word from me after that shift, thought the man, and Revenge was pleased no end. The next piece of the puzzle was already in place.

The night was going to be filled with wonderful chaos. And either a Paladin would lose their life *or* the survival chances of everyone on board would hang in the balance.

***

'Well, *I* wouldn't trust any of these mercenaries with my life,' grumbled Trogadon, his arms akimbo. 'They are only waiting for the chance to even things up after Mauk's death.'

'Trogadon is right,' said the First. 'As far as I'm concerned, these people are more dangerous than useful.'

'What else can we do?' asked Jelninolan soothingly as she looked at the others. 'We can hardly set them down here in the endless ice.'

'Why not?' replied the old warrior coolly.

'As if they would allow that to happen without a fight,' countered Bergen. 'It makes no sense to provoke a life-or-death squabble just because we don't trust them.'

'And it wouldn't be *right*,' added Hakanu, Ahren suddenly feeling very proud of his apprentice. The young warrior had been rummaging through his things when he made his throwaway comment.

'Can we help you?' asked Khara curiously, the boy shaking his head, however.

'It's just that I'm looking for my knife,' he murmured absently. 'I could have sworn I put in in my bunk so that I could sharpen it later.'

'Things are constantly getting lost in these cramped quarters,' grumbled Trogadon. 'One always ends up emptying rucksacks or chests whenever one needs something specific. I've been missing a bag of blacksmith's utensils for days now.'

'Once the storm has passed, we should see which of the provisions crates are empty and therefore expendable,' interjected Uldini. 'That way, we might be able to make more sleeping room for ourselves.'

'It *is* tight, but it's warm,' said Jelninolan, placing her hand on one of the iron braces which were set into the walls. 'The rest of Caldria's heat is transferred through the metal to down here.'

'Which is why there are no doors,' said Trogadon, nodding. 'So that the heat is distributed as evenly as possible.'

'Would it not make sense to close the hatch to the deck, then?' asked Ahren sceptically.

The dwarf shook his head. 'The trapped heat would cause us to bake in no time at all. The steel plates on the prow are red-hot, don't forget. A source of heat like that can transform the ship into an oven.'

'Being roasted in the endless ice certainly doesn't top my list of things that I would still like to experience,' said Uldini dryly. 'Maybe someone should advise Caldria to stop her efforts for the day? The storm will be upon us soon, and the ship is supposed to become ice bound.'

'I'll do that,' said Ahren. 'Ounlamun already advised me to do so, but the first thing I wanted to do was to discuss guard duty with you all.'

Bergen pointed at Hakanu and himself. 'We will take on the first watch,' said the Ice Lander. 'Since working together in the crow's nest, we have learned to communicate without words, so during the snowstorm, we will be able to use hand signals.'

Ahren considered for a moment if he himself should stand watch with his apprentice, but then he decided not to push Bergen aside. The more friendships that Hakanu formed, and the more varied these friendships were, the broader would be his view of the world. 'I will stay awake down below the hatch and keep an ear out for any sounds of alarm,' he said, silently compromising with himself.

'Khara and I will take over during the night,' said the First, the Swordsmistress immediately nodding her approval. The closeness that had developed between the pair during the Hjalgar campaign had manifested itself again on this voyage, and by now Ahren was well capable of being pleased on their behalf, without worrying that his beloved might be monopolised by the First's nefariousness. Her imprisonment within the Void lay a long time in the past and much water had passed under the bridge since then.

'Ahren,' murmured Jelninolan. 'You were going to visit the flame chamber, remember?'

The Forest Guardian nodded gratefully to her before making his way to the prow of the ship. He had hardly walked five paces when Khara was beside him, laying her arm around his waist.

'I'm coming too,' she chuckled. 'I would like to meet this mysterious woman who is sparing us a long and cold march through the snow.'

Ahren gave the Swordsmistress a quick peck on the cheek, then narrowed his eyes anxiously as they continued to walk. 'I still can't sense Culhen,' he murmured. 'He can hardly be that full that he is ignoring the weather.'

'I'm sure he will turn up,' said Khara in a gentle, reassuring voice. 'Muai isn't worried about your wolf, and she is normally the first who would be concerned.' Khara giggled. 'That's another secret I shouldn't have revealed.'

'Culhen considers Muai to be an honorary she-wolf,' countered Ahren with a grin.

Khara burst out laughing. 'She really didn't appreciate your remark. Cochan received a most proud cat as her companion animal.'

'I keep forgetting that she doesn't solely belong to you,' murmured Ahren thoughtfully.

Khara simply shrugged her shoulders, much to his surprise. 'Muai is one of the family,' she said simply. 'She is like my big sister, who looked after Cochan for a while and now she is doing the same thing with me.'

Ahren pointed at the heavy round door at the end of the corridor. The charm circle in the wood glimmered in a smouldering light, as though the magic signs were struggling to keep a lid on a blazing inferno within. 'Here we are,' he said, then cocking his head. 'Only having seen this door when it was dormant, I don't know if I can open it without coming to harm.' He stepped forward and knocked, taking care not to touch the glowing runes. The wood was uncomfortably hot to the touch.

'Yes?' sounded a loud and snorting voice from within.

'A storm is brewing?' called Ahren loudly. 'Ounlamun would like you to stop your work.'

'And about time,' came the relieved reply. 'A little cooling off would do me good.' Immediately, the charms on the door were extinguished.

'Princess Khara would like to take a look at the flame chamber!' added Ahren. 'Would it be possible for us to open the door?'

The sound of amused laughter ensued. 'Only if you would like to see me in all my glory – as the gods created me,' chuckled Caldria. 'It is far too warm in here to be wearing clothes. Call by later and I will gladly explain everything about this cabin to your spouse.'

'Of course,' said Ahren, looking apologetically at Khara.

'It doesn't matter,' said the Swordsmistress lightly, adding in a murmur: 'This Caldria seems to be a most affable person. I like her already. No wonder Falk and Trogadon have played dice with her so often.'

Ahren nodded. 'Her work is exhausting, forcing her as it does to work in a confined, overheated chamber,' he whispered as they made their way back. 'There are very few cut out for the job.' Then he chuckled. 'And regarding dice throwing – our two friends are dead set on winning back the money they have lost. Caldria fleeced them like a shepherd does his flock.'

The first snowflakes were falling through the hatch, melting in the warm air of the ship's interior even before they had reached the bottom steps of the wooden stairs. Ahren felt another pang of concern for Culhen in the pit of his stomach. 'I will go up and keep an eye out for my careless wolf,' he said.

Khara gave him a peck on the cheek and nodded towards the rear of the ship's interior, from where could be heard the sounds of heavy boxes being shifted and muffled curses. 'I had better help organise things. Storing all our worldly goods and still having enough room to sleep in is going to be a challenge.'

Ahren nodded before silently ascending the steps. The belief that they would in all probability spend the night fighting rather than sleeping he decided to keep to himself.

The wind howled like an unfettered beast through the rigging of *Alina's Rage*, and Ahren could see no further than five paces ahead thanks to the driving snow. There was still no sign of Culhen, the storm having now fully arrived. Behind the Paladin, the crew were making final preparations, battening down the hatches, checking the knots of the furled sails, and making sure that the hull was fully surrounded by ice. After all the days when the flame chamber had been active, the vessel seemed to Ahren in her stationary position like a cold, lifeless shell.

'Chin up, chin up,' he murmured to himself, pulling the cloak tightly around him. He exchanged worried looks with Hakanu and Bergen, who were already keeping first watch as well as maintaining a safe distance between themselves and the two mercenaries on the other side of the main deck. The heavy blanket of cloud made it well-nigh impossible to tell if the sun was already beginning to rise, but the hurricane lanterns on the masts of *Alina's Rage* had been lit in an attempt to defy the darkness that the storm was bringing with it.

'Still no sign of life?' bellowed Bergen across at him, Ahren shaking his head in response.

'He is a wolf the size of a horse!' shouted Hakanu. 'Nothing will happen to him!'

Ahren looked gratefully at his apprentice, then frowned when he saw the blue sheen on the boy's nose. 'You must wear your scarf properly,' he said, reaching down for his pouch of healing herbs. 'Otherwise, the tip of your nose will fall off, and your soul companion will run away from you should she ever meet you.'

The fingers of his apprentice's gloved hands flew up to his chilly nostrils, Ahren suppressing a chuckle. Bergen, however, had no such inhibitions, laughing uproariously at Hakanu's vanity. 'How bad does it look?' asked the boy fearfully.

'Bergen would certainly have warned you before it got too cold,' said Ahren, nonetheless scowling at the Ice Lander, who was still laughing gleefully. 'Still, better safe than sorry.' He took a tiny crucible containing a pale paste out of the pouch. 'Do you recognise this?' asked Ahren, his tone severe.

The apprentice sniffed at the oily mixture. 'It's Rooster Thistle, isn't it?' he suggested after a heartbeat.

'Precisely,' said Ahren, delighted with the answer. 'Do you remember when I plucked this plant in Eathinian and said it could prove useful to us sometime in the future in a distant land? Well, the time has come.' Then he smeared the tip of Hakanu's nose with the paste before carefully placing the crucible back in his herb pouch. 'As you can see, it always pays to think ahead...' he began, while Hakanu pulled his scarf over his nose and nodded respectfully only for Ahren to interrupt himself with a cry of joy, the Forest Guardian's heart skipping a beat as he sensed the first faint connection with Culhen's mind.

Come here right now, you fleabag! He scolded. *You frightened the living daylights out of me!*

The storm took me by surprise, admitted his four-legged friend regretfully. *The weather changes here so quickly.*

There are no forests, rivers, or mountains to slow down the fronts, said Ahren soothingly, having already given vent to his anger. *Only snow and ice.*

Culhen had by now reached the ship, and he leaped over a snowdrift directly onto the deck, thereby avoiding having to go up the gangplank of *Alina's Rage*. Ahren was preparing to take the wolf in his arms when two shadowy figures rushed from the far side of the deck, both of them screaming, their spears ready to strike.

'Culhen!' yelled Hakanu, throwing himself between the two shocked mercenaries and the supposed Dark One. 'It's only Culhen!'

'By the THREE!' screamed one of the two sentries, beside himself with fury. 'You could at least warn us beforehand if such a beast is going to jump on board deck like that! Especially as we are expecting an assault!'

'At least we can pull up the gangplank now that the creature is on board,' grumbled his associate.

Ahren swallowed his annoyance, nodding curtly. The two sentries resumed their posts, not without exchanging glares with Hakanu.

Assault? asked Culhen, confused. *What did I miss?*

'I will resume my sentry duty below!' the Forest Guardian called out to his friends as he went towards the hatch. *A pack of Snow Slashers has been spotted,* said Ahren in reply to his wolf's question. *Large, six-legged foxes. If they are hungry enough, or the storm becomes too violent, they may attempt to come on board.*

Should I stay out here? asked Culhen, but Ahren shook his head.

You can see how tense everyone is, countered the Forest Guardian. *It would be very easy for them to mistake you for a Dark One in this storm.*

Still, at least Deklar's men are useful for something now – apart from causing trouble for everyone, said Culhen, Ahren opening the hatch sufficiently for his friend to slip through.

'My wolf is coming!' he shouted down the steps, and judging by the terrified looks on the faces of the mercenaries, he hadn't spoken a moment too soon.

Ugh! exclaimed Culhen as he disappeared below deck. *It's so warm in here!*

It will take a while for the heat of the flame chamber to be cooled by the ice outside, said Ahren, who had pulled back his hood as an experiment on closing the hatch from within. *It's already cooler in the cabins.*

Once they reached the bottom of the steps, Ahren saw that the thick layer of ice on Culhen's armour was already beginning to melt. The air in the belly of the ship was already moist and sticky, the wolf's wet fur adding now to the already unpleasant aromas. 'Go to the others,' he said loudly. 'I will keep watch here.'

I wouldn't mind forty winks, said Culhen, the wolf's exhaustion clearly evident to Ahren. *Spending the whole day hunting and only half-filling my stomach – maybe I was too previous with my praise for this barren land.*

And that although it is spring here, Ahren reminded him with a grin. *In winter you would doubtless have to survive for days without nourishment.*

Culhen said nothing, but the Paladin was in no doubt that the wolf's admiration for the Ice Fields had already lessened considerably.

***

Revenge stretched his senses and recognised that the Snow Slashers were moving *past* the ship. The primitive brains of the Dark Ones were depressingly non-receptive to his feelings, which the child of the Dark god occasionally used to guide creatures effectively. Still, there were other pleasurable opportunities to influence the course of events as long as this mercenary, driven by scorn and rage, was still at his command.

Revenge plucked at his toy's memory of the last evening of throwing dice with Skiltous, the fellow that he was now on sentry duty with. It took the merest of impulses to spur on the vengefulness of his marionette sufficiently for the fellow to reach for the dagger on his belt.

Just look at his new shoes, whispered Revenge. *Bought with his ill-gotten gains!*

The blade slid out of the scabbard, unheard in the raging storm.

Pay him back, he whispered to his toy. *No-one will see you. And you will get one over those snotty-nosed Paladins!*

The marionette's hand moved uncertainly as the haunted mercenary silently approached the clueless Skiltous,

Do it for Mauk! snarled Revenge. And then it was over.

An almost inaudible crunching sound, a groan, and the thud of a heavy body falling – all under the protection of the howling wind and driving snow.

Horror at the deed took hold of the marionette, Revenge delighting at the man's panic. They always asked themselves afterwards *why* they had done it and even *what* they had done. Also – *how* they would get away with it.

Run to the hatch! urged Revenge, captivated by the blood of the victim, which was slowly spreading, the steam rising from it, only for it to freeze a moment later in the cold. *Give them your version of the story first, and all your comrades will believe you!*

Terrified of being found out, the mercenary hurried to the closed hatch. So panic-stricken was he that he never noticed the Snow Slashers, tempted by the smell of blood, now springing over the railings on his side and onto the deck. He had only managed to heave open the heavy timber hatch when a pony-sized creature attacked from behind.

'Skiltous!' screamed the tortured mercenary down the steps. 'The upstart Paladin murde—.' Then the sharp fangs closed around the man's neck, its claws tearing at his back.

Revenge quickly slipped out of the dying man and through the chink between the planks, down into the belly of the ship. Two mercenaries dead and more would follow this same night.

The child of the Adversary was certain that the Paladins would no longer find any allies among Deklar's men – assuming, of course, that they survived the chaos that was now unfolding on *Alina's Rage.*

***

Ahren stared for a heartbeat up at the figure of the panic-stricken mercenary who had heaved open the hatch and roared his strange message down the passageway, a slim, six-legged Dark One with a narrow nose and glimmering red eyes then leapt on the unfortunate from behind before pulling him out into the darkness and the raging snowstorm.

'Danger!' yelled the Forest Guardian, three Snow Slashers immediately leaping down the steps. "Dark Ones below deck!' Then he threw himself backwards, simultaneously extending *Fisiniell*, and using the *Han'halthin* technique to slay two of the ferocious creatures with one arrow. The third threw itself at the screaming spear carrier who was standing guard beside Ahren, but to the delight of the Forest Guardian, the man stretched out his long weapon in front of him, stabilising the bottom end of it on the timbers with his foot, so that the Snow Slasher skewered itself on the weapon.

Hearing the noise of fighting from above, Ahren shouted for Hakanu and Bergen, but already the next dark Ones were thundering down through the hatch, and although Ahren killed another three, both he and the mercenary had to retreat as the following Snow Slashers leaped elegantly over their dead companions, quickly lessening the distance between the monsters and the two defenders. An arrow whizzed over Ahren's shoulder, killing one of the beasts, a quick glance back revealing to the Forest Guardian that Falk, the First, and Khara were all standing in the corridor, ready to replace him and the mercenary.

Ahren shoved the man beside him into a cabin on the starboard side. 'In you go!' he roared, he himself then springing into an over-full cabin to the port side. 'We have to split them up or they will overrun us!' he screamed, hoping his friends would hear him.

Then several things happened at once. While Ahren extended *Fisiniell* so that he could defend himself against a Snow Slasher that had crept towards the doorway, another beast was preparing to attack the mercenary in the cabin across the way. Khara danced forward along the corridor, her blades creating a deadly cocoon around her lithe body, while another of Falk's arrows flew past her, giving the Swordsmistress additional cover.

'The flame chamber!' roared the First. 'A couple of them are on their way to Caldria. If they break through to her, we will never escape the eternal ice!'

Ahren cursed, letting his arrow fly, the attacking Snow Slasher managing to evade the missile, which flew on, slamming into the head of the Dark One in the opposite cabin. Then he dropped his bow and drew his Wind Blade at the very instant that the beast facing him lunged forward, its murderous jaws opened wide. Time seemed to slow down as the Wind Blade and the maw of the Dark One engaged in a race to see which would reach its target first.

It was the fraction of a heartbeat that made the difference. The fangs of the Snow Slasher were already sinking into Ahren's cheeks when the side of his blade met the neck of the creature, the young man drawing the steel back and in with all the power he could muster. This was followed by a dreadful sound as the monster was decapitated, its head falling uselessly onto the planks, its biting reflexes extinguished for ever.

Ahren gasped and cursed as the blood poured from his cheeks. Clearly, there was something in the spittle of the Snow Slashers that inhibited coagulation! He would have to be healed or the loss of blood would mean the end of him.

'Let me try and get through to Caldria,' his beloved cried as more and more Snow Slashers filled the corridor, where the First, Falk, and – having heard the cries of battle – Trogadon were all waiting for the enemy. Ahren stood in the frame of the doorway, fighting back any of the monsters that tried to trap him within the cabin, while his eyes urgently tried to make contact with those of his three friends.

'My heart!' bellowed Trogadon over his shoulder as he swung his hammer upwards, sending one of the Snow Slashers flying up to the ceiling of the corridor and causing the timbers to squeak and splinter. 'Throw us your healing canteen!'

Ahren couldn't see what was going beyond his immediate vicinity now, for he was concentrating fully on defending himself against a growling Snow Slasher which seemed to have been driven into a frenzy by the smell of the Paladin's blood. The six legs of the creature ensured that it was extraordinarily agile as it evaded several well-aimed blows with its slender build, while the Forest Guardian, having missed the target on several occasions, was forced to retreat a step so that he wouldn't be bitten again.

From down the passageway he could hear groaning and cursing, followed by a loud warning cry: 'Watch out back there!' screamed Falk through gritted teeth. 'Three of the monsters have gotten past us!'

They are spreading throughout the entire ship, said Culhen anxiously. Ahren was able to see through the eyes of his friend, how the wolf was engaged in a ferocious duel with one of the Snow Slashers, with fur and claws flying everywhere.

The Paladin groaned inwardly, deciding in a heartbeat that it was time for a daring manoeuvre as his rabid opponent prepared to jump. At the very instant that the six legs of the creature left the planks, Ahren threw himself into a forward roll, keeping himself as small as possible while allowing his Wind Blade to rotate above him. The Deep Steel weapon cut a swathe of destruction through the Snow Slasher flying above him, and a heartbeat later, it was only the Paladin who got to his feet. Cursing furiously, he ran ahead of the newest onslaught of Dark Ones and towards his friends, who let him pass, immediately blocking the passageway with their weapons and bodies.

'Catch, Ahren!' cried Jelninolan from the doorframe of a cabin four paces further on, against which she was leaning weakly, holding her staff uselessly with one hand. Yet despite her exhaustion, she still managed to gracefully toss her canteen of sacred water over a skirmish involving a Dark Ones that had broken through the defensive line and one of Deklar's men. The fact that Jelninolan was not magically engaged in the fighting revealed to him how weak the priestess still had to be.

Ahren plucked the priceless receptacle out of the air, pulled out the cork, and poured its entire contents quickly onto both his cheeks, whereupon his bite wounds immediately closed up. The welcome coolness and the disappearance of pain revivified his iron determination. Raising his Wind Blade, he launched himself into a creature directly in front of him.

'We fought our way through all Jorath to get here!' he roared. 'We are hardly going to allow ourselves to be beaten by the fangs of a few over-sized foxes!'

Trogadon's pealing laughter echoed down the corridor in response. 'Now that's what I call the fighting spirit!' the blacksmith called out. 'In fact, you're beginning to sound like Hakanu!'

'Less joking and more killing!' interjected the First, and as if to underline the grim words of the old warrior, the gurgled scream of a mercenary could be heard from the prow of the ship. Ahren sensed how Khara was strengthening the Blessing Band of the Paladins, the connection telling him that all the Champions of the gods were still standing. Falk, Bergen, and Hakanu, however, were all in considerable pain, while Khara was wounded too, and in the prow of the ship alone.

'You tidy up back here, and I will make my way forward!' shouted Ahren firmly, shoving his way past the First and Trogadon. It seemed that the entire pack had forced their way into the ship's interior, for there were no more Dark Ones coming down the steps. For a split second, Ahren imagined how this skirmish might have ended if they'd had to fight on the Ice Fields without the protection, the light, and the warmth of *Alina's Rage* – then he just as quickly put the thought out of his mind. This ship was more than worth her weight in gold, and he silently thanked Trimm, who was whiling away the time in Cape Verstaad, but whose cunning rise to the top had ensured the establishment of the Thirteenth Armada, the Flame Belly ships included.

By now, Ahren had picked up *Fisiniell* again and was making his way down the corridor, the bow extended before him as he concentrated on taking one step at a time. He glanced into every cabin that he passed, and whenever he came across a Snow Slasher duelling with a mercenary or victoriously ripping the flesh of a slain victim and gorging on the bloodied corpse, he killed it on the spot. Using arrow after arrow, he cleaned the forward part of the ship of Dark Ones, each and every one of them having been taken totally by surprise at the swiftness of his action. Following a multitude of such fleeting skirmishes, he finally found himself standing before the heavy round door of the flame chamber, which was scored with scratches and bites, Khara leaning against it with blood gushing from a nasty leg wound.

'These beasts have incredibly strong jaws,' gasped Khara, three lifeless Snow Slashers lying at her feet. 'They simply sank my Deep Silk into my flesh.'

'How bad is it?' asked Ahren anxiously, the Swordsmistress giving a dismissive wave.

'I certainly won't be dancing in the near future,' she said casually, but Ahren could hear the undertone of concern in her voice. 'Pelneng is making the pain bearable, but to be honest, it's beginning to hurt.'

'If I may?' he asked with a smile, picking her up in his arms.

'My knight in shining armour,' she murmured with a smile, looking at him yearningly with her eyes opened exaggeratedly wide. 'Does this mean that I have to allow myself to be bitten all over first before you begin to show your romantic streak?'

Her breathing was uneven, and the Paladin sensed that his beloved was using humour to fight against the pain – and that the latter was winning. He walked quickly towards the stern of the ship, all the while praying to the THREE that they wouldn't encounter a Snow Slasher along the way that he might have missed or that had straggled down after the others.

I'm on my way, said Culhen, and not ten heartbeats later the Paladin heard the growling of two animals, followed by a yelp, and then nothing. Culhen appeared in the light of one of the passageways storm lanterns, covered in blood. *There was one left over,* said the wolf with a quiet solemnity. *Your path is now clear.*

Accompanied by Culhen, Ahren finally brought Khara into the cabin where Jelninolan was waiting, the elf immediately attending to the Swordsmistress. While the Storm Weaver went about her healing business, the rest of the companions arrived in dribs and drabs. Ahren had to swallow hard when he saw that almost all his friends had suffered bites or slashes to their skin. This battle had been won, but it had also been a clear warning. The creatures of the Ice Fields were not to be trifled with – he and his friends would do well to weigh up their options carefully as they journeyed through the unwelcoming vastness.

He opened his mouth to express his thanks to Jelninolan when suddenly a scornful cry echoed down the corridor. 'That murderous Paladin is in front of you. *Grab him!*'

Chapter 16

'Not again,' groaned Trogadon, wearily raising his hammer. 'I thought these accusations had been dealt with.'

Ahren and the dwarf positioned themselves in the passageway before the companions' cabin, which the First was blocking with his impressive frame. The veteran warrior was holding Falk's shield and sword in his hands, both smeared with the old Forest Guardian's blood, the injured man now lying on one of the bunks in the cabin, while Uldini treated the bite wound to his neck.

'Are we the only three who haven't been seriously wounded?' murmured Ahren.

We four, interjected Culhen from one of the cabins that the furious gang were now rushing past, heading straight for Ahren, Trogadon, and the First. *And it isn't you they want to get to. They want to get past you.* With a quick glance, the animal showed Ahren that Bergen and Hakanu were wearily stumbling down the steps behind the Forest Guardian, bringing ice and blood with them. Ahren resisted the temptation to look over his shoulder, comforting himself with the fact that the pair were at least able to remain on their own two feet. Even if all the blood was their own, they would hopefully be able to persevere until Ahren had calmed the situation.

'Why are your people raising their weapons against one of ours again?' asked Ahren, forcing himself to sound calm. 'I gave you my word regarding what would happen if one of my companions was threatened again.'

To Ahren's relief, Deklar raised his hand, causing his mercenaries to come to an immediate halt. The troop leader still had control over his men.

'One of my boys found Skiltous on deck just now,' said the squat mercenary. Then he pulled an object from his belt – an object that Ahren recognised all too easily. 'This was sticking out of his back.' He casually threw the knife on the timbers between them – it belonged to Hakanu.

'Yes, my apprentice has been seeking it for quite a while,' said Ahren matter-of-factly, fixing his eyes on the troop leader. Although scornful muttering and mocking laughter could be heard coming from the mercenaries, their commander remained quiet and focused.

I can smell how tense he is, commented Culhen.

He knows that the next skirmish will finish with the total annihilation of one side or the other, said Ahren. *And considering how beaten up we are, I wouldn't bet on us being victorious.*

'He has already killed one of our men,' said Deklar gravely, his voice suggestion that violence could break out at any moment. 'And now I find one of my mercenaries with the dagger of this *Paladin* protruding from his back.' The way he pronounced Hakanu's title caused Ahren to prick up his ears. He decided to follow his instincts.

'You have just said it yourself – he is a Paladin,' replied the young Forest Guardian, lowering his weapon. 'We do not spend our time running around the place killing anyone who doesn't appeal to us.'

'Oh, you do more than that,' countered Deklar bitterly. 'You lot hide away from your responsibilities for centuries on end, instigating wars instead, wars in which generations of people lose their loved ones.'

'It was the Adversary who started this war—,' responded Ahren energetically only for the mercenary to interrupt him with a furious outburst.

'I AM NOT TALKING ABOUT THIS WAR!' The troop leader's face had turned purple, and Ahren minimally turned his wrist, preparing to turn a gesture of de-escalation into a quick attack, should it prove necessary. 'Was it the Dark god who started the war between the Sunplains and the Eternal Empire?!' spluttered the mercenary leader. 'Or was it not, indeed, a Paladin who was lounging around on her jade throne, totally bored?'

'You lost someone in that war, I see,' said Ahren soothingly, all the while aware of his gut feeling. 'And that is why you are contemptuous twoards us.'

'Three brothers, a sister, my spouse… The list is endless,' growled Deklar, looking over Ahren's shoulder and staring at Hakanu. 'At the time, I could do nothing against this blatant injustice, but now I will not let any of you escape the consequences of your blood-thirsty acts.' The mercenaries behind him cheered, and Ahren feared that it would not be long before Deklar lost control of the situation.

'Master, I swear that it wasn't me,' said Hakanu, who had now reached the Forest Guardian, as had Bergen. 'One moment we were staring out into the storm, and the next, we saw one of the mercenaries heaving the hatch open for the Snow Slashers before immediately falling victim to one of the beasts. Then we were all fighting to stay alive as more and more of the monsters flooded the inside of the vessel.'

'He knows nothing!' exclaimed Deklar, his voice dripping with disdain. *'How original!'*

'I am not trying to be original,' countered Hakanu coldly. 'I am merely being *honest.*'

'This isn't getting us anywhere,' sighed Ahren, pointing down at the knife. 'The crew quarters down here have no doors. Anyone could have taken the weapon. You believe that no-one but Hakanu could have murdered Skiltous, and we don't believe that my apprentice is capable of such a deed. We are all wounded, and there more than enough corpses strewn about this ship. A snowstorm is raging outside, and we are moons away from Cape Verstaad.' Ahren looked expectantly at Deklar. 'What do you plan on doing?'

The troop leader glared at the Forest Guardian, and Ahren could see in the man's eyes that an internal battle between common sense and rage was being waged within the squat mercenary.

'We shall no longer fight for you,' said Deklar finally, with so much gall in his voice that Ahren was surprised he hadn't choked on the words. 'We shall no longer stand guard beside you or rescue you in an emergency. And as soon as we get back to Cape Verstaad, we will inform all the bards who are willing to listen, how cowardly and murderous the august Paladins really are.'

Ahren's heart was sore, through both sadness and pity. Deklar was fully aware that a formal complaint would be useless while Trimm was principal grandee of the city, and he also clearly knew that open warfare here and now would lead to considerable losses on his side. The squat man was relying instead on a succession of hollow gestures that he thought he would be able to sell to his men.

Glancing at the spear carriers, Ahren realised that he had wasted his words when it came to at least four of them, but the Forest Guardian nodded nonetheless before pointing towards the front of the ship. 'We shall seek out a cabin in the prow – everything to the rear of the stairway belongs to you and your men,' said Ahren curtly. 'We will try to stay out of your way insofar as this is possible.'

'Space will be easier to find than you might think, Thirteenth.' It was Ounlamun's voice that echoed down the corridor.

Ahren glanced over his shoulder and saw the captain approaching. The man's robe was covered in blood, but he himself seemed uninjured. 'Half my crew were killed in the assault – including my first mate.'

Ahren felt for the captain as he remembered the always smiling Harrebon.

'If *Alina's Rage* is going to continue sailing anywhere, then I am going to need help.'

'Should we turn around on the spot, my men will be only too glad to assist you, captain,' said Deklar, crossing his arms belligerently. 'But if we keep on our southward course, then you had better turn to this gang of murderers.'

'Careful!' snarled the First in a low voice. 'The Thirteenth may indeed be trying to spare as many lives as possible, but that doesn't mean that I won't smash your jaw in if you continue to drag the honour of my brothers and sisters through the mud.'

'Well, if we are all willing to lay down our arms, we can settle our differences in a civilised brawl,' suggested Trogadon, putting his hammer on the timbers and cracking his knuckles. 'I would be only too happy to beat the crazy ideas out of our new friends' skulls.'

Ahren suppressed a smile as several of the spear carriers retreated a step. Culhen took advantage of the moment to accidentally yawn as he stepped out of the cabin where he had been waiting, thereby revealing his impressive fangs as he positioned himself behind the flinching mercenaries.

Daring, commented Ahren, full of admiration for his friend's manoeuvre.

I can smell that their fighting spirit has deserted them, countered Culhen, uttering a low growl to underling the danger the spear carriers were in.

'Then we are agreed?' asked Ahren, looking coolly at Deklar. 'You don't cross us by sitting this voyage out. In return, we will keep away from you.'

'Done!' snapped the troop leader, glaring at the Forest Guardian. Then he fixed his gaze on Culhen. 'And now get this fleabag out of *my* half of the ship.'

While the mercenaries made room so that the companions could pass, the First grabbed Ahren by the elbow and pulled him to the side. 'We cannot trust them,' he murmured. 'I've suspected as much for a lo—'

'I know,' whispered Ahren, interrupting the old warrior. 'But at the moment, it is Deklar's men who are lamenting the many deaths in their ranks, not us. Earlier I saw how one of the mercenaries got Falk out of a sticky situation with a valiant throw of his spear. We saved each other's lives in our skirmish with the Snow Slashers. If it weren't for this damn dagger in Skiltous's back, our two groups could have made a fine fighting force.'

The First narrowed his eyes and looked thoughtfully down the passageway, observing the mixture of soldiers. 'You're right,' he said absently.

'*Sabotage?*' asked Khara, repeating the suspicion of the First, the old warrior having explained his theory to Ahren and the others. 'Here? In the middle of nowhere?'

They were standing below deck in the prow of the ship, directly in front of the scratched door of the flame chamber, having requisitioned the two cabins on either side of them once they had carried the dead bodies up and thoroughly cleaned the cabins of any remaining bloodstains.

'You forget that we examined every soul on board this vessel,' said Jelninolan, her voice weak. She and Uldini had superficially patched up their companions' wounds, preparing a healing sleep for the injured instead – which explained the exhausted state of the two Ancients. 'I can guarantee that we have found neither High Fangs nor Dopplers on board.'

'At least, no *conventional* Dopplers,' interjected Bergen. 'What about the children of the Dark god, who escaped from the Obsidian Fortress? One of them was certainly spotted heading south.'

'You mean, he or she sneaked onto the ship in Cape Verstaad?' asked Uldini sceptically. 'And how would they know that *Alina's Rage* would be the ship that survived the leviathan's attack?'

'It is certainly…a possibility,' said Jelninolan hesitantly, breaking the silence that had ensued. 'The only thing we know is that these beings possess different powers, and that we still haven't identified the child who challenged us in Gol-Konar despite our spells.'

'Don't forget the simplest motive of all – greed,' muttered Trogadon grimly. 'These mercenaries aren't exactly models of respectability. Maybe one of them was offered a goodly pile of gold if he made sure that this expedition failed, and we were forced to return to Cape Verstaad early.'

'Then I would prefer to believe that one of the children was here on board,' said Hakanu with a sigh. 'That would be less depressing than us being betrayed for a handful of gold coins.'

'But how would a paid henchman force Mauk into attacking Hakanu?' interjected Khara, shaking her head.

'If it was a case of bribery, then at a minimum Mauk and another mercenary were paid,' concluded Bergen.

'Or Mauk and one of Ounlamun's crew, who is lying low,' suggested Trogadon darkly.

'Whichever it is, I think that the First has a point,' said Falk with a frown. 'I can certainly see how Mauk may have gone into a rage, but a murder committed with Hakanu's stolen knife? That stinks of a saboteur in our ranks.'

'And as we are on the topic,' began Ahren, glaring angrily at the young warrior, 'how often have I told you *never* to lose sight of your weapons? Especially your knife. You never know…'

'…when it can save your life,' added Hakanu, finishing off the Forest Guardian's sentence with his head bowed. 'I am so sorry, master. In the chaos below deck, I was sure that it has fallen into one of the rucksacks or into one of the crates that we are constantly moving hither and yon.' With that, he nodded towards the mountain of possessions which they had moved for the umpteenth time.

'If a child of the Dark god is behind all this, it is unbelievably devious,' said Uldini, rubbing his eyes wearily. 'It is driving a wedge between us and the mercenaries and creating enmity where there should be an alliance.'

'And don't forget Mauk's attack,' added Ahren. 'A perfect little trap. Either the mercenary would have been successful, and a Paladin would be dead now, or Hakanu defended himself, bringing the wrath of the other soldiers of fortune upon us. That doesn't sound like hired saboteurs – unless they were fanatics as well.'

'To my mind, we are looking for a servant of the Adversary,' said Jelninolan firmly. 'Now the only question is, where do we find them?'

Ahren looked pleadingly at his friends, their faces, however, reflecting his own cluelessness.

As the silence grew longer and longer, it dawned on Ahren that they had no plan to counter an enemy, who was proving to be both devious and highly intelligent.

***

Despite the events of the night, Revenge was discontented. This Deklar was a hard nut to crack, the child of Adversary not yet having managed to find a way into his stubborn head. He had watched on helplessly as Deklar and the Thirteenth Paladin agreed to their laughable truce. Thankfully, anger was seething in the minds of many of the troop leader's men, and Revenge knew he could pick almost all of them to be his new toys.

The night's haul hadn't been too bad, he reminded himself. Half the crew were dead *and* eight of the mercenaries. The fact that one of the Wind Sorcerers had also been slaughtered meant that *Alina's Rage* would progress at only half her normal speed. If he could only get one of the mercenaries to take action against either the captain or the wench in the flame chamber, but alas, they were too focused on getting their revenge on the Paladins. Revenge decided to keep his eyes peeled for any opportunity that would allow him to cause indirect damage to either the ship or her crew.

When the angry mercenary within whom he was ruminating suddenly had an idea, Revenge seized upon it, immediately bending it to suit his own, very particular, ends…

***

Ahren was awakened by sweat rolling down his body as he found himself panting for air in the sticky and unbearably hot cabin. Khara, Bergen, and Falk looked as overheated as he felt with their red cheeks and wide-open mouths, and when the Forest Guardian tried to sense Culhen, he realised instantly that the wolf had sought refuge in the fo'c'sle.

'Am I dreaming?' grunted Ahren numbly as he sat up.

'It only started now,' said Falk, who was wiping the sweat from his brow with an old shirt. 'One heartbeat, I'm lying here in a deep healing sleep, and the next, it's become suffocatingly hot.'

'It must have something to do with the flame chamber,' suggested Ahren, getting to his feet.

'The interior of the ship has always been only moderately heated,' said Khara sceptically. 'Why should it be any different now?'

'Maybe because we are sleeping directly beside the flame chamber?' interjected Bergen, drying his blonde beard with his sleeve.

Ahren shook his head and forced himself to put on his trousers. Then he had an idea and immediately wrapped himself in his magical cloak. It proved just as resistant to heat as it was to cold.

'Have you any room in there, little brother?' asked Bergen enviously, only for Khara to chuckle before positioning herself between the Forest Guardian and the Ice Lander.

'Don't even think of it,' she teased. 'If Ahren is going to let anyone under his cloak, then it's going to be his spouse.'

'Isn't it nice to be so popular?' interjected Falk, winking at the young Forest Guardian. 'The way they all want to be as close to you as possible?'

Ahren grinned before shrugging his shoulders apologetically towards both Khara and Bergen. 'I'm going to see if I can find out why we suddenly have temperatures like those in the Southern Jungles,' he said, slipping out of the cabin. A quick side glance revealed to him that the runes on the door to the flame chamber were glowing an angry red, which was far more powerful than the smouldering that he had seen before whenever Caldria had cast her spell to heat up the prow. On the other side of the passageway, Uldini, Jelninolan, and the other companions were stirring uneasily in their sweat-soaked sleep, while the corridor itself seemed so still and deserted that Ahren decided to talk to the flame sorceress herself before seeking the advice of the two Ancients.

'Caldria?' he asked in a low but urgent voice through the closed door, which was squeaking and crackling in the intense heat. 'Are you alright?'

'I have a hard day ahead of me, but otherwise, I can't complain,' said the woman cheerfully. 'The breakfast that the captain had delivered to me was splendid and my chamber pot has been slopped out. What more could a woman want?'

'And you are certain that she isn't a she-dwarf?' asked Trogadon, sleepily emerging from his cabin. 'She sounds like one, at any rate.'

'Maybe you would like to enter the bond with her?' hissed Jelninolan, looking at the dwarf irritably. 'Seeing as you have so much in common.'

'Why don't we go and get some fresh air, my heart?' countered Trogadon with untypical diplomacy. 'The heat isn't doing any of us any good.'

Ahren suppressed the urge to point out that the blacksmith was undoubtedly used to much higher temperatures on account of his profession. Instead, he concentrated on the sorcerous Caldria once Jelninolan had silently dismissed Trogadon's suggestion with a wave of her hand. 'You *do* know that the door to the flame chamber looks as though it is about to catch fire?' he asked. '*And* that it's hotter here than in the Nameless Desert?'

Ahren heard a continuous muttering of curses from within, followed by a loud rumble. The runes on the door were suddenly extinguished, Caldria then pulling open the heavy door, at which point a blast of heat so powerful poured out that even Ahren was aware of it as a pleasant summer's breeze from beneath his cloak. The sorceress's face was bright red, and the garment that she had hurriedly thrown over herself stuck to her body, she was sweating so much. Ahren looked at the woman expectantly, but she ignored him completely, so concerned was she for the outside of the door. She ran her fingers along the runes in the wood, grunting with displeasure after her examination.

'The charm circle has been broken,' announced Uldini from behind Ahren, a glance over his shoulder on the Forest Guardian's part revealing that the Ancient had floated silently over to them and was now performing his own examination. 'Up there, directly under the…'

'I see it,' grumbled Caldria without looking at Uldini. 'Never confuse insufficient power with insufficient knowledge, Ancient.'

'And don't confuse knowledge with arrogance,' countered Uldini suavely.

Now Caldria stared at Uldini, and Ahren was sure that he saw a flicker of amusement in her narrowed eyes. She pointed at a rune, still looking at the Arch Wizard. 'This nick here looks like a claw mark,' she murmured urgently. 'But it isn't – or at least, not only. I checked the bane charm last night again and although it was damaged, it was still usable. Someone lent a helping hand since then.'

Ahren leaned forward and looked closely at the spot that the sorceress had indicated. He noticed a small, straight, and deep notch engraved in one of the broad grooves that the claws of the Snow Slasher had left.

'This sign was deliberately altered,' said the Forest Guardian grimly. 'I think there was a dagger at work here.'

'I have mine with me, master,' Hakanu announced from the starboard cabin. 'I'm even sleeping on top of it so that it isn't taken a second time.'

'Our saboteur was at work again,' said Falk, 'and is clearly wasting no time.'

'A *saboteur?*' asked Caldria, taken aback. '*Here?*'

'That was how I reacted too, at first,' said Khara dryly. 'But the clues are indisputable.'

'And contradictory,' interjected the First irritably. 'On the one hand, Mauk's suicidal actions and the assassination of a comrade – actions that one could attribute to a fanatic or a child of the Adversary. On the other hand, needling like this – something that makes our life more difficult, encouraging us to abandon our mission. None of it makes sense.'

'It sounds as though you and this mysterious saboteur are playing a game, whose rules you don't understand,' commented Caldria, not in the least concerned. 'And that you have ruled me out as a suspect.'

'You have been in the flame chamber the entire period of our voyage,' said Falk, who had stepped out into the passageway. 'Which means that you could not have carried out half of the attacks. Furthermore, you would have damaged the flame chamber in a far subtler and more effective manner than by simply scratching the bane charm that protects the interior of *Alina's Rage* from the heat.'

The sorceress nodded approvingly as she once again studied the damage to the door. 'This was undoubtedly the work of an amateur,' she said finally. 'Your saboteur has no clue when it comes to sorcery. All they needed to do was to damage the rune a handspan further left and the charm would have been disabled. The entire belly of the ship would now be an inferno.'

'Could we discuss such possibilities in a lower voice, perhaps?' asked Trogadon, coughing nervously. 'We don't want to give anyone who might be eavesdropping ideas.'

Ahren glanced down the lantern-illuminated passageway. There was no-one to be seen, but the doorless cabins port and starboard offered plenty of hiding places for a possible spy.

'I will check to see if anyone is listening in,' whispered Khara, her hands on the hilts of her weapons.

Holding his axe firmly, Bergen pushed his way behind the Swordsmistress. 'I will go with you and watch your back.'

The pair carried out their search, cabin by cabin, and only when they had progressed ten paces along the passageway without encountering a soul did Ahren turn to Caldria and whisper: 'Can we reverse the damage?'

'Yes. By swapping the door for another one in Cape Verstaad and renewing the bane circle,' murmured the sorceress.

Uldini's and Jelninolan's nods confirmed the worst.

'The good news is that the plate-heating magic will still be channelled towards the prow. However, the bane circle that guides the rest of the heat via the iron braces to the individual cabins will not function properly anymore. Which means that summer temperatures will prevail down here whenever I do my work and ensure that the Wind Sorcerers are able to move the ship forward through the ice.'

'Are we talking about a pleasant summer like in the Knight Marshes or will it more resemble the Southern Jungles, where even a dwarf can't take a breath without breaking into a sweat?' asked Trogadon anxiously.

The apologetic look on the sorcerer's face was all too revealing, the blacksmith immediately reaching for his fur cloak.

'I will be up on deck,' he said, stomping down the passageway and muttering to himself.

'We should all wait outside whenever Caldria performs her work,' suggested Jelninolan. 'Sticky heat like that won't do any of us any good.'

'We cannot leave this door unguarded,' countered the First. 'If the saboteur turns up again and manages through chance or design to destroy the correct rune…'

'*I* will stay here,' said Ahren, straightening his cloak. 'The heat doesn't bother me.'

Uldini chuckled and shook his head. 'Once the bards start singing the praises of your cloak, Akkad will be overrun with orders for new ones.'

'Which is why *none* of those loudmouths will learn about it – *ever*,' warned Jelninolan. 'The Firesprays would be eradicated in no time at all, because those with enough money or influence would demand such a cloak for their collection.'

'Back to Ahren's idea,' growled the First. 'It makes sense and is easily doable. Ahren stands guard whenever Caldria is working, one of us will do it when she rests.'

'My charged magic is slowly losing power anyway,' said the woman, pointing back into her chamber, where the runes that decorated the interior were glimmering with far less energy than Ahren remembered from his first visit. 'That, allied with the loss of our first mate, suggests that Ounlamun and I will only be able to move the ship forward during the day, and we will have to rest at night.'

'And when your supplies peter out?' asked Jelninolan.

'Then progress will be even slower,' said Caldria with a shrug of her shoulders. 'You can add on another one or two moons for our return journey through the pack ice.'

Uldini opened his mouth to speak, then closed it again. He paused for a couple of heartbeats before making a second attempt: 'Jelninolan can conjure up the wind that we need, and I can enter this chamber when Caldria's supplies have been depleted. However, that will mean that we will be of little use in the event of a confrontation, our energy being worn out by the daily labour of driving the ship onward.'

'In other words, such actions can only be brought about as a last resort,' said Ahren, the First nodding emphatically. 'I shudder to think what might have happened last night if you and Jelninolan had been too worn out to perform your healing magic.'

'Perhaps this is our saboteur's plan,' interjected Khara, having just returned with Bergen. 'First, weaken the sorcerers and then launch a fresh attack.'

'By the way, the front part of the ship is devoid of people,' added Bergen. 'Ounlamun's crew are all on deck. Apparently, the heat was too much for them.'

Most of Deklar's men are here too,' said Culhen, Ahren then seeing through the eyes of his wolf that the main deck and part of the aft deck were filled with occupants. *They don't look too happy.*

The Forest Guardian cursed quietly. 'Culhen has identified at least four mercenaries, who are standing around Ounlamun, discussing something angrily with him.' *Go over to him and sit down,* commanded Ahren. *That should calm things down a little.* 'Culhen is taking care of it,' he said to his friends.

Khara grinned. 'Muai has seen what he's up to. And, of course, she doesn't want to forego the chance of appearing equally impressive and intimidating. She has sat down on the other side of Ounlamun.' She giggled as she continued: 'I don't know who is more nervous – the poor captain, finding himself between an armoured giant wolf and a majestic tigress, or the mercenaries who are now going to have to push their way past these unusual bodyguards if they want to continue harassing the captain.'

'We should all go on deck too,' sighed Falk. 'A short visit down here should suffice to warm us up if we get too cold up there.'

'I would advise against that,' warned Jelninolan. 'The difference in temperature between the air outside and the heat in here will be so great that experiencing both extremes in close proximity shall certainly pose a danger.'

'Which effectively means that we are barred from the interior of the ship once Caldria begins her work,' concluded the First. 'That doesn't appeal to me one little bit.'

'You could always stand guard beside your friend in your underclothes,' suggested Caldria, looking the First up and down salaciously. 'I promise that I won't secretly peer at you – at least, not very often.'

The war veteran blinked in surprise before wordlessly picking up his fur garment.

Ahren was sure that the age-old Paladin had not been addressed so cheekily by a mere mortal for centuries, the Forest Guardian secretly hoping that this little episode might make him just that little bit more approachable.

'Then be off with the lot of you!' commanded Ahren, giving Khara a peck on the cheek.

'We will ensure that no-one spends their time down here with you,' replied the Swordsmistress. 'Whoever this saboteur is, they will have to run around below deck in their underclothes or else be stuck on deck with us before *Alina's Rage* comes to a halt again.'

Ahren nodded at Caldria, who then closed the door to her little realm from within. The rest of the companions slipped into their fur garments to protect themselves from the Ice Field winds. When the bane circle on the door of the flame chamber began to glimmer angrily, Ahren's friends quickly bade their farewells and fled from the growing heat by scampering down the corridor and up the steps. Ahren stood with his back to the flame chamber, staring down the abandoned passageway before him. He couldn't help feeling that he was being watched by invisible eyes that were waiting for him to make one little mistake. He pulled his cloak closer around him and prepared for a long, and in all probability, uncomfortable watch.

It kind of looks as if the interior of the ship is on fire, said Culhen uneasily as he shared with Ahren his view of the open hatch in the mid deck, from where clouds of steam were billowing up.

The opposing air temperatures were engaged in bitter conflict wherever they met, creating in the process an impressive sight. Ahren saw, too, that his friends had either gathered around Ounlamun or had sought refuge in the fo'c'sle. The main deck, on the other hand, belonged to Deklar's men as well as to those mariners currently being commanded by the captain, who was steering *Alina's Rage* southward through the newly created channel.

What's the mood up there like? asked Ahren, concerned.

Not good, responded the wolf, his answer no surprise to the Forest Guardian. *The fact that the days must from now on be endured in either bitter cold or oppressive heat is causing considerable unrest, and not only among the mercenaries. Both the sailors and the spear carriers are muttering that we should turn around and get reinforcements as well as a fully functioning ship before returning here again.*

Ahren nodded in the silence and seclusion of the passageway. Even if he didn't quite understand the strategy of the saboteur, the results spoke for themselves – a crew that was at odds with itself and an only partially functioning flame chamber – *Alina's Rage* was beginning to resemble a volcano on the point of eruption.

He was about to share his thoughts with Culhen when Ahren suddenly saw a figure walking along the corridor towards him. His Wind Blade was already half drawn when the Forest Guardian recognised that the stranger was a lad of no more than fifteen or sixteen winters, dressed in light clothing, and carrying a water jug.

'I thought you might be thirsty,' said the youth, coming to a halt eight paces from Ahren and clearly intimidated by the Wind Blade glistening in the lantern light.

Ahren sheathed his weapon again before grunting irritably: 'You gave me a fright.' Then he added in a friendly tone: 'I expected everyone to be on deck. What are you doing down here?'

'I am Bahron, the cabin boy,' explained the lad, shrugging his shoulders awkwardly. 'Every morning I bring Caldria sufficient water in a closed pitcher so that she doesn't dry out while she works. She sweats so much, you know. And I thought you might like some too.'

The cabin boy's explanation made logical sense to Ahren, and now he remembered having seen him hurrying through the ship on several occasions, always carrying food, drink, or bundles of dirty clothing. His voice sounded honest, and the round, young face of the youth suggested that he was in awe of the Paladin. But there was something about Bahron's eyes that didn't quite seem to match the rest of his appearance.

'Come closer,' said the young Paladin after a pause. 'Put the pitcher down in front of me.'

Bahron nodded quickly and approached, his eyes fixed firmly on the planks below, as though he was aware that Ahren had noticed something. Two paces in front of the Paladin, he set down the receptacle.

'Closer,' said Ahren coldly.

Without looking up, Bahron shoved the pitcher forward until it was a pace before the waiting Forest Guardian. Still stooped, he was about to retreat only for Ahren to suddenly shoot his arm forward, grabbing the cabin boy by the chin, his other hand clutching the scabbard of his Wind Blade, ready to put it to deadly use in an instant if necessary. Then he forced Bahron to look up at him, the Paladin narrowing his eyes and peering into those of the quaking young man.

'Who *are* you?' whispered Ahren, trying to see if there were any signs of maliciousness in the eyes of his opposite number who didn't seem to quite fit the bill of a mere cabin boy. 'Are you a brother of Hate?'

It took no more than the briefest of moments, but there was a fleeting flash of amazement in the eyes of the lad, immediately followed by a look of confusion.

'Of…of *whom?*' stammered Bahron shifting his head uncomfortably, the Forest Guardian still holding the unfortunate lad's chin in a grip of steel.

Ahren couldn't be certain in the lantern light, but he thought he could make out a dark shadow – similar to a puff of smoke – rising from Bahron's face like the last fumes of a dying campfire. The pall forced its way through the gaps in the timbers above, disappearing so quickly that under normal circumstances, Ahren would be wondering if he had merely imagined the whole thing. He concentrated once more on the cabin boy now shaking like a leaf, who was now covering his tear-stained face with his hands as he kicked wildly at the pitcher, causing it to smash into smithereens, its contents spilling onto the timber floor.

'Don't drink it,' wailed Bahron, his voice betraying the terrible guilt that he was feeling. 'The water is poisonous! I don't know what came over me!' He stared at Ahren through his fingers with such a lost look that the Paladin could do nothing other than release his grip from the distracted lad's chin. 'All I want to do is go home! We are all going to die because of you!' Then he wept bitter tears, once again hiding his face in his hands.

Ahren wanted to take the grief-stricken boy in his arms and reassure him, but he didn't dare to for fear that the shadow would return and force the innocent cabin boy to do something reckless, like seize Ahren's knife. 'Sit down,' he said instead, his voice nonetheless friendlier now. 'Let us keep watch together until friends of mine come to find out what has happened to you and to see if you need help.'

Bahron looked at him in confusion, his eyes red from crying. '*Help?*' he asked. 'Although I tried to ensure that you would suffer the worst cramps of your life?'

Ahren suppressed a chuckle. This lad was certainly no murderer, nor even a bad person. Only a frustrated soul who had come up with a bad idea so that he could simply escape from an unpleasant situation.

And he had perhaps revealed to Ahren the first rule of this mysterious game that the child of the Dark god was playing with them on board *Alina's Rage.*

***

Revenge was beside himself with fury. What had he been thinking of – using this snivelling cabin boy! Bahron's vengeful streak had been far too weak to carry out such a grievous act, and it had taken all the child of Adversary's efforts to transform the lad's homesickness and helplessness into anger against the Paladins, on whose account *Alina's Rage* was cutting her way through the Ice Fields.

Revenge had been so proud of himself after the successful onslaught of the Snow Slashers and the damage done to the flame chamber door! So proud that he had decided to concentrate on a small deed as a reward – a deed which would ideally intensify the atmosphere of suspicion on board the vessel, not to mention draw everyone's attention to a Paladin, doubled over in agony as cramps assailed his guts, giving Revenge himself cover as he took his next step. Instead, it had had the opposite effect, and in all probability revealed his presence aboard *Alina's Rage*.

Revenge extended all his senses to everyone assembled on deck, searching for the darkest soul that he could find. He only had a few days before the Ancients would recognise what it was their charm nets should be trying to catch.

It was time for the decisive strike!

***

'The poor boy is beside himself,' said Jelninolan, who had just returned from Bahron's bunk. 'I had to put him into a deep sleep so that his spirit can heal. A night filled with pleasant dreams should give him the strength to be able to live with his feelings of guilt.'

Ahren and his companions were standing in the passageway in front of the cooled down flame chamber discussing the events of the day while the companion animals stood guard at the helm and the abandoned ship's wheel. Until they understood fully the saboteur's modus operandi, they were not going to take any risks. Ounlamun, Caldria, and Deklar were also present – the latter only because Ahren had insisted upon it.

'What's this all about?' snarled the squat mercenary. 'Did you lot bring me here to show me how sympathetic you are to Ounlamun's snotty-nosed brat, while my men are falling like flies all around you?'

'Why is this dirty swine here anyway?' asked Bergen, glaring down at the spear carrier. 'It's people like you who give honest mercenaries a bad name.'

'Not everyone can be *blessed* with a gods' *Blessing*,' snorted Deklar, his eyes narrowed belligerently. 'Some of us have to rely on our own natural ability to ensure the survival of our comrades.'

'That's enough!' barked Falk. 'Ahren, say what you have to say before we have another bloodbath here.'

'There was something in the way Bahron looked when he brought the pitcher,' explained the Forest Guardian, chewing his lower lip uncertainly. What he had experienced was difficult to explain, especially to someone as antagonistic as Deklar. 'Something that didn't *belong* there. A darkness that seemed too intense for someone of such tender years.'

'How poetic,' growled Deklar. 'Half of my men have enough darkness in them for three people. It's one of the perks of the job.'

'Whatever it was, it seemed to flee the moment it recognised that I was suspicious,' continued Ahren, ignoring the troop leader's comment. 'Immediately afterwards, the cabin boy broke down and confessed. He even smashed the pitcher to prevent me from consuming the poison.'

Uldini shook his head. 'According to Palnah, the *thing* influenced Reik deeply in Gol-Konar. If our opponent was similarly capable, then they would have set mercenary after mercenary on us – including our esteemed Deklar here.'

'Who says that won't happen?' asked Trogadon, glancing sideways at the squat troop leader while demonstratively leaning on his hammer.

'This is why both leaders of the ship are here now,' said Ahren before Deklar had a chance to rise to the dwarf's bait. 'If one knows that one is being manipulated, one can do something about it.'

'Has anyone under your command behaved in a peculiar manner?' asked Jelninolan, addressing both the captain and the mercenary simultaneously.

Ounlamun shook his head, Deklar reacting to the question as if he had bitten into a lemon, within which a Needle Spider was hiding.

'My people are not what you might call meek specimens,' muttered the mercenary irritably. 'Most of them behave more than a little strangely – it's their natural state.'

'The child is probably hiding amongst them,' said Falk, raising a warning hand as Deklar was on the point of protesting. 'You have just admitted that you have some pretty unsavoury characters in your troop. The ideal place for a child of the Adversary that wants to remain undiscovered.'

'Mauk's assassination attempt on me, the framed murder of Skiltous, the scratches to the flame chamber door, and then the rather harmless attempted poisoning of Ahren...' pondered Hakanu. 'If these were all the work of a child of the Adversary, then why such differing approaches?'

'The ability of the child to manipulate people must be impaired in some way,' interjected Uldini. 'He couldn't, for example, force Ounlamun to simply jump overboard into the icy waters – otherwise, he would have instigated such an action a long time ago to make our life more difficult.'

The captain went ashen faced on hearing these words.

'And I could overheat the flame chamber if this…child befogged *my* mind,' said Caldria, who was standing in the open doorway of the cabin that she was not permitted to leave. 'But my thoughts seem clearer than ever.' Then she grinned cheekily at the captain. 'All things considered, do you think I might be allowed to renegotiate my salary?' she asked in a sugary voice. 'You know yourself, my dear Ounlamun – it would keep me in my good mood and prevent me from coming up with any silly notions that the child might take advantage of.'

To everyone's surprise, Deklar laughed – even if somewhat grimly. 'Your priorities are almost as direct as your sense of humour.'

'We should do some delving into Mauk and the murdered Skiltous,' said Falk thoughtfully. 'Perhaps their comrades know something that will help us to recognise a pattern.'

Deklar hesitated before nodding. 'I can help you in this regard,' he said. 'By engaging my boys in conversation during the day, for example. Then the Swordsmistress and the elf could come by and collect the so-called research.'

'Why us specifically?' asked Khara coolly.

'You are not Paladins,' said Deklar before grinning shamelessly. 'And of course, for the reason that you suspect, princess – you two are pleasant on the eye. That will have a calming effect on my lads.'

'Can I smash his teeth in *now?* asked Trogadon, looking pleadingly at the priestess.

'No,' said the elf, fixing the grinning mercenary with a cold stare. 'If Deklar doesn't ensure that his *lads* behave themselves, then the predatory animals of the Ice Fields can pick up the remains of the mercenaries in our slip stream.'

Ahren chuckled silently to himself as all the colour drained from Deklar's face.

Chapter 17

The next five days followed the same pattern. Ahren stood guard before the flame chamber while Khara and Jelninolan sought – under Deklar's protection – answers to questions that they themselves did not quite know how to formulate. All the while they steadily approached the Frozen Teeth, Ahren reminding himself that despite all the problems they had encountered trying to locate Yollock, they were nearing their goal, nautical cable by nautical cable.

Uldini, meanwhile, cast several charm nets, each specifically aimed at sensing human minds at work, while Culhen, Muai, and the disguised Kamaluq listened intently for whispered conversations, while the rest of the companions concentrated on ensuring – insofar as this was possible – that the mercenaries behaved themselves.

Every evening they discussed the unfamiliar pattern that lay behind the acts of sabotage and pondered the importance of this or that piece of information which had been brought to their attention. They had found out that Mauk was wanted in another country for a knifing incident, and that Skiltous was such a notorious dice cheater that he would have even given Falk and Trogadon the shivers. Furthermore, they learned that many of the mercenaries were suspicious of the flame chamber, fearing that the runes on its door represented a curse to keep away curious eyes.

Having failed to make much progress in their investigations, Ahren's mood was not the best when one day at around noon Culhen suddenly slipped into his mind, behaving like a skittish whelp.

A clue, a clue! he gloated. *I think I've found a clue!*

Alright, alright, grumbled Ahren. *Do you want me to throw a damn stick for you as a reward or what?*

The term 'mortally offended' was insufficient to describe how Culhen felt on hearing his Paladin's huffy response. *Ahren – since when have I been your puppy dog?* asked the wolf, askance.

Apologies, muttered the Forest Guardian. *Five days of monotonous sentry duty added to a crippling uncertainty as to when the next calamity will fall upon us isn't doing me any good.*

Clearly not, said Culhen, still piqued.

Ahren sighed. *Tell me what you have heard? Please?*

Right, then, the wolf replied, resuming his cheerful disposition. *There is a rumour going round that Mendraal had a problem with Skiltous. Apparently, he had repeatedly accused the murdered fellow of cheating.*

Who is Mendraal? asked Ahren. *That name doesn't mean anything to me.*

This is where it gets exciting, explained Culhen, wagging his tail. *Mendraal was the mercenary who was on sentry duty with Skiltous on deck during the night of the Snow Slasher attack.*

Ahren remembered the unfortunate mercenary, who had been bitten by one of the Dark Ones before being pulled away just when he'd opened the hatch and roared something about Hakanu. Suddenly, the Paladin was all ears.

This Mendraal wanted to put the blame for Skiltous' murder on Hakanu! said Ahren excitedly, remembering the words of the deceased mercenary. *You think he killed his comrade and then fell victim to the Dark One before he had a chance to finish roaring his accusation?*

Even better, replied Culhen proudly. *I think I can now see through the scheming of this child of the Adversary.*

Ahren gasped. *Tell me more!* he urged his animal, the rest of the afternoon then being taken up with the exploration of various theories, which by the end of the day had hardened into a few relevant questions that Deklar, Khara, and Jelninolan would pose to the mercenaries the following morning.

***

Through the ears of his marionette, Revenge heard the information that the troop leader and the two females were gleaning from the mercenaries, and it wasn't long before he realised that they were on his trail. Meanwhile, this Uldini character was experimenting in the background with his charm nets, which were already tugging at Revenge's being, forcing the child of the Adversary to retreat to the most vicious mind that he could find – where he remained perfectly still, to avoid detection.

When the sorcerer temporarily suspended his search so that he could recharge his magic and get closer to the mystery that was Revenge, the child decided to go for broke. He flooded the mind of his marionette with images in an attempt to break his resistance. The man stumbled backward a step, and then forward into a cloud of steam that was climbing up the steps and out of the hatch. Revenge's plaything ran down the stairs and back to the stern of the ship. There he listened, gasping, to Revenge's words, which the child repeated, again and again: *They have you now! You are sitting in a trap! There is only one possibility of escape!*

Slowly, dreadfully slowly, the mercenary's eyes moved up until they were looking at one of the hurricane lamps hanging from the walls.

***

'So, *that's* it?' asked Falk, who was standing with the others on the aft deck. 'The key that we are looking for.'

Culhen, who was sitting beside the old man, woofed in affirmation. He was sharing his senses with Ahren, the young Forest Guardian standing guard in front of the flame chamber while excitedly listening in. He had been witness – thanks to his and the wolf's connection – to Deklar cajoling a piece of important information from one of his men on the main deck. The wolf was feeling incredibly proud of himself, having been the cause of all the questions that had at last led to this success.

'Let us summarise the situation,' murmured Uldini, beckoning his companions and Deklar to assemble around the expectant Ounlamun. 'Mauk bore a grudge against animals – that was why he kicked Kamaluq.'

The fox whimpered, and Culhen had the impression that the little fellow was relieved at the fact that the man's action had at least been based on some sort of reason, no matter how dark and twisted it may have been.

'After which, Hakanu broke the mercenary's ribs, which meant he was now revengeful towards the lad, too.'

'I should have stabbed him hard through the foot,' said the young warrior grimly. 'Maybe that would have put a stop to all our problems.'

'Don't interrupt me,' growled the Ancient irritably. 'I am trying to *think* here.'

Hakanu murmured something about crotchety sorcerers, causing Ahren to chuckle as he listened in on Uldini's explanation through Culhen's ears.

'Driven on by his scorn, Mauk finally tried to murder Hakanu. Mendraal, furthermore, despising Skiltous because he believed that his comrade had cheated him, killed his fellow mercenary during the night of the Snow Slasher assault,' continued Uldini in a droning, lecturing voice. 'Do we really need to torture ourselves over what is blindingly obvious?' he asked rhetorically. 'The being on board this ship can magnify the anger of anyone and everyone, and manipulate, at least partially, whoever is hosting them.' With that, the Arch Wizard tapped his temple meaningfully.

'Not *anger*,' said Khara thoughtfully. 'If that were so, he could just as easily have inhabited Deklar.'

'Indeed, you are right,' said the troop leader, grinning balefully. 'I am a *very* angry man.'

'I think it is the lust for revenge that we are seeking,' said Jelninolan. 'Both Mauk and Mendraal were hoping to get revenge for perceived slights.'

'And the flame chamber?' asked Bergen sceptically. 'Did that also treat someone badly?'

'I think it has less to do with the chamber,' replied the elf, 'but rather with its occupant.' She turned to Deklar. 'Is there anyone in your troop who had a bone to pick with Caldria?'

The troop leader thought for a moment before nodding. 'Old Caprum tried flirting with her moons ago,' he said, laughing coarsely. 'It didn't work out too well for him.' Then he nodded over at a weather-beaten man who was wearing a dented helmet from the Knight Marshes on top of his fur hat. 'He moaned and groaned for a moon about getting his revenge on her. But that was more than a summer ago.'

'It's the old scars that one feels the most,' said Falk sadly. 'And if you look at how the face of your mercenary has changed since he noticed that we are talking about him, I think we have the answer to our questions.'

The old soldier of fortune had turned as white as the Ice Fields, and his eyes were darting this way and that – as though he were looking for an escape route. Furthermore, his hand was resting on the hilt of his weapon, and Culhen could smell that the mercenary was on the point of doing something stupid. He growled in such alarm that Ahren couldn't decide whether to go to his friends' assistance or continue to guard the flame chamber.

'I'd bet anything that he carved at the door so that Caldria would burn herself the next time she cast her spell,' said Trogadon. 'Or worse.'

Deklar pointed at Caprum, then called him over by crooking his finger. The mercenary shook his head vehemently and immediately began whispering to one of his cronies, all the while gesticulating angrily over at the troop commander and the Paladins around him.

'Could it be that your fraternising with us dastardly Paladins is proving too much for your men?' asked Bergen ironically. 'This is beginning to look like a mutiny.'

Uldini looked in alarm at the whispering spear carriers and raised *Flamestar* to gaze through the crystal ball so that he could get a better view.

Culhen smelled the scents floating over from the mercenaries, the men glaring with hate-filled eyes in a strangely *synchronised* manner towards the fo'c'sle. Even their smells seemed remarkably similar…

Ahren, said the wolf. *Something is amiss here. I think you'd better join us.*

***

Revenge was proud of his work as he left the guffawing mercenaries beneath him in the belly of the ship and slipped up through the gaps in the timbered ceiling and onto the main deck. The idiot Caprum was delivering a passionate speech about the injustices of the world in general and Deklar's duplicitousness in particular. The moron stank of frustration and fear but not of vengeance – hence, he was useful but not controllable. Revenge sensed the Arch Wizard's charm net slowly spreading across the ship, its mesh woven so finely that it could feel the innermost mind of all on board.

No more hiding then, thought Revenge, the realisation bringing with it a sense of freedom. He stretched himself out as far as he could, touching each of the six mercenaries that he had been feeding with revenge fantasies for weeks now.

Look at them standing there, he whispered into their minds. *All of them huddled together and keeping you from your homeland and your richly deserved reward!*

Revenge sensed the charm net hitting him, but he cared not a whit. He laughed at the suddenly flinching sorcerer as he drove his marionettes forward. As they drew their weapons and launched themselves at the Paladins and those mercenaries that followed Deklar's orders, the expected cry of the Thirteenth Paladin sounded from below deck, Revenge revelling in it as if it were a resplendent banquet.

'Fire!' The lonesome warning sounded, but in the tumult, no-one heard it. 'Everything down here is blazing!'

***

Ahren coughed and gasped in the thick smoke. Following Culhen's warning, he had run to the hatch to find out what was going on up above, suddenly noticing the dark cloud that had formed in the stern of the ship and which was now creeping forward through the belly of the vessel like a living, all-consuming being. Behind it, and to his horror, he saw the flickering of flames and heard the bursting of over-heated hurricane lamps, their contents only feeding the rapidly growing inferno.

'Fire!' he bellowed again, but the only answer he received was the screaming of men and women, scornful and terrified, as well as the clash of blades and the groans of the dying. He glanced through Culhen's eyes and froze for a heartbeat. Mercenaries were fighting against other mercenaries who were attacking the Paladins and amidst the chaos, more and more bewildered sailors were falling victim to the weapons. Ounlamun was lying, lifeless, on the wheel, skewered by a spear which had either been expertly thrown or had completely missed its intended target.

Above Ahren's head, a bloodbath was unfolding while a raging fire blazed where he was – a fire that could mean death to all of them, for all their equipment and provisions for the Ice Fields lay in the stern of the ship!

Ahren took a desperate forward step into the thick smoke, but was immediately forced to retreat, coughing and spluttering. Although he could not feel the heat of the fire through his protective cloak, he fully realised the extent of the conflagration behind the smoke. His thoughts were racing, and instinctively he wanted to get back on deck to help his friends, but then he remembered the woman sitting in the prow of the ship, ignorant of what was happening behind her and certain to be burned to death if no-one warned her of the fire and its deadly fumes.

Cursing, the Paladin raced to the flame chamber and banged wildly on the door. 'Fire!' he screamed for a third time. The runes were immediately extinguished, and he heard Caldria approaching the door.

'The flames will soon reach the hatch at midship, and we won't be able to escape!' he shouted through the timbers.

'I'll quickly get dressed,' came the reply, Ahren not believing what he was hearing.

'Do we have time for such niceties?' he shouted, askance.

'No,' she replied dryly. 'But how long am I going to survive on the Ice Fields stark naked after our ship has been consumed by fire?'

Ahren grunted in agreement and waited. Then his eyes fell on the sleeping cabins port and starboard and he cursed again.

'For a sacred Champion of the gods you *do* use colourful language,' laughed Caldria from behind the door.

'You should hear Trogadon when he has a bee in his bonnet,' muttered Ahren absently as he began stuffing his friends' most valued possessions into their rucksacks. There were so many things, and he only had two hands...

Culhen! he yelled through their connection. *I need you down here!*

I'm a bit busy up here at the moment, came the reply, the wolf sending a fleeting image of insanely fighting mercenaries striking all around them without a care in the world despite themselves having been seriously wounded. *They don't seem to feel any sort of pain!*

The ship is ablaze and will sink, said Ahren, summarising the situation. *Either you come and assist me, or we are going to have to leave things behind us that are invaluable. Mirilan is lying here, for example, as well as a bundle of Deep Steel arrows for Fisiniell, not to mention the First's dragon helmet. Which of these things do you think I should sacrifice?*

I'm on my way, was the quick response.

Ahren was yanked from his connection when Caldria placed her hand on his shoulder.

'You're doing an impressive amount of daydreaming considering our lives are on the line,' she said impatiently.

Ahren opened his mouth to explain, then thought better of it. 'Throw everything on this bunk into a rucksack,' he ordered. 'Then do the same with those two chests over there.'

'You want to pack?' asked the Flame Sorceress, taken aback. 'Now?'

Ahren ran into the other cabin, where the rest of his and his companions' belongings were. 'Remember what you said about the Ice Fields and surviving on them?' he snapped. 'The more things we manage to pack and carry out of here, the greater the likelihood is that we will survive not only the cold but also the Dark Ones lurking out there. Oh, yes – *and* the dragon that we still think is alive.'

Ahren heard a snort from the other cabin. 'Whatever it was that the gods have promised you on completing the mission, it isn't enough.'

'They never offered us anything,' said the Forest Guardian, Culhen in his bloodstained armour then suddenly appearing in the passageway as the young man added in a whisper: 'But finding new friends has made it worth the dangers.'

I do value your thoughts, said Culhen, shaking himself and sending blood spatters everywhere. *But there is a mini war being waged up there, and the smoke has now reached the steps. Also, I've heard the sound of wood bursting at the stern. If we dawdle any longer, we will be left with the choice of either choking to death or drowning in icy water.*

Ahren heaved two heavy rucksacks onto Culhen, tying them to the pommel of his saddle. *Today, you will be the pack animal that you never wanted to be, big lad,* he joked, trying to distract himself from the knot in his stomach.

The wolf looked demonstratively back at the weighty baggage, then along the passageway that he had only now hurried down. *Maybe the water won't be that bad.*

***

Revenge revelled in the chaos of the bloody skirmish taking place below him, gleefully sucking the dark thoughts of the fighters as if they were a good wine.

Every thrust, every new wound, and every dead comrade inflamed the resentment and desire for revenge in his marionettes. Even if Revenge could no longer control the events of the ship, his influence was still sufficient for as many as possible of the passengers to slay one another while *Alina's Rage* was ablaze beneath their feet.

Revenge had, perhaps, revealed himself, but the reward for that was the fact that soon the Paladins and their friends would be well and truly stuck on the Ice Fields, *sans* ship, *sans* nourishment, *sans* weaponry.

Unwillingly, the child of the Adversary fled out into the cold vastness when the boy-like Arch Wizard began to construct a spell that would do

Revenge harm. The child sensed Dark Ones in the area and began to head towards them.

With a bit of luck, mother nature would finish off the rest of them.

***

Ahren looked at the wall of smoke looming ahead of him as he made his way along the passageway in the belly of *Alina's Rage*, the fire now having sprung further forward in the ship. Behind him struggled a heavily laden wolf, who – it had to be said – was bearing his load with considerable forbearance. Caldria made up the rear, anxiously holding onto Culhen's tail.

'We're going to have to go through the smoke and very probably the fire, too!' shouted Ahren over the noise of the crackling inferno.

'Do not worry about me, Thirteenth,' replied the Flame Sorceress. 'I have spent my whole life surrounded by fire. A few flames won't frighten me off.'

All very well for her, muttered Culhen. *I am wolf enough to admit that I have no desire to find out whether fur is combustible.*

Ahren pondered for a heartbeat and then shouted: 'Stay here, the two of you! My cloak will protect me. I'll see if I can get some sorcerous support!' Then he ran, keeping his hands and face covered as much as possible by the cloak, his hood pulled down to his nose. Flames darted up with every one of his blind, half-stumbling steps, and when he finally sensed the stairs in the thick, oily miasme, he almost yelled in delight. He managed to hold his breath as he ran up the steps towards the weak light of day, which seemed to be battling through the fog as if it were a glimmer of hope in a sea of despair.

Ahren took the final step before the deck – only to be yanked back by a calloused hand, which caused him to tumble down into the smoke and darkness. His armour had protected him from the hard steps, but his cloak was now swinging open, and the heat of the nearby fire enveloped his body. Sweat was starting to run out of every pore even as he slammed onto the planks, winding himself in the process.

Ahren, Culhen called, wishing to come to his friend's aid, the Paladin stopping his loyal friend with a quick thought, however. Fire was licking up from the timbers around him, and there was little doubt that the wolf would catch fire, should he try to help.

Ahren wanted to get to his feet, storm up the steps, escape from the smoke, find his bearings, and breathe in some fresh air, but already a nightmarish figure was throwing itself at him, a lantern shard in its bloodied hand. Instinctively, the Forest Guardian shoved the ball of his left hand up, smashing the nose of his attacker, whose burned features were marked with sheer insanity. One of man's ears was charred beyond recognition and he was seized with an uncontrollable, and clearly painful fit of coughing, his red eyes, their blood vessels burst, staring wildly at the Paladin.

'I warned you,' babbled the man, now trying to stab Ahren with the shard. 'Week after week, I kept telling Deklar I'd rather do nothing else but burn down this ship of incarceration! He wouldn't listen to me!' A gurgling chuckle could be heard coming from the throat of the lunatic while Ahren, whose view was considerably diminished by his lack of air, resorted to brute force rather than finesse. He drew his leg back from the man kneeling over him, then kicked him with all the force he could muster, sending him spinning away and into the flames, which were now rampant, all the way from the stern of the ship to the stairs.

The man continued to laugh as the fire consumed him, while Ahren now crawled up the steps on his hands and knees. His lungs were in dire need of a relieving intake of air, but the smoke was at its destructive worst. His body was so racked with relentless coughing that he feared his chest would rip open, and to his horror, he collapsed on the stairs, finding himself completely unable to crawl at all, his reflexes causing him to breathe in ever more smoke, which only worsened his coughing fit.

Ahren! It was Culhen's horrified voice in his fevered head. *I'm coming!*

The Forest Guardian imagined with horror the burns that his friend would suffer, but then two powerful hands grabbed him from above and dragged him out into the priceless, life-giving air.

'I thought I'd seen your shadowy figure in the smoke earlier,' grunted Bergen, whose right cheek was badly bruised. 'Did you stumble back down or what?'

Ahren was too concerned with coughing to provide an answer, only managing to gasp with great effort: 'Cul…Culhen!' With that he pointed below deck as he wheezed.

Bergen cursed and spun around. 'Uldini! Jelninolan! One of you has to help get Culhen out of the fire!'

Ahren saw through his tear-filled eyes that the deck of the Flame Belly ship had been transformed into a battlefield. The corpses of mercenaries and mariners lay scattered around, even seeming to have continued clawing at each other in the throes of dying, so possessed must they have been by madness. His companions came running to him on hearing Bergen's cry, and to Ahren's relief, he saw that his friends had emerged relatively unscathed from the massacre.

Uldini floated past him and into the smoke, causing *Flamestar* to hover over his child-sized open palm, the crystal ball creating a gold-shimmering circle which banished both flames and smoke from its field of light. 'Culhen!' shouted the Ancient curtly. 'Get your fur over here before I have second thoughts and allow it to be burned in the blaze!'

That's not one bit funny, complained the animal, as he struggled with his heavy load up the steps.

'What *have* you done with him?' asked Falk in amazement as he looked at Ahren, but already Caldria had come into view, the woman still holding Culhen's tail as she was pulled through the smoke. She stumbled sideways out of the hatch and struggled for breath.

'By the THREE…' she gasped. 'I…*never*…want…to see…a fire…again!'

'Surely that's going to be a bit tricky for you, seeing as you're a Flame Sorcerous?' asked Trogadon, who was checking the rucksacks on Culhen's back.

'Couldn't…care…less!' she spluttered.

'I don't want to hurry you along, but the ship is sinking,' interjected the First mockingly, nodding towards the stern of *Alina's Rage*, which was already submerged. 'We should get onto the ice as long as the prow is above the meltwater.'

'Put out the gangplank from there before Culhen and all his ballast tips us into the water,' added Jelninolan, placing her hand on Ahren's aching chest and closing her eyes for several heartbeats.

Immediately his paroxysmal coughing stopped, the grateful Paladin filling his lungs with icy air. Then he wrapped his cloak closer around him on feeling the merciless cold of the Ice Fields threatening to steal into his body.

'Is everyone fit and able?' asked Ahren, getting to his feet.

'Yes,' replied Khara gravely, looking at the fo'c'sle now rising into the air. 'Thanks to Deklar and a handful of loyal mercenaries.'

Ahren realised that the squat troop leader was among the dead. 'You're saying that he *defended* you?' he asked in disbelief.

'He had no choice,' interjected the First curtly as he heaved the heavy gangplank onto the ice. 'He saw himself being confronted by a mutiny and fought against those who were trying to seize control of the ship.'

'I would prefer to think that he decided to do the *right* thing in the end,' said Jelninolan, carefully running down the plank and stabbing her staff into the cool snow to support herself as soon as she reached the bottom. Ahren soon joined her, the others following suit.

'It's lucky that we are all wearing suitable clothing,' said Falk, who was the last to disembark. 'Imagine if we had lost our fur cloaks.'

Ahren pointed at the heavily laden Culhen. 'I think I managed to rescue the most important of our possessions. Alas, there were no provisions.'

Trogadon, the First, and Bergen surrounded the wolf and began to pass on the rucksacks to their owners while Muai and Kamaluq guarded the group, the two companion animals keeping their eyes and ears peeled a little distance away. 'Tell me, Ahren,' began the dwarf, now having an overview of the rescued pieces of equipment. 'Where is my new rucksack – the one I got in Cape Verstaad with all my blacksmith's tools?'

Ahren looked apologetically at his friend. 'It was simply too heavy, unfortunately. If I'd brought it with me, I would have had to leave three other bundles behind.'

'That's a pity…' began Trogadon, shrugging his shoulders, only for his eyes to widen as the colour drained from his face until it became as white as the ice that surrounded them. 'By the love of the THREE!' he suddenly roared. 'RUN!' Then he took to his heels as if all the Glower Bears in the world were after him. 'Come on! Stop dillydallying!' he commanded once more, waving furiously as he hurried away. 'If the fire ignites certain crucibles…'

Ahren remembered the hole that Trogadon's paraphernalia had blown into the wall of a rock tunnel in Gol-Konar, and imagined what such a force would do to a paltry wooden boat. Then he ran as fast as he could, thanking the THREE for the snow that was giving them the necessary grip on the pack ice. All around him, his friends were running through the whiteness too while on several occasions he heard cracking sounds under his feet, which he decided to ignore for the moment.

'Do we need to be worried about this crackling beneath us?' asked Khara, turning to look at Bergen as she pelted along, the Paladin waving his hand dismissively.

'As long as they don't get any louder, they are perfectly normal,' replied the Ice Lander, gasping. 'Afterwards, I will show you all—'

His sentence was interrupted by a loud bang from behind. This was immediately followed by a sudden blast of air that lifted Ahren and his companions into the air as if they were autumn leaves in a gale. Head over heels, the young Forest Guardian sailed through the air before coming down with a crash on the never-ending whiteness, along which he slid another five paces before coming to an undignified halt. All around him, he could hear the sounds of colourful curses, which suggested to him that none of his friends had been seriously injured.

'Trogadon,' muttered the First, his voice laden with tension. 'I think I speak for all of us when I make this command – no more blacksmith's powder in the rucksacks!'

'No-one ever complained in Gol-Konar,' grumbled the dwarf as he struggled to his feet.

Ahren, too, straightened himself up, and not ten heartbeats later, he and his somewhat battered looking companions were all upright and staring at the wreckage of *Alina's Rage,* which sank with breath-taking speed in the narrow channel of meltwater. No-one said a word until the vessel had disappeared beneath the surface, a layer of ice forming in no time at all, like fresh skin on a wound. Soon there was nothing there to suggest that a ship had ever been present. Ahren couldn't stop himself from wondering if a similar fate awaited them in this vastness of ice and snow.

'Right then,' said Falk, once Ahren and his friends had overcome their initial shock and provided Caldria with sufficient clothing from their own meagre supplies. 'Let us have a look at what Ahren managed to save.'

'No food or drink – that much is certain,' said the First, a look of perturbation on his face. 'All the provisions were stored at the stern of the ship.'

Ahren pointed at himself, Falk, and Bergen. 'Here are two Forest Guardians and one Ice Lander, who will ensure that we don't go hungry,' he said confidently.

Don't promise too much, warned Culhen. *If there are no prey in the vicinity, then there is nothing to catch. Muai and I were barely able to fill ourselves and we can cover far more ground than you three can.*

Ahren made sure that the increasing unease that he was feeling on account of the wolf's advice wasn't visible while Trogadon and the others examined the contents of the rucksacks and bags that he had recovered with Culhen's assistance.

'Well, at least we have enough furs,' said Bergen with relief once they had gotten an overview of everything. 'But not much rope and even less climbing gear.'

'They don't seem to me to be of much importance,' countered Khara stubbornly, looking demonstratively at the flat surface of snow and ice that surrounded them.

Bergen snorted. 'You will certainly see things differently if you fall into the water because the floes suddenly drift apart thanks to your weight. Just because everything *looks* stable around us, that does not necessarily mean that it *is*. Maybe with your very next step you will walk onto an extremely fine layer of ice and snow that will immediately give way.'

Khara said no more but bound one end of a rope around her waist before passing it on.

'Anything else missing?' asked Jelninolan, her cheeks pink. The protection against the elements afforded to the elves by HER, WHO FEELS, seemed to be assisting the priestess at least to some extent against the bitter cold, and unlike the rest of Ahren's companions, she hadn't resorted to covering her face with a thick woollen scarf.

'We have very few tents,' said Bergen. 'Once night sets in or when the next storm approaches, we will have to build snow dwellings in the manner of the *Hisunik*.'

'Won't that take forever?' asked Uldini irritably.

'You can freeze to death if that is what you prefer,' replied the Ice Lander matter-of-factly.

'I have a better idea,' grumbled the Arch Wizard, raising *Flamestar* with his hand and causing it to immediately glimmer. 'I should be able to manage the creation of a little heat from time to time.' Immediately, the snow around them began to melt, while Bergen cursed and knocked the crystal ball out of the childlike figure's palm.

'Do you want the ice to crack, and for us all to *drown?*' he asked sharply. 'Have you not been *listening?*' He gesticulated towards the mountains far to the south. 'The Ice Fields are nothing more than an enormous mass of ice, which were formed in that mountain range over there. We are standing on frozen water, and you want to melt the very ground beneath our feet?!'

Uldini glared at the Paladin, clicked his fingers, and directed *Flamestar* back up to his hand. 'You are exaggerating,' he snarled. 'The ice through which *Alina's Rage* was ploughing was at least two paces thick.'

Bergen rolled his eyes. 'But it's not like that *everywhere*,' he countered. 'There are also thin sheets, and even holes in the ice here and there – at least, if luck is on our side.'

'What do you mean?' asked Ahren, bemused.

Bergen nodded towards his rucksack. 'I have a fishing line, hooks, and bait with me. Fish live under the ice. If we have the opportunity to fish, we won't need to hunt.'

Muai growled contentedly and licked her chops, causing Khara to laugh. 'You are now officially my tigress's favourite Paladin,' she chuckled.

Ahren, meanwhile, had noticed how Uldini had with gentle words and various hand signals dimmed *Flamestar's* brightness to a warm glow, before grunting approvingly and sending it up a good pace above the group, where it remained hovering. The Arch Wizard pointed at the ice surrounding them, no longer warmed by the crystal ball. 'The charm will not heat us per se, but it will at least transform the merciless cold of this region into the chill of a typical Hjalgarian winter's day.'

Ahren noticed no difference on account of his cloak, but his friends were no longer hopping from one foot to the other or hiding their gloved fingers beneath their armpits.

Bergen stooped down and felt the snow before nodding sternly at Uldini. 'Very well,' he said after a heartbeat. 'But please, no warmer than this.'

Uldini saluted ironically before pointing south towards the peaks of the Frozen Teeth. 'The theme of coldness has hereby been dealt with,' he said smugly. 'If Falk, Ahren, and Bergen can provide us with food, then we should be able to continue with our expedition.'

'As if we had a choice,' snorted Caldria. 'Hasn't it occurred to anyone here that we *cannot* return to Jorath? Or were you all thinking of swimming back to Cape Verstaad?'

'She's right, you know,' said Jelninolan, turning to Uldini. 'You had better send for help as soon as possible so that the other Ancients will have come up with something by the time we find Yollock.'

'Perhaps they will send Sun Shimmer,' suggested Khara hopefully.

Uldini shook his head. 'The Roc is undoubtedly hardy, but with ballast on her back, Sunju's bird cannot fly for days on end without a break. She would undoubtedly crash into the sea with exhaustion before she has making it halfway here, never mind trying to make the return journey.'

Jelninolan nodded. 'Had that been an alternative, we would already have discussed it in Cape Verstaad.'

'The simplest solution is for Cape Verstaad to send another Flame Belly ship that can meet us on the ice,' mused Uldini. He ordered *Flamestar* down, and as it floated between his hands, the colours within it changed, while his friends began to shiver again.

'One gets used to the higher temperature too quickly,' said Falk, his teeth chattering as he pulled his woolly scarf closer around his face.

'Don't be such a sap,' said Bergen. 'We Ice Landers have endured such temperatures for centuries – and without any magic.'

'It's *such* a pleasure having you here,' snarled Falk.

'Enough now,' murmured Uldini absently. 'I'm trying to contact one of the Ancients…' The Arch Wizard grunted irritably and muttered: 'I should have known.'

'Lost son of the jungle surrounded by ice.' Ahren recognised the voice of Sleeps-in-Treetops whispering in the air surrounding Uldini. 'Has the final Champion been found?'

'No, dammit,' growled Uldini irritably. 'And stop alienating my charm. Speak *through* the crystal ball, please – you are giving me a headache.'

The Arch Wizard quickly detailed their situation, which didn't make for very good listening even in its abridged form. Then he grunted impatiently as he listened to the answers from the Ancient of the Northern Jungles. Ahren knew that Uldini despised Sleeps-in-Treetops' cryptic speech formulations. Having to confess to *her* of their critical state had to be physically painful to the first of the Ancients.

'Ye THREE, why do you send this woman to punish me?' asked Uldini dramatically as he looked towards the heavens, having concluded his charm. 'And why does she have to carry on as if she had predicted our fate all along?'

'If that were so, it would have been a good move on her part if she had ordered another Flame Belly ship for us,' said Caldria grimly.

'You don't know Sleeps-in-Treetops,' interjected Jelninolan with a grin. 'Pragmatism is *not* one of her strengths.'

'What *did* she say then?' asked Falk gruffly. 'And could you *please* resume your warming spell?'

Uldini tossed his crystal ball skywards, from where it cast its weak shine as the sorcerer pointed towards the south. 'She told us to keep on looking for Yollock. And then something else about the beginning being the end and vice versa.'

'That sounds like her alright,' groaned Bergen.

'The important thing is that she knows what's happening and has promised to inform the other Ancients,' muttered Uldini through gritted teeth. 'Akkad or Quin-Wa will think of some way of getting us back to the continent.'

'Right then,' said Ahren, rubbing his fingers under his cloak. 'We have asked for help and know that thanks to our armour and the Ancients' sorcery, we have a more than even chance of survival.' He nodded towards the line of Frozen Teeth stretching from east to west as far as the eye could see. 'Now we simply have to find out *if* and *where* Yollock is hiding out in this domain.'

The First stepped past Ahren, his dragon helmet on his head despite the present lack of danger. 'If we find Four Claws then we will find Yollock,' he said bluntly, pointing towards a peak in the distance, which – unlike the other jagged mountains – seemed strangely smooth. 'And *there* is where we will find the dragon.'

'Uh-huh,' muttered Trogadon before going on to ask the question that was on Ahren's lips: 'And *how* do you know that?'

The First turned to look at the dwarf, and whatever it was that the blacksmith saw in the eyes of the Paladin, he said no more but nodded. Then the war veteran stomped off in a south-south-westerly direction.

Cursing, Bergen moved to the front of the group. 'Everyone – rope yourselves up and pass the rope to the person behind you,' he barked, pressing the end of a rope into the First's hands. 'And you all follow *me!*'

he added brusquely. 'We don't want anyone falling into the icy water just because they are a little too *proud*, do we?'

Ahren looked at the First from behind, the seasoned warrior hardly listening to Bergen's instructions. The Forest Guardian was now certain that the veteran had good reason for protecting his head beneath his dragon helmet. Clearly, the First had an ulterior motive for coming on this expedition – one that he had not revealed to his companions – yet.

'This place radiates a mysterious peacefulness,' said Khara as she lay snuggled in Ahren's arms and under the protective warmth of the magic cloak. Culhen and Muai had, as was their wont, curled up on either side of the couple and were lying on a thick carpet of furs, Bergen having built a narrow wall of snow around their encampment, which protected them from the wind with remarkable success. Of course, there was no fire, so that it was only thanks to Uldini's sorcery that there was a minimum of heat, while the fact that neither Falk nor Ahren had found any trace of wild game meant that they had all settled down for the night on empty stomachs. Despite that, the absolute stillness of the Ice Fields, the utter clarity of the night sky, and the incredible purity of the air all combined to create a sensation of calm that led to Ahren relaxing far more than he would have expected, given their current situation. Dusk had long since set in, and Ahren was sure that he could see every star in the firmament with absolute clarity.

'Peace, my eye,' muttered Trogadon, who was lying with Jelninolan in one of the few tents that they had managed to save. 'We dwarves are used to the cold of the high mountain tops, and yet I am still freezing my you-know-whats off.'

'Some of us are trying to sleep,' muttered Falk from another tent. 'Ahren and I will have the thankless task of rustling up some food for you lot once dawn breaks. That will be hard enough without you keeping an old man from his well-earned sleep.' This was greeted by general guffawing, which was then followed by whispered conversations.

Are you certain that we don't need anyone to stand guard? the Forest Guardian asked Culhen anxiously.

For the tenth time, retorted the wolf irritably. *Muai, Kamaluq, and I are sleeping with one eye open – that should suffice. And anyway, what else can you do? Spend the whole night on sentry duty, go hunting at break of day, and then march for the whole day – following the same routine for weeks on end?*

Ahren heard Hakanu murmuring insistently to his fox in the singsong tongue of his people. The apprentice was sharing a tent with Falk, who reacted to the disturbance with a distinct sigh. Ahren was proud of his protégé. Although the boy seemed quieter and almost a little withdrawn, he seemed to have coped with the experiences of their journey well and was adjusting to their present situation with equal ease. He decided to take the young warrior with him on the morning hunt. Firstly, it would be an opportunity for Hakanu to learn something new, and secondly, another pair of eyes couldn't do any harm.

'I'm coming too,' said Bergen as the sun began to peek above the horizon. The Ice Lander pointed at the shadow circling above them. 'Karkas can help identify prey.'

'I am one step ahead of you,' announced Uldini smugly, directing *Flamestar* to a point ten paces to the left of their encampment. Then he waved his hand, causing the crystal ball to burn so brightly as if to shame the rising sun into yielding its supremacy to the little orb. Uldini then commanded *Flamestar* to sink onto the ice, whereupon there was an immediate hissing sound, accompanied by a fountain of steam lasting several heartbeats.

'What are you *doing?*' snarled Bergen furiously.

Flamestar rose heavenward again, Uldini then dimming its light. Slowly, the steam dissipated, revealing a circular hole in the ice – roughly two paces across. 'You wanted a waterhole for fishing,' said the Arch Wizard with a grin. 'Well – here you have one.'

Bergen opened his mouth to speak as all around them it began to crackle and snap, Ahren seeing to his horror how the artificial hole in the ice distended into an oval with the first pieces breaking away from its edge, while long zig-zag cracks spread out, soon dividing their encampment in two.

'No-one moves so long as fissures don't appear beneath their feet!' shouted Bergen in alarm. 'Wait and pray that the ice floes stabilise.'

Finally, the icy surface calmed down, and Ahren breathed a sigh of relief.

'How many times to I have to tell you that the Ice Fields are not simply a smooth layer of frozen ice into which one can punch holes at one's leisure?' snarled Bergen, glaring at Uldini. 'There are different layers and levels of purity ensuring that the individual floes...fight amongst each other, so to speak,' added the blonde Paladin in explanation. Then he pointed at the waterhole, which now looked more like an extended crack. 'If you bring chaos into the system of pressure and counter-pressure, this is what happens. So please *ask* me before you want to create a hole the next time and make it *considerably* smaller!'

Ahren was surprised to see that Uldini seemed indeed intimidated. 'Should I close it up again?' asked the Arch Wizard, meekly raising his hand.

'Not necessary,' grunted Bergen, taking his rucksack from his tent. 'We will all rope up and then fish. Your idea was a good one, it was merely the realisation that was less than...'

'Yes, yes – I understand,' said Uldini defensively before floating back into his tent. 'Catch a few big ones for me, alright?' he called as he closed the tent flap from within. 'I am going to lie down for a bit and recover from my sorcery.'

'Am I imagining things or is Uldini workshy?' asked Hakanu, who had followed Bergen's example by picking out a fishing line for himself, inspecting it, and attaching a bait to it before lowering it into the water.

'He was never very good at fishing,' chuckled Jelninolan as she and the others gathered around the waterhole.

Ahren was amazed to see so many shadows beneath the ice. For a heartbeat he remembered the skull-like head of the leviathan and prayed that only normal fish would be on their menus for the next few days.

Chapter 18

Revenge moved southward beneath the ice in search of a suitable host. He had drunk his fill on board *Alina's Rage* and could now dedicate himself completely to the task of delivering the death blow to the Paladins. The fools were now without a ship, without nourishment, and with only a minimum of supplies as they made their way across the Ice Fields. Revenge was determined to add to their list of woes by attracting the native Dark Ones to the unfortunates.

He sensed signs of hunger to the east and turned towards them. He could detect no desire for retribution in the dull-witted creatures, but he was his father's child, and they, too, were the patriarch's creations. His own power would surely be sufficient for them to understand his command.

Three simple words would do it: *Food! Go west!*

***

Day by day, their little group moved laboriously onward over the monotonous whiteness of the ice while Karkas warned them of potential dangers from his vantage point in the sky, at the same time guiding them towards the south-west and the blunted Frozen Tooth. Every second day, they found themselves hungry when the fish refused to bite, and their eyes hurt, the thin protective veils, which would have otherwise protected them against the reflecting snow, being, alas, among their lost belongings. During the brightest part of the day, Uldini would use *Flamestar* to dim the light immediately surrounding them, but this charm demanded its tribute, the Ancient suffering more and more from the effects of his sorcery.

Ahren, meanwhile, had tried repeatedly to lure the First into conversation, for the Forest Guardian was burning with curiosity – why was the age-old Paladin so sure that they would find Four Claws on this mountain in particular? What was he not telling them?

One sunny afternoon, Ahren tried his luck again, this time with Khara beside him, having already asked her to help him in his efforts. 'Who would have thought that good weather could be so dangerous in this region?' the young man asked innocently.

Bergen had already told them earlier that day that the sun had now melted the ice sufficiently for it to form a deceptive layer of meltwater, upon which no boot could keep a grip. There were, he said, special boards with nails that one could strap to the soles of one's shoes, but they were lying with *Alina's Rage* at the bottom of the sea – along with the tools that Trogadon would have needed to create such simple things as nails.

The First glanced over towards Ahren and sighed loudly. He was wearing his dragon helmet – he had been doing so ever since they had started their trek – his steely eyes gleaming through the eye slits and seeming to bore right into the young man's head. 'Well then, spit it out,' grumbled the old man. 'If both you and Khara are going to grill me, then I have no hope of avoiding your questions. Also, the way you keep glancing at me is becoming more than a little annoying.'

Out of the corner of his eye, Ahren could see that his other companions were all ears and drawing closer. Apparently, he was not the only one who could make neither rhyme nor reason out of the First's behaviour. Ahren wasn't sure if this was a good or a bad thing. How many secrets did the Paladins have, their early years lying hidden in the mists of time?

'Why exactly *this* mountain?' asked Ahren, deciding to come straight to the point.

'Because Four Claws prefers mountains with rounded tops,' was the curt response.

'And how do you know this?' probed Ahren.

'Because I know more about dragons than the oldest living dwarf,' said the First wearily.

'I wouldn't be so sure about that,' countered Trogadon dryly.

'Oh, *really?*' retorted the age-old Paladin venomously. 'Your folk know nothing regarding the habits of the northern dragons! If anyone asks you anything, it's always Dragon Ridge here and Dragon Ridge there!'

Trogadon scratched beneath his helmet. 'But they died out so long ago,' he said. 'I mean, who could possibly still know anything about…' He paused. 'Oh.'

'Precisely,' replied the First in a low voice. '*Elegance on sweeping wings, lost in time*'.

Ahren racked his brains. During the conclave on King's Island, Sunju had told him the First's dragon had been a northern one. 'They were smaller and more intelligent than their southern cousins, isn't that so?' he asked, remembering her words, the First then looking at him in surprise. The war veteran narrowed his eyes.

'It seems that not everything has been forgotten,' he said, his voice unusually soft. 'Although your statements are not quite correct – northern dragons are smaller than their southern counterparts at *birth* – but then they don't stop growing – unlike those from the south. A finger's width every year, so they say.'

'Were the northern dragons capable of speech?'

The First shook his head. 'They were as intelligent as companion animals, but their mouths were incapable of forming words,' he said. 'The older ones sometimes learned how to share their thoughts with other living beings. I think that they were the models through which the gods created all further companion animals, after they had united me and...' He paused before continuing. 'After they had united man and animal through mental communication for the first time.'

'And how come you know Four Claws and *his* preferences?' asked Hakanu.

The First began to stomp away, Ahren silently accepting that they wouldn't learn anymore for the time being, only for the war veteran to speak again.

'Four Claws was no foolish beast that the Adversary could corrupt,' said the man in a low voice. 'He attached himself *willingly* to the Dark god, a fact that I confronted him on many times but without success. Four Claws rampaged for dozens of centuries – with many interludes whenever he was defeated and had to lick his wounds. Why do you think that Yollock has followed him onto the Ice Fields? He simply *had* to make sure that Four Claws would never again make it back to the continent.' The First's words were followed by a short pause. 'And I must do so too.'

'So there is something personal between you and this dragon,' said Bergen, nodding. 'That is something that I can respect.'

Ahren suspected that the First had not yet revealed everything and that he was keeping a considerable portion of the story to himself. *Maybe Four Claws killed his companion animal,* thought the young man, Culhen silently transmitting his agreement on that point.

Then the wolf gasped. *I can see a wall far ahead – before the mountains,* he said, now somewhat confused.

Ahren frowned and used the wolf's sight to study the line in the distance, his own eyes not being powerful enough. 'Can anyone tell what that is ahead of us?' he asked, pointing towards the horizon. 'Is that a wall...of ice?'

'A glacier,' said Bergen, nodding in confirmation. 'Ice that piles up on other ice. According to Karkas, it forms a circle around the Frozen Teeth and is a good twenty leagues across, with the blunt mountain near its centre.' He looked at Uldini. 'As I have already said, with the forces of nature directly beneath our feet, we cannot take things lightly.'

'The edge of this glacier surrounds the Frozen Teeth like a very long ribbon,' said Khara, repeating what the tigress had told her. 'Is that normal?'

Bergen hesitated. 'It's unusual for one to be so broad,' he said uncertainly. 'Its symmetrical form, as described by Karkas, is also strange.'

'Perhaps it is a result of sorcery,' interjected Jelninolan. 'A centre of power might have formed this glacier – maybe the same one that controls the Ice Fields?'

'I sincerely hope not,' groaned Bergen. 'For if that is the case, then this place will not follow the patterns of the normal icy regions that I am familiar with.'

'This glacier seems to be very tall and steep,' mused Khara. 'However it came about, we still have to figure out a method for scaling it.'

An uneasy silence came over the group which remained for the rest of the day, Ahren repeatedly looking with concern at the glittering band of ice on the horizon. It seemed that nature herself was using this massive wall to remind the travellers that they were far from welcome in the icy south.

The howling in the distance made Ahren shiver. He, his companions, and Caldria looked towards the east and tried to work out what sort of creatures far beyond their encampment were producing such plaintive, extended tones. Suddenly, the wall of ice around their sleeping quarters seemed decidedly low and brittle as visions of their night-time skirmish with the Snow Slashers on board *Alina's Rage* came into his mind. How would they fare without the protection of the narrow passageways if a horde of similarly dangerous opponents should ambush them? 'Well, they are certainly not Snow Slashers,' he said, as much to reassure himself as the others.

'A pity,' countered the First grimly. 'I prefer to fight the enemy that I already know.'

'Which must be an experience that you have not enjoyed for a considerable time now,' said Caldria, speaking to the war veteran in her usual jocular tone. 'Fighting against someone that you have never encountered before, I mean.'

'Don't remind me,' was the old man's sober reply.

The howling sounds somewhat like a wolf, said Culhen, giving his evaluation. *But I can also make out another animal in their utterances – one that I simply cannot identify.*

'Culhen suspects that it is a composite creature. Half wolf and half something else.'

Jelninolan groaned. 'I hate it when the Dark god takes two separate species and fuses them forcibly into a new being. Such creations *always* mean trouble.'

'Can you fight, my heart?' asked Trogadon, looking anxiously at the elf. Ahren glanced over and spotted her worried nod.

'I will refrain from using magic and rely on my staff,' she said. 'I don't want to lose one of you because I am too weary to perform an urgent healing.'

'I, too, shall husband my magic,' said Uldini. 'My priority must be to keep you all alive with my sorcery over the next few days – or even weeks. No-one will gain anything if I use brute magic to keep Dark Ones at bay, only for you to stagger blindly and half-frozen through the Ice Fields because I have collapsed through sheer exhaustion.' With that, the Ancient pointed at the smouldering crystal ball, which was keeping them alive and just about warm enough thanks to its hint of warmth.

'In other words, we will fight unaided by magic – as so often over the last while,' said Falk, raising his shield.

'Why don't I slay any Dark One that crosses our path and then *you* deal with the next leviathan – is that a deal?' asked Jelninolan sharply. When Falk didn't reply, she nodded, her lips pursed. 'I thought as much.'

'Our teasing before the skirmishes is gradually becoming as brittle as crusted snow,' warned Bergen. 'Be careful that its coldness doesn't harden your hearts. The life that we knew so well still exists out there – with its hearths, its jocular drinking companions and its beds that are welcoming you home. It is only that we are so far from civilisation that we are finding it hard to remember them.'

'The creatures are approaching,' said Hakanu, alarmed. 'And their call has altered.'

'How many are there?' asked Falk, looking towards Muai and Culhen.

I think there are ten, said the wolf to Ahren.

'Muai reckons there are eleven,' reported Khara.

I'm sticking with ten, insisted Culhen sulkily, Ahren not having corrected the Swordsmistress.

'Too many for me, considering we don't know what these creatures are that are tearing along towards us,' said the young man.

'Or even if they have claws for tearing at all,' said Trogadon with a grin, testing his hammer out by swinging it in the air.

'Your good humour is ridiculous,' grunted the First.

The dwarf shrugged his shoulders nonchalantly. 'I am simple by nature. All this ice is getting on my nerves, and a few creatures are hurtling in from the east. I can vent my frustration by beating them to a pulp. That's all there is to it, really.'

'Do we have any choice *other* than fighting?' asked Caldria. 'And when I say *we*, I mean *you*, unless these creatures allow themselves to be intimidated by warm hands.' With that she raised both arms and waved them, her fingers glimmering weakly.

'We had better make a defensive circle,' muttered Falk grimly. 'Each look out for their neighbours, and if one of these creatures breaks through, shout loudly…'

'Hold on there,' said Uldini, his eyes fixed on Caldria's fingers. 'I *might* have an idea.'

The yelping and howling were drawing closer by the heartbeat, and Ahren now unshouldered *Fisiniell*. 'We have no more time for *mights*.'

Instead of retorting, Uldini took *Flamestar,* allowing it to hover above the squeaking Kamaluq. 'How brave has your fox become in the meantime, boy? he asked Hakanu.

The lad stuck out his chest proudly. 'My Kamaluq is the most valiant Glimmer Fox imaginable…' he began, Ahren interpreting through the little animal's irritated whimper that Hakanu hadn't translated precisely enough what his companion animal was thinking at that moment.

'Good,' said Uldini dryly. 'Then it is time for him to prove himself.' He pointed at *Flamestar*, the ever-brightening ball now hurtling northwards. 'He must remain *in* the light and make as much of a racket as he can,' said the sorcerer, looking at Ahren's protégé. 'With a little luck he will save all of us here from too much blood being spilt.'

'Ah come on now,' muttered Trogadon, lowering his hammer. 'Why do you have to spoil our fun like that?'

'And you want to enter the bond of matrimony with *him?*' asked Khara, turning towards Jelninolan.

The elf laughed. 'He has his good points – or so I've been told.'

'You lot are *very* strange when you are in mortal danger,' commented Caldria.

'We've been told so often enough,' said Bergen. 'Although, many mercenaries chat loudly before battle so that…'

'Not now,' hissed Falk, putting his finger to his lips in warning to the others.

Hakanu, meanwhile, was arguing silently with his bristling fox, the latter finally acquiescing and hurrying after *Flamestar,* whimpering loudly as he scampered along. Ahren could hardly believe his eyes when the fox finally reached the light of the crystal ball, suddenly increasing greatly in size and looking far more dangerous than he had done a heartbeat earlier. Uldini had somehow morphed the animal's distorted shadow with his actual figure, while the cute whimpering of the little fellow now sounded like a cacophonous, challenging howl.

'Neat little trick,' murmured the First appreciatively.

'Mere shadow play – a tiny illusion and the bending of light,' whispered Uldini. 'No self-respecting predatory animal worth their salt can resist an alien intruder that is challenging them. Jelninolan, would you be so kind as to conjure up a wind so that these creatures don't catch our scent?''

The elf plucked a single string on *Mirilan,* creating a sound so low as to be practically inaudible, and immediately Ahren felt the cold air under his hood, causing him to draw the material closer to maintain its protective effect.

Caldria sighed beside him, and when the Forest Guardian glanced at her, he could see the wounded, yearning expression in the eyes of the Flame Sorceress. 'What those two are capable of...' she whispered sadly.

'It is not our talents that make us into persons of true worth,' murmured Ahren, 'but rather how we use them. Your own sorcery, persistence, and determination have brought us many leagues into the ice. Without you, we would have already encountered dozens of these situations.'

The sorceress looked at him in surprise. 'The bards really *weren't* exaggerating when they sang your praises,' she said finally.

'Not when it came to the important things,' added Khara with a chuckle, gently stroking Ahren's cheek.

'If you lot are finished being all lovey-dovey,' snarled Uldini, 'I would like to concentrate on finding out if my plan is working.'

Poor Kamaluq, said Culhen, unable to take his eyes and ears off the whimpering fox. *All alone out there with those ghastly creatures.*

You're sounding like his granddad, teased Ahren, sinking into his friend's hearing. The barking sounds of the unknown creatures were as angry as before, but he had the feeling that they were moving away from the east and in a northerly direction.

'It's working,' he murmured to the group. 'They are following Kamaluq.'

'That's good,' said Hakanu proudly before adding hesitantly, 'isn't it?'

Uldini continued to stare after the ever-shrinking crystal ball in the distance. 'As soon as I give the word, Kamaluq must use his flash and come back to us, helter-skelter,' commanded the sorcerer, staring at the nervous Hakanu.

'I don't think that those Dark Ones are going to give up on us so easily,' muttered the First. 'As soon as the distraction provided by the fox is over, they will turn their attention in our direction again.'

Uldini said nothing, raising his hand instead. The first of the alien creatures had come into *Flamestar's* light field. Ahren could make out wolves the size of ponies with strangely awkward gaits, unusually hefty legs, and enormous trunks covered by thick, leathery skin decorated with fiery-red flecks. The most striking thing about these Dark Ones, however, were the pairs of long tusks protruding well beyond their upper jaws and towards the ground.

Ahren was still taking in what he had seen when Uldini lowered his arm and whispered: 'Now, Hakanu!'

Thinking quickly, Ahren closed his eyes to avoid looking straight at the flash. The hunting howls of the Dark Ones were suddenly transformed into confused whimpers and growls, while the groans of Caldria, now down on her hunkers beside the Forest Guardian, reminded him that he and his companions had not forewarned the Flame Sorceress. 'Kamaluq can defend himself with a flash of light,' he murmured apologetically to the old woman, who responded with a low curse.

'How far is your fox from the mob now?' asked Uldini urgently, Ahren opening his eyes again to follow the events.

'A good ten paces,' replied Hakanu, Uldini grunting impatiently.

'Too close,' he muttered. 'He must run as fast as he can.'

Flamestar was dancing furiously amongst the Dark Ones, the creatures not yet having begun to move, concentrating instead on biting wildly around them. The blinded horde snuffled as they threw their heads this way and that. Clearly, they were attempting to reorientate themselves, the First's warning coming true as more and more of the wolflike creatures turned towards the companions and began to trot cumbersomely forward.

'Hakanu?' asked Uldini tersely. 'His distance from them now?'

'Thirty paces,' replied the apprentice quickly.

'That should suffice,' muttered the sorcerer, spreading his hands.

Immediately, *Flamestar* sent out a harsh light causing Ahren to blink and groan, while tears ran down from his irritated eyes.

'May the *Three* do away with you all!' exclaimed Caldria furiously. 'And I had only just regained full use of my eyes…'

Ahren heard hissing and cracking sounds, followed immediately by the first terrified utterances of the Dark Ones. Struggling to see again through the sparks of light that were still dancing in front of his eyes, Ahren could just about make out *Flamestar*, surrounded by a powerful cloud of steam, rolling along the surface in a large circle, melting the ice at lightning speed, causing the ice floes to break and long fissures to appear in the frozen water. The alien Dark Ones found themselves in the middle of this deadly chaos, all of them struggling in vain to flee the icy depths which quickly swallowed them up.

'Kamaluq!' screamed Hakanu in terror, but as Ahren spun around in alarm to behold his protégé, the latter was already breathing a sigh of relief. 'A crack began appearing before him,' said the young warrior, spreading out his arms, 'but he was able to evade it.' The upper body of the apprentice shuddered, and when he closed his arms again, the shivering fox suddenly became visible – with a lightning flash, of course.

Ahren could do nothing but rub his pained eyes and laugh at the same time as Caldria announced with grim determination: 'That's *enough!* I shall try my luck alone. It couldn't be worse than being constantly blinded.'

She may not understand our humour, laughed Culhen, *but she has internalised it, nonetheless.*

A spirit of anxious silence pervaded the rest of the night. Ahren and his friends had not dared to move from the spot, fearing the damage that Uldini's spell had caused to the frozen landscape, and when the following morning's sun revealed the extent of the destruction, Ahren was relieved that they hadn't made any attempt to move further away from the hole, already covered by a new layer of ice. At noon they were still hunkered in the spider's web of cracks, whose centre was the point where the horde of Dark Ones had met their shivering deaths. The icy surface resembled a frozen puddle, onto whose centre a child had carelessly tossed a stone, which had smashed only that point but had nonetheless left its mark on the entire surface with a network of fissures.

A very big stone, commented Culhen, following Ahren's train of thought. *And one made entirely from magic.* The wolf paused before continuing: *Am I a bad Ice Wolf if I say that I have had it up to here with all this? I want to return to a nice, cool forest.*

Ahren stroked his friend's fluffy belly as he observed one of the nearby cracks, a mere five paces northwest of their encampment. 'Am I seeing things or is the damage to the ice getting more pronounced?' he asked nervously. 'I could swear that this gap was an inch narrower this morning.'

Bergen pointed up at the sky, from where the bright sun was shining down on them. 'If you ask me, I suspect that the ice will only refreeze in the course of the afternoon.'

'Then let us take advantage of the moment,' said Trogadon, pointing at the rucksack with the fishing hooks. 'The more fish we catch now, the less we have to worry about finding food later. I doubt that the Seal

Wolves will be lurking under the ice. They seem to like the ocean just about as much as I do.'

'*Seal Wolves?*' asked Falk wearily. 'You're not serious, are you?'

'Well, they looked like wolves – with the additional markings and tusks of the seals that we saw near the *Bay of Whiteness,*' replied Trogadon matter-of-factly. 'Ergo, they are Seal Wolves.'

'The first pair of eyes to recognise a new form of Dark One is allowed to name them,' said the First with a sigh. 'This rule is even older than me.'

'Yes, but whoever created the rule wasn't thinking of the creative limitations of a Dwarfish blacksmith,' muttered Falk, shaking his head. '*Seal Wolves*. I never heard the like!'

Ahren chuckled as he heard the bickering of his friends, while under Bergen's strict instruction, he widened the crack that the Ice Lander considered the safest. They had lost a day or so, thanks to Uldini's powerful spell, but by the time the sun began to rise again above the horizon, they had gained more fish – dried by sorcerous means – as they could possibly carry. For the first time in weeks, they'd had enough to eat, each of them having filled their stomachs to their heart's content. Even Culhen and Muai were replete and content as the little group finally moved off again – and Ahren could only be pleased at their latest achievement.

***

Revenge floated over the spot where the Ice Fields had not yet fully healed their fresh wounds, and he had to admit that he felt just a little tinge of respect for the Paladins and more especially for the Ancients among their number. Revenge's efforts on board ship had been considerably more subtle and therefore more effective than here in the icy vastness, where the Paladins were less susceptible to Revenge's favoured methods. The entire horde of Dark Ones had been swallowed whole by the greedy waters, meeting their deaths beneath the ice without a single hated Paladin having suffered so much as a scratch. Even the useless old woman was still alive.

Revenge scolded himself for his clumsy attempt at visiting suffering and death upon the travel party and he silently swore to approach things with more care the next time. He turned his attention southward to the glittering wall of ice now clearly visible ahead of him.

It was time to find out what would happen to the doughty Jorathian heroes when their attention was drawn to something quite different.

***

'This thing seems to be getting bigger by the day,' muttered Trogadon, using his chin to point at the glacier sparkling in all its glory under the glare of the afternoon sun. For two weeks now they had been marching stubbornly southward, one wearying step after another – sometimes over ice as flat as a mirror, sometimes through powdery snow up to their calves, but always under the protection of Uldini's sorcery which either provided warmth to the trudging group or offered them protection from the all too slippery ice, and occasionally did both simultaneously, all the while causing the Arch Wizard to become more weary and irritable. The companions kept their eyes fixed on the glacier soaring ahead of them, the next milestone on their journey. To Ahren's surprise, the ice of this natural phenomenon was not white but blue, containing within it patterns that resembled lines or shafts. Bergen had delivered a lecture on the topic, explaining how the appearance was down to the thickness and purity of the ice, but Ahren hadn't listened closely. For him, another question was far more relevant.

'Does anyone have *any* idea of how we are going to climb up there?' he asked, unburdening his worry to the others. 'We have no appropriate climbing apparatus and hardly enough rope even to secure us on our march across the ice.' He tugged at the now tattered hemp around his waist. 'I wouldn't like to trust it with my weight.'

'How about floating up?' asked the First, nodding towards Uldini. 'After all, we have an expert in our midst.'

The Arch Wizard turned his weary face to the age-old Paladin. 'Your *expert* has been juggling several life-saving spells both day and night for several weeks now,' snarled the childlike figure. 'I suggest that you find another way of getting us up there – or it will be decidedly cold around your little noses while you are hauling my exhausted, sleeping body blindly up the glacier.'

'Jelninolan?' asked Falk, narrowing his eyes. 'Can *you* do anything?'

The elf nodded hesitantly. 'I could float us all up – but only with the aid of *Mirilan*, or else I will be as exhausted as Uldini. And who will then help you if we meet Dark Ones...or worse?' With that, her eyes strayed towards the blunted Frozen Tooth.

'And what's wrong with using *Mirilan?*' asked Khara anxiously.

Without saying a word, Jelninolan put her Storm Fiddle to her shoulder and played a single, quiet note. The sound reverberated with unusual strength however, resulting in what sounded like a rumble of thunder in the distance – as if the skies were responding to the Elven magic.

'As I have already said, I believe that there is a centre of energy hidden out here somewhere.' She pointed at the mountains. 'Probably on one of the Frozen Teeth. Age-old and full of the original power from the time of Creation. My Storm Fiddle seems to whip it up.'

'So, no *Mirilan* then,' muttered Hakanu, disappointed.

'Not if there is another way,' explained Jelninolan, gesturing with a wave of her arm. 'The ice under our feet, the glacier, and even the air somehow...it all feels...connected somehow,' she said vaguely. 'Like invisible threads of a bane spell that we had better not break.'

'Was that why Master Uldini's sorcery caused such damage to the ice?' asked Caldria curiously.

'It's possible,' admitted the Arch Wizard. 'Less magic is more – until we *know* more, at any rate.' He pointed at *Flamestar* floating above their heads. 'It seems that sun magic is more alien than Storm Weaving in this place of energy. I'm delighted that my little sleight-of-hand doesn't seem to have had any disastrous side-effects here.'

Ahren saw how Caldria turned her head away in shame, the Arch Wizard having disparaged his own talent which was so much more powerful than any that she could conjure up. 'One thing is clear,' said the Forest Guardian, smiling encouragingly at the old woman. 'As soon as we get out of here, you can take up whatever position you wish as advisor regarding all things magical at any Jorathian court of your choosing. The bards will write songs in *your* honour too.'

The woman looked at him gratefully, then frowned. 'I'd rather not,' she said. 'I find some of their song texts quite unbearable.'

'I simply took what I could get,' interjected Uldini defensively. 'And the most successful bards are not always the most artistically talented.'

'As long as I can sing along to a ditty in my honour with a couple of beers in my stomach, I'll be happy,' added Bergen with a chuckle.

Jelninolan laughed. 'No wonder that human music is mocked at in Eathinian.'

Ahren was about to counter with a comment on the awful nature of Elven lyrics only to suddenly sense Culhen's unease, breaking in on top of him like a sudden downpour in the middle of summer. *What's up, big lad?* he asked anxiously.

I'll...I'll be back soon, came the reply, the wolf scooting off, spraying snow in his wake.

'What's wrong with *him?*' asked Falk. 'Did he get the whiff of roast beef?'

Muai growled and licked her chops, Khara then throwing the old Paladin a disapproving look. 'Thank you,' she said dryly. 'Now I am going to have to spend the next three days trying to distract our furry feline from images of a festive banquet.'

'I thought she liked the fish,' said Hakanu, taken aback.

Muai growled again, causing Khara to sigh. 'Indeed, she does. But not for weeks on end. My tigress is easily bored.'

Muai reacted to the Swordsmistress's final sentence by turning her head away and licking her front paws in a disdainful manner.

Ahren was only half-listening to the banter. He was trying to maintain his connection with Culhen, which was now decidedly weak – as though his friend was isolating himself. The Forest Guardian understood that it had been a distinctive smell which had provoked Culhen into action, but with the best will in the world he was unable to make out what the scent's origin was. At least he was satisfied that the wolf had seemed excited rather than fearful.

'Bergen, can you ask Karkas to keep an eye on Culhen?' he asked the blonde Paladin.

'Don't worry – he's already doing so,' said the Ice Lander, reassuring his fellow Paladin. 'Karkas is *very* fond of Culhen.'

Ahren raised his eyebrows in surprise. Bergen's falcon was a solitary creature, who loved being alone even more than the brooding Lanlion did, and Ahren wondered how his wolf and the bird of prey had become friends. He could only think of those times when Sun Shimmer had held court with the other companion animals. 'We shouldn't proceed without

Karkas' keen eyes guarding us,' he said finally. 'Let us wait here and fish until Culhen returns.'

'Your wolf had better have a good reason for holding us up,' grumbled the First grimly, his eyes firmly fixed on the distant blunted mountain on the far side of the wall of ice.

The nearer they had approached the glacier, the crotchetier the First had become, but all subsequent attempts at conversation on Ahren's part had failed to provoke the veteran into revealing more about his reasons for being here, or any more information regarding Four Claws or even dragons in general.

While fishing hooks were unpacked, Uldini busied himself with melting little holes into the ice, Muai expressing her displeasure at the prospect of yet more fish with a low snarl. Ahren, meanwhile, asked wondered what exactly it *was* that the First was hiding from them.

The night was accompanied by a light fall of snow, and the world seemed to Ahren remarkably quiet when Culhen returned at last to their encampment. Ahren, sharing his cloak with Khara and lying on a thick blanket of furs, stared in silence at his friend while he tried to assess the wolf through his mind. Culhen was being unusually secretive and feeling terribly sad, the Forest Guardian therefore refraining from giving the animal a lecture but pulling the wolf towards him instead and stroking him gently. The animal's fur felt wet – it was as though Culhen had wept copiously. Ahren knew, of course, that it was only melted snow, but the deep sorrow of his friend had given rise to this heart-breaking thought.

What is the matter? he asked gently.

Nothing, said the wolf. *I was just mistaken in something, that's all. Go back to sleep.* Then the animal curled up into a ball, a half a pace away from Ahren and Khara.

Ahren could hardly bear to see his beloved wolf in such distress, but when Culhen locked him out of his mind again, the Paladin decided to leave him in peace. It seemed that Culhen wanted to come to terms with whatever it was that was troubling him without any help, and Ahren couldn't help wondering if it was the cold, lifeless Ice Fields surrounding them that seemed to make each and every one of his companions increasingly withdraw into themselves as they brooded over their own personal concerns.

When they finally reached the foot of the glacier, Ahren could do nothing but admire the simple beauty of the pure ice soaring silently and majestically before them. The surface seemed polished smooth, doubtless an effect of the sun and the cool breeze, which melted the ice during the day, only to freeze it again at night.

Aaron looked around at his friends, whose faces, apart from the First's, bore the same reverential expression.

'I had hoped it would have had cracks or crevices,' muttered Bergen. 'Some kind of irregular structure that we could use to ascend it.'

'Could Karkas fly along the glacier and seek out such a weak point?' asked Khara.

Bergen hesitated before nodding. 'I don't like sending him away from us,' he said. 'Who knows – there may be airborne Dark Ones.'

'Apart from dragons, you mean?' asked Trogadon before flinching at Jelninolan's warning look.

Bergen grimaced, tilted his head back, and watched his falcon disappear into the west. 'This mountain that we are heading for lies to the southwest, far beyond the wall,' said the Ice Lander with a sigh. 'Karkas may as well search for a climbing route to the west while we continue to make our way along the base of the glacier. If we don't find any suitable spot for climbing beforehand, we can stop at the level of the blunted mountain and try our luck there.'

'I hate to say it, but without sorcery I don't see any chance of us being able to scale the wall of ice,' said Khara, running her gloved hand along the smooth surface. 'Not without a single climbing iron.'

'Let us first head west,' said Uldini uncertainly, weary after the days of marching. 'If the worst comes to the worst, we can discuss sorcery.'

Ahren had lost track of how far they had travelled, the days spent in the shadow of the glacier being so monotonous that he found himself constantly falling into a kind of trance as he walked along.

At least the long shadow of the wall ensured that their eyes did not have to suffer the bright reflection, while the travellers had agreed to preserve Uldini's energy as much as possible by only requesting that he put his crystal ball to work when the cold became unbearable, which usually happened when the wind was strong, when the snow was heavy, and when it was deep into the night. Twice they'd had to rest for a day so that Uldini could replenish his energy by having a deep sleep, but as far as Ahren could make out, these breaks were a drop in the ocean when it came to reinvigorating the childlike figure.

Jelninolan, too, had tried to take Uldini's sorcerous place, but every attempt to make use of *Mirilan*, had resulted in a roll of thunder, and the elf feared that any magical song on her part would end in a snowstorm. They had no choice but to stubbornly follow the base of the glacier in the hope of finding a crack in its armour, where they could make their ascent.

According to Bergen, the blunted Frozen Tooth was within striking distance when the Ice Lander let out a laugh, clapping his hands in glee as he did so. 'At last,' he said, breathing a sigh of relief. 'Karkas has found a crevice. A narrow one.'

'And narrow is good?' asked Trogadon sceptically.

'Narrow is *very* good,' explained Bergen. 'We will be able to support our backs against one side of the crevice while placing a counter-pressure with our hands and feet on the other side, thereby enabling us to move up, inch by inch.'

'*Support?*' asked Khara incredulously. 'On smooth ice? What you are suggesting would even make experienced acrobats break into a sweat.'

'It isn't as difficult as it sounds,' said Bergen, although not at all convincingly. 'The trick is to maintain the bodily tension at all times.'

'If that is all there is to it…' muttered Falk grumpily before shrugging his shoulders. 'We have come this far, we may as well take a look at this crevice.'

It took until noon before the group reached the crack in the glacier, which appeared like a wound in the otherwise perfect surface of the ice wall, as if a giant had brought his axe down on the massive blue of frozen water, creating in the glacier a gash of no more than one pace across, cutting a good eight paces deep into the wall of ice, tapering rapidly as it did so. The crack made its way upward, following a zigzag course as it approached the heavens, which had now taken on a dark grey hue. Ahren was familiar enough by now with the weather in this region to understand that there was snow in the offing.

'Should we wait until the clouds have passed?' he asked.

'Probably makes sense,' muttered Falk, but Bergen shook his head grimly.

'If we're unlucky, the snow might get compressed in the crevice, freezing hard. Then our chance will be gone.'

Trogadon positioned himself in the fissure, bracing his hands against its eastern wall, his biceps bulging beneath his heavy clothing. With his back pressed hard against the western wall, the dwarf lifted one foot and then the other until both were wedged hard against the frozen water. He looked triumphantly at Ahren and the others, grinning so broadly from beneath his scarf that the Forest Guardian was sure that he could make out the outline of his smile.

'It isn't difficult at all,' said the blacksmith, moving his right hand an inch up so that he could begin his slow, upward trajectory. Immediately, he slipped down, landing on his backside in the snow.

'Very impressive,' commented Falk dryly.

'Still, at least he made the effort,' commented the First with a perfectly straight face.

The dwarf got to his feet and stepped out from the crevice.

'Not a hope,' he muttered. 'I'm much too heavy for these circus tricks.'

'What if we hung a rope from the top?' suggested Khara. 'Then we would have something to cling onto that would not give way.'

'Using a rope on the glacier would be child's play if we had one long enough – even without a crevice,' muttered Bergen. 'But we don't.'

Khara pointed at the carefully stored supplies of the group. 'We could tie the straps of our rucksacks together,' she said. 'Those, combined with our rope, might extend far enough.'

'Such a contraption would be far from secure,' warned Falk. 'And we would also have to drag up all of our weighty supplies at the same time, for we can hardly empty them out down here – unless we decide to leave the contents behind us.'

'Not forgetting that someone would have to climb up first to secure the rope, knotting the straps of our rucksack together securely enough to hold all of us,' added Bergen, shaking his head.

'It's very steep, but I *could* hurl up our luggage,' suggested Jelninolan. 'Without using *Mirilan*, of course. The necessary sorcery would only exhaust me temporarily. I would be back to my normal self by tomorrow morning.'

'Can you not simply hurl all of *us* to the top of the glacier,' asked Hakanu with a twinkle in his eyes that made Ahren decidedly nervous.

The elf took off her rucksack, spinning it around her with a groan before sending it flying upwards. She pointed up at the leather bag, a shudder passing through the baggage as it shot skyward and over the top of the glacier, where it landed out of sight and with a loud crash on the ice. 'That could be you,' said Jelninolan, looking at Hakanu. 'I would like to state clearly that it will take me days to repair multiple fractures.'

'It didn't sound *that* bad,' said Trogadon doubtfully. 'Would you like to go first, Hakanu?'

The apprentice wrang his hands uncertainly before shaking his head, making an intervention by Ahren unnecessary.

You are forgetting something, said Culhen, positioning himself beside his Paladin. *There is no way that either Muai or I will be able to make our way up.*

'Oh dear,' said Jelninolan, looking thoughtfully at the wolf once Ahren had verbalised his friend's misgivings.

'I will manage the two of them,' said Uldini wearily. 'Myself and the two monsters. But the fox goes with one of the climbers.'

Monsters? Puh! muttered Culhen, Ahren nonetheless sensing the relief on the wolf's part at the fact that he and Muai did not have to figure out another way of getting to the top of the glacier.

'One of us still needs to climb up there first,' said Falk. 'Someone is going to have to secure the improvised climbing rope.'

'I will float up with Culhen and knot everything together,' suggested Uldini. 'I can secure the rope by tying it to his pommel.'

'Hm,' said Falk, shaking his head. 'I've seen your rope-tying abilities. A blind, one-handed drunkard who hasn't seen a drop of alcohol in a fortnight, would make a better job of it than you can.'

'I am the first among the Ancients!' snarled Uldini, but with his eyelids drooping. 'How often have I needed to use knots, having sorcery available to me?'

'There you have it,' replied Falk decisively. 'Anyway, Uldini is clearly exhausted. A simple mistake and one of us could fall should one of the knots open at the wrong moment.'

'One of us will do it,' said Ahren to his erstwhile master. 'Hakanu hasn't yet internalised his lessons on tying knots, but the two of us could tie these straps together in our sleep.'

Falk looked at his heavy fur clothing and then at Ahren, standing there in his magic cloak. 'Then you go,' said the old Paladin. 'This ascent will be tricky enough even without being weighed down by fur.'

'Will we give it a try then?' asked Jelninolan. 'First the equipment, then Uldini with Culhen, and then Ahren, who will prepare everything for the rest of us?'

'And while Ahren is sorting out his knots, I will float down to you, have a breather, and bring Muai back up with me,' murmured Uldini flatly.

Ahren frowned, then placed himself in the crevice. He pressed against the two walls as Trogadon had done, but he, too, met with no success against the smooth surfaces of ice. 'It's like trying to crawl up a well-oiled iron pipe,' he muttered as he struggled to think of his options. Finally, he drew *Sun*, and hacked a little at the ice. A few splinters flew this way and that, cracks appearing in the frozen blue. 'Not helpful at all,' said the young man, turning the blade thoughtfully in his hands.

'No matter what you *want* to do, you have to be *capable* of doing it,' said Bergen, shrugging his shoulders. 'I'm telling you – the method that I have already explained to you is the best for overcoming any obstacles.'

Ahren nodded absently. 'For well-trained Ice Landers perhaps,' he said. 'Maybe you would like to try your luck?'

'Uh,' said Bergen, his face turning a deep red. 'I've never been much good at this type of climbing,' he murmured, much to the amusement of the others.

Ahren shook his head in response and tut-tutted. 'Right,' he grunted, then, on impulse, he angled his blade and pushed it into the ice of the crevice. Despite his strength and the sharpness of the metal, it took a considerable effort to sink the Deep Steel blade in as far as its hilt. Once he had finished his labours and was panting for breath, he glanced at his friends, being immediately met by sceptical looks. Carefully, he stood on the horizontal hilt and checked his stance. 'Two of them and I will have supports to climb.' He allowed himself to tip rearward so that his back was now against the opposite wall of the crevice. 'And if I make a mistake or lose my balance, I can support myself here or even have a rest from time to time.'

'And now?' asked Trogadon, who was fascinated by the process.

'Now I need more blades,' said Ahren, looking pleadingly at Khara.

The Swordsmistress snorted as she drew her Wind- and Whisper Blade. 'If Fantui-Go finds out about this, he'll yank my Warrior Pin from my hair – with Cokuchan's help, I'll have you know.' Then she handed her weapons to Ahren, who pushed them into the ice above his own hilt so that there were now three steps in the ice. He stood on the top two before going down on his hunkers.

'Now for the tricky part,' said Ahren with a groan, slowly but surely pulling his own weapon out of the wall, while maintaining his balance on the other two handles with his back pressed against the opposite wall. Then he took his blade and again pushed it hard into the ice, this time a little above the top weapon.

'Well roast me a Swarm Claw!' said Trogadon with a chuckle. 'Our Ahren really *has* found a way of scaling this wall.'

'A way that will last the best part of the afternoon,' added the First with a frown before turning to face the Forest Guardian. 'I appreciate your creativity, but you are going to have to move more quickly or the rest of us will have to wait until after the snowstorm to join you.'

The climbing Paladin nodded curtly and redoubled his efforts. Meanwhile, Jelninolan catapulted one rucksack after another up to the stop while Ahren looked down at Hakanu from time to time, checking to make sure that his apprentice hadn't persuaded the elf to turn him into a human missile.

Chapter 19

By the time Ahren reached the crest of the glacier, panting and groaning with exhaustion, a contented Culhen was waiting for him, the wolf having already dragged the scattered rucksacks together before placing them into a pile. Every bone in the Paladin's body ached, and his limbs felt as if they had swollen to double their normal size. Again and again, he had been hit with blasts of cold whenever his cloak had flapped open, the air slipping past its protective charm and adding to the Forest Guardian's general feeling of misery – as if he'd been marching for three days without stopping to eat or sleep. His hands were trembling, and to cap it all, it had begun snowing again. He had to quickly take the straps off the rucksacks and knot them together, creating an improvised rope to add to the real one so that his friends could climb up to him. With a silent curse, he struggled to his feet and pulled Khara's weapons out of the ice.

'Watch out!' he shouted down to his companions before hurling down the blades. The others might find them useful during their ascent.

The weather is deteriorating, said Culhen, pointing his nose upwind. *It smells different up here than on the pack ice. Thicker...somehow.*

What do you mean? asked Ahren as he began to artfully tie the rope and the leather straps together.

There is no life form up here beneath the ice, said the wolf. *No fine cracks through which smells from the ocean arise.* The animal looked around. *And no fish. We will have to go hunting sooner or later.*

Ahren's practised fingers quickly tied one strap to the next while the Forest Guardian took in the view that the crest of the glacier offered. The plateau stretched as far as he could see to the southern horizon, and Ahren had the anxious feeling that the glacier formed an enormous circle, which stretched far beyond the limits of human comprehension. The Paladin remembered that Jelninolan had spoken of a place of power, and he wondered if it might not be located at the very centre of the glacier.

'*Today,* please, Ahren!' It was the impatient voice of his erstwhile master that was echoing up from below. 'This snowstorm is hardly going to make our ascent any easier.'

Ahren mumbled into his beard something about doddery, ungrateful old Paladins, causing Culhen to whimper with laughter, the young man then quickly re-tying a knot that his weary fingers had bungled. 'I'm working as fast as I can!' he bellowed. 'But I'm sure you don't want me to make a mess of my knotting – or *do* you?!'

'Quickly and thoroughly, boy!' yelled Falk from below. 'Just as I taught you!'

Ahren suppressed a retort, concentrating instead on his improvised rope before fastening it securely to Culhen's saddle pommel and throwing the other end down the crevice.

'At last!' grunted the First loudly, before Trogadon added, shouting up his advice.

'Culhen has to go closer to the edge!' yelled the blacksmith, 'We need more rope down here.'

The wolf trotted until he was a half pace from the edge of the crest, stopping when he heard 'perfect!' being yelled from below.

'Are you safe standing there?' the young man asked his wolf anxiously. 'I don't want the ice giving way beneath you.'

This glacier is almost as solid as rock, said Culhen reassuringly. *I would never have believed that ice could be so strong.*

Ahren smiled at the good-natured exaggeration of his friend, and when Khara began her ascent, he took advantage of the breathing space to have another look southward. Through the gathering snowstorm, he could just about make out the blunted mountain that they were heading for, as well as a strange flickering above the ice in the vicinity of the mountain which looked a little like…fog?

Before Ahren had a chance to mull over his discovery, Culhen's head spun around, and the animal pointed his nose into the wind.

Ahren! warned the wolf, suddenly panic-stricken. *Something is coming towards us through the snow!*

***

Revenge whipped his marionette onward, the creature's dull understanding little more than a glimmer in the darkest night, but all the more powerful, for it contained a thirst for revenge against all bipeds. Every step of his new plaything was a reminder to the beast that it had been a *human* that had rammed a spearhead into its hip where it had become embedded, deep in the creature's musculature, sending fiery waves of pain with every movement that the dim-witted creature made.

Pain that screamed for retribution. A feeling that the child of the Dark god understood only too well, and one that would be most suitably directed at the two figures on the edge of the glacial crest, isolated as they were from their friends below and so terribly exposed as well. Indeed, a length of rope was hanging from the body of the wolf, the hateful animal standing alluringly close to the abyss.

Revenge used all his might and cunning to goad his plaything into a frenzy, then lurked in the crazed understanding of the creature, waiting for the inevitable explosion of rage and violence.

***

What the... began Culhen, being the first with his keen senses to recognise what was approaching, only for Ahren to drown out his thought with a furious cry.

'WE'RE UNDER ATTACK!' he yelled down the glacier as he drew *Sun.* 'Khara – Culhen *must* get away from here! Ram your weapon into the ice – *now!*'

His beloved, midway through her ascent, reacted without hesitation. She rammed her Wind Blade up to its hilt into the glacier, and a heartbeat later Ahren had already severed the rope that had rooted Culhen to the spot. Khara was now hanging from the handle of her weapon a good twenty paces above the ice below, but the enormous ice bear, almost three paces high, with foam slavering from its mouth and racing at full pelt towards them along the crest of the glacier was of even more urgent concern.

Ahren swung himself into Culhen's saddle, the wolf immediately rushing off.

'Not *towards* it!' gasped the startled Forest Guardian, quickly changing from his Wind Blade to his bow. 'We have a better chance of defeating it from a distance!'

Good idea, replied Culhen, turning southward, forcing the furious animal away from the crevice as it hunted its prey.

Ahren had already extended *Fisiniell* while turning, insofar as this was possible, in the saddle. The ice bear was extraordinarily fast – faster even than Culhen, the Forest Guardian realised to his horror, while the hurtling speed of the wolf as well as the worsening snowstorm were not increasing Ahren's chances of a successful shot – despite his recently acquired ability to aim equally well with *both* eyes. Three arrows flew aimlessly into the stormy gloom before the Paladin finally landed a hit, the missile lodging in the left shoulder of the beast. *That should slow it down,* he said reassuringly to Culhen as he drew another arrow.

I hope you're not mistaken, countered the wolf anxiously. *This bear is out of its mind.*

When Ahren was about to dispatch his next shot, he understood what Culhen meant. The creature's eyes had widened unnaturally through agony and madness, and it seemed as if its rage at its torturers had only spurred it on. 'The child!' screamed the Forest Guardian, flabbergasted. 'I bet the child is in the bear's *mind!*'

I don't care if it's possessed, replied Culhen hectically. *The only thing that worries me is that it's getting closer all the time, and I'm beginning to get tired. Running on snow and ice is child's play to this bear. I've only been practising for a few weeks!*

Ahren dispatched another couple of arrows, yet despite the fact that the bear was nearing them all the time, a shot to the heart was still out of the question. Although the first missile had lodged in the beast's barrel-shaped chest which was the width of a carter's wagon, the second one went wildly astray, and the marksman was determined not to waste his supplies. Shouldering *Fisiniell*, he grabbed the sprinting rein at Culhen's neck, snuggled into the wolf as closely as possible, and spurred the wolf on. Culhen's relief was unmistakable, Ahren's repositioning enabling the wolf to break into an effortless sprint.

Get us away from here, big lad! yelled the Paladin as the bear snapped at them with its massive jaws, its teeth scraping loudly along the armour that protected the wolf's hindlegs. *I felt its fur on my thigh!* exclaimed Ahren in horror. *If it catches me, it will pull me off your back easily, and then...*

Culhen's paws were barely touching the ice now as he struggled to escape the ice bear. With graceful bounds, the wolf dived through the driving snow, slowly increasing the distance to half a pace between themselves and the snapping fangs of the salivating beast.

Ahren could sense that his friend was using up his last reserves of energy, yet their pursuer was neither slowing down nor showing any signs of weariness. The claws of the creature were so big that even Culhen would suffer considerable injury should the bear manage a successful swipe. Ahren shuddered to think of the beast's powerful fangs and the damage *they* could cause.

This monster is going to hunt us until its heart bursts, thought Ahren fearfully. *Can you do a loop and bring us back to our friends?*

I have no idea of where I am, retorted Culhen. *And neither the worsening snowstorm nor the insane bear are helping me to find my bearings. If I turn around and we're unlucky, we might easily hurtle over the edge of this glacier!*

Ahren looked left and right, but apart from the whirling snowflakes and their rabid pursuer, the only thing he could make out was the icy surroundings which seemed grey and without contours in the encroaching darkness. He gritted his teeth, his mind racing as he furiously sought a solution to their dilemma, but he and his friend were almost out of options. He didn't rate their chances of victory as particularly high if it came to close combat fighting, and if Culhen ran out of breath…

On your command I will spin around, said the wolf, his voice suddenly eerily calm. *I will bite into him and try to make room for a stab to the heart.*

Ahren's own heart stopped for a moment. Culhen had spoken in this tone only once before – during the skirmish on the bridge in Thousand Halls when they had been attacked by the hunter. Calm and courageous and…ready for death.

Once again, the bear was snapping at Culhen's hind legs, and Ahren only escaped the jaws of the beast by pulling back his own left leg at the last moment. He sensed his fingers, no longer protected by his magic cloak, getting number and number. Holding his Wind Blade would soon be impossible…

Let's do this, said Ahren, struggling to hold back tears of despair.

Three, he murmured, sensing the incredible bond between himself and his wolf, a bond that would last beyond their last breath.

Two. Ahren released his left hand from the rein and grasped his Wind Blade with his shivering, freezing fingers.

Culhen's thoughts were filled with peacefulness and gratitude for their shared time together.

One.

'What was *that* up there?!' yelled Falk in consternation. 'It sounded damn big – and *angry!*' He shielded his eyes from the snowflakes with his hand and looked up, but it seemed as if the developing storm was covering a blanket of whirling flakes over the entire world, and that everything two paces above them was nothing more now than a collection of barely distinguishable shadows.

'Ahren was panic-stricken, I can tell you that much!' yelled Khara from her position up in the crevice, and the fear in the voice of the Swordsmistress was impossible to miss. She was hanging from the hilt of her weapon halfway up the crevice and, considering her situation, was reacting with considerable courage.

'We have to help him!' urged Hakanu. '*Now!*'

'You are correct,' said the First matter-of-factly. 'So, why don't you bring us up to them?'

Ahren's apprentice threw the age-old Paladin a furious look, and Falk would have done the same but for the fact that this was a moment for pragmatism rather than reckless hot-headedness.

'Uldini…?' he began, only to break off as he saw the Arch Wizard trying, and failing, to float Khara up the last section of the crevice. The sorcerer was on the point of collapse having already started protecting the group from the icy temperatures with the onset of the snowstorm. 'Jelninolan!' shouted the old man instead. 'Now would be the right moment for a bit of derring-do! I suspect that things can hardly get worse!'

The elf frowned as she took *Mirilan* out of the bag, it being the one thing that she had not hurled up onto the ledge. She looked down at the instrument almost fearfully. Then she directed her gaze up to the sky. 'Are you sure?' she asked.

Falk nodded firmly. 'Yes, dammit,' he growled. 'We are stuck down here, Khara is swinging from the hilt of her sword, while Ahren is fleeing on Culhen from who knows what in the middle of a snowstorm. We can no longer afford the luxury of caution!'

'Give it a go, my heart,' said Trogadon. 'There is hardly a worse feeling in the world than the regret of wasted opportunities. Especially if it ends up that friends die.'

Jelninolan nodded, closed her eyes, and soon there was no longer *one* raging storm but *two*. Revealing the power of her True Form, Jelninolan stood there in a whirlwind of ice and snow, illuminated like a star descended from the firmament that was challenging the very essence of darkness. She lifted the Storm Fiddle to her shoulder and placed the bow on the strings.

She still hadn't sounded a single note, and yet already a shiver was running down Falk's spine. Had the glacier just shuddered?

'I'm not sure if...' he began to whisper as doubts began to creep into his mind, but already the first clear tone of the Storm Weaver's fiddle was rising upwards.

A scraping and cracking sound came from the glacier looming over them, and as the elf continued her powerful melody, violet-blue lightning flashes forked across the sky before seeking their way earthwards.

And suddenly Falk's world consisted of nothing but falling lumps of ice, screaming companions and splitting ice floes.

***

Revenge yielded all his power to the heart of the bear, now beating furiously with its extended effort. The creature would soon die, but before that it would fulfil its final, glorious task!

The child of the Adversary watched as the hand of the Thirteenth Paladin moved at snail's pace towards the hilt of the weapon. The inevitability of a bloody skirmish had at last sunk into the Forest Guardian's feeble mind.

Revenge released the last reserves of the bear.

In no more than a few heartbeats it would all be over...

***

Now! thought Ahren, Culhen spinning around in mid-flight, ready to bite into the rabid ice bear's throat and to engage in a furious skirmish with its fangs and lethal, over-sized paws. Ahren awkwardly pulled at *Sun's* hilt, grimly determined to save Culhen by driving the sword into the heart of the monster with a single, well-aimed thrust. First, he had to leap from Culhen's back, roll away, and find an opening while the larger, heavier, and stronger bear launched itself at the wolf... He forced himself not to think of the uncertain outcome of such a manoeuvre.

With a grunt, Ahren slipped into Pelneng, and prepared his legs, ready to launch himself from his friend, the wolf now spinning around on his own axis – when suddenly, the world was covered in a blinding whiteness that sent burning spasms through the Paladin and his animal companion.

Ahren could smell burnt hair and fur as he suddenly felt the heat of Deep Steel against his body, assuaged somehow by the all-encompassing mysterious force that surrounded them, both he and the wolf now tumbling through breaking ice and melting snow.

Ahren's dazzled eyes were as useless as Culhen's, and the only thing he could do was to curl up into a ball – insofar as this was possible, given his cramping muscles – as he spun through the snow, gaining momentum all the time. They were falling over the edge!

Culhen howled as his right foreleg snapped following an unlucky impact, while the air was driven out of Ahren's lungs every time he slammed against the ice. His hands were shaking and cramping and practically useless while he continued his inevitable downward trajectory. Above him, he could hear an enraged bellowing combined with a scream of pain, every time the heavy body of the bear slammed against the frozen water. The beast was falling with them and not yet dead!

Ahren tried in vain to make out details with his throbbing eyes but felt as powerless as a new-born babe. Culhen's pain combined with his own as the pair became increasingly bruised and battered. The Forest Guardian wondered what it was that was now afflicting them when suddenly their fall was brought to an end with a final, powerful impact. The Paladin felt the familiar pain of several breaking ribs, as well as Culhen's right thigh snapping loudly.

We must get away from here! thought the Forest Guardian despairingly, pulling himself painfully forward as he groaned in agony. They had to flee from the point where the bellowing ice bear would land – that was the main thing. Still blinded, Ahren was not sure of where the animal would end up, but if the furious sounds of the beast were anything to go by, it would soon slam into the ice beneath what was left of the glacier.

Ahren rolled despairingly to the side, amazement and horror combining as he encountered a smooth obstacle that stopped him in his tracks within a single pace. Culhen whimpered and howled as he crawled away from the place where *he* had landed, the courage of the desperate enabling him to do so, until he, too, met a wall of ice. Ahren uttered a prayer to the THREE as the bear tumbled closer and closer, the young man even managing to yank *Sun* into position. A loud cracking and the sound of snapping bones – music to Ahren's ears at that moment – signalled the arrival of the hundred-stone creature. Somehow forcing himself to gain control of his shivering, cramping hands, the Paladin threw himself in the direction of the growling and howling sounds, swinging and stabbing his sword with all his might. Claws scraped along his armour, and Ahren could feel the resistance against his blade, but he continued to thrust and swipe like a murderous lunatic. With every attack, his ribs would send waves of searing pain through his body, the agony having long since caused Pelneng to evaporate, but Ahren did not cease his bloody work. He knew that this was his only chance of overpowering the colossus, and if the THREE had decided that its claws were to be the weapons to send him to his death, well – so be it!

Having fully succumbed to his fatalistic state of mind, Ahren continued to hack and stab until he finally heard Culhen's voice in his head, the wolf repeating over and over again: *Stop, Ahren. It is over.*

***

'Take cover!' Falk heard Trogadon's call as Jelninolan's melody conjured up a maelstrom of lightning flashes that lit up the skies before slamming into the ice around them as well as into the glacier, enormous chunks of ice springing out of its once smooth and perfect surface. The pack ice broke under the tumbling clumps, the ice water spraying waves over the companions, who were left totally vulnerable to the extraordinary natural forces. By now, Jelninolan had ceased her playing, and Falk could see by the expression on her face that the elf was in a state of total shock.

'Too much power,' she stammered as the chaos unfolded around her. 'Far too much power.'

'Trogadon!' commanded Falk in a harsh voice. 'Grab Jelninolan! The First – do the same with Uldini. Whoever is wearing sufficient Deep Steel, protect the others from the lightning with your bodies…'

He got no further, being interrupted by a terrified scream. The ice had cracked beneath Hakanu's feet, and within a heartbeat the apprentice had sunk without trace into the water.

'NO!' bellowed Falk, racing to where Ahren's protégé had been standing. Kamaluq was whimpering in a heartrending manner, tilting his head as he attempted to spot his Paladin in the murky liquid while the growling Muai held back the little fox by placing her paw on his tail, thus preventing him from leaping in after Hakanu.

Falk looked too and cursed, unable to see the boy either.

'The current!' shouted Bergen. 'It's pulling him along! He is sure to be under the ice already!'

Falk's desperation was almost too much for him as he continued to search for the young warrior in the water. Suddenly, he *sensed* where Hakanu, Bergen, Khara, and the First were located!

'To the left of you!' screamed Khara, still hanging on desperately to the hilt of the blade, stuck into the crevice of the crumbling glacier. Her bracelet twinkled like a barely visible star in a foggy night. 'Follow the Blessing Band!'

Falk leaped from one ice floe to the next, almost losing his balance several times and slipping into the water before straightening up again as the icy water washed over the pieces of ice until he arrived at the point where he sensed Hakanu the most powerfully. The boy's rising terror was like a beacon in Falk's mind as he stood on a sheet of ice almost two paces thick, under which Hakanu was now struggling.

'Jelninolan!' he yelled. 'Uldini! Do something or the lad will be lost forever!' To Falk's horror, the Arch Wizard was floating erratically towards him, only the dregs of his magical powers remaining, while the shocked elf was still standing there, looking at the old Paladin with bewilderment. Out of pure frustration, Falk yanked his blade out and began hacking at the ice beneath his feet as if there were no tomorrow. Large splinters flew in every direction, but it was clear to the Paladin that Hakanu would long since have drowned by the time he reached the lad. 'No!' he pleaded in agony, sinking to his knees as the ice floe shuddered and Caldria landed beside him, having performed a most inelegant bellyflop, her arms and legs spread wide to stop her from slipping off the ice floe. The old woman pulled herself up onto her knees beside the grieving Falk before placing both hands on the hilt of his blade.

'What you need,' she gasped, 'is a little more warmth.'

***

Revenge struggled to come to terms with what had so recently transpired. Then he released himself, albeit with a feeling of utter frustration, from the hacked remains of his marionette.

A lightning flash, he thought, bewildered. *A damn lightning flash struck us!*

Even Revenge had not been spared the shock that had flowed into the bear. The child of the Adversary still could not comprehend how the tables had turned so suddenly as he struggled to orientate himself. Indeed, he was not even sure that the flash had been aimed at him, for the Paladin and his wolf had also been illuminated by a white light. They were lying there like two scorched chickens – battered, bruised, and unconscious.

Revenge finally got a grip on himself and whooshed quickly away through the cold sky. It was true that he had given some of his power to the bear, and lost yet more of it to the lightning, but all he needed was a nearby oafish Dark One and then he would make short shrift of the half-dead Paladin.

***

Falk stared down at his trusty broadsword, which was heating up and now beginning to glow in the grasp of the groaning Caldria. The cramped fingers of the woman were grasping his hands and the hilt as if in a vice. Falk sensed the strength draining from Hakanu in the bitterly cold water below and again he tried to wield his weapon against the ice floe, but Caldria shook her head.

'Patience,' she wheezed, her head suddenly tilting back as blood flowed out of her nose.

Falk was unsure as to whether the sorceress had been talking to him or to herself, but suddenly she froze before collapsing in a heap. The broadsword was glowing as if newly forged, while Falk struggled to hold onto the burning hot hilt of the weapon. After a heartbeat's hesitation, he struggled to his feet, took a step away from the prostrate Caldria and slammed the red-hot blade deep into the ice at his feet.

There was a sharp bang, then a crack, and finally, a breaking sound. Falk sensed the ice below him drifting apart and saw that the weapon had completely retuned to normal, having taken on, once again, the Deep Steel hue. He flung the blade to Trogadon on the neighbouring ice floe and shouted: 'Bergen, help Caldria!' Then he plunged his hand into the dark water beneath his feet, following the weakening Blessing Band. His fingers closed around the top of a spear shaft and with a groan, he pulled the coughing and spluttering Hakanu to the surface.

'I have you,' grunted Falk, weakly attempting a smile as he hauled the shivering apprentice out of the water.

'I...I...ra...rammed my sp...sp...spear into the ice from below,' stammered the young warrior. 'Current...too...str...str...strong.'

'Hush now,' said Falk reassuringly. Then he picked up the lad and flung him straight into the arms of the waiting First, who was standing on a nearby ice floe.

'I will bring him over to *Flamestar*,' said the war veteran. 'He should survive his ice bath with the help of the warming spell.'

'I'm coming too,' said Falk, suddenly overcome by a feeling of utter exhaustion. He helped Bergen with the limp Caldria, the companions then gathering in the light of the warmth-endowing crystal ball, in the midst of the shattered pack ice and the splintered glacier.

'At least there's no lightning anymore,' said Khara, her dripping features suggesting to Falk that the Swordsmistress had pulled her blade out of the ice and sprung out of the crevice and into the icy waters. Without armour and being a superb swimmer, she had been able to defy the current long enough to save herself.

'That was a lucky escape,' said Trogadon, shaking his head. 'Let us hope that Ahren and Culhen were similarly fortunate, wherever they are.

***

Wake up. It was Culhen's voice permeating the dullness of Ahren's mind. *Come on! Wake up!*

It was the frustration in his friend's tone, and the wolf's pain, rather than his own physical and mental state that caused the Forest Guardian to come to. Unconsciousness had been a blessing, allowing him to forget for a while the misfortune that had been visited upon them.

The Paladin opened his eyes and groaned with relief as he made out the dim outline of the moon. He could see again!

The storm had passed and been replaced by a clear sky, with strange streaks of light – blue, green, and purple – dancing as if they were long forgotten spirits performing a roundelay.

'You can see it too, can't you?' asked Ahren with a groan, silently cursing his aching ribs as he struggled to sit up. Speaking aloud to his wolf was helping him to focus. His voice bounced off the walls of the crevasse in a dull echo.

The lights? Asked Culhen. *Yes, I can see them too,*

'Good,' grunted Ahren. 'For a moment there, I thought that I had banged my head and was imagining things.' Blinking, he looked around, recognising more and more details of his surroundings, his eyes adjusting also to the bizarre play of lights above. 'We are at the bottom of a very deep glacial crevasse,' said Ahren, surprised, as he looked back up in the direction from where they had rolled. A zigzag crack, five paces wide, had opened up in the ice massif, the ice bear, Culhen, and he himself all having tumbled down the uneven edge, which now loomed, jagged, above the Paladin. Beneath their feet was what had to be primeval rock, a layer of ice already forming on its newly exposed surface. It seemed that they had neared the mountains of the far south and were now standing on one of their subterranean spurs. To his left and right soared the ice walls with all the ease of endless patience. The only way out for Ahren and Culhen was to walk forward, following the fissure, which had eaten its way through the ice, forming a narrow passageway.

I'm not going anywhere, said the wolf, and as the animal tried to stand up, the pain was almost unbearable, even for Ahren. *Just leave me here and get help.*

Ahren snorted in reply and struggled to his feet. He silently thanked Trogadon for his ribbon armour, which was giving support to his damaged ribs, and began to untie his vambraces and greaves of Deep Steel, quietly cursing at the pain he was feeling.

What are you doing there? asked Culhen in alarm.

'Improvising,' said Ahren. 'As we Forest Guardians always do.'

Show-off, said Culhen, the Paladin sensing that his companion was trying to hide his own pain from his friend.

'Don't worry,' said Ahren. 'We share everything – even the agony of the other.' With that, he carefully began to put Culhen's foreleg to right.

I'll remember that the next time you don't want to share your dinner with me, muttered the wolf. Then there was a low cracking sound as the bone sprang back into place. *Ouch!* complained the animal as he gazed at Ahren with his golden eyes. *I want Jelninolan or even Uldini. They are much gentler,* he added grimly.

'Stop complaining,' said Ahren, smiling. Then he took his vambraces and placed them like two halves of a shell around the break. 'This is going to hurt,' he warned his friend.

It was doing that already, countered the wolf sardonically.

Ahren took the straps of the vambraces, fastening them together from either side of Culhen's leg and pulling them towards each other before knotting them as best he could. Culhen whimpered quietly but remained still until Ahren nodded reassuringly.

'Some would see a pair of Paladin vambraces – I, however, consider them to be the most priceless protectors in all Jorath,' he commented, satisfied with his handiwork.

It wasn't that bad, lied Culhen bravely. *Let me check to see if this leg of mine is reliable.*

'Hold on there, big lad,' warned Ahren. 'You still have another break, and I have *these*.' With that, he picked up his greaves.

Ah, come on now, complained Culhen, but Ahren was already putting the next bone back in its proper place.

This time the wolf said nothing, which the Paladin took to be a bad sign. For a heartbeat he sank right into his friend's mind, realising immediately how weary and battered Culhen was. The exhausting attack, the two broken bones, and the countless bruises demanded their tribute of the stubborn, proud wolf, who was trying his best to shield Ahren from his own suffering.

The Forest Guardian completed his care of the broken thigh speedily but thoroughly, although he still looked sceptically down at his work once he had finished.

'Your leg is too thick,' he said, teasing Culhen. 'My greaves don't quite fit around it.'

It's all muscle and fur, said the wolf worthily. *And I must be strong – otherwise, I would not be able to carry a heavy Paladin on my back.*

Ahren chuckled, tickling his friend on the belly for a moment before straightening up with a groan. 'Be careful with this leg in particular,' he said in a serious voice. 'These guards are not as secure as those on your foreleg.'

Well, let us see if Falk hasn't wasted all his time on your education, shall we? said Culhen. The wolf tried to make his words sound as solemn as possible as he simultaneously tried to stand up.

'A consumptive foal is more elegant than you are,' mocked Ahren as he watched his wolf struggling.

Hold your horses, grumbled Culhen sulkily. It took him a painful ten heartbeats to finally get into a tottery upright position, Ahren generously sharing his friend's pain as much as possible by merging his own thoughts with those of the animal.

'Better than nothing,' said the Paladin once the wolf was standing. 'But I strongly advise you to remain on your feet for now. Watching you get up was *not* a pleasant sight.'

Go stick your head down a Glower Bear's throat, growled Culhen before becoming genuinely serious. *What do we do now? We don't know where we are, let alone our friends' location, and we have no food or supplies with us. We are injured and this child of the Adversary is still somewhere out there.*

'We will do what we always do,' said Ahren slowly putting one foot in front of the other. 'We will keep going.'

***

'*Everything* gone?' asked the First tersely, Falk nodding silently in response.

They had clambered up the glacier through a particularly craggy fracture and searched in vain for their equipment as soon as the skies had cleared to a starry, moonlit night.

The old Paladin pointed at the spot where he believed their pile of rucksacks had last been. 'This is where they must have stacked everything.'

Trogadon stood at the edge of the gaping fissure criss-crossing the glacier and looked down. 'There's water down there,' he sighed. 'Everything washed away. The tents, the fishing hooks, our provisions…'

'Listing them off is hardly going to improve things,' grumbled Bergen.

Falk shook off his shock at their latest setback and forced himself to think. 'What happened?' he asked Jelninolan bluntly, looking first up at the sky and then at the shattered Ice Fields all around them. Under the play of the coloured lights, they had a perfect view from their elevated vantage point, the old Paladin scanning the damage below with fear and trepidation. 'You almost caused the sky to fall down on top of us, and I'm talking literally.'

The elf wrang her hands before shaking her head helplessly. 'When I was playing, it felt as if I was calling something towards us that was far mightier than me,' she said uncertainly. 'It was neither an attack by the Adversary nor an evil trick of a goblin, but a pure, unsullied power – a power that wanted to meld with mine – a power that I could not control. I was like a fork trying to catch water. All the power was channelled through me and into my melody.'

'This will be fun,' said Bergen. 'One of our sorcerers is about to drop off to sleep, another one had better *not* lift a finger for fear of conjuring up the next disaster, and the third of their lot...' He looked quizzically at Caldria, whom they had placed on some furs and who hadn't moved an inch since then. 'What's wrong with *her?*' he asked cautiously.

Jelninolan went down on her knees beside the old woman, demonstratively putting *Mirilan* back in its bag before she whispered some words to the Fire Sorceress, placing a finger on the woman's forehead at the same time. 'Oh,' she said sadly. 'How tragic.'

'Is she dead?' asked Hakanu fearfully, the boy still shivering, and hugging the quietly whimpering Kamaluq, who was providing him with another heat source.

'There are *some* who might describe her as such,' said Jelninolan, glancing over at Uldini. 'She is burnt out. She used all the sorcery that she possessed for this one spell on Falk's sword. The deed was a particularly unpredictable form of Unleashing.' The elf looked at each of her companions in turn. 'Caldria has cast her last spell.'

'And all because of me,' whispered Hakanu morosely, Kamaluq then rubbing his little head against the Paladin's neck.

'Your extreme situation was *my* fault,' said the elf, getting back to her feet. 'I was incapable of controlling the power that seems to reign supreme here.'

'But where is it coming from?' mumbled Uldini, his eyes almost completely closed. 'Can you sense that?'

Jelninolan shook her head. 'Not without a charm net,' she said. 'And considering the situation we find ourselves in, I would prefer not to risk searching for this mysterious power source by casting one.' Falk noticed how the Ancient had shivered. 'I shudder to think of what might happen if my net makes contact with this power, and their combined energy runs along the threads and back to us…'

'Not a good idea, my heart,' said Trogadon firmly. 'Let us first concentrate on finding our lost Paladin and his wolf.'

Falk saw how Khara closed her eyes, rubbing her bracelet simultaneously. Immediately, he sensed the Blessing Band, but Ahren was not a part of it. 'Nothing,' said the Swordsmistress curtly.

'We would have sensed if he had sunk beneath the ice,' said the First matter-of-factly, Falk suppressing the desire to wring his eldest brother's neck for his lack of subtlety.

'The First is right,' he said instead. 'Let us assume that both Ahren and Culhen are still alive.'

'This is great,' muttered Bergen, his hands on his hips. 'We came here to find a Paladin, instead of which we have *lost* one.'

Trogadon kicked a little lump of ice into the nearest crevice, where it tumbled out of sight with a dull din. Then he succinctly expressed what Falk was thinking: 'I hate these Ice Fields.'

***

At last, Revenge could sense life ahead of him and he quickly felt for the animal's mind. Its greed would suffice to send the creature to the crevasse, the child of the Dark god immediately moving onwards. If he sent enough predatory animals or Dark Ones to this crack in the glacier, the injured Paladin would never emerge from it alive.

***

'Would you look at the state of us two scarecrows,' said Ahren wearily, pulling his cloak in closer. Had Akkad's leather not been magically treated, it would surely be little more than a tattered rag by now. It was the corpulent Ancient's magic that was keeping Ahren from freezing to death. Every now and then, the Forest Guardian would cut little pieces of ice from the walls right and left and either push them into the wolf's mouth or suck on them himself so that they would at least consume enough liquids. He sensed both his own hunger and that of the animal, but they could survive a few days without food until they found their friends, at which point they would feast on fish while Jelninolan or Uldini could treat them with some healing magic…

Ahren! Culhen's note of alarm startled the Paladin. *Something is coming towards us in the fissure!* The wolf had pricked up his ears, and his body was as tense as his two broken bones would allow.

Ahren unshouldered *Fisiniell* and took an arrow from his quiver as his fingers instinctively counted his remaining missiles. After this one, there would be four left. The Forest Guardian practised extending the bow, doubling over in pain as he did so. Slowly, he released the tension again. *I won't manage more than half the normal extension thanks to my broken ribs,* Ahren warned his friend. *I don't want to risk the ribs digging into my lungs.*

Half-strength is more than I can do at the moment, muttered the wolf. *If we are to be jumped on, I'm more likely to flatten myself to the floor rather than risk being eaten alive.*

Now Ahren could make out a snuffling sound in front of them, and gritting his teeth, he went down on one knee beside Culhen. He positioned his bow so that it faced forward, not extending it yet to preserve his remaining strength.

Whatever is coming, it's very near, announced Culhen, who then lifted his nose to sniff the air. *Alas, it has the scent advantage, and I can smell nothing, for the wind is coming from the north.*

Ahren heard a growling sound, which he reckoned to be about ten paces away. The crevice curved a little so that for now, he could not make out his target. In order to ameliorate the pain, the Forest Guardian slipped into Pelneng, concentrating fully on his breathing.

The first arrow must hit home, he told himself, thereby simultaneously informing Culhen. *It will take me so long to extend the bow that I will hardly manage a second shot.*

The wolf didn't reply but continued to sniff the air, a mild irritation beginning to trouble his mind. *Ahren…* he began, but already the Forest Guardian could make out the first outline of something large. Bared fangs glistened in the moonlight, claws scraped along the ice, and within a heartbeat, the figure was ready to pounce.

Ahren's heart was beating wildly as he extended the bow and fixed his aim on a point between two glimmering eyes. *Only one chance…* he repeated.

NO! screamed Culhen suddenly as he unceremoniously pushed the Forest Guardian sideways with his head, causing the Paladin to slam against the wall of ice and slip to the ground. At that same moment, their attacker launched its attack, its jaws opened wide, and its front legs outstretched.

Culhen howled with all his might and stumbled forward a step, his head high and his eyes fixed on those of the enemy. Ahren struggled to his feet with the intention of aiming *Fisiniell* once more when the creature slammed into Culhen's armour, almost causing the injured wolf to fall. But Ahren's animal only growled in warning and bit half-heartedly at the attacker's neck, relying then on grunting and barking.

Ahren still wanted to use *Fisiniell* when a reflection of light in the ice gave him a better view of the alien creature, the bow immediately falling out of the Paladin's hand as he looked in astonishment. 'An Ice Wolf?' he said, flabbergasted. 'Here?'

A she-wolf, explained Culhen, who was still trying to persuade the animal not to attack. *She is hungry and remarkably stubborn. As if she is fully convinced that there is good food to be found here.* This was followed by more warning bites, loud growling, and the occasional whimper – on both sides. Ahren shouldered *Fisiniell* but kept a hand on his Wind Blade's hilt – just to be on the safe side. After all, the she-wolf could well be too hungry for their liking.

At last, she is listening to me, said Ahren's friend, clearly relieved. *She says that I look weird for a wolf but that my size is impressive.*

She can talk? asked the Paladin, confused.

Of course not, chuckled Culhen. *But I can figure out what she's trying to communicate through her body language and the noises that she's making.*

The she-wolf barked and growled with her head cocked, while Culhen's mood was improving all the time. *At first, she thought that I was some sort of exotic bear,* he boasted.

Then tell your new girlfriend that she isn't allowed to gobble up either of us, you limping bear, you, commanded Ahren impatiently.

I've already done so, said Culhen, delighted with himself. *She said that she'll leave me in peace but that she's not so sure about you. She's already asked me twice if you are my booty and if that's so, can she eat you.*

Tell her to help herself, countered Ahren dryly. *You've been fraying my nerves and testing my patience for years anyway.*

Oh, you're so funny. Culhen pushed his head against the she-wolf and growled once. The other animal took a backward step before lowering her head a little. *She speaks with a funny accent,* said Culhen curiously.

Ahren didn't understand the world anymore. *I'm sorry, what?*

I mean her body language is...distorted. Not completely wolfish if you see what I mean.

I can imagine that her pack have been isolated from the continent for a long time now, mused Ahren. *Maybe they have developed their own dialect.*

Culhen growled and barked a couple of times, then pointed with his head towards Ahren. The she-wolf then retreated another step and glanced behind her. Ahren could sense the excitement in his friend. *I had an idea,* he proudly announced. *I asked her if she saw other creatures like you, and she said yes.*

Ahren was suddenly filled with joyful anticipation, as if he had been struck by lightning, this time of a beneficent kind. *That had to be Khara and the others! Ask her if she can lead us to them.*

Again, there was an exchange of animal sounds before the she-wolf turned on her heels and trotted along the crevice with Culhen limping after her, while Ahren shuffled along in the rear. *I take it that she's helping us then?* he asked.

But of course, said Culhen cockily. *Why wouldn't she help a prime specimen like me?*

Ahren sensed that his friend was hiding something from him. *Come on, Culhen! Spit it out!* he commanded.

Well, you see, it's like this, began the wolf hesitantly. *I had to promise that she would get whatever was left of you once I've had my fill.*

She's going to pay dearly for your joke, countered Ahren sulkily. *If she knew you at all, then she would understand that you never leave anything on your plate.*

You have a point, you know, agreed Culhen generously, moving up closer to the Ice Wolf so that she could see him out of the corner of her eye.

Ahren wearily rubbed his face and pulled his cloak tighter around his broken ribs. This was going to be a most uncomfortable stroll.

Chapter 20

'So, Ahren *is* still alive?' asked Falk, his relief resembling a refreshing morning swim after a good night's sleep. Hakanu cried with relief beside him and even Kamaluq whimpered with delight.

Jelninolan nodded, pointing at Khara's bracelet. 'The miniscule charm net that I cast on her trinket leaves me in no doubt,' said the elf, who had anxiously glanced skyward several times. She hadn't used *Mirilan* in her efforts as she was clearly wary of the mysterious power that had reacted so furiously to her Stormweaving.

'He is somewhere in that direction,' said Khara with remarkable equanimity as she pointed in a south-south-westerly direction. 'It is so good to sense him – even if it is only a weak echo of his presence.'

'Let us hope that Culhen is alive too,' interjected Bergen, who had sent Karkas off into the clear blue sky to figure out a way over the cracked glacier for them.

'Well, *I* preferred the original lump of pure ice, I have to say,' grumbled Trogadon, pointing at the countless fissures decorating the surface of the deep blue surface now sprinkled with powdery snow – all a result of the previous night's storm. 'It is going to take us forever to make our way south to the Frozen Teeth over this labyrinth of rifts.'

'Karkas will guide us,' said Bergen reassuringly. 'And even if it takes us a long time, he will bring us to our destination.'

'Your prediction is so comforting,' interjected Falk. 'Especially as Uldini is in a state of total exhaustion and more or less continuously asleep, while Muai and I are the ones who have to search for food so that none of us starve to death.'

'Not to mention this ballast,' added the First matter-of-factly, who had thrown the unconscious Caldria over his left shoulder. Falk was relieved that the war veteran hadn't proposed leaving the old woman behind them altogether. 'Our progress will be snail's pace.'

Khara gazed into the distance as though she were trying to see her beloved through sheer willpower alone. 'We can follow Ahren's route and pray that he will already have found Yollock by the time we reach him.'

***

Ahren continued to stagger through the snow, panting as he did so. For a while now they had been making their way on top of the glacier instead of struggling along down one of its fissures, their new leader having led them up a gently rising snow drift, thereby enabling them to escape their ice-bound prison. The searing pain in his chest was now accompanied by a gnawing hunger, and no matter how flatly he tried to breathe, his ribs shot fiery darts of pain through his entire body, while his eyes were hurting from the blinding sunlight reflected from the surfaces around him. Then there were also Culhen's injuries, which he felt almost as much as his own. His wolf, on the other hand, was cheerful despite their plight – a fact which would have drawn a smile from the Forest Guardian were it not for the fact that their current situation precluded such a gesture.

She's very impressive and yet she's still so young, said his friend admiringly, who was now trotting along directly beside the Ice Wolf and looking at her repeatedly in the bright midday sunshine.

Her fur glistens in the light like snow, her gait has something playfully elegant about it, and don't you agree that her claws are perfectly formed and symmetrical? added Culhen, listing off the positive attributes of their new acquaintance.

I didn't notice her paws, said the Forest Guardian, trying to maintain his patience. *My attention is taken up with the fact that we have no food, warmth or Healing Water.* Much as his magic cloak protected Ahren when the Paladin retreated beneath it, he felt more and more the bitter cold every time he took his arms out from under it, the lack of food and sleep ensuring that his body was becoming less and less resistant to the elements. *Can your girlfriend please tell us where she spotted Falk and the others? And how long it will take us to reach them?*

No, was the wolf's unsatisfactory response. *Despite her undoubted cleverness and her extraordinary beauty, her sense of time is still that of a normal animal, while her manner of expression is somewhat limited.*

Ahren groaned and tried to orientate himself yet again. Judging by the position of the sun, they were going west, but their unusual guide kept changing direction, their way being constantly impeded by rocky spurs that were now breaking through the ice plateau. The Forest Guardian reckoned that they were now making their way over a mountain ridge which surely had to be part of the Frozen Teeth, the range that dominated the endless ice of the south.

The thought that there was solid rock beneath the frozen water at his feet was strangely comforting even if it didn't alter the precariousness of their situation. With ever increasing weariness and a growing feeling of weakness, Ahren shuffled after the she-wolf and the smitten Culhen, always seeking out any clue that might increase their chances of survival. He didn't share the unshakeable confidence of his four-legged friend in their new companion, as he pretty much knew what emotion Culhen was succumbing to.

On recognising Ahren's thought, the wolf snorted and refused to talk to the Forest Guardian for the rest of the day.

***

Revenge *hated* the Ice Fields. He flourished in the company of humans with their petty fits of jealousy, their imagined slights, and their dogmatic viewpoints. Any little deviation from what was deemed normal behaviour could lead to lifelong vendettas in one small village, while one poor business deal could result in open warfare between two lords. But out here he only had dull animals with their limited impulses to play with. This good-for-nothing she-wolf was practically useless.

Revenge had weakened considerably by the time he at last found some Dark Ones. Thankfully, they reacted to the dark call of his father, which he had by now learned to imitate.

As the howling pack of Snow Slashers began to make their way eastward, Revenge hoped earnestly that at last, he would complete his woeful task.

***

Oh no, gasped Culhen, the words ringing in Ahren's head as the night was drawing in.

The Paladin listened with the ears of the alarmed wolf and groaned.

At least six Snow Slashers were approaching, but neither he nor Culhen were in any state to fight. A glance at the nervous she-wolf confirmed to Ahren that she had instinctively understood the danger, but to his surprise, she was remaining by their side. *By Culhen's side, he corrected himself.*

No surprise there, said his friend, who had decided that the silent treatment towards the Forest Guardian had lasted long enough. *She surely has never encountered such a mightily impressive Ice Wolf before.*

And because she can't hear your voice, she has no idea of how incorrigibly boastful that same preening Ice Wolf is, added Ahren sarcastically. Of course, he was relieved that the she-wolf had not made her escape in view of the approaching danger, but he was under no illusions as to what the outcome of the imminent skirmish would be.

He glanced at a rock rising out of the glacial ice like a natural ramp. A good four paces high and double that in length and width, Ahren reckoned that he would be able to scale it easily enough even with his injuries, and it might offer them some tactical advantage.

I'll climb to the top, and you two give me cover, said Ahren curtly before making his laborious ascent, cursing under his breath. Every upward step was torture, the young man praying that none of the broken ribs would puncture his lungs.

Having arrived at the top, the Forest Guardian settled down on the front edge and placed *Fisiniell* across his knees, his remaining arrows lined up neatly beside him. He could see the white outlines of the six-legged Dark Ones in the distance, leaping at speed towards them. *Five arrows for six Snow Slashers,* he calculated grimly. *If I were in good health, they would certainly suffice.*

Don't forget, we are here too, said Culhen, who was standing guard with the she-wolf at the base of the rock. Ahren could sense his friend's concern for their new companion, which only gave him an additional pain in the pit of his stomach.

Culhen, he said gently, *she must be able to look after herself...*

Would you say the same thing about a female biped too? retorted the wolf, the instant Ahren's silent communication had reached him.

No, admitted the Paladin, checking his gloves before testing his ability to extend *Fisiniell.* The result was even more disappointing than the night before. *We will protect her as well as we can,* he said wearily. *Of course, we will.*

Together, not alone, intoned Culhen, surprising his friend with the slogan.

Together, not alone, repeated Ahren with tears of exhaustion in his eyes. Then the Snow Slashers were sufficiently close. The Forest Guardian weakly raised his bow, extended it as far as he possibly could, and dispatched the arrow.

***

'I sense something,' said Khara, anxiously looking at Falk and the others. 'It is Ahren – and he is afraid.'

'Is that a good sign, my heart?' asked Trogadon, looking at Jelninolan. 'I don't mean the fear but the fact that Khara can sense his emotions?'

The elf shrugged her shoulders sadly. 'It can either mean that he is nearby,' she said after a prolonged pause. 'Or that his emotions are so powerful that she can pick them up even over a great distance.'

'The first option sounds good. The second one…not so much,' murmured Hakanu, whose concern for his master was clear for all to see. Falk had noticed that the young warrior had been unusually silent and focused since the Forest Guardian had gone missing. The old Paladin was painfully aware of the irony that Hakanu was behaving most as his master would wish it now that Ahren was *not* present.

'Can Karkas see anything unusual?' asked the First gruffly.

Bergen pointed towards the quickly encroaching dusk. 'With every heartbeat, his view is diminishing,' he said apologetically. 'But he thinks that he spotted some sort of rushing movement ahead.'

'Then let us hope that it is our wandering Paladin,' said Falk, breaking into a steady trot, hoping to progress as quickly as the slippery ice would allow. After all, it would give him great pleasure first to rescue his former apprentice and then to tease him about it mercilessly.

***

The first arrow met its target, Ahren feeling a grim sense of satisfaction as the Snow Slasher collapsed on the ice as if struck by lightning, where it remained motionless.

Four more hits and we will have survived this assault, he thought hopefully.

As long as you leave one of them for me, said Culhen. *After all, we want her to see how superb a fighter I am.*

Ahren didn't need to turn his head to understand that his friend was totally besotted by the she-wolf at his side, the Forest Guardian deciding, however, to refrain from commenting. Anything that distracted Culhen from his broken legs was a godsend. The young man aimed another arrow and shot it at the next Snow Slasher. The Dark One changed direction at the last moment, the missile failing to slam into its head, but hitting a shoulder instead. Which meant that they would have to encounter at least two of the beasts in close combat.

Ahren suppressed his increasing frustration, slipping into the Void instead. The all-embracing coolness that accompanied the letting go of his emotions *and* physical sensations enabled him to shoot the next arrow cleanly, the missile slamming perfectly into the chest of the snuffling Snow Slasher.

Two arrows to go and four Snow Slashers left.

The Dark Ones had spotted the little travel party by now and were bearing down on them, making good use of the rocks and snow drifts as protective shields. Ahren realised that the foes were behaving more cleverly than he would have expected, concluding in the silence of the Void, that the child of the Adversity was somehow involved.

Ahren extended his bow again, noticing as he did so that his hands were trembling badly. It was true that he couldn't sense his exhaustion or his wounds while in the Void, but it was now clear to him that he was very close to collapsing. He aimed slowly and deliberately as the Snow Slashers turned to prepare for their assault on the rock. Then he let his arrow fly, incorporating the *Han'halthin* technique in the process in the hope of felling two Snow Slashers with one shot. Totally emotionless, he followed the course of his arrow with his eyes, his daring meeting with only partial success as one of the Snow Slashers gracefully feinted, the Dark One behind it being mortally wounded in its stead.

Quickly, Ahren picked up the last arrow in the hope of dispatching one last missile before the Dark Ones would leap up the rock, forcing him to engage the two growling wolves in close combat, but he found that the projectile had slipped from his fingers and was tumbling uselessly down onto the ice. First, it was only a vague sense of confusion that penetrated the Void, but soon the warrior felt weak all over and a piercing pain was exploding in his chest.

Ahren spat up blood and the Void shattered like a sheet of glass under a powerfully swung hammer. Every breath sent a burning flame through the right side of his chest. One of his ribs must have punctured a lung while Ahren had been extending himself in the Void!

With a piping gasp, the Forest Guardian drew his Wind Blade and saw from his hunkered position on the top of the rock how the three Snow Slashers began their gallop which would bring them past the two snarling wolves and onto the rock...

***

Khara clutched her bosom and gasped. 'I think...' she began uncertainly, and when she looked around, Falk could see the terror in her eyes. 'I think that Ahren is injured – badly injured.'

Muai uttered a low growl, her large body keeping the Swordsmistress from collapsing.

Khara's words weighed like a bad omen on the hurrying group, no-one daring to reply to her suspicions. Instead, Falk, Trogadon, Hakanu, and Bergen picked up speed, leaving Uldini's warming crystal ball in their wake as they skilfully negotiated snowdrifts, fissures, and jutting rocks while the First with the unconscious Caldria slung over his back, and the two Ancients fell further behind.

Falk prayed to the THREE that they wouldn't arrive too late as a succession of horrible images flashed across his mind.

Those images that had been burned into his imagination since the previous Thirteenth Paladin had died.

***

Much to Ahren's relief, it didn't take long after the onset of the skirmish for Culhen to bite into one of the attacker's throats, but the she-wolf was already on the defensive. The animal was not as big as Culhen, nor did she possess his armour, his experience, or his guile, so the most she could manage was to keep the furious Snow Slasher at bay as she slowly moved sideways, step by step – thereby creating a space for the third Dark One, which leaped into the air, sailed towards Ahren, and landed a quarter pace in front of the Paladin. The fox-like head of the creature lunged forward, its needle-sharp fangs ready to tear and rip.

Ahren drew *Sun* across the throat of the beast – or that had been his *plan*. In fact, all he could manage was a weak, inaccurate thrust, which did little more than injure one of the Dark One's front legs. The creature flinched, but his jaws closed around its prey, nonetheless, then swung the helpless Paladin this way and that – as if he were nothing but a rag doll.

Ahren heard Culhen howl, the canine struggling to gain the upper hand against the third Snow Slasher, while the she-wolf snapped at one of the Dark One's hindlegs. Somehow, Ahren managed to keep hold of *Sun*, stabbing weakly at the creature which had him in its fangs a second time. Blood spurted out of a wound in the Snow Slasher's flank, the beast then dropping him with a yelp of pain – down off the rock towards the hard ice below.

Ahren felt a brief moment of terror before he hit the surface, pain exploding like a thousand flames from his chest. Gasping and coughing up blood – which only made things worse – the Paladin looked up through a veil of red at the Snow Slasher leaning over the edge of the rock staring greedily down at him. Then the monster sprang, the Forest Guardian only hearing Culhen's howl of horror in his head.

Ahren despairingly tried to hold up *Sun*, in the desperate hope that his opponent would be skewered through the force of its jump, but the Paladin was no longer able to lift the hilt of his weapon. He could do nothing but watch as the murderous creature fell – with the clear intention of finishing him off.

***

'Over *there!*' roared Trogadon, hurtling off as though a tableful of beer and roast meat were waiting for him, 'I saw something ahead of us!'

Falk broke into a sprint but was still overtaken by Khara, who was uttering silent prayers as she ran, accompanied by Hakanu, his spear at the ready in his hand. Maybe the THREE really were showing their mercy!

'We're coming, Ahren,' murmured the old Paladin, drawing his broadsword as he ran. Meanwhile, he swore to himself that he would tie his former apprentice to him for the rest of their journey through the Ice Fields so that the young man wouldn't go astray again.

***

AHREN! yelled the despairing Culhen as the Snow Slasher slammed down towards the Paladin like an executioner's axe, with the added impact of fangs and claws. Baring his teeth in fury and clenching his fists in a futile gesture, being unable to lift them through weakness and pain, the Thirteenth Paladin awaited his death. His final attempt at raising his Wind Blade having ended in failure, Ahren was unable to do anything more than breathe out in exhaustion.

The Dark One was not more than two handspans above him when there was a sudden whizzing sound as a shadowy object shot across Ahren's field of vision, smashing into the head of the Snow Slasher, causing it to jerk violently. The Paladin heard a cracking sound above him, then another one as the beast fell on top of him.

The last thing he was aware of was the rumbling voice of a dwarf, which caused him first to smile and then to frown before darkness overcame his consciousness.

***

'I wasn't expecting this,' said Trogadon morosely, as he retrieved the hammer that he had thrown and cleaned the blood off it. Falk and the others were all standing around a dead Seal Wolf, their disappointment and confusion evident on their faces. The blacksmith's weapon had done its work, finishing off the creature, but there was no sign at all of Ahren or Culhen.

'Oh, yes. Karkas spotted this fellow in the distance, too,' said Bergen sadly. 'And he was on his own.'

'I can't sense Ahren anymore,' said Khara, her normally calm demeanour replaced by a look of sheer panic. 'Not even a faint echo to confirm that he is still alive!'

'There can be many reasons for that,' said Jelninolan, sounding less than convincing. 'A deep sleep or perhaps this power that seems to be everywhere here,' she said. 'Maybe it's simply interfering with the charm net.'

Falk rubbed his face wearily and said nothing. Then he pointed down at Uldini, who was sitting on the floor, his crystal ball barely flickering and producing almost no heat. 'It is dark, Uldini can no longer cast spells, and the night is getting colder. 'As long as my heart doesn't tell me that Ahren is dead, I refuse to believe that he is. Let us concentrate for the time being on taking care of ourselves by setting up camp here – otherwise, *he* may well end up mourning *our* deaths.' He pointed at the companions, one at a time. 'Bergen, grab the First and Trogadon and build us an ice hut. Khara – you and Muai stand guard and keep your senses about you in case you receive any signs of life coming from Ahren. Jelninolan, see what you can do for Uldini and Caldria. Hakanu, you can help me gut this Dark One. Let's hope it tastes better than it looks.'

No-one bickered over the instructions, with even the First following his orders without complaint. Proof to Falk if he needed it, that his companions feared for the worst regarding Ahren's fate.

***

'Menek'malor thurm Paladrim,' said an unfamiliar voice as Ahren struggled to escape from the deep sleep to which he had succumbed. Breathing was proving difficult, with every inhalation filling the lungs of the Forest Guardian with a heavy and even *bitter* taste. He was so weak, he could hardly open his eyes, and when he eventually did manage to do so, all he could see were two braziers filled with glimmering red coals in pitch black surroundings.

His skin felt damp, the Paladin then noticing that he was stripped almost naked as well as being bound. His chest hurt at the smallest movement, but for the moment, Ahren was pleased that at least he was no longer coughing up blood, and his ribs seemed back in place.

He gathered his senses insofar as he could, concentrating primarily on his connection with Culhen and satisfying himself that at least his friend was still alive, even if he seemed *very* far away, for Ahren could only sense the presence of the wolf as a distant echo, and speaking to him was out of the question. Perhaps Culhen was being kept prisoner in a similar manner?

The Forest Guardian decided to keep his speculations for later, focusing instead on the voice that had aroused him from his slumber. He could still hear it, talking in the gravelly, rumbling Dwarfish tongue, but despite Ahren's rudimentary knowledge of the language, he couldn't understand a single word. He tried crawling closer to the door but abandoned the idea after a couple of heartbeats. His hands were tied behind his back, and his legs were bound together, too. For now, he would concentrate on listening to the voices while trying to familiarise himself with the room that he was in.

His half-opened eyes were slowly becoming accustomed to the very faint light cast by the braziers, and he began to make out a few details. His clothing – but not his armour – was lying in a heap in a corner of the square shaped room. The ceiling was low, while the walls were of smooth, innocuous stone, a fur cloth hanging before the single opening in the room and serving as a curtain. Apart from his clothing and the two coal burning bowls, there were no other objects in the room, not even a straw mat. Ahren was lying on cold stone, which, however, felt less cold than he would have expected.

Because his eyes were beginning to ache, he closed them again and heightened his other senses. He slowly breathed in the unusual smelling air – which was difficult enough to inhale – his lungs protesting as he tried to figure out what exactly it was that he was smelling. To his surprise, he first identified ground Wolf Herb, then dried Life Fern, and finally charred Low Herb. It seemed that someone had helped themselves to his herb pouch!

Ahren continued to sniff the air, and it wasn't long before he was identifying more healing herbs. Whoever had mixed the plants and thrown them onto the coals must have been an expert, making sure that the sleeping Paladin had breathed in the fumes, which had dried any bleeding in his lungs. Ahren was amazed that anyone could possess such knowledge, which was far beyond any herbalism that he had learned. Whoever it was that had taken him prisoner, they clearly hadn't wanted him to die.

Had it been *Hisunik* who had killed the Snow Slasher and rescued him? Perhaps they were suspicious of an armed stranger travelling in the company of two wolves, and that was why they had tied him up. But why were they speaking this peculiar Dwarfish?

The conversation on the other side of the curtain having concluded, Ahren decided that it was time for him to seize the initiative – insofar as such a thing was possible, considering he was lying half naked on the floor, bound with thin leather straps like an autumn festival present.

'Hello?' he asked weakly. 'Is there anyone there?'

Ahren flinched in shock as the curtain was pulled roughly aside the instant that he had uttered his words. The Paladin then stared, dumbstruck, when he saw the figure at the entrance. He *really* didn't understand the world anymore.

***

Revenge floated over the spot onto which the Paladin had fallen and tried to make sense of what he was looking at. Here a puddle of blood had seeped into the cracks in the ice and frozen, directly under the Snow Slasher with its broken neck. There were drag marks leading away from the scene of the skirmish, yet Revenge could make out no footprints that might have given him a clue as to what might have happened to the body of the Paladin.

The child of the Adversary cursed his own cowardice, for he had observed the fight from a safe distance, once the Dark Ones had located the presence of the Paladin with his oversized fools and then launched their assault. After Ahren had fallen, Revenge had refrained from floating over to him, for the Paladin's accursed wolf had rounded the corner at lightning speed once he had slain the last Dark One on the rock, the sound of growling and yelping immediately announcing the next skirmish. Only when things had quietened down again did Revenge consider it safe to move in to examine the scene. The child had felt too weak, and he been fearful that the two Ancients who had been among the Paladin's companions might have set a trap for him.

Thus, Revenge hovered uncertainly above the frozen red spot coloured by Paladin blood, the child of the Adversary asking himself if he had been successful or not. Father was too far away for him to sense whether his progenitor was gleefully rejoicing or not, Revenge quickly deciding that he had no choice but to kill another Paladin in case this particular one hadn't yet met his makers.

These cursed, cursed, *cursed* Champions of the Gods had more lives than a damn *cat!*

***

The dwarf looked at Ahren through narrowed eyes, which were surrounded by complicated patterns, as were the lines around the mouth of the squat figure, whose face was for the most part clean-shaven. The stranger had shorn his head completely of hair, with only an extraordinarily thin but long goatee reminding Ahren of the dwarves that he had encountered in the Silver Cliff and Thousand Halls. Bone earrings bedecked both ears, right up to their tips, thereby providing a kind of frame to the wild looking figure wrapped in heavy fur who was examining the young man keenly.

A sudden thought flashed through Ahren's mind. This fellow had to be a dwarf of the Wild Clans! But surely they only lived in the Claw Pass?

The stranger pointed at the opposite wall of the other, larger chamber, illuminated by a brazier, where Ahren's armour and weapons were lying. Then the Wild Dwarf posed a question that the Paladin couldn't understand.

Ahren shrugged his shoulders in so far as he could manage to do so, before slowly saying: 'I do not understand your language. Can you speak in the trading tongue?'

His opposite number frowned so hard that Ahren thought he could see the fellow's eyebrows tickling the bridge of his nose, but then the dwarf uttered a few words that the Paladin finally understood.

'Spy?' growled the Wild Dwarf. 'Thousand Halls. Weapons and armour.'

Ahren looked at the dwarf helplessly, the latter then nodding.

'Spy,' he repeated, as if in confirmation, making a move to pull the fur curtain shut again.

'Wait!' said Ahren desperately, unsure as to what the Wild Dwarf's hasty judgement implied. 'I am no spy. I am a Paladin. This is why I possess weapons and armour of Deep Steel.' He fixed his eyes firmly on the confused look of the guard and repeated slowly: Pa-la-din,' making sure to stress each syllable.

'Paladrim?' asked the dwarf as he pointed at Ahren. 'Nok Paladrim. Thur'baon fuul.' Then he waved his hand in what seemed to be a dismissive manner as he laughed heartily.

Thoroughly confused, Ahren could only watch as the Wild Dwarf drew the curtain again from the other side only to chuckle from behind it, as he said 'Eom Paladrim. Meon tuturur.'

Then he guffawed loudly, the young man now convinced that his title of Paladin bore no weight here at all.

Not being able to do anything other than breathe in the healing vapours of the herbs, he could only agree with the judgement of the strange dwarf.

***

Falk and the others had now spent three days in the little ice hut, nourishing themselves on the foul-smelling meat of the Seal Wolf. The mood was so depressing that the friends had passed the time in morose silence.

Apart from occasionally glancing nervously or pleadingly over at Khara, they even avoided making eye contact with each other. The Swordsmistress spent her time sitting cross-legged and concentrating fully on the charm net in her bracelet – that is, when she wasn't outside, the ice hut, taking out her frustration on imaginary enemies or practising with the grim-looking Hakanu.

Caldria had at last re-awakened, but the old woman's zest for life seemed to have vanished along with her gift of magic, the old woman merely staring out at the white walls from under her fur blanket.

Uldini recovered more and more with every passing day, for he had not been forced to use his magic for a while now, Falk secretly wishing that the Arch Wizard would have an extended sleep, for the mood of the Ancient was worsening with every heartbeat, and the stronger he became, the more he criticised the decisions that the others had taken while he had been dozing.

The First bore the waiting around with his usual stoicism, while Jelninolan succumbed to Hakanu's pleadings and carried out a succession of tests to see how much magic she could use without it becoming dangerous. The results were as disappointing as they were predictable. If the elf used but a hint of Storm Weaving, the skies above them immediately became threatening, and the ice beneath their feet began to crack. It seemed that they were condemned to having to wait for a sign of life from Ahren via the already existing charm net – the only thing for it was for them to rest as much as possible in the meantime while Muai and Karkas alternated as sentries.

Falk himself put on a brave face, while internally he veered between fearing for the safety of Ahren and yearning for the company of Selsena. He was in no doubt that his Titejunanwa would have cheered everyone up, and on more than one occasion he found himself wishing that he had accompanied Lanlion in his search for the deities rather than trek vast distances only to finally find himself freezing half to death in the crowded confines of an ice hut, smack-bang in the middle of nowhere.

***

Ahren woke at irregular intervals from a deep sleep, which he assumed was part of the unusual recovery treatment he was undergoing. Slumber Poppy had also been one of the healing plants in his pouch, and it seemed that every time he dropped off, more of it was being added to the glowing coals of the two braziers.

The Wild Dwarf and whoever it was that Ahren had also heard speaking took special care not to enter his chamber when he was awake, the Paladin spending his time dozing and laboriously inhaling the smoky vapours into his lungs as his mind searched for Culhen whenever he managed to concentrate for long enough. Often, he would sense his friend feeling for him, but neither he nor the wolf managed to communicate with each other in any meaningful way.

Ahren was completely unable to tell whether he had been lying in the chamber for days or weeks when at last the fur curtain was roughly pulled aside, the Wild Dwarf entering the room quickly with a long spear which seemed to have been fashioned from the bone of some enormous creature.

Ahren quickly rolled away from the weapon, reaching a position at the end wall, which he then pressed against as he got to his feet. The Wild Dwarf looked at him in astonishment, Ahren finding himself equally flabbergasted – only now did he realise how much strength he had recovered.

'I am a Pa-la-din,' repeated the Forest Guardian, the stranger having tested his spear by poking it in Ahren's direction.

The dwarf gestured with his hand that the young man should sit down, again thrusting his weapon towards the Paladin, but Ahren's patience had come to an end during his imprisonment, and his mood was far from cheerful. He was not going to rely solely on the mercy of this dwarf who seemed rather too quick to judge – at least, not if there were other options!

Ahren shifted his weight as if to move forward, provoking yet another threatening spear thrust from the Wild Dwarf, the Forest Guardian then turning in so that the sharp point rubbed along the leather binding around his wrists. Yanking his arms up, he heard the leather tear as he freed his hands.

The Wild Dwarf jumped back a step in wide-eyed surprise before attempting another, far less playful thrust, but Ahren had already dropped down on his hunkers to evade the lunging weapon.

'Face the fact!' he warned the guard. 'Your next attack will only cut through my ankle fetters.'

Even if the stranger hadn't understood Ahren's words, he still looked the Forest Guardian up and down, then hesitated. Finally, he rested his spear against the wall, threw his head back and laughed uproariously, holding his stomach with his hand. Then a she-dwarf stepped in, slapped the first dwarf hard on his upper arm, scolded him severely, and pointed at Ahren.

Finally, the guard stopped laughing, and engaged in a furious argument with the she-dwarf, the pair of them speaking far too quickly for Ahren to make out anything more than the oft-repeated 'Paladrim'. He took the opportunity to untie the knots on his ankle fetters before slowly straightening up again, enjoying greatly his ability to stretch himself. He let his hands hang loosely and remained as relaxed as he could while the mysterious couple argued.

The she-dwarf looked almost as exotic as her male companion, with the paintings on her face, her bald head, her eccentric earrings and her thick fur clothing. Only the goatee was missing, a painted line fulfilling that role by running from her chin down to her throat. Ahren could see a bone dagger hanging from the woman's leather collar, her hand reaching down to its grip from time to time as the couple's argument developed into an ear-splitting screaming match with spittle flying from the mouths of the verbal sparrers.

Trogadon had told Ahren once that the Wild Clans rejected all forms of the original Dwarfish traditions, this heated argument and the appearance of the two strangers confirming the statement. But when it came to temperament and stubbornness, these two dwarves certainly couldn't deny their origins, even if their conflict was far less frightening, although far louder than what Ahren had experienced in Thousand Halls or the Silver Cliff.

The longer the dispute continued, the more amusing the Paladin found the vision of the two dwarves yelling at each other, until he could no longer refrain from giggling. The heads of the two squabblers turned towards him in unison, their eyes boring into his, which only made the couple seem more hilarious. Ahren tried, and failed, to stop chuckling, but already the two dwarves had thrown back their heads and burst out laughing. Ahren laughed with them, hoping at the same time that they had taken the first tentative steps to perhaps even forging some sort of friendship with him.

'Fire Falcon says you too weak for Paladin,' explained the she-dwarf, who had introduced herself as Moss Rose.

Ahren and the two Wild Clan members were sitting on a large ice bear rug and drinking melted water from roughly hewn stone mugs in the chamber adjoining his prison cell.

'He think you spy from Thousand Halls. Come to look for Wild Clans on ice.'

Ahren was relieved that the she-dwarf's mastery of the trading tongue was better than her companion's, Fire Falcon still staring sceptically at Ahren as he murmured something in his peculiar dialect which didn't sound at all like Dwarfish.

'He say you inferior, puny...*Shuol'Bror?*'

Ahren frowned, confused. 'Does he mean "Slow Slasher"?' he asked. 'Like a large, six-legged fox?'

Moss Rose nodded with a smile, Fire Falcon then grinning mockingly at Ahren.

'I was injured,' explained Ahren. 'I had been fighting an enormous ice bear,' he added, patting the fur that they were sitting on, 'and then I fell off a glacier.' On seeing the perplexed look on Moss Rose's face, he added: 'The great wall of ice.'

The she-dwarf translated, and Fire Falcon nodded approvingly. Then he drained his mug and left the cave through the exit at the back without saying a word. 'I say for nine days you Paladin, but Fire Falcon, he our *Yan'yalk.*' She pondered before adding: 'Sentry who sees before danger.'

'A scout?' asked Ahren, the she-dwarf grunting her approval.

'You quick heal,' she said, tapping Ahren on his chest. 'And you heal wounds kill nine of ten dwarves would. And you human only. Paladin you be. Doubt no.'

'Thank you,' said Ahren, smiling weakly, then repeating the gesture, this time with an air of solemnity and a bow. 'Thank you for healing me.'

Moss Rose slapped him hard on the cheek with the back of her hand, a look of disgust on her face. 'Bow *never*,' she scolded. 'All equal. Never anyone bow. No bow head. *Never!*'

Ahren nodded cautiously. 'Understood,' he said. Then he stuck out his bare chest and put his hands on his hips. 'I thank you,' he said in a loud, firm voice.

Moss Rose clapped her hands in delight and grinned. 'Now you sound like Free Dwarf. Proud like mountain…soon cold like ice if not you dress.'

Ahren grinned in return before responding to her warning by quickly slipping into his clothes and putting his cloak on, wondering all the while why he had only been a little cold in the cave beyond the coal braziers. He placed his hand on the wall and felt a certain warmth, not enough to make the room comfortable, but intense enough to take the bite out of the granite's natural coldness. He wondered if the Free Dwarves – as they called themselves – had brought with them the Thousand Halls' skills of heated caves.

Before Ahren had a chance to verbalise his question, Culhen came storming cheerfully into his mind like a whelp, accompanied by the sound of an Ice Wolf in full armour squeezing his way through what seemed like a terribly narrow tunnel. It sounded as if a handful of knights had been simultaneously grasped by the hand of a giant, and Ahren could only stand, and laugh, and listen as his four-legged friend showered him with all the love and joy of the world while at the same time peppering him with dozens of questions.

Finally, the wolf barged through the entrance to the chamber, throwing himself at his friend as he whimpered, the Paladin, for his part, digging his hands deep into the fur of his companion animal, swearing out loud that he and Culhen would never be parted again. Tears of relief ran down Ahren's cheeks, and as he stood there soaking up the presence of his loyal wolf, he could see out of the corner of his eye, Moss Rose and the newly returned Fire Falcon grinning broadly as they stood there, watching the reunion of man and animal as if they were admiring a beautiful sunset.

Chapter 21

They put me up in their stall cave, where my fractures were given time to knit, said Culhen excitedly for the umpteenth time as he continued to sing the praises of those who had given him so much careful attention. *Their hands are so skilled! Every day fur massages and herb poultices for my wounds! Not to mention the food! As much seal meat to eat as I wanted! And that was a lot!*

Ahren smiled indulgently. 'Culhen tells me that you looked after him *very* well.'

The two dwarves sighed melancholically. 'You really *can* talk to animals,' said Moss Rose, her eyes welling up with tears.

Wild...sorry, I mean Free Dwarves are like a mixture of...uh, let me think...yes...of Wrath Elves, of the horse people we met in the Green Sea, and of the grumpy lads we know from Thousand Halls, explained Culhen. *They are proud, they really love animals, and not laughing is practically sacrilegious as far as they're concerned.* The wolf cocked his head. *In fact, they hate it if you nurture any sorts of feelings but don't reveal them. As far as I can see, they see themselves as free from all the constrictions that Dwarfish tradition has smothered them with. They choose their own names, and if they don't like them anymore, they simply find new ones for themselves!*

'Our companion animals are a gift from the deities,' said Ahren to Moss Rose, patting Culhen's head. 'Without this fellow's help, I would have been in trouble even more often than the number of times *he* got me into scrapes,' he teased, the wolf responding by giving the Forest Guardian a slobbery lick across the face.

'I not talk with Xandrolfor,' said Fire Falcon stiffly, struggling to master the trading language. 'But connection close is – yes.'

'Xandrolfor?' asked Ahren, puzzled.

'*Oh,* said Culhen, prancing excitedly on the spot. *I forgot to tell you.* The wolf then closed off his mind, Ahren immediately recognising that his friend wanted to surprise him with something. 'Come you,' said Fire Falcon, stepping with Moss Rose into the only passageway that led outside. 'Wolf too. He not scratch walls more with armour.'

As if it would make any difference, muttered Culhen snootily. *The caves here are so badly finished that even a Dwarfish child would be ashamed of the outcome.*

Ahren suspected that some of the traditional Dwarfish skills had somehow been lost along the way by the Free Dwarves. Everything had its price, and those who wanted maximum freedom without responsibility could hardly complain if there was no-one left who possessed the fundamental skills. He followed his two leaders through several decidedly crooked tunnels which tested Culhen's powers of contortion. From time to time, they passed chambers, all of which seemed deserted, however.

'At moment, we only two – Fire Falcon and me,' said Moss Rose airily. 'Time for summer flight but Xandrolfor no can fly moment now…'

Ahren tried to make sense of the she-dwarf's utterance only for it to become apparent once he had followed her and Fire Falcon out of the tunnel, where he almost stumbled into a large cave and was presented with a sight that made him gasp in surprise. 'But that's a…that's a *dragon!*' he exclaimed, staring wide-eyed at the sleeping creature that took up much of the enormous chamber with its jagged hole in the ceiling. Snow was falling through the opening, immediately turning into steam as soon as it came into contact with the breath of the creature, which was sleeping on an enormous pile of furs.

'Xandrolfor wings in storm broken,' explained Fire Falcon sadly. 'No summer flight to Dragon Ridge.'

'You belong to the Dragon Ridge tribe then?' asked Ahren, the faces of the two dwarves immediately hardening.

'We no-one *belong* to,' said Moss Rose sternly. 'This mountain called Ripe Jags. Here colony Free Dwarves. Not heat like Dragon Ridge – better life, far away other clans from.'

'Free Dwarves places seek…remote,' explained Fire Falcon, still struggling for words. 'Others where *not* live. Make us home at ourselves. With summer flight, new dwarves from Dragon Ridge mountain come. Unhappy dwarves fly there back to.' The dwarf shrugged his shoulders matter-of-factly. 'Moss Rose and stay I – others get new dwarves with different dragon.' Fire Falcon suddenly guffawed. 'Few dwarves long stay. Sun on stomach tempting. Less ice on beard.'

'Why no other clan here,' added Moss Rose. 'Peace. No rules.'

Fire Falcon raised his hand defensively. 'Me stay. You know.'

'Ripe Jags here young colony. Will grow,' said Moss Rose firmly. 'Soon our own clan we have.' The she-dwarf spoke with such passion that Ahren fully understood her motivation for making such a long journey here. If *all* the Free Dwarves were driven by their own *personal* beliefs, they would hardly stick living together in a larger community in the one place for an extended period.

At least now we know why the Clans of Thousand Halls don't acknowledge the existence of the Wild Dwarves, thought Ahren, hiding his ruminations with an implacable face. *Their practices are in direct contrast to all known Dwarfish traditions, and yet their clansmen- and women are equally as stubborn and quarrelsome as their cousins.*

'How many of you are there in Dragon Ridge?' asked Ahren curiously.

'Many,' said Fire Falcon. 'Two times hundred hands.'

If you think of how many dwarves have left the old colonies to go south over the years, then that doesn't sound like many at all, interjected Culhen. *Life on Dragon Ridge must be harder than they are suggesting.*

Ahren looked around the cave, not taking long to recognise the spot where Culhen must have rested and recovered. There was a pile of furs surrounded for the most part by gnawed seal bones. *Where is your girlfriend?* asked the Paladin cautiously. *She survived the Snow Slashers, surely?*

Gone, said Culhen, his mood immediately altering. *No sooner did we arrive at the cave with Fire Falcon when she disappeared.*

Ahren cuddled the now morose wolf, sending him waves of sympathy. *There are other nice she-wolves out there,* he said, immediately regretting conveying such cliched words of comfort.

No-one is like her, sighed Culhen, turning his head away with a whimper. *Her coat was so soft, her fangs so straight, her...*

'What Paladin in Ice Fields do?' asked Fire Falcon, inadvertently putting an end to the unspoken dialogue between the Forest Guardian and his wolf.

'We are looking for one of my brothers,' said Ahren absently. 'His name is Yollock. He travelled here a long time ago – to hunt a dragon.'

'Hunt *dragon!*' exclaimed Moss Rose and Fire Falcon in unison, their faces expressing their horror at the very idea of such a thing, Ahren groaning inwardly in response. He really should have formulated the phrase more diplomatically.

He took a deep breath and began explaining the story from the beginning.

'Hmm,' said Fire Falcon, having listened to Ahren's account of things. 'Free Dwarves know Four Claws of. Mightiest dragon of north. Not like cousins peaceful.' With that he nodded towards the sleeping Xandrolfor, whose breath and body temperature were keeping the cave at a comfortable temperature. Ahren suspected that the Free Dwarves had some method of transmitting the heat down to the lower chambers – even if he couldn't make out any tunnels or shafts that could perform such a function.

'But not him chase to end of world,' said Moss Rose implacably. 'He old dragon. Rest in peace.'

'He *northern dragon*, murmured Fire Falcon gently.

'Oh. Yes,' said the she-dwarf before falling silent.

'What do you mean?' asked Ahren, all ears. This was the ideal opportunity to find out more about the dragons that were unknown in Thousand Halls.

'Dragon Ridge not *first* choice,' said Fire Falcon cautiously. 'Free Dwarves north went many hundred ago years. All dwarves admire flying creatures big – roc be or dragon. Wanted friends be with northern dragons.' He looked down at the ground. 'One dragon not in favour. Waged war against dwarves. They fled south towards. Northern dragons not fighting stop. Kill many humans. Humans kill dragons. Northern dragons gone. Southern dragons different.' He pointed at Xandrolfor. 'Not so clever. Tame easier.'

'I always thought that the cleverer the animal, the easier they are to teach,' countered Ahren.

Because it worked so well with me, you mean? interjected Culhen with a laugh.

'If one clever, no need train,' mused Fire Falcon.

You see? said Ahren, continuing his silent conversation with his friend. *Listen to the dwarf. You are simply too clever – and that's my problem. I must give you more of Trogadon's Dwarfish schnapps. Maybe that will make you sense how I feel.*

Oh, stop trying to ingratiate yourself with me and listen to the dwarves yourself, countered Culhen, playfully head-butting the Paladin. Ahren began to tousle the wolf's fur as he turned his full attention once again to Fire Falcon.

'Northern Dragons not get weak when old,' explained the dwarf. 'Get bigger. Cleverer. Stronger.'

'Four Claws so old, he mightiest dragon Jorath,' added Moss Rose, drawing the only logical conclusion to her partner's statement.

Ahren's hands instinctively went up to his face before he said in a low voice: 'And it has to be him of all dragons who is colluding with the Dark god.'

***

Revenge was *afraid*. Not only was he dangerously weak, but there was nothing far and wide that he could satiate himself on. Hunger was a poor substitute for that urge for retribution that the child of the Adversary needed to nourish himself on if he was going to survive. Revenge feared death and fervently prayed that the Thirteenth Paladin had passed away – which would mean that the child had *not* failed. He threw himself against the wind, towards the south in the faint hope of finding *something* to feed on...

Like a sun of naked energy, something within his mind lit up to the southwest, something that drew Revenge towards it as though he were nothing more than a moth attracted to a flame. There was something resting there – a mighty spirit haunted by visions of violence, of death and destruction.

Visions of *revenge*.

***

'Ahren!' screamed Khara, leaping up, only to bang her head off the low ceiling of their ice hut before she fell on the floor with a curse.

'You can complain later, girl,' said Falk, trying to contain his excitement. 'Tell us – have you found Ahren or not?'

The Swordsmistress got to her feet and shook her head, visibly stunned. 'Well – yes and no,' she said, her voice quivering with frustration. 'I sensed him for a heartbeat – but now I can't again.'

Falk uttered a stream of oaths, only stopping when Jelninolan gave him a warning look. 'If she can do it, then so can I!' he grumbled, pointing at Khara. 'Anyway,' he added after a pause before clapping once. 'Enough resting! Uldini has recovered his strength sufficiently, and Caldria can walk on her own two feet again. We have our improvised fur rucksacks…'

'…which are already stinking to high heaven…' interjected Trogadon.

'…and enough provisions for an extended march,' added Falk, finally completing his sentence with an air of determined stubbornness. Muai and he had turned out to be a better hunting combination than the old man had expected. 'Khara can at least tell us where she sensed Ahren is located, and hopefully, the charm net will pick something up again soon.' He looked forcefully at Uldini and Jelninolan. 'You two clever clogs had better come up with an ingenious way that we can track Ahren down without either Uldini having to abandon his use as a heat source or Jelninolan having us all struck dead by a bolt of lightning.'

'And who made *you* into our leader all of a sudden, if I may ask?' countered the Arch Wizard bitingly.

Well, as far as I can see, no-one else wanted to seize the reins of power over the last couple of weeks,' snapped Falk, glancing over at the First as he did so, the war veteran seemingly interested in doing nothing but sitting and waiting.

At first, Falk had thought that the First had merely been at peace with himself, but now he was certain that the senior Paladin's mind was somewhere else entirely.

The veteran's eyes met Falk's for the briefest of moments, the old Forest Guardian being certain that he recognised a flash of *fear*. A shudder immediately ran down Falk's spine as he quickly stepped outside in the hope that nobody saw the change in his countenance.

If there was anything or anyone that caused the First to be afraid, then it was surely time for his companions to make a run for it.

***

Ahren stepped back into the cave and away from the narrow, windswept rocky ledge that served as sort of lookout point near the top of the Ripe Jags, offering a splendid view of the surrounding area. From up here, there was snow and ice for as far as the eye could see – except where the view was interrupted by the mountainous colossi to the south. It was from this ledge that Fire Falcon had looked west and spotted Ahren, Culhen, and the she-wolf in their fight to the death with the Snow Slashers. Ahren was only too glad that the individualistic streak of the Free Dwarves hadn't developed to the point where they would simply leave endangered strangers to their fate on the dwarfish doorsteps.

And it's lucky that Fire Flame didn't recognise your Deep Steel from a distance, said Culhen, genuinely relieved. *Or he might have searched for clues regarding your identity and reason for being here among your mortal remains instead of keeping you alive to quiz you.*

The Paladin didn't react to his friend's words. A few heartbeats earlier, when he had been out on the ledge in the freezing wind and swirling snow, he had been sure that he'd heard Khara's voice. But he hadn't seen anything, and the moment had passed like the briefest of gusts.

Ahren felt his ribs and cast a keen eye on Culhen's legs. 'We are ready, he said finally, sighing sadly. 'Ready to take on the ice again. The only decision that remains is who we will search for first – Yollock, Four Claws, or our friends?'

The wolf snorted loudly and looked past Ahren out into the stormy desert of ice. *What makes you so sure that we will be able to decide for ourselves who we should stumble on first?*

'We not know Yollock,' said Moss Rose.

Ahren nodded with a weary smile. 'It was worth asking you anyway.' The Forest Guardian had decided to carry on looking for Yollock rather than try to track down Khara and the others. The risk was simply too great that he might accidentally march past without noticing them, and anyway, he had no idea how far south they had progressed during his enforced rest. If, however, he shared the same goal as they did, then the chances would be much higher that it wouldn't be too long before he could wrap Khara and the others in his warm embrace.

Ahren and Culhen were standing there, laden down with bags of smoked seal meat at the exit of the Ripe Jags, dallying before the moment of departure. Neither the Forest Guardian nor his wolf were at all happy about venturing out into the vast whiteness without the assistance of Uldini's protective charm, but somewhere out there on the snow, on the rocks and on the ice, their friends were doubtless looking for *them*, and it would be the height of irresponsibility to delay their departure for even one more day.

'Maybe in Fog Fields look,' suggested the she-dwarf, Ahren immediately becoming all ears.

'The *Fog Fields?* he asked.

'The south in,' explained Fire Falcon, pointing towards the blunted mountain, whose slopes were already dominating the horizon ahead. 'Heat from volcano earth under meets ice. Fog much. Dangerous. Lava. Ice. Hot water.'

That sounds like the last place I would like to visit, said Culhen sardonically. *But knowing you, we will be going there directly.*

'Before go,' countered Moss Rose sharply. 'Even not friends. Too we hide from *Hisunik*. Dragons big detour make when summer flight.' The she-dwarf's features were so grim now that Ahren could do nothing but nod submissively. 'And herbs remaining bag from payment save you for,' she added more cheerfully, having noticed his acquiescence.

'My lovely collection,' sighed the Forest Guardian. 'I suppose I will have to start gathering them all again from scratch.'

'Few left plants,' replied the she-dwarf in a gentle voice, moved by his sadness. 'Lungs yours and fingers herbs up used most.'

'My *fingers?*' countered Ahren, taken aback.

'Fingers blue when found you I,' said Fire Falcon. 'We from use bag Rooster Thistle.'

Ahren remembered having principally added the plant to his pouch to use as a lesson for Hakanu, but now it had saved his own fingers.

He pensively put his hands beneath his cloak, nodded appreciatively to the two dwarves one last time, and stepped out onto the snow. The next time he drifted into unconsciousness, he would try to remember to make sure his fingers were well protected by his outer garment.

The next time?! exclaimed Culhen angrily before lowering his head against the blasts of snow. *Please ensure that there is no next time. Remember, this time we have no enchanting she-wolf with us who can lead us to a mysterious Dwarfish enclave.*

***

'I can sense Ahren again,' said Khara excitedly as she looked from one to the other within the group. 'His presence is very strong and clear to me.'

Falk smiled at the Swordsmistress before turning to Jelninolan. 'Does this mean that we are approaching him?'

The elf shook her head sadly. 'The fact that his presence is more intensively tangible simply means that he is uninjured and fully rested. Only when Khara has the feeling that he is actually standing beside her, can we be sure that we have neared him significantly.'

'Still great news,' said Hakanu with an encouraging smile. 'My master can survive anything, it seems.'

'The problem is,' said the First cagily, 'that your master cannot survive *anything*. Which is why we had better locate him before he internalises this bitter truth in a particularly unpleasant manner.' Then the war veteran stamped on ahead leaving Falk and the others looking at each other in bafflement.

Bergen pointed at the blunted mountain, whose base was shrouded in some sort of fog. 'The nearer we approach this massive rock, the grumpier he is getting,' said the Ice Lander in a low voice. 'Does anyone else here also feel that something is going on here that we don't understand?'

Falk answered with nothing other than a nod before walking on. The First was not going to answer their questions before he was ready to, while the old Forest Guardian had other things that he was currently more concerned with. Ahren was struggling through the snow somewhere, and Falk wouldn't rest easy until he located his former protégé safe and well.

***

On the third day of their travelling, Ahren and Culhen found themselves on a little rock that stood a few paces above the smooth ice- and snow landscape. A thick, low blanket of cloud hung from the sky, as though looking down onto a natural mirror. Clouds and ice seemed to merge into each other on the horizon, turning the entire world into a single mass of white.

Oh, come on now – don't be getting all moody on me again, commented Culhen, having recognised Ahren's thought processes. *It's only a few clouds, after all.*

All this ice and snow gets one down in the end, said Ahren, shaking his head as if trying to banish his ill temper. Then he pointed to the southwest, where after two furlongs or so the ice seemed to fall into a sort of crater, disappearing into an area of bubbling fog extending for at least half a league. Here and there, flashes lit up the billowing plumes, making the whole natural spectacle even more bizarrely dramatic. 'It seems as though we have reached the Fog Fields,' said Ahren.

And they look even less inviting than I'd feared, commented Culhen. *I wonder if those flashes of light that we see are magma?*

There is only one way of finding out, said Ahren, descending from the rock. He glanced south beyond the Fog Fields to the blunted mountain, which had seemed to be their guide for the previous few weeks – or was it months? Ahren's sense of time had certainly taken a battering.

I wonder if the First is right, and we really will find Four Claws on this mountain? mused Culhen, as the two doughty travellers continued to make their way towards the edge of the Fog Fields.

We will soon find out if he knows the dragon as well as he claims to, said Ahren, looking more closely at the massive rock. The mountain seemed so blunted because its peak was so rounded, while its slopes were less acute, extending unusually far in each direction.

As if the mountain were slowly dying of old age, thought Ahren gloomily.

Really! complained Culhen. *We are about to enter an enormous area that looks like the Adversary's worst nightmare, and you insist on filling my head with visions of our downfall?*

Ahren didn't get the chance to utter a rebuke, for he suddenly began to slip down the sloping ice and instinctively tried to grab hold of Culhen's saddle. The wolf yelped in fright, his claws causing a scraping sound on the smooth surface as the animal tried to stop himself and his companion. At first very slowly, but then with gathering speed, Ahren and his wolf slid down the mirrorlike icy surface, formed by the fog that condensed on the surface.

This is pointless, commented the wolf, failing completely to get a grip with his claws as they continued their accelerating slide.

What are you doing? asked Ahren, now terrified, as their controlled descent turned into a seemingly reckless, hurtling glissade.

I am trying to ensure as soft a landing as possible, said Culhen grimly, his heavier mass causing him to disappear before Ahren into the Fog Fields. *If you can manage it, stay directly behind me. Then your journey will finish with a delicious fall into my fur.*

By now, Ahren had reached a terrifying speed, and it took all his skill to position his arms and legs so that he could remain behind the wolf vanishing ahead of him.

Yaaaaaaaaay! howled Culhen gleefully. *This is so much fun!*

As long as we don't fall into a river of magma, yes, it certainly is! countered Ahren, who could make out among the frozen edges and ancient rock, the tell-tale glimmering of tiny fissures filled with magma, the animal's exuberant mood suddenly bursting like a bubble of air on a surface of agitated water.

You really know how to take the fun out of a wolf's life, don't you? countered the animal sulkily. Then Ahren heard the scraping of metal in front of him and a muffled woof. *Ow,* said Culhen as Ahren, too, hurtled into the mist, slamming after a few paces into the wolf, who had come to a shuddering halt at a lump of rock.

You're absolutely right, said Ahren, getting to his feet and shaking his head in an effort to orientate himself. *Your soft stomach brought my fall to a wonderfully soft end!*

Only too happy to help, grunted Culhen as he got up in a rather less dignified manner. Still, Ahren sensed that the wolf hadn't suffered any serious injuries as he ruffled his friend's fur.

Great reactions, he said, teasing the animal gently. *Your armour protected you from the worst, and your fat tummy did the same for me.*

Remember that I'm not in the mood for second helpings, retorted Culhen before sneezing loudly. *This fog is annoying and cold. I can't help feeling that it's already freezing on my fur.*

Ahren looked more closely at his friend, then glanced quickly at his own cloak. *This fog could prove deadly if it soaks though your fur and cools you more and more!* The Paladin quickly checked around them, his sight limited to only a few paces thanks to the thick plumes of mist. Then he pointed at where he could see distinct glowing. *There!* he said, signalling Culhen to follow him. *That is where the magma seems to come* to the surface. *The first thing we need to do is to save ourselves from this frost.*

Oh, great, commented the wolf sarcastically. *Yes – let's approach the volcanic centre. I mean, what could possibly go wrong?*

Ahren ignored his friend's barbs, slipping before the wolf's very nose instead while trying to concentrate on the ground beneath his feet. The dark rock was continually interrupted by strips of smooth ice which seemed to form wherever the bubbling heat of the volcano submitted to the all-embracing cold of the Ice Fields. The Paladin did his best not to step onto the smooth surfaces, following instead a zigzag course towards the glimmering in the distance.

My paws are either terribly cold or uncomfortably warm, complained Culhen from behind. *I wish this place would decide on one of the extremes and then stick to it.*

You mean a volcanic eruption, for instance? teased Ahren.

As they continued their cautious advance, the glimmering shone more and more intensely through the swathes of fog that surrounded them, which were becoming ever steamier. The heat was intensifying as the red, gaping fissure peeled out of the murky whiteness like open wounds in the rock. Ahren pulled back his hood as he reached the edge of the crevice in which semi-molten rock was being slowly turned this way and that, occasionally being transformed into a bubble of the purest magma, its crust tearing open with effort. The heat that hit the young man's face was so forceful that he immediately covered it with his magic cloak again, drawing the protective leather as tightly around his head as he could manage.

'Is there magic at work here?' he asked aloud. 'Can fire and ice exist so closely together?' With that, he pointed down at the narrow stream of molten rock, then at the irregular glimmering around about, suggesting many more fissures in the valley of the crater.

That is a question that perhaps a dwarf or a scholar might answer, suggested Culhen, who had placed first one of his flanks, and then the other towards the fissure, so that all the hoarfrost would melt from his fur. *Ooh, this is nice and warm,* he added. *I'd almost forgotten what it feels like, not having any ice in my fur.* Then he sneezed. *But the steam rising from the fissure cannot be healthy. I don't think we should hang around here for too long.*

Ahren nodded and gazed out into the clouds of whiteness where the coldness of the Ice Fields gained the upper hand again with its plumes of thick fog. Was that a moving shadow there within the plumes?

The young man unshouldered *Fisiniell* and reached back to his quiver, only to clutch thin air. Cursing, he shouldered the bow again. He had completely forgotten that he'd planted the last of his arrows in the Snow Slashers several leagues to the north! He drew *Sun* instead and stared once more at the darker spot, which he was certain had moved only a moment earlier.

I hope that you are well thawed, warned Ahren, his wolf cowering beside the fissure. *I fear that we will shortly have company.*

***

Falk could hardly believe his eyes when he spotted the three figures making their way in the distance through the bleak, icy landscape, each of them well wrapped up in their furs. They were using their spears to maintain their foothold on the treacherous ground, driving the tips of the hunting weapons deep into the ice. When they spotted Falk and the others, they came to a sudden stop.

'*Hisunik*,' said Bergen, positioning himself beside Falk.

'Hunters, I would say,' added the old Forest Guardian. 'But what has brought them so far south?'

'Let us find out,' said Khara impatiently, making her way towards the still impassive strangers. 'They may have seen Ahren or Culhen.'

'Hang on a heartbeat,' gasped Uldini, rolling his eyes as he floated towards the Swordsmistress. 'It might be an idea to have someone *with* you who *understands* their language.'

Bergen pondered as he observed the trio of hunters, who still had not stirred from the spot, but who seemed to be waiting for the others to take the initiative. 'You know,' he said, winking at Falk, 'experience has taught me that offering food is a very good ploy if you want to glean information from strangers – especially when food is such a rare treat, like in this wasteland.'

'Once again, your mind is ruled by your stomach,' scolded the First. 'A few short, sharp questions would do just as well. We are in the majority and better armed.'

Falk pointed with his thumb at Kamaluq and Muai, both of whom had begun to drool at the prospect of eating. Threads of ice were hanging from their chops. 'Now you have been outvoted,' he said curtly.

Falk didn't give the First's particularly harsh behaviour a second thought – they had enough problems to deal with as it was.

Grinning broadly, and with laughing heartily, the three *Hisunik* sat around *Flamestar*, which was emitting as much heat as Bergen would permit without melting the ice beneath where they were resting. The strangers had merely laughed on being offered food, producing their own rations which smelled of mysterious herbs and made Falk's mouth water, they seemed so delicious.

'Two of them are hunters,' said Uldini, who was conscientiously translating both Khara's impatient questions and the calm responses of the *Hisunik*. 'The young woman, on the other hand, is a trainee shaman,' said the Arch Wizard, nodding towards the smallest of the figures, who was neither speaking nor eating, but was staring wide-eyed into the core of *Flamestar*. 'She seems to be on some sort of spiritual journey while the hunters are providing an escort for her.'

'Do they know anything about Ahren?' asked Jelninolan, repeating Khara's question.

Uldini shook his head, Falk immediately muttering a curse.

'Is there *nothing* that they can tell us?' grumbled the old Paladin. 'Surely *something* in this godsforsaken landscape of ice has struck them as being out of the ordinary?'

With decidedly little enthusiasm, the Ancient translated the question. It was clear to Falk that the Arch Wizard wasn't holding out much hope for a revelatory reply. Suddenly, he tilted his head back and listened with renewed enthusiasm as one of the hunters spoke, pointing towards the west at the same time.

'Well, then,' said Uldini once the stranger had finished speaking. 'I have good news and I have bad...'

'Ahren was undoubtedly here,' murmured Falk, pulling a Deep Steel arrow from the frozen cadaver of a Snow Slasher. He looked around anxiously, hoping to find further clues that might reveal more information regarding the outcome of the skirmish that had clearly unfolded here a considerable time earlier.

The *Hisunik* had told them of this place, and following some hasty expressions of gratitude, the companions had set off immediately. The young shaman had watched them with a particularly sad look on her face as they had departed – the woman's unspoken fear shaking Falk to his very core.

'These corpses have been lying here for an extended period,' said Bergen, who had been examining another dead Snow Slasher on his hunkers and was now getting back to his feet.

'Since roughly the time that our contact with Ahren was broken, would you say?' asked Jelninolan, having completed a whispered spell while feeling the snow with her staff until she hit upon a layer of red ice. 'This is *his* blood,' she murmured. 'And there is an awful lot of it.'

'Whatever *happened* here?' asked Hakanu, nonplussed. 'If my master was slain during the fight, then why did we sense him again? And if he won, then why did he leave his arrows behind?'

'Maybe his greedy wolf saved his bacon and hauled him away,' suggested the First, whose eyes were once more fixed on the mountain in the distance. 'The only thing that matters is that we don't have to recover any bodies. All the Paladins are still living.'

'He is *more* than merely a part of the Thirteen,' said Khara through gritted teeth. Falk had never heard the Swordsmistress speak in such an accusatory manner towards the First. 'Whatever it is that is torturing you, you had better tell, because you are quickly becoming again that unbeloved cold-hearted figure who is only too willing to sacrifice whole nations to gain a tactical advantage.'

The First looked at Khara and blinked, Falk immediately seeing the hurt the veteran was feeling behind his mask of inscrutability. The age-old Paladin put on his helmet and pointed towards the mountain. 'Let us continue,' he said brusquely. 'None of us can possibly want Ahren to encounter Four Claws without our presence.'

Falk exchanged glances with the others and shrugged his shoulders. They moved on in silence, hoping that the ominous words of the First would not become reality.

***

I can't smell anything, muttered Culhen. *The air here is swirling around like mad while the vapours rising from the magma aren't exactly helping either.*

Ahren still had his eyes fixed on the dark spot, which hadn't moved since the Paladin had first noticed it. The Forest Guardian hardly dared to blink for fear that he would lose sight of it. Somehow, he couldn't escape the feeling that this shadowy figure hidden by the swirling fog was a lurking predatory animal waiting for its prey to look away. Did this place of extremities shelter special Dark Ones? And what did they really look like? Suddenly, the Paladin's mind was filled with countless images of nightmarish figures, Ahren now slowly moving forward with his weapon drawn until Culhen mentally cleared his throat, bringing to an end the terrifying images.

Slowly but surely, Paladin and Wolf moved closer to the outline, which became more manifest and real with every step. The feeling of threat from the figure became evermore tangible, too, Ahren keeping close beside Culhen, who was now uttering a low, continuous growl, ready to pounce in a heartbeat as he placed one paw in front of another, while Ahren gripped his Wind Blade, alert to the first sign of an assault. The swathes of fog between the two friends and the figure seemed to have developed a life of their own, thickening all the time until it became impossible to make out details of the threatening presence until a sudden gust of wind sliced through the fog and divided it as a knife would. Ahren stared open-mouthed at the figure, while Culhen was now rooted to the spot at the vision that presented itself to them.

'Oh,' said the old, one-armed man, covered in a multitude of furs with his short spear at the ready, having been waiting perfectly still, ready to launch his weapon at the opportune moment. Having looked Ahren and Culhen up and down, he lowered his spear and beckoned with his chin, well covered in a woolly scarf, to follow him. 'Then come along with me,' he said in a deep and remarkably easy-going voice. He turned and pointed down at a battered, fur-covered wooden bucket with an improvised lid. 'Carry this, lad,' said the stranger. 'And make life a little easier for an old man.' Then he disappeared into the swirling fog without turning to look at them again. Ahren and Culhen exchanged quizzical looks, the Forest Guardian then sheathing his weapon.

'Either we have just discovered Yollock, or the Ice Fields have more eccentric recluses than I'd imagined,' murmured Ahren, picking up the pail, wisps of steam escaping from under its lid. Then he stomped after the stranger, accompanied by his wolf, the man seemingly adjusting his pace so that he was always a dozen paces in front of them, no matter that they were negotiating fissures of magma, sheets of ice, and pools of bubbling water.

The longer Ahren walked behind the one-armed man, the more he felt himself like an apprentice again, hurrying to keep up with his master. This feeling, and the manner in which the stranger picked his way through the Fog Fields left the Paladin in no doubt – in front of them walked Yollock, the very first Forest Guardian.

Their long search for the thirteen Paladins had come to an end!

***

Revenge slaked on the irresistible urge for retribution that the sleeping figure emitted, the child of the Adversary having eventually located it in the cave. The mind of the creature was age-old, and its slumber had been deep and surrounded by magic. Normally, control of such a powerful mind lay beyond the ken of the weakened child, but a deep rancour jutted out through the mighty spiritual barriers of the creature like a burning needle, offering a way in for Revenge.

The child of the Dark god slipped unnoticed into the essence of the sleeping creature and began to disturb its dreams. Slowly but surely, the sleeping dragon would awaken – and then it would be in the sole possession of Revenge!

Chapter 22

Panting for breath, Ahren abandoned his latest attempt at catching up with the probable Paladin on foot, swinging himself into Culhen's saddle instead, so that the wolf could bring him alongside the striding figure. Hardly had his mount arrived by the one-armed man, when the latter glanced sideways up at Ahren.

'Good training,' he commented in so relaxed a manner that it seemed as if they had spent years in one another's company, and they were now chatting about the weather. 'But you are out of practice – after all, your animal had to *help* you.' The deep, calm, self-confidence of the old man was almost tangible, while his economical use of words suggested that he was used to speaking only the pure, unvarnished truth. 'You *are* a Forest Guardian, are you not?'

Ahren nodded. 'And a Paladin,' he replied.

There was no reaction from the stranger.

'Just like you.'

The one-armed man merely grunted in response. Nevertheless, a heavy weight was lifted off the young man's shoulders on receiving this less than spectacular confirmation that what the Forest Guardian had suspected for the league or so that they had travelled was, in fact, correct.

'You are Yollock,' he said with a grin, before whooping for joy and ruffling Culhen's fur. 'We did it!' he exclaimed. 'After all these years, we finally have all of the Paladins!'

Culhen's thoughts were filled with pride and not a little conceit as he shared with Ahren this moment of pure joy. After all the long and tortuous journeys with all their attendant dangers, they were now closer to victory over the Adversary than at any time since the erection of the Pall Pillar!

The young man's euphoria cooled somewhat as Yollock cast him a more critical look from the side. 'You are too *loud*,' he said. 'Who trained you?'

'Falk,' said Ahren.

The one-armed man frowned. 'Young *Falkenstein*, you mean?' grunted Yollock after a pause. 'His ridiculous nickname has stuck, I see.' The founder of Forest Guardianship chuckled. 'So, Falk is trying to fill my boots. I never thought I'd see the day. The THREE really *do* have a sense of humour.' Yollock looked at Ahren again – this time it was a thorough visual inspection. 'And how is Selsena?'

It was the first time that Ahren sensed a hint of emotion in the calm voice of the man. 'She is not with us,' said Ahren. 'But she is keeping well. Otherwise, Falk would have told us.'

'Yes,' said Yollock with a hint of sorrow in his deep green eyes, the emotion recognisable despite most of his face being hidden by his woolly scarf. 'Yes. He would have *sensed* it if the situation were otherwise.'

Ahren observed the one-armed figure more closely, soon recognising that it was more than a limb that he was missing. Yollock was *alone* because he had no animal by his side. 'I am so sorry,' was all that he could say, the one-armed man nodding. For a while they proceeded along in silence until Yollock suddenly grasped Culhen by the chin and began to tickle him.

Oh, yes! exclaimed the enchanted wolf. *Oh, yes – he really knows where to tickle. This man knows his wolves!*

'A splendid animal,' said the one-armed man, continuing to pet Culhen as he strode onwards. He seemed to have no problem anticipating any possible problems underfoot. 'An Ice Wolf?'

'Blood Wolf,' replied Ahren, instinctively falling into the economical speech pattern of his opposite number. Unlike the First, the frugal way with words of this old Paladin had something incredibly attractive about it. It was almost as though he had met for the first time Falk's tough yet serene grandfather.

That would make Yollock your foster great-grandfather, teased the wolf before snorting disdainfully. *Ye gods, what complicated words you humans think out for yourselves when it comes to naming things. He is simply an Alpha through and through. And that is good enough for me.* Then the animal concentrated completely on having his fur tousled.

'A *Blood* Wolf?' repeated Yollock, coming to a sudden halt. For the briefest of moments, Ahren feared that the one-armed man would reject Culhen on the spot, but instead, he stared up at Ahren. 'You won him over before he had his first taste of blood? How, by the THREE, did you manage that?'

Ahren thought back to one of the most intense memories of his life. 'Falk helped me. And so did Selsena. And it cost me a lot of sweat and tears,' he said summarising that fateful night in the Eastern Forest hut. Culhen sulked a little at the fact that the heroic rescue mission had been so abridged in the telling of it, but Yollock nodded approvingly at the Thirteenth. 'You have summed it up well.' Then he marched on, leaving Ahren to wonder if he had passed some sort of test.

'Are you staying in this place because of Four Claws?' asked the young Forest Guardian, hoping that he had somehow gained the right to pose such a question.

'Hence the bucket,' was the cryptic response of the one-armed man. 'And whose boy *are* you?' asked Yollock after another period of silent marching. 'Bergen's? Or maybe Fisker's? Only a fop like him would venture onto the eternal ice with nothing but a cloak for protection.'

Ahren was delighted that Yollock was opening up and had abandoned his single-syllable answers. He shivered inwardly at the thought of having the irresponsible Fisker as his father. The blonde-locked Paladin would have been a terrible example for any child before Ahren had gotten him to see the error of his ways. Being Bergen's son, on the other hand, would have been ideal, thought Ahren. 'I am the Thirteenth,' he said in response. 'And this cloak has magic powers. Firespray leather – strengthened through Akkad's magic.'

Yollock closed one eye and peered closely with the other up at Ahren. 'Magic, hmm? I was never that interested in such frippery.'

Ahren blinked in dismay before seeing a flash of amusement cross the man's face. By deliberately ignoring his mention of the Thirteenth, Yollock was testing Ahren's reactions. And the young man was certain that he had failed because of the look of disappointment that he had exhibited. 'The war has begun again,' he added, trying to sound considerably less proud. 'All the Paladins are gathering together.'

Damn and blast it – why do I want so desperately to impress this grumpy old codger? he scolded himself.

Because it doesn't bother him one way or the other, said Culhen effusively. *I have never encountered anyone who lives so much in the here and now as this man. He does not care about impressing anyone nor does he expect anything from the world around him. If he has to do something, then he does it, and he rejects the superfluous.*

Then he would surely be less generous with tickling your fur if he knew that you were as proud as a peacock and that you loved the sound of your own howling, countered Ahren mockingly.

Yollock had observed the silent dialogue between the pair, and he now nodded approvingly. 'Your wolf loves you,' he said simply, before adding: 'And that says something for you.'

'Thank you,' murmured Ahren, taken aback. It would take him a while yet to figure out Yollock, even if Culhen had apparently done so.

The Master of the Forest Guardians nodded down at the bucket that Ahren was still carrying. 'First, we have to take care of Four Claws.'

Ahren decided to refrain from asking about the receptacle and said nothing, merely nodding instead. Again, Yollock's eyes expressed wry amusement, Ahren realising that he had passed *this* test, at least.

'Those who ask too many questions fail to listen to the answers,' said Yollock, repeating one of the many wise saws that had been drummed into him by Falk. 'Those who listen closely and observe, on the other hand, rarely need to pose questions.'

'The first expression is one that probably all Forest Guardian apprentices in Jorath learn,' said Ahren dryly. 'Although I must admit, the second one is new to me.' He tried to sound as matter of fact as possible as he glanced quickly at Yollock to see if he could see any hint of pride in the man's reaction. The news that his maxim was now a commonplace in the traditions of Forest Guardianship was greeted, however, with nothing more than a grunt of acknowledgment.

'How come you two are alone?' asked Yollock as they finally approached the southern edge of the Fog Fields, the blunted mountain soaring up out of the fog in front of them like a sleeping giant. 'You spoke of "us" earlier.'

'Dark Ones were the cause,' said Ahren curtly. 'My friends are somewhere out there and they, too, are making their way to this mountain.'

Yollock stopped suddenly. 'Why *this* mountain?'

Ahren shrugged his shoulders. 'It was the First's idea.'

The Master of the Forest Guardians spun around, his eyes suddenly as hard and unforgiving as two green crystals. 'He is *here?*' snarled Yollock. 'After all this time?'

Stunned, Ahren could do no more than nod, the one-armed man then uttering a grunt before marching on again. A casual onlooker would never have noticed the flicker of fury that he had manifested so briefly. The Thirteenth thought back to the First's peculiar behaviour on their journey. It seemed that Yollock knew the real reason for the age-old Paladin's presence in the travel party.

'Is it *bad* that the First is here?' he asked.

'Everything comes to an end at some point,' replied the man cryptically. 'Our task is to ensure that the *right* things end.'

I wonder is he related to Sleeps-in-Treetops? asked Culhen, whose unquestioning admiration for the taciturn man was beginning to crumble just a little.

I would certainly like to eavesdrop on a conversation between the two of them, murmured Ahren, suppressing a chuckle.

Yollock looked at him sideways with one eyebrow raised, causing the young Forest Guardian to wonder if the one-armed man knew what they had been talking about, the Paladin quickly turning away to study his unfamiliar surroundings in an effort to deflect attention. *By the THREE, I am behaving like an apprentice on the first day of training,* he thought. Then he saw beyond the southern edge of the Fog Fields and gasped.

The blunted mountain rose a little beyond the last wisps of mist, its gently rising stone slope revealing an entrance that was blocked by a wall of solid ice. The chamber glittered behind the deep, transparent blue mass of frozen water. Beside the cave, a crude and almost indistinguishable set of steps led up the slope to an artificial looking ledge that was set above the cave, stretching all the way across it.

'We have arrived,' announced Yollock, pointing at the bucket in Ahren's hand. 'Follow me. And don't spill anything.'

The Forest Guardian dismounted and, completely taken aback, walked after the one-armed man, who effortlessly and agilely climbed up the stairs and walked along the stone ledge until he was standing in the middle of it. Ahren followed rather more uncertainly, concerned as he was with not spilling the contents of the heavy bucket that he had been carrying for some time now. The steps were not particularly deep and certainly not straight, while a layer of ice had already formed on them. When he finally caught up with Yollock, the latter tut-tutted disapprovingly.

'You ride too much,' he said before pointing at a spot on the ledge to his right. 'Stand there,' he added.

Ahren did as he was told, still baffled as to what he was supposed to do.

'Now take the lid off the bucket,' said the one-armed man.

The Forest Guardian placed the container down between his feet and loosened the leather straps that kept the round piece of wood secured to the top of steel bucket. Immediately, steam hit his face, and Ahren was astounded to find himself looking down at a pailful of clear, hot water.

Yollock grunted approvingly, went down on his hunkers beside Ahren, and leaned over the edge with one eye closed as he examined the wall of ice below.

'Precisely here,' he said, tapping his finger at a point on the ledge. 'This is where you pour out the water. Be careful that it doesn't spill on the rock that we are standing on but directly onto the ice below us.'

Ahren raised an eyebrow and exchanged a look with Culhen, who was waiting below. Was it possible that the many centuries of solitude on the eternal ice had changed Yollock from being a mere eccentric into nothing short of a lunatic? Had the old Paladin decided not to return to the continent because he preferred to live here on the Ice Fields where he could play with dented buckets and heated springs?

'The water is cooling down too quickly!' snarled Yollock. 'Do it *now!*'

Ahren took great care to ensure that he was holding the bucket in precisely the right place before he began to carefully pour the warm water onto the wall of ice below. He had expected the heated liquid to thaw the ice below, but instead it froze in no time at all, adding a thin layer of ice to the already solid wall of frozen water.

'Good,' said Yollock cheerfully. 'It always thaws a little here. It must have something to do with the angle of the summer sun.' Then he beckoned Ahren to leave the ledge, the pair of them descending the steps until they joined Culhen at the bottom. Yollock nodded towards the low sun. 'If we hurry, we might manage another bucket,' he announced before turning to go.

'Wait!' said Ahren loudly. 'First, I would like to know what is going on here.'

Yollock nodded but began to stride away. 'Look through the ice,' he said curtly. 'Then you and your wolf can catch up with me once you have understood what it is that I am doing here.' The Master of the Forest Guardians strode on another few paces before adding: 'And bring the bucket with you.' Then the one-armed man was swallowed up by the billowing clouds of fog, leaving Ahren to ask himself if they had found a

Paladin who, when it came down to it, had been so spiritually damaged by the experiences of his life that he had lost all connection to reality.

Now filled with doubts, Ahren stepped towards the smooth, transparent wall of ice and stared into it. The weak rays of the late afternoon sun shone deep into the cave, illuminating different parts of the chamber, which extended a good thirty paces in. Slowly, Ahren was able, by virtue of the individual beams, to make out more and more of the interior, as if he were a thief tiptoeing to a bulging treasure chest.

Then the Paladin recognised what was hidden behind the thick wall of ice. And suddenly, he understood *everything*.

***

'Well, isn't this *perfect*,' growled Trogadon as they looked at the Fog Fields stretched out before them. Night had fallen, and the diffuse glimmering of the magma-filled crevices veiled by the swirling vapours competed with the purple-green sheen of those mysterious heavenly lights that had been visible to them so often in the night sky above the Ice Fields.

'I would much rather be looking at the face of a stubborn Paladin,' muttered Falk grimly.

'Then why not look over there at the ice,' replied Bergen with a grin. 'I'm sure you will see it in your own reflection.'

'Very funny,' retorted the old Paladin before turning to Khara. 'What is your bracelet saying?'

'This afternoon, I was sure that I felt a shock coming from Ahren, but since then…no emotions whatsoever,' said the Swordsmistress, clearly frustrated.

'Then we must be considerably closer to him now,' said Jelninolan reassuringly. 'If Ahren's shock was strong enough to register with you, then you would certainly know if he was in any real danger.'

'It somehow fits with what we all know of Ahren that he would enter such a place,' said Trogadon, shaking his head as he peered into the dark, glimmering field of vapours. 'Why walk around it if you can barrel your way straight through?'

'And that's exactly what we will do tomorrow!' interjected Hakanu excitedly.

'Oh, no, we won't!' growled the First, his voice reminding the others of the cold authority he normally radiated. 'This crater of ice looks slippery. Without proper protection, we would never get out of it. We shall circumvent this volcanic field and approach the mountain from the side. There we will certainly find Ahren.'

Falk pricked up his ears – this was the first time in a long time that the war veteran had assumed his traditional position when it came to reaching decisions. The words of the man sounded so absolute that everyone in the group nodded instinctively. Falk knew, of course, that the First had his own agenda, but when he opened his mouth to protest, the Forest Guardian saw Jelninolan shaking her head at him surreptitiously, causing him to stop in his tracks, acceding to the elf's request instead. Something told him that the First would not be able to keep his secret from them for much longer, and it seemed that Jelninolan believed that they would find out what was troubling the war veteran if they yielded to his wishes.

He sat down with a sigh beside Khara and Hakanu, both of whom were watching the flickering shadows of the Fog Fields, the two of them playing a melancholy game of trying to ascertain which of the fleeting shadows could be Ahren and which Culhen.

***

It was already late evening by the time Ahren, Culhen, and Yollock arrived at the sealed cave again. This time the one-armed man took the bucket silently from Ahren and brought the container up to the stone ledge. Then he walked from one side to the other and back again until he finally picked out a suitable spot. He then untied the lid, humming quietly as he did so, before carefully pouring the contents of the bucket down the wall of ice where it froze as it descended the thick sheet.

'Within a moon, this interplay of sun and wind should cause it to flow down at precisely the *right* spot,' he murmured as if to himself before climbing down the steps again. These were the first words that Yollock had spoken since Ahren had caught up with him during the afternoon. The one-armed man had been radiating an aura of aloofness which now seemed to be broken at last, giving Ahren the opportunity to ask the question that had been on the tip of his tongue since he had looked into the cave.

'That *is* him, isn't it?' he asked in a low voice – as if he feared that the sleeping creature on the other side of the slab of ice might awaken at the words. 'You are holding *Four Claws* prisoner, aren't you?'

Yollock snorted. 'His prison is here,' he said, tapping his forehead with a finger. 'And it has been here for aeons.' He threw the bucket at Ahren, who caught it, then he nodded towards the Fog Fields. 'Time to go home.'

Ahren jutted out his chin belligerently. Did Yollock want to send him packing with his business yet unfinished as if he was nothing more than an inattentive godsday pupil? 'If you think I'm going to traipse across all Jorath only to return without you, then…' he began, only to trail off as he heard Yollock laughing for the first time. It was a sound as deep and down to earth as the man himself.

'*My* home, not *yours*,' he chuckled before moving off again.

Ahren tied the bucket to Culhen's saddle and rode after the one-armed man. He wondered where in this wasteland Yollock lived and could only imagine that it had to be a utilitarian hideaway under a fallen rock or suchlike.

Let us simply play along with him until our friends get here, suggested Ahren to his wolf.

Culhen was by now negotiating the crevices, sheets of ice, and magma fissures with considerable confidence – it was almost as though he were native to the Fog Fields. *And then what?* asked the animal. *You saw the beast with your own eyes.*

The memory of the dragon's form emerged in Culhen's memory. Claws as long as a fully grown man. A head that was larger than two carts put side by side. Wings that surely had a span of sixty paces when extended.

The creature sleeping in the Ice Cave can only be defeated by an army, continued Culhen. *And that says the wolf who never admits defeat!*

Ahren didn't know how to respond to that and therefore remained silent as they continued to follow the one-armed Paladin. He could only hope and pray that his friends knew how to handle a monstrous dragon.

When the unlikely trio finally reached Yollock's lodgings, Ahren couldn't believe his eyes. Extremely narrow, perfectly sculpted stone steps curved gently down the rock past a pool of hot, murky water, leading to a coarse but tightly woven tapestry – which would have suited a castle wall in the Knight Marshes – hanging at the end of the descent before the entrance to a warm, cosy cave.

While Culhen preferred to make himself comfortable by the warm pool, Ahren stepped after Yollock into the lodgings' interior, which consisted of a single chamber with two horizontal stone plinths, clearly serving as beds. Moss grew in tiny stone alcoves, which were neatly arranged around the walls, seemingly with the purpose of offering plants a place to grow and flourish. There was also a crooked wooden table, cobbled together from remnants of other furniture, along with two chairs constructed in the same improvisatory manner. On one of them sat a young woman, holding a longbow in her hand. The arrow placed on it was aiming directly at Ahren's heart.

'Uh,' began Ahren, as he struggled to introduce himself only for Yollock to intervene.

'He is a Paladin,' said the one-armed man before plonking himself down on the chair that was free. 'He carried one or two buckets for me. He talks too much.' He paused. 'His wolf is nice.'

The stranger lowered her weapon and eyed Ahren closely. 'So, has the time *come*, father?' she asked, Yollock nodding in response.

'*Father?*' asked Ahren in disbelief, immediately regretting sounding so much like an idiot. Clearing his throat, he pulled himself together and asked: 'How is that possible?'

'Abandoned at sea,' said Yollock, leaving it at that.

Ahren looked almost pleadingly at the stranger, who chuckled as she lay her bow aside. 'Father doesn't like to talk,' she said.

'I *had* noticed,' responded Ahren dryly. 'And what about you?'

'You can gossip outside,' grunted Yollock. 'Can a man not have some peace in his own cave?'

The woman raised her eyebrows and gave her father a chiding stare, then pointed at a stone pitcher in one of the corners of the northern wall of the cave. 'I managed to shoot an Ice Bird, you old curmudgeon,' she said affectionately. 'You will find the stew over there.'

Ahren's stomach began to rumble at the mention of food, the woman looking at him with her piercing eyes. 'What will it be?' she asked mischievously. 'A full stomach or the story of my birth?'

It took quite an internal struggle before Ahren finally replied: 'I'll take the story, please. My wolf would never forgive me, anyway, if I managed to get some food and he didn't.'

The stranger burst out laughing, causing Yollock to flinch and grumble, Ahren now finding the woman extraordinarily friendly.

'It has been a long time since I have eaten so much meat,' said the young woman who had introduced herself as Lyssin. She was sitting with Ahren and Culhen at the edge of the steaming spring, which seemed to also heat the cave below them, and she was enjoying one of the pieces of smoked meat that the Forest Guardian had remembered was stored in his rucksack.

Ahren observed Yollock's daughter more closely now from his position, nestled into Culhen's tummy fur. Her thick, unruly locks of red hair were somehow kept in check by a leather thong at the nape of her neck. Her eyes were as deep green as her father's, while her cheekbones were so high that Ahren suspected that there was some Elven blood in her forebears. It was difficult to make out her build beneath her many furs, but she was smaller than Khara, and Ahren suspected that she was more muscular than his beloved from the way that she ripped the piece of meat apart with her bare hands, throwing Culhen half of it.

'He has had enough already,' said Ahren with a grin. 'Culhen would continue to beg for meat even if he was full to the gills.'

Don't be so cheeky, countered his friend, chewing on the treat before swallowing it a heartbeat later. *You know full well that I am still two seals short of being full.*

You have seen how Lyssin and her father live, scolded Ahren. *I suspect that they would survive an entire moon on what you have just gulped down.*

The wolf did not reply but neither did he plague Lyssin anymore with begging looks, Ahren then tousling his neck-fur lovingly as a reward.

'Such a lovely animal,' said the woman, stretching out her hand to touch Culhen's pelt. 'I have seen only very few wolves in the Ice Fields. They are too shy for one to approach them,' she said. 'They must be descendants of those my father brought here.'

Ahren stopped eating and looked sharply at Lyssin. '*Yollock* introduced the wolves to the Ice Fields?'

The woman grinned and waved her finger in front of Ahren's nose, a gesture that reminded him so much of Khara that his heart was suddenly sore with yearning for his beloved. 'Now you want to have it both ways,' she laughed, 'food *and* a story.'

'*I* provide the meal, and *you* the story,' countered Ahren with a smile.

'You *are* a cheeky fellow,' said Lyssin, the young man immediately blushing at his own directness.

'You wanted to tell me more about your father, and your own birth,' he asked, having regained his composure. 'And don't forget the bit about the wolves,' he added, nodding humorously at Culhen. 'If you don't, he will probably bite you,' he said, now enjoying the light-heartedness of their banter.

'Puh,' said Lyssin. 'I usually only have conversations with the rocks around here. They are *very* good listeners. Better than father at any rate – even if he says otherwise. Too many words wear him out.'

'Take your time,' said Ahren, snuggling down in Culhen's fur. Then he patted on the wolf's belly beside him. 'Make yourself at home,' he chuckled, Lyssin immediately taking up the offer and settling into Culhen's underside with a sigh of contentment.

Only this once, muttered the wolf. *This is Khara's place, remember? But I want to find out if she knows anything about the young she-wolf who led us to the dwarves.*

Ahren wondered if Yollock and his daughter knew anything of their peculiar neighbours, but as he had promised to keep the secret of the Ripe Jags, he didn't mention the Free Dwarves.

'Father arrived here in the deep south with the intention of hunting Four Claws, a mighty northern dragon,' began Lyssin, who was now gazing up at the stars and the heavenly lights which streaked across the firmament like shimmering ribbons, dissolving and forming again, making Ahren feel as though he was watching entire worlds being born and vanishing in a never-ending succession of moving images while he, too, leaned back and looked up, listened intently now to Lyssin relating her story.

'Ice Wolves have amazingly sensitive noses, and father brought a pack of them with him as well as a small section of Four Claws' wing, which he let the animals sniff when he arrived on the Ice Fields, so that the animals could pick up the dragon's scent now that they were on terra firma again. The *Hisunik* told him of a village where there had been a massacre, from where he then began his hunt. It led him towards the Fog Fields, and it wasn't long before father had figured out where his prey had fled to. Four Claws loves dying mountains, and this one here is so old it must have formed at the beginning of time.' She pointed south to the massive rock in whose sealed cave Four Claws lay imprisoned. 'Alas, the land was more barren than father had anticipated, and food was scarce. Hence, he had to let the wolves free once he had reached the glacier, after which time he concentrated completely on constructing traps with which he could capture Four Claws.'

'*Traps?*' asked Ahren in surprise. 'For a *flying* dragon?'

'You don't know much about dragons, do you?' asked Lyssin with a chuckle. 'But then again, you are merely a Paladin and *not* a Forest Guardian like me.'

Ahren pursed his lips and silently suffered Culhen's guffawing in his head.

'Four Claws' left pinion had been damaged during a skirmish, and that is why he flew here – to recover.' She cleared her throat, and Ahren understood that she hadn't been lying – talking this much *was* new to her. 'Dragons are highly magical creatures. They recover by falling into a deep sleep from which they only awaken to eat. Then they slumber again. This pattern of ravenousness and deep sleep repeats itself until their injuries have healed. At first, father wanted to execute Four Claws while he was asleep, but the dragon woke up in the nick of time, severing father's arm in the ensuing fight. Father then reverted to a simple yet effective tactic. While Four Claws was sleeping, father sealed up the cave with the thickest layer of ice that he could manage. Then he set traps in the ice all around it – in places where he reckoned Four Claws would land during his hunting forays. Because of his damaged wing, he can only fly short distances and needs a sufficiently large, smooth area for taking off and landing. Sharp stone spears hidden under soft mounds of snow, poisonous cave lichen ground to a fine powder and hidden in fish bladders, which explode when touched… Father had plenty of nasty tricks prepared so that Four Claws would weaken every time he went hunting until the dragon retired to his cave at last and father would reseal the entrance. Four Claws never weakened significantly, but his many minor injuries and illnesses brought about through father's cunning meant that the dragon's wing could never fully heal. For centuries now, there has been no direct skirmish involving the two of them.' The young woman fell silent, giving Ahren the chance to digest what he had just heard. It reminded him of Trogadon and his Long Watch in the tunnels of the Silver Cliff. He, too, had been faced with a task that he simply could not have successfully completed on his own – merely managing stalemates in his struggle against the Ore Worm, ones that were renewed on a daily basis. It was true that Yollock didn't have to test his strength against Four Claws quite so often, yet he was at a considerably greater disadvantage when one compared the relative sizes of hunter and hunted.

'But how did a man like Yollock produce a daughter in a place like this?' asked Ahren, his curiosity getting the better of him.

'Through the THREE,' chuckled the young woman. 'Father grew weary of his task, and it was my *mother* who heard the call of the soul companions except that it reached her in a most unusual manner. She was a noblewoman from the Knight Marshes who suddenly had a burning desire to explore the Ice Fields and find out more about its mysteries. Using her wealth and influence, she organised an expedition that was to bring her to the pack ice beyond the Ravenous Maw. Alas, the ship was infected by the plague before she had reached her destination, and the captain had all those who were stricken put onto a tender and left to fend for themselves. Mother was one of the afflicted, but was already recovering, yet no-one else on board the ship cared. Neither her wealth nor her societal position were of any assistance as she and five dying companions were cut loose on their boat in the current of the Ravenous Maw. She was driven eastward for over a week, and day by day, she had to deliver a newly deceased sailor to the sea. Her tender eventually passed by a *Hisunik* village where father was bartering with the locals – something he always did in the summer when Four Claws had fallen into a deep sleep again. Knowing that this village presented her with the only chance of survival, she dived into the icy waters and tried to reach the shore. The *Hisunik* saved her from drowning by fishing her out of the water, and father could tell from her symptoms that she had barely survived the plague. Fearing that the stranger might infect the whole village, and confident that his gods' Blessing would protect him, he took her with him.' Lyssin shrugged her shoulders and snuggled deeper into Culhen's fur. 'Then fate took its course. I was born, while mother died as a result of an eruption of magma in the Fog Fields, father then bringing me up and teaching me everything that a Forest Guardian needs to know.'

Ahren was not surprised that the young woman had related only a truncated version of her childhood. It must have been a hard life, having no mother, and living in the middle of an icy wasteland with a taciturn father. She seemed to possess a sociable, chatty personality, her openness suggesting that she and father were like fire and water.

Both of which seem to live relatively harmoniously together in this place, commented Culhen.

It doesn't look like harmony to me, countered Ahren, gazing at the bubbling water, the mist that smelled of seething rock, and the greedy ice that sought to cover everything that came into its path. *More like a never-ending battle.*

'Did you never want to leave here?' asked Ahren curiously.

'Of course, I did,' replied Lyssin, nodding vigorously. 'But father told me that Paladins would come to visit us at some point, and that I could then head off with *them.*'

Ahren grunted in surprise. 'He *knew* that we were coming?'

'The appearance of a soul companion was a sure sign that the Thirteenth would soon be found,' she said lightly. 'Hence, I knew that my time would come.'

No surprise then that Yollock didn't react when you mentioned your title, said Culhen. *He'd been expecting you for ages, anyway.*

And he is less than impressed by the result, it seems, thought Ahren, self-ironically.

I don't think that there is anything in all Jorath that can impress him, countered Culhen. *The more I hear about him, the more I recognise that he is an Alpha, waiting for the chance to be replaced. Experienced, yes, but also weary beyond measure.*

Culhen's animal instincts hit the mark more often than not, and what he said tallied with Ahren's observations of many of the older Paladins that he had encountered during the course of his adventures. 'Nevertheless, I admire your patience,' he said to Lyssin, not wanting to neglect her by engaging in too much conversation with his wolf.

'It wasn't *that* bad,' said Lyssin, shrugging her shoulders. 'Father taught me well in the meantime, I trained a lot and hunted, and once I go through the Naming ceremony, I will no longer age. Then I will have all the time in the world – the THREE willing – to explore Jorath from top to bottom.'

Ahren stared at the young woman as if she had suddenly turned into a Glower Bear. 'Did you say *Naming?!*' he gasped. 'You mean that Yollock wants to pass on his *Blessing* to *you?*'

The young woman nodded. 'He is tired,' she explained, her voice reverberating with all the love that a daughter has for her father. 'He has been fighting for so long that all he wants now is to be at peace – and anyway, his missing arm would be a great disadvantage in the war against the Adversary.' Lyssin grinned at him, then stretched out her hand, protected by a fur mitten. 'Hello, Ahren,' she said with a chuckle. 'I am Lyssin, and I will soon be your sister.'

Ahren took her hand in his, unable to desist from smiling at the open, friendly young woman. Lyssin had grown up far away from other humans, only knowing the *directness* of her father – a trait that she had inherited and combined with her own obvious sincerity to create a cheerfully honest amicability. Now that he understood that she was going to become a Paladin, he found himself thinking of her as his little sister, a confusing mixture of emotions suddenly almost overcoming him.

A battle-hardened Paladin, whose age and experience can only be surpassed by the First, exchanging roles on the verge of the final assault with none other but his innocent young successor who has only ever known the Ice Fields? said Culhen, summarising the latest revelations with a chuckle. *Uldini will be charmed beyond all measure.*

***

'I am charmed beyond all measure,' growled Uldini sarcastically as he glared at the First, tramping silently ahead of them, the old veteran's eyes fixed on the mountain before them as he led the group at such a tempo that Caldria – who still hadn't spoken – could hardly keep up. 'The First was always the personification of cool, clear, rational thinking,' muttered the Arch Wizard to Falk beside him, 'and suddenly he has turned into the exact opposite.'

'I would never have guessed that there was something so personal regarding his relationship with Four Claws,' mused the old Forest Guardian. 'In fact, I thought that he would simply be delighted to see Yollock again. After all, the pair of them are the oldest living Paladins and they were always very close.'

'They experienced so many things together,' admitted Uldini. 'But remember that they very often had opposing views on issues.'

Falk nodded. 'It was very rare for the First to lose arguments, and when he did, it was generally Yollock's dogged determination that wore him down. He was one of the few who could change the First's mind once the veteran was fixed in his opinion regarding one thing or another.'

Uldini chewed on the inside of his cheek, a habit of the Arch Wizard that always made him seem particularly childish as far as the old Forest Guardian was concerned. 'Did they fight over Four Claws, I wonder?' mused the Ancient. 'Is that why the First wants to find the dragon so much – even more so than he does Ahren or Yollock? So that he can do whatever it is that he wants to do without having to explain himself to his old friend?'

'What *is* going on?' asked Falk, verbalising the question that had been bothering the group for weeks.

'I can sense Ahren!' exclaimed Khara, pointing joyfully down into Ice Fields. 'He is nearby and remarkably happy.' Her eyes widened in surprise. 'And there is someone *with* him,' she added, her face beaming. 'A *Paladin* whose Blessing I am unfamiliar with.'

Falk and the others stopped in their tracks, but the First continued to move belligerently onwards – as though he hadn't heard Khara at all. In fact, it seemed as if the First was *increasing* his speed.

Cursing, Falk ran after him, almost slipping on a sheet of ice which had been uncovered by the wind before grabbing the stubborn war veteran's arm and spinning him forcefully around. 'Ahren is down there, and with a bit of luck, Yollock,' fumed the Forest Guardian. 'They are so close that we should try calling them to us. So, please stop!'

The eyes staring out at him from beneath the dragon helmet seemed drained of all human emotion, causing the old Forest Guardian to flinch in shock. He might just as easily have been looking at a pair of *very* cold stones. He had never seen the man like this before – not even during the darkest moments that they had shared in their long lives.

'Then call them,' said the war veteran coldly. 'I, however, will keep going.' With that, he pulled his arm roughly away and resumed his onward march.

Falk scratched his beard in consternation. The First was clutching onto a secret for dear life – one that was so old that not even the Forest Guardian or Uldini had an inkling of what it was,

He hurried back to Khara and the others, all of them then calling out Ahren's name as loudly as they could.

***

When Ahren had woken up by the steaming spring the following morning, he had found Yollock already standing there and looking down at him expectantly with the bucket firmly in his grip. It seemed that the one-armed man was not going to let the sudden appearance of the Thirteenth Paladin upset his normal routine. Ahren had silently and dutifully gotten to his feet, had nodded amicably at his fellow Paladin, and had quickly nibbled on some smoked meat, before finally following Yollock as the latter began his march,

Culhen had remained behind to spend more time with Lyssin, who had promised him before they had settled down for the night that she would show him the hunting grounds of the local ice wolves. Clearly, Culhen was determined to find his she-wolf again, and as they had to wait for the arrival of their friends anyway, Ahren had not objected. Now, he and Yollock were tramping through the fog, with a clear sky above them, the morning sun beaming down on the steaming fields trapped in a never-ending battle between heat and cold.

'Your daughter likes to chat,' said Ahren finally, having had enough of the brooding silence. There were simply too many questions that he wanted to ask.

'No-one is perfect,' said the one-armed man curtly.

'Indeed, you yourself are a good example of that,' snapped Ahren. He *liked* Lyssin, and the thought that thanks to the old man's influence she might end up a tight-lipped recluse like her father almost made his blood boil.

'True,' said the one-armed man, thereby taking the wind out of Ahren's sails. Yollock gave him a sideways glance. 'Glad you're here,' he said after a pause, smiling briefly from beneath his woolly scarf. 'She can talk away to you instead.'

It was only the faintest hint, hidden in the words of the one-armed man, but it was as clear as the first sign of spring on a dreary winter day – Yollock had just revealed the love he felt for his daughter, and also his relief that Ahren and his friends would soon release her from the existence which had imprisoned her since birth. The Thirteenth Paladin was surprised by this revelation, understanding now, too, that Yollock was right in one respect – the less one spoke, the more one could hear the hidden messages in the few words that were uttered.

The Master of the Forest Guardians nodded at Ahren as though acknowledging a powerful, shared secret before falling broodingly silent again. Ahren, meanwhile, ran over the questions occupying his mind, filtering them out until only the most important ones were left. As he was doing so, it dawned on him how this method was freeing up his head and allowing him to concentrate only on what was *essential*.

'Do you think that we can conquer Four Claws?' he asked, sure that this man knew the beast like no other.

Yollock hesitated for the first time before replying, making Ahren somewhat uneasy. Suddenly, a voice called out in the distance – a voice which belonged to someone who the Forest Guardian yearned for more than anyone in the world.

'Ahren!' the voice called out again, the young man turning on his heels in delight and astonishment.

'KHARA!' he yelled at the top of his voice. Then he began to run, all the worries that had been afflicting him dissolving into insignificance.

Chapter 23

Ahren ran westward through the fog until it thinned out, calling Khara by name again and again. Soon, the Swordsmistress's voice was joined by those of Hakanu, Trogadon, Falk, and Bergen.

Once the last plumes of fog had parted, and the Forest Guardian saw his friends at the upper edge of the extended ice crater, he jumped for joy like an excited foal. He waved his arms wildly, wiping away his tears as his fears for the safety of Khara and the others, which he had tried so desperately to suppress, were washed away in a heartbeat. Quickly, he counted their number as he neared the cheering group, only to conclude as he met them, that there was someone missing. An icy shiver ran down his spine.

'Where is the *First!*' he shouted.

'Further ahead!' bellowed Falk. 'He seems to have taken leave of his senses. The only thing that matters to him are this mountain and the dragon, which he suspects to be there!'

Ahren heard a gasp of dismay from behind, and when he turned to look back through the fog, he saw Yollock making a run directly for the ice cave. He had carelessly dropped his precious bucket, and Ahren's stomach did a somersault, so gripped he was by fear. Suddenly, he wondered if Yollock was doing something more here than simply guarding Four Claws – was *he*, perhaps, hiding from something in these fog-shrouded fields as well? What *was* it that seemed to connect the dragon and the two aeon-old Paladins in so ominous and mysterious a manner? Ahren's instincts were now pressing upon him the fact that he and his companions had better move heaven and earth *not* to be the last to reach the ice cave.

'Run after him!' he yelled. 'Stop him if you can. Do *not* let him get inside the cave!'

Then he spun around and vanished into the fog.

***

Falk stared furiously at the spot where his former apprentice had been standing only a heartbeat earlier. Had everyone in this godsforsaken region lost their minds? Maybe too much ice affected one's sanity, he wondered grimly.

'You all heard him!' he shouted, shooing the disappointed Khara along the edge of the crater, as well as Trogadon and the rest of the companions. 'Let's grab the First, and by the THREE, he is then going to tell us the *real* reason for his being here – even if I have to beat the answer out of his stubborn skull!'

***

Revenge had been trying for days, but the dragon's mind was stuck unshakeably in a deep healing sleep – like a rock lodged deep in the bed of a lake. The child of the Adversary had been able to fill the creature's dreams with visions of bloody retribution but waking it up was another matter entirely. The injured wing of the dragon sent fiery impulses coursing through its body with every heartbeat, but even when Revenge magnified the pain, Four Claws slumbered on. The first pangs of doubt regarding the practicalities of his plan were beginning to overtake the child when suddenly there was a loud hammering on the outside of the ice wall which shielded the cave from the world beyond, an age-old instinct then beginning to rouse the sleeping dragon into a state of preparedness.

Revenge laughed out loud when he saw the carry-on outside the cave. Sometimes it was his greatest enemies who did the heaviest lifting for him.

***

'First! *No!*' roared Yollock, Ahren immediately picking up speed as he began to sprint. Fiery crevices filled with magma, sheets of ice as smooth as glass, and treacherous fissures in the ground had to be negotiated first, not to mention the lakes of seething hot water which spewed up dangerous fountains high into the air from time to time.

Once Ahren reached the southern end of the Fog Fields, where the age-old mountain began its ascent, he was greeted by the very sight that he had feared so much. The First was standing there with his two-hander held high, while Yollock struggled to lower the heavy weapon with his one arm. A spider's web of thin fissures already decorated the carefully conceived ice wall which Yollock had maintained and renewed, century after century. Again, the First let out a roar as he slammed his weapon against the obstruction, the sheer force of his effort sending shards of ice flying in every direction.

Ahren doubted that the age-old Paladin would be able to destroy the wall within a day, but he greatly feared the awakening of the creature that slumbered not ten paces behind the sealed entrance to the cave.

He hurried over to the First and Yollock, making short shrift of the situation. Using the one-armed man as a distraction, he whooshed behind the First, and as the sword bearer again raised his two-handed weapon above his head, the Forest Guardian slammed his back into that of the war veteran, grabbed his upstretched arms by the wrists, yanking them sideways and down, while swivelling on his hips. With a strangled groan and a loud clatter, the heavily armed man with his dragon helmet fell onto the cold stone, and even before the veteran could react, Ahren had him pinned to the ground in an arm lock.

'You will hardly be able to manipulate your two-hander if your arm is broken,' said Ahren severely, the age-old Paladin struggling to free himself. 'So, stop squirming and *yield,* dammit!'

'Well, I'm sure that Falk didn't teach you *that,* said Yollock, kicking the First's weapon away.

Ahren smiled grimly. 'My wife is a Swordsmistress and one-time fighting slave in the arenas,' he replied.

'*And* she is a princess, don't forget, gasped Trogadon, before breathing a sigh of relief. The dwarf was still a good twenty paces away, having just rounded a rocky spur. He grinned at Ahren, then bellowed over his shoulder: 'They are here!'

Ahren still had the First pinned to the rocky floor, but he was now beaming as, one by one, his friends came from behind the rock as they ran towards him. Tears were flowing down Khara's cheeks as Ahren began to laugh helplessly while sitting on the First's back, keeping the war veteran's arm twisted as he did so.

'I would give you all a decent welcome,' he said, his voice shaking. 'But unfortunately, I have a troublesome Paladin to control.'

Khara snorted as she laughed. 'That's easy,' she said, winking at him lovingly, 'after all, that's something I have to do on a daily basis.'

Ahren gave her a loving glance, then concentrated on the First again, who was still trying to free himself, cursing all the while under his breath. 'It is over,' said the Forest Guardian in as gentle a voice as he could muster. 'Either you explain your behaviour, or I will have Trogadon put you in shackles.'

'*None* of you understand,' muttered the First furiously. 'I must bring it to an end. Yollock is *protecting* Four Claws!'

Ahren blinked up at the one-armed man, recognising the silent admission in his eyes, without a word being spoken.

'Come,' said the Paladin wearily from behind his scarf. 'There are too many words to be spoken for this story to be related before the cave of a dragon.' Then he turned and walked away, leaving Ahren and his friends to look at each other in bemusement.

'Has he *always* been that recalcitrant?' asked Ahren irritably, looking at Falk.

'But of course,' grinned Falk. 'How do you think *I* learned such behaviour?'

This was greeted by muted laughter, Falk and Trogadon then helping Ahren pull the First to his feet before guiding him away from the cave.

While Ahren led his friends into the fog, he glanced back from time to time at the wall of ice, now decorated with a deep, splintered gash. And every time he heard a pool bubbling, magma hissing, or ice cracking, he flinched, so fearful was he now that the massive wall of ice might have shattered.

Yollock was waiting for them at his improvised table with wary eyes, his body the picture of anxiety.

This was the first time that Ahren had seen the Paladin without his fur hat and woolly scarf, which meant that it was his earliest opportunity to get a good look at his face. Deep furrows decorated the one-armed man's face, while his black hair streaked with grey had been plaited into countless braids, which clearly hadn't been tended to for a considerable time. A wild, dark beard completed the picture of the man, who lived here at the end of the world with no particular interest in his outward appearance. Lyssin and Culhen were nowhere to be seen, Ahren suspecting that the pair were still out hunting for a bride for his wolf.

'Bergen, please tell Karkas to keep an eye out for Culhen and a young woman,' he murmured to the blonde Paladin once all the companions had squeezed into the compact cave.

Bergen raised his eyebrows in surprise, but merely nodded. Trogadon, meanwhile, was making sure that there was sufficient distance between Yollock and the First, while Falk carried the First's weapon on his back, just to be on the safe side.

'You look tired,' said Jelninolan gently, breaking the heavy silence.

'And you, happy,' replied the one-armed man, the corners of his mouth twitching as if he were trying to smile. 'You have found your True Form, I see.'

'We had to travel a long way to find you,' said Falk, Ahren realising from the look on his erstwhile master's face that he was happier to see his long-lost brother than his words suggested.

'I had no choice,' said Yollock, the First snorting loudly in response.

'*One* of you two had better start talking now,' said Ahren irritably. 'Or we will shackle you both and hope that we can get back to the continent before Four Claws wakes up.'

'No!' retorted the two wranglers in unison, Falk laughing bitterly.

'And already they are in agreement,' growled the old Paladin.

'Well?' grunted Trogadon. 'Who will start?' When both remained silent, he demonstratively produced his rope and stepped towards the First.

'It was *my* fault!' yelled the war veteran. 'It was *my* fault that Four Claws waged war on the Jorathian tribes! Are you all happy now!' The First was breathing heavily, as though his confession had taken more out of him than a day's uninterrupted marching.

'I think you had better explain yourself more clearly,' said Uldini, after which an expectant silence descended on the room, which was eventually broken when the first of all the Paladins began telling his story.

'When the gods created us Paladins – no, when they created *me* – they were following the plan that they had thought up in their deep sleep. A man, given and adjusted by HIM, WHO FORMS, weapons and armour provided by HIM, WHO IS…and a companion animal from HER, WHO FEELS. Awe-inspiring and mighty we were to be – at least, that is how I saw it – and so, the deities even giving me the largest and cleverest animal Creation had to offer – a dragon.'

I have never understood why these oversized lizards are praised to high heaven so often, grumbled Culhen, who had by now arrived back with Lyssin and was waiting with her outside the overcrowded cave so as not to interrupt proceedings. *What's wrong with an impressive wolf – or even a mangy tigress for that matter?*

Shush, said Ahren, turning his attention back to the First and his story.

'Alas, the most striking quality of the northern dragons is their independent streak – they can hardly even bear the presence of their *own* kind. They are clever enough to possess a sharp understanding and they are capable of complex emotions. When *she* was bound to me, *she* was not well pleased. The gods didn't repeat the mistake when the next Paladin was created. Indeed, they never made that mistake again. *Her* disgust had been so great.'

'Your dragon's?' asked Hakanu, who had been listening with bated breath, and was squeezing the whimpering Kamaluq tightly to his chest.

'*She* had no name. According to *her,* no dragon did. They didn't believe in such a thing.' The First was struggling for words. 'It's…it's…difficult to explain. *She* always said that a name constricts one, makes one smaller than one might be.'

Trogadon snorted in disdain but decided to say nothing.

'It took many years before *she* accepted *her* role, and I, in my pride, learned that *she* was not merely there to serve me. None of us had a role model, for there had been no Paladin before us from whom we could have learned.' The First swallowed hard, and Ahren felt for the otherwise so emotionless man. The scars, both inside and out, that the veteran had carried with him for so long would have destroyed many others. 'When *she* finally died…' the First's voice cracked with emotion as he struggled to keep control of the story, '…I had no idea what *her* death would devastate along with my heart.' The war veteran looked at Yollock, the latter merely nodding in response. All hostility seemed to have softened into an expression of fraternal concern on the face of the one-armed man. 'There were then rumours about a northern dragon that was attacking soldiers, merchants, and farmers. One that laid waste to entire villages, and later even cities, and on account of whom *all* the northern dragons suddenly began to behave aggressively, which led to them being hunted and slaughtered. This dragon was given a name – and his name was *Four Claws…*' The First could go on no longer, his eyes now looking pleadingly over at Yollock.

'Four Claws is *her* grandfather,' said the one-armed man simply. 'He blames the First for *her* death. And the gods. And every living being that is waging war against the Adversary.'

The ensuing silence was laden with tension. Falk was the first to find his voice. 'Are you saying that Four Claws is *not* under the spell of the Dark god *at all?*' he asked scornfully. 'He is *only* furious because his granddaughter was a *victim* in this war?'

The First nodded. 'At first, I merely looked on him as a servant of the Dark god and took no more notice of him than the other horrific creatures that I and the other Paladins were confronted with during the first centuries of our existence. It was only when he spared five hundred soldiers and two other Paladins to hunt *me* down that I began to suspect that he was something more than an enslaved creature to HIM, WHO FORCES. I studied him more closely and recognised elements of *her* character again. I knew enough about dragons to identify several inherited features that they both shared.'

'Shouldn't we perhaps discuss for a moment the fact that the First said a moment ago that the supposed Dark One had *spared* five hundred soldiers and two Paladins?' interjected Bergen. 'And *why* this thing is slumbering less than half a league from us in a cave?'

'He isn't a *thing!*' snapped Yollock. 'But a *being* who is grieving. Who has had too much taken away from him during his life.'

'And this is where we come to the bit where the two of you are *not* in agreement, right?' asked Uldini caustically.

Ahren took Khara's hand and squeezed it hard. Feelings of loss and sorrow had destroyed many a life, some of the Paladins being badly affected in this manner, as the young man had seen when he had found them.

And some of them still are, added Culhen.

'I tried to hunt Four Claws down and bring his campaign of violent revenge to an end, but I failed,' said the First. 'I was too emotional in his presence…he reminded me too much of…' he trailed off, shaking his head.

'The First sought me out,' said Yollock, taking up the story. 'The best tracker and slayer of Dark Ones that he knew.' The Paladin looked regretfully at the First. 'Alas, he only told me half the story. And I hunted a Dark One that *wasn't* one.'

'And *you* failed,' concluded Hakanu. 'Know your prey or you fail,' he added, quoting one of the saws of Forest Guardianship.

Yollock nodded. 'Well learned off by heart, little foal,' he said. 'But nevertheless true. The creature I was hunting down was no servant of the Dark god, and therefore my efforts missed the mark – again and again.' Yollock sighed and closed his eyes. 'It was Sleeps-in-Treetops who finally recognised the problem when she realised that Four Claws fled like a *normal* animal after we had tracked him down and wounded him in the Sunplains. He didn't fight us to the bitter end as any Dark One would.'

'And then you simply followed him,' added Falk, remembering back to Yollock's actions at the time. 'Of course, we all thought that you were going to kill him – a dreadful mistake on our part.'

Yollock shrugged his shoulders. 'He bit off my arm when I tried to negotiate in a friendly manner with him. Then I changed my strategy and successfully stopped him from returning to the mainland,' he said. 'And for a *very* long time.'

'He must *die*,' said the First, his voice dripping with hatred. 'His feelings of grief and suffering alone cannot justify what he has done. After all, he has slaughtered thousands, many thousands in his madness, and there is a price to be paid for that.'

'A price that he is already paying. He is locked away and sleeping – and his wound will never heal,' countered Yollock. 'After all this time without treatment, his wing is going to hurt him for evermore – even if his bones somehow manage to knit fully together again. He has been paying a terrible price ever since I have locked him in this cage of ice. Do you not see that he has suffered enough – every day now for hundreds of years? You know perfectly well that northern dragons are very sensitive creatures. Fragile, even. Their bodies crave for harmony and understanding. If *one* of those two are in a state of unbalance…' The Paladin paused for a moment before adding: 'Why should death *always* be the answer? He is *not* a Dark One!'

'This discussion is going nowhere,' muttered Uldini. 'We need Yollock for the final battle against the Adversary. Which means that Four Claws will get out sooner or later. Ergo, we will have to kill him before his pinion heals and he destroys Cape Verstaad first before wreaking revenge on all Jorath.'

'It is not *me* that you need,' replied Yollock instantly before calling out Lyssin's name. 'It is *another* Paladin that you require.'

All eyes other than Ahren's turned to the tapestry hanging in the doorway, which was duly pulled back with a considerable amount of energy before Yollock's daughter stopped in surprise as she was greeted by the eyes of an unexpectedly large number of guests.

'So many visitors?' she asked, beaming and blinking as she looked at the stunned faces of Ahren's companions. 'Have I missed something?

Jelninolan and Falk handed the stew out to all those in the chamber, having rustled it up in no time at all by combining their own provisions and the bird soup into a tasty dish, while the companion animals stood guard outside. Ahren and Lyssin had related that part of Yollock's story that involved his soul companion and his daughter, the newcomers now gratefully eating their stew and mulling over the recent revelations.

Lyssin kept trying to make eye contact with her father, now that she finally knew how he had lost his arm and what the Master of the Forest Guardians *really* thought of the sleeping dragon. Ahren could make out only compassion and absolutely no anger in her reaction, which only increased his admiration for the young woman.

The Forest Guardian finally took his stone bowl and beckoned Khara to follow him outside, where they cuddled up to Culhen and Muai, with the bubbling of the hot spring sounding behind them. Hardly had they sat down when Ahren kissed Khara passionately, his beloved responding in kind.

'I am so happy that you are safe and sound,' he whispered after a time, the Swordsmistress nodding in return, tears filling her eyes.

'And likewise,' she laughed, her voice quivering. Then she gestured down the steps towards the cave. 'That was an *awful* lot to take in.'

Ahren nodded. 'If you consider how long Yollock and the First have already lived, we must be grateful if this is the only secret they share.' They both took a mouthful of stew and pondered for a moment.

'What's wrong with Caldria?' asked Ahren, breaking the pleasant silence that had ensued. 'She seems distant somehow. Since I have met you all again, she hasn't said a single word.'

'Ah,' said Khara sadly. 'She sacrificed her ability to cast spells in order to save Hakanu's life. She has been silent since then.'

Ahren looked at his beloved in dismay. '*Sacrificed?* Does that mean that…' He trailed off, unable to finish the question.

'Exactly,' said Khara morosely. 'Her talent is gone. Burned out in a great sacrificial deed.'

Ahren's eyes welled up with tears, but he refused to weep. 'I will fix this,' he said firmly, and it was more an oath to himself rather than to the Swordsmistress. 'As a reward, she will live out the evening of her life in the manner that she would wish. She will lack for *nothing*.'

'That is sweet of you,' said Khara, kissing him fleetingly on his cheek, an action which failed to cover the fact that his promise would never fully compensate for that which the woman had sacrificed. The young couple fell silent again for a time.

'And what do you think of Lyssin?' asked Khara finally, unable to contain her curiosity, while also changing the subject, much to the relief of Ahren. 'She seems so…friendly.'

Ahren grinned. 'You mean *not* like her father?' Then he took a deep breath and looked up at the stars. 'They love and care for each other,' he said after a pause. 'The fact that he says little, and she talks all the more seems to suit them to the ground.'

'Still,' said Khara. 'Growing up in this wasteland…'

'There *are* people who spent their childhoods in fighting arenas,' said Ahren with a chuckle. 'And even some of *them* have developed into halfway decent human beings.'

'Only *halfway* decent?' countered Khara, setting down her stone bowl, her eyes now glittering dangerously. Ahren grinned at her and did the same. 'Then let me show you how a *halfway* decent woman ca…'

Trogadon interrupted the Swordsmistress by clearing his throat loudly. 'Perhaps the two of you might like to come in,' he said in a solemn tone. 'A Naming is about to take place.'

Ahren and Khara exchanged knowing looks before leaping to their feet, while Culhen snorted audibly.

Of course, we companion animals are not invited – as usual.

You can see everything through my eyes, said Ahren comfortingly as he descended the steps, and when he heard Muai's low growl, he concluded that Khara was engaged in a similar conversation.

'Yollock doesn't seem to believe in wasting any time,' whispered Khara once they had reached the cave, nodding towards Uldini, Trogadon, and Jelninolan, who were already standing around the one-armed Paladin and his daughter, an improvised charm circle already drawn on the floor with ashes.

'I think that he has been waiting for this day a *long* time,' murmured Ahren in response. 'And because we have brought enough of the Einhans with us, he will get his way, and we will have our Paladin.'

'Silence, please!' said Falk severely. 'You two are whispering like a pair of godsday pupils.'

Ahren watched eagerly as Uldini intoned the introductory liturgy, while it suddenly struck him that this was the first time that he was going to experience a peaceful Naming, in the manner of the ones traditionally performed in the past. There had been nothing normal about his own one, while with Hakanu's, the boy's physical father had only just been slain, his gods' Blessing manifesting itself just before his father's one had dissolved. Here in this dim, crowded cave beneath the ice, Yollock was smiling affectionately at his daughter, who was calmly awaiting her new life, her eyes bright with anticipation, her entire young existence having been spent in preparation for this moment.

'We have gathered here today to see how the burden of the Paladin passes from father or mother to daughter or son,' intoned Uldini in a solemn voice. 'We ask the gods to bless this transference and to grant their true servant a long and happy life, he having served THE THREE so truly.'

Falk placed his hand on the shoulder of Yollock's missing arm, his fellow Paladin reacting as if a heavy burden had suddenly been taken from him.

'We further ask for the Blessing of THE THREE on their new champion, who is now taking on the heavy burden to fight for creation, to halt the progress of HIM, WHO FORCES, and to wipe HIM off the face of Jorath,' added Uldini.

Lyssin wiped a tear from the corner of her eye, her broad grin revealing to Ahren, however, that it wasn't a tear of sorrow. The young woman was ready for her calling, and Ahren could only feel delight for her at this precious moment. It was lovely to see how *differently* the career of a Paladin could be launched. In harmony and confidence rather than in despair and bloodshed.

'To show that she is worthy, the Einhans have gathered to intercede on her behalf, and also a Paladin, who will welcome her into the circle of their kind.' Uldini glanced around the room, Bergen then raising his hand and chuckling. There was certainly no lack of Paladins in this little cave.

'May the Einhan of the dwarves impart to us if he supports the selection of the aspirant here present, and if he considers said aspirant to be worthy of bearing the burden of a Paladin conscientiously and diligently,' intoned the Arch Wizard.

Trogadon raised himself to his full height, his hands on the grip of the hammer set before him. 'The Einhan of the dwarves considers the aspirant to be worthy.'

'May the Blessing of HIM, WHO IS be upon the aspirant, and may the sacred armour and weapons serve the Paladin well,' continued Uldini.

Yollock caught Ahren's attention, then nodded towards a bundle in the corner of the room, which still had signs of fresh ice on it. It seemed that Yollock had hidden his treasures underground, just as Falk had once done in the Eastern Forest.

Ahren took a Deep Steel short sword from the bag as well as a buckler made from the same material, before finally pulling out a leather jerkin, vambraces, and greaves. Each leather piece was decorated with thin ribbons of Deep Steel. Ahren frowned in surprise as he held out the armour for Lyssin, the young woman grinning at the Thirteenth in return.

'Father had the heart of a legionary before he matured into a Forest Guardian,' she said with a wink. 'We all have to start somewhere and see where the journey takes us.'

Then without a care in the world she stripped off her furs until she was only in her undergarments, then slipped on her new armour, and fixed both sword and armour to her back.

Ahren sighed when he saw that poor Hakanu was totally smitten by the newest Paladin. It was clear that a heart to heart with his apprentice was going to be necessary sooner rather than later.

Uldini, meanwhile, was waiting patiently – totally untypical behaviour for the first among the Ancients. Ahren was sure that the Arch Wizard, too, wanted Lyssin to have the best possible start to her sacred mission, the childlike figure now continuing with his intoning.

'May the Einhan of the elves impart to us if she supports the selection of the aspirant here present, and if she considers said aspirant to be worthy of bearing the burden of a Paladin conscientiously and diligently.'

Jelninolan flicked her wrist, the illusion of a glow-worm immediately lighting up the room as the priestess winked at Lyssin. 'The Einhan of the elves considers the aspirant to be worthy.'

Uldini nodded approvingly while the newest Champion of the gods watched the glow-worm, enchanted. 'May the Blessing of HER, WHO FEELS be upon the aspirant, and may her servant protect her from all dangers on her travels, be they physical or spiritual,' said the Arch Wizard gently.

There followed a silence lasting several heartbeats before Falk cleared his throat discreetly. 'There are…very few animals in this wasteland…' he began in a soft voice, only for Ahren to grin like a village idiot as Culhen began howling in an over-dramatic manner.

It is she, it is she, Ahren, it is she! called the wolf, his emotions overwhelming Ahren's mind like waves crashing onto rocks. *Oh, you merciful goddess, accept the thanks of your unworthy wolf!* prayed Culhen with a ridiculous amount of pathos as the young she-wolf who had led them to the dwarves began to make her way slowly down the steps, snuffling as she proceeded.

'I think we had better make some space,' said Ahren, tears now running down his cheeks. He could hardly contain himself at the prospect of seeing the new Paladin and her companion animal meeting each other for the first time.

Lyssin screamed with joy as the impressive ice wolf stepped into the cave, while her father had to grab her to stop her from breaking out of the charm circle. The she-wolf stretched out her head, and when Lyssin did the same until they were forehead to forehead, it was complete. The she-wolf sat down beside Lyssin with a whimper and looked at her quizzically.

'She isn't talking,' said the young woman, taken aback. 'What is the matter with me that I can't hear her?'

'She will be conversing with you soon enough, especially considering the fact that she is quite mature for a companion animal,' said Ahren. 'Don't worry – you will be cursing this aspect of being a Paladin before you know it.'

The young man's companions laughed at what he had said, Culhen renewing his joyful howl of approval.

Oh, her voice is bound to be wonderful, take my word for it, said the wolf excitedly in praise of the newly chosen companion animal.

Ahren could do nothing else but tease his friend. *You've had it far too easy up to now,* he said. *All you had to do was to grow bigger and stronger than the other wolves around you. But this she-wolf is no fool, and you are going to have to make considerably more effort if you want to impress her.*

Culhen's disenchantment was instant. *Oh, no,* he murmured. *Oh, no,* he repeated.

Ahren silently swore to himself that he would give his wolf new courage later, but now he turned his attention fully back to the ceremony, which was coming to an end, with Uldini beginning the final prayer.

'I, as human Einhan, consider the aspirant to be worthy of bearing the burden of a Paladin conscientiously and diligently. May the Blessing of HIM, WHO FORMS be upon the aspirant, and her form prove itself against coercion from within or without,' he said.

Lyssin stiffened for an instant, as did Yollock, who now took his hand away from his daughter. For a fraction of a heartbeat, Ahren thought he saw a golden shimmer passing from the old Paladin to the new one, but then the moment was past as father and daughter smiled affectionately at one another.

Behind him, Ahren heard a little sound, and when he glanced back, he saw Caldria standing there with tears in her eyes as she took in the ceremony, her eyes shining with yearning. Her look seemed softer, less harried as she almost lovingly ran her fingers along the icy surface of the cave wall.

Uldini was clearly more than satisfied with his own performance as he intoned the closing litany. 'Bergen Olgitram, do you accept this aspirant as Paladin, and will you teach her everything that she needs to know?'

The blonde man nodded. 'I accept the aspirant as one of our own.'

Yollock snorted in amusement. 'As if *you* could teach her anything that she hasn't learned from me ten times already.'

The leader of the Blue Cohorts grinned. 'It depends on what you're talking about. Do you have any alcohol here?'

Yollock frowned and shook his head, Bergen's grin growing wider. 'Well now, she really *must* learn how to *drink* like a Paladin!'

Trogadon, who was looking pityingly at Lyssin, tapped her hand. 'Poor child,' he said. 'Not a single drop of alcohol? Don't worry – we'll sort that out. You can trust your Uncle Trogadon.'

'Then I hereby seal the Naming,' intoned Uldini as he waved his arm dismissively, clearly annoyed by his fellow travellers' irreverence.

'I congratulate you!' called out Ahren above the cheers of his friends. 'Considering that they have already educated you *during* your Naming, there is no doubt but that you are already a Paladin through and through.'

This was greeted by laughter and more cheers, Ahren now inwardly preparing for an evening of joyful celebration. His thoughts, however, were suddenly interrupted by a loud gasp from Bergen, whose face had drained of all colour.

'You remember our plan – that Yollock would remain here and keep Four Claws imprisoned?' asked the leader of the Blue Cohorts, the others now staring with uneasy anticipation at the Ice Lander.

'Come on, spit it out!' snarled Uldini.

'I let Karkas have a sleep on the mountain slope at a safe distance from the Ice Cave,' said the Paladin, Ahren's heart suddenly missing a beat. Then he heard the dreadful words.

'Well – the dragon has smashed through the glass wall,' whispered Bergen. 'Four Claws is free.'

Chapter 24

Revenge bathed in the feeling of power that his marionette was radiating forth.

Freshly anchored in the midst of the injuries and losses that the dragon had suffered at the hands of humans and their actions, it had been child's play for Revenge to steer the monster towards the glimmering Fog Fields, where the child of the Adversary had sensed several gods' Blessings at once, among whom there seemed to be one as fresh and innocent as a new-born babe.

While the dragon's mighty wings, which caused the beast so much pain, beat mightily nonetheless, carrying the child towards the volcanic fields of ice, steam, and fire, Revenge found himself revelling at the prospect of snuffing out the life of a freshly baked Paladin before it had even properly begun. He caused the dragon to utter a bone-shattering scream, audible for leagues around, expressing the very scorn that the child of the Adversary himself was feeling.

Tonight, all Jorath would tremble!

***

'What are our options?' asked Falk breathlessly while the Forest Guardian and his companions scanned the heavens for any sign of the escaped dragon.

Following Bergen's warning, they had all run outside and stared up at the night sky, from where snow was gently falling, creating a white powder, billowing steam, and sometimes even a low hissing sound, depending on where the flakes had come to rest. The individual magma fissures cast the clouds of fog in a sombre red, which sometimes changed into a powerful orange, whenever one of the magma bubbles burst and molten lava brightened up the night sky.

'He doesn't know where Lyssin and I live,' said Yollock hastily. 'If anyone wants to hide themselves, now is the time to do it.' No-one moved until the First gave Caldria a gentle push.

'No-one will think ill of you, my good woman,' said the war veteran in a surprisingly gentle voice. 'Not after the sacrifice you have made for us.'

The burnt-out sorceress nodded before tiptoeing down into the cave, closing the tapestry behind her.

'Yollock, perhaps you, too, might consider…' began Falk, but the one-armed man responded with such a withering look that the old Paladin immediately fell silent.

'I know this dragon better than anyone else here,' he said. 'I may not be a Paladin anymore, but my mind and my mouth may still come in useful.'

A second scream filled the night sky, this time considerably closer than the previous one. Ahren still couldn't make out any shadow among the clouds, but already he could hear the irregular beating of enormous wings. 'What can we do?' he asked Yollock. 'Apart from hide.'

'His scales are too thick for us to penetrate them,' declared the Master of the Forest Guardians. 'They have hardened even more over the centuries, since the skirmishes that the First had with Four Claws. The best way of hurting the dragon is through his wings. If we can incapacitate them, then his flying ability will be nullified.'

'Uldini? Jelninolan? asked Bergen, looking at the Ancients.

The Arch Wizard shook his head. 'Magic is practically ineffective against dragons – they possess such a large amount themselves.' He let *Flamestar* ignite, causing the core of the crystal ball to cast a powerful white light. 'The best I can do is to equip your weapons and armour with a raw, unformed power, which will hopefully even things up a little.'

'Magical steel meets magical scales?' asked Hakanu. 'Something like that?'

'It's more a case of evening out the differences between the two magical *potentials*. When looked at mathematically—' began Uldini, only for the First to grab the Ancient by the shoulder, giving the sorcerer a thorough shaking.

'Just *do* it!' snarled the veteran, the childlike figure then muttering to himself as he rubbed the orb along the armour and weapons, the pieces immediately taking on a shimmer reminiscent of distant candlelight.

'My magic is too dangerous,' murmured Jelninolan sadly. '*Mirilan* would create a storm instantly.'

'If I had to choose between a dragon's maw or a thunderbolt, I would undoubtedly choose the latter,' said Trogadon soberly. 'If I were you, my heart, I would be at the ready.'

The priestess nodded her agreement before placing her Storm Fiddle on her shoulder, though without playing it. Ahren could see that she was now terrified of her instrument, the young man suddenly being overcome by a feeling of compassion for the Storm Weaver, only for Culhen to let out a low howl that shook him to the core.

The dragon is coming, warned the wolf, and now Ahren, too, could see the silhouette of the enormous creature above them, illuminated at irregular intervals as it approached them in a sweeping arc. Four Claws was still two lengths of an arrow shot away, but that left them little time for preparations.

'Any last ideas?' he called out to his companions.

'I have a quick question,' said Trogadon, raising his hammer and instinctively moving protectively before Jelninolan. 'They say that very old dragons can spit fire. Is that true?'

'No,' replied Yollock.

Trogadon breathed a sigh of relief. 'I'm glad to hear it.'

'But their body temperature is so high that their scream can spew out a stream of seething hot air. Hence, the fire-breathing legend.'

'Oh,' said Trogadon with a shiver. 'That's *not* so good.'

'Aim first at the wings,' said the First, his voice funereal. 'Then at his eyes or into his open mouth. You can also try any gaps between his scales near his joints. Anywhere where the flesh is unprotected you should stab.'

'My magic will not last for ever,' warned the Arch Wizard. 'Once your armour and weapons have been hit a few times, they will lose their power. Then you will be little more than a handful of mortal warriors fighting against a mighty dragon.'

Watch out!' yelled Khara, pointing upwards with her Whisper Blade, her Wind Blade held close to her body. 'He is preparing to plummet!'

'Fan out!' screamed Yollock.

Ahren jumped to the left. Thanks to the Blessing Band, which Khara had caused at this moment to spring into action, he sensed his companions scattering to all the points of the compass, disappearing for the most part into the swirling fog as Four Claws screamed violently, dropping headfirst at an alarming speed.

Hakanu alone did not flee. His courage and determination were like a beacon in the Blessing Band which connected Khara and the Paladins. With his chest expanded and his spear at the ready, he stood there and murmured more loudly than he must have intended: 'Hakanu, the dragon slayer.' Then the apprentice flung his weapon, even before Ahren had the chance to shout at him to make a run for it, the young warrior's glove glowing brightly as the spear flew forward with power and speed, resembling a shaft of light beaming through the blanket of fog, leaving wafts of mist spinning in its wake.

Ahren held his breath as the spear shot directly towards one of the dragon's eyes – the beast turning its head at the last moment so that the missile scraped along Four Claws' cheek before disappearing harmlessly into the night.

'Get away from there!' screamed Ahren, his protégé now standing there in shocked bemusement, watching the downward hurtling dragon. But just before the colossus slammed into the earth with a bone-shaking shudder, boring its man-size claws into the earth where Hakanu had even now been standing, the apprentice sprinted forward with his head lowered, subverting the dragon.

Hope welled up within Ahren when he saw Hakanu reappear on the other side of Four Claws' hindlegs and sprint to the side only for the dragon's tail to whip across with incredible speed, sweeping Hakanu off his feet. The metal plates of his armour flashed and expired like dying stars, Uldini's magic exploding. The apprentice was catapulted far into the fog, performing several unwitting somersaults before coming to a shuddering halt.

Ahren changed course and raced towards where the Blessing Band suggested that Hakanu had landed, while behind him Four Claws' deafening screams seemed to cause the fog surrounding the Forest Guardian to spin furiously before violently dispersing. Despite his cloak, the Paladin could feel his back heating up as he grimly recognised that were it not for Akkad's present, his entire body would now be burned to a cinder thanks to the ferocious temperature of the dragon's breath.

He reached the apprentice, quickly reassuring himself that although the young warrior had lost consciousness, he seemed to be generally unharmed. The fact that the lad's breastplate was no longer shimmering suggested that the remnants of Uldini's magic had saved the boy from serious injury.

How can we conquer a beast like that? asked Culhen, who was pushing the confused she-wolf this way and that, the companion animal still unused to her new role and torn between defending her Paladin and her natural flight instinct.

I've no idea, admitted Ahren in frustration. *Shove the she-wolf into Yollock's cave as soon as the dragon is distracted,* he commanded as Four Claws prepared for another aerial attack. The Forest Guardian had noticed that the creature was behaving so cleverly that it only took off when the First, Trogadon, and Khara came within striking distance, thereby ensuring that they had no chance of causing further damage to the dragon's wings. For half a heartbeat, he looked directly into the eyes of the dragon, whose eyes were glimmering red as they reflected the magma, and he recognised the expression that was peering out at him.

'He is playing with us!' shouted Ahren as the creature above disappeared into the low-hanging clouds. The Forest Guardian ran over to his friends, who were huddled together and gasping, trying to figure out what to do before the next attack.

'This is *not* his style,' said Yollock, shaking his head. 'Especially not considering that the First is among us.' He nodded towards the war veteran, whose eyes promised blue murder.

'Did you see the look on Four Claws' face?' asked Khara. 'He looked so…well…*human.*'

'It is the child,' said Jelninolan grimly. 'I am certain that the child has the dragon under his control. The mercenaries on *Alina's Rage* had exactly the same expression on *their* faces towards the end.'

'Because we would never be a sufficient challenge for a *normal* dragon,' groaned Trogadon, scanning the heavens above them.

'I don't want to spoil the party,' said Bergen with an ironic grin. 'But I have the feeling that we may have bitten off more than we can chew here.'

From the clouds above, they heard another scream, and this time it sounded as if Four Claws was *mocking* the Paladins and their friends.

'Does anyone have a plan?' asked Falk hurriedly. 'I am open to any ideas – even one from Ahren.'

Immediately, the young man's thoughts went back to the battle of Gol-Konar and of how it was only Trimm's and Kamaluq's valour that had saved him from his own miscalculation. 'Yollock and the First know Four Claws best,' he said hesitatingly before looking beseechingly at the two Paladins.

'Anyone who *cannot* attack him, withdraw into the cave,' retorted the First. 'The wounded among us will only distract from our battle with the dragon.'

Khara immediately sent Muai away, the Arch Wizard, exhausted from having expended so much sorcery, accompanying the tigress.

Out of the corner of his eye, the Forest Guardian saw Four Claws break through the clouds, he and his friends once again scattering in all directions. Feverishly, Ahren wondered what they could do differently this time, quickly deciding to use what he had learned from the first aerial attack. He unshouldered *Fisiniell* and took three arrows from his quiver, running as he did so to the edge of a magma fissure. From there, he spun around and shot off the three projectiles at the plummeting dragon in quick succession, trying to catch the beast's eye with his own.

I am here, he thought grimly. *Come and get me!*

What are you doing? asked Culhen fearfully, who was, much against his wishes, lying low in Yollock's cave with Uldini, Muai, Caldria, and the she-wolf.

Making myself into an easy target, was Ahren's reply, which only made the wolf more anxious.

As the Forest Guardian had feared, Four Claws evaded the arrows sufficiently to cause them to glance off his scaley body as he screamed directly at Ahren with his steaming breath. The Paladin turned away so that his cloak protected him before springing sideways, Four Claws almost landing on him. For a fraction of a heartbeat, he believed that he had escaped the beast, only for something to connect so forcefully with his back that his world turned into a spinning spiral of heaven and earth until he landed with a clatter and a groan on the ground, sliding several paces on a sheet of ice. Gasping, Ahren tried to focus his eyes on Four Claws again, cursing quietly when he saw the result of his manoeuvre. The dragon had tumbled into the magma fissure on landing, but the quickly cooling magma on the beast's skin seemed to have had no effect on his scales!

When Four Claws soared up towards the heavens again with a scream of triumph, the cooled magma simply cracked and fell from him like the shell of a newly hatched chick.

Ahren got to his feet, and once again, the companions gathered to confer.

'Your magic is gone,' said Falk earnestly, pointing at Ahren's ribbon armour. The younger Forest Guardian snorted as he looked down and saw that the glimmering on his protective bands had been extinguished.

'So much for Uldini's claim that we can withstand several strikes of the dragon with his magic,' growled the First.

'The child,' said Khara. 'He is driving Four Claws to peak performance and is strengthening his power. Remember how the mercenaries fought with such extraordinary fury.'

'That knocks any hope on the head that this dragon might get bored eventually and fly away,' said Trogadon with a sigh. 'My crossbow is in the cave,' he added. 'Do you think a bolt might penetrate the scales?'

'Not a hope,' replied Yollock, the dwarf's shoulders slumping in disappointment.

When the next scream from the dragon announced another attack, Bergen snorted irritably. 'At least, he is predictable,' he muttered.

'Dragons are creatures of habit,' explained Yollock. 'It has something to do with their desire to find an inner as well as an outer balance.'

Ahren thought furiously about how they could make use of any newly learned knowledge. The dragon was well-nigh unbeatable, especially now that he was under the control of the child, who – and they were all in agreement on this – was undoubtedly nourishing himself on the creature's desire for retribution.

Unbeatable.

The word echoed in Ahren's head, provoking an idea so hair-raising that he, himself, quaked at the thought of it.

When the dragon broke out of the cloud cover yet again and began his downward plummeting strafe, which would weaken them yet further, the Forest Guardian began to speak at a furious pace.

'Why don't we do the following...' he murmured conspiratorially, his friends' eyes growing wider and wider as they looked at him in utter disbelief.

You know that this is madness, said Culhen yet again while Ahren waited for the dragon, his two remaining arrows in his hand. Once more, the Paladin stood in front of a magma fissure, hopefully giving the downward racing creature the idea that his opponents were already running out of ideas.

But this time it is our common madness, countered Ahren. *This time, no-one can say that I hadn't forewarned them or asked for advice. In the end, we all agreed.*

Because the others only had ten heartbeats to lodge an objection, replied Culhen nervously.

The Blessing Band is the key, said Ahren reassuringly. *Through our connection to each other, we will know when to act, and in a coordinated manner.*

Ahren shot off his two last arrows, making sure to appear as if he was concentrating completely on the job in hand, although his mind was already on the next part of his mission. He even displayed a mask of desperation on his face as he reached for his empty quiver after both missiles again ricocheted off Four Claws' scales, the malicious look in the eyes of the dragon sparkling with just a little more mocking glee. The child in the mind of the oversized animal was clearly revelling in Ahren's presumably critical situation, Four Claws then hurtling down with a furious cry on the cowering Paladin, who had spread out his cloak to protect himself and his immediate environs from the scorching dragon-breath.

Again, Ahren felt the searing heat, again, the magic leather held fast, and again, the Forest Guardian prepared for his sideways leap – which, however, he did not carry out. Instead, Falk sprang out at the last moment from behind a nearby rock, beside which Ahren had positioned himself, the old Forest Guardian now shielding both himself and his friend from the dragon's attack with his Deep Steel shield so recently charmed by Uldini. The metal made a loud, bell-like sound as Four Claws slammed into it, Falk being immediately flung up in a wide backward arc like a malformed crossbow bolt, the dragon, meanwhile, stumbling under the influence of Uldini's dispersing magic. Kamaluq, who had been cowering invisibly before Ahren, whimpered bravely as he suddenly became discernible, his flash blinding Four Claws before the young fox bounded away towards his still unconscious Paladin, who Falk had dragged into the safety of the cave following the dragon's previous aerial assault.

Ahren took advantage of Four Claws' moment of weakness to sprint forward and use the crook of the mighty creature's bent foreleg to hoist himself onto the beast's shoulder. Four Claws shook his head while bellowing a further cry, which this time was filled more with fury rather than triumph, but Ahren was already running determinedly along the left side of the dragon's back, sensing Khara running up the trembling tail while masterfully maintaining her balance before she sprinted along the right side of Four Claws' back. Less than ten heartbeats after Kamaluq's flash had extinguished, Ahren and his beloved were in position. They exchanged a quick yet intense look, and then – having agreed on their tactic via the Blessing Band – began striking, each one aiming at one of the dragon's wing-bones, just above the beast's shoulder joints.

While Khara used both her weapons on the already injured spot that had caused Four Claws to flee Jorath all those years before, and whose healing Yollock had prevented over many centuries, Ahren stabbed *Sun* into the healthy wing. Thanks to Uldini's magic, the Deep Steel blade sank deep into the cartilaginous tissue, Ahren breathing a sigh of relief once he realised that after one blow, *Sun* still maintained a little of the Arch Wizard's magic. Ahren had been fairly certain that his blade, thanks to its mysterious affinity for Uldini's sun magic, would maintain a little more power than Khara's weapons, which had lost all sheen after their first attacks. Ahren quickly struck a second time, cutting the bird-bone clean through, the magical sheen on *Sun* becoming extinguished in the process.

Four Claws screamed in naked fury as both wings dropped to the ground on either side of him, robbing him of any possibility of ever becoming airborne again. On hearing the cry of raw scorn, Ahren suddenly doubted if his plan could be successfully concluded, for the plain unvarnished truth was that they would still be defeated by an earth-bound dragon so long as the beast was under the control of Revenge.

'Make yourself scarce!' he yelled at Khara as he leaped sideways off the dragon's back, Four Claws turning his long neck this way and that as he tried to snap at his two torturers.

The Swordsmistress threw herself off from the other side, but although the jaws narrowly failed to connect with her, the dragon's furiously raised claws did not. Khara was caught like a ball in mid-flight, the dragon's blow striking her dead centre and sending her, accompanied by a little flash of light – the protective magic clearly dissolving – flying out into the night. The Blessing Band went out with a flicker as the Swordsmistress lost consciousness.

'KHARA!' roared Ahren, yearning to get to her, but now the wounded dragon was between them, and the beast was incandescent with rage.

I will look after her, volunteered Culhen. *If I can manage it, I will drag her by her tunic into the cave. No-one else in the lodgings is capable of helping you. Hakanu's ribs are broken, while Falk has been scalded by the dragon's breath and is the picture of misery.*

Ahren sent his wolf his deepest gratitude, while the knowledge that his loyal companion would bring Khara to safety was such a relief to him that now he could concentrate on the next phase of their plan. *Bodily harmony* – the thought shot through Ahren's mind as he tried to catch Jelninolan's eye while Bergen and Trogadon distracted the flailing Four Claws with clever feints, their main goal being not to be hit by the dragon. He nodded once at the elf to give her encouragement, the priestess holding *Mirilan* in her hands as if the fiddle were a poisonous snake. 'It must be so!' screamed the Paladin above the noise of battle.

While Jelninolan raised her bow painfully slowly, *Mirilan* secure on her shoulder, Ahren made use of the ever so brief moment of recovery to see through Culhen's eyes, the wolf now dragging Khara by the collar of her garment, down the steps to the cave. Ahren's heart was sore when he saw the blood, seeping from a nasty cut to her head.

Uldini will take care of it, said the wolf comfortingly. *Just make sure that Four Claws doesn't find this cave. One exhalation down here and we'll all be toast.*

The brutal warning was effective, Ahren immediately gritting his teeth as he gave the signal to retreat, at which point Jelninolan played her first note on the Storm Fiddle.

The heavens seemed to have been only waiting for the sign, the dark clouds now lighting up. Dozens of lightning flashes streaked across the sky, as if warning the elf that she should immediately cease her playing.

Ahren, meanwhile, scooted to an angled rock that he had selected as cover, his friends, too, having sought out natural nooks and crannies in anticipation of the imminent performance. Only Jelninolan remained where she was, thereby becoming the sole focus of the raging dragon.

Ahren held his breath, for the next critical moment of his plan was about to reveal itself, one that would either turn the tide of battle in their favour or else put the elf's life in mortal danger.

Already, Jelninolan was again drawing her bow across the strings, the heavens responding to her challenge with a lightning storm the likes of which the Forest Guardian had never experienced. He screamed defiance at his own fear as within a radius of half a league, hundreds of flashes of lightning forked their way to the ground, while more seemed to wander across the sky, as if they were aimlessly searching for the cause of their creation so that they could punish her forthwith.

Ahren saw the elf being struck by at least two of the discharges, but her own destructive power seemed to flow directly into *Mirilan*, the fiddle beginning to both glow dangerously and smoulder.

Jelninolan uttered a cry of terror and pain before playing on, her notes following in such quick succession and with such a furious speed and complexity that it seemed as if every discharge from the seething heavens was a note of her furious melody.

Four Claws, the mighty dragon of the north and vessel of the Adversary's child, stamped forward towards the elf, step by shuddering step, struck again and again by bolts of lightning, which caused him to jerk and shiver, but failed to fell him. For every discharge that slammed into Jelninolan now, a dozen struck the dragon, as the pair conducted their unequal duel, whose horrific ending Ahren could now see. *Mirilan's* wooden body was smoking and glowing a cherry red, while the dragon, on the other hand, seemed at most to be weakened and stunned – like a warrior whose helmeted head has just been hit by a flying rock.

Ahren pleaded silently to the priestess to concentrate as hard as she could, for the flashes of lighting were a necessary evil but not the be-all and end-all of her magic. Yes, the dragon was weakened, and his wings were gone, but still the child raged within him, giving him his unholy strength.

A shudder went through Jelninolan's body as the elf's song now reached its climax, causing the sluice-gates of the heavens to open and the icy rain to hammer down.

Healing rain, cleaning the gaping wounds on Four Claws' back, sealing them, closing them until there was nothing there but smooth, unmarked, scaly skin – as though Four Claws had *never* possessed wings.

'Outer harmony,' whispered Ahren fearfully.

Jelninolan abruptly ceased her playing and fled from the dragon and into the fog, but the creature had already come to a halt and turned his head to peer back at himself, a look of wonder in his eyes as he stared, first at the wings that had been separated from him, then at his perfectly formed back, beneath which his muscles worked without pain. Pain, which the creature had had to bear alone for hundreds of years.

'We are *not* your enemy!' shouted Ahren, coming out from behind the rock to face the dragon. 'Your *true* enemy is lurking within you! He is playing you like a puppet on a string! He wants to corrupt you, so that the last dragon of the north will be nothing but a Dark One in the army of the Adversary! Fight against *him*, not against *us!*' Ahren threw his Wind Blade to the ground and stretched his arms out to both sides. 'Banish the child of the Adversary from your mind, and the icy spaces of the south will be your home, far away from humans and their wars!'

Ahren watched as Four Claws stumbled and shook his head. With all his power, the Paladin prayed to the gods that his plan would work this time. He had been unable to free Reik Silvercape from the influence of the shadow that had lain over him, but perhaps he would succeed with this creature, whose understanding was surely so much greater than that of the Dark children who the Adversary had created and let loose on Jorath.

***

Revenge clawed, panic-stricken, at the understanding of his marionette.

Healed!

These dastardly fools really *had* cut away the dragon's scarred nerve pathways and healed his stumps! And that in the *middle* of a life-or-death skirmish!

The child of the Adversary *could* not and *would* not understand such an action – it went against his very being! You *smashed* your hated enemy to *smithereens!* Making things alright again? Reaching out the hand of *friendship? IMPOSSIBLE!*

Revenge sensed how he was losing control of the dragon, whose powerful spirit was tightening around him like thunderclouds before a cleansing storm. Terrified now, the child sought some way of turning the wheel of fortune in his favour again, when suddenly, a shadow appeared out of the fog, a shadow which stared malevolently at the dragon. Triumphantly, Revenge threw himself into Four Claws' seething memories.

Kill him! screamed the child with glee. *Avenge the death of your granddaughter!*

***

Ahren groaned in frustration as the First stumbled – as if driven by some inner urge – towards the dragon, who, on seeing his age-old enemy, seemed suddenly to have lost the battle against the presence inside his head. With wild thrusts and snapping jaws, the veteran and the dragon went for each other, and had the First not been proven himself a master of war in the course of a thousand successful skirmishes, then undoubtedly the enormous creature would have ripped him to pieces on the spot. Ducking, spinning, and parrying with his magically enhanced blade, the First bobbed and weaved around Four Claws, getting closer and closer to the head of the creature.

Ahren sensed that the Paladin was preparing a thrust into one of the eyes of the dragon, while recklessly disregarding the danger to his own life. The dragon, too, seemed to have lost his mind. His inability to fly any more, and his blind rage made Four Claws vulnerable to the deadly dance that the First was weaving with his moves and parries, and yet he still attacked the veteran relentlessly.

Ahren saw how his own plan, which had met with so much success against all expectations, was now rapidly unravelling. 'First!' he called out despairingly. '*Don't!*'

The man couldn't or wouldn't hear him, and when Four Claws struck a mighty blow into the ground, ripping open a hole where the war veteran had been dancing only an instant earlier, the veteran had already sprung sideways, the dragon's head now snapping furiously at the First, and Ahren suddenly understanding the war veteran's ruse. Drawing his two-hander along his body in preparation for a lunge, the age-old Paladin had expected the attack and now prepared to ram the long blade into the eye of the dragon.

Ahren took a helpless step forward, too far away to intervene, when suddenly a small, wiry figure leaped forward from the far side of Four Claws, diverting the First's weapon just far enough with an almost playful thrust of the short sword, causing the two-hander to drive harmlessly over the scaly cheek of the dragon.

Time, seemed to stand still as Ahren tried in vain to run forward. In rapid succession, the dragon's jaws found their next, unintended target, the First tumbled back thanks to a claw-swipe, and Yollock appeared out of the swirling fog, screaming in horror.

'LYSSIN!'

Four Claws recoiled as if he had been punched by an invisible fist, the bloodied body of the young Forest Guardian falling out of his mouth and slamming onto the ground.

'Are you happy now?!' screamed Yollock as he threw himself protectively over his daughter. 'Are we going to carry on *killing* and *killing?* Daughter after granddaughter after son after brother? Do you want to be the murderous monster that the Adversary is intent on turning you into?' Yollock stared at the dragon – now rooted to the spot – with tears streaming down his cheeks, the glimmering of the magma fissures and the billowing fog giving the unfolding drama an aura of mystery. 'All I wanted to do over all these years was to grant you *sleep!*' wailed the former Paladin, his voice raw, hiding the bloody horror that he held in his arms. 'I wanted to give *you* just a breath of peace in your cave of silence and ice!'

By now, Ahren had almost reached Yollock and the First, who was standing there in utter shock, and only now did it dawn on him that he had thrown his Wind Blade away. If Four Claws was to get over his shock, then…

'Say it,' pleaded Ahren, glaring at the overwhelmed First. 'Say what *he* must hear!'

'I…' the war veteran's mouth turned into a grimace, as though he had to clear a thousand stones of age-old rubble from his soul with every muscle he moved, 'I…I'm *sorry*,' he finally managed to whisper. And – as if those words were like a magical incantation that simply had to be spoken, other words followed, filled with honesty and generosity. 'If I had been able to, I would have taken *her* place,' said the First, his voice breaking with grief and weariness. 'I miss *her*, too, you know. I think about *her* every day.'

Four Claws looked into the age-old Paladin's eyes and blinked once. And when the lids of the dragon were raised again, the louring expression of a lust for blood and revenge had completely vanished.

***

Revenge knew that he'd lost, as soon as the stupid Paladin had apologised – and yet, that delicious moment when the might of the dragon had turned *against* the child of the Adversary had given him a clarity of vision that he now wished that he had possessed earlier. Again and again, the Paladins had thwarted his plans, nourishing the very feeling in him that he had so often sought in others. In a single, defiant act of self-destruction, Revenge gathered together all his *own* revenge fantasies against the Paladins, then devoured *himself* for his *own* final call of utter ruination.

Pure, unsullied Revenge would survive his own death and carry his deadly seed even *after* his disappearance out into the world.

***

Four Claws crouched and looked at the Paladins with stoical, yet penetrating eyes which had seen more in their lives than many a mountain. Everywhere on the Ice Fields for as far as ears could hear and beyond, Dark Ones began to howl and yelp, and still Yollock held Lyssin's body in his arms. Ahren tried to check on the young Forest Guardian, but the one-armed man shielded her with his body, not wanting anyone else to so much as touch his daughter.

'Is she dead?' whispered Khara, who had silently stolen up to Ahren and watched the tragic drama unfold with tears in her eyes. Blood still stuck to her hair, but the skin beneath was unharmed.

'Not yet,' murmured Falk, his eyes overshadowed by his memories of the Night of Blood. 'Otherwise, her Blessing would have made its way back to Yollock again.'

Ahren blinked and looked at Falk and Khara in surprise. 'How come you are both so well?' he asked in a daze.

Falk pointed at Caldria, who standing silently in the background. 'She ran out into the healing storm and caught enough of the rain to treat us with.'

'Jelninolan?' whispered Falk, turning to the elf before nodding meaningfully down at Lyssin's body. The priestess held *Mirilan* up, an expression of weary resignation on her face, and Ahren saw immediately that her Storm Fiddle was no more than a charred wooden box, and completely unusable. Jelninolan, herself, was clearly in a state of shock, her mouth opening before closing again, the priestess unable to utter a word.

It was Hakanu who had the wherewithal to loosen the bottle of healing water from the Ancient's belt, presenting it then to Yollock. 'Pour this on her wounds,' he said gently. 'It might help.'

The one-armed man wasted no time, and within five heartbeats, the receptacle was completely empty. Still, Lyssin didn't move, Yollock then shaking his head sadly. 'Not enough,' he said. 'It is not enough.'

'Let me have a look,' muttered Uldini, pushing his little figure past the protective embrace of Yollock. 'Ah, no,' said the Arch Wizard sadly. 'If we only had *Mirilan*.'

The howling of the Dark Ones was growing closer, and Trogadon looked irritably at his hammer. 'Usually, I like introducing Dark Ones to my blacksmith's tool, but this night has seen enough suffering, and anyway, that which is approaching us sounds like an army.'

'We need to get away from here,' added Bergen superfluously.

'But where do we go?' asked Khara, non-plussed 'We are stranded in the middle of nowhere.'

'Stranded,' muttered Uldini through gritted teeth, only to click his fingers a heartbeat later. Then he spun his crystal ball on the palm of his hand as if it were a spinning top, whereupon it took on a flickering yellow hue as if they were all sitting around a crackling campfire. 'Sleeps-in-Treetops,' he snarled. 'We are up to our necks in horse manure here.'

'Help ye have requested, help ye shall receive,' intoned the oracular Ancient. 'Find the beginning!'

'Something a *little* more substantial would help,' countered Uldini venomously. 'We have a dying Paladin here, and an enormous horde of Dark Ones is approaching.'

'Find the *beginning*,' repeated Sleeps-in-Treetops, this time with yet more urgency in her voice. 'I can only see the *end*. Both are one and must be united.' *Flamestar* then dimmed as the Ancient's final few words were carried by the wind: 'The broken elf knows the way.'

Immediately, all eyes turned to the Priestess, who still stood there in silence, now turning what remained of *Mirilan* in her hands.

'Jelninolan,' pleaded Ahren, taking a step towards his companion, but already Trogadon was with her and taking her face between his calloused hands.

'My heart,' he whispered. 'We *need* you. I understand why you are feeling like this now, but you must fight your way through your pain and troubles,' he said gently but firmly. 'You are the strongest female that I have ever encountered, and I want you to prove this now. Your friends are here with you, *and* a young Champion of the gods – we *all* need your help. I know that you will never forgive yourself if you do not act now, and I want to spare you this sorrow.'

Ahren watched as the eyes of the blacksmith locked with those of the priestess.

'Jelninolan.' He said her name so lovingly. '*Please.*'

'We were both tested and found to be impure,' said the elf in a flat whisper. '*I* was too weak.' Jelninolan raised *Mirilan's* remains ever so slightly. '*She* was too weak.'

'Then be *stronger*,' implored Trogadon. 'Stand tall and prove that you are the elf who is stubborn enough to love a dwarf.'

It was only the faintest hint of a smile that decorated Jelninolan's features but, like a fresh breeze on a warm summer morning, it was enough to blow away the lifelessness from her face. The priestess closed her eyes, her fingers now gripping hard the charred wood in her hands. 'South,' she whispered. 'We must go *south*'.

Ahren looked questioningly at Uldini, the Arch Wizard merely shaking his head in bafflement. The childlike figure placed his crystal ball into Lyssin's hands, spreading her fingers around it. Immediately, the faintest of glimmers flickered in *Flamestar's* core, Ahren flinching in horror.

'You haven't *trapped* her Blessing, have you?' he asked, Yollock turning fearfully to look at Uldini.

The Arch Wizard shook his head indignantly, then muttered something incomprehensible. Immediately, Lyssin's fingers clasped the crystal, and Uldini pointed at the now stiff figure of the young woman. 'I have joined *her* spark of life with *Flamestar's* power,' he said. 'As long as she has enough strength to hold the orb in her hands, she will survive. After that…' His voice trailed off, but an element of confidence had already manifested itself on Yollock's features.

'Save her,' said the suffering father, placing her in Hakanu's waiting arms. 'Save her, for I shall never fight again as a Paladin. Then Yollock got to his feet with a determined look on his face and began to trudge back towards his cave. 'Only if my daughter lives will you be able to conquer the Adversary,' he said as he walked. 'So, do what you can to protect her.' The final words that Ahren heard seared his very heart. 'I will sense it if you *fall short.*'

'YOU ALL HEARD THE MAN!' bellowed Bergen after a heartbeat of silence, his voice reminiscent of how he had sounded in his days as a mercenary leader, rousing Ahren and the rest of the group out of their lethargy in no uncertain terms. 'I, for my part, am fond of Lyssin, and have no attention of allowing her Blessing to travel back to the end of the world and into the body of this old curmudgeon, so let us bring her to safety and hope that Sleeps-in-Treetops wasn't just babbling utter gibberish!'

The blonde Paladin grabbed by the shoulder those who were reacting too slowly, and Ahren felt inside him the warmth of gratitude towards the powerful figure. Bergen's natural gift for leadership transformed the mood, helping the Forest Guardian to shrug off the numbness that had held him prisoner since Lyssin had been wounded.

'Culhen, Muai – you go up front!' shouted Ahren. 'Find us the quickest way south, and with as few Dark Ones as possible between us and…' he hesitated a moment before continuing, '…whatever it is that we are looking for.' Then he pointed at Hakanu. 'You stay in the middle. No more deeds of derring-do. Lyssin is counting on you!' The apprentice nodded firmly. 'Khara, cover our backs – you are the fastest, and can always catch up with us if necessary. Trogadon, Falk – the flanks, *please!*' Ahren glanced at Bergen, who nodded back, having allowed him to issue the orders. 'You stay with me and use Karkas' advice to discover where exactly we are going to. I know that it is still night, but I am sure that he will know what it was that Sleeps-in-Treetops meant once he spots it.'

The Ice Lander saluted ironically, Ahren then turning to Caldria. 'You…' he began, then stopping in surprise as he saw the silent woman walking towards the steps leading down to Yollock's dwelling before waving weakly back at him. Her mouth opened, but instead of hearing words, the young Paladin saw a weary yet warm smile. Then she descended and was soon hidden by the fog that covered those lodgings which now would be sheltering two souls again – two souls that would hopefully find peace in each other's company.

Ahren hesitated for a heartbeat before beginning to march, following the route that Culhen was mentally sharing with him. It was only when he had walked a dozen paces that he heard the claws of the dragon following them on the ice at a respectful distance, the beast bellowed his challenge to the approaching Dark Ones.

It felt to Ahren that it had been an eternity since he had last broken into a smile.

The march across the never-ending ice was as monotonous as it was nerve-wracking. First, they had rounded the blunted mountain, and then placed one exhausted foot after the other onto the crusted snow. Muai and Culhen not only kept their eyes and ears peeled for potential Dark Ones, but also sought out the best ground underfoot for the little travel party to proceed safely. The servants of the Dark god were steadily catching up with them, but Four Claws used his powerful claws and snapping teeth to eliminate those creatures that had hurried on ahead of the howling horde. Ahren could already see in the dawn's early light how their pursuers had now ganged together into a snapping, drooling mass of bodies, trotting a good two hundred paces or so behind Four Claws, waiting for the right moment to overpower the dragon or to simply stream past him with the aim of eliminating the little band of exhausted fighters.

Neither Karkas nor Culhen nor Muai had spotted anything exceptional on the white plains stretching towards the horizon, while Ahren's anxiety was now growing at the same speed as the flickering fire in *Flamestar* was diminishing. The Forest Guardian didn't for a moment doubt Yollock's intention never to carry the burden of being a Paladin again should his daughter die, and the young man was now seriously beginning to question whether they would ever reach the place that Sleeps-in-Treetops had so cryptically described. They were almost out of provisions. They were exhausted and shattered, literally making their way to the end of the world, pursued by a hostile army on sheets of ice that seemed to stretch to eternity. Uldini was unable to provide them with protection from the cold, so focused was he on maintaining the charm for Lyssin, while every step on the ice was now robbing Ahren and his companions of life-saving warmth. Ahren wondered if, after all, they would suffer ignominious deaths, worn down by a thousand needling barbs rather than sacrificing themselves in any glorious battle.

Suddenly, Jelninolan stopped dead in her tracks – as if an icy wind had frozen her solid – Ahren having to force himself to break his own monotonous stride through the never-ending, barren wilderness.

'What's wrong?' asked Trogadon anxiously, pre-empting Ahren's similar question. 'Why did you stop, my heart?'

'We have arrived,' said the elf in a trancelike voice as she pointed down to the ice at their feet. 'The *beginning*. It is here.'

'What…?' began Uldini, only for Jelninolan to make the faintest of gestures with one hand, her other one still clasping the charred Storm Fiddle. A faint gust of wind emanated from the elf and swept the snow, gently but firmly aside, revealing a quickly expanding circle of the purest ice.

Ahren peered around him in surprise before looking down into the depths of the frozen water beneath him, which seemed in some inexplicable manner to be so pure that it surely must have been like this, unmoving and unseen in its stillness since the first day of Creation.

Jelninolan closed her free hand into a fist, the magical gust of wind ending as abruptly as when it had first appeared. Ahren studied the perfect circle of perfect ice, and blinked in surprise as a suspicion began to dawn on him.

'Is it…is it a pool of the Goddess?' he whispered, breaking the almost reverential silence that now reigned over the place.

'SHE, WHO FEELS became one with the wind, whispering to every living being their task and their place in the world, so that all would manifest itself into a harmonious whole,' intoned Jelninolan in a voice that seemed greater than the elf herself – almost, indeed, as if her voice was an echo of the deity's recitation. 'Three breaks she took as she performed her great task. Three breaks between the end of her journey – and its *beginning*.'

Uldini groaned and slapped his hand against his forehead. 'Of *course!*' he exclaimed. 'This is the very spot from where the goddess took flight – to present creation with the gift of *feeling*. This was the source of her travelling on the winds.'

'And *how* is all this going to help us now?' asked the First, who seemed to have recovered from the shock of what had happened during the night and returned to his pragmatic, cool self. 'Because by continuing to stand here, we are undoubtedly helping the Dark Ones.' With that, he pointed at the horde of creatures, which were now fanning out, clearly intent on storming past the protection that the dragon was offering the companions by launching their attack from all sides. 'Another couple of hundred heartbeats and we will be up to our necks in Snow Slashers, Frost Bears, and Wolf Seals.'

'Seal Wolves,' said Trogadon, correcting the war veteran, much to the annoyance of the others. 'Well, it was *me* who came up with the name,' grumbled the dwarf. 'Those who first see a new Dark One are allowed to name it. That's the *rule*.'

Ahren turned pleadingly to Jelninolan. 'Is there anything that we can do?' he asked. '*Why* are we here?'

'I know what is to be done,' said Jelninolan with a sorrowful look. 'But I have *failed*.' With that she raised the charred remains of *Mirilan*. 'She was not strong enough.'

Bergen cursed, while Ahren looked questioningly at his friends to see if anyone had an idea of how to assist the elf. Meanwhile, the Dark Ones were moving into position, the first of them even trying to slip past Four Claws, who was bellowing his challenge.

'I suddenly wish that we'd left him his wings,' murmured Trogadon. 'Then none of these Dark Ones would escape him.'

'Jelninolan, *now* would be the right time to ask your goddess to stand by you,' urged Uldini, the elf merely holding out the charred remains of her Storm Fiddle for all to see.

'She was not strong enough,' she murmured again, as if in a trance.

'What does that *mean,* dammit?!' snarled the First. 'You Ancients and your constant riddling…'

Uldini raised his hand for silence, then looked at the remnants of *Mirilan* more closely. 'Not a riddle!' he suddenly exclaimed, then clapping his hands together. 'But the pure, unvarnished truth! Oh, what a fool I am!' Then he grabbed what was left of the charred Storm Fiddle and tossed it into the air, where it broke into a dozen pieces, the sections then floating before the childlike figure as if trapped in time. Uldini pointed his finger sharply at Trogadon. 'You! Blacksmith!' he thundered in a tone that brooked no dissent. 'Tell me that you, stubborn fellow as you are, have *some* Deep Steel on your person – even here on the eternal ice.'

Trogadon looked at the Arch Wizard in wide-eyed surprise as he fumbled at his belt bag. 'Not much,' he said uncertainly before producing three ingots, each one no longer and no wider than the average finger. 'One never knows when one might...'

Uldini snapped his fingers, the priceless metal then floating over to the broken shards of the Storm Fiddle. The Arch Wizard grunted in satisfaction, then looked over at Lyssin's body. 'I need *Flamestar*,' he said. 'When I take it, her life force will evaporate quickly.'

'Does it even matter anymore?' asked Bergen wearily, nodding towards the horde of Dark Ones, which had almost formed a perfect circle around them. 'Either you and Jelninolan perform a miracle, or *all* our life forces will evaporate faster than you can say "grub for Dark Ones".'

Uldini nodded curtly, then uttered a single word unknown to the others. Immediately, *Flamestar* shot onto his outstretched hand while Lyssin began to tremble in Hakanu's arms. Ahren whipped off his cloak and placed it on top of the dying girl, ignoring the biting cold that suddenly enveloped him.

'Ke...eep,' he said, his teeth already chattering, 'keep her warm.'

Khara passed him a fur blanket that looked the worse for wear, but which had, nonetheless, survived all the travails of their long trek, Ahren then gratefully wrapping it around himself. He glanced from the Dark Ones – who seemed to be gaining more and more courage – to Uldini, who was now surrounded by the floating remains of the Storm Fiddle and the Deep Steel ingots.

'HE, WHO FORMS, hear your servant!' intoned the Arch Wizard suddenly, Ahren's eyes widening in astonishment. The number of times that he had heard Uldini recite a genuine prayer, he could count on the fingers of one hand. 'Let me *bring* together that which *belongs* together!' The sorcerer closed his eyes, *Flamestar* burning so brightly now that it seemed to the companions as if a second sun had just been born.

'And again, I say – a warning would have been helpful,' muttered Falk grouchily.

Ahren shielded his eyes with his hands as he blinked and tried to make out what Uldini was up to. Finally, he fled into Culhen's senses, the wolf standing with Muai a little away from the group, steadfastly watching the approaching Dark Ones.

There are simply too many of them, said the wolf. *If they reach us, then we're all dead.*

We must have faith, countered Ahren. He wasn't sure himself whether he was suggesting faith in the two Ancients or in the gods.

Culhen sent him a feeling of fatalistic agreement, then looked over at Uldini and his magicking, having already been warned by Ahren to narrow his eyes. In this way, Ahren was able to watch on incredulously as the Arch Wizard reshaped the ingots of pure Deep Steel with his nimble fingers, spinning the pieces of *Mirilan* simultaneously, stretching or compressing the materials as if they were nothing more than hot bees' wax complying willingly to the commands of the sorcerer. The hands of the Ancient worked with such skill and precision that even an Elven charm-craftsman would pale with envy. As if in a dream, Ahren observed how individual splinters formed into little platelets, and several platelets were combined into little boards, until finally, these little boards were joined together, creating the beautifully carved outline of a Storm Fiddle with a metallic sheen.

Uldini stroked and plucked and smoothed and bent, his fingers performing dozens and dozens of acrobatic tricks as he worked at the form, bathed in the warm glow of *Flamestar*, until he finally stopped, suddenly dropping his arms. The light in the core of the crystal ball was extinguished and Uldini's newly created artwork fell with a metallic crash onto the ice. Ahren could see how ashen-faced the Arch Wizard was, and he hurried over to help the Ancient remain on his feet.

'Thankshh, lad,' mumbled the childlike figure, his voice slurred. Then he spread his fingers above the inert Storm Fiddle and its accompanying bow, whose wooden surface betrayed the whitish hint of unalloyed Deep Steel.

Ahren sensed the heat that was still emanating from the instrument, which was slowly melting the pure ice on which it lay, thereby turning it into the clearest water that Ahren had ever beheld.

The aroma of springtime seemed to rise from the liquid, Uldini now whispering flatly: 'Essence of HIM, WHO IS, moulded by HIM, WHO FORMS, clarified in the icy waters of HER, WHO FEELS.' Uldini fished the Storm Fiddle out of the melted ice and pressed it into the hands of Jelninolan, who seemed to be awakening from a dream. 'Now, play, Auntie,' said the sorcerer with a smile, his eyes rolling of their own volition. 'Play us out of here.' Then Uldini collapsed into Ahren's arms and instantly fell asleep.

The furious cry of Four Claws heralded the beginning of the Dark Ones' onslaught, the dragon doing his impressive bit to keep the creatures at bay by sweeping dozens of them off their feet with his powerful claws, tearing others apart with his ferocious fangs, the drooling, deformed monsters unable to bite or claw through his thick scaly armour, which had even withstood Deep Steel that hadn't been magically treated. Their eyes knew only one prey, and they seemed to be sensing what Ahren sensed – an age-old power was beginning to heave within them, causing their very bones to vibrate.

When the Paladin looked around, he spotted Jelninolan, who was standing there with her eyes closed, her bow tightened with its countless threads of Deep Steel which she now drew ever so gently across the strings of her newly recreated *Mirilan*. The very sky seemed to surge for a moment, as though the clouds wished to protest against the tone, but now the elf was caught up in the strains of a melody, light and plaintive, and as the first of the Dark Ones reached the weary group of travellers, Ahren's world exploded, transforming into a single whirlwind of white.

Into the pure, *unvarnished* eternity of ice.

Epilogue

Ahren's mind was filled with visions of the time *before* time itself. A divine presence seemed to be floating beside him, too powerful for any mortal understanding to comprehend and seeming to prepare for a task so monumental that it threatened to shatter the limits of her own power. The whole world lay before her – a sterile construct of substance and form, waiting to be filled with emotions, with a feeling for life, and with a sense of *being*.

It was as if Ahren was flying with the immortal presence over the vast expanse of Jorath in a northern direction as she touched the souls of a myriad of living creatures. The complex pattern of Creation slipped from the grasp of his mortal understanding, but he sensed the growing weariness of the presence, whose journey he, too, was experiencing.

Three times she rested and three times she soared again, defying the leaden weight that troubled her entire being. Her exhausted brothers were waiting patiently for her. It was now *her* task to contribute *her* portion so that Creation would finally be complete. And so onward she flew – Ahren's benumbed understanding beside her – north and then further north until every last Jorathian soul had received her blessing. Only then did she float down onto a low hill, where she closed her eyes, feeling the welcoming embrace of her brothers.

It was completed.

Ahren gasped for breath – it was as if his body had forgotten to breathe for an entire moon as he looked around him urgently.

The first thing he recognised were the icy plains around him. Then his astounded friends. And finally, those changes in the landscape that his spirit could not *quite* comprehend.

Far to the south was a wall of trees, only visible as a hazy green ribbon, but filled with the promise of a place to call home – a place that promised protection.

Eathinian.

Then his gaze fell on Lanlion, Haminul, and Selsena, all three of them laden down with bundles and rucksacks. And beside them a laughing Sleeps-in-Treetops who called out loudly: 'The beginning is the end – found in sand, strengthened in moor, refined in ice.' Then she chuckled quietly to herself, waiting for Ahren and his friends to arise from the snow.

'Did you...' began Ahren but his words were failing him. What he had experienced was so anchored in his soul that words would never do them justice. He looked his companions in the eye and understood that they were experiencing the same sense of wonder as he was. Whatever they had experienced, it had been so unreal and earth-shattering that the mortal world simply did not have enough room for it. He knew that he would be taking these impressions with him to the grave, and that he was not the only one who would be doing so.

'Is that *Eathinian* back there?' asked Bergen, scratching his head in bemusement. 'Or did one of the Dark Ones hit me so hard that I am now dreaming?'

'We have travelled,' said Jelninolan with an unearthly serenity. 'You *know* from where –and you *know* with whom – and you *know* where to.' Then she packed *Mirilan* into her bag with almost ritualistic attention before turning to Uldini – who only now had woken up – and kissed him affectionately on his forehead.

'Thank you,' she murmured. 'Thank you for the gift you have twice given me. First, out of wood, and then out of belief and steel woven together.'

Uldini seemed embarrassed as he mumbled: 'If you think that I am about to start praying on a *regular* basis—'

Hakanu's whoop of joy interrupted the sorcerer. 'Lyssin! She's *moving!*'

'Mischief stayed behind,' said Sleeps-in-Treetops, pointing at the snow that they were lying on. Looking more closely now, Ahren recognised a complicated bane circle of finely ground ice. 'What travelled here was pure, completely...refined,' added the enigmatic Ancient.

Ahren looked around to see if Four Claws, too, had survived the journey to the north from the far south, but there was no sign of the age-old dragon. The Paladin pondered over the long overdue peace that Yollock had wanted to realise for the creature. Through Ahren's plan, Four Claws had recovered, albeit without his wings. The Ice Fields were now his homeland, his refuge – his place of rest.

With a satisfied smile, Ahren imagined the dragon eating his fill on the Dark Ones of the far south, while keeping a protective eye on

Yollock and Caldria. The Ice Fields now had their new, powerful guard, while the Wild Dwarves would certainly be delighted to make his acquaintance.

Falk, meanwhile, stumbled over to Selsena, placing his head on her neck. 'You'll never believe all the things that happened to us,' said the old Paladin. 'Or how much I missed you with every step of the journey.'

Ahren sensed the warmth of the Titejunanwa as her waves of love touched him, too. 'We *all* missed you,' he said to the Elven charger.

Haminul snorted loudly, Lanlion then guffawing. 'Yes, you are right, my dear,' he said, his voice completely devoid of the melancholy that so often coloured it. 'We are carrying all these provisions *and* the tents, not to mention warm clothing – just because Sleeps-in-Treetops has commanded it – and as a reward, we are completely ignored.'

Ahren slipped his arm around Khara's waist, the Swordsmistress smiling as they strolled over to the pale Paladin who, at first glance, looked the same as ever. 'Have you completed your search?' asked Ahren curiously.

Lanlion nodded and grinned, showing off his striking teeth. 'The way was long and wondrous, and I finally landed here.' With that, he pointed at the snow-covered hill that glistened an unearthly white. 'At the end of a journey which *wasn't* mine after all.'

Ahren frowned. 'You mean, the gods *didn't* cure you?' he asked. 'They *haven't* forgiven you?'

Lanlion smiled gently, a hint of his normal moodiness reappearing in his features, nonetheless. 'They have taught me to trust myself. *This* is the path that I first must follow.' He sighed. 'And it is longer than I expected.'

'Schnapps!' exclaimed Trogadon, reaching for a barrel that was sticking out of one of the bundles on Selsena's back. 'This pale golden boy has brought schnapps along. The day truly *has* been saved!'

His companions burst out laughing, Ahren then turning to face Evergreen, as a truth dawned on him. A truth that warmed him more than the most beautiful summer's morning could ever hope to do.

Thirteen Paladins had been found.
Thirteen gods' Blessings stood united.
The time for the final battle was nigh.

United at last, the Thirteen Paladins embark on their final battle against the Adversary, knowing that victory is within their grasp. Experience the exciting finale to the saga of the Thirteenth Paladin.

The 13th Paladin – the final volume
The Adversary
Available latest February 2024

A small request to my loyal readers:

If you are enjoying the saga of Ahren and his friends, please leave a short review on the product page of the volume that you have read or on your favourite social media platform.

Thank you for helping me to guide Ahren's adventure towards its exciting ending.

As always, I am grateful to my German editor Janina Klinck, to my illustrator Petra Rudolf, and to my translation team who works tirelessly to create the english version of Ahrens adventures.

about the author

Torsten Weitze (b. 1976) is a native of Krefeld in Germany, where he still resides.

Having trained as a publishing assistant, he organised so many pen and paper role-plays that he was inexorably drawn to the creative side of the business. He now spends his time dreaming up new worlds and characters and using them to breathe life into his fantasy fiction.

He relaxes by regular Jiu-Jitsu training and learning to master traditional Japanese weapons.

His debut novel, *Ahren: The Thirteenth Paladin,* appeared first in German in February, 2017

Published books:

The Thirteenth Paladin

Volume I	Ahren
Volume II	the Naming
Volume III	the Brazen City
Volume IV	the Sleeping Mother
Volume V	the Isles of the Cutlass Sea
Volume VI	the Battle for Hjalgar
Volume VII	the Eternal Empire
Volume VIII	the Father of the Mountain
Volume IX	the Forest of Ire
Volume X	the Green Sea
Volume XI	the City of Cutthroats
Volume XII	the Call of the Ice Fields

Printed in Great Britain
by Amazon